ELIZABETH GEORGE

Careless in Red

HODDER &
STOUGHTON

First published in Great Britain in 2008 by Hodder & Stoughton
An Hachette Livre UK company

I

Copyright © Susan Elizabeth George 2008

The right of Elizabeth George to be identified as the Author of the Work has
been asserted by her in accordance with the Copyright,
Designs and Patents Act 1988.

A CIP catalogue record for this title is available from the British Library

Trade Paperback ISBN 978-0-340-92297-2

Typeset in Plantin Light by
Palimpsest Book Production Limited, Grangemouth, Stirlingshire

Printed and bound by Griffin Press

Hodder & Stoughton's policy is to use papers that are natural, renewable and
recyclable products and made from wood grown in sustainable forests. The
logging and manufacturing processes are expected to conform to the
environmental regulations of the country of origin.

Hodder & Stoughton Ltd
A division of Hodder Headline
338 Euston Road
London NW1 3BH

www.hodder.co.uk

To the memory of Stephen Lawrence and 22 April 1993,
when he was murdered in Eltham, southeast London, by five men
who have gone unpunished by the British judicial system to this day.

If thou art indeed my father,
then thou hast stained thy sword
in the lifeblood of thy son.
And thou didst it of thine own obstinacy.
For I sought to turn thee into love . . .

From the *Shahnama*

I

He found the body on the forty-third day of his walk. By then, the end of April had arrived, although he had only the vaguest idea of that. Had he been capable of noticing his surroundings, the condition of the flora along the coast might have given him a broad hint as to the time of year. He'd started out when the only sign of life renewed was the promise of yellow buds on the gorse that grew sporadically along the cliff tops, but by April, the gorse was wild with colour, and yellow archangel climbed in tight whorls along upright stems in hedgerows on the rare occasions when he wandered into a village. Soon foxgloves would be nodding on roadside verges, and lamb's foot would expose fiery heads from the hedgerows and the drystone walls that defined individual fields in this part of the world. But those bits of burgeoning life were in the future, and he'd been walking these days that had blended into weeks in an effort to avoid both the thought of the future and the memory of the past.

He carried virtually nothing with him. An ancient sleeping bag. A rucksack with a bit of food that he replenished when the thought occurred to him. A bottle that he filled with water in the morning if water was to be had near the site where he'd slept. Everything else, he wore. One waxed jacket. One hat. One tattersall shirt. One pair of trousers. Boots. Socks. Underclothes. He'd come out for this walk unprepared and uncaring that he was unprepared. He'd known only that he had to walk or he had to remain at home and sleep, and if he remained at home and slept, he'd come to realise that eventually he would will himself not to awaken again.

So he walked. There had seemed no alternative. Steep ascents to cliff tops, the wind striking his face, the sharp salt air desiccating his skin, scrambling across beaches where reefs erupted from sand and stone when the tide was low, his breath coming short, rain soaking his legs, stones pressing insistently against his soles . . . These things would remind him that he was alive and that he was intended to remain so.

He was thus engaged in a wager with fate. If he survived the walk, so be it. If he did not, his ending was in the hands of the gods. In the plural, he decided. He could not think that there might be a single Supreme Being out there, pressing fingers into the keyboard of a divine computer, inserting this or forever deleting that.

His family had asked him not to go, for they'd seen his state although, like so many families of his class, they'd not made any direct mention of it. Just his mother saying, 'Please don't do this, darling,' and his brother suggesting, with his face gone pale and always the threat of another relapse hanging over him and over them all, 'Let me go with you,' and his sister murmuring with her arm round his waist, 'You'll get past it. One does,' but none of them mentioning her name or the word itself, that terrible, eternal, definitive word.

Nor did he mention it. Nor did he mention anything other than his need to walk.

The forty-third day of this walk had taken the same shape as the forty-two days that had preceded it. He'd awakened where he'd fallen on the previous night, with absolutely no knowledge where he was aside from somewhere along the South-West Coast Path. He'd climbed out of his sleeping bag, donned his jacket and his boots, drunk the rest of his water, and begun to move. In mid-afternoon the weather, which had been uneasy most of the day, made up its mind and blew dark clouds across the sky. In the wind, they piled one upon the other, as if an immense shield in the distance were holding them in place and allowing them no further passage, having made the promise of a storm.

He was struggling in the wind to the top of a cliff, climbing from a V-shaped cove where he'd rested for an hour or so and watched the waves slamming into broad fins of slate that formed the reefs in this place. The tide was just beginning to come in, and he'd noted this. He needed to be well above it. He needed to find some sort of shelter as well.

Near the top of the cliff, he sat. He was winded, and he found it odd that no amount of walking these many days had seemed sufficient to build his endurance for the myriad climbs he was making along the coast. So he paused to catch his breath. He felt a twinge that he recognised as hunger, and he used the minutes of his respite to draw from his rucksack the last of a dried sausage he'd purchased when he'd come to a hamlet along his route. He gnawed it down to nothing, realised that he was also thirsty, and stood to see if anything resembling habitation was nearby: hamlet, fishing cottage, holiday home, or farm.

There was nothing. But thirst was good, he thought with resignation. Thirst was like the sharp stones pressing into the soles of his shoes, like the wind, like the rain. It reminded him, when reminders were needed.

He turned back to the sea. He saw that a lone surfer bobbed there, just beyond the breaking waves. Whether it was a man or woman, he could not tell. The figure was entirely clothed in black neoprene. At this time of year, it was the only way to enjoy the frigid water.

He knew nothing about surfing, but he knew a fellow cenobite when he saw one. There was no religious meditation involved, but they were both alone in places where they should not have been alone, in conditions that were not suited for what they were attempting. For him, the coming rain – for there could be little doubt that rain was moments away from falling – would make his walk along the coast slippery and dangerous. For the surfer, the exposed reefs on shore demanded an answer to the question that asked why he surfed at all.

He had no answer and little interest in developing one. His inadequate meal finished, he resumed his walk. The cliffs were friable in this part of the coast, unlike the cliffs where he'd begun his walk. There they were largely granite, igneous intrusions into the landscape, forced upon ancient lava, limestone, and slate. Although worn by time, weather, and the restless sea, they were nonetheless solid underfoot, and a walker could venture near the edge and watch the roiling sea or observe the gulls seeking perches among the crags. Here, however, the cliff edge was culm: slate, shale, and sandstone, and cliff bases were marked by mounds of the stony detritus called clitter that fell regularly to the beach below. Venturing near the edge meant a certain fall. A fall meant broken bones or death.

At this section of his walk, the cliff top levelled out for some one hundred yards. The path was well marked, moving away from the cliff's edge and tracing a line between gorse and thrift on one side and a fenced pasture on the other. Exposed here, he bent into the wind, and moved steadily forward. He became aware that his throat was painfully dry, and his head had begun to fill with a dull ache just behind his eyes. He felt a sudden bout of dizziness as he reached the far end of the cliff top. Lack of water, he thought. He would not be able to go much farther without doing something about it.

A stile marked the edge of the high pasture he'd been following, and he climbed it and paused, waiting for the landscape to stop swimming in front of him long enough for him to find the descent to what would be yet another cove. He'd lost count of the inlets he'd come upon in his walk along the undulating coast. He had no idea what this one was called, any more than he'd been able to name the others.

When the vertigo had passed, he saw that a lone cottage stood at the edge of a wide meadow beneath him, perhaps two hundred yards inland from the beach and along the side of a twisting brook. A cottage meant potable water, so he would make for that. It wasn't a great distance off the path.

He stepped down from the stile just as the first drops of rain fell. He wasn't wearing his hat at the moment, so he shrugged his rucksack from his shoulders and dug it out. He was pulling it low onto his fore-head – an old baseball cap of his brother's with *Mariners* scrolled across it – when he caught sight of a flash of red. He looked in the direction from which it had seemed to come, and he found it at the base of the cliff that formed the far side of the inlet beneath him. There, a sprawl of red lay across a broad plate of slate. This slate was itself the land-ward end of a reef, which crept from the cliff bottom out into the sea.

He studied the red sprawl. At this distance it could have been anything from rubbish to laundry, but he knew instinctively that it was not. For although all of it was crumpled, part of it seemed to form an arm, and this arm extended outward onto the slate as if supplicating an unseen benefactor who was not nor would ever be there.

He waited a full minute that he counted off in individual seconds. He waited uselessly to see if the form would move. When it did not, he began his descent.

A light rain was falling when Daidre Trahair made the final turn down the lane that led to Polcare Cove. She switched on the windscreen wipers and created a mental note that they would have to be replaced, sooner rather than later. It wasn't enough to tell herself that spring led to summer and windscreen wipers wouldn't actually be necessary at that point. April had been notoriously unpredictable as usual and while May was generally pleasant in Cornwall, June could be a weather night-mare. So she decided then and there that she had to get new wipers, and she considered where she might purchase them. She was grateful for this mental diversion. It allowed her to push from her mind all consideration of the fact that, at the end of this journey south, she was feeling nothing. No dismay, confusion, anger, resentment, or compas-sion, and not an ounce of grief.

The grief part didn't worry her. Who honestly could have expected her to feel it? But the rest of it . . . to have been bled of every possible emotion in a situation where at least marginal feeling was called for . . . That concerned her. In part it reminded her of what she'd heard too many times from too many lovers. In part it indicated a regression to a self she thought she'd put behind her.

So the nugatory movement of the windscreen wipers and the resulting smear they left in their wake distracted her. She cast about for potential purveyors of car parts: in Casvelyn? Possibly. Alsperyl? Hardly. Perhaps she'd have to go all the way to Launceton.

She made a cautious approach to the cottage. The lane was narrow, and while she didn't expect to meet another car, there was always the possibility that a visitor to the cove and its thin strip of beach might barrel along, departing in a rush and assuming no one else would be out here in this kind of weather.

To her right rose a hillside where gorse and yellow wort made a tangled coverlet. To her left the Polcare valley spread out, an enormous green thumbprint of meadow bisected by a stream that flowed down from Stowe Wood, on higher ground. This place was different from traditional combes in Cornwall, which was why she'd chosen it. A twist of geology made the valley wide as if glacially formed – although she knew this could not be the case – instead of canyon-like and constrained by river water wearing away aeons of unyielding stone. Thus, she never felt hemmed in in Polcare Cove. Her cottage was small, but the environment was large, and open space was crucial to her peace of mind.

Her first warning that things were not as they should have been occurred as she pulled off the lane onto the patch of gravel and grass that served as her drive. The gate was open. It had no lock, but she knew that she'd left it securely closed for that very reason the last time she'd been here. Now it gaped the width of a body.

Daidre stared at this opening for a moment before she swore at herself for being timid. She got out of the car, swung the gate wide, then drove inside.

When she'd parked and went to shut the gate behind her, she saw the footprint. It pressed down the soft earth where she'd planted her primroses along the drive. A mansized print, it looked like something made by a boot. A hiking boot. That put her situation in an entirely new light.

She looked from the print to the cottage. The blue front door seemed unmolested, but when she quietly circled the building to check for other signs of intrusion, she found a window pane broken. This was on a window next to the door that led outside to the stream, and the door itself was off the latch. Fresh mud formed a clump on the step.

Although she knew she should have been frightened, or at least cautious, Daidre was, instead, infuriated by that broken window. She pushed the door open in a state of high dudgeon and stalked through the kitchen to the sitting room. There she stopped. In the dim light of the tenebrous day outside, a form was coming out of her bedroom. He was tall, he was bearded, and he was so filthy that she could smell him from across the room.

She said, 'I don't know who the hell you are or what you're doing here, but you *are* going to leave directly. If you don't leave, I shall become violent with you, and I assure you, you do *not* want that to happen.'

Then she reached behind her for the switch to the lights in the kitchen. She flipped it and illumination fell broadly across the sitting room to the man's feet. He took a step towards her, which brought him fully into the light, and she saw his face.

She said, 'My God. You're injured. I'm a doctor. May I help?'

He gestured towards the sea. From this distance, she could hear the waves as always, but they seemed closer now, the sound of them driven inland by the wind. 'There's a body on the beach,' he said. 'It's up on the rocks. At the bottom of the cliff. It's . . . he's dead. I broke in. I'm sorry. I'll pay for the damage. I was looking for a phone to ring the police. What is this place?'

'A body? Take me to him.'

'He's dead. There's nothing—'

'Are you a doctor? No? I am. Take me to him. We're losing time when we could otherwise be saving a life.'

The man looked as if he would protest. She wondered if it was disbelief. You? A doctor? Far too young. But he apparently read her determination. He took off the cap he was wearing. He wiped the arm of his jacket along his forehead, inadvertently streaking mud on his face. His light hair, she saw, was overlong, and his colouring was identical to hers. Both trim, both fair, they might have been siblings, even to the eyes. His were brown. So were hers.

He said, 'Very well. Come with me,' and he came across the room and passed her, leaving behind the acrid scent of himself: sweat, unwashed clothing, unbrushed teeth, and something else, more profound and more disturbing. She backed away from him and kept her distance as they left the cottage and started down the lane.

The wind was fierce. They struggled against it and into the rain as they made their way swiftly towards the beach. They passed the point where the valley stream opened into a pool before tumbling across a natural breakwater and rushing down to the sea. This marked the beginning of Polcare Cove, a narrow strand at low water, just rocks and boulders when the tide was high.

The man called into the wind, 'Over here,' and he led her to the north side of the cove. From that point, she needed no further direction. She could see the body on an outcropping of slate: the bright red windcheater, the loose dark trousers for ease of movement, the thin and exceedingly flexible shoes. He wore a harness round his waist and from this dangled numerous metal devices and a lightweight bag from which a white substance spilled across the rock. Chalk for his hands, she thought. She moved to see his face.

She said, 'God. It's . . . He's a cliff climber. Look, there's his rope.'

Part of it lay nearby, an extended umbilical cord to which the body was still attached. The rest of it snaked from the body to the bottom of the cliff, where it formed a rough mound, knotted skilfully with a carabiner protruding from the end.

She felt for a pulse although she knew there would be none. The cliff at this point was two hundred feet high. If he'd fallen from there – as he most certainly had – only a miracle could have preserved him.

There had been no miracle. She said to her companion, 'You're right. He's dead. And with the tide . . . Look, we're going to have to move him or—'

'No!' The stranger's voice was harsh.

Daidre felt a rush of caution. 'What?'

'The police have to see it. We must phone the police. Where's the nearest phone? Have you a mobile? There was nothing . . .' He indicated the direction they'd come. There was no phone in the cottage.

'I haven't a mobile,' she said. 'I don't bring one when I come here. What does it matter? He's dead. We can see how it happened. The tide's coming in, and if we don't move him the water will.'

'How long?' he asked.

'What?'

'The tide. How long have we got?'

'I don't know.' She looked at the water. 'Twenty minutes? Half an hour? No more than that.'

'Where's a phone? You've got a car.' And in a variation of her own words, 'We're wasting time. I can stay here with the . . . with him, if you prefer.'

She didn't prefer. She had the impression he would depart like a spirit if she left things up to him. He would know she'd gone to make the phone call he so wanted made, but he himself would vanish, leaving her to . . . what? She had a good idea and it wasn't a welcome one.

She said, 'Come with me.'

She took them to the Salthouse Inn. It was the only place within miles that she could think of that was guaranteed to have a phone available. The inn sat alone at the junction of three roads: a white, squat thirteenth-century hostelry that stood inland from Alsperyl, south of Shop, and north of Woodford. She drove there swiftly, but the man didn't complain or show evidence of worry that they might end up down the side of a hill or headfirst into an earthen hedge. He didn't use his seat belt, and he didn't hold on.

He said nothing. Nor did she. They rode with the tension of strangers between them and with the tension of much unspoken as well. She was relieved when they finally reached the inn. To be out in the air, away from his stench, was a form of blessing. To have something in front of her – immediate occupation – was a gift from God.

He followed her across the patch of rocky earth that went for a car park, to the low hung door. Both of them ducked to get inside the inn. They were at once in a vestibule cluttered with jackets, rainwear, and sodden umbrellas. They removed nothing of their own as they entered the bar.

Afternoon drinkers – the inn's regulars – were still at their normal places: round the scarred tables nearest the fire. Coal, it put out a welcome blaze. It shot light into the faces bent to it and streamed a soft illumination against soot-stained walls.

Daidre nodded to the drinkers. She came here herself, so they were not unfamiliar to her nor she to them. They murmured, 'Ms Trahair' and one of them said to her, 'You come down for the tournament, then?' but the question fell away when her companion was observed. Eyes to him, eyes to her. Speculation and wonder. Strangers were hardly unknown in the district. Good weather brought them to Cornwall in droves. But they came and went as strangers and they did not generally show up in the company of someone known.

She went to the bar. 'Brian, I need to use your phone. There's been a terrible accident. This man . . .' She turned from the publican. 'I don't know your name.'

'Thomas.'

'Thomas. Thomas what?'

'Thomas,' he said.

She frowned but said to the publican, 'This man Thomas has found a body in Polcare Cove. We need to phone the police. Brian,' and this she said more quietly, 'it's . . . I think it's Santo Kerne.'

Constable Mick McNulty was performing patrol duty when his radio squawked, jarring him awake. He considered himself lucky to have been in the panda car at all when the call came through. He'd recently completed a lunchtime quickie with his wife, followed by a sated snooze with both of them naked beneath the counterpane they'd ripped from the bed ('We can't *stain* it, Mick. It's the only one we've *got*!'), and only fifty minutes earlier he'd resumed cruising along the A39 on the lookout for potential malefactors. But the warmth of the car in combination with the rhythm of the windscreen wipers and the fact that his two-year-old son had kept him up most of the previous night weighed down his eyelids and encouraged him to look for a lay-by into which he could pull the car for a kip. He was doing just that – napping – when the radio burst into his dreams.

Body on the beach. Polcare Cove. Immediate response required. Secure the area and report back.

Who phoned it in? he wanted to know.

Cliff walker and a local resident. They would meet him at Polcare Cottage.

Which was where?

Bloody hell, man. Use your effing head.

Mick gave the radio two fingers. He started the car and pulled onto the road. He'd get to use the lights and the siren, which generally happened only in summer when a tourist in a hurry made a vehicular misjudgment with dire results. At this time of year, the only action he usually saw was from a surfer anxious to blast into the water of Widemouth Bay: too much speed into the car park, too late to brake, and over the edge onto the sand he'd go. Well, Mick understood that urgency. He felt it himself when the waves were good and the only thing keeping him from his wetsuit and his board were the uniform he wore and the thought of being able to wear it – right here in Casvelyn

– into his dotage. Messing up a sinecure was not in his game plan. They did not refer to a posting in Casvelyn as the velvet coffin for nothing.

With siren and lights, it still took him nearly twenty minutes to reach Polcare Cottage, which was the only habitation along the road down to the cove. The distance was less than five miles as the crow flies – but the lanes were no wider than a car and a half, and, defined by farmland, woodland, hamlet, and village, not a single one of them was straight.

The cottage was painted mustard yellow, a beacon in the gloomy afternoon. It was an anomaly in an area where nearly every other structure was white, and in further defiance of local tradition, its two outbuildings were purple and lime, respectively. Neither of them was illuminated, but the small windows of the cottage itself streamed light onto the garden that surrounded it.

Mick silenced the siren and parked the car, although he left the headlights on and the roof lights twirling, which he considered a nice touch. He pushed through a gate and passed an old Vauxhall in the drive. At the front door, he knocked sharply on the bright blue panels. A figure appeared quickly on the other side of a stained glass window high on the door, as if she'd been standing nearby waiting for him. She wore snug jeans and a turtleneck sweater; long earrings dangled as she gestured Mick inside.

'I'm Daidre Trahair,' she said. 'I made the call.'

She admitted him to a small square entry crammed with Wellingtons, hiking boots, and jackets. A large egg-shaped iron kettle that Mick recognised as an old mining kibble stood to one side, filled with umbrellas and walking sticks instead of with ore. A gouged and ill-used narrow bench marked a spot for changing in and out of boots. There was barely space to move.

Mick shook the rain water from his jacket and followed Daidre Trahair into the heart of the cottage, which was the sitting room. Here, an unkempt bearded man was squatting by the fireplace, taking ineffective stabs at five pieces of coal with a duck-headed poker. They should have used a candle beneath the coal until it got going, Mick thought. That was what his mum had always done. It worked a treat.

'Where's the body?' he said. 'I'll want your details as well.' He took out his notebook.

'The tide's coming in,' the man said. 'The body's on the . . . I don't know if it's part of the reef, but the water . . . You'll want to see the body surely. Before the rest. The formalities, I mean.'

Being given a suggestion like this – by a civilian who no doubt obtained all his information about procedure from police dramas on ITV – got right up Mick's nose. As did the man's voice, whose tone, timbre, and accent were completely out of keeping with his appearance. He looked like a vagrant but certainly didn't talk like one. He put Mick in mind of what his grandparents referred to as 'the old days' when people always known as 'the quality' cruised down to Cornwall in their fancy cars and stayed in big hotels with wide verandas before the days of international travel. 'They knew how to tip, they did,' his granddad would tell him. ''Course things were less dear in those days, weren't they, so tuppence went a mile and a shilling'd take you all the way to London.' He exaggerated like that, Mick's granddad. It was, his mother said, part of his charm.

'I wanted to move the body,' Daidre Trahair said. 'But he' – with a nod at the man— 'said not to. It's an accident. Well, obviously, it's an accident, so I couldn't see why . . . Frankly, I was afraid the surf would take him.'

'Do you know who it is?'

'I . . . no,' she said. 'I didn't get much of a look at his face.'

Mick hated to cave in to them, but they were right. He tilted his head in the direction of the door. 'Let's see him.'

They set off into the rain. The man brought out a faded baseball cap and put it on. The woman used a rain jacket with the hood pulled over her sandy hair.

Mick paused at the police car and fetched the small flash camera that he'd been authorised to carry, its purchase intended for a moment just like this. If he had to move the body, they'd at least have a visual record of what the spot had looked like before the waves rose to claim the corpse.

At the water's edge, the wind was fierce, and a beach break was coming from both left and right. These were rapid waves, seductive swells building offshore. But they were forming fast and breaking faster: just the sort of surf to attract and demolish someone who didn't know what he was doing.

The body, however, wasn't that of a surfer. This came as something of a surprise to Mick. He'd assumed . . . But assuming was an idiot's game. He was glad he'd jumped only to mental conclusions and said nothing to the man and woman who'd phoned for help.

Daidre Trahair was right. It looked like an accident. A young climber – most decidedly dead – lay on a shelf of slate at the base of the cliff.

Mick swore silently when he stood over the body. This wasn't the best place to cliff climb, either alone or with a partner. While there were swathes of slate, which provided good handholds, toeholds, and cracks into which camming devices and chock stones could be slid for the climber's safety, there were also vertical fields of sandstone that crumbled as easily as yesterday's scones if the right pressure was put upon them.

From the look of things, the victim had been attempting a solo climb: an abseil down from the top of the cliff, followed by a climb up from the bottom. The rope was in one piece and the carabiner was still attached to the rewoven figure eight knot at the end. The climber himself was still bound to the rope by a belay device. His descent from above should have gone like clockwork.

Equipment failure at the top of the cliff, Mick concluded. He'd have to climb up via the coastal path and see what was what when he was finished down here.

He took the pictures. The tide was creeping towards the body. He photographed it and everything surrounding it from every possible angle before he unhooked his radio from his shoulder and barked into it. He got static in return.

He said, 'Damn,' and clambered to the highpoint of the beach where the man and woman were waiting. He said to the man, 'I'll need you directly,' took five steps away, and once again shouted into his radio. 'Phone the coroner,' he told the sergeant manning the station in Casvelyn. 'We need to move the body. We've got a bloody great tide coming in, and if we don't move this bloke, he's going to be gone.'

And then they waited, for there was nothing else to do. The minutes ticked by, the water rose, and finally the radio bleated. 'Coroner's . . . okay . . . from surf . . . road,' the disembodied voice croaked. 'What . . . site . . . needed?'

'Get out here and bring your rain kit with you. Get someone to man the station while we're gone.'

'Know . . . body?'

'Some kid. I don't know who it is. When we get him off the rocks, I'll check for i.d.'

Mick approached the man and woman who were huddled separately against the wind and the rain. He said to the man, 'I don't know who the hell you are, but we have a job to do and I don't want you doing *anything* other than what I tell you. Come with me,' and to the woman, 'You as well.'

They picked their way across the rock-strewn beach. No sand was left down near the water; the tide had covered it. They went single file across the first slate slab. Halfway across, the man stopped and extended his hand back to Daidre Trahair to assist her. She shook her head. She was fine, she told him.

When they reached the body, the tide was lapping at the slab on which it lay. Another ten minutes and it would be gone. Mick gave directions to his two companions. The man would help him move the corpse to the shore. The woman would collect anything that remained behind. It wasn't the best situation, but it would have to do. They could not afford to wait for the professionals.

2

Cadan Angarrack didn't mind the rain. Nor did he mind the spectacle that he knew he presented to the limited world of Casvelyn. He trundled along on his freestyle BMX, with his knees rising to the height of his waist and his elbows shooting out like bent arrows, intent only on getting home to make his announcement. Pooh bounced on his shoulder, squawking in protest and occasionally shrieking 'Landlubber scum!' into Cadan's ear. This was decidedly better than applying his beak to Cadan's earlobe, which had happened in the past before the parrot learned the error of his ways, so Cadan didn't try to silence the bird. Instead he said, 'You tell 'em, Pooh,' to which the parrot cried, 'Blow holes in the attic!' an expression whose provenance was a mystery to his master.

Had he been out working with the bicycle instead of using it as a means of transport, Cadan wouldn't have had the parrot with him. In the early days, he'd taken Pooh along, finding a perch for him near the side of the empty swimming pool while he ran through his routines and developed strategies for improving not only his tricks but the area in which he practised them. But some damn teacher from the infants' school next door to the leisure centre had raised the alarm about Pooh's vocabulary and what it was doing to the innocent ears of the seven-year-olds whose minds she was trying to mould, and Cadan had been given the word. Leave the bird at home if he couldn't keep him quiet and if he wanted to use the empty pool. So there had been no choice in the matter. Until today, he'd had to use the pool because so far he'd made not the slightest inroad with the town council about establishing trails for air jumping on Binner Down. Instead, they'd looked at him the way they would have looked at a psycho, and Cadan knew what they were thinking, which was just what his father not only thought but said: Twenty-two years old and you're playing with a *bicycle*? What the hell's the matter with you?

Nothing, Cadan thought. Not a sodding thing. You think this is *easy*? Tabletop? Tailwhip? Try it sometime.

But of course, they never would. Not the town councillors and not his dad. They'd just look at him and their expression would say, Make something of your life. Get a job, for God's sake.

And that was what he had to tell his father: Gainful employment was his. Pooh on his shoulder or not, he'd actually managed to acquire another job. Of course, his dad didn't need to know *how* he'd acquired it. He didn't need to know it was really all about Cadan asking if Adventures Unlimited had thought about the use to which its decrepit crazy golf course could be put and ending up with a brokered deal of maintenance work in the old hotel in exchange for utilising the crazy golf course's hills and dales – minus their windmills, barns, and other assorted structures, naturally – for perfecting air tricks. All Lew Angarrack had to know was that, sacked once again, for his myriad failures in the family business – and who the *hell* wanted to shape surf-boards anyway? – Cadan had gone out and replaced Job A with Job B within seventy-two hours. Which was something of a record, Cadan decided. He usually gave his dad an excuse to remain in a state of cheesed-off-at-him for five or six weeks at least.

He was jouncing along the unpaved lane behind Victoria Road and wiping the rain from his face when his father drove past him on the way to the house. Lew Angarrack didn't look at his son although his expression of distaste told Cadan his father had clocked the sight he presented, not to mention been given a reminder of why his progeny was on a bicycle in the rain and no longer behind the wheel of his car.

Up ahead of him, Cadan saw his father get out of the RAV4 and open the garage door. He reversed the Toyota into the garage and when Cadan wheeled his bicycle through the gate and into the back garden, Lew had already hosed off his surfboard. He was heaving his wetsuit out of the 4 x 4 to wash it off as well, while the hosepipe burbled fresh water onto the patch of lawn.

Cadan watched him for a moment. He knew that he looked like his father, but their similarities ended with the physical. They had the same stocky bodies, with broad chests and shoulders so they were built like wedges, and the same surfeit of dark hair, although his father was growing more and more of it over his body so that he was starting to look like what Cadan's sister privately called him, which was Gorilla Man. But that was it. As to the rest, they were chalk and cheese. His father's idea of a good time was making sure everything was perman-ently in its place with nothing changing one iota till the end of his days while Cadan's was . . . well, decidedly different. His father's world was

Casvelyn start to finish and if he ever made it to the north shore of Oahu – big dream, Dad, and you just keep dreaming – that would be the world's biggest all time miracle. Cadan, on the other hand, had miles to go before he slept and the end of those miles was going to be his name in lights, the X-games, gold medals, and his grinning mug on the cover of *Ride BMX*.

He said to his father, 'Onshore wind today. Why'd you head out?'

Lew didn't reply. He streamed the water over his wetsuit, flipped it over, and did the same to the other side. He washed out the boots, the hood, and the gloves before he looked at Cadan and then at the Mexican parrot on his shoulder.

'Best get that bird out of the rain.'

Cadan said, 'It won't hurt him. It rains where he comes from. You didn't get any waves, did you? Tide's just now coming in. Where'd you go?'

'Didn't need waves.' His father scooped the wetsuit from the lawn and hung it where he always hung it: over an aluminium lawn chair whose webbed seat caved in with the ghost weight of a thousand bums. 'I wanted to think. Don't need waves for thinking, do I?'

Then why go to the trouble of getting the kit ready and hauling it down to the sea? Cadan wanted to ask. But he didn't because if he asked the question, he'd get an answer and the answer would be what his father had been thinking of. There were three possibilities, but since one of them was Cadan himself and his list of transgressions, he decided to forego further conversation in this area. Instead, he followed his father into the house, where Lew dried his hair off with a limp towel left hanging for this purpose on the back of the door. Then he went to the kettle and switched it on. He'd have instant coffee, one sugar, no milk. He'd drink it in a mug that said *Newquay Invitational* on it. He'd stand at the window and look at the back garden and when he'd finished the coffee, he'd wash the mug. Mr Spontaneity himself.

Cadan waited till Lew had the coffee in hand and was at the window as usual. He used the time to establish Pooh in the sitting room at his regular perch. He returned to the kitchen himself to say, 'Got a job, then, Dad.'

His father drank. He made no sound. No slurp of hot liquid and no grunt of acknowledgement. When he finally spoke, it was to say, 'Where's your sister, Cade?'

Cadan refused to allow the question to deflate him. He said, 'Did you hear what I told you? I've got a job. A decent one.'

'And did you hear what I asked you? Where's Madlyn?'

'As it's a workday for her, I expect she's at work.'

'I stopped there. She's not.'

'Then I don't know where she is. Moping into her soup somewhere. Crying into her porridge. Whatever she might be doing instead of pulling herself together like anyone else would. You'd think the bloody world has ended.'

'Is she in her room?'

'I *told* you—'

'Where?' Lew still hadn't turned from the window, which was maddening to Cadan. It made him want to down six pints of lager right in front of the man, just to get his attention.

'I said I didn't know where—'

'Where's the job?' Lew pivoted, not just a turn of his head but of his whole body. He leaned against the window sill. He watched his son and Cadan knew he was being read, evaluated, and found wanting. It was an expression on his father's face he'd been looking at since he was six years old.

'Adventures Unlimited,' he said. 'I'm to do maintenance on the hotel till the season starts.'

'What happens then?'

'If things work out, I'll became an instructor.' This last bit was a stretch, but anything was possible, and they *were* in the process of interviewing instructors for the summer, weren't they? Abseiling, cliff climbing, sea kayaking, swimming, sailing . . . He could do all of that and even if they didn't want him in those activities, there was always freestyle BMX and his plans for altering the crazy golf course. He didn't mention this to his father, though. One word about the freestyle bicycle and Lew would read Ulterior Motive as if the words were tattooed on Cadan's forehead.

'"If things work out."' Lew blew a short breath through his nose, his version of a derisive snort, which said more than a dramatic monologue and all of it based upon the same subject. 'How're you intending to get there, then? On that thing outside?' By which he meant the bike. 'Because you won't be getting your car keys back from me, nor your driving licence. So don't start thinking a job'll make a difference.'

'I'm not asking for my keys back, am I?' Cadan said. 'I'm not asking for my licence. I'll walk. Or I'll ride the bike if I have to. I don't care what I look like. I rode it there today, didn't I?'

That breath again. Cadan wished his father would just *say* what he was thinking instead of always telegraphing it through facial expressions and not-so-subtle sounds. If Lew Angarrack just came out and declared You're a loser, lad, Cadan would at least have something to row with him about: failures as son set against a different sort of failure as father. But Lew always took the indirect route, and this was one that generally used the vehicle of silence, heavy breathing, and, at a pinch, outright comparisons of Cadan and his sister. She was the sainted Madlyn, of course, a world class surfer, headed for the top. Until recently, that is.

Cadan felt bad for his sister and what had happened to her, but a small, nasty part of him crowded in joy. For such a small girl, she'd been casting a large shadow for far too many years. He said, 'So that's it, then? No, "Good job of it, Cade," or "Congratulations," or even "Well, you've surprised me for once." I find a job – and it's going to pay good money, by the way – but that's sod all to you because . . . what? It's not good enough? It's got nothing to do with surfing? It's—'

'You had a job, Cade. You cocked it up.' Lew downed the rest of his coffee and took his mug to the sink. There, he scoured it out as he scoured out everything. No stains, no germs.

'That's bollocks,' Cadan said. 'Working for you was always a bad idea, and we *both* know that, even if you won't admit it. I'm not a detail person. I never was. I don't have the . . . I don't know . . . the patience or whatever.'

Lew dried the mug and the spoon. He put them both away. He wiped down the scratched, old stainless steel work top, although there wasn't a crumb upon it. 'Your trouble is you want everything to be fun. But life's not that way, and you don't want to see it.'

Cadan gestured outside, towards the back garden and the surfing kit that his father had just rinsed off. 'And that's *not* fun? You've spent all your free time for your entire life riding waves, but I'm supposed to see that as what? Some noble endeavour like curing AIDS? Putting an end to world poverty? You give me aggro about doing what *I* want to do, but haven't you done the very same? But wait. Don't answer. I already know. What you do's all about grooming a champion. Having a goal. While what I do—'

'There's nothing wrong with having a goal.'

'Right. Yes. And I have mine. It's just not the same as yours. Or Madlyn's. Or what Madlyn's *were*.'

'Where is she?' Lew asked.

'I *told* you . . .'

'I know what you told me. But you must have some idea where your own sister might have taken herself off to if she didn't go to work. You know her. And him. You know him as well, if it comes down to it.'

'Hey. Don't put that on me. She knew his reputation. *Everyone* knows it. But she wasn't having any words of wisdom from anyone. And anyway, what you *really* care about is not where she is at this exact moment but that she got derailed. Just like you.'

'She isn't derailed.'

'She bloody well is. And where does that leave you, Dad? You pinned your dreams on her instead of living your own.'

'She'll get back to it.'

'Don't put money on that.'

'And don't *you*—' Abruptly, Lew bit off whatever it was he'd intended to say.

They faced each other then across the width of the kitchen. It was an expanse of less than ten feet, but it was also a chasm that grew wider every year. Each of them stood at his respective edge, and it seemed to Cadan that the time would come when one of them was going to topple over the side.

Selevan Penrule took his time about getting over to Clean Barrel Surf Shop, having quickly decided it would be unseemly to bolt out of the Salthouse Inn the moment the whisper went round about Santo Kerne. He certainly had reason to bolt, but he knew it wouldn't look good. Apart from that, at his age he was beyond bolting anywhere. Too many years milking cows, not to mention herding the bloody bovines in and out of pastures, and his back was permanently bent and his hips were done for. Sixty-eight years old, he felt like eighty. He should have sold out and opened up the caravan park thirty-five years earlier, and he would have done so had he only had the cash, the bollocks, the vision, no wife, and no kids. They were all gone now, the house was torn down, and the farm was converted. Sea Dreams, he'd called it. Four neat rows of holiday caravans like shoe boxes perched on the cliffs above the sea.

In his car, he was careful. There were dogs occasionally on the country lanes. Cats, too. Rabbits. Birds. Selevan hated the thought of hitting something, not so much because of the guilt or responsibility he might feel having brought about a death but because of the inconvenience it would cause him. He'd have to stop and he hated to stop once he set out on a course of action. In this case, the course of action was getting himself over to Casvelyn and into the surf shop where his granddaughter worked. He wanted Tammy to hear the news from him.

When he reached the town, he parked on the wharf, the nose of his antique Land Rover pointing towards the Casvelyn Canal, a narrow cut that had once connected Holsworthy and Launceton with the sea but that now meandered inland for seven miles before ending abruptly like an interrupted thought. This put him across the River Cas from the centre of town where the surf shop was, but finding a spot for the car was always too much trouble over there, no matter the weather or the time of year, and, anyway, he wanted the walk. Tracing a path back along the crescent of road that defined the southwest edge of the town, he would have time to think. He had to have an approach that would play the information out and allow him to gauge her reaction to it. For what Tammy *said* she was and who Tammy *really* was were, as far as Selevan Penrule was concerned, in outright contradiction to each other. She just didn't know that yet.

He set off into the heart of town, going towards it along a string of shops. He stopped for a takeaway coffee at Jill's Juices and then again for a packet of Dunhills and a roll of breath mints at Pukkas Pizza Slices Et Cetera (the accent being on the *et cetera*, for their pizza was rubbish in a shoe), which was where the Crescent made its turn up into the Strand. Here the road created a slow climb to the top of the town, and Clean Barrel Surf Shop stood on a corner half the distance up, just along a route that offered a hair salon, a decrepit nightclub, two extremely down-at-heel hotels, and a fish and chip shop.

He finished his coffee before he got to the surf shop. There was no bin nearby, so he folded the takeaway cup and put it in the pocket of his rain jacket. Ahead of him, he could see a young man with Julius Caesar hair having an earnest conversation with Nigel Coyle, Clean Barrel's owner. This would be Will Mendick, Selevan thought. He'd had high hopes of Will, but so far they'd come to nothing.

Selevan heard Will saying to Nigel Coyle, 'I *admit* I was wrong, Mr Coyle. I shouldn't even have suggested it. But it's not like it's something I ever did before,' to which Coyle replied, 'You're not a very good liar, are you,' before walking off with his car keys jingling in his hand.

Will said darkly, 'Sod you, man.' And as Selevan came up to him, 'Hullo, Mr Penrule. Tammy's inside.'

Selevan found his granddaughter restocking a rack with colourful brochures. He observed her the way he always observed her, like a

species of mammal he'd never come upon before. Most of what he saw
he disapproved of: She was skin and bones in black: black shoes, black
tights, black skirt, black jersey. Hair too thin and cut too short and not
even a bit of that sticky goo in it to make it do something other than
lie lifelessly against her skull.

Selevan could have coped with the black and the skin and bones of
the girl if she'd given the slightest bit of evidence that she might be
normal. Ring her eyes with kohl and plant silver rings through her
eyebrows and her lips and a stud in her tongue, and he understood
that. Mind, he didn't *like* it, but he understood. That was the fashion
among certain people her age and they'd come to their senses, one
hoped, before they disfigured themselves entirely. When they hit twenty-
one or maybe twenty-five and they discovered that gainful employment
wasn't beating a path to their doorsteps, they'd sort themselves out.
Like Tammy's father. And what was he now? Lieutenant colonel in the
Army with a posting in Rhodesia or wherever because Selevan could
never keep track of him (and it would *always* be Rhodesia to Selevan,
never mind what it wanted to call itself) and a distinguished career
stretching out before him.

But as for Tammy? Can we send her to you, Dad? her father had
asked Selevan, his voice coming over the phone line as true as if he'd
been standing in the very next room and not in an African hotel where
he'd parked his daughter prior to flying her out to England. And what
was her granddad to do, then? She had her ticket. She was on her way.
We *can* send her to you, can't we, Dad? This isn't the right environment for her. She sees too much. We think that's the problem.

Selevan himself had his own ideas of what the problem was, but he
liked the idea of a son relying on his father's wisdom. Send her, Selevan
told David. But mind, I'll not have any of her nonsense if she's going
to stop with me. She'll eat her meals and clean up after herself and—

That, his son told him, would not be a problem.

True enough. The girl barely left a wake behind her. If Selevan had
thought she would cause him trouble, what he'd come to learn was that
the trouble she caused came from not causing trouble at all. *That* wasn't
normal, which was the heart of the matter. For damn it all, she was his
granddaughter. And *that* meant she was meant to be normal.

She tapped the final brochure into place and straightened the rack.
She stepped back as if to see its effect just as Will Mendick came into
the shop. He said to Tammy, 'No bloody good. Coyle won't take me
back,' and then to Selevan, 'You're early today, Mr Penrule.'

Tammy swung round at this. She said, 'Grandie. Didn't you get my message?'

'Haven't been home,' Selevan told her.

'Oh. I was . . . Will and I were meaning to have a coffee after closing.'

'Were you now?' Selevan was pleased. Perhaps, he thought, he'd been incorrect in his assessment of Tammy's regard for the younger man.

'He was going to drive me home afterwards.' Then she frowned as she seemed to realise it was too early for her grandfather to be there to fetch her home anyway. She looked at a watch that flopped round on her thin wrist.

'Come from the Salthouse Inn,' Selevan said. 'Been an accident out round Polcare Cove.'

'Are you all right?' she asked. 'Did you get in a smash with the car or something?' She sounded concerned, and this gratified Selevan. Tammy loved her old granddad. He might be short with her, but she never held it against him.

'Not me,' he said, and here he began to watch her closely. 'It was Santo Kerne.'

'Santo? What's happened to him?'

Was there a rise to her voice? Panic? A warding off of bad news? Selevan wanted to think so, but he couldn't reconcile the tone of her voice with the look that she exchanged with Will Mendick.

'Fell off the cliff, way I understand it,' he said. 'Down Polcare Cove. Ms Trahair brought some coast walker to the inn to phone the police. This bloke – the walker – he found the boy.'

'Is he all right?' Will Mendick asked even as Tammy said, 'Santo's all right, though, isn't he?'

Selevan was *definitely* gratified at this: the rush of Tammy's words and what that indicated about her feelings. No matter that Santo Kerne was about as worthless an object for a young girl's affections as could be found. If affection was present, that was a positive sign, and Selevan Penrule had recently allowed the Kerne boy access to his property at Sea Dreams for just this reason. Give him a shortcut across to the sea cliffs or the sea itself and who knew what might blossom in Tammy's heart? And that had been the objective, hadn't it? Tammy, blossoming, and a diversion.

'Don't know,' Selevan told her. 'Just that Ms Trahair came in and told Brian over Salthouse that Santo Kerne was down on the rocks 'n Polcare Cove. That's all I know.'

'That doesn't sound good,' Will Mendick said.

'Was he surfing, Grandie?' Tammy asked. But she didn't look at her grandfather when she spoke; she kept her eyes on Will.

This made Selevan look more closely at the young man. Will, he saw, was breathing oddly, a bit like a runner, but his face had lost colour. He was a ruddy boy naturally, so it was noticeable when the blood drained away.

'Don't know what he was doing, do I?' Selevan said. 'But something's happened to him, that's for certain. And it looks bad.'

'Why?' Will asked.

'Cos they'd've hardly left the boy on the rocks alone if he'd only been hurt and not . . .' He shrugged.

'Not dead?' Tammy said.

'Dead?' Will repeated.

Tammy said, '*Go*, Will.'

'But how can I—'

'You'll think of something. Just go. We'll have coffee another time.'

That was apparently all he needed. Will nodded at Selevan and headed for the door. He touched Tammy on the shoulder as he passed her. He said, 'Thanks, Tam. I'll ring you.'

Selevan tried to take this as a positive sign.

Daylight was fast fading by the time Detective Inspector Bea Hannaford arrived in Polcare Cove. She'd been in the midst of buying football boots for her son when her mobile had rung, and she'd completed the purchase without giving Pete a chance to point out that he'd not tried on every style available, as was his habit. She'd said, 'We buy now or you come back later with your father,' and that had been enough. His father would force him into the least expensive pair, brooking no arguments.

They'd left the shop in a hurry and dashed through the rain to the car. She'd rung Ray from the road. It wasn't his night for Pete, but Ray was flexible. He was a cop as well, and he knew the demands of the job. He'd meet them in Polcare Cove, he said. 'Got a jumper?' he'd asked her.

'Don't know yet,' she'd said.

Bodies at the base of cliffs were not rare in this part of the world. People climbed foolishly on the culm, people wandered too near the edge of cliffs and went over, or people jumped. If the tide was high, the bodies sometimes were never found. If it was low, the police had a chance to sort out how they had got there.

Pete was saying enthusiastically, 'I bet it's all bloody. I bet its head cracked open like a rotten egg and its guts 'n' brains're all over the place.'

'Peter.' Bea cast him a glance. He was slouched against the door, the shopping bag containing his boots clutched to his chest as if he thought someone might rip it from him. He had spots on his face – the curse of the young adolescent, Bea remembered, although her own adolescence was forty years long gone – and braces on his teeth. Looking at him at fourteen years old, she found it impossible to imagine the man he might one day become.

'What?' he demanded. 'You *said* someone went over the cliff. I bet he went headfirst and splattered his skull. I bet he took a dive. I bet he—'

'You wouldn't talk that way if you'd ever seen someone who's fallen.'

'Wicked,' Pete breathed.

He was doing it deliberately, Bea thought, trying to provoke a row. He was angry that he had to go to his father's and angrier still about the disruption to their plans, which had been the rare treat of takeaway pizza and a DVD. He'd chosen a film about football, which his father would not be interested in watching with him, unlike his mother. Bea and Pete were as one when it came to football.

She decided to let his anger go unconfronted. There wasn't time to deal with it and, anyway, he had to learn to cope when plans got changed because no plan was ever written in concrete.

The rain was coming down in sheets when they finally reached the vicinity of Polcare Cove. This wasn't a place Bea Hannaford had been to before, so she peered through the windscreen and crawled along the lane. This descended through a woodland in a series of switchbacks before shooting out from beneath the budding trees, climbing up once again into farmland defined by thick earthen hedgerows, and descending a final time towards the sea. Here, the land opened to form a meadow at the northwest edge of which stood a mustard-coloured cottage with two nearby outbuildings, the only habitation in this place.

A panda car jutted partially into the lane from the cottage drive with another police vehicle sitting directly in front of it, nudging against a white Vauxhall near the cottage, itself. Bea didn't stop since to do so would have blocked the road entirely, and she knew there would be many more vehicles arriving and needing access to the beach long before the day was done. She went farther along towards the sea and found what went for a car park: a patch of earth that was pot-holed like a piece of Swiss cheese. There she stopped.

Pete reached for the handle of his door. She said, 'Wait here.'

'But I want to see—'

'Pete, you heard me. Wait here. Your father's on his way. If he shows up and you're not in the car . . . Do I need to say more?'

Pete threw himself back against the seat, looking sulky. 'It wouldn't hurt if I looked. And it's *not* my night to stay at Dad's anyway.'

Ah. He knew how to choose his moment, so like his father. She said, 'Flexibility, Pete. As you well know, it's the key to every game, including the game of life. Now wait here.'

'But, Mum . . .'

She pulled him towards her. She kissed him roughly against the side of the head. '*Wait,*' she told him.

A knock on her window drew her attention. A constable stood there in rain gear, his eyelashes spiked by water, a torch in his hand. She got out into the gusting wind and the rain, zipped her jacket, pulled up her hood, and said, 'DI Hannaford. What've we got?'

'Kid. Dead.'

'Jumper?'

'No. There's rope attached to the body. I expect he fell during an abseil down the cliff. He's got a belay device still on the rope.'

'Who's up at that cottage? There's another panda car.'

'Duty sergeant from Casvelyn. He's with the two who found the body.'

'Show me what we've got. Who are you, by the way?'

He introduced himself as Mick McNulty, constable from the Casvelyn station. There were only two of them manning the place: himself and a sergeant. It was a typical set-up for the countryside.

McNulty led the way. The body lay some thirty yards from the breaking waves, but a good distance from the cliff itself from which it must have fallen. The constable had had the presence of mind to cover the corpse with a sheet of bright blue plastic, and he'd been prescient enough to arrange it so that – with the aid of rocks – the sheet didn't touch the body.

Bea nodded and McNulty lifted the sheet to expose the corpse while protecting it from the rain. The plastic crackled and snapped like a blue sail in the wind. Bea squatted, raised her hand for the torch, and shone its light onto the young man, who lay on his back. He was blond, with sun-streaked hair that curled cherubically round his face. His eyes were blue and sightless, and his flesh was excoriated from hitting against the rocks as he fell. He was bruised as well – an eye was blackened – but this looked like an older injury. The colour had yellowed as the skin healed. He was dressed for climbing: He still had his step-in harness fastened round his waist with at least two dozen metal bits and bobs hanging from it, and a rope was coiled on his chest. This remained knotted to a carabiner. But what the carabiner had been attached to, that was the question.

'Who is this?' Bea asked. 'Do we have an i.d.?'

'Nothing on him.'

She looked towards the cliff. 'Who moved the body?'

'Me and the bloke who found it.' He went on quickly lest she reprimand him, 'It was that or drag it, guv. I couldn't've moved it on my own.'

'We'll want your clothes, then. His as well. He's up at the cottage, you say?'

'My clothes?'

'What did you expect, Constable?' She pulled out her mobile and flipped it open. She looked at the screen and sighed. No signal.

Constable McNulty, at least, wore a radio on his shoulder, and she told him to make the arrangement for a Home Office pathologist to get down here as soon as possible. This, she knew, wasn't going to be soon at all as the pathologist would have to come from Exeter. And that would be only if he or she was actually *in* Exeter and not involved in something somewhere else. It was going to be a long evening and a longer night.

While McNulty radioed as ordered, she gazed once more at the body. He was a teenager. He was very good looking. He was fit, muscular. He was kitted out to climb, but like so many climbers his age, he wore no headgear. That might have saved him, but it might have been superfluous. Only a postmortem would be able to tell.

Her gaze went from the body to the cliff from which the young man had fallen. She could see that the coastal path – a walking trail in Cornwall that began in Marsland Mouth and ended in Cremyll – marked a twisting passage up from the car park to the top of this rise, just as it did along much of the Cornish coast. The sea cliff climber who lay at her feet had to have left something up there. His identification, one hoped. A car, a motorcycle, a bike. They were out in the middle of nowhere, and it was impossible to believe he'd come here on foot. They'd know who he was soon enough. But one of them was going to have to go up there to see.

She said to Constable McNulty, 'You'll need to climb up and see what he's left on the cliff top. Have a care, though. That path's going to be murder in the rain.'

They exchanged looks at her choice of words: *murder*. It was too early to tell. But they would know eventually.

3

Since Daidre Trahair lived by herself, she was used to silence, and because at work she was most often surrounded by noise, when she had the opportunity to exist for a while where the only sound was that which was ambient, she experienced no anxiety even when she found herself in a group of people with nothing to say to one another. In the evenings, she rarely turned on a radio or the television. When the phone rang at her Bristol home, she often didn't bother to answer it. So the fact that at least an hour had passed in which not a word had been spoken by either of her companions did not trouble her.

She sat near the fire with a book of Gertrude Jekyll's garden plans. She marvelled at them. The plans themselves were done in watercolours, and where there were gardens available to photograph, those accompanied the plans. The woman had understood much about form, colour, and design, and as such, was Daidre's goddess. The Idea – and Daidre always thought of it in upper case – was to turn the area round Polcare Cottage into a garden that Gertrude Jekyll might have fashioned. This would be a challenge because of the wind and the weather and it might all come down to succulents in the end, but Daidre wanted to have a go. She had no garden at her home in Bristol, and she loved gardens. She loved the work of them: hands in the soil and something growing as a result. Gardening was to be her outlet. Staying busy at work wasn't enough.

She looked up from her book and considered the two men in the sitting room with her. The policeman from Casvelyn had introduced himself as Sergeant Paddy Collins, and he had a Belfast accent to prove the name was genuine. He was sitting upright in a straight-back chair that he'd brought from the kitchen table, as if to take one of the armchairs in the sitting room would have indicated a dereliction of duty. He still had a notebook open on his knee and he was regarding the other man as he'd regarded him from the first: with undisguised suspicion.

Who could blame him? Daidre thought. The hiker was a questionable character. Aside from his appearance and his odour, which in and of themselves might not have raised doubts in the mind of a policeman querying his presence in this part of the world since the South-West Coast Path was a well-used trail at least in fair weather months, there was the not small detail of his voice. He was obviously well educated and probably well bred, and Paddy Collins had done more than raise an eyebrow when the man had told him he had no identification with him.

'What d'you mean, you've no identification? You got no driving licence, man? No bank cards? Nothing?'

'Nothing,' Thomas said. 'I'm terribly sorry.'

'So you could be bloody anyone, that it?'

'I suppose I could be.' Thomas sounded as if he wished that were the case.

'And I'm meant to believe whatever you say about yourself?' Collins asked him.

Thomas appeared to take the question as rhetorical. But he hadn't seemed bothered by the threat implied in the sergeant's tone. He'd merely gone to the small window and gazed out towards the beach although it couldn't actually be seen from the cottage. There he'd remained, motionless and looking as if he were barely breathing.

Daidre wanted to ask him what his injuries were. When she'd first come upon him in her cottage, it hadn't been blood on his face or his clothes nor had it been anything obvious about his body that had prompted her to offer him her aid as a doctor. It had been the expression in his eyes. He was in inconceivable agony: an internal injury but not a physical one. She could see that now. She knew the signs.

When Sergeant Collins stirred, rose, and made for the kitchen – probably for a cuppa as Daidre had shown him where her supplies were kept – Daidre took the opportunity to speak to the hiker. She said, 'Why were you walking along the coast alone and without iden-tification, Thomas?'

Thomas didn't turn from the window. He made no reply although his head moved marginally, which suggested that he was listening.

She said, 'What if something had happened to you? People fall from these cliffs. They put a foot wrong, they slip, they—'

'Yes,' he said. 'I've seen the memorials, all along the way.'

They were up and down the coast, these memorials: sometimes as ephemeral as a bunch of dying flowers laid at the site of a fatal fall, sometimes a bench carved with a suitable phrase, sometimes something as lasting and permanent as a marker akin to a tombstone with the deceased's name engraved upon it. Each was something to note the eternal passage of surfers, climbers, walkers, and suicides. It was impossible to be out hiking along the coastal path and not to come upon them.

'There was an elaborate one that I saw,' Thomas said, as if this were the one subject above all that she wished to discuss with him. 'A table and a bench, this was, both done in granite. Granite's what you want if standing the test of time is important, by the way.'

'You haven't answered me,' she pointed out.

'I rather thought I just had.'

'If you'd fallen—'

'I still might fall,' he said. 'When I walk on. When this is over.'

'Wouldn't you want your people to know? You have people, I dare say.' She didn't add 'Your sort usually do,' but the remark was implied.

He didn't respond. The kettle clicked off in the kitchen with a loud snap. The sound of pouring water came to them. She'd been correct: a cuppa for the sergeant.

She said, 'What about your wife, Thomas?'

He remained completely motionless. 'My wife.'

'You're wearing a wedding ring, so I presume you have a wife. I presume she'd want to know if something happened to you. Wouldn't she?'

Collins came out of the kitchen then. But Daidre had the impression that the other man wouldn't have responded, even had the sergeant not returned.

Collins said with a gesture of his teacup that sloshed liquid into its saucer, 'Hope you don't mind.'

Daidre said, 'No. It's fine.'

From the window Thomas said, 'Here's the detective.' He sounded indifferent to the reprieve.

Collins went to the door. From the sitting room, Daidre heard him exchange a few words with a woman. She was, when she came into the room, an utterly unlikely sort.

Daidre had only ever seen detectives on the television on the rare occasions when she watched one of the police dramas that littered the airwaves. They were always coolly professional and dressed in a tediously similar manner that was supposed to reflect either their psyches or their personal lives. The women were compulsively perfect, tailored to within an inch of their lives and not a hair out of place, and the men were dishevelled. One group had to make it in a man's world. The other had to find a good woman to act the role of saviour.

This woman, who introduced herself as DI Beatrice Hannaford, didn't fit that mould. She wore an anorak, muddy trainers, and jeans, and her hair – a red so flaming that it very nearly preceded her into the room and shouted 'Dyed and what do you have to say about it?' – stood up in spikes that were second cousins to a mohawk, despite the rain. She saw Daidre examining her and she said, 'As soon as someone refers to you as *gran*, you rethink the whole growing old gracefully thing.'

Daidre nodded thoughtfully. There was sense to this. 'And are you a gran?'

'I am.' The detective made her next remark to Collins. 'Get outside and let me know when the pathologist gets here. Keep everyone else away, not that anyone's likely to show up in this weather, but you never know. I take it the word's gone out?' This last she said to Daidre as Collins left them.

'We phoned from the inn, so they'll know up there.'

'And everywhere else no doubt, by now. You know the dead boy?'

Daidre had considered the possibility that she might be asked this question again. She decided to base her answer on her personal definition of the word *know*. 'I don't,' she said. 'I don't actually live here, you see. The cottage is mine, but it's my getaway. I live in Bristol. I come here for a break when I have time off.'

'What d'you do in Bristol?'

'I'm a doctor. Well, not actually a doctor. I mean, I *am* a doctor, but it's . . . I'm a veterinarian.' Daidre felt Thomas's eyes on her, and she grew hot. This had nothing to do with shame about being a vet, a fact about which she was inordinately proud, considering how difficult it had been to reach that goal. Rather, it was the fact that she'd led him to believe she was another sort of doctor when she'd first come upon him. She wasn't quite sure why she had done it although to tell someone she could help him with his supposed injuries because she was a vet had seemed ludicrous at the time. 'I do larger animals mostly.'

DI Hannaford had drawn her eyebrows together. She looked from Daidre to Thomas, and she seemed to be testing the waters between them. Or perhaps she was testing Daidre's answer for its level of veracity. She looked like someone who was good at that, despite her incongruous hair.

Thomas said, 'There was a surfer. I couldn't tell if it was male or female. I saw him – I'll call him *him* – from the cliff top.'

'What? Off Polcare Cove?'

'In the cove before Polcare. Although he could have come from here, I suppose.'

'There was no car, though,' Daidre pointed out. 'Not in the car park. So he had to have gone into the water at Buck's Haven. That's the cove to the south. Unless you meant the north cove. I've not asked you what direction you were walking in.'

'From the south,' he said. And to Hannaford, 'The weather didn't seem right to me. For surfing. The tide was wrong as well. The reefs weren't covered completely. If a surfer came to close to them . . . Someone could get hurt.'

'Someone did get hurt,' Hannaford pointed out. 'Someone got killed.'

'But not surfing,' Daidre said. Then she wondered why she'd said it because it sounded to her as if she were interceding for Thomas when that hadn't been her intention.

Hannaford said to both of them, 'Like to play detectives, do you? Is it a hobby of yours?' She didn't seem to expect a response to this. She went on to Thomas, saying, 'Constable McNulty tells me you helped him move the body. I'll want your clothes for forensics. Your outer clothes. Whatever you had on at the time, which I presume is what you have on now.' And to Daidre, 'Did you touch the body?'

'I checked for a pulse.'

'Then I'll want your outer clothing as well.'

'I've nothing to change into, I'm afraid,' Thomas said.

'Nothing?' Again, Hannaford looked from the man to Daidre. It came to Daidre that the detective had assumed that she and the stranger were a couple. She supposed there was some logic in this. They'd gone for help together. They were together still. And neither of them had said anything to dissuade her from this conclusion. Hannaford said, 'Exactly who might you two be and what brings you to this corner of the world?'

Daidre said, 'We've given our details to the sergeant.'

'Humour me.'

'I've told you. I'm a veterinarian.'

'Your practice?'

'At the zoo in Bristol. I've just come down this afternoon for a few days. Well, for a week this time.'

'Odd time of year for a holiday.'

'For some, I suppose. But I prefer my holidays when there are no crowds.'

'What time did you leave Bristol?'

'I don't know. I didn't actually look. It was morning. Perhaps nine. Ten. Half past.'

'Stop along the way?'

Daidre tried to work out how much the detective needed to know. She said, 'Well . . . briefly, yes. But it hardly has to do with—'

'Where?'

'What?'

'Where did you stop?'

'For lunch. I'd had no breakfast. I don't, usually. Eat breakfast, that is. I was hungry so I stopped.'

'Where?'

'There was a pub. It's not a place I usually stop, but there was a pub and I was hungry and it said "pub meals" out front, so I went in. This would be after I left the M5. I can't remember its name. The pub's. I'm sorry. It was somewhere outside of Crediton. I think.'

'You think. Interesting. What did you eat?'

'A ploughman's.'

'What sort of cheese?'

'I don't know. I didn't pay attention. It was a ploughman's. Cheese, bread, pickle, onion. I'm a vegetarian.'

'Of course you are.'

Daidre felt her temper flare. She hadn't *done* anything, but the detective was making her feel as if she had. She said with some attempt at dignity, 'I find that it's rather difficult to care for animals on the one hand and eat them on the other, Inspector.'

'Of course you do,' DI Hannaford said thinly. 'Do you know the dead boy?'

'I believe I already answered that question.'

'I seem to have lost the plot on that one. Tell me again.'

'I didn't get a good look at him, I'm afraid.'

'And I'm afraid that isn't what I asked you.'

'I'm not from around here. As I said, this is a getaway place for me. I come on the occasional weekend. Bank holidays. Longer holidays. I know a few people but mostly those who live close by.'

'This boy doesn't live close by?'

'I don't *know* him.' Daidre could feel the perspiration on her neck and she wondered if it was on her face as well. She wasn't used to speaking to the police, and speaking to the police under these circumstances was especially unnerving.

A sharp double knock sounded on the front door, then. But before anyone made a move to answer it, they heard it open. Two male voices – one of them Sergeant Collins – came from the entry, just ahead of the men themselves. Daidre was expecting the other to be the pathologist who Inspector Hannaford had indicated was on the way, but this was apparently not the case. Instead, the newcomer – tall, grey haired, and attractive – nodded to them and said to Hannaford, 'Where've you got him stowed, then?' to which she answered, 'He's not in the car?'

The man shook his head. 'As it happens, no.'

Hannaford said, 'That bloody child. I swear. Thanks for coming at such short notice, Ray.' Then she spoke to Daidre and Thomas. To Daidre she repeated, 'I'll want your clothes, Ms Trahair. Sergeant Collins will bag them, so sort yourself out about that.' And to Thomas, 'When SOCO arrives, we'll get you a boiler suit to change into. In the meantime, Mr . . . I don't know your name.'

'Thomas,' he said.

'Mr Thomas, is it? Or is Thomas your Christian name?'

He hesitated. Daidre thought for a moment that he meant to lie because that was what it looked like. And he could lie, couldn't he, since he had no identification with him. He could say he was absolutely anyone. He looked at the coal fire as if meditating on all the possibilities. Then he looked back at the detective. 'Lynley,' he said. 'It's Thomas Lynley.'

There was a silence. Daidre looked from Thomas to the detective, and she saw the expression alter on Hannaford's face. The face of the man she'd called Ray altered as well, and oddly enough, he was the one to speak. What he said was completely baffling to Daidre:

'New Scotland Yard?'

Thomas Lynley hesitated once again. Then he swallowed. 'Until recently,' he said. 'Yes. New Scotland Yard.'

'Of *course* I know who he is,' Bea Hannaford said tersely to her former husband. 'I don't live under a stone.' It was just like Ray to make the pronouncement as if from on high. Impressed with himself, he was. Devon and Cornwall Constabulary. Middlemore. Mr Assistant Chief Constable. A pencil pusher, really, as far as Bea was concerned. Never had a promotion affected anyone's demeanour so maddeningly. 'The only question is what the hell is he doing *here*, of all places?' she went on. 'Collins tells me he isn't even carrying identification with him. So he could be anyone, couldn't he?'

'Could be. But he isn't.'

'How d'you know? Have you met him?'

'I don't need to have met him.'

Another indication of self-satisfaction. Had he always been like this and had she never seen it? Had she been so blinded by love or whatever it had been that had propelled her into marriage with this man? She hadn't been ageing and Ray her only chance at having a home and family. She'd been twenty-two. And they had been happy, hadn't they? Until Pete, they'd had their lives in order: one child only – a daughter – and that had been something of a disappointment but Ginny had given them a grandchild soon enough into her own marriage and she was at this moment on her way to giving them more. Retirement had been beckoning them from the future and all the things they planned to do with retirement had been beckoning as well. And then there was Pete, a complete surprise. Pleasant to her, unpleasant to Ray. The rest was history.

'Actually,' Ray said in that way he had of outing himself, which had always made her forgive him in the end for his worst displays of self-importance, 'I saw in the paper that he comes from round here. His family are in Cornwall. The Penzance area.'

'So he's come home.'

'Hmm. Yes. Well, after what happened, who can blame him for wanting to be done with London?'

'Bit far from Penzance, here, though.'

'Perhaps home and family didn't give him what he needed. Poor sod.'

Bea glanced at Ray. They were walking from the cottage to the car park, skirting past his Porsche, which he'd left – foolishly, she thought, but what did it matter since she wasn't responsible for the vehicle – half on and half off the lane. His voice was moody and his face was moody. She could see that in the dying light of the day.

'It touched you, all that, didn't it?' she said.

'I'm not made of stone, Beatrice.'

He wasn't, at that. The problem for her was that his all too compelling humanity made hating him an impossibility. And she would have vastly preferred to hate Ray Hannaford. Understanding him was far too painful.

'Ah,' Ray said. 'I think we've located our missing child.' He indicated the cliff rising ahead of them to their right, beyond the Polcare Cove car park. The coastal path climbed in a narrow stripe sliced into the rising land, and descending from the top of the cliff were two figures. The one in front was lighting the way through the rain and the gloom with a torch. Behind him a smaller figure picked out a route among the rain-slicked stones that jutted from the ground where the path had been inadequately cleared.

'That bloody child,' Bea said. 'He's going to be the death of me.' She shouted, 'Get the hell down from there, Peter Hannaford. I *told* you to stay in the car and I damn well meant it and you bloody well know it. And you, Constable. What're the *hell* are you doing, letting a child—'

'They can't hear you, love,' Ray said. 'Let me.' He bellowed Pete's name. He gave an order only a fool would have failed to obey. Pete scurried down the remainder of the path and had his excuse ready by the time he joined them.

'I didn't go near the body,' he said. 'You said I wasn't meant to go near and I didn't. Mick c'n tell you that. All I did was go up the path with him. He was—'

'Stop splitting hairs with your mother,' Ray told him.

Bea said, 'You know how I feel when you do that, Pete. Now say hello to your father and get out of here before I wallop you.'

'Hullo,' Pete said. He stuck out his hand for a shake. Ray accommodated him. Bea looked away. She wouldn't have allowed a handshake. She would have grabbed the boy and kissed him.

Mick McNulty came up behind them. 'Sorry, guv,' he said. 'I didn't know—'

'No harm done.' Ray put his hands on Pete's shoulders and firmly turned him in the direction of the Porsche. 'I thought we'd do Thai food,' he said to his son.

Pete hated Thai food, but Bea left them to sort that out for themselves. She shot Pete a look that he could not fail to read: *Not here*, it said. He made a face.

Ray kissed Bea on the cheek and said, 'Take care of yourself.'

She said, 'Mind how you go, then. Roads're slippery.' And then because she couldn't help herself, 'I didn't say before. You're looking well, Ray.'

He replied, 'Lot of good it's doing me,' and walked off with their son. Pete stopped at Bea's car. He brought forth his football boots. Bea didn't call out to tell him to let them be.

Instead she said to Constable McNulty, 'So. What've we got?'

McNulty gestured towards the top of the cliff. 'Rucksack up there for SOCO to bag. I expect it's the kid's.'

'Anything else?'

'Evidence of how the poor sod went down. I left it for SOCO as well.'

'What is it?'

'There's a stile up top, some ten feet or so back from the edge of the cliff. Marks the far west end of a cow pasture up there. He'd put a sling round it, which was supposed to be what his carabiner and rope were fixed to for the abseil down the cliff.'

'What sort of sling?'

'Made of nylon webbing. Looks like fishing net if you don't know what you're looking at. It's supposed to be a long loop. You drape it round a fixed object and each end is fastened with the carabiner, making the loop into a circle. You attach your rope to the carabiner and off you go.'

'Sounds straightforward.'

'Should have been. But the sling's been taped together, presumably over a weak spot to strengthen it, and that's exactly where it's failed.' McNulty gazed back the way he'd come. 'Bloody idiot. I can't think why anyone'd just not get himself another sling.'

'What kind of tape was used for the repair?'

McNulty looked surprised by the question. 'Electrical tape, this was.'

'Kept your digits off it?'

'Course.'

'And the rucksack?'

'It was canvas.'

'I reckoned as much,' Bea said patiently. 'Where was it? Why do you presume it was his? Did you have a look inside?'

'Next to the stile, so I reckon it was his all right. He probably carried his kit in it. Nothing in it now but a set of keys.'

'Car?'

'I reckon.'

'Did you have a look for it?'

'Thought it best to report back to you.'

'Think again Constable. Get back up there and find me the car.'

He looked towards the cliff. His expression told her how little he wanted to make a second climb up there in the rain. Well, that couldn't be helped. 'Up you go,' she told him pleasantly. 'The exercise will do you a world of good.'

'Thought p'rhaps I ought to go by way of the road. It's a few miles, but—'

'Up you go,' she repeated. 'Keep an eye out along the trail as well. There may be footprints not already destroyed by the rain.' Or by you, she thought.

McNulty did not look happy, but he said, 'Will do, guv,' and set off back the way he'd come with Pete.

Kerra Kerne was exhausted and soaked to the skin because she'd broken her primary rule: Head into the wind on the first half of the ride; have the wind at your back on your route home. But she'd been in a hurry to be gone from Casvelyn, so for the first time in longer than she could remember, she hadn't checked the internet before donning her cycling kit and pedalling out of town. She'd just set off in her Lycra and her helmet. She'd clicked into the pedals and pumped so furiously that she was ten miles out of Casvelyn before she actually clocked her location. Then it was the location alone that she took into consideration and not the wind, which had been her error. She'd just kept riding vaguely east. When the weather rolled in, she was too far away to do anything to escape it other than seek shelter, which she did not want to do. Hence, muscle weary and wet to the bone, she struggled with the last of the thirty-five miles she needed to cover on her return.

She blamed Alan, blind and foolish Alan Cheston, who was supposed to be her life partner with all that being a life partner implied but who'd decided to go his own bloody-minded way in the one situation that she couldn't countenance. *And* she blamed her father who was also blind and foolish – as well as stupid – but in a completely different manner and for a completely different set of reasons.

At least ten months earlier, she'd said to Alan, 'Please don't do this. It won't work out. It'll be—'

And he'd cut into her words, which he rarely did, which should have told her something about him that she hadn't yet learned, but which did not. 'Why won't it work out? We won't even see each other much, if that's what worries you.'

It wasn't what worried her. She knew what he was saying was true. He'd be doing whatever one did in the marketing department – which was less a department and more an old conference room located behind what used to be the reception desk in the mouldy hotel – and she'd be doing her thing with the trainee instructors. He'd be sorting out the chaos that her mother had wrought as the nominal director of the non-existent marketing department while she, Kerra, tried to hire suitable employees. They might see each other at morning coffee or at lunch, but they might well not. So rubbing elbows with him at work and then rubbing other body parts later in the day was not what concerned her.

He'd said, 'Don't you see, Kerra, that I've got to get some solid employment in Casvelyn? And this is it. Jobs aren't dangling from trees round here, and it was decent of your dad to offer it to me. I'm not about to look a gift horse.'

Her father was hardly a gift horse, Kerra thought, and decency had nothing to do with why he'd offered the marketing job to Alan. He'd made the offer because they needed someone to promote Adventures Unlimited to the masses but they also needed a certain *kind* of someone to do that marketing, and Alan Cheston appeared to be the kind of someone Kerra's father had been looking for.

Her father was deciding based on appearance. To him, Alan was a type. Or perhaps better said, Alan was *not* a type. Her father thought the type to be avoided at Adventures Unlimited was a manly sort: grit under the fingernails, throw a woman across the bed, and have her till she saw stars. What he didn't understand, and had never understood, was that there actually *was* no type. There was just maleness. And despite the rounding of his shoulders, the spectacles, the bobbing Adam's apple, the delicate hands with those long probing spatulate fingers, Alan Cheston was male. He thought like a male, he acted like a male, and most important, he *re*acted like a male. That was why Kerra had put her foot down, which had ultimately done no good because she wouldn't say more than, 'It won't work out.' That proving useless, she'd done the only thing she could do in the situation, which was to tell him they'd likely have to end their relationship. To this, he'd calmly replied without the slightest tinge of panic to his words, 'So that's what you do when you don't get what you want? You just cut people off?'

'Yes,' she'd declared, 'that's what I do. And it's not when I don't get what I want. It's when they won't listen to what I'm saying for their own good.'

'How can it be for my own good not to take the job? It's money. It's a future. Isn't that what you want?'

'Apparently not,' she'd told him.

Still, she hadn't *quite* been able to make good on her threat because in part she couldn't imagine what it would be like to have to work with Alan daily but not see him nightly. She was weak in this and she despised her weakness, especially when she'd chosen him primarily because *he'd* seemed like the weak one: considerate, which she'd taken for malleable, and gentle, which she'd taken for diffident. That he'd proved himself exactly the opposite since coming to work at Adventures Unlimited scared the hell out of her.

One way to terminate her fear was to confront it, which meant confronting Alan himself. But really, how could she? So at first she'd fumed, and then she'd waited, watched, and listened. The inevitable was just that – inevitable – and since it had always been that way, she spent the time attempting to harden herself, becoming remote within while playing the part of certain without.

She'd carried the act off until today when his announcement of 'I'll be gone a few hours down the coast' set the alarm off in her brain. At that point her only choice was to ride fast and far, to exhaust herself beyond thinking so that she exhausted herself beyond caring as well. Thus, despite her other responsibilities that day, she'd gone on her way: along St Mevan Crescent and over to Burn View, down the slope of Lansdown Road and the Strand, and from there out of town.

She'd kept riding eastward, long after she should have turned back for home. For this reason, darkness had fallen by the time she'd geared down to make the final climb up the Strand. Shops were closed; restaurants were open although meagerly peopled at this time of year. A dispirited line of bunting crisscrossed the street, dripping water, and the lone traffic light at the crest of the hill cast a streak of red in her direction. No one was out on the soaked pavement, but in another two months that would all change when summer visitors filled Casvelyn to take advantage of its two broad beaches, of its surf, of its sea pool, of its fun fair, and, one hoped, of the experiences offered by Adventures Unlimited.

This holiday business was her father's dream: taking the abandoned hotel – a 1933 derelict structure sitting on a promontory above St Mevan Beach – and turning it into an activities-oriented destination. It was an enormous risk for the Kernes, and if it didn't work out, they'd be destitute. But her father was a man who'd taken risks in the past and had seen them bear fruit because the one thing he wasn't afraid of in life was hard work. As to other things in her father's life . . . Kerra had spent too many years asking why and receiving no answers.

At the top of the hill, she turned into St Mevan Crescent. From there, along a line of old B & B's, older hotels, a Chinese takeaway, and a newsagent's shop, she reached the drive to what had once been the Promontory King George Hotel and what was now Adventures Unlimited. The old hotel stood, barely illuminated, with scaffolding fronting it. Lights were on in the ground floor, but not at the top where the family quarters were.

In front of the entry a police car was parked. Kerra drew her eyebrows together when she saw it. At once she thought of Alan. She didn't consider her brother at all.

Ben Kerne's office at Adventures Unlimited was on the first floor of the old hotel. He'd fashioned it out of a single room that had once undoubtedly been used by a lady's maid since directly next door to it – and formerly with an adjoining door – was a suite. That, he'd had converted to a unit suitable for one of the holidaying families upon whom he'd bet his economic future.

The time had seemed right to Ben for this, his biggest venture ever. His children were older and at least one of them – Kerra – was self-sufficient and completely capable of obtaining gainful employment elsewhere should this venture go under. Santo was a different matter for more than one reason that Ben preferred not to consider, but he had become more dependable of late, thank God, as if he finally understood the weighty nature of their undertaking. So Ben had felt the family was with him. It wouldn't be just himself upon whose shoulders the responsibility rested. They were fully two years into it now: the conversion complete save for the exterior painting and a few final interior details. By the middle of June, they would be up and running. The bookings had been coming in for several months.

Ben was looking through these when the police arrived. Although the bookings represented the fruits of his family's labours, he hadn't been thinking of the bookings. Instead he'd been thinking of red. Not red as being in the red, which he certainly was and would be for any number of years until the business earned back what he'd spent upon it, but red as the colour of nail varnish or lipstick, of a scarf or a blouse, of a dress that hugged the body.

Dellen had been wearing red for five days. First had come the nail varnish. Lipstick had followed. Then a jaunty beret over her blonde hair when she went out. Soon, he expected a red sweater would top snug black trousers as it also revealed just a bit of cleavage. Ultimately, she would wear the dress, which would show more cleavage as well as her thighs, and by that time, she'd be in full sail and his children would be looking at him as they had looked at him forever: waiting for him to do something in a situation in which he could do nothing at all.

Despite their ages – eighteen and twenty-two – Santo and Kerra persisted in thinking that he was capable of changing their mother. When he did not do so, having failed at the effort when he was even younger than they were now, he saw the *why* in their eyes, or at least in Kerra's eyes. Why do you put up with her?

When Ben heard the slam of a car door, then, he thought of Dellen. When he went to the window and saw it was a police car below and not his wife's old BMW, he still thought of Dellen. Later, he realised that thinking of Kerra would have been more logical since she'd been gone for hours on her bicycle in weather that had been growing ever worse since two o'clock. But Dellen had been the centre of his thoughts for twenty-eight years and since Dellen had gone off at noon and had not yet returned, he assumed she'd got herself into trouble.

He left his office and went to the ground floor. When he got to reception, a uniformed constable was standing there. The constable was male, young, and vaguely familiar. He'd be from the town, then. Ben was getting to know who lived in Casvelyn and who was from the outlying area.

The constable introduced himself: Mick McNulty, he said. And you are, sir?

Benesek Kerne, Ben told him. Was something wrong? Ben switched on more lights. The automatic ones had come on with the end of daylight, but they cast shadows everywhere, and Ben found he wanted to dispel those shadows.

Ah, McNulty said. Could he speak to Mr Kerne, then?

Ben realised the constable meant could they go somewhere that was not the reception area, so he took him one floor above to the lounge. This overlooked St Mevan Beach, where the swells were of a decent size and the waves were breaking on the sand bars in rapid sets. They were coming in from the southwest, but the wind made them rubbish. No one was out there, not even the most desperate of the local surfers.

Between the beach and the hotel, the landscape was much changed from what it had been during the heyday of the Promontory King George. The pool was still there, but in place of the bar and the outdoor restaurant, a rock climbing wall now stood. As did the rope wall, the swinging bridges, and the pulleys, gears, cords, and cables of the Canopy Experience. A neat cabin housed the sea kayaks and another contained the diving equipment. Constable McNulty took all of this in, or at least he appeared to be doing so, which gave Ben Kerne time to prepare himself to hear what the policeman had come to say. He thought about

Dellen in bits of red, about the slippery roads and Dellen's intentions, which likely had been to get out of town entirely, to go along the coast, and perhaps to end up at one of the coves or bays. But getting there in this weather, especially if she hadn't stuck to the main road, would have exposed her to danger. Of course danger was what she loved and wanted, but not the sort that led to cars skidding off roads and down the side of cliffs.

When the question came, it was not what Ben expected. McNulty said, 'Is Alexander Kerne your son?'

Ben said 'Santo?' and he thought, Thank God. It was *Santo* who had got himself into trouble, no doubt arrested for trespassing, which Ben had warned him about time and again. He said, 'What's he done, then?'

'He's had an accident,' the constable said. 'I'm sorry to tell you that a body's been found that appears to be Alexander's. If you have a photo of him . . .'

Ben heard the word *body* but did not allow it to penetrate. He said, 'Is he in hospital, then? Which one? What happened?' He thought of how he would have to tell Dellen, of what route the news would send her down.

'. . . awfully sorry,' the constable was saying. 'If you've a photo, we—'

'What did you say?'

Constable McNulty looked flustered. He said, 'He's dead, I'm afraid. The body. The one we found.'

'Santo? Dead? But where? How?' Ben looked out at the roiling sea just as a gust of wind hit the windows and rattled them against their sills. He said, 'Good Christ, he went out in this. He was surfing.'

'Not surfing,' McNulty said.

'Then what happened?' Ben asked. 'Please. What happened to Santo?'

'He's had a climbing accident. Equipment failure. On the cliffs at Polcare Cove.'

'He was climbing?' Ben said stupidly. 'Santo was *climbing*? Who was with him? Where—'

'No one, as it seems at the moment.'

'*No* one? He was climbing alone? At Polcare Cove? In this weather?' It seemed to Ben that all he could do was repeat the information like an automaton being programmed to speak. To do more meant he would have to embrace it, and he couldn't bear that because he knew what embracing it was going to mean. 'Answer me,' he said to the constable. 'Bloody *answer* me, man.'

'Have you a picture of Alexander?'

'I want to see him. I must. It might not be—'

'That's not possible just now. That's why I need the photo. The body . . . He's been taken to hospital in Truro.'

Ben leapt at the word. 'So he's *not* dead, then.'

'Mr Kerne, I'm sorry. He's dead. The body—'

'You said *hospital.*'

'To the mortuary, for postmortem,' McNulty said. 'I'm very sorry.'

'Oh my God.'

The front door opened below. Ben went to the lounge doorway and called out, 'Dellen?' Footsteps came in the direction of the stairs. But it was Kerra and not Ben's wife who appeared. She dripped rainwater onto the floor, and she'd removed her bicycle helmet. The very top of her head was the only part of her that appeared to be dry.

She looked at the constable, then said to Ben, 'Has something happened?'

'Santo.' Ben's voice was hoarse. 'Santo's been killed.'

'Santo.' Then, '*Santo*?' Kerra looked round the room in a kind of panic. 'Where's Alan? Where's Mum?'

Ben found he couldn't meet her eyes. 'Your mother's not here.'

'What's *happened*, then?'

Ben told her what little he knew.

She said as he had, 'Santo was *climbing*?' and she looked at him with an expression that said what he himself was thinking: If Santo had gone climbing, he'd likely done so because of his father.

'Yes,' Ben said. 'I know. I *know.* You don't need to tell me.'

'Know what, sir?' It was the constable speaking.

It came to Ben that these initial moments were critical ones in the eyes of the police. They would always be critical because the police didn't yet know what they were dealing with. They had a body and they reckoned having a body equated to an accident, but on the chance that it wasn't an accident, they had to be ready to point the finger and ask relevant questions and for the love of God, *where* was Dellen?

Ben rubbed his forehead. He thought, uselessly, that all of this was down to the sea, coming back to the sea, never feeling completely at ease unless the sound of the sea was not far off and yet being forced into feeling at ease for years and years while all the time longing for it and the great open heaving mass of it and the noise of it and the excitement of it and now *this*. It was down to him that Santo was dead.

No surfing, he had said. I do not want you surfing. D'you know how many blokes throw their lives away just hanging about, waiting for waves? It's mad. It's a waste.

'. . . act as liaison,' Constable McNulty was saying.

Ben said, 'What? What's that? Liaison?'

Kerra was watching him, her blue eyes narrowed. She looked speculative, which was the last way he wanted his daughter to look at him just now. She said carefully, 'The constable was telling us they'll send a liaison officer round. Once they have the picture of Santo and they know for certain.' And then to McNulty, 'Why d'you need a picture?'

'He had no identification on him.'

'Then how—'

'We found the car. A lay-by near Stowe Wood. His driving licence was in the glove box, and the keys in his rucksack fitted the door lock.'

'So this is just a formality,' Kerra pointed out.

'Essentially, yes. But it has to be done.'

'I'll fetch a photo then.' She went off to do so.

Ben marvelled at her. All business, Kerra. She wore her competence like a suit of armour. It broke his heart.

He said, 'When can I see him?'

'Not until after the postmortem, I'm afraid.'

'Why?'

'It's regulations, Mr Kerne. They don't like anyone near the . . . near him . . . till afterwards. Forensics, you see.'

'They'll cut him up.'

'You won't see. It won't be like that. They'll fix him up after. They're good at what they do. You won't see.'

'He's not a God damn piece of meat.'

''Course he's not. I'm sorry, Mr Kerne.'

'Are you? Have you children of your own?'

'A boy, yes. I've got a boy, sir. Your loss is the worst a man can experience. I know that, Mr Kerne.'

Ben stared at him, hot eyed. The constable was young, probably under twenty-five. He thought he knew the ways of the world, but he had no clue, absolutely not the slightest idea, what was out there and what could happen. He didn't know that there was no way to prepare and no way to control. At a gallop, life came at you on horseback and there you were with two options only. You either climbed up or you were mown down. Try to find the middle ground and you failed.

Kerra returned, a snapshot in hand. She gave it to Constable McNulty, saying, 'This is Santo. This is my brother.'

'Handsome lad,' he said.

'Yes,' Ben said heavily. 'He favours his mother.'

4

'Formerly.' Daidre chose her moment when she was alone with Thomas Lynley, when Sergeant Collins had ducked into the kitchen to brew himself yet another cup of tea. Collins had so far managed to swill down four of them. Daidre hoped he had no intention of sleeping that night because, if her nose was not mistaken, he'd been helping himself to her very best Russian Caravan tea.

Thomas Lynley roused himself from staring at the coal fire. He was seated near it, not comfortably with his long legs stretched out as one might expect of a man enjoying the warmth of a fire, but elbows on knees and hands dangling loosely in front of him. 'What?' he said.

'When he asked you, you said formerly. He said New Scotland Yard and you said formerly.'

'Yes,' Lynley said. 'Formerly.'

'Have you quit your job? Is that why you're in Cornwall?'

He looked at her. Once again she saw the injury that she had seen before in his eyes. He said, 'I don't quite know. I suppose I have. Quit, that is.'

'If you don't mind my asking, what sort of policeman were you?'

'A fairly good sort, I think.'

'Sorry. I meant, well, there're lots of different sorts, aren't there? Special Branch, protecting the Royals, vice, walking the beat . . .'

'Murder,' he said.

'You investigated murders?'

'Yes. That's exactly what I did.' He looked back at the fire.

'That must have been difficult. Disheartening.'

'Seeing man's inhumanity? It is.'

'Is that why you quit? I'm sorry. I'm being intrusive. But, had you had enough trials on your heart?'

He didn't reply.

The front door opened with a thud, and Daidre felt the wind gust into the room. Collins came out of the kitchen with his cup of tea as

Detective Inspector Hannaford returned to them. She carried a white boiler suit over her arm. This she thrust at Lynley.

'Trousers, boots, and jacket,' she said. It was clearly an order. And to Daidre, 'Where're yours, then?'

Daidre indicated the carrier bag into which she'd deposited her outer clothing when she'd changed into blue jeans and a yellow jumper. She said, 'But he'll have no shoes.'

'It's all right,' Lynley said.

'It isn't. You can't go round—'

'I'll get another pair.'

'He won't need them just yet anyway,' Hannaford said. 'Where can he change?'

'My bedroom. Or the bathroom.'

'See to it, then.'

Lynley had already risen when the DI had joined them. Less anticipation, this seemed, than years of breeding and good manners. The DI was a woman. One rose politely when a woman came into the room.

'SOCO's arrived?' Lynley said to her.

'And the pathologist. We've a photo of the dead boy as well. He's called Alexander Kerne. A local boy from Casvelyn. D'you know him?' She was speaking to Daidre. Sergeant Collins hovered in the kitchen doorway, as if not quite sure he was meant to be having tea while on duty.

'Kerne? The name's familiar, but I can't say why. I don't think I know him.'

'Have a vast acquaintance round here, do you?'

'What d'you mean?' Daidre was pressing her fingernails into her palms, and she made herself stop. She knew the detective was attempting to read her.

'You say you don't think you know him. It's a strange way of putting it. Seems to me, you either know him or you don't. Are you getting changed?' This last to Lynley, an abrupt shift that was as disconcerting as her steady and inquisitive gaze.

He cast a quick look at Daidre and then away. He said, 'Yes. Of course,' and ducked through the low doorway that separated the sitting room from a passage created by the depth of the fireplace. Beyond it lay a tiny bathroom and a bedroom big enough for a bed and a wardrobe and nothing else. The cottage was small and safe and snug. It was exactly the way Daidre wanted it.

She said to the detective, 'I believe one can know someone by sight

– actually have a conversation with him, if it comes down to it – without ever knowing that person's identity. Their name, their details, anything. I expect your sergeant here can say the same and he's a local man.'

Collins was caught, teacup halfway to his mouth. He shrugged. Agreeing or discounting. It was impossible to tell.

'Takes a bit of exertion, that, wouldn't you say?' Hannaford asked Daidre shrewdly.

'I've found the exertion worth it.'

'So you knew Alexander Kerne by sight?'

'I may have done. But as I said earlier and as I've told the other policeman, Sergeant Collins here, and you as well, I didn't get a good look at the boy when I first saw the body.'

Thomas Lynley returned to them, then, sparing Daidre any further questions as well as any further exposure to DI Hannaford's pene-trating stare. He handed over the clothing the DI had asked for. It was absurd, Dairdre thought. He was going to catch his death if he wandered round like that: no jacket, no shoes, and just a thin white boiler suit of the type worn at crime scenes to ensure the official investigators did not leave trace evidence behind. It was ridiculous.

DI Hannaford spoke to him. 'I'm going to want to see your identi-fication as well, Mr Lynley. It's form and I'm sorry, but there's no way round it. Can you get your hands on it?'

He nodded. 'I'll phone—'

'Good. Have it sent. You're not going anywhere for a few days, anyway. This looks like a straightforward accident, but till we know for certain . . . Well, I expect you know the drill. I'll want you where I can find you.'

'Yes.'

'You'll need clothing.'

'Yes.' He sounded as if he didn't care one way or the other. He was something windblown, not flesh, bone, and determination, but rather an insubstantial substance, desiccated and helpless against the forces of nature.

The detective looked round the cottage sitting room, as if assessing its potential to produce a set of clothes for the man as well as to house him. Daidre said hastily, 'He'll be able to get clothing in Casvelyn. Not tonight, of course. Everything'll be closed. But tomorrow. He can stay there as well. Or at the Salthouse Inn. They've rooms. Not many. Nothing special. But they're adequate. And it's closer than Casvelyn.'

'Good,' Hannaford said. And to Lynley, 'I'll want you there at the inn, then. I'll have more questions. Sergeant Collins can drive you.'

'I'll drive him,' Daidre said. 'I expect you'll want everyone you can get your hands on to do whatever it is you do at the scene when someone dies. I know where the Salthouse Inn is, and if they've no rooms, he'll need to be taken to Casvelyn.'

'Don't trouble—' Lynley began.

'It's no trouble,' Daidre said. What it was was a need to get Sergeant Collins and DI Hannaford out of her cottage, something that she could effect only if she had a reason to get out of the cottage herself.

After a pause, DI Hannaford said, 'Fine,' and, handing over her card to Lynley, 'Phone me when you're established somewhere. I'll want to know where to find you, and I'll be along directly we have matters sorted out here. It'll be some time.'

'I know,' he said.

'I expect you do.' She nodded and left them, taking with her their clothing stuffed into bags. Sergeant Collins followed her. Police cars were blocking Daidre's access to her own Vauxhall. They would have to be moved if she was to get Thomas Lynley to the Salthouse Inn.

Silence swept into the cottage with the departure of the police. Daidre could feel Thomas Lynley looking at her, but she was finished with being looked at. She went from the sitting room into the entry, saying over her shoulder, 'You can't go out in your stocking feet like that. I have wellies out here.'

'I doubt they'll fit,' he said. 'It doesn't matter. I'll take the socks off for now. Put them back on when I get to the inn.'

She stopped. 'That's sensible. I hadn't thought of it. If you're ready, then, we can go. Unless you'd like something . . . ? A sandwich? Soup? Brian does meals at the inn, but if you'd rather not have to eat in the dining area . . .' She didn't want to make the man a meal, but it seemed the proper thing to do. They were somehow bound together in this matter: partners in suspicion, perhaps. It felt that way to her, because she had secrets and he seemed to have them, too.

'I expect I can have something sent up to my room,' Lynley said, 'providing they have rooms available tonight.'

'Let's be off then,' Daidre said.

They made their second drive to the Salthouse Inn more slowly as there was no rush, and they encountered two more police vehicles and an ambulance on the way. They didn't speak and when Daidre glanced over at her companion, she saw that his eyes were closed and his hands rested easily on his thighs. He looked asleep, and she didn't doubt that he was. He'd seemed exhausted. She wondered how long he'd been hiking along the coastal path.

At the inn, she stopped the Vauxhall in the car park, but Lynley didn't move. She touched him gently on the shoulder.

He opened his eyes and blinked slowly as if clearing his head of a dream. He said, 'Thank you. It was kind—'

'I didn't want to leave you in the clutches of the police,' she cut in. Then, 'Sorry. I forget you're one of them.'

'After a fashion, yes, I am.'

'Well, anyway, I thought you might like a respite from them. Although from what the inspector said it doesn't appear you've escaped them for long.'

'No. They'll want to talk to me tonight. The first person on the scene is always suspect. They'll be intent on gathering as much information as possible as quickly as possible. That's the way it's done.'

They were silent then. A gust of wind, stronger than any so far, rocked the car. It stirred Daidre to words once more. She said, 'I'll come round for you tomorrow, then.' She made the declaration without thinking through all the ramifications of what it meant, what it could mean, and what it would look like. This wasn't like her, and she shook herself mentally. But the words were out there, and she let them lie. 'You'll need to get things from Casvelyn, I mean. I don't expect you want to walk round in that boiler suit for long. You'll need shoes as well. And other things. Casvelyn's the closest place to get them.'

'That's good of you,' Lynley told her. 'But I don't want to trouble you.'

'You said that earlier. But it isn't and you're not. It's very strange, but I feel that we're in this together although I don't quite know what *this* is.'

'I've caused you a problem,' he said. 'More than one. The window in your cottage. Now the police. I'm sorry about it.'

'What else were you to do? You could hardly walk on once you'd found him.'

'No. I couldn't walk on, could I?'

He sat for a moment. He seemed to be watching the wind play with the sign hanging above the inn's front door.

He finally said, 'May I ask you something?'

'Certainly.'

'Why did you lie?'

She heard an unexpected buzzing in her ears. She repeated the last word, as if she'd misheard him when she'd heard him only too clearly.

He said, 'The first time we came here, you told the publican that the boy in the cove was Santo Kerne. You said his name. Santo Kerne. But when the police asked you . . .' He gestured, a movement saying *finish the rest for yourself*.

The question reminded Daidre that this man, dishevelled and filthy though he was, was himself a policeman and a detective at that. From this moment, she needed to take extraordinary care.

She said, 'Did I say that?'

'You did. Quietly, but not quietly enough. And now you've told the police at least twice that you didn't recognise the boy. When they've said his name, you've said you don't know him. I'm wondering why.'

He looked at her, and she instantly regretted her offer to take him into Casvelyn for clothing in the morning. He was more than a sum of his parts, and she hadn't seen that in time.

She said, 'I've come for a holiday. At the time what I said to the police seemed the best way of ensuring I have one. A holiday. A rest.'

He said nothing.

She added, 'Thank you for not betraying me to them. Of course, I can't stop you from betraying me when you speak to them again. But I'd appreciate it, if you'd consider . . . There're things the police don't need to know about me. That's all, Mr Lynley.'

He didn't reply. But he didn't look away from her and she felt the heat rising up her neck to her cheeks. The door of the inn banged open, then. A man and a woman stumbled into the wind. The woman twisted her ankle, and the man put his arm round her waist and then kissed her. She shoved him away. The gesture was playful. He caught her up again and they staggered in the wind towards a line of cars.

Daidre watched them as Lynley watched her. She finally said, 'I'll come for you at ten, then. Will that do for you, Mr Lynley?'

His response was a long time in coming. Daidre thought he must be a good policeman.

'Thomas,' he said to her. 'Please call me Thomas.'

It was like an old time film about the American west, Lynley thought. He ducked into the inn's public bar, where the local drinkers were gathered, and silence fell. This was a part of the world where you were a visitor until you had become a permanent resident and you were a newcomer until your family had lived in the place for two generations. So he went down as a stranger among them. But he was more than that. He was also a stranger dressed in a white boiler suit and wearing nothing but socks on his feet. He had no coat against the cold, the wind, and the rain, and if that were not enough to make him a novelty, had anyone other than a bride entered this establishment in the past wearing white from shoulder to ankle, it probably hadn't happened in the living memory of anyone present.

The ceiling – stained with the soot of fires and the smoke of cigarettes and crossed with black oak beams from which horse brasses were nailed – hung less than twelve inches above Lynley's head. The walls bore a display of ancient farm implements, given mostly to scythes and pitchforks, and the floor was stone. This last was uneven, pockmarked, scored and scoured. Thresholds made of the same material as the floor were cratered by hundreds of years of entrances and exits, and the room itself that defined the public bar was small and divided into two sections described by fireplaces, one large and one small, which seemed to be doing more to make the air unbreathable than to warm the place. The body heat of the crowd was seeing to that.

When he'd been at the Salthouse Inn earlier with Daidre Trahair, just a few late afternoon drinkers had been present. Now, the place's nighttime crowd had arrived, and Lynley had to work his way through them and through their silence to get to the bar. He knew it was more than his clothing that made him an object of interest. There was the not small matter of his smell: unwashed from head to toe for seven weeks now. Unshaven and unshorn as well.

The publican – Lynley recalled that Daidre Trahair had referred to him as Brian – apparently remembered him from his earlier visit because he said abruptly into the silence, 'Was it Santo Kerne out there on the cliffs?'

'I'm afraid I don't know who it was. But it was a young man. An adolescent or just older than that. That's all I can tell you.'

A murmur rose and fell at this. Lynley heard the name *Santo* repeated several times. He glanced over his shoulder. Dozens of eyes – young and old and in between – were fixed on him.

He said to Brian, 'The boy, Santo, he was well-known?'

'He lives hereabouts,' was the unhelpful reply. That was the limit of what Brian appeared to be willing to reveal to a stranger. He said, 'Are you after a drink, then?'

When Lynley asked for a room instead, he recognised in Brian a marked reluctance to accommodate him. He put this down to a logical unwillingness to allow an unsavoury stranger such as himself access to the inn's sheets and pillows. God only knew what vermin might be crawling upon him. But the novelty he represented at the Salthouse Inn was in his favour. His appearance was in direct conflict with his accent and his manner of speaking and if that were not enough to make him an object of fascination, there was the intriguing matter of his finding the body that had likely been the subject of conversation inside the inn before he entered.

'A small room only,' was the publican's reply. 'But that's the case with all of 'em. Small. Wasn't like people needed much when the place was built, did they.'

Lynley said that the size didn't matter and he'd be happy with whatever the inn could give him. He didn't know how long he'd actually need the room, he added. It seemed that the police were going to require his presence until matters about the young man in the cove had been decided.

A murmur rose at this. It was the word *decided* and everything that the word implied.

Brian used the toe of his shoe to ease open a door at the far end of the bar, and he spoke a few words into whatever room existed behind it. From this a middle-aged woman emerged, the inn's cook by her garb of stained white apron, which she was hastily removing. Beneath it she wore a black skirt and white blouse. Sensible shoes as well.

She would take him up to a room, she said. She was all business, as if there was nothing strange about him. This room, she went on, was above the restaurant, not the bar. He'd find it quiet there. It was a good place to sleep.

She didn't wait for his reply. His thoughts likely didn't interest her anyway. His presence meant custom, which was hard to come by until late spring and summer. When beggars went begging, they couldn't exactly choose their benefactors, could they?

She headed for another door at the far side of the public bar. This gave onto an icy stone passage. The inn's restaurant operated in a room off this passage, although no one was seated within it, while at the far end a stairway the approximate width of a suitcase made the climb to the floor above. It was difficult to imagine how furniture had been carried up the stairs.

There were three rooms only on the first floor, and Lynley had his choice although his guide – her name was Siobhan Rourke and she was Brian's longtime and apparently longsuffering partner – recommended the smallest of them as it was the one she'd mentioned earlier as being above the restaurant and quiet at this time of year. They all shared the same bathroom, she informed him, but that ought to be of no account as no one else was staying.

Lynley wasn't particular about which room he was given so he took the first one whose door Siobhan opened. This would do, he told her. It suited him. Not much larger than a cell, it was furnished with a single bed, a wardrobe, and a dressing table tucked under a tiny casement window with leaded panes. Its only bow to mod cons were a washbasin in a corner and a telephone on the dressing table. This last was a jarring note in a room that could have done for a serving maid two hundred years earlier.

Only in the centre of the room could Lynley actually stand upright. Seeing this, Siobhan said, 'They were shorter in those days, weren't they? P'rhaps this isn't the best choice, Mr . . . ?'

'Lynley,' he said. 'This is fine. Does that phone work?'

Indeed, it did. Could she bring him anything? There were towels in the wardrobe and soap as well as shampoo in the bathroom – she sounded encouraging as she said this last bit – and if he wanted a meal, that could be arranged. Up here. Or in the dining room below, naturally, if that was what he wanted. She added this last as a hasty afterthought although it was fairly clear that the more he kept to his room, the happier everyone would be.

He said he wasn't hungry, which was more or less the truth. She left him, then. When the door closed behind her, he gazed at the bed. It was nearly two months since he'd slept in one, and even then he'd not done much sleeping. When he slept, he dreamed and he dreaded his dreams. Not because they were disturbing but because they ended. It was, he'd found, more bearable not to sleep at all.

Because there was no point in putting it off, he went to the phone and punched in the numbers. He was hoping that there would be no answer, just a machine picking up so that he could leave a brief message without the human contact. But after five double rings, he heard her voice. There was nothing for it but to speak.

He said, 'Mother. Hullo.'

At first she said nothing and he knew what she was doing: standing next to the phone in the drawing room or perhaps her morning room or elsewhere in the grand sprawling house that was his birthright and even more his curse, raising one hand to her lips, looking towards whoever else was in the room and that would likely be his younger brother or perhaps the manager of the estate or even his sister in the unlikely event that she was still down from Yorkshire. And her eyes – his mother's eyes – would communicate the information before she said his name. It's Tommy. He's phoned. Thank God. He's all right.

She said, 'Darling. Where are you? *How* are you?'

He said, 'I've run into something. It's a situation up in Casvelyn.'

'My God, Tommy. Have you walked that far? Do you know how—' But she didn't say the rest. She meant to ask whether he knew how worried they were. But she loved him and she wouldn't burden him further.

As he loved her, he answered her anyway. 'I know. I do. Please understand that. It's just that I can't seem to find my way.'

She knew, of course, that he wasn't referring to his sense of direction. 'My dear, if I could do anything to remove this from your shoulders . . .'

He could hardly bear the warmth of her voice, her unending compassion, especially when she herself had borne so many of her own tragedies throughout the years. He said to her, 'Yes. Well,' and he cleared his throat roughly.

'People have phoned,' she told him. 'I've kept a list. And they've not stopped phoning, the way you think people might. You know what I mean: One phone call and there I've done my duty. It hasn't been like that. There has been such concern for you. You are so deeply loved, my dear.'

He didn't want to hear it, and he had to make her understand that. It wasn't that he didn't value the concern of his friends and associates. It was that their concern, and what was worse, their *expression* of it, rubbed a place in him that was already so raw that having it touched by anything was akin to torture. He'd left his home because of this, because on the coast path there was no one in March and few enough people in April and even if he ran across someone on his walk, that person would know nothing of him, of what he was doing trudging steadily forward day after day, or of what had led up to his decision to do so.

He said, 'Mother . . .'

She heard it in his voice, as she would do. She said, 'Dearest, I'm sorry. No more of it.' Her voice altered, becoming more businesslike, for which he was grateful. 'What's happened? You're all right, aren't you? You've not been injured?'

No, he told her. He wasn't injured. But he'd come upon someone who *had* been. He was the first to come upon him, it seemed. A boy. He'd been killed in a fall from one of the cliffs. Now the police were involved. As he'd left at home everything that would identify him, could she send him his wallet? 'It's a formality, I dare say. They're just in the process of sorting everything out. It looks like an accident but, obviously, until they know, they won't want me going off. And they do want me to prove I am who I say I am.'

'Do they know you're a policeman, Tommy?'

'One of them, apparently. Otherwise, I've told them only my name.'

'Nothing else?'

'No.' It would have turned things into a Victorian melodrama: My good man – or in this case woman – do you *know* who you're talking to? He'd go for the police rank first and if that didn't impress, he'd try the title next. *That* should produce some serious forelock tugging if nothing else. Only, DI Hannaford didn't appear to be the sort who tugged forelocks, at least not her own. He said, 'So they're not willing to take me at my word and who can blame them. I wouldn't take me at my word. Will you sent the wallet?'

'Of course. At once. Shall I have Peter drive it up to you in the morning?'

He didn't think he could bear his brother's anxious concern. He said, 'Don't trouble him with that. Just put it in the post.'

He told her where he was and she asked if the inn was pleasant, at least, if his room was comfortable, if the bed would suit him. He told her everything was fine. He said that he was, in fact, looking forward to having a bath.

His mother was reassured by that, if not entirely satisfied. While the desire for a bath did not necessarily indicate a desire to continue living, it at least declared a willingness to muddle forward for a while. That would do. She rang off after telling him to have a good, long, luxurious soak and hearing him say that a good, long, luxurious soak was exactly his intention.

He replaced the phone on the dressing table. He turned from the table and, because there was no help for it, he looked at the room, the bed, the tiny washbasin in the corner. He found that his defences had fallen – his mother's conversation had done it to him – and there was her voice, with him suddenly. Not his mother's voice this time, but Helen's voice. *It is a bit monastic in here, isn't it, Tommy? I feel absolutely nunlike. Determined to be chaste but faced with such* horrific *temptation to be very very naughty indeed.*

He heard her so clearly. The Helen-ness of her. The nonsense that drew him out of himself when he most needed to be drawn. She'd been intuitive that way. One look at his face in the evening, and she'd known exactly what was required. It had been her gift: a talent for observation and insight. Sometimes it was the touch of her hand on his cheek and the three words *tell me, darling*. Other times it was the superficial frivolity that dissipated his tension and brought forth his laughter.

He said into the silence, 'Helen,' but that was all that he said, and certainly the extent to which he could, at the moment, acknowledge what he'd lost.

Daidre didn't return to the cottage when she'd left Thomas Lynley at the Salthouse Inn. Instead, she drove east. The route she took twisted like a discarded spool of ribbon through the misty countryside. It passed through several hamlets where lamps shone at windows in the dusk, then dipped through two woodlands. It divided one farmhouse from its outbuildings, and ultimately it came out on the A388. She took this road south and veered off on a secondary road that tracked east through pastureland where sheep and dairy cows grazed. She turned off where a sign pointed to *Cornish Gold* with *Visitors Welcome* printed beneath the name of the place.

Cornish Gold was half a mile down a very narrow lane, a farm comprising vast apple orchards circumscribed by stands of plum trees, these last planted years ago as a windbreak. The orchards began at the crest of a hill and spread down the other side in an impressive fan of acreage. Before them, in a stair-step fashion, stood two old stone barns, and across from these, a cider factory formed one side of a cobbled courtyard. In the centre of this, an animal pen traced a perfect square and within that square, snuffled and snorted the ostensible reason for Daidre's visit to this place, should anyone other than the farm's owner ask her. This reason was an orchard pig, a huge and decidedly unfriendly Gloucester Old Spot that had been instrumental in Daidre's meeting the owner of the cider farm soon after the woman's arrival in this part of the world, a journey she'd made over thirty years from Greece to London to St Ives to the farm.

At the side of the pen, Daidre found the pig waiting. He was named Stamos after his owner's former husband. The porcine Stamos, never a fool and always an optimist, had anticipated the reason for Daidre's visit and had lumbered to the rail fence cooperatively, once Daidre came into the courtyard. She had nothing for him this time, however. Packing peeled oranges into her bag while still at her cottage had seemed a questionable activity while the police were hanging about, intent upon watching and noting everyone's movements.

She said, 'Sorry, Stamos. But let's have a look at the ear all the same. Yes, yes. It's just routine. You're quite recovered, and you know it. You're too clever for your own good, aren't you?'

The pig was known to bite, so she took care. She also looked round the courtyard to see who might be watching because, if nothing else, one had to be diligent. But no one was there, and that was reasonable. For it was late in the day, and all employees of the farm would have long gone home.

She said, 'Looking perfect now,' to the pig and then she crossed the remainder of the courtyard where an arch led to a small rain-sodden vegetable garden. Here she followed a brick path – uneven, overgrown, and pooled with rainwater – to a neat white cottage from which the sound of classical guitar came in fits and starts. Aldara would be practising. That was good, as it likely meant that she was alone.

The playing stopped instantly when Daidre knocked on the door. Steps hurriedly approached across the hardwood floor inside.

'Daidre! What on earth . . . ?' Aldara Pappas was backlit from within the cottage, so Daidre couldn't see her face. But she knew the great dark eyes would hold speculation and not surprise, despite her tone of voice. Aldara stepped back from the door, saying, 'Come in. You are so very welcome. What a lovely surprise that you should come to break the tedium of my evening. Why didn't you phone me from Bristol? Are you down for long?'

'It was a sudden decision.'

Inside the cottage it was quite warm, the way Aldara liked it. Every wall was washed in white, and each one of them displayed highly-coloured paintings of rugged landscapes, arid and possessing habitations of white – small buildings with tile on their roofs and window boxes bursting with flowers, with donkeys standing placidly against their walls and dark-haired children playing in the dirt before their front doors. Aldara's furniture was simple and sparse. The pieces were brightly upholstered in blue and yellow, however, and a red rug covered part of the floor. Only the geckos were missing, their little bodies curving against the surface of whatever their tiny suctioned feet could cling to.

A coffee table in front of the sofa held a bowl of fruit and a plate of roasted peppers, Greek olives, and cheese: feta, undoubtedly. A bottle of red wine was still to be opened. Two wine glasses, two napkins, two plates, and two forks were neatly positioned. These gave the lie to Aldara's words. Daidre looked at her. She raised an eyebrow.

'It was a small social lie only.' Aldara was, as ever, completely un-embarrassed to have been caught out. 'Had you walked in and seen this, you would have felt less than welcome, no? And you are always welcome in my home.'

'As is someone else, apparently, tonight.'

'You are far more important than someone else.' As if to emphasise this, Aldara went to the fireplace, where a fire was laid and matches remained only to be used. She struck one on the underside of the mantle and put it to the crumpled paper beneath the wood. Apple wood, this was, dried and kept for burning when the orchard trees were pruned.

Aldara's movements were sensuous, but they were not studied. In the time Daidre had known the other woman, she'd come to realise that Aldara was sensual as a result of simply being Aldara. She would laugh and say, 'It's in my blood' as if being Greek equated to being seductive. But it was more than blood that made her compelling. It was confidence, intelligence, and complete lack of fear. Daidre admired this final quality most in the other woman, aside from her beauty. For she was forty-five and looked ten years younger. Daidre was thirty-one and, without the olive skin of the other woman, knew she would not be so lucky in fourteen years' time.

Having lit the fire, Aldara went to the wine and uncorked it, as if underscoring her declaration that Daidre was as valued and important a guest as whomever Aldara was actually expecting. She poured, saying, 'It's going to have a bite. None of that smooth French business. As you know, I like wine that challenges the palate. So have some cheese with it, or it's likely to take the enamel from your teeth.'

She handed over a glass and scooped up a chunk of cheese, which she popped into her mouth. She licked her fingers slowly, then she winked at Daidre, mocking herself. 'Delicious,' she said, 'Mama sent it from London.'

'How is she?'

'Still looking for someone to kill Stamos, of course. Sixty-seven years old and *no* one holds a grudge like Mama. She says to me, "Figs. I shall send that devil figs. Will he eat them, Aldara? I'll stuff them with arsenic. What d'you think?" I tell her to dismiss him from her thoughts. I have, I tell her. "Do not waste energy on that man," I tell her. "It's been nine years, Mama, and that is sufficient time to wish someone ill." She says, as if I had not spoken, "I'll send your brothers to kill him." And then she curses him in Greek at some length, all of which I'm paying for, naturally, as I'm the one who makes the phone calls, four times a week like the dutiful daughter I have always been. When she's finished, I tell her at least to send Nikko if she truly intends to kill Stamos because Nikko's the only one of my brothers who's actually good with a knife and a decent shot. And then she laughs. She launches into a story about one of Nikko's children and that is that.'

Daidre smiled. Aldara dropped onto the sofa, kicking off her shoes and tucking her legs beneath her. She was wearing a dress the colour of mahogany, its hem like a handkerchief, its neckline V-ing towards her breasts. It had no sleeves and was fashioned from material more suitable to summer on Crete than spring in Cornwall. Little wonder that the room was so warm.

Daidre took some cheese and wine as instructed. Aldara was right. The wine was rough.

'I think they aged it fifteen minutes,' Aldara told her. 'You know the Greeks.'

'You're the only Greek I do know,' Daidre said.

'This is sad. But Greek women are much more interesting than Greek men, so you have the best of the lot with me. You've not come about Stamos, have you? I mean Stamos the lower case pig, of course. Not Stamos the upper case Pig.'

'I stopped to look at him. His ears are clear.'

'They would be. I did follow your instructions. He's right as rain. He's asking for a girlfriend as well although the last thing I want is a dozen orchard piglets round my ankles. You didn't answer me, by the way.'

'Did I not?'

'You did not. I'm delighted to see you as always, but there's something in your face that tells me you've come for a reason.' She took another piece of cheese.

'Who're you expecting?' Daidre asked her.

Aldara's hand, lifting the cheese to her mouth, paused. She cocked her head and regarded Daidre. 'That sort of question is completely unlike you,' she pointed out.

'Sorry. But . . .'

'What?'

Daidre felt flustered, and she hated that feeling. Her life experience

– not to mention her sexual and emotional experience – placed in opposition to Aldara's left her seriously wanting and even more seriously out of her depth. She shifted gears. She did it baldly, as baldness was the only weapon she possessed. 'Aldara, Santo Kerne's been killed.'

'What did you say?'

'Are you asking that because you didn't hear me or because you want to think you didn't hear me?'

'What happened to him?' Aldara said, and Daidre was gratified to watch her replace her bit of cheese onto the plate, uneaten.

'He was climbing, apparently.'

'Where?'

'The cliff in Polcare Cove. He fell and was killed. A man out walking the coastal path was the one to find him. He came to the cottage.'

'You were there when this happened?'

'No. I drove down from Bristol this afternoon. When I got to the cottage, the man was inside. He was looking for a phone. I came upon him.'

'You came upon a man inside your cottage? My God. How frightening. How did he . . . ? Did he find the extra key?'

'He broke a window to get in. He told me there was a body on the rocks and I went down to it with him. I said I was a doctor—'

'Well, you *are* a doctor. You might have been able to—'

'No. It's not that. Well, it is in a way because I could have done something, I suppose.'

'You must more than *suppose*, Daidre. You've been educated well. You've qualified. You've managed to acquire a job of enormous responsibility and you cannot say—'

'Aldara. Yes. All right. I know. But it was more than wanting to help. I wanted to see. I had a feeling.'

Aldara said nothing. Sap crackled in one of the logs and the sound drew her attention to the fire. She looked at it long, as if checking to see that the logs remained where she had originally placed them. She finally said, 'You thought it might be Santo Kerne? Why?'

'It's obvious, isn't it?'

'Why is it obvious?'

'Aldara. You know.'

'I don't. You must tell me.'

'Must I?'

'Please.'

'You're being—'

'I'm being nothing. Tell me what you want to tell me about why things are so obvious to you, Daidre.'

'Because even when one thinks everything has been seen to, even when one thinks every *i* has been dotted, every *t* has been crossed, even when one thinks every sentence has a full stop at the end—'

'You're becoming tedious.'

Daidre took a sharp breath. 'Someone is dead. How *can* you talk like that?'

'All right. *Tedious* was a poor choice of words. *Hysterical* would have been better.'

'This is a human being we're talking about. This is a teenage boy. Not nineteen years old. Dead on the rocks.'

'Now you *are* hysterical.'

'How can you be like this? Santo Kerne is *dead*.'

'And I'm sorry about that. I don't want to think of a boy that young falling from a cliff and—'

'*If*, he fell, Aldara.'

Aldara reached for her wine glass. Daidre noted – as she sometimes did – that the Greek woman's hands were the only part of her that was not lovely. Aldara herself called them peasant's hands, made for pounding clothes against rocks in a stream, for kneading bread, for working the soil. With strong, thick fingers and wide palms, they were not hands made for delicate employment. 'Why "if he fell"?' she asked.

'You know the answer to that.'

'But you said he was climbing. You can't think someone . . .'

'Not someone, Aldara. Santo Kerne? Polcare Cove? It's not difficult to work out who might have harmed him.'

'You're talking nonsense. You go to the cinema far too often. Films make one start believing that people act like they're playing parts devised in Hollywood. The fact that Santo fell while he was climbing—'

'And isn't that a bit odd? Whyever would he climb in this weather?'

'You ask the question as if you expect me to know the answer.'

'Oh, for heaven's sake, Aldara!'

'Enough.' Aldara firmly set her wine glass down. 'I am *not* you, Daidre. I've never had this . . . oh, what shall I call it . . . this awe of men that you have, this feeling that they are somehow more significant than they actually are, that they are necessary in life, essential to a woman's completion. I'm terribly sorry that the boy is dead, but it's nothing to do with me.'

'No? And this?' Daidre indicated the two wine glasses, the two plates, the two forks, the endless repetition of what should have been but never quite was the number two. And there was the additional matter of Aldara's clothing: the filmy dress that embraced and released her hips when she moved, the choice of shoes with toes too open and heels too high to be practical on a farm, the earrings that illustrated the length of her neck. There was little doubt in Daidre's mind that the sheets on Aldara's bed were fresh and scented with lavender and there were candles ready to be lit in her bedroom.

A man was at this moment on his way to her. He was even now pondering the removal of her clothes. He was wondering how quickly upon his arrival he could get down to business with her. He was thinking of how he was going to take her – rough or tender, up against the wall, on the floor, in a bed – and in what position, of whether he'd be up for the job of doing it more than twice because he knew merely twice would not be enough, not for a woman like Aldara Pappas. Earthy, sensual, ready. He damn well *had* to give her what she was looking for because if he didn't, he'd be tossed aside and he didn't want that.

Daidre put her palm on the table between them. She repeated her earlier question. 'Who're you expecting tonight?'

'That doesn't concern you.'

'Are you completely mad? I had the police in my cottage.'

'And that worries you. Why?'

'Because I feel *responsible*. Don't you?'

Aldara seemed to consider the question because it was a moment before she replied. 'Not at all.'

'And that's that, then?'

'I suppose it is.'

'Because of this? The wine, the cheese, the lovely fire? The two of you? Whoever he is?'

Aldara rose. 'You must leave. I've tried to explain myself to you time and again. But you see how I am as a moral issue and not what it is, which is just a manifestation of the only way I can function. So yes, someone is on his way and, no, I'm not going to tell you who it is, and I'd vastly prefer it if you were not here when he arrives.'

'You refuse to be touched by anything, don't you?' Daidre asked her.

'My dear, that is definitely the pot and the kettle,' was Aldara's reply.

5

Cadan had high hopes that the Bacon Streakies would do the trick. He also had high hopes that Pooh would do the trick. The Bacon Streakies, which were the bird's favourite treat, were supposed to encourage and reward him. The system was to let the parrot see the bag of goodies dangling from Cadan's fingers – a manoeuvre sufficient to get the bird's interest – and then put him through his paces. The reward would follow, and there was absolutely no need to show Pooh the crunchy substance itself. He might have been a parrot, but he was no dummy when it came to food.

But tonight, distractions diverted him. He and Cadan were not alone in the sitting room, and the other three individuals were proving more interesting to the parrot than the food on offer. So balancing on a small rubber ball and walking said ball across the length of the mantelpiece did not hold the same promise that a lolly stick in the hands of a six-year-old girl held. A lolly stick carefully applied to the parrot's feathered head, rubbed gently back and forth in the region where one assumed his ears to be, guaranteed ecstasy. A Bacon Streakie, on the other hand, effected only momentary gustatory satisfaction. So although Cadan made a heroic attempt to get Pooh to provide some entertainment for Ione Soutar and her two young daughters, entertainment was not forthcoming.

'Why's he not want to *do* it, Cade?' Jennie Soutar asked. She was the younger of the two. Her older sister Leigh – who was, at ten, already wearing glittery eye shadow, lipstick, and hair extensions – looked as if she'd never expected the bird to do anything extraordinary in the first place and who cared anyway as the bird was neither a pop star nor someone likely to become a pop star. Instead of paying attention to the failed bird show, she'd been flipping through a fashion magazine, squinting at the pictures because she refused to wear her specs and was campaigning for contact lenses.

Cadan said, 'It's the lolly stick. He knows you've got it. He wants to be petted again.'

'C'n I pet him, then? C'n I hold him?'

'Jennifer, you know how I feel about that bird.' These words were spoken by her mother. Ione Soutar was standing in the bay window, gazing out at Victoria Road. She'd been doing that for thirty minutes, and she didn't look like a woman who intended to stop doing it anytime soon. 'Birds carry germs and diseases.'

'But Cade touches him all the time.'

Ione shot her daughter a look that seemed to say, 'And just *look* at Cade, will you?'

Jennie interpreted the expression on her mother's face in whatever way Ione intended. She scooted back on the sofa, her legs sticking out in front of her, and she puffed out her lips in disappointment. It was, Cadan saw, a facial expression unwittingly identical to Ione's.

No doubt the feeling behind it was the same as well: disappointment. Cadan wanted to tell Ione Soutar that she was going to be endlessly disappointed as long as she had his father in her marital sights. On the surface it looked as if they were perfect for each other: two independent business people with workshops on Binner Down, two parents years without partners, two parents who surfed, two children for each of them, two little girls interested in surfing, with a third older girl their role model and instructor, two family-oriented families. There was probably also good sex involved as well, but Cadan didn't like to speculate about that as the thought of his father in a carnal embrace with Ione made his skin go prickly. Nonetheless, superficially it appeared to be logical that nearly three years in, this association ought to have resulted in something akin to a commitment from Lew Angarrack. But it hadn't done, and Cadan had heard enough of his father's end of telephone conversations to know Ione was no longer happy with the situation.

She was currently annoyed as well. Two takeaway Pukka's pizzas had long since gone cold in the kitchen while she waited in the sitting room for Lew's return. It was a wait that was beginning to seem futile to Cadan, for his father had showered and changed and rushed off on what Cadan saw as a real fool's errand.

It seemed to Cadan that a visit from Will Mendick had prompted Lew's departure. Will had rumbled up Victoria Road in his wheezing old Beetle and as he'd unfolded his wiry frame from the car and approached the front door, Cadan could see from his ruddy face that something was troubling him.

He'd asked for Madlyn directly and said curtly, 'Where is she, then?

She wasn't at the bakery either,' when Cadan revealed that she wasn't at home.

'We don't have her on the GPS yet,' Cadan told him. 'That's next week, Will.'

Will hadn't seemed to appreciate the humour. 'I need to find her.'

'Why?'

So he'd told him the news he'd had off the bird at Clean Barrel Surf Shop: Santo Kerne was dead as a doornail, his head mashed in or whatever it was that happened when one fell during a cliff climb.

'He was climbing alone?' Climbing at all was the real question since Cadan knew what Santo Kerne *really* preferred doing, which was surf and shag, and shag and surf, both of which came quite easily to him.

'I didn't say he was alone,' Will pointed out sharply. 'I don't know who was with him or even if there was someone with him. Why d'you think he was alone?'

Cadan didn't have to reply at that point because Lew had heard Will's voice and had apparently read something dire from the tone. He'd come from the back of the house where he'd been working on the computer and Will had brought him into the picture as well. 'I've come to tell Madlyn,' Will explained.

Too right, Cadan thought. The way to Madlyn was open, and Will was not a man to ignore a gaping doorway.

'Damn,' Lew said in a thoughtful tone. 'Santo Kerne.'

Not one of them was exactly in extremis over the news, Cadan admitted to himself. He reckoned that he was the one who probably felt the worst, but that was likely because he had the least at stake in the matter.

'I'll go and look for her, then,' Will Mendick had said. 'Where do you think . . . ?'

Who bloody knew? Madlyn's emotions had been running their usual mad course since her break-up with Santo. She'd started with devastation and moved on to blind and unreasonable anger. As far as Cadan was concerned, the less he saw of her the better until she'd gone through her last stage – it was always revenge – and then got back to normal again. She might have been anywhere: robbing banks, breaking windows, pulling men in pubs, tattooing her eyelids, beating up small children, or off to regions unknown for a surf. With Madlyn, you just never knew.

Lew said, 'We've not seen her since breakfast.'

'Damn.' Will bit the side of his thumb. 'Well, someone's got to tell her what's happened.'

Why? Cadan thought, but didn't say. Instead, he asked, 'Think it should be you?' Adding foolishly, 'Wise up, mate. You're not her type.'

Will's face flared. His skin was spotty anyway, and the spots enflamed. Lew said, 'Cade.'

'But it's true. Come on, man—'

Will didn't wait to hear the rest. He was out of the room and out of the door before Cadan could say another word.

Lew said, 'Christ, Cade,' as apparent commentary on Cadan's finesse. Then he went upstairs for his shower.

He hadn't had one after his surf, so Cadan had first assumed his father was just doing what he ordinarily did: getting the sand and salt-water off. But then, he'd left the house and he'd not returned. This had put Cadan in the position of trying and failing to entertain Ione and her daughters as they waited for his father.

'Looking for Madlyn,' was what Cadan had told his father's girl-friend. He'd explained about Santo and said nothing more. Ione was already fully in the picture about the Madlyn-Santo situation. She could not have been involved with Lew Angarrack and *not* known; Madlyn's well-developed sense of drama would have made that completely impossible.

Ione had gone into the kitchen, where she'd deposited the pizzas on the work top, set the table, and made a salad. Then she'd returned to the sitting room. After forty minutes, she'd rung Lew's mobile. If he had it with him, he didn't have it on.

'How stupid of him,' Ione said. 'What if she comes home while he's out looking for her? How're we to let him know?'

'He probably didn't think of that,' Cadan said. 'He went out in a rush.'

This wasn't exactly true, but it seemed more . . . well, more *likely* that a worried father would depart in a rush than as Lew had departed, which was quite calmly, as if he'd made a grim decision about some-thing or as if he knew something that no one else knew.

Now, having finished studying her fashion magazine, Leigh Soutar piped up in her usual fashion, with that bizarre cadence peculiar to young girls with too much exposure to adolescent films on satellite tele-vision. 'Mum, I'm *hungry*?' she said. 'I'm *starving*? Lookit the *time*, okay? Aren't we having *dinner*?'

'Want a Bacon Streakie?' Cadan asked her.

'Yuck,' Leigh said. '*Junk* food?'

'And pizza is what?' Cadan inquired politely.

'Pizza,' Leigh told him, 'is highly *nutritious*? There are at least two food groups involved and anyway I'm only having one slice, *okay?*'

'Right,' Cadan said. He'd seen Leight at the trough before and when it came to pizza she regularly forgot her intention of becoming the Kate Moss of her generation. The day she stopped at one slice of pizza would be the day pigs took to the air in droves.

'I'm hungry, too,' Jennie said. 'Could we not eat, Mummy?'

Ione cast one last agonised look at the street. 'I suppose so,' she said.

She headed in the direction of the kitchen. Jennie followed, scratching her bum as she went. Leigh practised a catwalk prance in her sister's wake, casting a baleful look at Cadan as she passed him.

'Stupid *bird*?' she said. 'He doesn't even *talk*? What sort of parrot doesn't even *talk*?'

'One who saves his vocabulary for useful conversations,' Cadan said.

Leigh stuck out her tongue and left the room.

After a dreary meal of pizza left too long on the work top and salad left to the ministrations of a preoccupied chef wielding too much vinegar, Cadan offered to do the washing up and hoped that Ione would take her offspring and depart. No such luck. She hung about for another ninety minutes, exposing Cadan to Leigh's withering comments about the quality of his dishwashing and drying. She phoned Lew's mobile four more times before taking herself and the girls home.

This left Cadan in his least favourite position: alone with his thoughts. He was thus relieved to field a phone call at long last revealing Madlyn's whereabouts, but he was less relieved when the caller wasn't his father. And he became downright concerned when a casual question on his part revealed that his father had not even been round seeking to discover Madlyn for himself. This concern led Cadan directly to being unnerved – a condition he didn't care to speculate upon – so when his father finally turned up shortly after midnight, Cadan was fairly cheesed off at the bloke for causing him sensations he preferred not to feel. He was watching telly when the kitchen door opened and shut. Thereafter Lew appeared in the doorway to the lounge, standing in the shadows of the corridor.

Cadan said briefly, 'She's with Jago.'

Lew blinked. 'What?'

'Madlyn. She's with Jago. He rang. He said she's asleep.'

No reaction from his father. Cadan felt an unaccountable chill at this. It ran up and down his arms like a dead baby's fingers. He reached for the telly remote and clicked the off button.

'You were looking for her, right?' Cadan didn't wait for an answer. 'Ione was here. Her and the girls. Crikey, that Leigh's a cow, you ask me.' Silence. 'You *were*, right?'

Lew turned and went back to the kitchen. Cadan heard the fridge opening and something being poured into a pan. His father would be heating milk for his nightly Ovaltine. Cadan decided he wanted one himself, so he shuffled to the kitchen to join him.

He said, 'I asked Jago what she was doing there. You know what I mean. Just, "What the heck's she doing there, mate?" because first of all why would she want to spend the night with Jago . . . What is he, seventy years old? It's not like he's a relative or anything . . . and second of all . . .' But he couldn't remember what the *second of all* was. He was babbling because his father's obdurate silence was unnerving him. 'And Jago said he was up at the Salthouse with Mr Penrule when this bloke came in with that woman who's got the cottage in Polcare Cove. She said there was a body out there and Jago heard her say that she reckoned it was Santo. So Jago went to fetch Madlyn from the bakery to break the news to her. He didn't phone here at first because . . . I don't know. I s'pose she went dead mental on him when he told her and he had to cope with her.'

'Did he say that?'

Cadan was so relieved that his father was finally speaking that he said, 'Who? Say what?'

'Did Jago say Madlyn went mental?'

This seemed such an unlikely choice of queries that Cadan said, 'You were looking for her, right? I mean that's what I told Ione. Like I said, she was here with the girls. Pizza.'

'Ione,' Lew said. 'I'd forgotten the pizza. I expect she left in a state.'

'She tried to ring you. Your mobile . . . ?'

'I didn't have it on.'

The milk steamed on the cooker. Lew got his Newquay mug and spooned Ovaltine into it. He used a generous amount, added the milk, and handed the jar over to Cadan, who'd got his own mug down from the shelf above the sink.

'I'll ring her now,' Lew said.

'It's after midnight,' Cadan told him unnecessarily.

'Believe me, better late than tomorrow.'

Lew left the kitchen and went to his room. Cadan felt an urgent need to know what was going on, so after a moment he climbed the stairs in his father's wake.

His intention was to listen at Lew's door, but he found that wasn't going to be necessary. He'd barely reached the top step when he heard Lew's voice rise and could tell the conversation was going badly. Lew's end consisted mostly of, 'Ione . . . Please listen to me . . . So much on my mind . . . Overloaded with work . . . Completely forgot . . . Because I'm in the middle of shaping a board, Ione, with nearly two dozen more . . . Yes, yes. I *am* sorry, but you didn't actually tell me . . . Ione . . .'

That was it. Then silence. Cadan went to the doorway of his father's room. Lew was sitting on the edge of the bed. He had one hand on the phone's receiver, which he'd just replaced in its cradle. He glanced at Cadan, but he didn't speak. Instead, he got up and went for his jacket, which he'd thrown over the seat of a ladder-back chair in the corner of the room. He began to put it on. Apparently, he was going out again.

Cadan said, 'What's happening?'

Lew didn't look at him as he replied with, 'She's had enough. She's finished.'

He sounded . . . Cadan thought about this. Regretful? Tired? Heavy-hearted? Accepting of the fact that as long as one remained unchanged, the past would accurately predict the future? Cadan said philosophically, 'Well, you cocked things up. Forgetting her and everything.'

Lew patted his pockets as if looking for something. 'Yes. Right. Well. She didn't want to listen.'

'To what?'

'It was a pizza dinner, Cade. That's all. Pizza. I could hardly be expected to remember a pizza dinner.'

'That's a bit heartless isn't it?' Cadan said.

'It's also none of your business.'

Cadan felt his belly grow tight and hot. He said, 'Well, when you want me to entertain your girlfriend while you're out doing whatever, then it is my business.'

Lew dropped his hand from the search of his pockets. He said, 'Christ. I'm sorry, Cade. I'm on edge. So much is going on. I don't know how to explain myself to you.'

But that was just it, Cadan thought. What *was* going on? True, they'd heard from Will Mendick that Santo Kerne was dead – and yeah that was unfortunate, wasn't it? – but why would the news throw their lives into chaos, if chaos was indeed where they were?

* * *

The equipment room of Adventures Unlimited had been constructed in a former dining hall and the former dining hall had itself once been a tea dancing pavilion in the heyday of the Promontory King George Hotel, a heyday that had occurred between the two world wars. Often when he found himself in the equipment room Ben Kerne tried to imagine what it had been like when the parquet floor wore a gloss, the ceiling glittered with chandeliers, and women in frothy summer frocks floated in the arms of men wearing linen suits. They'd danced with a blissful lack of awareness then, believing that the war to end all wars had actually ended all wars. They'd learned otherwise, and far too soon, but the thought of them had always been soothing, as was the music Ben imagined he heard: the orchestra playing as white-gloved waiters passed finger sandwiches on silver trays. He considered the dancers – nearly saw their ghosts – and felt a poignancy about times that had passed. But at the same moment he always felt comfort. People came and went from the Promontory King George, and life continued.

In the equipment room now, however, the tea dancers of 1933 didn't enter Ben Kerne's mind. He stood in front of a row of cabinets, one of which he'd unlocked. Inside this cabinet, climbing equipment hung from hooks, lay neatly in plastic containers, and was coiled on shelves. Ropes, harnesses, slings, belay and camming devices, chock stones, carabiners . . . everything. His own equipment he stored elsewhere because he didn't like the inconvenience of coming down here to sort out what he wanted to take with him if he had a free afternoon for a climb. But Santo's kit had a prominent place, and above it Ben himself had proudly fixed a sign that said Do Not Take From This. Instructors and students alike were to know those pieces of gear were sacrosanct, the accumulation of three Christmases and four birthday celebrations.

Now, however, all of it was missing. Ben knew what this meant. He understood that the absence of Santo's equipment constituted Santo's final message to his father, and he felt the impact of that message, just as he felt the weight and experienced the sudden illumination that the message provided as well: his own remarks, made unthinkingly and born of pigheaded self-righteousness – had effected this. Despite his every effort, despite the fact that he and Santo could not possibly have been more unlike each other in everything from personality to appearance, history had repeated itself, in form if not in substance. His own history spoke of wrong-headed judgement, banishment, and years of estrangement. Santo's now spoke of denunciation and death. Not in so many words but, rather, with an open acknowledgement of a heaviness of heart that in and of itself had uttered a single damning question as loudly as if Ben had shouted it: *What sort of miserable excuse for a man are you, to have done such a thing?*

Santo could not have failed to interpret this unspoken query as anything other than what it was, and any son of any father would have likely reacted out of the same sense of outrage that had taken Santo out to the cliffs. Ben himself had reacted to his own father in much the same manner at much the same age: *You talk about* man, *I'll give you* man.

But the underlying *reason* for Ben's interaction with Santo remained unexamined although the superficial *why* of it didn't need to be addressed at all, because Santo knew exactly what it was. The historical reason for their interaction, on the other hand, was far too frightening to contemplate. Instead of doing so, Ben had eternally told himself only that Santo was – always and merely – who Santo was.

'It just happened,' Santo had confessed to Ben. 'Look, I don't want—'

'*You?*' Ben said, incredulous. 'You stop right there, because what you want doesn't interest me. What you've done, on the other hand, does. What you've accomplished. The sum total of your bloody self-interest—'

'Why the hell do you care so much? What is it to you? If there was something to be handled, I would have handled it, but there was nothing. There *is* nothing. *Nothing*, okay?'

'Human beings,' Ben said, 'are *not* to be handled. They're not pieces of meat. They're not merchandise.'

'You're twisting my words.'

'You're twisting people's lives.'

'That's unfair. That's so fucking unfair.'

As Santo would find most of life, Ben had thought. Except he hadn't lived long enough to do so.

And whose fault was that, Benesek? he asked himself. Was the moment worth the price you're paying?

That moment had been a single remark, said partly in anger but in larger part bleak fear: 'Unfair is having a worthless piece of manure as a son.' Once said, the words hung there, like black paint tossed at a clean, white wall. His punishment for having said them was going to be the memory of what they had produced, which was Santo's face gone white and the fact that a father had turned his back on his son. *You want* man, *I'll show you* man. *In spades if I must.*

Ben didn't want to think of what he'd said. If he had his preference, it would be that his mind would go blank and thus remain, allowing him to go through the motions of living until his body gave out and eternal rest claimed him.

Ben closed the cupboard and looped the padlock back into place. He breathed slowly through his mouth till he'd mastered himself, and his guts were easy again. Then he went to ring for the lift. It descended at a dignified, antique speed that matched its appearance of open iron fretwork. It creaked to a stop and he rode it to the top of the hotel where the family flat was and where Dellen waited.

He didn't go to his wife at once. Instead, he went first to the kitchen. There, Kerra sat at the table with her partner. Alan Cheston was watching her, and Kerra herself was listening, her head tilted in the direction of the bedrooms. She was, Ben knew, waiting for a sign of how things would be.

Her gaze took in her father as he came through the doorway. Ben's eyes questioned. She responded. 'Still,' was her answer.

'All right,' he said.

He went to the hob. Kerra had boiled a kettle there, and the fire was still on beneath it, low so the steam escaped soundlessly and the water stayed just beneath a boil. She'd set up four mugs, each with a teabag. He poured water in two of them and stood there, watching the tea brew. His daughter and her lover sat in silence. He could feel their eyes upon him, though, and he could sense the questions they wanted to ask. Not only of him but of each other. There were matters to discuss in every corner.

He couldn't bear the thought of talking, so when the tea was sufficiently dark, he poured milk and added sugar to one and nothing to the other. He carried both from the kitchen and set one on the floor momentarily in front of Santo's door which was closed but not locked. He opened it and went inside, into the dark with two cups of tea that he knew neither of them would be able to drink.

She'd switched on no lights, and as Santo's room was at the back of the hotel, there were no street lamps from the town that illuminated the darkness within. Across the curved expanse of St Mevan Beach, the lights at the end of the breakwater and atop the canal lock glittered through the wind and the rain, but they did nothing to expel the gloom in here. A milky shaft of light from the corridor, however, fell across the rag rug on the bedroom floor. On this, Ben saw that his wife was foetally curled. She'd ripped sheets and blankets from Santo's bed and she'd covered herself with them. Most of her face was in shadow but where it was not, Ben could see it was stony. He wondered if the thought was in her mind: If I had only been here, if only I hadn't gone off for the day . . . He doubted it. Regret had never been Dellen's style.

With his foot, Ben closed the door behind him. Dellen stirred. He thought she might speak, but instead she drew the linens up to her face. She pressed them to her nose, taking in Santo's scent. She was like a mother animal in this, and like an animal she operated on instinct. It had been her appeal from the day he'd met her: both of them adolescents, one of them randy and the other one willing.

All she knew so far was that Santo was dead, that the police had been, that a fall had taken him, and that the fall was during a seacliff climb. Ben had got no further than that with the information because she'd said, 'A *climb*?' after which she'd read her husband's face as she'd long been capable of doing and she'd said, 'You did this to him.'

That was it. They'd been standing in the reception area of the old hotel because he'd not managed to get her any farther inside. Upon her return, she'd seen at once that something was wrong and she'd demanded to know, not as a way of deflecting the obvious question of where she herself had been for so many hours – she wouldn't think anyone actually had a right to know that – but because something was wrong on a much larger scale than curiosity over her whereabouts. He'd tried to get her upstairs to the lounge, but she'd been immovable. So he told her there.

She went for the stairs. She stopped momentarily at the bottom step, and she clutched at the railing as if to keep herself upright. Then she climbed.

Now, Ben set the milk-and-sugar tea on the floor near her head. He sat on the edge of Santo's bed.

She said, 'You're blaming me. You reek of blaming me, Ben.'

'I don't blame you,' he said. 'I don't know why you'd think that.'

'I think it because we're here. Casvelyn. That was all about me.'

'No. It was for all of us. I'd had enough of Truro as well.'

'You would have stayed in Truro forever.'

'That's not the case, Dellen.'

'And if you'd had enough – which I don't believe anyway – it hadn't to do with you. Or Truro. Or any town. I can feel your loathing, Ben. It smells like sewage.'

He said nothing. Outside a gust of wind hit the side of the building, rattling the windows. A fierce storm was brewing. Ben knew the signs.

The wind was onshore. It would bring in heavier rain from the Atlantic. They were not yet out of the season of storms.

'It's myself,' he said. 'We had words. I said some things—'

'Oh, I expect you did. You saint. You bloody *saint*.'

'There's nothing saintly about following through. There's nothing saintly about accepting—'

'That's not what things were about between you and Santo. Don't think I don't know. You're a real bastard.'

'You know why.' Ben set his mug of tea on the bedside table. Deliberately, then, he switched on the lamp. If she looked at him, he wanted her able to see his face and to read his eyes. He wanted her to know that he spoke the truth. 'I told him he needed to take more care. I told him people are real, not toys. I wanted him to see that there's more to life than seeking pleasure for himself.'

Her voice was scorn. 'As if that's how he lives.'

'You know that it is. He's good with people. All people. But he can't let that, that skill of his lead him to do wrong by them. But he doesn't want to see—'

'*Doesn't?* He's dead, Ben. There *is* no *doesn't*.'

Ben thought she might weep then, but she did not. He said, 'There is no shame in teaching one's children to do right, Dellen.'

'Which means *your* right, yes? Not his. Yours. He was supposed to be made in your likeness, wasn't he? But he wasn't you, Ben. And nothing could make him in your likeness.'

'I know that.' Ben felt the words' intolerable weight. 'Believe me, I know that.'

'You don't. You didn't. And you couldn't cope with it, could you? You had to have him the way you wanted.'

'Dellen, I know I'm to blame. Do you think that I don't? I'm as much to blame for this as—'

'No!' She rose to her knees. 'Do not dare,' she cried. 'Don't bring that back to me just now because if you do, I swear, if you even mention, if you bring it up, if you try to, if you . . .' Words seemed to fail her. Suddenly, she reached for the mug he'd placed on the floor and she threw it at him. Hot tea stung his chest; the rim of the mug struck his breastbone. 'I hate you,' she said and then louder with each successive word, 'I hate you, I hate you. I hate you.'

He dropped off the bed and onto his knees. He grabbed her then. She was still shrieking her hate as he pulled her to him, and she beat on his chest, his face, and his neck before he was able to catch her arms.

'Why didn't you *let* him just be who he was? He's dead and all you ever *needed* to do was just to let him be. Was that too much? Was that *asking* too much?'

'Shh,' Ben murmured. He held her; he rocked her; he pressed his fingers to her thick blonde hair. 'Dellen,' he said. 'Dellen, Dell. We can weep for this. We can. We must.'

'I won't. Let me go. Let. Me. Go!'

She struggled but he held her firmly. He knew he couldn't let her leave the room. She was on the edge and if she went over, they all would go with her and he couldn't have that. Not in addition to Santo.

He was stronger than she, so he began to move her even as she fought him. He got her to the floor, and he held her there with the weight of his body. She writhed, trying to throw him off.

He covered her mouth with his. He felt her resistance for a moment and then it was gone, as if it had never been. She tore at him, but it was clothing now: She ripped at his shirt, at the buckle of his belt; she pushed his jeans desperately over his buttocks.

He thought, Yes, and he showed no tenderness as he pulled her sweater over her head. He shoved up her bra and fell on her breasts. She gasped and lowered the zip on her trousers. Savagely, he slapped her hand away. He would do it, he thought. He would own her.

In a fury, he made her naked. She arched to accept him and cried out as he took her.

Afterwards, both of them wept.

Kerra heard it all. How could she help it? The family flat had been transformed as inexpensively as possible from a collection of rooms on the hotel's top floor. Because it was needed elsewhere, very little money had gone into the insulation of the walls. They weren't paper thin, but they might as well have been.

She heard their voices first – her father's soft and her mother's rising – then the shrieking, which she could not ignore, and then the rest. Hail the conquering hero, she thought.

Dully, she said to Alan, 'You need to go,' although part of her was also saying, Do you understand *now*?

Alan said, 'No. We need to talk.'

'My brother has died. I don't think we *need* to anything.'

'Santo,' Alan said quietly. 'Your brother's name was Santo.'

They were still in the kitchen although not at the table where they'd

been sitting when Ben had joined them. With the rising noise from
Santo's bedroom, Kerra had shoved away from the table and gone to
the sink. There she'd turned on the water to fill a pan, although she
had no idea what she would do with it.

She'd remained there after she'd turned off the taps. Outside, she
could see Casvelyn, just the top of it where St Issey Road met St Mevan
Crescent. An unappealing supermarket called Blue Star Grocery
sprawled like a nasty thought at this V-shaped junction, a bunker of
brick and glass that made her wonder why modern conveniences had
to be so ugly. Its lights were still on for evening shopping, and just
beyond it, more lights indicated cars moving carefully along the northwest and southeast boundaries of St Mevan Down. Workers were heading
home for the evening, to the various hamlets that for centuries had
popped up like toadstools along the coast. Smugglers' havens, Kerra
thought. Cornwall had always been a lawless place.

She said, 'Please go.'

'Do you want to tell me what this is about?'

'Santo' – and she said his name with deliberate slowness – 'is what
this is about.'

'You and I are a couple, Kerra. When people—'

'A couple,' she cut in. 'Oh, yes. How true.'

He ignored her sarcasm. 'When people are a couple, they face things
together. I'm here. I'm staying. So you can choose which thing you'd
like to face with me.'

She shot him a look. She hoped he read in it derision. He wasn't
supposed to *be* like this, especially now. She hadn't taken him on as her
partner only to have him reveal a side of himself that proved he was
someone she didn't actually know. He was Alan, wasn't he? *Alan.* Alan
Cheston. Bit of a weak chest so winters were tough on him, often
cautious to a maddening extreme, church-going, parents-loving, un-
athletic, sheep not shepherd. Respectful as well. *And* respectable. He
was the sort of bloke who'd said May I . . . ? before he'd tried to hold
her hand. But now, this person just now . . . This was not the Alan
who'd never missed a Sunday dinner at his mum and dad's since he'd
left university and the London Bloody School of Economics. This was
not the floppy-haired and white-skinned Alan who practised yoga and
served meals-on-wheels and was *never* known to dive into the Sea Pit
just above St Mevan Beach without sticking his toes in first to test the
temperature of the water. *He* wasn't supposed to be telling *her* how
things were going to be.

Yet he stood there doing it. He stood there in front of the stainless-steel fridge and he looked . . . *implacable*, Kerra thought. The sight of him made her veins feel icy.

He said, 'Talk to me.' His voice sounded firm.

The firmness undid her. So what she said in reply was, 'I can't.'

Even this wasn't what she intended to say. But his eyes, which were generally so deferential, were compelling at the moment. She knew that came from power, knowledge, and lack of fear and where *that* had come from was what made Kerra turn from him. She would cook, she decided. They were all going to have to eat eventually.

'Fine,' Alan said to her back. 'I'll talk, then.'

'I have to make a meal,' she told him. 'We all have to eat. If we lose our strength, things will get worse. In the next few days, there's going to be so much to do. Arrangements, phone calls. Someone has to call my grandparents. Santo was their favourite. I'm the oldest of the grandkids – there're twenty-seven of us, isn't that obscene, what with overpopulation and that sort of thing? – but Santo was their favourite. We spent time with them, Santo and I. Sometimes a month. Once nine weeks. They need to be told and my father won't do it. They don't speak, he and Granddad. Not unless they have to.'

She reached for a cookbook. She had a collection of them, all kept in a stand on the work top, the product of cookery classes she'd taken. One of the Kernes had to learn how to plan nutritious, inexpensive, and tasty meals for the large groups who'd book into Adventures Unlimited. The Kernes would hire a cook, of course, but they'd save money by having the meals planned by someone other than an executive chef. Kerra had volunteered for the job. She wasn't interested in anything to do with a kitchen, but she knew they couldn't rely on Santo and relying on Dellen would have been ridiculous. The former was a passable cook on a small scale, but easily distracted by everything, from a piece of music on the radio to the sight of a gannet flying in the direction of Sawsneck Down. As for the latter, everything about Dellen could alter in a second, including her willingness to participate in matters familial.

Kerra flipped open the book she'd chosen at random. She began leafing through pages to find something complicated, something requiring every bit of her attention. The list of ingredients needed to be impressive, and what they didn't have in the kitchen, she would send Alan out to purchase at Blue Star Grocery. If he refused, she would go herself. In either case, she would be busy and busy was what she wanted to be.

Alan said, 'Kerra.'

She ignored him. She decided on jambalaya with dirty rice and green beans, along with bread pudding. It would take hours, and that was fine with her. Chicken, sausage, prawns, green peppers, clam juice . . . The list stretched on and on. She'd make enough for a week, she decided. The practice would be good, and they could all dip into it and reheat it in the microwave whenever they chose. And *weren't* microwaves marvellous? Hadn't they simplified life? God, wouldn't it be the answer to a young girl's prayers to have an appliance like a microwave into which *people* could be deposited as well? Not to heat them up, but just to make them different from what they were. Whom would she have shoved in first? she wondered. Her mother? Her father? Santo? Alan?

Santo, of course. It was always Santo. In you go, brother. Let me set the timer and twirl the dial and wait for someone new to emerge.

No need for that now. Santo was decidedly altered now. No more will o' the wisp, no more tripping without a care in the world along the paths that opened up before him, no more thoughtless chase of if-it-feels-good-do-it. There's more to life than that and I suppose you know it now, Santo. You knew it in the final moment. You *had* to know it. You crashed towards the rocks without a last minute miracle in sight and in the precise instant before you struck bottom, you finally knew that there were actually other people in your world and that *you* were answerable for the pain you caused them. It was too late then to amend yourself, but it was always better late than never when it came to self-knowledge, wasn't it?

Kerra felt as if bubbles were rising inside her. They were hot, like the bubbles of water boiling, and just like boiling water they burned to get out. She hardened herself against letting them escape, and she grabbed a litre of olive oil from another cupboard, above the work top. She turned to scoop up measuring spoons, thinking How much oil? and the bottle slipped from her fingers. It hit the floor just right – naturally – and broke into two neat pieces. The oil pooled out in a viscous mess. It splashed the cooker, the cupboards, and her clothes. She leapt to one side, but she didn't escape.

'Damn!' She finally felt the threat of tears and said to Alan, 'Would you just please *leave*?' She snatched up a roll of kitchen towels and began to unspool them into the oil. Completely unequal to the task at hand, they were soaked to mush the instant they touched the liquid.

Alan said, 'Let me, Kerra. Sit down. Let me.'

She said, 'No! I made the mess. I'll clean it up.'

'Kerra—'

'I said no. I don't need your help. I don't want your help. I want you to leave. *Go.*'

On a stand near the door a dozen or more copies of the *Watchman* had been piled. Alan reached for this. He put Casvelyn's newspaper to good use. Kerra watched the oil soak into the newsprint. Alan did the same. They stood at opposite sides of the pool. She considered it a chasm but he, she knew, saw it as a momentary inconvenience.

He said, 'You don't need to feel guilty because you were angry with Santo. You had a right to anger. He may have thought it was irrational, even stupid of you to care about something that seemed silly to him. But you had a reason for what you felt and you had a right. You always have a right to *whatever* you feel, if it comes down to it. That's how it is.'

'I asked you not to work here.' Her voice was expressionless; her emotion was spent.

He looked puzzled. It was a remark, she realised, coming out of nowhere as far as he knew, but at the moment it summed up everything she was feeling but could not say.

'Kerra, jobs aren't falling from the sky. I'm good at what I do. I'm getting this place noticed. The *Mail on Sunday*? There're bookings coming in every day as a result of that piece. It's tough out here, and if we mean to make a life in Cornwall—'

'We don't,' she said. 'We can't. Not now.'

'Because of Santo?'

'Oh come on, Alan.'

'What are you afraid of?'

'I'm not afraid. I'm *never* afraid.'

'Bollocks. You're angry *because* you're afraid. Anger is easier. It makes more sense.'

'You don't know what you're talking about.'

'Accepted. So tell me.'

She couldn't. Too much hung in the balance to speak: too much seen and too much experienced for too many years. To explain it all to Alan was beyond her. He needed to take her word as the truth and he needed to act accordingly.

That he had not done so, that he was going to continue his refusal to do so rang the death knell over their relationship. Kerra told herself that, because of this, nothing that had happened that day actually mattered.

Even as she thought this, though, she knew that she was lying to herself. But that was something that also didn't matter.

Selevan Penrule thought it was rubbish, but he joined hands with his granddaughter anyway. Across the narrow table in the caravan, they closed their eyes and Tammy began to pray. Selevan didn't listen to the words although he caught the gist of them. Instead, he considered his grandchild's hands. They were dry and cool but so thin that they felt like something he could crush simply by closing his own fingers roughly over them.

'She's not been eating right, Father Penrule,' his daughter-in-law had told him. He hated what she called him – 'Father Penrule' made him feel like a renegade priest – but he'd said nothing to correct Sally Joy since speaking to him at all was something that she and her husband hadn't bothered with for ages. So, he'd grunted and said he'd fatten the girl up. It's being in Africa, woman, don't you know that? You cart the girl off to Rhodesia—

'Zimbabwe, Father Penrule. And we're actually in—'

'Whatever the hell they want it to be called. You cart her off to Rhodesia and expose her to God only knows what and that would kill anyone's appetite, let me tell you.'

Selevan realised he was taking things too far at that point because Sally Joy said nothing for a moment. He imagined her there in Rhodesia or wherever she was, sitting on the porch in a rattan chair with her legs stretched out and a drink on the table next to her . . . lemonade, it would be, lemonade, with a dash of . . . what is it, Sally Joy? What's in the glass that would make Rhodesia go down a treat for you?

He harrumphed noisily and said, 'Well, never mind then. You send her along. I'll get her sorted.'

'You'll watch her food intake?'

'Like a peregrine.'

Which he had done. She'd taken thirty-nine bites tonight. Thirty-nine spoonfuls of a gruel that would have made Oliver Twist lead an armed rebellion. No milk, no raisins, no cinnamon, no sugar. Just watery porridge and a glass of water. Not even tempted by her grandfather's meal of chops and veg, she was.

'. . . for Your will is what we seek. Amen,' Tammy said, and he opened his eyes to find hers on him. Her expression was fond. He dropped her fingers in a rush.

He said roughly, 'Bloody stupid. You know that, eh?'

She smiled. 'So you've told me.' But she settled in so that he could tell her again, and she balanced her cheek on her palm.

'We pray before the bloody meal,' he groused. 'Why've we got to bloody pray at the bloody end as well?'

She answered by rote, but with no indication that she was tiring of a discussion they'd had at least twice a week since she'd come to Cornwall. 'We say a prayer of thanks at the beginning. We thank God for the food we have. Then at the end we pray for those who don't have enough food to sustain them.'

'If they're bloody alive they have enough bloody food to bloody sustain them, don't they?' he countered.

'Grandie, you know what I mean. There's a difference between just being alive and having enough to be sustained. Sustained means more than just living. It means having enough sustenance to *engage*. Take the Sudan, for example—'

'Now you hang on right there, missy-miss. And don't move either.' He slid out from the banquette. He carried his plate the short distance to the caravan's sink as a means of feigning other employment, but instead of beginning the washing up, he snatched her rucksack from the hook on the back of the door and said, 'Let's just have a look.'

She said, 'Grandie,' in a patient voice. 'You can't stop me, you know.'

He said, 'My duty to your parents is what I know, my girl.'

He brought the sack to the table and emptied its contents and there it was: on the cover a young black mother in tribal dress holding her child, one of them sorrowful and both of them hungry. Blurred in the background were countless others, waiting in a mixture of hope and confusion. The magazine was called *Crossroads*, and he scooped it up, rolled it up, and slapped it against his palm.

'Right,' he said. 'Another bowl of that mush for you, then. Either that or a chop. You can take your pick.' He shoved the magazine into the back pocket of his drooping trousers. He would dispose of it later, when she'd gone to bed.

'I've had enough,' she said. 'Truly. Grandie, I eat enough to stay alive and well, and that's what God intended. We're not meant to carry round excess flesh. Aside from being not good for us, it's also not right.'

'Oh, a sin, is it?'

'Well . . . it can be, yes.'

'So your grandie's a sinner? Going straight to hell on a plate of beans while you're playing harps with the angels, eh?'

She laughed outright. 'You know that's not what I think.'

'What you think is a cartload of bollocks. What I *know* is that this stage you're in—'

'A stage? And how do you know that when you and I have been together . . . what? Two months? Before that you didn't even *know* me, Grandie. Not really.'

'Makes no difference, that. I know women. And you're a woman despite what you're doing to make yourself look like a twelve-year-old girl.'

She nodded thoughtfully, and he could tell from the expression on her face that she was about to twist his words and use them against him as she seemed only too expert at doing. 'So let me see,' she said. 'You had four sons and one daughter, and the daughter – this would be Aunt Nan, of course – left home when she was sixteen and never returned except at Christmas and the odd bank holiday. So that leaves Gran and whatever wife or girlfriend your sons brought round, yes? So how is it that you know women in general from this limited exposure to them, Grandie?'

'Don't you get clever with me. I was married to your gran for forty-six years when the poor woman dropped dead, so I had plenty of time to know your sort.'

'My "sort"?'

'The female sort. And what I know is that women need men as much as men need women and anyone who thinks otherwise is doing their thinking straight through the arse.'

'What about men who need men and women who need women?'

'We'll not talk about that!' he declared in outrage. 'There'll be no perversion in *my* family and have no doubt about *that.*'

'Ah. That's what you think, then. It's per*version*.'

'That's what I *know*.' He shoved her possessions back into the rucksack and he'd replaced it on the hook before he saw how she'd diverted them from his chosen topic. The damn girl was like a freshly hooked fish when it came to conversation. She flipped and flopped and avoided the net. Well, that would *not* be the case tonight. He was a match for her wiliness. The cleverness in *her* blood was diluted by having Sally Joy for a mother. The cleverness in his blood was not.

He said, 'A stage. Full stop. Girls your age, they all have stages. This one here, it might look different from another girl's, but a stage is a stage. And I know one when I'm looking it in the eyes, don't I?'

'Do you?'

'Oh aye. And there've been signs, by the way, in case you think I'm blowing smoke in the matter. I saw you with him, I did.'

She didn't reply. Instead, she carried her glass and bowl to the sink and began the washing up. She scraped the bone from his chop into the rubbish, and she stacked the cooking pots, the plates, the cutlery, and the glasses on the work top in the order in which she intended to wash them. She filled the sink. Steam rose. He thought she was going to scald herself some night, but the heat never seemed to bother her.

When she began to wash but still said nothing, he picked up a tea towel for the drying and spoke again. 'You hear me, girl? I saw you with him, so do *not* be declaring to your granddad that you have no interest, eh? I know what I saw and I know what I know. When a woman looks at a man in the way you were looking at him . . . That tells me you don't know your own mind, no matter what you say.'

'And where did this seeing take place, Grandie?'

'What does it matter? There you were, heads together, arms locked the way *lovers* do, by the way.'

'And did that worry you? That we might be lovers?'

'Don't try that with me. Don't you bloody try that again, missy-miss. Once a night is enough and your granddad isn't fool enough to fall for it twice.' She'd done her water glass and his lager pint, and he snatched up the latter and pushed the tea towel into it. He screwed it around and gave it a polish. 'You were *interested*, you bloody were.'

She paused. She was looking out of the window towards the four lines of caravans below their own. They marched towards the edge of the cliff and the sea. Only one of them was occupied at this time of year – the one nearest the cliff – and its kitchen light was on. This winked in the night as the rain fell against it.

'Jago's home,' Tammy said. 'We should have him over for a meal soon. It's not good for elderly people to be on their own so much. And now he's going to be . . . He'll miss Santo badly, though I don't expect he'll ever admit it.'

Ah. There. The name had been said. Selevan could talk about the boy freely now. He said, 'You'll claim it was nothing, won't you. A what d'you call it? A passing interest. A bit of flirting. But I saw and I know you were willing. If he'd made a move . . .'

She picked up a plate. She washed it thoroughly. Her movements were languid. There was no sense of urgency in anything that Tammy did. She said, 'Grandie, you misconstrued. Santo and I were friends. He talked to me. He *needed* someone to talk to, and I was the person he chose.'

'That's him not you.'

'No. It was both. I was happy with that. Happy to be someone he could turn to.'

'Bah. Don't lie to me.'

'Why would I lie? He talked, I listened. And if he wanted to know what I thought about something, I told him what I thought.'

'I saw you with your arms *linked*, girl.'

She cocked her head as she looked at him. She studied his face and then she smiled. She removed her hands from the water and, dripping as they were, she put her arms around him. She kissed him even as he stiffened and tried to resist her. She said, 'Dear Grandie. Linking arms doesn't mean what it might have meant once. It means friendship. And that's the honest truth.'

'Honest,' he said. 'Bah.'

'It is. I always try to be honest.'

'With yourself as well?'

'Especially with myself.' She went back to the washing up and cleaned her gruel bowl carefully, and then she began on the cutlery. She'd done it all before she spoke again. And then she spoke in a very low voice, which Selevan might have missed altogether had he not been straining to hear something quite different from what she next said.

'I told him to be honest as well,' she murmured. 'If I hadn't, Grandie . . . I'm rather worried about that.'

6

'You and I both know that you can arrange this if you want to, Ray. That's all I'm asking you to do.' Bea Hannaford raised her mug of morning coffee and watched her ex-husband over the rim of it, trying to determine how much further she could push him. Ray felt guilty for a number of things, and Bea was never beyond a session of button pressing in what she considered a good cause.

'It's just not on,' he said. 'And even if it was I don't have those kinds of strings to pull.'

'Assistant Chief Constable? Oh please.' She refrained from rolling her eyes. She knew he hated that, and he'd score a point if she did it. There were times when having experienced nearly twenty years of marriage with someone came in very useful, and this was one of those times. 'You can't intend me to take that on board.'

'You can do with it what you will,' Ray said. 'Anyway, you don't know what you've got yet, and you won't know till you hear from forensics, so you're jumping the gun. Which, by the way, you're very good at doing.'

That, she thought, was below the belt. It was one of those ex-husband kinds of remarks, the sort that lead to a row in which comments are made with the intention of drawing blood. She wasn't about to participate. She went to the coffee maker and topped up her mug.

He'd shown up at her door at eight-twenty. She'd assumed the courier from London had arrived far earlier than expected, but she'd opened the door to find her former husband on the step. He was frowning in the direction of her front window, where a three-tiered plant stand displayed a collection of pot plants going through the death throes of the sadly neglected. A sign above them was printed with the words: *Fund Raiser for Home Nurses/Leave Money in Box*. Clearly, the poor home nurses were not going to benefit from Bea's attempt to add to their coffers.

Ray said, 'Your black thumb, I see, has not become greener recently.'

She said, 'Ray. What're you doing here? Where's Pete?'

'At school. Where else would he be? And deeply unhappy at having been forced to eat two eggs this morning instead of his regular. Since when is he allowed cold pizza for breakfast?'

'He's lying to you. Well . . . essentially. It was only once. The problem is he has an unfailing memory.'

'He comes by *that* honestly.'

She returned to the kitchen rather than reply. He followed her, a carrier bag in his hand, and he placed this on the table. It was the reason for his call: Pete's football boots. She didn't want him leaving the shoes at his dad's house, did she? Nor did she want him to take them to school, yes? So his father brought them by.

She sipped her coffee and offered him one if he wanted. He knew where the mugs were, she'd told him.

But she'd made the offer before she thought about it. The coffee maker squatted next to her calendar and what was on this calendar was not only Pete's schedule, but also her own. Given, her own was cryptic enough, but Ray was no fool.

He'd read a few of the notations inside the boxed dates. She knew what he was seeing: *Motor-mouth Wanker, Big Trouble Wanker.* There were others as well, as he would note if he flipped back to the previous three months. Fifteen weeks of internet dating: There might be millions of fish in the sea, but Bea Hannaford kept hooking crab pots and seaweed.

It was largely to forestall a conversation about her decision to re-enter the world of dating yet again that prompted Bea to bring up having the incident room in Casvelyn. It should, of course, have been in Bodmin where the set-up would be minimal, but Bodmin was miles and miles from Casvelyn with only tediously slow-moving two-lane country roads between them. She wanted, she explained to him, an incident room that was nearer to the crime scene.

He made his point once again. 'You don't know it's a crime scene. It might be the scene of a tragic accident. What makes you think it's a crime? This isn't one of your "feelings", is it?'

She wanted to say I don't have feelings, as you recall, but she didn't. Over the years she'd become so much better at letting go of matters over which she had no control, one of which was her former husband's assessment of her. She said, 'The body's a bit marked His eye was blackened – healing now, so I'd guess he'd had a bust-up with someone last week or earlier. Then there was the sling, that webbing-thing they use for slinging round a tree or some other stationary object.'

'Hence its name,' Ray murmured.

'Bear with me, Ray, as I know nothing about cliff climbing.' Bea kept her voice patient.

'Sorry.'

'Anyway, the sling broke, which was how he fell, but I think it may have been nobbled. Constable McNulty – who, by the way, has absolutely *no* future in criminal investigations – pointed out that the sling was being held together with electrical tape over a tear and is it any wonder the poor lad took a fatal tumble as a result. *But* every single piece of the boy's equipment had electrical tape wrapped round it at some point, and I think the tape's used to identify the equipment for some reason. If that's the case, how difficult would it have been for someone to remove the tape, weaken the sling however it was weakened, and then replace the tape without the boy ever knowing it?'

'Have you had a look at the rest of the equipment?'

'Every piece is with forensics, and I have a fairly good idea what they're going to tell me. And *what* they tell me is why I'll need an incident room.'

'But not why you need one in Casvelyn.'

Bea downed the rest of her coffee and placed the mug in the sink. She neither rinsed nor washed it and she realised this was yet another benefit to life-without-husband. If she didn't feel up to doing the washing up, she didn't have to do the washing up just to soothe the savage breast of the compulsive personality.

She said, 'The principals are there, Ray, in Casvelyn. Not in Bodmin, not even here in Holsworthy. They have a police station, small but adequate, and it's got a conference room on the first floor that's perfectly adequate as well.'

'You've done your homework.'

'I'm trying to make it easier for you. I'm giving you details to support the arrangement. I know you can do this.'

He studied her. She avoided studying him back. He was an attractive man – hair going a bit thin but that didn't detract – and she didn't need to compare him to *Motormouth Wanker* or any of the others. She just needed him to cooperate or leave. Or cooperate *and* leave, which would be even better.

'And if I arrange this for you, Beatrice?'

'What?'

'What's the quid pro quo?' He was standing by the coffee maker and he gave another look to the calendar. '*Big Trouble Wanker*,' he read. '*Motormouth Wanker*. Come on, Beatrice.'

She said, 'Thanks for bringing Pete's football boots. Finished with your coffee?'

He let a moment go by. Then he took a final gulp and handed the mug over to her, saying, 'There had to have been less expensive shoes.'

'He has expensive taste. How's the Porsche running, by the way?'

'The Porsche,' he said, 'is a dream.'

'The Porsche,' she reminded him, 'is a car.' She held up a finger to stop him from retorting. 'Which brings to mind . . . the victim's car.'

'What about it?'

'What does an unopened package of condoms in the car of an eighteen-year-old boy suggest to you?'

'Is this rhetorical?'

'They were in his car. Along with a blue grass CD, a blank invoice from something called LiquidEarth, and a rolled up poster for a music festival last year in Cheltenham. And two dog-eared surfing magazines. I've got my fingers on everything but the condoms—'

'Well, thank God for that,' Ray said with a smile.

'—and I'm wondering if he was about to get lucky, getting lucky, or hoping to get lucky.'

'Or just eighteen,' Ray said. 'All boys that age should be so adequately prepared. What about Lynley?'

'Condoms. Lynley. Where're we going with this?'

'What was your interview like?'

'He's hardly going to be intimidated by being in the presence of a cop, so I'd have to say the interview was fine. No matter which way I flipped the questions, his answers were consistent. I think he's playing it straight.'

'But . . . ?' Ray prompted.

He knew her too well: her tone of voice, the expression that she tried and obviously failed to control on her face. 'The other one concerns me,' she said.

'Ah. The woman at the cottage. What was her name?'

'Daidre Trahair. She's a vet from Bristol.'

'And what concerns you about the vet from Bristol?'

'I've a sense about things.'

'I know that well enough. And what's the sense about things telling you this time?'

'That she's lying about something. I want to know what.'

*   *   *

Daidre neatly situated her Vauxhall in the car park at the town end of St Mevan Crescent, which made a slow curve towards St Mevan Beach and the old Promontory King George Hotel sitting well above the sand with a line of decrepit blue beach huts below it. When she'd dropped him at the bottom of Belle Vue Lane and pointed him in the direction of the shops, she and Thomas Lynley had agreed on two hours.

He'd said politely, 'I'm not inconveniencing you, I hope.'

He was not, she assured him. She had several things to do in town anyway. He was to take his time and purchase what he needed.

He'd protested this idea initially, when she'd first fetched him from the Salthouse Inn. Although he was considerably more fragrant than on the previous day, he was still wearing the ghastly white boiler suit, still with nothing but socks on his feet. He'd carefully removed these to cross the muddy path to her car and he'd tried to insist that buying new clothing could wait when she pressed two hundred pounds upon him.

She said, 'Please. Don't be ridiculous, Thomas. You can't continue to walk round the area like . . . well, like someone from a hazardous chemicals squad, or whatever they call it. You can repay me the money. Besides,' and here she smiled, 'I hate to be the one to inform you, but white doesn't suit you in the least.'

'It doesn't?' He'd smiled in turn. He had quite a pleasant smile, and it came to her that she'd not seen him smile until that moment. Not that there had been anything in particular to grin about on the previous day, but still. Smiling was virtually an automatic response in most people, a reaction indicative of nothing other than passing courtesy, so it was unusual to find someone so grave.

'Not in the least,' she told him. 'So buy something suitable for your-self.'

'Thank you,' he'd said. 'You're very kind.'

'I'm only kind to the wounded,' she told him.

He'd nodded thoughtfully and looked out of the windscreen for a moment, perhaps meditating on the way Belle Vue Lane climbed in a narrow passage to the upper reaches of the town. He'd finally said, 'Two hours then,' and got out, leaving her wondering what else he had on his mind.

She'd driven off as he'd walked barefoot on a route towards the outdoor outfitter's shop. She'd passed him with a wave and had seen from her rearview mirror that he'd watched from the pavement as she made her way up the hill to where the street curved out of sight and split off in one direction to the car park and in the other towards St Mevan Down.

This was the highest point in Casvelyn. From here, one could take in the charmless nature of the little town. It had seen its heyday more than seventy years earlier when holidaying at the sea had been the height of fashion. Now it existed largely at the pleasure of surfers and other outdoor enthusiasts, with tea shops long ago morphed into T-shirt boutiques, souvenir shops, and surfing academies, and post-Edwardian homes serving as doss houses for a peripatetic population who followed the seasons and the swells.

Across Belle Vue Lane from the car park, Toes on the Nose Café was doing a good morning's business from the local surfers, two of whom had left their cars parked illegally along the kerb as if with the intention of tearing out of the establishment at the first sign of a change in conditions. The place was crowded with them: They were a close community. Daidre felt the prick of absence – how different it was from the sorrow of loss, she realised – as she passed by and saw them huddled round tables and no doubt telling tales of derring do in the waves.

She headed for the offices of the *Watchman*, which hunkered in an unattractive cube of blue stucco at the junction of Princes Street and Queen Street, in an area of Casvelyn that the locals jokingly called the Royal T. Princes Street served as the cross piece of the T, with Queen Street the trunk. Below Queen was King Street and nearby were Duke Street and Duchy Row. In Victorian times and earlier, Casvelyn had longed to append *Regis* to it name, and its streets' appellations bore historical testimony to this fact.

When she'd told Thomas Lynley that she had things to do in town, she hadn't been lying, exactly. There were arrangements to be made eventually about the broken window at the cottage, but beyond that there was the not insignificant matter of Santo Kerne's death. The *Watchman* would be covering the teenager's fall in Polcare Cove, and as she did not take a newspaper in Cornwall, it would be perfectly logical that she might stop by the offices of the paper to see if an issue with this story in it was soon going to be available.

When she entered, she saw Max Priestley at once. The place was quite small – consisting of Max's own office, the layout room, a tiny newsroom, and a reception area – so this was no surprise. He was in the layout room in the company of one of the paper's two reporters, and they were bent over what appeared to be a mock-up of a front page, which Max seemed to want changed and which the reporter – who looked like nothing so much as a twelve-year-old girl in flip flops – apparently wanted to remain the same.

'People'll *expect* it,' she was insisting. 'This's a community paper, and he was a member of the community.'

'The Queen dies and we go three inches,' Max replied. 'Otherwise we don't get carried away.' He looked up then and fixed on Daidre.

She raised a hand hesitantly and studied him as closely as she could without being obvious about it. He was an outdoorsman, and he looked it: weathered skin making him seem older than his forty years, thick hair permanently bleached from the sun, trim from regular coastal walking. He seemed normal today. She wondered about that.

The receptionist, who tripled as copy editor and secretary to the publisher, was in the process of politely enquiring after Daidre's business when Max came out to join them, polishing his gold-rimmed spectacles on his shirt. He said to Daidre, 'I just sent Steve Teller to interview you not five minutes ago. It's time you had a phone like the rest of the world.'

'I do have a phone,' she told him. 'It's just not in Cornwall.'

'That's hardly convenient to our purpose, Daidre.'

'So you're working on the story about Santo Kerne?'

'I can't exactly avoid it and still call myself a newsman, can I?' He tilted his head towards his office, saying to the receptionist, 'Get Steve on his mobile if you can, Janna. Tell him Ms Trahair's come into town and if he manages to get back quick enough, she might consent to an interview.'

'I've nothing to tell him,' Daidre told Max Priestley.

'"Nothing" is our business,' he replied affably. He held out his hand, a gesture telling Daidre to go into his office.

She cooperated. Beneath his desk, his golden retriever snoozed. Daidre squatted by the dog and caressed her silky head. 'Looking well,' she said. 'The medication's working?'

He grunted in the affirmative and said, 'But you aren't making a house call, are you.'

Daidre made a cursory exam of the dog's belly, more a matter of form than from any real need. All signs of the skin infection were gone. She rose and said, 'Don't let it go on so long next time. Lily could lose her fur in gobs. You don't want that.'

'Won't be a next time. I'm actually a fast learner, despite what my history suggests. Why're you here?'

'You know how Santo Kerne died, don't you?'

'Daidre, you know that I know. So I suppose the real question is why're you asking. Or stating. Or whatever you're doing. What do you want? How can I help you this morning?'

She could hear the irritation in his voice. She knew what it meant. She was merely an occasional holiday maker in Casvelyn. She had entrée to some places and not to others. She changed gears. 'I saw Aldara last night. She was waiting for someone.'

'Was she indeed?'

'I thought it might have been you.'

'That's not very likely.' He looked round the office as if for employment. 'And is that why you've come? Checking up on Aldara? Checking up on me? Neither seems like you, but I'm not much good at reading women, as you know.'

'No. That's not it.'

'Then is there more? Because as we want to get the paper out earlier today . . .'

'I've actually come to ask a favour.'

He looked immediately suspicious. 'What would that be?'

'Your computer. The internet actually. I've no other access, and I'd rather not use the library. I need to look up . . .' She hesitated. How much to say?

'What?'

She cast about and came up with it, and what she said was the truth despite its being incomplete. 'The body, Santo . . . Max, Santo was found by a man doing the coastal walk.'

'We know that actually.'

'All right. Yes. I suppose you do. But he's also a detective from New Scotland Yard. Do you know that as well?'

'Is he indeed?' Max sounded interested.

'So he says. I want to find out if that's true.'

'Why?'

'*Why*? Well, goodness, think of it. What better claim to make about yourself if you don't want people looking at you too closely?'

'Thinking of going into police work yourself? Thinking of coming to work for me? Because otherwise, Daidre, I don't see what this has to do with you.'

'I found the man inside my cottage. I'd like to know if he is who he says he is.' She explained how she'd come to be acquainted with Thomas Lynley. She made no mention, however, of how the man seemed: like someone carrying across his shoulders a yoke studded with protruding nails.

Her explanation apparently seemed reasonable to the newsman. He tilted his head towards his computer terminal. 'Go on then. Print up what you find because we may well use it. I've work to do. Lily'll keep you company.' He started to leave the room but paused at the door, one hand on the jamb. 'You haven't seen me,' he said.

She'd moved to the terminal. She looked up, frowning. 'What?'

'You haven't seen me, should anyone ask. Are we clear on that?'

'You do know what that sounds like, don't you?'

'Frankly, I don't care what it sounds like.'

He left her, then, and she mulled over what he'd said. Only animals, she concluded, were safe for one's devotion.

She logged onto the internet and then a search engine. She typed in Thomas Lynley's name.

Daidre found him waiting at the bottom of Belle Vue Lane. He looked completely different from the bearded stranger she'd driven into town, but she had no trouble recognising him since she'd spent over an hour gazing on a dozen or more news photos of him, generated by the investigation of a serial killing in London and by the tragedy that had supervened in his life. She now knew why she had seen him as an injured man carrying a tremendous burden. She merely didn't know what to do with her knowledge. Nor with the rest of it: who he actually was, what comprised his background, the title, the money, the trappings of a world so far different from her own that they might have come from different planets and not merely from different circumstances in different parts of the very same county.

He'd had his hair cut, and he'd had a shave. He wore a rain jacket over a collarless shirt and pullover. He'd bought sturdy shoes and corduroy trousers. He carried a waxed rain hat in his hand. Not, she thought grimly, exactly the getup one expected to see on a belted earl. But that's what he was. Lord Whoever with a murdered wife, done in on the street by a twelve-year-old boy. She'd been pregnant as well. It was little wonder to Daidre that Lynley was among the injured. The real miracle was that the man was capable of functioning at all.

When she pulled to the kerb, he got into the car. He'd bought a few items from the chemist as well, he told her, indicating a bag he brought forth from the capacious inner pocket of his jacket. Razor, toothbrush, toothpaste, shaving cream—

'You've no need to account to me,' she told him. 'I'm only glad you had enough funds.'

He gestured to his clothes. 'On sale. End of the season. A real bargain. I've even managed' – he reached into the pocket of his trousers and brought out a few notes and a handful of coins 'to bring you change,' he said. 'I never thought I'd . . .' He drifted off.

'What?' She stuffed the notes and coins into the unused ashtray. 'Shop for yourself?'

He looked at her, clearly assessing her words. 'No,' he said. 'I never thought I'd enjoy it.'

'Ah. Well. It's retail therapy. Absolutely guaranteed to lift one's spirits. Women know this at birth, somehow. Men have to learn it.'

He was quiet for a moment, and she caught him doing it another time, looking out of the car, through the windscreen, at the street. In a different place and a different time. She heard her words again and bit the inside of her lip. She hastened to add, 'Shall we top off your experience with a coffee somewhere?'

He considered this. He answered slowly. 'Yes. I think I'd like a coffee.'

Detective Inspector Hannaford was waiting for them at the Salthouse Inn when they returned. Lynley decided that the inspector had been watching for Daidre's car, for as soon as they pulled into the inn's lumpy car park, she came out of the building. It had begun to rain again, March's ceaseless bad weather having segued into April and now May, and she pulled up the hood of her rain jacket and marched across to them, moving briskly.

She knocked on Daidre's window and, when it was lowered, said, 'I'd like a word. Both of you, please.' And then directly to Lynley, 'You're looking more human today. It's an improvement.' She turned and headed back into the inn.

Lynley and Daidre followed. They found Hannaford in the public bar where she'd been – as Lynley suspected – occupying a window seat. She shed her rain jacket onto a bench and nodded for them to do the same. She led them to one of the larger tables on which a magazine-size *A to Z* was opened.

She spoke expansively to Lynley, which made him immediately

suspicious about her motives. When cops were friendly, as he well knew, they were friendly for a reason and it wasn't necessarily a good one. Where, she asked him, had he begun his coastal walk on the previous day? Would he show her on the map? See, the path's well-marked with a green dotted line, and if he'd be so kind as to point out the spot . . . It was all a matter of tying up the loose ends of his story, she said. He would know the dance, of course.

Lynley brought out his reading spectacles and leaned over the road atlas. The truth of the matter was that he hadn't the slightest idea where he'd begun his walk on the South-West Coast Path on the previous day. If there had been a landmark he hadn't taken note of it. He remembered the names of several villages and hamlets he'd come upon along the coast, but as to when on his walk he'd passed through them, he couldn't say. He also didn't see that it mattered, although DI Hannaford cleared the air on that concern in a moment. He took a stab at placing himself some twelve miles southwest of Polcare Cove. He had no idea if this was accurate.

Hannaford said, 'Right,' although she made no note about the location. She went on pleasantly with, 'And what about you, Ms Trahair?'

The vet stirred next to Lynley. 'I did tell you I came down from Bristol.'

'You did indeed. Mind showing me the route? C'n I assume you follow the same route each time, by the way? Straightforward matter and all that?'

'Not necessarily.'

Lynley noted how Daidre drew out the final word, and he knew that Hannaford would not miss it either. Drawing a reply out like that generally meant certain mental hoops were being jumped through. Whatever those hoops were and why they existed at all, Hannaford would be fishing for the reason.

Lynley took a moment to evaluate the two women. From head to toe, they couldn't have been more dissimilar: Hannaford's flaming mop done up in wild spikes, Daidre's sandy hair drawn back from her face and held at the crown of her head with a tortoiseshell slide; Hannaford dressed to mean business in a suit and court shoes, Daidre wearing jeans, pullover, and boots. Daidre was lithe, like a woman who took regular exercise and watched what she ate. Hannaford looked like someone whose busy life precluded both regular meals and regular work-outs. There were also several decades between them. The detective could have been Daidre's mother.

She wasn't acting motherly now. She was waiting for an answer to her question, as Daidre looked at the atlas to explain the route she'd followed from Bristol to Polcare Cove. Lynley knew why the cop was asking. He wondered if Daidre was working that out as well before she replied.

The M5 down to Exeter, she said. Over to Okehampton and north-west from there. There was no completely easy way to get to Polcare Cove, she pointed out. Sometimes she did the Exeter route, but other times she worked her way over from Tiverton.

Hannaford made much of studying the map before she said, 'And from Okehampton?'

'What d'you mean?' Daidre asked.

'One can't leap from Okehampton to Polcare Cove, Ms Trahair. You didn't come by helicopter from there, did you? What was the route you took? The exact route please.'

Lynley saw a flush rise up the vet's neck. She was lucky that her skin was lightly freckled. Had it not been, she would have coloured to puce.

She said, 'Are you asking me this because you think I had some-thing to do with that boy's death?'

'Did you?'

'I did not.'

'Then you won't mind showing me your route, will you?'

Daidre pressed her lips together. She pushed an errant lock of hair behind her left ear. Her lobe, Lynley saw, was pierced three times. She wore a hoop, a stud, but nothing else.

She traced the route: A3079, A3072, A39, and then a series of smaller roads until she reached Polcare Cove, which earned barely a speck in the *A to Z*. As she pointed out the journey she'd made, Hannaford took notes. She nodded thoughtfully and thanked the other woman when Daidre had completed her answer.

Daidre didn't look pleased to have the detective's thanks. She looked, if anything, angry and trying to master her anger. This told Lynley that Daidre knew what the detective was up to, though not where her anger was being directed: at DI Hannaford or herself.

'Are we released now?' Daidre asked.

'You are, Ms Trahair,' Hannaford said. 'But Mr Lynley and I have further business.'

'You *can't* think he—' She stopped. The flush was there again. She looked at Lynley and then away.

'He what?' Hannaford asked politely.

'He's a stranger round here. How would he have known that boy?'

'Are you saying you yourself knew that boy, Ms Trahair? He might have been a stranger here as well. Our Mr Lynley – for all we know – may have come along precisely to toss Santo Kerne – that's his name, by the way – right down the face of that cliff.'

'That's ridiculous. He's said he's a policeman.'

'He's said. But I've no actual proof of that. Have you?'

'Never mind.' She'd placed her shoulder bag on a chair, and she scooped it up. 'I'm leaving now, as you said you were finished with me, Inspector.'

'As indeed I am,' Bea Hannaford said pleasantly. 'For now.'

They exchanged only a brief few remarks in the car afterwards. Lynley asked Hannaford where she was taking him, and she replied that she was taking him with her to Truro, to the Royal Cornwall Hospital, to be exact. He then said, 'You're going to check all the pubs on the route, aren't you?' To which she archly replied, 'All the pubs on the route to Truro? Not very likely, my good man.'

He said, 'I'm not talking about the route to Truro, Inspector.'

She said, 'I knew that. And do you really expect me to answer that question? You found the body. You know the game if you're who you say you are.' She glanced his way. She'd put on sunglasses although there was no sun and, indeed, it was still raining. He wondered about this and she answered his wonder. 'Corrective,' she told him. 'For my driving. My others are at home. Or possibly in my son's rucksack at school. Or one of the dogs could have eaten them, for all I know.'

'You have dogs?'

'Three black labs. Dog One, Two and Three.'

'Interesting names.'

'I like to keep things simple at home. To balance all the ways things are never simple at work.'

That was the extent of what they said. The rest of the drive they made in silence broken by radio chatter and two calls Hannaford took on her mobile phone. One of them apparently asked for her approximate time of arrival in Truro, barring traffic problems, and the other was a brief message from someone to whom she responded with a terse, 'I *told* them to get it to *me*. What the hell's it doing with you in bloody Exeter? And how'm I supposed to . . . That is *not* necessary and yes you're right before you say it: I don't want to owe you. Oh, grand. Do what you like, Ray.'

At the hospital in Truro, Hannaford guided Lynley to the mortuary, where the air smelled headily of disinfectant and an assistant was hosing off the trolley on which a body had been cut open for inspection. Nearby, the forensic pathologist – thin as an ageing spinster's marital hopes – was downing a large tomato juice over a stainless-steel sink. The man, Lynley thought, had to have a stomach of iron and the sensitivity of a stone.

'This is Gordie Lisle,' Hannaford said to Lynley. 'Fastest Y incision on the planet and you don't want to know how quickly he can shear ribs.'

'You do me too much honour,' Lisle said.

'I know. This is Thomas Lynley,' she told him. 'What've we got?'

Finishing his juice, Lisle went to a desk and picked up a document to which he referred as he began his report. This he prefaced with the information that the injuries were consistent with a fall. He went about relating them. Pelvis broken, he said, and right medial malleolus shattered. He added, 'That's ankle to the layman.'

Hannaford nodded sagely.

Right tibia and right fibula fractured, Lisle continued. Compound fractures of the ulna and radius, also on the right, six ribs broken, left greater tubercle crushed, both lungs pierced, spleen ruptured.

'What the hell is a tubercle?' Hannaford asked.

'Shoulder,' he explained.

'Nasty business, but is all that enough to kill him? What sent him to the other side, then? Shock?'

'I was saving the best for last. Enormous fracture of the temporal bone. His skull broke like an eggshell. See here.' Lisle set his document on a work top and strolled over to a wall on which the human skeletal system was displayed on a large chart. 'When he fell, I reckon he hit an outcrop on the way down the cliff. He flipped at least once, picked up speed with the rest of the descent, landed heavy on the right side and crushed his skull on the slate. When the bone fractured, it sliced into the middle meningeal artery. That produced an acute epidural haemotoma. Pressure on the brain and no place for it to go that's not lethal. He'd have died in about fifteen minutes although he would have been unconscious throughout. I take it there was no helmet nearby? No other headgear?'

'Kids,' Hannaford said. 'They think they're invincible.'

'This one wasn't. Anyway, the extent of the injuries suggests he fell the moment he began the abseil.'

'Which itself suggests the sling broke the instant it took his full weight.'

'I'd agree with that.'

'What about the black eye? It was healing, yes? What's it consistent with?'

'A bloody good punch. Someone gave him a decent one that likely floored him. You can still see the impression of the knuckles.'

Hannaford nodded. She gave a glance at Lynley who'd been listening and simultaneously wondering why Hannaford was making him part of this. It was more than irregular. It was foolhardy of her, considering his position in the case, and she didn't seem like a foolhardy woman. She had a plan of some sort. He would have laid money on that.

'When?' Hannaford asked.

'The punch?' Lisle said. 'I'd say a week ago.'

'Does it look like he was in a fight?'

Lisle shook his head.

'Why not?'

'No other marks on him of a similar age,' Lynley put in. 'Someone got one good blow in and that was that.'

Hannaford looked at him, quite as if she'd forgotten she'd brought him. Lisle said, 'I'd agree. Someone snapped or someone was giving him discipline of some sort. It either resolved things, knocked him flat, or he wasn't the type to be provoked, even by a punch in the face.'

'What about sado-masochism?' Hannaford asked.

Lisle looked thoughtful, and Lynley said, 'I'm not sure sado-masochists like being punched in the face.'

'Hmm. Yes,' Lisle said. 'I'd think your common S and M freak would be looking to have himself tweaked round his privates. Spanked as well. Maybe whipped for good measure. And we've got nothing on the body consistent with that.' He returned to his tomato juice. All three of them stood for a moment, staring at the chart of the skeletal system. Lisle finally said to Hannaford, 'How's the dating coming along? Internet made your dreams come true yet?'

'Daily,' she told him. 'You must try it again, Gordie. You gave up far too soon.'

He shook his head. 'I'm finished there. Case of looking for love in all the wrong places, if I might coin a phrase.' He gazed mournfully round the mortuary. 'Puts them right off, this does, no getting away from it. No dolling it up. I spill the beans and there you have it.'

'What d'you mean?'

He gestured to the room. Another corpse was waiting nearby, a sheet covering its body, a tag on its toe. 'When they learn what I do. No one fancies it much.'

Hannaford patted him on the shoulder. 'Well, no matter there, Gordie. You fancy it and that's what counts.'

'You want to give us a try, then?' He looked at her differently, assessing and weighing.

'Don't tempt me, dear. You're far too young, and anyway I'm a sinner at heart. I'll need the paperwork on this' – using her chin to indicate the trolley that had been washed off – 'as quickly as possible.'

'I'll sweet talk someone,' Lisle said.

They left him. Hannaford examined a hospital plan nearby and ushered Lynley to the cafeteria. He couldn't think she intended to have a meal after their visit to the mortuary and he found he was correct in this assessment. Hannaford paused in the doorway and looked round the room till she spied a man at a table alone, reading a newspaper. She led Lynley to him.

It was the man, Lynley saw, who'd come to Daidre Trahair's cottage on the previous night, the same man who'd asked him about New Scotland Yard. He hadn't been identified then, but Hannaford did the honours now. This was ACC Ray Hannaford from Middlemore, she told him. The assistant chief constable stood and courteously offered his hand.

'Yes,' DI Hannaford then said to Lynley.

'Yes?' Lynley asked.

'He's a relation.'

'Former,' Ray Hannaford said. 'Regrettably.'

'You flatter me, darling,' DI Hannaford said.

Neither of them elucidated further, although the word *former* spoke a volume or two. More than one cop in the immediate family, Lynley concluded. It couldn't have been easy.

Ray Hannaford picked up a manila envelope that had been sitting on the table. 'Here it is,' he said to his former wife. 'Next time you insist on a courier, do tell them where you are for delivery, Beatrice.'

'I did tell them,' the DI replied. 'Obviously, whoever the sod was who brought this down from London didn't want the bother of going all the way to Holsworthy or the Casvelyn station. Or,' she asked shrewdly, 'did you put in a call for this as well?' She gestured with the manila envelope.

'I didn't,' he said. 'But we're going to have to talk about a quid pro quo. The account's growing. The drive from Exeter was bloody murder. You owe me on two fronts now.'

'What's the other?'

'Fetching Pete last night. Without complaint, as I recall.'

'Did I drag you from the arms of a twenty-year-old?'

'I believe she was at least twenty-three.'

Bea Hannaford chuckled. She opened the envelope and peered inside. She said, 'Ah yes. I take it you've had a look yourself, Ray?'

'Guilty as suspected.'

She brought the contents out. At once Lynley recognised his own police identification from New Scotland Yard.

He said, 'I handed that in. It should have been . . . What do they do to those things when someone quits? They must destroy them.'

Ray Hannaford was the one who replied. 'Apparently, they weren't willing to destroy yours.'

'*Premature* was the word they used,' Bea Hannaford added. 'A hasty decision made at a bad time.' She offered the Scotland Yard ID to Lynley.

He didn't take it. Instead he said, 'My identification is on its way from my home. I did tell you that. My wallet, along with everything in it, will be here by tomorrow. This' – he indicated his warrant card – 'was unnecessary.'

'On the contrary,' DI Hannaford said, 'it was entirely necessary. Phony IDs, as you well know, are as easy to get as the clap. For all I know, you've spent the morning scouring the streets for the goods.'

'Why would I want to do that?'

'I expect you can work that out for yourself, Superintendent Lynley. Or do you prefer the aristo title? And what the hell is someone like you doing working for the Bill?'

'I'm not,' he said. 'Not any longer.'

'Tell that to the Yard. You didn't answer. Which d'you prefer? Personal or professional title?'

'I prefer Thomas. And now that you know I am who I said I was last night, which I suspect you knew already or why else would you have allowed me into the mortuary with you, may I presume I'm free to resume my walk along the coast?'

'That's the very last thing you may presume. You're not going anywhere till I tell you otherwise. And if you're thinking of scurrying off in the dark of night, think again. You've a usefulness now I have the proof you are who you claimed to be.'

'Usefulness as a policeman or as a private citizen?'

'As whatever works, Detective.'

'Works for what?'

'For our good doctor.'

'Who?'

'The vet. Ms Trahair. You and I both know she's lying through those pretty white teeth of hers. Your job is to find out why.'

'You can't possibly require me—'

Hannaford's mobile rang. She held up a hand and cut him off. She dug the phone from her bag and walked off a few paces, saying 'Tell me' into the mobile as she flipped it open. She bent her head as she listened. She tapped her foot.

'She lives for this,' Ray Hannaford said. 'She didn't, at the beginning. But now, it's what makes her alive. Foolish, isn't it?'

'That death would make someone alive?'

'No. That I let her go. She wanted one thing; I wanted another.'

'That happens.'

'Not if I'd had my head on straight.'

Lynley looked at Hannaford. Earlier, he'd said *regrettably* about his status as the inspector's former husband. 'You could tell her,' Lynley said.

'Could and did. But sometimes when you demean yourself in another's eyes, you can't recover. I'd like to turn back time, though.'

'Yes,' Lynley said. 'Wouldn't we both.'

The DI returned to them, then. Her jaw was set. She gestured with her mobile and said to the ACC, 'It's murder. Ray, I want that incident room in Casvelyn. I don't care what you have to do to get it and I don't care what the quid pro quo is going to be either. I want HOLMES set up, an MCIT in place, and an evidence officer assigned. All right?'

'You don't ask for much, Beatrice, do you?'

'On the contrary, Raymond,' she replied levelly. 'As you well know.'

'We'll sort out a car for you,' Bea Hannaford said to Lynley. 'You're going to need one.'

They stood outside the entrance to the Royal Cornwall Hospital. Ray had gone on his way, after telling Bea that he couldn't promise her anything and after hearing her retort of 'how true.' She knew it was an unfair dig but she'd long ago learned that when it came to murder, the end of charging someone with a homicide justified any means one employed to get there.

Lynley replied with what sounded to Bea like care. 'I don't believe you can ask this of me.'

'Because you outrank me? That's not going to count for much out here in the hinterlands, Superintendent.'

'Acting, only.'

'What?'

'Acting Superintendent. I was never promoted permanently. I was just filling in a need.'

'How good of you. The very sort of bloke I'm looking for. You can fill in another rather burning need now.' She felt him glance her way as they proceeded towards her car, and she laughed outright. 'Not that need,' she said, 'though I expect you offer a decent shag when a woman puts a gun to your head. How old are you?'

'The Yard didn't tell you?'

'Humour me.'

'Thirty-eight.'

'Star sign?'

'What?'

'Gemini, Taurus, Virgo, what?'

'Is this somehow important?'

'As I said, humour me. Going along with the moment is so inexpensive, Thomas.'

He sighed. 'Pisces, as it happens.'

'Well, there you have it. It would never work between us. Besides, I'm twenty years older than you and while I fancy them younger than myself, I don't fancy them that young. So you're entirely safe in my company.'

'Somehow that's not a soothing thought.'

She laughed again and unlocked the car. They both climbed in, but she didn't insert the ignition key at once. Instead, she looked at him seriously. 'I need you to do this for me,' she told him. 'She wants to protect you.'

'Who?'

'You know who. Ms Trahair.'

'She hardly wants that. I broke into her house. She wants me around to pay for the damage. And I owe her money for the clothing.'

'Don't be obtuse. She jumped to your defence earlier, and there's a reason for that. She's got a vulnerable spot. It may have to do with you. Or it may not. I don't know where it is or *why* it is, but you're going to find it.' ·

'Why?'

'Because you *can*. Because this is a murder investigation, and all the nice social rules fly out of the window when we start looking for a killer. And *that's* something you know as well as I do.'

Lynley shook his head, but it seemed to Bea Hannaford that this movement wasn't one of refusal so much as one that acknowledged a regretful understanding and acceptance of a single immutable fact: She had him by the short and curlies. If he did a runner, she'd fetch him back and he knew it.

He said at last, 'Was the sling cut, then?'

'What?'

'The phone call you received. You came away from it calling the situation murder. So I'm wondering if the sling was cut or if they've dug up something else at forensics.'

Bea thought about whether to answer the question and what it would signal to him if she did so. She knew little enough about the man, but she also knew when a leap of faith was needed. 'It was cut.'

'Obviously so?'

'Microscopic examination helped push the decision, if you will, over the edge.'

'So not terribly obvious, at least to the naked eye. Why do you think it's murder?'

'And not what?'

'Suicide played out to look like an accident to spare the family additional pain.'

'What do we know so far that could possibly lead you there?'

'He was hit. Punched.'

'And?'

'It's stretching, but perhaps he wasn't in a position to defend himself. He wanted to but couldn't. Who knows why. He felt unable or at least unwilling, which resulted in a sense of uselessness. He projects that uselessness onto the rest of his life, onto all his relationships, no matter how illogical the projection is . . .'

'And Bob's your mother's you-know-what? I don't think so and neither do you.' Bea shoved her car key into the ignition and thought about what these remarks suggested, not so much about the victim but about Thomas Lynley himself. She gave him a wary look and wondered if she'd been wrong in her assessment of him. 'D'you know what a chock stone is?' she asked him.

He shook his head. 'Should I? What is it?'

'It's what makes this a murder investigation,' she said.

7

The rain stopped in Casvelyn not long after midday, and for this Cadan Angarrack was grateful. He'd been painting radiators in the guest rooms of Adventures Unlimited since his arrival that morning, and the fumes were causing his head to pound. He couldn't sort out why they had him painting radiators anyway. Who was going to notice them? Who *ever* noticed whether radiators were painted when they were in a hotel? No one except perhaps a hotel inspector and what did it amount to if a hotel inspector noticed a bit of rust? Nothing. Abso-bloody-lutely nothing. And anyway, it wasn't like the decrepit Promontory King George Hotel was being taken back to its former glory, was it? It was merely being made habitable for hordes interested in a holiday package on the sea that consisted of fun, frolic, food, and some kind of instruction in an outdoor activity. And *that* lot didn't care where they stayed at night, as long as it was clean, served chips, and stayed within the budget.

So when the skies cleared, Cadan decided that a bit of fresh air was just the ticket. He would have a look at the crazy golf course, future location of the BMX trails, future site of the BMX lessons that Cadan was certain would be requested of him once he had a chance to show his stuff to . . . That was the problem of the moment. He wasn't quite sure to whom he would be showing anything.

Indeed, he hadn't been certain he was even supposed to come into work on this day as he wasn't sure that he had a job, after what had happened to Santo. At first, he'd thought he simply wouldn't show up. He'd let a few days roll by and then he'd phone and express whatever condolences he could come up with and ask did they still want him to do maintenance work. But then he reckoned a phone call like that would give them a chance to sack him before he'd even had a chance to demonstrate how valuable he could be. So he'd decided to put in an appearance and to look as doleful as possible round any Kerne he might run into.

Cadan hadn't yet seen a hair of either Ben or Dellen, but his arrival had coincided with Alan Cheston's and when Cadan brought Alan into the picture about his employment at Adventures Unlimited, Alan said he'd fetch someone at once to see what Cadan was meant to be doing. He'd stridden off after unlocking the front door, letting them both in, and pocketing the keys with the air of a man who knew exactly where his place was in the scheme of things.

The old hotel was as silent as a graveyard. It was cold as well. Cadan shivered – he felt Pooh do likewise on his shoulder – and he waited in the new reception area, where a bulletin board displayed the words *Your Instructors*, along with head shots of the six staff members so far hired. These all pyramided down from a picture of Kerra Kerne, who was identified as *Director of Instruction*.

It was, Cadan thought, a decent picture of Kerra. She was no great beauty – ordinary brown hair, ordinary blue eyes, and stockier than Cadan fancied in a woman – but there was no doubt she was in the best physical condition of any female her age in Casvelyn. It was just unfortunate that her roll of the genetic dice had given Kerra her father's looks instead of her mother's. Santo had inherited every one of those, a fact which some might refer to as lucky. Cadan, however, reckoned most blokes didn't fancy being pretty like Santo. Unless, naturally, one knew how to use it.

'Cade?'

He swung round. Pooh squawked and shifted position.

Kerra had materialised from somewhere. Alan was with her. Cadan knew they were a couple, but he couldn't reconcile the matter. Kerra was sun and sinew with, unfortunately, tree trunk ankles. Alan looked like someone who'd take exercise as a last resort and then only if threatened with disembowelment.

A few words among them had sorted things. Although Alan on the surface might have looked like small change, it turned out he was on top of almost all that was going on at the place. So before Cadan knew enough to make a spurious excuse about the delicate condition of his lungs should they *ever* be exposed to paint fumes, he found himself with drop cloths and a paint brush in one hand and two gallons of white glossy in the other. Alan made an introduction between Cadan and the project, and that was that.

Four hours later saw Cadan deciding he was owed a break outdoors. Pooh, he noted, had grown ominously silent. Likely the parrot had a headache as well.

The ground was still sopping round the crazy golf course, but Cadan didn't let that deter him. Guiding his bike, he climbed the slope to hole number one, where he quickly saw that doing a few tabletops just now in this location had been something of a pipedream. He set his bike to one side, established Pooh on the handlebars, and gave the crazy golf course a closer look.

This wasn't going to be a simple project. The course looked at least sixty years old. It also looked as if it hadn't been maintained in the last thirty of those years. This was too bad because otherwise crazy golf could have been a little money maker for Adventures Unlimited. On the other hand, this was also a plus because an unmaintained course made it far likelier than otherwise that anyone in the position of making a decision about the future would climb on board once Cadan laid out his plans. But the idea of laying out plans necessitated *having* plans, and Cadan wasn't a having-plans sort of person. So he walked round the first five holes of the course and tried to reckon what needed to be done aside from ripping out miniature windmills, barns, and school-houses and filling in the holes.

He was still considering all this when he saw a panda car pulling into the car park of the old hotel from St Mevan Crescent. The driver, a uniformed constable, got out and went inside. A few minutes later he departed.

Shortly thereafter, Kerra came out of the building. She stood in the car park, hands on hips, and she looked about. Cadan was squatting next to a tiny shipwrecked rowing boat that acted as an obstacle on hole number six, and it came to him that she was searching for someone, possibly him. His modus operandi was generally to hide, since if someone was seeking him, it was usually because he'd bollocksed something up and was presently going to hear about it. But a quick evaluation of his performance in the painting department told him he'd been doing a Class A job, so he rose and made his presence known.

Kerra headed in his direction. She'd changed from what she'd been wearing earlier. She was decked out in Lycra, and Cadan recognised the kit: She had on her long distance cyclist's gear. Odd time of day to be going for a ride, he thought, but when you were the boss's daughter, you made your own rules.

Kerra spoke to him without preamble when she reached the ruins of the crazy golf course. Her voice was clipped. 'I phoned the farm, but they told me she doesn't work there any longer. I phoned your house, but she's not there either. D'you know where she is? I want to speak to her.'

Cadan took a moment to think about the remarks, the question, and the implications of each. He bought time by going to his bike, removing Pooh from the handlebars, and settling the bird on his shoulder.

'Blow holes in the attic,' Pooh remarked.

'Cade.' Kerra's voice was patient but with an edge. 'Please answer me. Now would be preferable to sometime in the future.'

'It's weird you want to know, that's all,' Cadan told her. 'I mean, it's not like you're friends with Madlyn any longer, so I was wondering . . .' He cocked his head so that his cheek touched Pooh's side. He liked the feeling of the bird's feathers against him.

Kerra's eyes narrowed. 'You were wondering what?'

'Santo. The cops showing up. You coming out here to talk to me. Asking me about Madlyn. Is all this related?'

Kerra had her hair in a ponytail and she unbanded it so that it fell to her shoulders. She shook it out, then tied it back up. It seemed as much a gesture to buy time for her as rescuing Pooh from the bike had been for Cadan. Then she looked at him and seemed to focus more clearly. 'What happened to your face?'

'Plain old luck,' he said. 'It's the one I was born with.'

'Don't joke, Cadan. You know what I mean. The bruises, the scratches.'

'I slipped. Occupational hazard. I was doing a no-footed can-can, and I hit the side of the pool wrong way. Over at the leisure centre.'

'You did that swimming?' She sounded incredulous.

'Pool's empty. I was practising there. On the bike.' He felt himself colour, and this irritated him. He made it a point *never* to be embarrassed about his passion, and he didn't want to think why he was embarrassed now. 'What's going on?' he asked, with a nod at the hotel.

'It wasn't an ordinary fall. He was murdered. That's what the police came to tell us. They sent their . . . whatever he is . . . their liaison officer. I think he's meant to hang about serving us tea and biscuits to keep us from, I don't know, what do people generally do when a member of the family is murdered? Go mad to get vengeance? Shoot up the town? Gnash their teeth? And what the hell *is* that, gnashing the teeth? Where is she, Cade?'

'She already knows he died.'

'That he died or that he was murdered? Where *is* she? He was my brother, and as she was his girlfriend—'

'Your friend as well,' Cadan reminded her. 'At least at one time.'

'Don't,' she said. 'Just don't, all right?'

He shrugged. He directed his attention back to the crazy golf course and said, 'This needs to go. It's a wreck. You could repair it, but my guess is the cost would exceed the benefits. In the short term. In the long run, who knows?'

'Alan knows the long run. Profit and loss, long term projections. He knows it all. But none of that matters because just now there may not be a reason to worry.'

'About?'

'About anything related to Adventures Unlimited. I doubt my father will have the stomach to open after what's happened to Santo.'

'What's next, then, if you don't open?'

'Alan would say we try to find a buyer and recoup our investment. But then, that's Alan. A mind for the figures if nothing else.'

'Sounds like you're cheesed off at him.'

She didn't take up the remark. 'Is she at home and just not answering the phone? I can go over there but I don't want to take the trouble if she's not there anyway. So d'you mind telling me that much?'

'I expect she's still with Jago,' he said.

'Who's Jago?'

'Jago Reeth. Bloke that works for my dad. She was with him all night. She's still with him, for all I know.'

Kerra laughed shortly, without amusement. 'Well, she's moved on, hasn't she? That was quick. Miraculous recovery from complete heart-break. How very nice for her.'

Cadan wanted to ask what it was to her, whether his sister moved on to another man or not. But instead he said, 'Jago Reeth's maybe seventy or something. He's like a granddad to her, okay?'

'What's he do for your dad, then, some seventy year old?'

She was definitely annoying him. She was being the boss's daughter and you-better-treat-me-as-I'm-meant-to-be-treated, and that rubbed Cadan up the wrong way. He said, 'Kerra, does that matter? Why the hell d'you want to know?'

And just like that, she altered. She gave a weird little cough and he saw the glitter of tears in her eyes. That glitter reminded him that her brother was dead, that he'd died only on the previous day, and that she'd just learned he'd been murdered.

He said, 'A glasser.' When she looked at him in confusion, he added, 'Jago Reeth. He does the fibreglass on the boards. He's an old surfer my dad picked up . . . I don't know . . . six months ago maybe? He's a detail man like Dad. And, what's important, not like me.'

'She spent the night with a seventy-year-old bloke?'

'Jago phoned and said she was there.'

'What time?'

'Kerra . . .'

'This is important, Cadan.'

'Why? D'you think she gave your brother the bump? How was she supposed to do that? Shove him over the cliff?'

'His equipment was messed about with. That's what the cop told us.'

Cadan widened his eyes. 'Hang on, Kerra. No way. And I mean *no* way. She may have been off her nut with everything that happened between them, but my sister is *not*—' He stopped himself. Not because of what he'd intended to say about Madlyn but because as he'd been speaking, his gaze had moved from Kerra to the beach below them and across that beach a surfer was jogging, his board under his arm and its leash trailing behind him in the sand. He was fully garbed as he would be at this time of year, for the water was still quite cold. Head to toe in black. You couldn't, in fact, tell if the surfer was male or female from this distance.

'What?' Kerra said.

Cadan shuddered. He said quietly, 'Madlyn may have been all over the map with how she reacted after what happened between her and Santo. I give you that.'

'That and then some,' Kerra remarked.

'But killing off her ex-boyfriend wouldn't be part of her repertoire, okay? Jesus, Kerra, she kept thinking he was just going through a *stage*, you know.'

'At first,' Kerra clarified.

'Okay. Maybe only at *first* she thought that. But it doesn't mean she'd finally get to the point of understanding how things really were and deciding the only reasonable thing to do was to kill him. Does that make sense to you?'

'Love,' Kerra said, 'never makes sense to me. People do all sorts of mad things when they're in love with someone.'

'Yeah?' Cadan said. 'So, what about you?'

She made no reply.

'I rest my case,' he told her, and added, 'Sea Dreams, if you have to know.'

'What's that?'

'Where she is. Jago's got a caravan at that holiday park where the dairy used to be. Out beyond Sawsneck Down. If you want to grill her, grill her there. For what it's worth, though, you'll be wasting your time.'

'What makes you think I want to grill her?'

'You sure as hell want something.'

Once Bea Hannford had him in possession of a hired car, she told Lynley to follow her. She said to him, 'I expect this isn't your typical heap,' in reference to the Ford, 'but at least you'll fit it. Or it'll fit you.'

Under other circumstances, Lynley might have told her that she was being more than generous. Indeed, his breeding generally made that sort of remark second nature to him. But under the present circumstances, he merely told her that his usual mode of transport had been written off in February and he hadn't yet replaced it with something else, so the Ford was fine.

She said, 'Good,' and advised him to mind his driving since he would be doing so without a licence until his wallet arrived. 'It'll be our little secret,' she said. She told him to follow her. She had something to show him.

What she had to show him was in Casvelyn, and he obediently trailed her there. He drove trying to keep his mind simply on the driving but he found the strength draining out of him with the sheer effort he made to hold his thoughts in check.

He'd told himself he was finished with murder. One did not watch a beloved wife die, the victim of an utterly senseless street killing, and walk away from that to think that tomorrow was simply another day. Tomorrow was, instead, something to be endured. So far he'd endured the endless succession of tomorrows he'd been living through, by doing what was set in front of him and nothing more.

At first it had been Howenstow: seeing to matters on and around the land that was his legacy and the great house sitting upon that land. No matter that his mother, his brother, and an estate manager had been handling Howenstow matters for ages. He'd thrown himself into them to keep from throwing himself elsewhere, until half of what he'd taken on was a muddle and the other half was a wreck. His mother's gentle admonition of 'Darling, let me handle this,' or 'John Penellin's been working on this situation for weeks, Tommy,' or anything of a similar persuasion was something he brushed aside with a remark so terse that the dowager countess had sighed, pressed his shoulder, and left him to it.

But he found that Howenstow matters ultimately brought Helen into his mind, whether he wanted her there or not. The half-finished nursery had to be dismantled. Countryside clothing she'd left in their bedroom had to be gone through. A plaque for her resting place in the estate chapel – for the resting place she shared with their never-born son – had to be designed. And then there were the reminders of her: where he and she had walked together on the path from the house through the wood and over to the cove, where she'd stood in front of pictures in the gallery and light-heartedly commented on the physical attributes of some of his more questionable ancestors, where she'd browsed through ancient editions of *Country Life* in the library, where she'd curled up with – and ultimately dozed off over – a thick biography of Oscar Wilde.

Because reminders of Helen were everywhere at Howenstow, he'd begun his walk. Trudging along the entire South-West Coast Path was the last possible challenge Helen would ever have undertaken ('My God, Tommy, you've got to be mad. *What* would I do for shoes that aren't utterly appalling in appearance?'), so he knew he could walk the length of it with impunity, should he choose to do so. There would be not a single reminder of her along the way.

But he'd not counted on the memorials he'd come across. Nothing he'd read about the path prior to walking it had prepared him for those. From simple bunches of dying flowers to wooden benches engraved with the names of the departed, death greeted him nearly every day. He'd left the Yard because he could not face another sudden brutal passing of a human being, but there it was: confronting him with a regularity that mocked his every attempt to forget.

And now this. DI Hannaford wasn't exactly involving him in the murder investigation itself, but she was putting him close to it. He didn't want that, but at the same time, he didn't know how he could avoid it because he read the inspector as a woman who was as good as her word: Should he conveniently disappear from the region of Casvelyn, she would happily fetch him back and not rest till she'd done so.

As to what she was asking him to do . . . Like DI Hannaford, Lynley believed Daidre Trahair was lying about the route she'd taken from Bristol to Polcare Cove on the previous day. Unlike DI Hannaford, Lynley also knew Daidre Trahair had lied more than once about knowing Santo Kerne. There were going to be reasons behind both of these lies – far beyond what the vet had told him when he'd confronted her about her knowledge of the dead boy's identity – and he didn't know if he wanted to uncover them. Her reasons for obfuscation were doubtless personal, and the poor woman was hardly a killer.

Yet why did he think that? he asked himself. He knew better than anyone that killers wore a thousand different guises. Killers were men; killers were women. Killers, to his anguish, were children. And victims everywhere – no matter how foul they might actually be – were not meant to be dispatched by anyone, whatever the motive for untimely sending them to their eternal reward or punishment. The whole basis for their society rested upon the idea that murder was wrong, start to finish, and that justice had to be served so that closure, if not satisfaction, not relief, and certainly not an end to grief, might at least be achieved on the entire event. Justice equated to naming and convicting the killer, and justice was what was owed to those the victim summarily left behind.

Part of Lynley cried out that this was not his problem. Part of him knew that now and forever and more than ever, it would always be.

By the time they reached Casvelyn he was, if not reconciled to the matter, then at least in moderate accord with it. Everything needed to be accounted for in an investigation. Daidre Trahair was part of that everything, having made herself so the moment she lied.

Casvelyn's police station was in Lansdown Road in the heart of the town, directly at the bottom of Belle Vue's course up the town's main acclivity, and it was here in front of the plain, grey two-storey structure that Bea Hannaford parked. Lynley thought at first that she meant to take him inside and introduce him around, but instead she said, 'Come with me,' and she put a hand on his elbow and guided him back the way they had come.

At the junction of Lansdown Road and Belle Vue, they crossed a triangle of land where benches, a fountain, and three trees provided Casvelyn with an outdoor gathering place in good weather. From there they headed over to Queen Street, which was lined with shops like Belle Vue Lane: everything from purveyors of furniture to chemists. There, Bea Hannaford paused and peered in both directions till she apparently saw what she wanted, for she said, 'Yes. Over here. I want you to see what we're dealing with.'

Over here referred to a shop selling sporting goods: both equipment and clothing for outdoor activities. Hannaford did an admirably quick recce of the place, found what she wanted, told the shop assistant they needed no help, and directed Lynley to a wall. Upon it were hung various metallic devices, mostly of steel. It wasn't rocket science to sort out they were used for climbing.

She chose a package that held three devices constructed of lead, heavy steel cable, and plastic sheathing. The lead was a thick wedge at the end of a cable perhaps one quarter inch thick. This looped through the wedge at one end and also formed another loop at the other end. In the middle was a tough plastic sheath, which wrapped tightly round the cable and thus held the two sides of it closely together. The result was a sturdy cord with a slug of lead at one end and a loop at the other.

'This,' Hannaford said to Lynley, 'is a chock stone. D'you know how it's used?'

Lynley shook his head. Obviously, it was meant for cliff climbing. Equally so, its loop end would be used to connect the chock stone to some other device. But that was as much as he could work out.

DI Hannaford said, 'Hold up your hand, palm towards yourself. Keep your fingers tight. I'll show you.'

She slid the cable between his upright index and middle fingers, so that the slug of lead was snug against his palm and the loop at the other end of the cable was on her side of his hand.

She said, 'Your fingers are a crack in the cliff face. Or an aperture between two boulders. Your hand is the cliff itself. Or the boulders themselves. Got it?' She waited for his nod. 'The lead piece – that's the chock stone – gets shoved down the crack in the cliff or the aperture between the boulders as far as it can go, with the cable sticking out. In the loop end of the cable' – Here she paused to scan the wall of climbing gear till she found what she wanted and scooped it up – 'you clip a carabiner. Like this.' She did so. 'And you fix your rope to the cara- biner with whatever sort of knot you've been taught to use. If you're climbing up, you use chock stones on the way, every few feet or what- ever you're comfortable with. If you're abseiling, you can use them at the top instead of a sling to fix your rope to whatever you've chosen to hold it in place while you descend.'

She took the chock stone from him and replaced it along with the carabiner on the wall of goods. She turned back and said, 'Climbers mark each part of their kit distinctly because they often climb together. Let's say you and I are climbing. I use six chock stones or sixteen chock stones; you use ten. We use my carabiners but your slings. How do we sort it all out quickly and without discussion in the end? By marking each piece with something that won't easily come off. Bright tape is just the ticket. Santo Kerne used black electrical tape.'

Lynley saw where she was heading with this. He said, 'So if someone wishes to play fast and loose with someone else's kit, he merely needs to get his hands on the same kind of tape?'

'And the equipment itself. Yes. That's right. You can damage the equipment, put identical tape over the damage, and no one is the wiser.'

'The sling, obviously. It would have been the easiest to damage although cutting it would have shown, if not to the naked eye, at least to the microscope.'

'Which is exactly what happened. As we've discussed earlier.'

'But there's more, isn't there, or you wouldn't have shown me this.'

'Forensics went though Santo's kit,' Hannaford said. Hand on his elbow again, she began to guide him out of the shop. She kept her voice low. 'Two of the chock stones had been seen to. Beneath the marking tape, both the plastic sheathing and the cable had been damaged. The sheathing was cut through; the cable was hanging on by a metaphorical thread. If the boy used either one for an abseil, he was done for. Same thing applied to the sling. He was a dead man walking. A dead climber climbing. Whatever. It was only a matter of time before he used the right piece of equipment at the worst possible moment.'

'Fingerprints?'

'Galore,' Hannaford said. 'But I'm not sure how useful they're going to be since most climbers don't go solo all the time, and we're likely to find that's the case with Santo.'

'Unless there's a print on the damaged pieces that doesn't exist on any others. That would be difficult for someone to explain away.'

'Hmm. Yes. But that whole bit has me wondering, Thomas.'

'What whole bit is that?' Lynley asked.

'Three damaged pieces instead of only one. What does that suggest to you?'

He said thoughtfully, 'Only one bad piece was needed to send him to his death. But he was carrying three. You might conclude that the killer didn't care when it happened or if the fall even killed him since he could have used the damaged chock stones quite low on an upward route and not used the sling at all.'

'Any other conclusions?'

'If he usually abseiled first and climbed back up afterwards, you might conclude that three pieces of damaged equipment indicate the killer was in a hurry to do away with the boy. Or, as difficult as it might be to believe . . .' He pondered a moment, wondering about the final likelihood and what that final likelihood suggested.

She prompted him. 'Yes?'

'Damaging three pieces . . . You might also conclude the killer wanted everyone to *know* it was murder.'

She nodded. 'Bit mad, isn't it, but that's what I was thinking.'

It was the sheer madness of love that had made Kerra want to get out of the hotel and onto her bike. She'd changed into her riding kit because of it and she'd determined that twenty miles or so would be sufficient to clear her head of the thought. A twenty-mile ride wouldn't take her terribly long, either, not if the weather continued to improve, and not for someone in her condition. On a good day with the weather co-operating, she could do sixty miles with one hand tied behind her back, so twenty was child's play. It was also highly *necessary* child's play, so she'd made herself ready and headed for the door.

The arrival of the police officer had stopped her. It was the same bloke as the previous night, Constable McNulty, and he had on his face such a lugubrious expression that Kerra knew the news would be bad before he uttered it.

He'd asked to see her parents.

She'd told him that was impossible.

They're not here? he'd asked. It was a logical question.

Oh, they were at home. Upstairs but unavailable. You can tell me what you've come to tell them. They've asked not to be disturbed.

I'm afraid I need to ask you to fetch them, the officer said.

And I'm afraid I have to refuse. They've asked to be left alone. They've made it clear. They're finally resting. I'm sure you understand. Have you any children, Constable? Because when one loses a child, one reels and they're reeling.

This wasn't exactly true, but the truth would hardly garner sympathy. The thought of her mother and her father going at each other in Santo's bedroom like randy adolescents made the contents of Kerra's stomach curdle. She didn't want anything to do with them just now. Especially she didn't want anything to do with her father whom she was growing to despise more and more with each passing hour. She'd despised him for years, but nothing he'd so far done or failed to do held a candle to what was going on at the moment.

Constable McNulty had reluctantly left the information once Alan had come out of the marketing office where he'd been reviewing a commercial video. Alan had said, 'What is it, Kerra? May I help?' and he sounded firm and sure of himself, as if the past sixteen hours were continuing to transform him. 'I'm Kerra's fiancé,' he told the policeman. 'Is there something I can do for you?'

Fiancé? Kerra had thought. Kerra's *fiancé*? Where was *that* coming from?

Before she'd been able to correct him, the cop had given them the information. Murder. Some pieces of Santo's kit had been tampered with. The sling and two chock stones as well. The police were going to want to interview the family first.

Alan had managed to sound perplexed and outraged simultaneously. 'You aren't supposing one of the family . . . ?'

Everyone who knew Santo would be interviewed, Constable McNulty told them. He appeared rather excited about this, and it had struck Kerra how tediously boring the policeman's life must be in Casvelyn in the off-season, with three-quarters of the summer population gone and those who remained either in their houses huddling against the Atlantic storms or committing only the occasional minor traffic violation to break the monotony of a constable's life. All of Santo's belongings would need to be examined, the constable told them. A family history would be constructed, and—

That had been enough for Kerra. Family history? *That* would certainly be illuminating. A family history would show it all: bats in the belfry and skeletons in the closet, people who were permanently estranged and people who were just permanently strange.

All of this gave her another reason to ride. And then came the conversation with Cadan, which left her feeling to blame.

After her words with him, she fetched her bike. Her father met her outside, Alan coming out behind him with an expression that said he'd passed along the information about Santo. So Alan didn't need to mouth the words *he knows* although that's what he did. Kerra wanted to tell him he'd had no right to tell her father anything. He wasn't a member of the family.

Ben Kerne said to Kerra, 'Where are you going? I'd like you to stay here.' He sounded exhausted. He looked it, too.

Did you fuck her again? was what Kerra wished to reply. Did she slip on her little red negligee and crook her finger and did you melt and not see anything else not even that Santo is *dead*? Good way to forget for a few minutes, eh? Works a treat. Always has done.

But she said none of that although she was positively itching to flay him. She said, 'I need a ride just now. I've got to—'

'You're needed here.'

Kerra glanced at Alan. Surprisingly, he indicated by cocking his head in the direction of the road that she should ride, no matter her father's desires. Although she didn't want to be, she was grateful for this display of understanding. Alan was, in this at least, fully on her side.

'Does she need something from me?' Kerra asked her father.

He looked behind him, up at the windows of the family's flat. The curtains of the master bedroom were blocking out the daylight. Behind them, Dellen was coping in her Dellen way: on the crushed spines of her near relations.

'She's in black,' Kerra's father said.

'That'll doubtless be a large disappointment to any number of people,' Kerra replied.

Ben Kerne looked at her with eyes so anguished that for a moment Kerra regretted her words. *Not his fault* came to her. But at the same time there were things that *were* her father's fault, not the least of which was that they were even talking about her mother and, in doing so, that they were reduced to using a carefully chosen set of words like semaphores and they two distant communicators with a secret language all their own.

She sighed, an aggrieved party unwilling to apologise. That he too was aggrieved could not be allowed to count. She said, 'Do you?'

'What?'

'Need something from me. Because she doesn't. She'll be wanting you. And no doubt vice versa.'

Ben went back into the hotel without another word, shouldering past Alan who looked rather like a man trying to decipher the Dead Sea Scrolls.

Alan said, 'A little harsh, that, Kerra. Don't you think?'

The last thing Kerra wanted to show Alan was gratitude for his previous understanding, so she welcomed the criticism. She said, 'If you've decided to remain at work here, you need to become a little more familiar with the mechanism of your employment, okay?'

Like her father, he looked struck. She was happy he felt the sting of her words. He said, 'I've got it that you're angry. But what I haven't got is why. Not the anger part of it, but the afraid part of it that's fuelling the anger. I can't suss that one. I've tried. I spent most of last night awake, trying.'

'Poor you,' she said.

'Kerra, none of this is like you. What're you frightened about?'

'Nothing,' she said. 'I'm not frightened at all. You're trying to talk about subjects you don't understand.'

'Then help me understand.'

'Not my job,' she said. 'I warned you off.'

'You warned me off working here. This – you, what's happening with you, and what happened to Santo – isn't part of my employment here.'

She smiled briefly. 'Stay around, then. If you haven't already, you'll soon find out what's part and parcel of your employment. Now if you'll excuse me, I want a ride. I doubt you'll still be here when I return.'

'Are you coming over tonight?'

She raised her eyebrows. 'I think that part might be finished between us.'

'What are you saying? Something's happened since yesterday. Beyond Santo, something's happened.'

'Oh, I do know that.' She mounted her bike, gearing it to take the rise of the driveway, heading into town.

She coursed along the southeast edge of St Mevan Down where unmowed grass bent heavily with a weight of raindrops and a few dogs romped, grateful for a respite in the rain. She too was grateful, and she decided she'd head roughly in the direction of Polcare Cove. She told herself she had no intention of going to the place where Santo had died, but if she ended up there by chance, she would consider it meant to be. She wouldn't pay attention to the route. She would merely blast along the lanes as fast as she could, turning when she felt like turning, continuing straight on when she fancied that.

She knew she needed a source of energy to do the sort of ride she had in mind, however, so when she saw Casvelyn of Cornwall (County's Number One Pasty) to the right on the corner of Burn View Lane, she coasted over to the bakery, a large operation that supplied pasties up and down the coast to restaurants, shops, pubs, and smaller bakeries unable to bake their own. The business comprised an industrial-sized kitchen at the back and a shop at the front: with ten bakers working in one area and two shop assistants in the other.

Kerra leaned her bike against the front window, a stunning monument to pasties, loaves, pastry, and scones. She ducked inside, deciding in advance that she would have a steak and beer pasty and she'd eat it on her way out of town.

At the counter, she placed her order with a girl whose impressive thighs looked like the result of their owner having sampled the products far too often. The requested pasty was being bagged and rung up at the till when the other shop assistant emerged with a tray of fresh goods to go into the display case. Kerra looked up as the kitchen door swung closed. At the same moment as her glance fell on the girl with the tray, that girl's glance fell upon Kerra. Her steps faltered. She stood expressionless with the tray extended in front of her.

'Madlyn,' Kerra said. It came to her much later how stupid she sounded. 'I didn't know that you worked here.'

Madlyn Angarrack went to one of the display cases and opened it, sliding fresh pasties from the tray she held. She said to the other girl, who was in the process of bagging Kerra's purchase, 'What sort is that, Shar?' Her voice was curt.

'Steak and beer.' Kerra was the one to answer. And then, 'Madlyn, I was asking Cadan about you only twenty minutes ago. How long've you been—'

'Give her one of these, Shar. They're fresher.'

Shar looked from Madlyn to Kerra, as if taking a reading off the tension in the air and wondering from which direction it was flowing. But she did as she was told.

Kerra took her pasty over to where Madlyn was lining up display trays neatly. She said to her, 'When did you start working here?'

Madlyn glanced her way. 'Why d'you want to know?' She shut the lid of the display case with a decisive snap. 'Would that make some sort of difference to you?' She used the back of her wrist to move some hair from her face. It was short, her hair, quite dark and curly. At this time of year, the copper that streaked it from exposure to the summer sun was missing. It came to Kerra how remarkably like Cadan his sister looked: the same colour of hair that was thick with curls, the same olive skin, the same dark eyes, the same shape of face. The Angarracks were thus nothing like the Kerne siblings. Physically, as well as in every other way, Kerra and Santo had been nothing alike.

The sudden thought of Santo made Kerra blink, hard. She didn't *want* him there: not in her mind and definitely not near her heart. Madlyn seemed to take this as a reaction to her question and to its inimical tone because she went on to say, 'I heard about Santo. I'm sorry he fell.'

Yet it seemed too much an obligation performed. Because of this, Kerra said more brutally than she otherwise would have done, 'He didn't fall. He was murdered. The police came to tell us a little while ago. They didn't know at first, when he was found. They couldn't tell.'

Madlyn's mouth opened as if she would speak, her lips clearly forming the first part of *murdered*, but she did not say it. Instead she said, 'Why?'

'Because they had to look at his climbing kit, didn't they. Under their microscopes or whatever. I expect you can work out the rest.'

'I mean why would someone murder Santo?'

'I find it hard to believe you, of all people, would even ask that question.'

'Are you saying . . .' Madlyn balanced the empty tray vertically, against her hip. 'We were friends, Kerra.'

'I think you were a lot more than friends.'

'I'm not talking about Santo. I'm talking about you and me. We were close friends. You might say best friends. So how you can think that I'd *ever*—'

'You ended our friendship.'

'I started seeing your brother. That was all I did. Full stop.'

'Yes. Well.'

'And you defined *everything* after that. No one sees my brother and remains my friend. That was your position. Only you didn't even say that much, did you? You just made the cut with your rusty scissors and that was it. No more friendship when someone does something you don't want them to do.'

'It was for your own good.'

'Oh really? What? Getting cut off from someone, getting cut off from a sister? Because that's what you were to me, all right? A sister.'

'You could have . . .' Kerra didn't know how to go on. She also couldn't see how they'd come to this. She'd wanted to talk to Madlyn, it was true. That was why she'd earlier gone to Cadan about his sister. But the conversation she'd been having with Madlyn Angarrack in her brain had not resembled the conversation she was having with Madlyn Angarrack now. That mental conversation had not taken place in the presence of a second shop assistant who was attending their colloquy with the sort of rabid spectator's interest that precedes a girl fight at a secondary school. Kerra said quietly, 'It's not as if I didn't warn you.'

'Of what?'

'Of what it would be like for you if you and my brother . . .' Kerra glanced at Shar. There was a glitter to her eyes that was discomfiting. 'You know what I'm talking about. I told you what he was like.'

'But what you *didn't* tell me was what you were like. What you *are* like. Mean and vindictive. Look at you, Kerra. Have you even cried? Your own brother dead and here you are, right as could be, going about on your bike without a care in the world.'

'You seem to be coping well enough yourself,' Kerra pointed out.

'At least I didn't want him to die.'

'Didn't you? Why're you here? What happened to the farm?'

'I quit the farm. All right?' Her face had gone red. Her grip on the tray she'd brought with her from the kitchen had become so tight that her knuckles were white as she went on. 'Are you happy now, Kerra? Have you learned what you wanted to know? I sorted out the truth. And do you want to know how I did that, Kerra? He claimed that he'd always be honest with me, of course, but when it came to this . . . Oh get out of here. Get *out*.' She raised the tray as if to throw it.

'Hey, Mad,' Shar spoke uneasily. Doubtless, Kerra thought, the other girl had never seen the rage of which Madlyn Angarrack was fully capable. Doubtless Shar had never opened a postal package and discovered within it pictures of herself with her head cut off, pictures of herself with her eyeballs stabbed by the lead of a pencil, handwritten notes and two birthday cards once saved but now smeared with faeces, a newspaper article about the head of instructors at Adventures Unlimited with *bollocks* and *shit* written in red pencil across it. No return address, but none had been needed. Nor had been any other sort of message, when the intentions of the sender were so clearly illustrated by the contents of the envelope in which they'd come.

This quality in her former friend comprised another reason that Kerra had wanted to talk to Madlyn Angarrack. Kerra might have hated her brother, but she loved him still. It wasn't a matter of blood being thicker. But it was still and always a matter of blood.

8

'I know this isn't a good time to talk about it,' Alan Cheston said. 'There's not going to *be* a good time to talk about anything for a long while to come, and I think we both know that. The thing is, though, these guys have a diary to fill and if we're going to commit, we need to let them know, or we're going to lose out.'

Ben Kerne nodded numbly. He couldn't imagine conversing rationally about any subject, let alone about business. All he could imagine was a further walking of the corridors inside the Promontory King George Hotel, one shoulder against the wall and his head aimed down to study the floor. Down one corridor and up another, through a fire door and up the stairs to begin another corridor. On and on, spectre-like, into infinity. Occasionally thinking about how much they had spent on the old hotel's transformation and wondering what the purpose might be in spending any more. Wondering what the purpose might be in anything at this point, and then trying to stop thinking altogether.

He'd done all that on the previous night. Dellen had pills but he would not take them.

Ben looked at Alan. He saw him through a fog, as if a veil existed between his eyeballs and his brain. He could take in the younger man, but he had no ability to process what he was taking in. So he said, 'Go on. I understand,' although he didn't want the first and didn't mean the second.

They were in the marketing office, a small former conference room that opened off the erstwhile reception area. It had likely been used for staff meetings when the hotel was in operation. An ancient blackboard still hung on the wall, stained with ghostly copperplate, undoubtedly the work of a manager stirring his troops to action if the excessive underlining was anything to go by. Beneath this writing surface and encircling the room, the walls were covered with gouged wainscoting, above it faded wallpaper featuring hunting scenes. The Kernes had determined to leave all this as it was when they'd taken over the hotel.

No one would see it but themselves, they'd decided, and the money could be more profitably spent elsewhere.

Which was the purpose of this meeting with Alan. Ben tuned in to what the young man was talking about and heard '. . . must consider the cost as an investment towards returns. Additionally, it's a onetime cost but not a onetime use of the product so we'd amortise what we spent producing it. If we're careful to avoid a look that will date the piece, we'll be fine. You know what I mean: keep away from shots of vehicles, avoid sites likely to demonstrate anachronicity in five years and *use* sites likely to demonstrate their history. That sort of thing. Here. This sample came the other day. I've already shown Dellen, but she probably . . . well, understandably she probably won't have mentioned it to you.' Alan rose from the conference table, a pitted and scratched pine affair with countless burns from forgotten cigarettes, and went to the video player. He had coloured in a febrile manner as he spoke, and not for the first time Ben speculated about his daughter's relationship with this man. He reckoned he knew the reason behind Kerra's choice of Alan, and he was fairly certain she was wrong about him in more ways than one.

He and Alan were having their regular meeting about marketing strategies. Ben hadn't possessed the will to cancel it. He sat in mute attendance now, considering which of them was the more heartless bastard: Alan for ostensibly carrying on as if nothing had happened or himself for being present. Dellen was meant to be in attendance as she too worked in marketing, but she'd not risen from bed.

On the video monitor, a promotional film began. It featured a resort in the Scilly Isles: a luxury hotel and spa with golf course attached. It wouldn't attract the same sort of clientele as Adventures Unlimited, but that wasn't the point of Alan's showing it to him.

A suave voiceover provided the commentary, a sales pitch for the resort. While the voice recited the expected panegyric, the accompanying film featured shots of the hotel sitting atop white sands, spa goers basking under the ministrations of lithesome and tanned masseuses, golfers whacking away at balls, diners on terraces and in candlelit rooms. This was, Alan said, the type of film one showed at travel venues. They could do that as well, but with a much broader base of appeal. This, then, was what Alan was after: Ben's permission to pursue yet another way to market Adventures Unlimited.

'As you've mentioned, we've got bookings coming in,' Alan said once the film had finished, 'which is brilliant, Ben. That piece in the *Mail on*

Sunday helped enormously as a promotional vehicle. But it's time we looked at the potential we have for a larger market.' He ticked items off on his fingers. 'Families with children from six to sixteen, independent schools with programmes taking pupils for weeklong maturing courses, singles looking to meet life mates, mature travellers in good condition who don't want to while away their golden years rocking on a veranda somewhere. Then there are drug rehab programmes, early release programmes for young offenders, inner city youth programmes. We've an expansive market out there, and I mean to see us tap into it.'

Alan's face was shiny, his ears were red, and his eyes were bright. Enthusiasm and hope, Ben thought. Either that or nerves. He said to Alan, 'You've got big plans.'

'I hope that's why you took me on. Ben, what you have here, This place. Its location. Your ideas for it. With an investment in areas likely to be fruitful, you're looking at the goose and gold eggs. I swear it.'

Alan seemed to study him, then, just as Ben had himself studied Alan. He ejected the video from the machine and handed it over, putting a hand on Ben's shoulder for a moment. 'Watch it again with Dellen when you're both up to it,' he said. 'We've no need to make a decision today. But, soon, though.'

Ben's fingers closed round the plastic case. He felt its little ridges press against his skin. He said, 'You're doing a good job. Organising the *Mail on Sunday* piece . . . That was brilliant.'

'I wanted you to see what I could do,' Alan told him. 'I'm grateful you took me on. Otherwise, I'd probably have been forced to live in Truro or Exeter, which I wouldn't much like.'

'Much larger places than Casvelyn, though.'

'Too large for me if Kerra's not there.' Alan gave a laugh, which sounded embarrassed. 'She didn't want me to come on staff here, you know. She said it wouldn't work out, but I mean to show her otherwise. This place' – He extended his arms to take in the hotel as a whole – 'this place *fills* me with ideas. All I need is someone to listen and okay them when the time is right. I mean, have you thought about everything the hotel can actually *be* in the off season? It's got room for conferences and with a little tweaking of the promotional film . . .'

Ben tuned out, not because he wasn't interested but because of the painful contrast to Santo that Alan Cheston was presenting. Here was the zeal Ben had hoped for in Santo: a wholehearted embracing of what would have been Santo's inheritance and that of his sister. But Santo hadn't seen things that way. He'd hungered for experiencing life instead of for building life. That was how he and his father had differed. True, he'd been only eighteen years old and with maturity might have come interest and commitment. But if the past was the best indicator of the future, didn't it stand to reason that Santo would have continued to engage in more of what had already begun to define him as a man? Charm and pursuit, charm and pleasure, charm and enthusiasm for what enthusiasm could gain him and not what enthusiasm could produce.

Ben wondered if Alan had seen all this when he'd asked for employment at Adventures Unlimited. For Alan had known Santo, had spoken to him, had seen him, had watched him. Thus Alan had known a gap was present. He'd assessed this gap and had deemed himself the man to fill it.

Alan was saying, 'So if we combine our assets and present a plan to the bank—' when Ben interrupted, *our* having broken into his thoughts like a sharp rap on the door of his consciousness.

'Do you know where Santo kept his climbing kit, Alan?'

Alan stopped dead in his verbal tracks. He looked at Ben in apparent confusion. It was feigned; it was not feigned. Ben couldn't tell. Alan said, 'What?' And when Ben repeated the question, Alan appeared to think about his reply before making it. 'I expect he kept it in his bedroom, Ben, didn't he? Or perhaps wherever you keep yours?'

'Do you know where mine is?'

'Why would I know?' Alan went about putting away the video recorder. A silence hung between them. In it, a car drove up outside and Alan walked to the window as he said, 'Unless . . .' But his answer was lost as two doors slammed on the other side of the window. 'Police,' Alan said. 'It's that constable again. The one who came earlier. He's got some woman with him this time.'

Ben left the conference room at once and went to the entrance as the front door opened and Constable McNulty came inside. He was preceded by a tough-looking woman with Sid Vicious hair dyed a shade of red that bordered on purple. She wasn't young, but she wasn't old. She looked at him directly, but not without compassion.

'Mr Kerne?' she said and went on to introduce herself as Detective Inspector Hannaford. She was there to interview the family, she told him.

All of the family? Ben wanted to know. Because his wife was in bed and his daughter was off on a bicycle ride. He felt this last made Kerra sound heartless, so he added, 'Stress. When she feels pressure, she needs an outlet.' And then he felt he'd said too much.

They would get to the daughter later, Hannford told him. In the meantime, they would wait while he roused his wife. This was preliminary stuff, she added. They would not take up too much of his time just now.

Just now meant there would be a later. With the police, what was implied was generally more important than what was said.

'Where are you with the investigation?' he asked.

'This is the first step, Mr Kerne, aside from forensics. They're beginning with fingerprints: his equipment, his car, the contents of his car. They'll move on from there. You' – and with a gesture that took in the hotel and obviously meant everyone within it – 'will need to be fingerprinted. But for the moment, it's questions. So if you'll fetch your wife . . .'

There was nothing for it but to do as she requested. Anything else and he'd look uncooperative, so Dellen's state couldn't be allowed to matter.

Ben went up the stairs instead of taking the lift. He wanted to use the climb to think. There was so much he didn't want the police to know, consisting of matters both buried and private.

At their bedroom, Ben knocked on the door softly, but he didn't wait to hear his wife's voice. He went into the darkness and moved towards the bed, where he switched on a lamp. Dellen lay as she'd lain when he'd last seen her. She was supine, one arm crooked across her eyes. Next to her on the bedside table were two bottles of pills and a glass of water. The glass's rim bore a crescent of red lipstick.

He sat down on the edge of the bed, but she didn't alter her position although her lips moved convulsively so he knew she wasn't asleep. He said, 'The police have come. They want to talk to us. You'll have to come down.'

Her head moved fractionally. 'I can't.'

'You must.'

'I can't let them see me like this. You know that.'

'Dellen—'

She lowered her arm. She squinted in the light and turned her head away from it and from him. 'I can't and you know it,' she said again. 'Unless you *want* them to see me like this. Is that it?'

'How can you say that, Dell?' He put his hand on her shoulder. He felt the answering tension run through her body.

'Unless,' she said again and she turned her head towards him, 'you want them to see me like this. Because we know you prefer me this way. You love me this way. You want me this way. I could almost think you arranged Santo's death just to send me in this direction. It's so useful to you, yes?'

Ben rose abruptly. He swung round so that she might not see his face.

She said at once, 'I'm sorry. Oh God, Ben. I don't know what I'm saying. Why don't you leave me? I know you want to. You've wanted to forever. You wear our marriage like a hair shirt. *Why*?'

He said, 'Please, Dell.' But he didn't know what he was asking her for. He wiped his nose on the arm of his shirt and went back to her. 'Let me help you. They're not going to leave till they've spoken to us.' He didn't add that the police were likely going to come back later to talk to Kerra and they could as well talk to Dellen then. That, he determined, could not be allowed to happen. He needed to be there when they spoke to Dellen and if the investigators came back later, there was always a chance they'd catch Dellen alone.

He went to the wardrobe and pulled clothes out for her. Black trousers, black jersey, black sandals for her feet. He sorted out underwear and carried everything back to the bed.

'Let me help you,' he said.

It had been the imperative of their years together. He lived to serve her. She lived to be served.

He drew the blankets and sheet away from her body. Beneath them, she was nude, and her scent was rank, and he looked on her with no stirring of lust. No longer the form of the fifteen-year-old girl he'd rolled with in the marram grass between the dunes, her body expressed the loathing that her voice wouldn't speak. She was pitted and stretched. She was dyed and painted. She was simultaneously barely real and all too corporeal. She was the past – embroilment and estrangement – made flesh.

He put his arm beneath her shoulders and he raised her. She'd begun to weep. It was a silent crying, ugly to watch. It stretched her mouth. It reddened her nose. It slit her eyes.

She said, 'You want to, so do it. I'm not holding you here. I've never held you.'

He murmured, 'Shhh, now. Put this on,' and he slid arms through the straps of her bra. She was no help to him, despite his encouragement. He was forced to cup her heavy breasts in his hands and fit the bra around them before he hooked it at the back. Thus he dressed her, and when he had her in her clothing, he urged her to her feet and she finally came to life.

She said again, 'I can't let them see me like this,' but her tone was different this time. She went to her dressing table and from among its clutter of cosmetics and costume jewellery, she brought forth a brush. This she vigorously ran through her long blonde hair till she had it untangled and fashioned into a passable chignon. She switched on a little brass lamp that he'd given her one long ago Christmas, and she bent to the mirror to examine her face. She used powder and a bit of mascara, and then she rustled among the lipsticks to find the one she wanted, which she applied.

'All right,' she said, and she turned to him.

Head to toe in black, but her lips were red. They were as red as a rose might be. They were as red as blood indeed was.

In conducting the preliminaries of the investigation with the assistance of Constable McNulty and Sergeant Collins, Bea Hannaford learned soon enough that she had as helpmates the indisputable police equivalents of Stan Laurel and Oliver Hardy. This realisation had abruptly descended upon her when Constable McNulty informed her, with a suitably lachrymose expression, that he'd give the family the information about Santo Kerne's death likely being murder. While this in itself could not be called execrable police work, having gone on blithely to share with the Kernes the facts about the dead boy's climbing equipment definitely was.

Bea had stared at McNulty, disbelieving at first. Then she'd understood that he was not misspeaking, that he *had* actually disclosed vital particulars of a police investigation to individuals who very well might be suspects. She'd exploded first. She'd wanted to strangle him second. Exactly what do you *do* all day, she'd inquired third in a nasty tone, toss off in public lavatories? Because, my man, you are the most *wretched* excuse for a police officer I've yet to meet. Are you aware that now we have *nothing* known only by ourselves and the killer? Do you understand the position that puts us in? After that, she'd told him to come with her and keep his mouth shut unless she told him he had permission to speak.

He'd shown good sense in this, at least. From the moment they'd arrived at the Promontory King George Hotel – a crumbling heap of derelict art deco that needed to be pulled down, in Bea's opinion – Constable McNulty had uttered not a word. He'd even taken notes, never once looking up from his pad as she spoke to Alan Cheston while they waited for the return of Ben Kerne, one hoped with his wife in tow.

Cheston was not a niggard with details: He was twenty-five, he was putatively the partner of the Kerne daughter, he'd grown up in Cambridge as the only child of a retired physicist ('That's Mum,' he explained with no little pride) and a retired university librarian ('That's Dad,' he added unnecessarily). He'd studied at Trinity Hall, gone on to the London School of Economics, and worked in marketing in a Birmingham redevelopment corporation until his parents' retirement to Casvelyn at which point he moved to Cornwall to be close to them in their latter years. He owned a terraced house in Lansdown Road that was being renovated, making it suitable for the wife and family he hoped for, so in the meantime he was living in a bedsit at the far end of Breakwater Road.

'Well, not exactly a bedsit,' he added after watching Constable McNulty's industrious scribbling for a moment. 'It's rather a room in that house – the large pink cottage? – at the end of the road, opposite the canal. I've kitchen privileges and . . . well, the landlady's quite liberal with how I use the rest of the house.'

By which, Bea assumed, he meant that the landlady had modern ideas. By which, she assumed, he meant that he and the Kerne daughter bonked there with impunity.

'Kerra and I intend to marry,' he added, as if this fine detail might smooth the troubled waters of what he mistakenly saw as Bea's ostensible concern for the young woman's virtue.

'Ah. How nice. And Santo?' she asked him. 'What sort of relationship did you have with him?'

'Terrific lad,' was Alan's reply. 'He was hard not to like. He was no great intellectual, mind you, but he had a happiness about him, a playfulness that was infectious and from what I could see, people liked to be around him. People in general.'

Joie de vivre, Bea thought. She pressed on. 'And what about you in particular? Did you like to be around him?'

'We didn't spend much time together. I'm Kerra's partner, so Santo and I were more like in-laws, I suppose. Cordial and friendly in conversation, but not anything else. We didn't have the same interests. He was very physical. I'm more . . . cerebral?'

'Which makes you better suited to run a business, I expect,' Bea noted.

'Yes, of course.'

'Like this business, for example.'

The young man was no idiot. He, unlike the Stan and Ollie she was saddled with, could tell a hawk from a handsaw no matter the direction of the wind. He said, 'Actually Santo was a bit relieved when he knew I was going to work here. It took an unwanted pressure off him.'

'What sort of pressure?'

'He'd have had to work with his mum in this part of the business, and he didn't want to. At least, that's what he led me to believe. He wasn't suited for this end of the operation.'

'But you don't mind it? Working this end of things. Working with her?'

'Not at all.' When he said this last bit, he kept his eyes fixed on Bea's and his entire body motionless. That alone made her wonder about the nature of his lie.

She said, 'I'd like to look at Santo's climbing kit if you'll point out where I can find it, Mr Cheston.'

'Sorry. Thing is, I don't actually know where he kept it.'

She had to wonder about that as well. He'd answered rather promptly, hadn't he, as if he'd been expecting the question.

She was about to press him further on this topic when he said, 'Here's Ben with Dellen,' into the sound of the old cage-like lift descending. She told the young man they'd speak again, no doubt. He said, Absolutely. Whenever the inspector wished.

He returned to his office before the lift reached the ground floor and disgorged the Kernes. Ben came out first and held his hand out to assist his wife. She emerged slowly, looking rather like a somnambulist. Drugs, Bea thought. She'd be sedated, which was hardly unexpected in the mother of a dead child.

The rest of her appearance, however, *was* unexpected. The polite term for it would have been *faded beauty*. Somewhere in her mid-forties, she suffered from the voluptuous woman's curse: the luscious curves of her youth having given way to the spread and the sag of advancing middle age. She'd been a smoker as well and perhaps she still was, for her skin was heavily webbed round the eyes and creviced round the lips. She wasn't fat, but she lacked the toned body that her husband possessed. Too little exercise and too much indulgence, Bea concluded.

And yet the woman had a way about her: pedicured feet, manicured hands, sumptuous blonde hair with a pleasing sheen, large violet eyes with thick dark lashes, and a manner of movement that asked for aid.

Troubadours would have called her a damsel. Bea called her Big Trouble and waited to find out why.

'Mrs Kerne,' she said. 'Thank you for joining us.' And then to Ben Kerne, 'Is there somewhere we could talk? This shouldn't take overly long.' The last bit was typical police casuistry. It would take however long it took for Bea to be satisfied.

Ben Kerne said they could go up to the first floor, the residents' lounge. They'd be comfortable there.

They were. The room overlooked St Mevan Beach, and it was fitted out with plush but durable new sofas, a large screen television, a DVD player, a stereo, a pool table, and a kitchenette. This last feature possessed tea-making facilities and a shiny stainless steel cappuccino machine. The walls displayed vintage posters of athletic scenes from the 1920s and 30s: skiers, hikers, cyclists, swimmers, and tennis players. It was well thought out and nicely done. A lot of money had gone into it.

Bea wondered where the money for such a project had come from, and she was not shy about asking. Rather than reply, however, Ben Kerne asked if the police wanted a coffee. Bea demurred for both of them before Constable McNulty – who'd raised his head from his pad with what she considered precipitate enthusiasm – could accept. Kerne went to the machine anyway, saying, 'If you don't mind . . .' and going on to make some sort of concoction, which he pressed upon his wife. She took it from him with no enthusiasm. He asked her to have a bit of it, and he sounded solicitous. Dellen said she didn't want it, but Ben was obdurate. 'You must,' he told her. They looked at each other and seemed to engage in a battle of wills. Dellen was the one to blink. She raised the cup to her lips and didn't lower it till she'd drunk it all, leaving a disturbing smear of red where her lips had touched the stoneware.

Bea asked how long they'd been in Casvelyn, and Ben told her they'd arrived two years earlier. They'd come from Truro, he said, and he went on to explain that he'd owned two sporting goods shops in that town, which he'd sold, along with the family house, in order to finance, if only partially, the project of setting up Adventures Unlimited. Further money had come from the bank, naturally. One did not take on a venture like this without more than one source of finance. They were due to open in mid-June, he said. At least, they *had* been due to open. Now, he didn't know.

Bea let that go for the moment. She said, 'Grow up in Truro, did you, Mr Kerne? Were you and your wife childhood sweethearts?'

He hesitated at this, for some reason. He looked to Dellen as if considering how best to phrase his answer. Bea wondered which of the questions was giving him pause: the growing up in Truro part or the childhood sweethearts part.

'Not in Truro, no,' he finally answered. 'But as to being childhood sweethearts . . .' He looked at his wife again, and there was no doubt that his expression was fond. 'We've been together more or less since we were teenagers: sixteen and fifteen, wasn't it, Dell?' He didn't wait for his wife to reply. 'We were like most kids, though. Together for a bit, broken up for a bit. Then forgiveness and getting back together. We did that for six or seven years before we got married, didn't we, Dell?'

Dellen said, 'I don't know. I've forgotten all that.' She had a husky voice, a smoker's voice. It suited her. Anything else would have been wildly out of character.

'Have you?' He turned from her to Bea. 'It seemed to go on forever: the drama of our teenage years. As these things do, when you care for someone.'

'What sort of drama?' Bea asked as next to her Constable McNulty kept up a gratifying scribbling against his pad.

'I slept around,' Dellen said bluntly.

'Dell . . .'

'She'll likely find out the truth, so we may as well tell it,' Dellen said. 'I was the village tart, Inspector.' And then to her husband, 'C'n you make me another coffee. Ben? And hotter, please. The last was rather lukewarm.'

Ben's face had altered to granite as she'd spoken. After a fractional hestitation, he rose from the sofa where he'd placed himself and his wife, and he went back to the cappuccino maker. Bea let the silence continue, and when Constable McNulty cleared his throat as if to speak, she knocked her foot against his to keep him quiet. She liked tension during an interview, especially if one of the suspects was inadvertently providing it to the other.

Dellen finally spoke again, but she looked at Ben, as if what she said comprised a hidden message for him. 'We lived down the coast, Ben and I, but not in a place like Newquay, where there're at least a few diversions. We were from a village, where there was nothing to do besides the beach in summer and sex in winter. And sometimes sex in summer as well if the weather wasn't good enough for the beach. We ran in packs then – a gang of kids – and we mixed it up with each other. Pairing off this way for a bit, pairing off that way for a bit. Till we got to Truro, that is. Ben went first and I, clever girl, followed him directly. And that made all the difference. Things changed for us in Truro.'

Ben returned with her drink. He also brought with him a packet of cigarettes that he'd taken from somewhere in the kitchenette, lit one for her and handed it over. He sat next to her, quite close.

Dellen downed the second coffee much as she'd done the first, as if her mouth were lined with asbestos. She took the cigarette from him and drew in on it expertly, doing what Bea always thought of as that double inhaling bit: drawing smoke in, letting a bit out, drawing it all back in again. Dellen Kerne made the act look unique. Bea tried to get a bead on the woman. Dellen's hands were unsteady.

'Bright lights, big city?' she asked the Kernes. 'Is that what took you to Truro?'

'Hardly,' Dellen said. 'Ben had an uncle who took him in when he was eighteen. He kept rowing with his dad. Over me. Dad thought – this is Ben's, not mine – that if he got him out of the village, he'd get him out of my hair as well. Or get me out of his. He didn't reckon I'd follow. Did he, Ben?'

Ben covered her hand with his. She was saying too much and all of them knew it, but only Ben and his wife knew *why* she was doing it. Bea considered what all this had to do with Santo as Ben endeavoured to wrest control of the conversation from Dellen by saying, 'That's a reinvention of history. Truth of the matter' – and this he said directly to Bea – 'is that my dad and I never got on very well. His dream was to live entirely off the land, and after eighteen years of that, I'd had enough. I made arrangements to live with my uncle. I took off for Truro. Dellen followed me in . . . I don't know . . . What was it? Eight months?'

'Seemed like eight centuries,' Dellen said. 'For my sins, I knew a good thing when I saw it. For my sins, I still do.' She kept her gaze on Ben Kerne as she said to Bea, 'I've a wonderful husband whose patience I've tried for many years, Inspector Hannaford. Could I have another coffee, Ben?'

Ben said, 'Are you sure that's wise?'

'But make it hotter still, please. I don't think that machine is working very well.'

And it came to Bea that that was it: the coffee and what the coffee stood for. She hadn't wanted it, and he'd insisted. Coffee as metaphor, and Dellen Kerne was rubbing his face in it.

She said, 'I'd like to see your son's room, if I may. As soon as you've finished with your coffee, of course.'

Daidre Trahair was walking back towards Polcare Cove along the cliff top when she saw him. A brisk wind was blowing and she'd just stopped to refasten her hair in its tortoiseshell slide. She'd managed to capture most of it, and she'd shoved the rest of it behind her ears, and there he was, perhaps a hundred yards to the south of her. He'd obviously just climbed from the cove, so her first thought was that he was on his way again, resuming his walk, having been released from all suspicion by Detective Inspector Hannaford. She concluded that this release was reasonable enough: As soon as he'd said he was from New Scotland Yard, he'd probably been absolved from suspicion. If only she herself had been half so clever . . .

Except she had to be truthful, at least with herself. Thomas Lynley had never told them he was from New Scotland Yard, had he? It had been something assumed the moment he'd said his name.

He'd said Thomas Lynley. One of them had said, and she couldn't remember which one it had been, New Scotland Yard? in such a way that seemed to speak volumes among them. He'd said something to indicate they were correct in their assumption and that had been it.

She knew why now. For if he was Thomas Lynley of New Scotland Yard then he was also Thomas Lynley whose wife had been murdered in the street in front of their Belgravia home. Every cop in the country would know about that. The police were, after all, a brotherhood of sorts. She needed to remember that, and she needed to be careful round him, no matter his pain and her inclination to assuage it. Everyone had pain, she told herself. Life was all about learning to cope with it.

He raised an arm to wave. She waved in turn. They walked towards each other across the top of the cliff. The path here was narrow and uneven, with shards of carboniferous stone tipping up from the soil, and along its east side gorse rustled thickly, a yellow intrusion standing hardily against the wind. Beyond the gorse, grass grew abundantly although it was closely cropped by the sheep that grazed freely upon it.

When they were close enough to be heard by each other, Daidre said to Thomas Lynley, 'So. You're on your way, then?' But as soon as she spoke, she realised this was not the case, and she went on to add, 'Except you've not got your rucksack with you, so you aren't on your way at all.'

He nodded solemnly. 'You'd make a good detective.'

'A decidedly elementary deduction, I'm afraid. Anything more would escape my notice. Are you out for a walk?'

'I was looking for you.' The wind tossed his hair and he brushed it away from his forehead. Again, she thought how like hers it was. She assumed that he went quite blond in summer.

'How did you know where to find me? Beyond knocking at the door of the cottage, I mean. Because I hope I can presume you *did* knock this time. I don't have many more windows to offer up to you.'

'I knocked,' he said. 'When no one answered, I had a look round and saw the fresh footprints. I followed them. It was simple enough.'

'And here I am.'

'And here you are.'

He smiled and seemed to hesitate, which surprised Daidre as he didn't seem the type of man who'd hesitate at anything. She said, 'And?' and cocked her head. He had, she noted, a scar on his upper lip which relieved his otherwise offputting appearance, which was handsome in that classical sense: He had strong features that were well defined. No indication of inbreeding here.

'I've come to ask you to dinner,' he said. 'I'm afraid I can only offer you the Salthouse Inn as I've no funds of my own yet, and I can hardly invite you for a meal and ask you to pay for it, can I? But at the inn, they'll put our meal on the bill and as breakfast was excellent – well, at least it was filling – I suspect dinner will be adequate as well.'

'What a dubious invitation,' she said.

He seemed to think about it. 'D' you mean the "adequate" part?'

'Yes. "Join me for an adequate albeit far-from-sumptuous meal." It's one of those gallant post-Victorian requests one can only respond to with "Thank you, I think."'

He laughed. 'Sorry. My mother would roll in her grave, were she dead, which she isn't. Let me say, then, that I've had a look at tonight's menu, and it appears, if not brilliant, then at least swell.'

She laughed in turn. '*Swell?* Where on earth did that come from? Never mind. Don't tell me. Have supper here instead. I've something already prepared and there's enough for two. It only needs baking.'

'But then I'll be doubly in your debt.'

'Which is exactly where I want you, my lord.'

His face altered, all amusement drained away by her slip of the tongue. She cursed herself for her lapse in circumspection and what it presaged about her ability to keep other things to herself in his presence.

'Ah. So you know.'

She sought an explanation and decided one existed that would be reasonable, even to him. 'When you said last night that you were from Scotland Yard, I wanted to know if that was the case. So I set about finding out.' She looked away from him for a moment. She saw that the herring gulls were settling in on the nearby cliff face for the night, pairing off onto ledges and into crevices, ruffling their wings, huddling against the wind. 'I'm terribly sorry, Thomas,' she said.

After a moment during which more gulls landed and others soared and cawed, he said, 'You've no need to apologise. I would have done the same in your situation. A stranger in your house claiming to be a policeman. Someone dead outside. What are you to believe?'

'That's not what I meant.' She looked back at him. He was into the wind; she was against it. It played havoc with her hair, whipping it into her face despite the slide.

'Then what?' he said.

'Your wife. I'm so terribly sorry about what happened to her. What a wrenching thing for you to have to go through.'

'Ah yes.' He moved his gaze to the seabirds. He would see them, Daidre knew, as she saw them, pairing off not because there was safety in numbers but because there was safety in just one other gull. 'It was far more wrenching for her than for me.'

'I don't believe that.'

'Don't you? Well, there's little more wrenching than death by gunshot, I dare say. Especially when death is not immediate. I didn't have to go through that. Helen did. She was there one moment, just trying to get her shopping in the front door. She was shot the next. That would be rather wrenching, wouldn't you say?' He sounded bleak, and he didn't look at her as she spoke. But he'd misunderstood her meaning, and Daidre sought to clarify it.

'I believe that death is the end of this *part* of our existence, Thomas: the spiritual being's human experience. The spirit leaves the body and then goes on to what's next. And what's next has to be better than what's here or what's the point, really?'

'Do you actually believe that?' His tone walked the line between bitterness and incredulity. 'Heaven and hell and nonsense in a similar vein?'

'Not heaven and hell. That all seems rather silly, doesn't it. God or whoever up there on a throne, casting this soul downward to eternal torment, tossing this soul upward to sing hymns with the angels.

That can't be what this' – Her arm took in the cliff side and the sea – 'is all about. But that there's something else beyond what we understand in this moment . . . ? Yes, I do believe that. So for you . . . You're still the spiritual being undergoing and attempting to understand the human experience while she now knows—'

'Helen,' he said. 'Her name was Helen.'

'Helen, yes. Forgive me. Helen now knows what it was all about. But there's little peace of mind in that. For you, I mean, knowing that Helen's moved on.'

'It wasn't her choice,' he said.

'Is it ever, Thomas?'

'Suicide.' He looked at her evenly.

She felt a chill. 'That's not a choice. That's a decision based upon the belief that there are no choices.'

'God.' A muscle moved in his jaw. She so regretted her slip of the tongue. A simple expression, *my lord*, had reduced him to his wound. These things take time, she wanted to tell him. Such a cliché but so much truth within it.

She said to him, 'Thomas, do you fancy a walk? There's something I'd like to show you. It's a bit of a way, perhaps a mile up the coast along the path, but it'll give us an appetite for dinner.'

She thought he might refuse, but he nodded and she gestured him to follow her. They headed in the direction from which she'd just come, dipping down at first into another cove, where great fins of slate shot out of the encroaching surf and reached towards a treacherous cliff top of sandstone and shale. The wind and the waves made talking difficult, as did their positions, one behind the other, so Daidre said nothing, nor did Thomas Lynley. It was, she decided, better this way. Letting a moment pass without acknowledging it further was sometimes a more efficacious approach to healing than troubling a developing scar.

Spring had brought wildflowers into areas more protected by the wind, and along the way into combes, the yellow of ragwort mixed with the pinks of thrift and heather while bluebells still marked the spots where ancient forests had once stood. There was scant habitation in the immediate environs of the cliffs when they ascended, but in the distance stone-built farmhouses crouched alongside their greater-sized barns, and the cattle these served grazed in paddocks that were marked by Cornwall's earthen hedgerows with their rich vegetation where dogrose and pennywort grew.

The nearest village was a place called Alsperyl, which was also their destination. This comprised a church, a vicarage, a collection of cottages, an ancient schoolhouse, and a pub. All fashioned from the unpainted stone of the district, they sat some half mile to the east of the cliff path beyond a lumpy paddock. Only the church spire was visible. Daidre pointed this out and said, 'St Morwenna's, but we're going this way just a bit farther if you can manage.'

He nodded, and she felt foolish with her final remark. He was hardly infirm and grief did not rob one of the ability to walk. She nodded in turn and led him perhaps another two hundred yards where a break in the wind-tossed heather on the seaside edge of the path gave way to steps hewn into stone.

She said, 'It's not much of a descent, but take care. The edge is still deadly. And we're . . . I don't know . . . perhaps a hundred and fifty feet above the water?'

Down a set of steps, which curved with the natural form of the cliff side, they came to another little path, nearly overgrown with gorse and patches of English stonecrop that somehow thrived here despite the wind. Perhaps twenty yards along, the path ended abruptly, but not with a preciptious cliff edge as one might expect. Rather, a small hut had been hewn into the cliff face. It was fronted with the old driftwood of ruined ships and sided – where such sides emerged beyond the cliff face itself – with small blocks of sandstone. Its wooden face was grey with age. The hinges that served its rough Dutch door bled rust onto pitted panels.

Daidre glanced back at Thomas Lynley to see his reaction: such a structure in such a remote location. His eyes had widened, and a smile crooked his mouth. His expression seemed to say, What *is* this place?

She replied to his unasked question, speaking above the wind that buffeted them. 'Isn't it marvellous, Thomas? It's called Hedra's Hut. Evidently, if the journal of the Reverend Mr Walcombe is to be believed, it's been here since the late eighteenth century.'

'Did he build it?'

'Mr Walcombe? No, no. He wasn't a builder, but he was quite a chronicler. He kept a journal of the doings round Alsperyl. I found it in the library in Casvelyn. He was the vicar of St Morwenna's for some forty years. He tried to save the tormented soul who did build this place.'

'Ah. That would be the Hedra from Hedra's Hut, then?'

'The very woman. Apparently, she was widowed when her husband, who fished the waters out of Polcare Cove, was caught in a storm and drowned, leaving her with one young son. According to Mr Walcombe, who does not generally embellish his facts, the boy disappeared one day, likely having ventured too near the edge of the cliff in an area too friable to support his weight. Rather than confront the deaths of both husband *and* son within six months of each other, poor Hedra chose to believe a selkie had taken the boy. She told herself he'd wandered down to the water – God knows how he managed it from this height – and there the seal waited in her human form and beckoned him into the sea to join the rest of the . . .' She frowned. 'Blast. I've quite forgotten what a group of seals is called. It can't be a herd. A pod? But that's whales. Well, no matter at the moment. That's what happened. Hedra built this but to watch for his return, and that's what she did for the rest of her life. It's a poignant story, isn't it?'

'Is it true?'

'If we can believe Mr Walcombe. Come inside. There's more to see. Let's get out of the wind.'

The upper and lower doors closed by means of wooden bars that slid through rough wooden handles and rested on hooks. As she pushed the top one back and then the bottom one, and swung the doors open, she said over her shoulder, 'Hedra knew what she was doing. She gave herself quite a sturdy place to wait for her son. It's framed in timber all round. Each side has a bench, the roof has quite decent beams to hold it up, and the floor is slate. It's as if she knew she'd be waiting for a while, isn't it?'

She led the way in, but then stopped short. Behind her, she heard him duck under the low lintel to join her. She said, 'Oh blast,' in disgust and he said, 'Now, that's a shame.'

The wall directly in front of them had been defaced and defaced recently if the freshness of the cuts into the wooden panels of the little building were anything to go by. The remains of a heart which had been earlier carved into the wood, no doubt accompanied by lovers' initials, curved round a series of vicious hack marks that now gouged deeply as if into flesh. No initials were left.

'Well,' Daidre said, trying to sound philosophical about the mess, 'I suppose it's not as if the walls haven't *already* been carved up. And at least it isn't spray paint. But still. Why do people do such things?'

Thomas was observing the rest of the hut, with its more than two hundred years of carvings: initials, dates, other hearts, the occasional name. He said thoughtfully, 'Where I went to school, there's a wall . . . It's not too far from the entrance, actually so no visitor can ever miss it . . . Pupils have put their initials into it since the time of Henry VI. Whenever I go back – because I do go back occasionally – I look for mine. They're still there. They somehow say I'm real, I existed then, I exist even now. But when I look at all the others – and there are hundreds, probably thousands of them – I can't help thinking how fleeting life is. It's the same thing here, isn't it?'

'I suppose it is.' She ran her fingers over several of the older carvings: a Celtic cross, the name Daniel, B.J. + S.R. 'I like to come here to think,' she told him. 'Sometimes I wonder who were these people all coupled together so confidently. And did their love last?'

Lynley touched the poor gouged heart. 'Nothing lasts,' he said. 'That's our curse.'

9

Bea Hannaford saw much that seemed typical in Santo Kerne's bedroom, and for the first time she was glad to have Constable McNulty doing penance as her dogsbody. For the walls of Santo's bedroom bore a plethora of surfing posters and, from what Bea could tell, what McNulty didn't know about surfing, the locations of the photos and the surfers themselves, didn't actually bear knowing. She couldn't conclude that his knowledge was in any way relevant to anything, however. She was merely relieved that, at the end of the day, McNulty did know something about *something*.

'Jaws,' he murmured obscurely, gazing awestruck at a liquid mountain down which a thumb-size madman rushed. 'Bloody hell, *look* at that bloke. That's Hamilton, off Maui. He's dead mad, that bloke. He'll do anything. Christ, this looks like a tsunami, doesn't it?' He whistled low and shook his head.

Ben Kerne was with them, but he didn't venture into the room. His wife had remained below in the lounge. It had been obvious that Kerne hadn't wanted to leave her on her own, but he'd been caught between the police and his spouse. He couldn't accommodate one while attempting to monitor the other. He'd had little choice in the matter, then. They would either wander the hotel till they found Santo's bedroom while he saw to his wife, or he would have to take them there. He'd chosen the latter, but it was fairly clear that his mind was elsewhere.

'So far we've heard nothing about Santo and surfing,' Bea said to Ben Kerne, who stood in the doorway.

'He started surfing when we first came to Casvelyn.'

'Is his surfing kit here? Board, wetsuit, whatever else.'

'Hood,' McNulty murmured. 'Gloves, boots, extra fins—'

'That'll do, Constable,' Bea told him sharply. 'Mr Kerne probably gets the point.'

'No,' Ben Kerne said. 'He kept his kit elsewhere.'

'Did he? Why?' Bea said. 'Not exactly convenient, is it?'

Ben looked at the posters as he replied. 'I expect he didn't like to keep it here.'

'Why?' she repeated.

'He likely suspected I'd do something with it.'

'Ah. Constable . . . ?' Bea was gratified to see that Mick McNulty took the hint and once more attended to his note taking, although Ben Kerne couldn't say, when asked, where Santo had indeed kept his gear. 'Why would Santo think you might do something with his kit, Mr Kerne? Or do you mean *to* his kit?' And she thought, If the surfing kit, why not the cliff climbing kit?

'Because he knew I didn't particularly want him surfing.'

'Really? It seems a harmless enough sport, compared to cliff climbing.'

'No sport is completely harmless, Inspector. But it wasn't that.' Kerne seemed to be looking for a way to explain, and he came into the bedroom to do so. He observed the posters. His face was stony.

Bea said, 'Do you surf, Mr Kerne?'

'I wouldn't prefer Santo not surf if I did it myself, now would I?'

'I don't know. Would you? I still don't see why you approved of one sport but not another.'

'It's the type, all right?' Kerne gave an apologetic glance to Constable McNulty. 'I didn't like him mixing with surfers because for so many of them it's their only world. I didn't want him adopting it: the hanging about they do, waiting for the opportunity for a surf, their lives defined by isobar charts and tide tables, driving up and down the coast to find perfect waves. And when they're not having a surf, they're talking about it or smoking cannabis while they stand round in their wetsuits afterwards, *still* talking about it. There're blokes – and lasses as well, I admit it – whose entire worlds revolve round riding waves and travelling the globe to ride more waves. I didn't want that for Santo. Would you want it for your son or daughter?'

'But if his world revolved round cliff climbing?'

'It didn't. But at least it's a sport where one depends upon others. It's not solitary, the way surfing generally is. A surfer alone on the waves: You see it all the time. I didn't want him out there alone. I wanted him to be with people. So if something happened to him . . .' He moved his gaze back to the posters, and what they depicted was, even to an unschooled observer like Bea, absolute danger embodied in an unimaginable tonnage of water: exposure to everything from broken bones to certain drowning. She wondered how many people died each year, coursing a nearly vertical declivity that, unlike the earth with its knowable textures, changed within seconds to trap the unwary.

'Yet Santo was climbing alone when he fell. Just as he might have been had he gone for a surf. And anyway, surfers don't always do this alone, do they?'

'On the wave itself. The surfer and the wave, alone. There may be others out there, but it's not about them.'

'With climbing it is, though?'

'You depend on the other climber, and he depends on you. You keep each other safe.' He cleared his throat roughly. 'What father wouldn't want safety for his son?'

'And when Santo didn't agree with your assessment of surfing?'

'What about it?'

'What happened between you? Arguments? Punishment? Do you tend towards violence, Mr Kerne?'

He faced her, but in doing so he put his back to the window so she could no longer read his face. He said, 'What the hell sort of question is that?'

'One that wants answering. Santo's eye was blackened by someone recently. What d'you know about that?'

His shoulders dropped. He moved again, but this time out of the light of the window and towards the other side of the room, where a computer and its printer sat on a single plywood sheet across two saw horses forming a primitive desk. There was a stack of papers face down on this desk; Ben Kerne reached for them. Bea stopped him before his fingers made contact. She repeated her question.

'He wouldn't tell me,' Kerne said. 'Obviously, I could tell he'd been punched. It was a bad blow. But he wouldn't explain it, so I was left to think . . .' He shook his head. He seemed to have information he was loath to part with.

Bea said, 'If you know something, if you suspect something . . .'

'I don't. It's just that the young women liked Santo, and Santo liked the young women. He didn't discriminate.'

'Between what?'

'Between available and unavailable. Between attached and unattached. Santo was like pure mating instinct given human form. Perhaps an angry father punched him. Or a furious boyfriend. He wouldn't say. But he liked the lasses and the lasses liked him. And the truth of the matter is that he was easily led where a determined young woman wanted him to go. I'm afraid he was always that way.'

'Anyone in particular?'

'His last was a girl called Madlyn Angarrack. They'd been an item for more than a year.'

'Is she also a surfer by any chance?' Bea asked.

'A brilliant one, if Santo was to be believed. National champion in the making. He was quite taken with her.'

'And she with him?'

'It wasn't a one-way street.'

'How was it for you, watching your son become involved with a surfer, then?'

Ben Kerne answered steadily. 'Santo was always involved somewhere, Inspector. I knew it would pass, whatever *it* was. As I said, he liked the ladies. He wasn't ready to settle. Not with Madlyn, not with anyone. No matter what.'

Bea thought that last was a strange expression. She said, 'You wanted him to settle, though?'

'Like any father, I wanted him to keep his nose clean and stay out of trouble.'

'Not overly ambitious for him, then? Those are fairly limited as expectations go.'

Ben Kerne said nothing. Bea had the impression he was keeping something to himself, and it was her experience that in a murder inquiry, when someone did that, it was generally out of self-interest.

'Did you ever beat Santo, Mr Kerne?'

His gaze on her didn't waver. 'I've answered that question already.'

She let a silence hang there, but this one lacked fecundity. She was forced to move on. She did so by giving her attention to Santo's computer. They would have to take it with them, she told Kerne. Constable McNulty would unplug it all and carry the components out to their car. Having said this, she reached for the stack of papers that Kerne had been going for on the desk. She flipped them over and spread them out.

They were, she saw, a variety of designs that incorporated *Adventures Unlimited* into each of them. In one the two words themselves formed into a curling wave. In another they made a circular logo in which the Promontory King George Hotel stood centrally. In a third they became the base upon which a variety of athletic feats were being accomplished by buffed out silhouettes both masculine and feminine. In another they made a climbing apparatus.

'Oh God.'

Bea looked up from the designs to see Kerne's stricken face. 'What is it?' she asked.

'He designed T-shirts. On his computer. He was . . . Obviously, he was working on something for the business. I'd not asked him to do it. Oh God, Santo.'

He said the last like an apology. In reaction, Bea asked him about his son's climbing equipment. Kerne told her that all of it was missing, every belay device, every chock stone, every rope, every item he would need for any climb he might make.

'Would he have needed all of it to make that climb yesterday?'

No, Kerne told her. He either began keeping it elsewhere without his father's knowledge or he'd taken it all on the previous day when he set off to make his fatal climb.

'Why?' Bea asked.

'We'd had harsh words. He'd have reacted to them. It would have been an "I'll show you" sort of statement.'

'One that led to his death? Too much in a state to examine his kit closely? Was he the type to do that?'

'Impulsive, you mean? Impulsive enough to climb without looking over his equipment? Yes,' Kerne said, 'he was exactly the type to do that.'

It was, praise God or praise whomever one felt like praising when praise was called for, the last radiator. Not the last radiator as in the *last* radiator of all radiators in the hotel, but the last radiator he would have to paint for the day. Given half an hour to clean the brushes and seal the paint tins – after years of practise while working for his father, Cadan knew he could stretch out *any* activity as long as was necessary – it would be time to leave for the day. Halle-fucking-lujah. His lower back was throbbing and his head was reacting to the fumes once again. Clearly, he *wasn't* meant for this type of labour. Well, that was hardly a surprise.

Cadan squatted back on his heels and admired his handiwork. It was dead stupid of them to put down the fitted carpet *before* they'd had the radiators painted, he thought. But he'd managed to get the most recent spill cleaned up with a bit of industrious rubbing, and what he'd not got up he reckoned the curtains would hide. Besides, it had been his only serious spill of the day, and that was saying something.

He declared, 'We are out of here, Poohster.'

The parrot adjusted his balance on Cadan's shoulder and replied with a squawk followed by, 'Loose bolts on the fridge! Call the cops! Call the cops!' yet another of his curious remarks.

The door to the room swung open as Pooh flapped his wings, preparatory either to making a descent to the floor or to performing a less than welcome bodily function on Cadan's shoulder. Cadan said, 'Don't you *bloody* dare, mate,' and a female voice said in concerned reply, 'Who are you, please? What're you doing here?'

The speaker turned out to be a woman in black, and Cadan reckoned that she was Santo Kerne's mother, Dellen. He scrambled to his feet. Pooh said, 'Polly wants a shag. Polly wants a shag,' displaying, not for the first time, the level of inapposition to which he was capable of sinking at a moment's notice.

'What is that?' Dellen Kerne asked.

'A parrot.'

She looked annoyed. 'I can see it's a parrot, I'm not stupid or blind. What sort of parrot and what's he doing here and what're *you* doing here, if it comes to that?'

'He's a Mexican parrot.' Cadan could feel himself getting hot, but he knew the woman wouldn't twig his discomfiture as his olive skin didn't blush when blood suffused it. 'His name is Pooh.'

'As in Winnie-the?'

'As in what he does best.'

A smile flickered round her lips. 'Why don't I know you? Why've I not seen you here before?'

Cadan introduced himself. 'Mr Kerne hired me yesterday. He probably forgot to tell you because of . . .' He saw the way he was headed too late to avoid heading there. He quirked his mouth and wanted to disappear since – aside from painting radiators and dreaming about what could be done to the crazy golf course – his day had been spent in avoiding a run-in precisely like this: face to face with one of Santo Kerne's parents in a moment when the magnitude of their loss was going to have to be acknowledged with an appropriate expression of sympathy. He said, 'Sorry about Santo.'

She looked at him evenly. 'Of course you are.'

Whatever that was supposed to mean. Cadan shifted on his feet. He had a paintbrush still in his hand and he wondered suddenly and idiotically what he was meant to do with it. Or with the tin of paint. No one had said where to put them at the end of the work day. He'd not thought to ask.

'Did you know Santo?' Dellen Kerne said abruptly.

'A bit. Yeah.'

'And what did you think of him?'

This was rocky ground. Cadan didn't know how to reply other than to say, 'He bought a surfboard from my dad.' He didn't mention Madlyn, didn't want to mention Madlyn, and didn't want to think *why* he didn't want to mention Madlyn.

'I see. Yes. But that doesn't actually answer the question, does it?' Dellen came farther into the room. She went to the fitted clothes cupboard, opened it, looked inside. She spoke, oddly, into the cupboard's interior. She said, 'Santo was a great deal like me. You wouldn't know that if you didn't know him. And you didn't know him, did you? Not actually.'

'Like I said. A bit. I saw him, around. More when he was first learning to surf than later on.'

'Because you surf as well?'

'Me? No. Well, I mean I've *been*, of course. But I've got other interests.'

She turned from the cupboard. 'What are they? Sport, I expect. You look quite fit. And women as well. Young men your age generally have women as one of their main interests. Are you like other young men?' She frowned. 'Can we open that window, Cadan? The smell of paint . . .'

Cadan wanted to say it was her hotel so she could do whatever she wanted to do, but he set down his paint brush carefully, went to the window, and wrestled it open, which wasn't easy. It needed adjusting or greasing or something. Whatever one did to rejuvenate windows.

She said, 'Thank you. I'm going to have a cigarette now. Do you smoke? No? That's a surprise. You have the look of a smoker.'

Cadan knew he was meant to ask what the look of a smoker was, and had she been somewhere between twenty and thirty years old, he would have done so. His attitude would have been that questions like that one, of a potentially metaphoric nature, could lead to interesting answers which in turn could lead to interesting developments. But in this case, he kept his mouth shut and when she said, 'You won't be bothered if I smoke, will you?' he shook his head. He hoped she didn't expect him to light her cigarette for her – because she *did* seem the sort of woman round whom men leapt like jackrabbits – since he had neither matches nor lighter with him. She was correct in her assessment of him, though. He was a smoker but he'd been cutting back recently, inanely telling himself it was tobacco and not drink that was the real root of his problems.

He saw that she'd brought a packet of cigarettes with her and she had matches as well, tucked into the packet. She lit up, drew in, and let smoke drift from her nostrils.

'Whose shit's on fire?' Pooh remarked.

Cadan winced. 'Sorry. He's heard that from my sister a million times. He mimics her. He mimics everyone. Anyway, she hates smoking.' And then again, 'Sorry,' because he didn't want her to think he was being critical of her.

'You're nervous,' Dellen said. 'I'm making you that way. And the bird's fine. He doesn't know what he's saying, after all.'

'Yeah. Well. Sometimes, I'd swear he does.'

'Like the remark about shagging?'

He blinked. 'What?'

'"Polly wants a shag,"' she reminded him. 'It was the first thing he said when I came into the room. I don't, actually. Want a shag, that is. But I'm curious why he said that. I expect you use that bird to collect women. Is that why you brought him with you?'

'He goes most everywhere with me.'

'That can't be convenient.'

'We work things out.'

'Do you?' She observed the bird, but Cadan had the feeling she wasn't really seeing Pooh. He couldn't have said what she *was* seeing but her next remarks gave him at least an idea. 'Santo and I were quite close. Are you close to your mother, Cadan?'

'No.' He didn't add that it was impossible to be close to Wenna Rice Angarrack McCloud Jackson Smythe, aka the Bounder. She had never remained stationary long enough for closeness to be anywhere in the deck of cards she played.

'Santo and I were quite close,' Dellen said again. 'We were very alike. Sensualists. Do you know what that is?' She gave him no chance to answer, not that he could have given her a definition, anyway. She said, 'We live for sensation. For what we can see and hear and smell. For what we can taste. For what we can touch. And for what can touch us. We experience life in all its richness, without guilt and without fear. That's what Santo was like. That's what I taught Santo to be.'

'Right.' Cadan thought he'd like to get out of the room, but he wasn't certain how to effect a departure that wouldn't look like running away. He told himself there was no *real* reason to turn tail and disappear through the doorway, but he had a feeling, nearly animal in nature, that danger was near.

Dellen said to him, 'What sort are you, Cadan? Can I touch your bird or will he bite?'

'He likes to be scratched on his head. Where you'd put his ears if birds had ears. I mean ears like ours, because they can hear, obviously.'

'Like this?' She came close to Cadan, then. He could smell her scent. Musk, he thought. She used the nail of her index finger, which was painted red. Pooh accepted her ministrations as he normally did. He purred like a cat, yet another sound he'd learned from a previous owner. Dellen smiled at the bird. She said to Cadan, 'You didn't answer me. What sort are you? Sensualist? Emotionalist? Intellectual?'

'Not bloody likely,' he replied. 'Intellectual, I mean. I'm not intellectual.'

'Ah. Are you emotional? Bundle of feelings? Raw to the touch? Inside, I mean.'

He shook his head.

'Then you're a sensualist, like me. Like Santo. I thought as much. You have that look about you. I expect it's something your girlfriend appreciates. If you have one. Do you?'

'Not just now.'

'Pity. You're quite attractive, Cadan. What do you do for sex?'

Cadan felt ever more the need to escape, yet she wasn't doing a single thing except petting the bird and talking to him. Still, something was very off with the woman.

Then it came to him at a gallop that her son was dead. Not only dead but murdered. He was gone, kaput, given the chop, whatever. When a son died – or a daughter or a husband – wasn't the mother supposed to rip up her clothes? tear at her hair? shed tears by the bucketful?

She said, 'Because you must do something for sex, Cadan. A young virile man like you. You can't mean me to think you live like a celibate priest.'

'I wait for summer,' he finally told her.

Her finger hesitated, less than an inch from Pooh's green head. The bird sidestepped to get back within its range. 'For summer?'

'Town's full of girls then. Here on holiday.'

'Ah. You prefer the short-term relationship, then. Sex without strings.'

'Well,' he said. 'Yeah. Works for me, that.'

'I expect it does. You scratch them and they scratch you and everyone's happy with the arrangement. No questions asked. I know exactly what you mean. Although I expect that surprises you. A woman my age. Married with children. Knowing what it means.'

He offered a half-smile. It was insincere, just a way to acknowledge what she was saying without having to acknowledge what she was saying. He gave a look in the direction of the doorway. He said, 'Well,' and tried to make his tone decisive, a way of saying That's that, then. Nice talking to you.

She said, 'Why haven't we met before this?'

'I just started—'

'No. I understand that. But I can't sort out why we haven't met before. You're roughly Santo's age—'

'Four years older, actually. He's my—'

'—and you're so like him as well. So I can't sort out why you've never come round with him.'

'— sister's age. Madlyn,' he said. 'You probably know Madlyn. My sister. She and Santo were, well, they were whatever you want to call it.'

'What?' Dellen asked blankly. 'What did you call her?'

'Madlyn. Madlyn Angarrack. She and Santo were together for . . . I don't know . . . Eighteen months? Two years? Whatever. Madlyn's my sister.'

Dellen stared at him. Then she stared past him, but she appeared to be looking at nothing at all. She said in a different voice altogether, 'How very odd. She's called Madlyn, you say?'

'Yeah. Madlyn Angarrack.'

'And she and Santo were, what, exactly?'

'Boyfriend and girlfriend. Partners. Lovers. Whatever.'

'You're joking.'

He shook his head, confused, wondering why she'd think he was joking. 'They met when he came to get a board from my dad. Madlyn taught him to surf. Santo, that is. Well, obviously, not my dad. That's how they got to know each other. And then I s'pose you could say they started hanging about together and things went from there.'

'And you called her Madlyn?' Dellen asked.

'Yeah. Madlyn.'

'Together for eighteen months?'

'Eighteen months or so. Yeah. That's it.'

'Then why did I never meet her?' she said.

*   *   *

When DI Bea Hannaford returned to the police station with Constable McNulty in tow, it was to find that Ray had managed to fulfil her wish for an incident room in Casvelyn and that Sergeant Collins had set the room up with a degree of expertise that surprised her. He'd somehow managed to get the upper floor conference room in order, and now it was ready with china boards upon which pictures of Santo Kerne were posted both in death and in life and on which activities could be listed neatly. There were also desks, phones, computers with HOLMES at the ready, printers, a filing cabinet, and supplies. The only thing the incident room didn't have was, unfortunately, the most vital part of any investigation: the MCIT officers.

The absence of a murder squad was going to leave Bea in the unenviable position of having to conduct the investigation with McNulty and Collins alone until such a time as a murder squad got there. Since that squad should have arrived along with the contents of the incident room, Bea labelled the situation unacceptable. It was also annoying because she knew very well that her former husband could get a murder squad from Land's End to London in less than three hours if he was pressed to do so.

'Damn,' she muttered. She told McNulty to type up his notes officially and she went to a desk in the corner where she quickly discovered that having a phone within sight did not necessarily mean that it was connected to an actual telephone line. She looked meaningfully at Sergeant Collins who said apologetically, 'BT says another three hours. There's no hook-up up here, so they're sending someone over from Bodmin to put one in. We have to use mobiles or the phones downstairs till then.'

'Do they know this is a murder inquiry?'

'They know,' he said, but his tone suggested that, murder or not, BT also didn't much care.

Bea said, 'Hell,' and took out her mobile. She walked to a desk in the corner and punched in Ray's work number.

'There's been something of a cock-up,' she told him.

He said, 'Beatrice. Hullo. You're welcome for the incident room. Am I having Pete for the night again?'

'I'm not phoning about Pete. Where're the MCIT blokes?'

'Ah,' he said. 'That. Well, we've a bit of a problem.' He went on to lower the boom. 'Can't be done, love. There's no MCIT available at the moment to be sent to Casvelyn. You can ring Dorset or Somerset and try to get one of theirs, of course, or I can do it for you. In the meantime, I do have a TAG team I can send you.'

'A TAG team,' she said. 'A *TAG* team, Ray? This is a murder inquiry. Murder. Major crime. Requiring a Major Crime Investigating Team.'

'Blood from a stone,' he returned. 'There's not much more I can do. I did try to suggest you maintain your incident room in—'

'Are you punishing me?'

'Don't be ridiculous. You're the one who—'

'Don't you dare go there. This is professional.'

'I think I'll have Pete with me till you've got a result,' he said mildly. 'You're going to be quite busy. I don't want him staying on his own. It's not a good idea.'

'You don't want him staying . . . *You* don't . . .' She was left speechless, a reaction to Ray that was so rare that its presence now left her even *more* speechless. What remained was ending the conversation. She should have done so with dignity but all she managed was to punch him off the mobile and throw the mobile onto the closest desk.

When it rang a moment later, she thought her former husband was phoning to apologise or, more likely, to lecture her about police procedure, about her propensity for myopic decision making, about perpetually crossing the boundaries of what was allowed while expecting someone to run interference for her. She snatched up the mobile and snapped. 'What? *What?*'

It was the forensic lab, however. Someone called Duke Clarence Washoe – and was *that* name bizarre enough? What in God's name had his parents been thinking? – ringing up with the fingerprint report.

'Got a real stew, Mum,' was how he broke the news to her.

'Guv,' she said. 'Or DI Hannaford. Not ma'am, madam, mum, or anything suggesting you and I are related or I've got royal connections, all right?'

'Oh. Right. Sorry.' A pause. He seemed to need a moment to adjust his approach. 'We've got dabs from your vic all over the car—'

'Victim,' Bea said, and she thought wearily about what American television had done to normal communications. 'Not vic. Victim. Or Santo Kerne, if you prefer. Let's show a little respect, Mr Washoe.'

'Duke Clarence,' he said. 'You c'n call me Duke Clarence.'

'That delights me no end,' she replied. 'Go on.'

'Eleven other different sets of prints as well. This is outside of the car. Inside, we've got seven sets. The vic . . . The dead boy's. And six others who also left prints on the passenger door, fascia, window handles, and glove box. There's prints on the CD cases as well. The boy and three others.'

'What about on the climbing equipment?'

'The only decent prints're on that tape wrapped round it. But they're Santo Kerne's.'

'Damn,' Bea said.

'There's a nice clear set on the boot of the car, though. Fresh ones, I'd guess. But I don't know what good that'll do you.'

None at all, Bea thought. Someone crossing the bloody road in town could've touched the damn car in passing. She would send forensics the prints gathered from everyone remotely connected to Santo Kerne, but the truth was that identifying whose fingers left dabs on the boy's car probably wasn't going to get them anywhere. This was a disappointment.

'Let me know what else you turn up,' she told Duke Clarence Washoe. 'There's got to be something from that car we can use.'

'Well, we've got some hair caught up in the climbing equipment. That might turn up something.'

'Tissue attached?' she asked hopefully.

'Yes, indeed.'

'Keep it safe, then. Carry on, Mr Washoe.'

'You c'n call me Duke Clarence,' he reminded her.

'Ah yes,' she said. 'I'd forgotten that.'

They rang off. Bea sat down at the desk. She watched Constable McNulty across the room attempting to type up his notes, and realised that he didn't actually know how to type. He was hunting for every letter to tap upon with his index fingers, with prodigious pauses between each tap. She knew if she watched him for longer than thirty seconds, she would scream, so she rose and began to head out of the room.

Sergeant Collins met her at the door. He said, 'Phone's below.'

She said fervently, 'Thank God. Where are they?'

'Who?'

'BT.'

'BT? They've not arrived yet.'

'Then what—'

'The phone. You've a call downstairs. It's an officer from—'

'Middlemore,' she finished. 'That would be my former husband. Assistant Chief Constable Hannaford. Head him off for me. I need some time.' Ray, she decided, had tried on her mobile, and now he was trying to get through on the land line. He'd have built a head of steam at this point. She didn't particularly want to experience it. She said, 'Tell him I've just left on some business. Tell him to phone me back tomorrow. Or at home later.' She would give him that much.

'It's not ACC Hannaford,' Collins said. 'It's someone called Sir David—'

'What *is* it with people?' Bea demanded. 'I've just got off the phone with a Duke Clarence up in Chepstow and *now* it's Sir David?'

'Hillier, he's called,' Collins said. 'Sir David Hillier. Assistant Commissioner up at the Met.'

'Scotland Yard?' Bea asked. 'Now, isn't *that* just what I need.'

By the time his regular drinking hour at the Salthouse Inn had rolled round, Selevan Penrule was in need of one. He also was, at least to his way of thinking, deserving of one. Something strong from the sixteen men of Tain. Or however the hell many there were.

Having to cope with both his granddaughter's pig-headedness and her mother's hysteria in a single day would have been too much for any bloke. No wonder David had moved them all off to Rhodesia. He'd probably thought a good bout of heat, cholera, TB, snakes, and tsetse flies would sort both of them out. But it hadn't done so if Tammy's behaviour and Sally Joy's voice on the phone were anything to go by.

'Is she eating properly?' Sally Joy had demanded from the bowels of Africa, where a decent connection on a telephone line was, apparently, something akin to the spontaneous transmogrification of tabby cat into two-headed lion. 'Is she still *praying*, Father Penrule?'

'She's—'

'Has she put on any weight? How much time is she on her knees? What about the Bible? Does she have a Bible?'

Jaysus in a sandwich, Selevan thought. Sally Joy made his bloody head swim. 'I told you I'd watch over the girl. That's what I'm doing. 'S there anything else, then?'

'Oh I'm tedious. I'm *tedious*. But you *don't* understand what it's like to have a daughter.'

'I had one myself, didn't I? Four sons as well if you're interested.'

'I know. I *know*. But in Tammy's case—'

'You either leave her to me or I send her back, woman.'

That got through. The last thing Sally Joy and David wanted was their daughter back in Africa, exposed to its hardships and believing that she could single-handedly do something about them.

'All right. I know. You're doing what you can.'

And better than you did, Selevan thought. But that was before he'd caught Tammy on her knees. She'd fashioned herself what he called a prayer bench – she'd referred to it as a *pree*-something but Selevan was not one for fancy terms – in her bitsy sleeping area in the caravan and he'd thought at first she meant to hang her clothing from the back of it, the way gents did with their suits in posh hotels. But not long after breakfast when he'd gone in search of her in order to drive her into work, he'd found her kneeling in front of it with a book open on its narrow shelf, and she was reading studiously. This he'd discovered too late – the reading – because the first thing he'd assumed was that the girl was at her God damn beads again, and this despite the fact that he'd already removed two sets of them from her belongings. He'd pounced and hauled her back by her shoulders, saying, 'We'll none of *this* nonsense,' and then had seen that she was merely reading.

It wasn't even a Bible. But it also wasn't much better. She was soaking up some saint's writing. 'St Teresa of Avila,' she revealed. 'Grandie, it's just *philosophy*.'

'If it's some saint' scribbles, it's religious muck,' was what he told her as he snatched up the book. 'Filling your head with rubbish, you are.'

'That's not fair,' she said, and her eyes became moist.

They'd driven to Casvelyn in silence, afterwards, with Tammy turned away from him so all he could see was the curve of her stubborn little jaw and the sheenless fall of her hair. She'd sniffed and he'd understood she was crying and he'd felt . . . He didn't know *how* he felt because – and he cursed her parents soundly for sending her to him – he was trying to *help* the girl, to bring her to whatever senses she had left, to get her to see she was meant to be *living* her life and not spending it reading about the doings of saints and sinners.

He felt irritated with her, then. Defiance he could deal with. He could shout and be rough. But tears . . . 'They're lezzies, you know, the lot of them, girl. You got that, don't you?'

She said in a small voice, 'Don't be stupid,' and she cried a little harder.

He was reminded of Nan, his daughter. A ride in the car and Nan in this same position, turned away from him. 'It's just Exeter,' she'd said. 'It's just a *club*, Dad.' And his reply, 'We'll be having none of that nonsense while you're under *my* roof. So dry your eyes or feel my palm and it won't be drying them for you.'

Had he really been so hard with the girl when all she'd wanted to do was go clubbing with her mates? But he had, he *had*. For clubbing with mates was how things started, and where they ended was in disgrace.

All of that seemed so innocent now. What had he been thinking of denying Nan a few hours of pleasure because he'd had none when he was her age?

The day passed slowly, with Selevan's internal skies quite clouded. He was more than ready for the Salthouse Inn by the time the appointed hour rumbled round for his embrace of the sixteen men of Tain. He was also ready for some conversation, and this would be provided by his regular companion of the spirits, who was waiting for him in the smoky inglenook of the Salthouse Inn's public bar when he arrived late in the afternoon.

This was Jago Reeth, and he sat with his regular pint of Guinness cupped in his hands, his ankles hooked round the legs of his stool, and his back hunched over so that his spectacles, repaired at the temple with a twist of wire, slid to the end of his bony nose. He was wearing his usual get-up of crusty jeans and sweatshirt, and his boots were, as always, grey with the dust of carved polystyrene from the surfboard maker's workshop where he was employed. He was beyond pensionable age but as he was fond of putting it when asked: Old surfers did not die *or* fade away; they merely looked for regular jobs when their days of riding waves were finished.

Jago's had concluded because of Parkinson's, and Selevan always felt a gruff sympathy for his contemporary when he saw how the shakes had come into his hands. But any expression of concern was always brushed aside by Jago. 'I had my day,' he was fond of saying. 'Time to let the youngsters have theirs.'

Thus he was the perfect confessor for Selven's current situation, and once Selevan had his Glenmorangie in hand, he told his friend about his morning skirmish with Tammy in answer to the question, 'How's tricks?' which Jago asked as he raised his own glass to his mouth. He used two hands to do it, Selevan noted.

'She's going over to the lezzies,' Selevan told him as a conclusion to his tale.

Jago shrugged. 'Well, kids're meant to do what they want to do, mate. Anything else, and you're buying trouble. Don't see any point to that, do I.'

'But her parents—'

'What do parents know? What did *you* know if it comes down to it? And you had, what? Five yourself? Did you know your arse from a pickle when you dealt with them?'

He hadn't known his arse from a pickle when he'd dealt with anything,

Selevan had to admit, even when he'd dealt with his wife. He'd been too caught up in being cheesed off at having to cope with the bloody dairy instead of doing what he'd wanted to do, which had been joining the Navy, seeing the world, and getting the hell away from Cornwall. He'd made a dog's dinner of his role as father and husband, and he hadn't done much better with his role as dairyman.

He said, but not in an unfriendly fashion, 'Easy for you to say, mate.' For Jago had no children, had never had a wife, and had spent his youth and his middle age following waves.

Jago smiled, showing teeth that had seen hard use and little maintenance. 'Too right,' he admitted. 'I ought to keep it plugged.'

'And how's a duffer like me supposed to understand a lass anyway?' Selevan asked.

'Just keep'm from getting stuffed too soon, 'n my opinion.' Jago downed the rest of his Guinness and pushed away from the table. He was tall, and it took a moment for him to untangle his long legs from the stool. While Jago went to the bar for another drink, Selevan considered what his friend had said.

It was good advice, except it didn't apply to Tammy. Getting stuffed was *not* her interest. What hung between men's legs had not so far beguiled her in the least. Should the girl ever come up pregnant, there'd be cause for celebration, not the general outcry one might assume would normally rise from outraged parents and relations.

'Never been a lezzie in my house,' he said when Jago returned.

'Why'n't you ask her about it, then?'

'Now how the hell am I s'posed to put it?'

'"Like the bush better'n the prong, my sweet? Why would that be?"' Jago offered, and then he grinned. 'Look, mate, you're meant to keep the doors open between you by pretending what's in front of your face i'n't in front of your face. Kids're different to what they were like when we were young. Get started early and don't know what they're about, do they. You're there to guide them, not to direct them.'

'That's what I'm trying to do,' Selevan said.

'It's the *how* of it, man.'

Selevan couldn't argue with this. He'd mucked up the how of it with his own children and now he was doing the same with Tammy. In contrast, he had to admit, Jago Reeth did have a way with the youngsters. Selevan had seen both of the Angarrack young people come and go from Jago's hired caravan at Sea Dreams and when the dead boy, Santo Kerne, had dropped by to ask Selevan's permission for beach access from his property, he'd ended up spending more time with the ancient surfer than in the water when that permission was given: waxing Santo's board together, setting its fins, examining it for dings and imperfections, sitting in deck chairs on the patch of scrub grass next to the caravan and talking. About *what*? Selevan wondered. How *did* one talk to another generation?

Jago answered as if the questions had been asked aloud, saying, "'S more about listening than anything else, not speechifying when all you itch to *do* is make a speech. Or give a lecture. Bloody hell, how I want to give a lecture. But I wait till they finally say to me, "So what d'you think?" and there's the opening. Simple as that.' He winked. 'But not easy, mind you. Quarter hour with them and the last thing you want is having your youth back. Trauma and tears.'

'That'd be the girl,' Selevan said wisely.

'Oh, aye. That'd be the girl. She fell and fell hard. Didn't ask for my advice in the befores. Didn't ask for my advice in the afters. But—' Here he took a hefty swig of his stout and sloshed it round his mouth which was, Selevan thought, probably his only bow to oral hygiene '— I broke my own rule at the end of the day.'

'Speechifying?'

'Telling her what I'd do in her place.'

'Which was?'

'Kill the bastard.' Jago spoke casually, as if Santo Kerne were not as dead as a Christmas goose on the table. Selevan raised both eyebrows at this. Jago went on. 'That not being possible, course, I told her to do it like a symbol. Kill off the past. Wave it goodbye. Make a bonfire of it. Toss in everything that bore on the two of them together. Diaries. Journals. Letters. Cards. Photos. Valentines. Paddington bears. Used condoms from their very first shag if she'd been feeling sentimental at that juncture. Everything. Just get rid of it all and move along.'

'Easy enough to say.'

'Truth there. But when it's a lass's first and they've gone the full mile, it's the only way when things go bad. Clean house of the bloke, you ask me. Which she was finally on her way to doing when . . . well . . . when it happened.'

'Bad, that.'

Jago nodded. 'Makes it worse for the girl. How's she supposed to see Santo Kerne in a real light now? No. She's got her work cut out, getting over this. Wish it hadn't happened, none of it. He wasn't a bad lad, but he had his ways, and she didn't see that till too bleeding late.

By that time the locomotive was steaming out of the station, and all that was left to do was step out of the way.'

'Love's a bitch of a thing,' Selevan said.

'It's a killer, that,' Jago agreed.

10

Lynley looked through the Gertrude Jekyll book, at the photos and drawings of gardens that were vibrant with English springtime colours. Their palettes were soft and soothing, and gazing at them he could almost feel what it would be like to sit on one of the weathered benches and let the pastel blanket of petals wash over him. Gardens, he thought, were meant to be like these. Not the formal parterres of the Elizabethans, planted with careful displays of constipated shrubbery and clipped vegetation, but rather the exuberant mimicry of what might occur in a nature from which weeds were banished but other plant life was allowed to flourish: banks of colour tumbling unrestrained onto lawns and herbaceous borders bowing onto paths that themselves *wandered* as a path would in nature. Yes, Gertrude Jekyll had known what she was about.

'Lovely, aren't they?'

Lynley looked up. Daidre Trahair stood before him, a small stemmed glass in her extended hand. She made a moue of apology as she gave a glance in its direction, saying, 'I've only sherry for an aperitif. I think it's been here since I got the cottage, which would be . . . four years ago?' She smiled. 'I'm not much of a drinker, so I don't actually know. Does sherry go bad? I can't even tell you if this is dry or sweet, to be honest. I suspect sweet, though. It said *cream* on the bottle.'

'That would be sweet,' Lynley said. 'Thank you.' He took the glass. 'You're not drinking?'

'I've a small one in the kitchen.'

'You won't allow me to help you?' He nodded in the direction from which domestic sounds had been coming. 'I'm not very good at it. Truthfully, I'm fairly wretched at it. But I'm sure I could chop something if something needs to be chopped. And measuring also. I can tell you unblushingly that I'm a genius with measuring cups and spoons.'

'That's comforting,' she replied. 'Are you capable of a salad if all the ingredients are set out on the work top and you've no critical decisions to make?'

'As long as I don't have to dress it. You wouldn't want me wielding . . . whatever it is one wields to dress a salad.'

'You can't be that hopeless,' she told him with a laugh. 'Surely your wife—' She stopped herself. Her expression altered, probably because his own had altered, she thought. She cocked her head ruefully. 'I'm sorry, Thomas. It's difficult not to refer to her.'

Lynley rose from his chair, the Jekyll book still in hand. 'Helen would have loved a Gertrude Jekyll garden,' he said. 'She used to dead head our roses in London because, she said, it encouraged more blooms.'

'She was right. Did she like to garden?'

'She liked to *be* in gardens. I think she liked the effect of *having* gardened.'

'But you don't know for sure?'

'I don't know for sure.' He'd never asked her. He'd have just come home from work to find her with secateurs in hand and a bucket of clipped and spent roses at her feet. She'd look at him and toss her dark hair off her cheek and say something about roses, about gardens in general, and *what* she'd say would force him to smile. And the smile would force him to forget the world outside the brick walls of their garden, a world that *needed* to be forgotten and locked away so it didn't intrude on the life he shared with her. 'She couldn't cook, by the way,' he told Daidre. 'She was dreadful at it. Completely appalling.'

'Neither of you cooked, then?'

'Neither of us cooked. I could do eggs and toast, of course, and Helen was brilliant at opening tins of soup and beans although she could easily pop a tin in the microwave and possibly blow the entire electrical system in the house. We employed someone to cook for us. It was that, takeaway curry, or starvation. And one can only eat so much takeaway curry.'

'You poor things,' Daidre said. 'Come along, then. I expect you can learn at least something.'

He followed her into the kitchen. From a cupboard, she took a wooden bowl, carved with primitive dancing figures round its rim, and she rustled up a chopping board and a number of, thankfully, recognisable foodstuffs meant to be combined into a salad. She set him to his task with a knife, saying, 'Throw in anything. That's the beauty of a salad. When you've got enough in the bowl, I'll show you a simple dressing that won't tax your sadly meagre talents. Any questions, then?'

'I'm sure I'll have them as I go along.'

They worked in companionable silence, Lynley upon the salad and

Daidre Trahair upon a dish with string beans and mint. Something was baking away in the oven – emitting the fragrance of pastry – while something else simmered in a pan. In time, they had a meal assembled, and Daidre instructed him in the art of laying a table, which he *did*, at least, know how to do but which he allowed her to demonstrate for him because allowing her that allowed *him* to watch and evaluate her.

He was acutely aware of DI Hannaford's instructions and while he didn't like the idea of using Daidre Trahair's hospitality as a device of investigation instead of a means of friendly entrée into her world, the part of him that was a policeman trumped the part of him that was a social creature in need of communing with other like creatures. So he watched and waited and he remained alert for what crumbs he could gather about her.

There were few enough. She was very careful. Which was, in itself, a valuable crumb.

They tucked into their meal in her tiny dining room, where a piece of cardboard fixed over a window reminded him of his duty to repair it for her. They ate something she called Portobello Wellington, along with a side dish of couscous with sun dried tomatoes, green beans done up with garlic and mint, and his salad dressed with oil, vinegar, mustard, and Italian seasoning. They had no wine to drink, merely water with lemon. She apologised for this, much as she had over the sherry.

She said she hoped he didn't mind a vegetarian meal. She wasn't vegan, she explained, for she saw no sin in consuming animal *products* like eggs and such. But when it came to the flesh of her fellow creatures on the planet, it seemed . . . well, too cannibalistic.

'Whatever happens to the beasts, happens to man,' she said. 'All things are connected.' It sounded like a quote, and even as he thought as much, she unblushingly told him it was. She said, appealingly. 'Those aren't my words, actually. I can't remember who said them or wrote them, but when I first came across them years ago, they had the ring of truth.'

'Isn't there an application to zoos?'

'Imprisoning beasts leading to man's imprisonment, you mean?'

'Something like that. Forgive me, I don't much care for zoos.'

'Nor do I. They hearken back to the Victorians, don't they? That excited quest for knowledge about the natural world without an accompanying compassion for that world. I myself loathe zoos, to be quite honest.'

'But you choose to work in them.'

'I choose to be committed to improving conditions for the animals therein.'

'Subverting the system from within.'

'It makes more sense than carrying a protest sign, doesn't it.'

'Rather like going on a fox hunt with a kipper attached to your horse.'

'Do you like fox hunting?'

'I find it execrable. I've been only once, one Boxing Day. I must have been eleven years old. My conclusion was that Oscar had it right, although I couldn't have said as much at the time. Just that I didn't like it and the idea of a pack of dogs on the trail of a terrified animal, and then being allowed to tear it to pieces if they find it . . . It wasn't for me.'

'You've a soft heart, then, for the animal world.'

'I'm not a hunter, if that's what you mean. I would have made a very bad prehistoric man.'

'No killing woolly mammoths for you.'

'Evolution, I'm afraid, would have ground to a precipitate halt had I been at the tribal helm.'

She laughed. 'You're very droll, Thomas.'

'Only in fits and starts,' he told her. 'Tell me how you subvert the system.'

'The zoo? Not as well as I would like to.' She helped herself to more green beans and passed the bowl to him, saying, 'Have some more. This is my mother's recipe. The secret is what you do with the mint, popping it into the hot olive oil just long enough to wilt it, which releases its flavour.' Her nose wrinkled. 'Or something like that. Anyway, the beans you boil only five minutes. Any longer and they'll be mushy, which is the last thing you want.'

'Nothing being worse than a mushy bean,' he noted. He took another helping. 'All praise to your mother. These are very good. You've done her proud. Where is she, your mother? Mine's just south of Penzance. Near Lamorna Cove. And I fear she cooks about as well as I do.'

'You're a Cornwall man, then?'

'More or less, yes. And you?'

'I grew up in Falmouth.'

'Born there?'

'Well, yes, I *suppose* so. I mean, I was born at home and at the time my parents lived just outside Falmouth.'

'Were you really? How extraordinary,' Lynley said. 'I was born at home as well. We all were.'

'In more rarefied surroundings than my own birthing chamber, I dare say,' Daidre pointed out. 'How many of you are there?'

'Just three. I'm the middle child. I've an older sister, Judith, and a younger brother, Peter. You?'

'One brother. Lok.'

'Unusual name.'

'He's Chinese. We adopted him when I was seventeen.' She cut a wedge of her Portobello Wellington neatly and held it on her fork as she went on. 'He was six at the time. He's reading maths at Oxford at the moment. Quite brainy.'

'How did you come to adopt him?'

'We saw him on the telly, actually, a programme on BBC1 about Chinese orphanages. He was handed over because he has spina bifida. I think his parents thought he'd not be able to care for them in their old age – although I don't know that for sure, mind you – and they didn't have the wherewithal to care for him either, so they gave him up.'

Lynley observed her. She seemed completely without artifice. Everything she said could be easily verified. But still . . . 'I like the *we*,' he told her.

She was spearing up some salad. She held the fork midway to her mouth, and she coloured lightly. 'The *we*?' she said, and it came to Lynley that she thought he was referring to the two of them, at that moment, seated at her little dining table. He grew hot as well.

'You said "we adopted him." I liked that.'

'Ah. Well, it was a family decision. We always reached big decisions as a family. We had Sunday afternoon family meetings, right after the roast beef and Yorkshire pud.'

'Your parents weren't vegetarians, then?'

'Goodness no. It was meat and veg. Lamb, pork, or beef every Sunday. The occasional chicken. Sprouts – Lord, I do hate sprouts, always did and always will – boiled into submission, as well as carrots and cauliflower.'

'But no beans?'

'Beans?' She looked at him blankly.

'You said your mother taught you to cook green beans.'

She looked at the bowl, where ten or twelve remained uneaten. She said, 'Oh yes. The beans. That would have been after her cookery course. My father went for Mediterranean food in a very big way and Mum decided there had to be life beyond spaghetti Bolognese, so she set about finding it.'

'In Falmouth?'

'Yes. I did say I grew up in Falmouth.'

'Go to school there as well?'

She observed him openly. Her face was kind, and she was smiling, but her eyes were wary. 'Are you interrogating me, Thomas?'

He held up both hands, a gesture meant to be read as openness and submission. 'Sorry. Occupational hazard. Tell me about Gertrude Jekyll.' For a moment, he wondered if she would do so. He added helpfully, 'I saw you've a number of books about her.'

'The very antithesis of Capability Brown,' was her answer, given after a moment of thought. 'She understood that not everyone had sweeping landscapes to work with. I like that about her. I'd have a Jekyll garden if I could but I'm probably doomed to succulents here. Anything else in the wind and the weather . . . well, one has to be practical about some things.'

'If not about others?'

'Definitely.' They'd finished their meal during their conversation and she stood, preparatory to gathering up the dishes. If she'd taken offence at his questioning of her, she hid it well, for she smiled at him and told him to come along as he was meant to help with the washing up. 'After that,' she said, 'I shall thoroughly scour your soul and reduce you to rubble, metaphorically speaking of course.'

'How shall you manage all that?'

'In a single evening, you mean?' She cocked her head in the direction of the sitting room. 'With a game of darts,' she told him. 'I've a tournament to practise for and while I expect you'll not be much of a challenger, you'll do at a pinch.'

'My only reply to that must be that I'll trounce you and humiliate you,' Lynley told her.

'With a gauntlet like that thrown down, we must play at once, then,' she told him. 'Loser washes up.'

'You're on.'

Ben Kerne knew he would have to phone his father. Considering the old man's age, he also knew that he ought to drive the distance to Pengelly Cove and break the news about Santo in person, but he hadn't been to Pengelly Cove in years, and he couldn't face going there just now. It wouldn't have changed at all, partly due to its remote location and even more due to the commitment of its citizens to never altering

a thing, including their attitudes, and the lack of change would cata-
pult him back into the past, which was the penultimate place in which
he wished to dwell. The last place was in the present. He longed for a
limbo of the mind, a mental Lethe in which he could swim until memory
itself no longer concerned him.

Ben would have let the entire matter go had Santo not been beloved
of his grandparents. He knew it was unlikely they would ever contact
him. They hadn't done so since his marriage, and the only time he'd
spoken to them at all was when he'd phoned occasionally, holding a
stilted conversation with them at holiday time or speaking more freely
to his mother when he phoned her office, or desperate for a place to
send Santo and Kerra when Dellen was in one of her bad periods.
Things might have been different had he written to them. He may have
worn them down over time. But he was no writer and even if he had
been, there was Dellen to consider and his loyalty to Dellen and
everything that loyalty to Dellen had demanded of him since his adolescence. So he'd relinquished all attempts at reconciliation, and they had
done the same. And when his mother had suffered a stroke suddenly
in her late fifties, he'd only learned of her condition because the event
had occurred during a period when Santo and Kerra had been staying
with their grandparents, and they'd brought the news with them upon
their return. Even Ben's own brothers and sisters had been forbidden
from passing the information along.

Another man might have extended the same treatment to his parents
now, allowing them to learn of Santo's death in whatever way fate
allowed them to learn it. But Ben had tried – and failed in so many
ways – to be a man unlike his father, and that meant creating a breach
in the wall that surrounded his heart at this moment, allowing some
form of compassion to enter it, despite his need to hide himself away
in a place where it would be safe for him to grieve all the things he
needed to grieve.

At any rate, the police were going to contact Eddie and Ann Kerne,
because that was what the police did. They delved into the lives and
histories of everyone associated with the deceased – God, he was calling
Santo *the deceased* and what did that mean about the state of his heart?
– and they looked for anything that could be used to assign blame.
Doubtless his father's grief upon hearing about Santo would propel
him into expletive first and accusation second, with a wife unwilling or
unable to act as a moderating influence upon his words, but rather with
Ann Kerne standing nearby looking what she felt, tormented after years

with a man whom she loved but could do little to temper. And although there was nothing for Ben to be accused of in Santo's death, the job of the police was to make deductions, connecting dots no matter how unrelated they were one to another. So he didn't need them talking to his father with his father unaware of what had happened to his favourite grandchild.

Ben decided to make the call from his office and not from the family's flat. He went down by means of the stairs because doing so prolonged the inevitable. When he was in his office, he didn't at once pick up the phone. Instead, he looked at the china board upon which the weeks prior to and after Adventures Unlimited's opening day were marked in the fashion of a calendar and filled with both activities and bookings. He could see their need of Alan Cheston displayed on this board. For months before Alan's advent, Dellen had been in charge of marketing Adventures Unlimited, but she'd not made much of a job of it. She had ideas but virtually no follow through. Organisational skills were not her strength.

And what is *her strength, if you don't mind my asking?* his father would have inquired. *But never mind that, no answer required. The whole effing village knows what she's good at and make no mistake about* that, *my boy.*

Untrue, of course. It was just his father's way of taking the piss because he believed that children were meant not to get puffed up, which was translated in Eddie Kerne's mind to children not being meant to have confidence in their own decisions. He wasn't a bad man, just set in his ways and his ways were not Ben's ways, so they'd come into conflict.

Not unlike Ben himself and Santo, Ben realised now. The very hell of being a father was realising one's own father cast a shadow one could not hope to escape.

He studied the calendar. Four weeks to opening and they *had* to open although he couldn't see how they would be able to do so. His heart wasn't in it, but they had so much money invested in the business that not to open or to postpone opening wasn't an alternative he could choose. Besides, to Ben the bookings they had were covenants that could not be broken, and while there weren't as many as he'd dreamed of having at this point in the business's development, he had faith that bringing on Alan Cheston was going to take care of that. Alan had ideas and the wherewithal to make them into realities. He was clever and a leader as well. Most important, he was not a bit like Santo.

Ben hated the disloyalty of the thought. In thinking it, he was doing what he vowed he would never do: repeat the past. *You're following your effing prong, boy!* had been his father's words, intoned with variation only in the emotion that underscored them: from sadness to fury to derision to contempt. Santo had done much the same, and Ben didn't want to think what lay behind his son's proclivity for sexual dalliance or where such a proclivity might have taken him.

Before he could avoid it any longer, he picked up the phone on his desk. He punched in the numbers. He had little doubt his father would still be up and about the ramshackle house. Like Ben, Eddie Kerne was an insomniac. He'd be awake for hours yet, doing whatever it was one did at night when committed to a green lifestyle as his father long had been. Eddie Kerne and his family had electricity only if he could produce it from the wind or from water; they had water only if he could divert it from a stream or bring it up from a well. They had heat when solar panels produced it, they grew or raised what they needed for their food, and their house had been a derelict farm building, bought for a song and rescued from destruction by Eddie Kerne and his sons: granite stone by granite stone, whitewashed, roofed, and windowed so inexpertly that the winter wind hissed through the spaces between the frames and the walls.

His father answered in his usual way, with the barked greeting, 'Speaking.' When Ben didn't say anything at once, his father went on with, 'If you're there, start yapping. If not, get off the line.'

'It's Ben.'

'Ben who?'

'Benesek. I didn't wake you, did I?'

After a brief pause, 'And what if you did? You caring for anyone 'sides yourself these days?'

Like father, like son, Ben wanted to reply. I had a very good teacher. Instead he said, 'Santo's been killed. It happened yesterday. I thought you'd want to know as he was fond of you and I thought perhaps the feeling was mutual.'

Another pause. This one was longer. And then, 'Bastard,' his father said. His voice was so tight that Ben thought it might break. '*Bastard.* You don't effing change, do you?'

'Do you want to know what happened to Santo?'

'What'd you let him get up to?'

'What did I do this time, you mean?'

'What happened, damn you? What God damn happened?'

Ben told him as briefly as possible. In the end he added the fact of murder. He didn't call it murder. He used *homicide* instead. 'Someone damaged his climbing kit,' he told his father.

'God damn.' Eddie Kerne's voice had altered, from anger to shock. But he shifted back to anger quickly. 'And what the hell were you doing while he was climbing some bloody cliff? Watching him? Egging him on? Or having it off with *her*?'

'He was climbing alone. I didn't know he'd gone. I don't know why he went.' The last was a lie, but he couldn't bear to give his father any additional ammunition. 'They thought at first it was an accident. But when they looked at his equipment, they saw it had been tampered with.'

'By who?'

'Well, they don't know that, Dad. If they knew, they'd make an arrest and matters would be settled.'

'*Settled*? That's how you talk about the death of your son? Of your flesh and blood? Of the means of carrying on your name? *Settled*? Matters get settled and you just go on? That it, Benesek? You and what-sername just stroll into the future and put the past behind you? But then, you're good at doing that, aren't you? So is she. She's bleeding *brilliant* at doing that, 'f I recall right. How's she taking all this? Getting in the way of her *lifestyle*, is it?'

Ben had forgotten the nasty emphases in his father's speech, loaded words and pointed questions, all designed to carve away one's fragile sense of self. No one was meant to be an individual in Eddie Kerne's world. *Family* meant adherence to a single belief and a single way of life. Like father, like son, he thought abruptly. What a cock-up he'd made of the rough form of paternity he'd actually been granted.

Ben said, 'There's no funeral planned yet. The police haven't released the body. I've not seen him, even.'

'Then how the hell d'you know it's Santo?'

'As his car was at the site, as his identification was in the car, as he hasn't returned home yet, I think it's safe to assume the body is Santo.'

'You're a piece of work, Benesek. Talking about your own son like that.'

'What do you want me to say when nothing I say is going to be right? I phoned to tell you because you're going to learn about it anyway from the police, and I thought—'

'You don't want *that*, do you? Me 'n' cops in a converse. My jaw wagging and their ears perked up.'

'If that's what you believe,' Ben said. 'What I was going to say is that

I reckoned you'd appreciate hearing the news from me and not from the police. They'll be talking to you and Mum. They'll be talking to everyone associated with Santo. I thought you'd want to know what they were doing on your property when they finally show up.'

'Oh, I'd reckon it'd have to do with you,' Eddie Kerne said.

'Yes. I suppose you would.'

Ben rang off then, no farewell given. He'd been standing, but now he sat at his desk. He felt a great pressure building inside, as if a tumour within his chest was growing to a size that would cut off his breath. The room seemed close. Soon the air within it would be used up.

What he needed was escape. Like always, his father would have said. His father: a man who rewrote history to suit whatever purpose the moment demanded. But there was no history to this moment. There was only getting through the now.

He rose. He went along the corridors to the equipment room, where he'd earlier gone himself and where he'd taken DI Hannaford. This time, though, he didn't approach the row of long cupboards where the climbing equipment was stored. Rather, he went through the room to a smaller one, where a storage cupboard the size of a large wardrobe had a padlock hanging from a hasp. He possessed the only key to this lock, and he used it now. When he swung it open, the scent of old rubber was strong. It had been more than twenty years, he thought. Before Kerra's birth, even. Likely the thing would fall apart.

But it didn't. He was in the wetsuit before he had a clear thought as to *why* he was in it, shoulders to ankles in neoprene, pulling the zip up his back by its cord, one hard tug and the rest was easy. No corrosion because he'd always taken care of his kit.

'Come on, come on, let's bloody get *home*,' his mates would say to him. 'Don't be such a wanker, Kerne. We're freezing our arses out here.'

But there was a hosepipe available, and he used it to rinse the salt-water off. Then he did the same when he got his kit home. Surfing kits were expensive and he had no intention of needing to purchase another because salt water had corroded and rotted the one he owned. So he washed the wet suit thoroughly, its boots, gloves, and hood as well, and he washed the board. His mates hooted and called him a poofter, but he would not be moved from his intentions.

In that and in everything else, he thought now. He felt cursed by his own determination.

The board was in the cupboard as well. He eased it out and examined it. Not a ding anywhere, the deck still waxed. A real antique by the standards of today, but perfectly suitable for what he intended. Whatever that was, because he didn't quite know. He just wanted to be out of the hotel. He scooped up boots, gloves, and hood. He tucked the surfboard under his arm.

The equipment room had a door that led to the terrace and from there to the empty swimming pool. A concrete stairway at the far end of the pool area took one up to the promontory for which the old hotel had been named, and a path along the edge of this promontory followed the curve of St Mevan Beach. A line of beach huts was tucked into the cliff here, not the standard huts which were generally free standing, but rather a joined rank of them, looking like a long and low-slung stable with narrow blue doors.

Ben followed this route, breathing in the cold salt air and listening to the crash of the waves. He paused above the beach huts to don his neoprene hood, but the boots and gloves he would pull on when he got to the edge of the water.

He looked out at the sea. The tide was high, so the reefs were covered, and the reefs would keep the waves consistent. From this distance five feet seemed their size, with swells coming from the south. They were breaking right, with an offshore wind. Had it been daylight – or dawn or dusk – conditions would be considered good, even at this time of year when the water would be as cold as a witch's heart.

No one surfed at night. There were too many dangers, from sharks to reefs to rips. But this wasn't so much about surfing as it was about remembering, and while Ben didn't want to remember, talking to his father was forcing him to do so.

He descended the steps to the beach. There were no lights here, but tall streetlamps that followed the path along the promontory above shed at least some illumination onto the rocks and sand. He picked his way through hunks of slate and sandstone boulders, clitter from the cliff top that now formed the base of the promontory, and he stepped at last onto the sand. This wasn't the soft sand of a tropical isle, but rather the grit produced over eons as a frozen land of permafrost warmed till slow moving landslides left coarse gravel in their wake and water forever beating upon these stones reduced them to hard little grains that glittered in sunlight but shone dull otherwise, grey and dun coloured, unforgiving upon flesh and abrasive to the touch.

To his right was the Sea Pit, high tide filling it with new water now, nearly submersing it in order to do so. To his left was the tributary of the River Cas and beyond it what remained of the Casvelyn Canal.

In front of him was the sea, restless and demanding. It drew him forward.

He set his board on the sand and donned his boots and gloves. He squatted for a moment, a huddled figure in black with his back to Casvelyn, and he watched the phosphorescence in the waves. He'd been to the beach at night as a youth, but those visits had not been for a surf. With their surfing done for the day, they'd make a fire ring. When embers were all that was left of the blaze, they'd pair off and if the tide was low, the great sea caves of Pengelly Cove beckoned. There they'd make love. On a blanket or not. Semi-clothed or nude. Drunk, slightly tipsy, or sober.

She'd been younger then. She'd been his. She was what he wanted, all that he wanted. She had known it as well, and the trouble had come from that knowing.

He rose and approached the water with his board. He had no leash for it, but that didn't matter. If it got away from him, it got away from him. Like so much else in his life, keeping the board close by should he fall from it was a concern beyond his control just now.

His feet and ankles felt the shock of the cold first and then his legs and thighs and upwards. It would take a few moments for his body temperature to warm the water within his wet suit, and in the meantime the bitter cold of it reminded him he was alive.

Thigh deep, he eased onto the board and began to paddle out through the white water towards the right hand reef break. The spray hit his face and the waves washed over him. He thought, briefly, he might paddle forever, straight into morning, paddle until he was so far from shore that Cornwall itself would be only a memory. But instead, bleakly governed by love and by duty, he stopped beyond the reef at the swells, and there he straddled his board. He sat first with his back to the shore, looking out at the vast and undulating sea. Then he turned the board round and saw the lights of Casvelyn: the line of tall lamps shining whitely along the promontory and then the amber glow behind the curtained windows of the houses in town, like the gaslights of the nineteenth century, or the open fires of an earlier time.

The swells were seductive, offering him a hypnotic rhythm that was as comforting as it was false. It felt, he thought, like a return to the womb. One could stretch out on the board, bob in the sea, and sleep forever. But swells broke, the sheer volume of the water collapsing in on itself, as the land-mass beneath it sloped up into the shore. There was danger here as well as seduction. One had to act or one submitted to the force of the waves.

He wondered if, after all these years, he would recognise the moment: that confluence of shape, force, and curl telling the surfer it was time to drop in. But some things ultimately were second nature, and he found that taking a wave was one of them. Understanding and experience coalesced into skill, and the passage of time had not robbed him of that.

The peak built, and he rose with it: paddling first, then up on one knee, and then erect. No deck grip at the tail of the board, holding the back foot in position because on this board, on *his* board, such a device had never been placed. He skimmed for a second across the wave's shoulder. He dropped into its face. He carved, getting high and fast, with his muscles acting on memory alone. Then he was in the barrel and it was clean. *Green room, mate,* they would have yelled. *Sheeee-it! You're in the green room, Kerne.*

He rode until there was only white water, and there he stepped off, thigh deep in the shallows once again, catching the board before it got away from him. He paused with the inside waves breaking against him. His breath came hard, and he stood there till the pounding of his heart grew slower.

Then he walked towards the beach, the sea water pouring off him like a discarded cape. He trudged in the direction of the stairs.

As he did so, a figure – midnight silhouette – came forward to meet him.

Kerra had seen him leave the hotel. At first she hadn't known it was her father. Indeed, for a mad moment her leaping heart had declared it to be Santo beneath her, striding across the terrace and up the steps towards the promontory and St Mevan Beach to have a secret surf at night. She'd watched from above and seeing only the black-garbed figure and knowing that figure had come out of the hotel . . . There was nothing else for her to think. It had all been a mistake, she'd thought nonsensically. A terrible, ghastly, horrible mistake. There was some other body discovered at the base of that cliff in Polcare Cove, but it was not her brother.

So she'd hurried to the stairs and she'd clattered down them, as the antique lift would have been too slow. She dashed through the dining hall which, like the equipment room, opened onto the terrace, and she set across this and flew up the stairs. By the time she reached the promontory, the figure was down on the beach, squatting next to the surfboard. So she waited there and there she watched. Only as he approached her after riding a single wave did she realise it was her father.

She was filled with questions and then with fury, with the eternal and unanswerable *why*s of nearly everything that had defined her childhood. Why did you pretend? Why did you argue with Santo about . . . ? And beyond that, the *who* of it all. Who are you, Dad?

But she asked none of these half-formed questions as her father reached her position at the base of the steps. Instead she tried in the semi-darkness to read his face.

His expression seemed to soften and he looked as if he intended to speak. But when he finally opened his mouth, it was only to say, 'Kerra, love,' and then he passed her. He climbed the steps to the promontory path, and she followed him. Wordlessly, they approached the hotel, where they descended towards the empty swimming pool. At a hose pipe, her father paused and washed the sea water from his surf board. Then he went on, into the hotel.

In the equipment room, he stripped off his wet suit. He was wearing his undershorts beneath it, and his skin was pimpled with the cold. But this didn't seem to bother him because he didn't shiver. Instead, he carried the wet suit to a large, heavy plastic rubbish bin in the corner of the room, and he dumped it inside without ceremony. The dripping surfboard he carried into another room – an inner room, Kerra saw, a room she had not yet investigated in the hotel – and there he put it into a cupboard. This he locked with a padlock, which he then tested as if to make sure the cupboard's contents were safe from prying eyes. From family eyes, she realised. From her eyes and from Santo's eyes because her mother must have known this secret all along.

Santo, Kerra thought. The sheer hypocrisy of it all. She simply did not understand.

Her father used his T-shirt to dry himself off. He tossed it to one side and donned his pullover. He motioned for her to turn her back, which she did and heard the sound of him removing his undershorts, plopping them onto the floor, and then zipping his trousers. Then he said, 'All right.' She turned back to him, and they faced each other. He waited, clearly, for her questions.

She determined to surprise him as he'd surprised her. So what she said was, 'It's because of her, isn't it?'

'Who?'

'Mum. You couldn't surf and keep an eye on her at the same time, so you stopped surfing. That's why, isn't it? I saw you, Dad. How long has it been? Twenty years? More?'

'Yes. Since before you were born.'

'So you put on your wetsuit, you went out there, you took the first wave that came along, and that was it. No trouble. It was easy for you. It was child's play for you. It was nothing. Like walking. Like breathing.'

'Yes. All right. It was.'

'How long had you surfed when you stopped?'

Her father picked up his T-shirt and folded it neatly, despite its condition, which was damp through. He said, 'Most of my life. It's what we did in those days. There was nothing else. You've seen how your grandparents live. We had the beach in the summer and school the rest of the time. There was work at home trying to keep that bloody house from falling apart and when there was free time, we surfed. There was no money for holidays. No cheap flights to Spain. It wasn't like today.'

'But you stopped.'

'Things change, Kerra.'

'Yes. She came along. That was the change. You got caught up in her, and by the time you saw what she's really like, it was too late. You couldn't get away. So you had to make a choice and you chose her.'

'It's not that simple.' He moved past her, into the larger equipment room. He waited for her to follow him and when she was with him, he shut and locked the smaller room's door.

'Did Santo know?'

'About?'

'This.' She gestured to the door he'd locked. 'You were good, weren't you? I saw enough to know that. So why . . . ?' Suddenly, she was as close to weeping as she'd come in the last terrible thirty hours or so.

He looked ineffably sad, and in that sadness she understood that while they were a family – the four of them then, the three of them now – they were a family in name only. Beyond a common surname, they were and had always been merely a repository of secrets. She'd believed that all these secrets had to do with her mother, with her mother's troubles, her mother's periods of bizarre alteration. And these were secrets to which she herself had long been a party because there was no way to avoid knowing them when the simple act of coming home from school might put her in the midst of what had always been referred to as 'a bit of an embarrassing situation'. *Don't breathe a word to Dad, darling.* But Dad knew anyway. All of them knew by the clothes she wore, the tilt of her head when she was speaking, the rhythm of her sentences, the tap of her fingers on the table during dinner, and the restlessness of her gaze. And the red. They knew from the red. For Kerra and Santo, what came on the heels of that colour was a prolonged visit to the elder Kernes and 'What's the cow up to now?' from her granddad. But 'Say nothing to your grandparents about this, understand?' was the injunction that Kerra and Santo had lived by. Keep the faith, keep the secret, and eventually things would return to normal, whatever normal was.

But now Kerra understood there were even more secrets than those which she'd kept about her mother: arcane bits of knowledge that went beyond Dellen's convoluted psyche and touched upon Kerra's father as well. Embracing this stinging piece of truth, Kerra realised there was no solid place to put down her foot if she wished to walk forward and pass into the future.

'I was thirteen years old,' she said. 'There was a bloke I liked, called Stuart Mahler. He was fourteen and he had terrible spots, and I liked him. The spots made him seem safe, you know? Only he wasn't safe. It's funny actually because all I'd done was go to the kitchen to fetch us some jam tarts and a drink – less than five minutes – and that's all it took. Stuart didn't understand what was going on. But I knew, didn't I, because I'd grown up knowing. So had Santo. Only he *was* safe because, let's face it, he was just like her.'

'Not in all ways,' her father said. 'No. Not that.'

'That,' she said. 'You know it. *That*. And in ways that affected me.'

'Ah. Madlyn.'

'We were best friends. Before Santo got his hands on her.'

'Kerra, Santo didn't intend—'

'Yes, he did. He bloody well did. And the worst part of it was that he didn't need to pursue her. He was already pursuing . . . what . . . three other girls? Or was it that he'd already been *through* three other girls?' She knew that she sounded bitter. But it seemed to her in that moment that nothing in her life had ever been secure from depredation.

Her father said, 'Kerra, people go their own way. There's nothing you can do about it.'

'Is that how you defend her? Defend him?'

'I'm not—'

'You *are*. You always have done, at least when it comes to her. She's made a fool of you for my entire life and I'll put money on it she's made a fool of you since the day you met her.'

If Ben was offended by Kerra's remark, he didn't say so. Rather he said, 'It's not your mother I'm talking about, love, and it's not Santo. It's this Stuart lad, whoever he was. It's Madlyn Angarrack.' He paused before finishing with, 'It's Alan, Kerra. It's everyone. People *will* go their own way. You're best off to let them.'

'Like you did, you mean?'

'I can't explain things further.'

'Because it's a secret?' she asked, and she did not care that the question sounded like a taunt. 'Like everything else in your life? Like the surfing?'

'We don't *choose* where to love. We don't choose *who* to love.'

'I don't believe that for a moment,' she said. 'Tell me why you didn't like Santo surfing.'

'Because I believed no good would come of it.'

'Is that what happened to you?'

For a moment, Kerra thought he would not reply. But at last he said what she knew he would say. 'Yes. Not a single good came of it for me. So I laid down the board and got on with my life.'

'With her,' Kerra noted.

'Yes. With your mother.'

D I Bea Hannaford arrived at the police station late, in a foul mood and with Ray's parting words still gnawing at her. She didn't want anything Ray had to say taking up residence in her consciousness, but he had a way of transmuting *goodbye* from an innocuous social moment into the bolt from a crossbow, and one had to be quick to avoid getting hit. She was fast on her verbal feet when there was nothing else on her mind. But that was impossible in the middle of a murder inquiry.

She'd had to cave in on the issue of Pete, another reason she was late to the station. Given the absence of MCIT officers to work on the case, given only the loan of a TAG team – and who the bloody hell knew when *they* were going to be withdrawn? – she would be putting in long hours, and someone had to look after Pete. Not so much because Pete couldn't look after himself – he'd been cooking for years and he'd mastered the art of laundry the first time his mother had turned a beloved Arsenal T-shirt purple – but because he had to be ferried about from school to football coaching to this or that appointment and his time on the internet had to be watched and his homework had to be monitored or he wouldn't bother to do it. He was, in short, an average fourteen-year-old boy who needed regular parenting. Bea knew she ought to be grateful that her former husband was willing to step up to the challenge.

Except that she was convinced Ray had orchestrated the entire situation just for that reason: to obtain unimpeded access to Pete. He wanted a more definite inroad with their son, and he'd seen this as an opportunity to make one. Pete's new enthusiasm for staying at his father's house suggested Ray was having some success in this area as well, which caused Bea to question exactly what constituted Ray's approach to fatherhood: from the meals he served Pete to the freedom he gave him.

So she'd grilled her former husband as Pete had trotted off to the spare room – *his* room, he had referred to it – to stow his belongings, and Ray had tunnelled his way through her questions to their root, in his typical fashion. 'He's happy to be here because he loves me,' was his reply. 'Just as he's happy to be with you because he loves you. He has two parents, not one, Beatrice. All things in the balance, this is good, you know.'

She wanted to say, 'Two parents? Oh, right. That's brilliant, Ray,' but instead she said, 'I don't want him exposed to any—'

'Naked twenty-five-year-old women running about the house?' he asked. 'Fear not. I've told my stable of beauties normally in residence here at the Playboy Mansion that the orgies are postponed indefinitely. Their hearts are broken, my own is devastated, but there you have it. Pete comes first.' He'd leaned against the kitchen work top. He'd been sorting through yesterday's post, and there was no indication that anyone else was present in the house. She'd checked this as surreptitiously as possible, telling herself she did not want Pete exposed to *anyone's* casual sex, not at his age and not before she'd had the opportunity to explain to him each one of the sexually transmitted diseases he could end up with if he played fast and loose with his body parts.

'You have,' Ray told her, 'the oddest damn ideas of how I spend what little free time I possess, my dear.'

She didn't engage. Instead she gave him a bag of groceries because she was damned if she was going to be in debt to him for having Pete to stay during a time when he was not scheduled to do so. Then she'd barked out their son's name, hugged him goodbye, kissed him on the cheek with the loudest smack she could manage despite his squirming and his 'oh *Mum*,' and she'd left the house.

Ray had followed her to her car. It was windy and grey outside, beginning to rain as well, but he didn't hurry or seek shelter from the weather. He waited till she got in and he motioned for her to lower the window. When she'd done so, he leaned down and said, 'What's it going to take, Beatrice?'

'What?' She didn't bother to hide her irritation.

'For you to forgive me. What do I need to do?'

She shook her head, reversed down the driveway, and drove off. But she'd not been able to shake his question.

She was predisposed to be annoyed with Sergeant Collins and Constable McNulty when she finally strode into the station, but the two miserable louts made it impossible for her to feel anything close to annoyance. Collins had somehow risen to the occasion of her tardiness, deploying half of the TAG officers to canvass the area within a three mile radius of Polcare Cove to see if they could come up with anything of note from those few who lived in the several hamlets and on the farms. The others he'd told to work on background checks of everyone so far connected to the crime: each of the Kernes – and especially Ben Kerne's financial status and whether that status was altered by his son's demise – Madlyn Angarrack, her family, Daidre Trahair, Thomas Lynley, and Alan Cheston. Everyone was being asked for fingerprints, and the Kernes had been given the word that Santo's body was ready for formal identification in Truro.

In the meantime, Constable McNulty had been engaged with Santo Kerne's computer. When Bea arrived, he was checking through all the deleted emails ('Going to take bloody *hours*,' he informed her, sounding as if he hoped she'd tell him to forego the tedious operation, which she had no intention of doing), and before that he'd pulled from the computer's files what seemed to be more designs for T-shirts.

McNulty had divided them into categories: local businesses whose names he recognised (largely pubs, hotels, and surf shops), rock bands both popular and extremely obscure, festivals from music to the arts, and those designs that were questionable because he 'had a feeling about them,' which Bea interpreted to mean he didn't know what they were. She was wrong, as she soon discovered.

The first questionable T-shirt design was for LiquidEarth, a name Bea recognised from the invoice left in Santo Kerne's car. This, McNulty explained, was the name of a surfboard shaper's business. The board shaper was called Lewis Angarrack.

'As in Madlyn Angarrack?' Bea asked him.

'As in her dad.'

This was interesting. 'What about the others?'

Cornish Gold was the second design he'd singled out. This belonged to a cider farm, he told her.

'How's that important?'

'It's the only business from outside Casvelyn. I thought that was worth looking into.'

McNulty, she thought, might not be as useless as she'd earlier concluded. 'And the last one?' She gave the design a scrutiny. It appeared to be two-sided. The obverse declared 'Commit an Act of Subversion' above a rubbish bin, which was suggestive of everything from bombs in the street to delving into the bins of celebrities for information to sell to the tabloids. On the reverse, however, things became clear. 'Eat Free' declared an Artful Dodger urchin, who was pointing to the same rubbish bin which had been upended, spilling its contents onto the ground.

'What d'you make of this?' Bea asked the constable.

'Don't know,' he said, 'but it seemed worth looking into because it's got nothing to do with an organisation, unlike the others. Like I said, I had a feeling. What can't be identified needs to be examined.'

He sounded like someone quoting a manual. But it was good sense, the first she'd heard from him. It gave her hope.

'You might have a future in this business,' she told him.

He didn't look entirely pleased with the idea.

Tammy was quiet in the morning, which concerned Selevan Penrule. She was always on the quiet side anyway, but this time her lack of conversation seemed to indicate a pensiveness she hadn't previously been caught up in. Before, it always looked to her grandfather as if the girl was just preternaturally calm, yet another indication that something was off about her because, at her age, she wasn't *supposed* to be calm about anything. She was supposed to be worrying about her complexion and her figure, about having the right clothes and the perfect haircut, and other such nonsense. But this morning, she looked caught up in considering something. To Selevan, there could be little doubt about what that something was.

Selevan contemplated his approach. He thought about what Jago Reeth had said on the subject of guiding and not directing a young person. Despite Selevan's earlier reaction of easy-for-you-to-say-mate, he had to admit that Jago had spoken good sense. What *was* the point of trying to impose one's will upon an adolescent when that adolescent had a will as well? It wasn't as if people were all *meant* to do the same thing as their parents, was it? If they did, the world would never change, would never develop, would perhaps never even be interesting. It would all be lock-step, one generation after another. But, on the other hand, was *that* so bad?

Selevan didn't know. What he did know was that he'd ended up, despite his own wishes in the matter and because of a cruel twist of fate in the person of his father's ill health, doing the same thing as his parents. He'd given in to duty, and the end result had been carrying on with a dairy farm that he'd intended to escape as soon as possible. He'd never thought that situation was fair, so he had to ask himself how fair the family were being on Tammy, opposing *her* desires.

On the other hand, what if her desires weren't her desires at all but only the result of her fear? Now *that* was a question that wanted answering. But it couldn't be answered unless it was asked.

He waited, though. First, he had to keep his promise to her and her parents, and that meant he had to go through her rucksack before he drove her to work. She submitted to the search with resignation. She watched him in silence. He could feel her gaze as he pawed through her belongings for contraband. Nothing. A meagre lunch. A wallet holding the five pounds he'd given her for spending money two weeks earlier. Lip balm and her address book. There was a paperback novel as well, and he leapt upon this as evidence. But the title, *Shoes of the Fisherman*, suggested she was reading at last about Cornwall and her heritage, so he let it go. He handed the rucksack over to her with a gruff, 'See you keep it this way,' and then he noted she was wearing something he'd not seen before. It wasn't a new garment. She was still in unrelieved black from head to toe like Queen Victoria in the post Albert period, but she had something different round her neck. It was inside her jersey, its green cord the only part he could see.

He pulled it out. 'What's this, then?' Not a necklace, he realised. Because if it was, it was the oddest necklace he'd ever looked at.

It had two ends, each of which was identical. They had small squares of cloth attached to them. These were embroidered with an ornamental *M* above which was embroidered a small gold crown. Selevan examined the cloth squares suspiciously. He said to Tammy, 'What's this, then, girl?'

'Scapular,' she told him.

'Scapper-what?'

'Scapular.'

'And the *M* means?'

'Mary.'

'Mary who?' he demanded.

She sighed. 'Oh, Grandie.'

This response didn't exactly fill him with relief. He pocketed the scapular and told her to get her arse out to the car. When he joined her, he knew it was time, so he spoke.

'Is it the fear?'

'What fear?'

'You know what fear. Men,' he said. 'Has your mum . . . You know. You bloody well know what I'm talking about, girl.'

'I don't, actually.'

'Has your mum *told* you . . . ?'

His wife's mum hadn't. Poor Dot knew nothing. She'd come to him not only a virgin but as ignorant as a newborn lamb. He'd made a mess of things because of his inexperience and his nerves, which had come across as impatience and reduced her to frightened tears. But modern girls weren't like that, *were* they? They knew it all before they were ten.

On the other hand, ignorance and fear explained a lot about Tammy. For they could be what lay at the root of how she was living at present, all huddled into herself.

'Has your mum told you 'bout *it*, girl?'

'About what?'

'Birds and bees. Cats and kittens. Has your mum told you?'

'Oh Grandie,' she said again.

'Stop the oh grandie and put me in the bloody picture. Because if she hasn't . . .' Poor Dot, he thought. Poor ignorant Dot. The oldest girl in a family of girls, never having seen a grown naked man except in museums and hadn't the poor fool woman actually believed that the male genitalia were shaped like fig leaves? God what a horror the wedding night had been and what he'd learned from it all was the idjit he'd been to have been respectful and waited for marriage because if they'd done it beforehand at least she would have *known* whether she wanted to marry at all. Only she would have insisted upon marriage at that point so any way you looked at, he'd have been caught. As he was always caught: by love, by duty, and now by Tammy.

'So what's oh grandie meant to mean?' he asked her. 'You know? You're embarrassed? What?'

She lowered her head. He thought she might be about to cry, and he didn't want that, so he started the car. They rumbled up the slope and out of the caravan park. He saw that she was not going to speak. She intended to make this difficult for him. Damn and blast her, she was a stubborn little thing. He couldn't reckon where she got *that* from, but it was no wonder her parents had reached the point of despair with her.

Well, there was nothing for it but to hammer away if she wasn't going to answer him. So out of the caravan park and up the lane on the way into Casvelyn, Selevan got out his tools. 'It's the natural order of things,' he told her. 'Men and women together. Anything else is unnatural and I mean *anything* else, if you receive my meaning, girl. Nothing to be worried over because we got separate parts, don't we, and our separate parts're meant to be joined. You got man on top and woman on bottom. They put their things together because that's how it goes. He slides in and they rustle about and when it's all said and done, they go to sleep. Sometimes they get a baby out of it. Sometimes they don't. But it's all the way it's supposed to be and if a man's got any wits about him, it's a jolly nice thing that they both enjoy.'

There. He'd said it. But he wanted to repeat one part, to make certain she understood. 'Anything else,' he said with a tap on the steering wheel, 'isn't in the natural order of things, and we're meant to be natural. Natural. Like nature. And in nature, what you *don't* see and don't *ever* see is—'

'I've been talking to God,' Tammy said.

Now that was a real conversation stopper. Straight out of the blue, like he hadn't been trying to make a point with the girl. He said, 'Have you, now? And what's God been saying back? Nice that he's got time for you, by the by, 'cause the bugger's never had time for me.'

'I've tried to listen.' Tammy spoke like a girl with things on her mind. 'I've *tried* to listen for his voice,' she said.

'God's voice? From where? You expecting it out of the gorse or something?'

'God's voice comes from within,' Tammy said, and she brought a lightly clenched fist to her skinny chest. 'I've tried to listen to the voice from inside myself. It's a quiet voice. It's the voice of what's right. You know when you hear it, Grandie.'

'Hear it a lot, do you?'

'When I get quiet I do. But now I can't.'

'I've seen you quiet day and night.'

'But not inside.'

'How's that?' He looked over at her. She was concentrating on the rain-streaked day, hedgerows dripping as the car skimmed past them, a magpie taking to the sky.

'My head's full of chatter,' she said. 'If my head won't be silent, I can't hear God.'

Chatter? he thought. What was the maddening girl *on* about? One moment he thought he had her sorted, the next he was flummoxed again. 'What d'you got up there, then?' he asked, and he poked her head. 'Goblins and ghoulies?'

'Don't make fun,' she told him. 'I'm trying to tell you. But there's nothing and no one that I can ask, you see. So I'm asking you as it's the only thing left that I can think to do. I s'pose I'm asking for help, Grandie.'

Now they were down to it. This was the moment the girl's parents had hoped for, time with her granddad paying off. He waited for more. He made a *hmph* noise to indicate his willingness to listen. The moments ticked by as they approached Casvelyn. She said nothing more till they were in town.

Then it was brief. He'd pulled in to the kerb in front of Clean Barrel Surf Shop before she finally spoke. 'If I know something,' she said to him, her eyes fixed on the shop's front door, 'and if *what* I know might cause someone trouble, what should I do, Grandie? That's what I've been asking God, but he hasn't answered. What should I do? I could keep asking because when something bad happens to someone you care about, it seems like—'

'The Kerne boy,' he interrupted. 'D'you know something about the Kerne boy, Tammy? Look at me square, girl, not out of the window.'

She did. He could see she was troubled beyond what he had thought. So there was only one answer, and despite the irritations it might cause in his own life, he owed it to her to give it. 'You know something, you tell the police,' he said. 'Nothing else to it. You do it today.'

12

S he excelled at darts. Lynley had learned that quickly enough on the previous evening, and he'd added the information to what little he knew about Daidre Trahair. She had a dart board mounted on the back of the sitting room door, something he'd not noticed before because she'd kept the door open instead of closing it against the cold wind that could sweep into the building from the tiny vestibule when someone entered the cottage.

He should have known he was in trouble when she used a tape measure to create a distance of exactly seven feet, nine and one quarter inches from the back of the closed door. Here she placed the fireplace poker on a parallel, calling it their oche. When he said, 'Okkey?' and she'd said, 'The oche marks where the player has to stand, Thomas,' he had his first real clue that he was probably in over his head. But he'd thought How difficult can it possibly be? and he'd gone like a lamb to the metaphorical slaughter, agreeing to a match called 501 about which he knew nothing at all.

He said, 'Are there rules?'

She'd looked at him askance. 'Of course there are rules. It's a game, Thomas.' And she'd gone about explaining them to him. She began with the dart board itself, losing him almost immediately when she began to refer to treble and double rings and what it meant to one's score to land in one of them. He'd never thought of himself as an idiot – it had always seemed to him that knowing how to identify a bull's eye was the limit of what one needed to embrace when it came to darts – but within moments, he was entirely lost.

It was simple, she told him. 'We each start with a score of five-oh-one, and the object is to reduce that to nought. We each throw three darts. A bull's eye scores fifty, the outer ring twenty-five and anything in the double or treble ring is double or treble the segment score. Yes?'

He nodded. He was almost altogether uncertain what she was talking about, but confidence, he reckoned, was the key to success.

'Good. Now, the caveat is that the last dart thrown has to land in a double or in the bull's eye. And additionally, if you reduce your score to one or it actually goes *below* nought, your turn ends immediately and the play is turned over to the other thrower. Follow?'

He nodded. He was even more uncertain at that point, but he decided it couldn't be that difficult to hit a dart board from less than eight feet away. Besides, it was only a game and his ego was strong enough to emerge undamaged should she win the match. For another could follow. Two out of three. Three out of five. It didn't matter. It was all in an evening's diversion, yes?

She won every match. They could have gone on all night and she probably would have continued to win. The vixen – for so he was thinking of her by then – turned out to be not only a tournament player but the sort of woman who did not believe a man's ego had to be preserved by allowing him moments of specious supremacy over her.

She had the grace to be at least moderately embarrassed. She said, 'Oh my. Oh dear. Well, it's just that I never actually just *let* someone win. It's never seemed right.'

'You're . . . quite amazing,' he said. 'My head is spinning.'

'It's that I play a lot. I didn't tell you that, did I, so I'll pay the penalty for unspoken truths. I'll help you with the washing up.'

She was as good as her word, and they saw to the kitchen in companionable fashion, with him doing the washing and her doing the drying. She made him clean the cooker top – 'It's only fair,' she told him – but she herself swept the floor and scoured the sink. He found himself enjoying her company and, as a result, felt ill at ease when it came to his appointed task.

He did it nonetheless. He was a cop when everything got reduced to essentials, and someone was dead through murder. She'd lied to an investigating officer and no matter his personal enjoyment of the evening, he had a job to do for DI Hannaford and he intended to do it.

He set about it the following morning, and he was able to get a fair distance right there from his room in the Salthouse Inn. He discovered through a few simple phone calls that someone called Daidre Trahair was indeed one of the veterinarians at Bristol Zoo Gardens. When he asked about speaking to Ms Trahair, he was told that she was on emergency leave, dealing with a family matter in Cornwall.

This bit of news didn't give him pause. People often claimed that family matters needed to be taken care of when what those family matters were was simply a need to get away for a few days of decompression from a stressful job. He decided that couldn't be held against her.

Her claims about her adopted Chinese brother held up as well. Lok Trahair was indeed a student at Oxford University. Daidre herself had a first in biological science from the University of Glasgow, having gone on from there to the Royal Veterinary College for her advanced degree. Well and good, Lynley had thought. She might have had secrets that she wished to keep from DI Hannaford, but they weren't secrets about her identity or that of her brother.

He delved back further into her schooling, but this was where he hit the first snag. Daidre Trahair had been a pupil at a comprehensive in Falmouth, but before that there was no record of her. No primary school in Falmouth would claim her. State or private, day school, boarding school, convent school . . . There was nothing. She either had not lived in Falmouth for those years of her education, or she'd been sent far away for some reason, or she'd been schooled at home.

Yet surely she would have mentioned being schooled at home since, by her own admission, she'd been born at home. It was a logical follow-up, wasn't it?

He wasn't sure. He also wasn't sure what more he could do. He was pondering his options, when a knock at his bedroom door roused him from his thoughts. Siobhan Rourke presented him with a small package. It had just arrived in the post, she told him.

He thanked her and when he was alone again, opened it to find his wallet. This he opened as well. It was a knee jerk reaction but it was more than that. He was – unprepared for the fact of it all – suddenly restored to who he was. Driving licence folded into a square, bank card, credit cards, picture of Helen.

He took this last in his fingers. It was of Helen at Christmas, less than two months away from dying. They'd had a hurried holiday, with no time to visit her family or his because he'd been in the midst of a case. 'Not to worry, there'll be other Christmases, darling,' she'd said.

Helen, he thought.

He had to force himself back to the present. He carefully placed the photo of his wife – cheek in her hand, smiling at him across the breakfast table, hair still uncombed, face without makeup, the way he loved her – back into its position in his wallet. He put the wallet onto the bedside table, next to the phone. He sat in silence, hearing only his own breathing. He thought of her name. He thought of her face. He thought of nothing.

After a moment, he continued his work. He considered his options. Further investigation into Daidre Trahair was needed but he didn't want to be the one who did it, loyalty to a fellow cop or not. For he *wasn't* a cop, not here and not now. But there were others.

Before he could stop himself, because it would be so easy to do so, he picked up the phone and punched in a number more familiar to him than his own. And a voice as familiar as a family member's answered. Dorothea Harriman, departmental secretary at New Scotland Yard.

At first he wasn't sure he could speak, but he finally managed to say, 'Dee.'

She knew at once. In a hushed voice she said, 'Detective Superintendent . . . Detective Inspector . . . Sir?'

'Just Thomas,' he said. 'Just Thomas, Dee.'

'Oh goodness no, sir,' was her reply. Dee Harriman, who had never called anyone by anything less than his or her full title. 'How are you, Detective Superintendent Lynley?'

'I'm fine, Dee. Is Barbara available?'

'Detective Sergeant Havers?' she asked. Stupid question, which wasn't like Dee. Lynley wondered why she had asked it. 'No. No, she isn't, Detective Superintendent. She isn't here. But Detective Sergeant Nkata is around. And Detective Inspector Stewart. And Detective Inspec—'

Lynley spared her the endless recitation. 'I'll try Barbara on her mobile,' he said. 'And Dee . . . ?'

'Detective Superintendent?'

'Don't tell anyone I've phoned. All right?'

'But are you—'

'Please.'

'Yes. Yes. Of course. But we hope . . . not just me . . . I speak for everyone, I know I do, when I say . . .'

'Thank you,' he said.

He rang off. He thought about making the call to Barbara Havers, longtime partner and fractious friend. He knew that she would offer her help gladly, but it would be too gladly and if she was in the middle of a case, she'd offer her help anyway and then suffer the result without mentioning it to him.

He didn't know if he could do it for other reasons that he'd felt the moment he'd heard Dorothea Harriman's voice. It was obviously far too soon, perhaps a wound too deep to heal.

Yet a boy was dead, and Lynley was who he was. He picked up the phone again.

'Yeah?' The answer was vintage Havers. She shouted it as well, for she was obviously rattling along somewhere in her death trap of a car if the background noise was anything to go by.

He drew a breath, still unsure.

She said, 'Hey. Someone there? I can't hear you. C'n you hear me?'

He said, 'Yes. I can hear you, Barbara. The game's afoot. Can you help me out?'

There was a long pause. He could hear noise from her radio, the distant sound of traffic passing. Wisely, it seemed, she'd pulled to the side of the road to talk. But still she said nothing.

'Barbara?' he said.

'Tell me, sir,' was her reply.

LiquidEarth stood on Binner Down, among a collection of other small manufacturing businesses in the grounds of a long-decommissioned Royal Air Force station. This was a relic of World War II, reduced all these decades later to a combination of crumbling buildings, rutted lanes, and masses of brambles. Between the abandoned buildings and along the lanes, the area resembled nothing so much as a rubbish tip. Disused lobster traps and fishing nets formed piles next to lumps of broken concrete; discarded tyres and mouldering furniture languished against propane tanks; stained toilets and chipped basins became contrasting elements that fought with wild ivy. There were mattresses, black rubbish sacks stuffed with who-knew-what, three-legged chairs, splintered doors, ruined casings from windows. It was a perfect spot to toss a body, Bea Hannaford concluded. No one would find it for a generation.

Even from inside the car, she could smell the place. The damp air offered fires and cow manure from a working dairy farm at the edge of the down. Added to the general unpleasantness of the environment, pooled rain water that was skimmed by oil slicks sat in craters along the tarmac.

She'd brought Constable McNulty with her, both as navigator and notetaker. Based on his comments in Santo Kerne's bedroom on the previous day, she decided he might prove useful with matters related to surfing, and as a longtime resident of Casvelyn, at least he knew the town.

They'd come at LiquidEarth by a circuitous route that had taken them by the town wharf, which formed the northeast edge of the disused Casvelyn Canal. They gained Binner Down from a street called Arundel, off which a lumpy track led past a grime-streaked farmhouse. Behind this, the decommissioned air station lay, and far beyond it in the distance a tumbledown house stood, a mess of a place taken over by a succession of surfers and brought to wrack as a result of their habitation. McNulty seemed philosophical about this. What else could one expect? he seemed to say.

Bea saw soon enough that she was lucky to have him with her, for the businesses on the erstwhile airfield had no addresses affixed to them. They were nearly windowless cinderblock buildings with roofs of galvanised metal overhung with ivy. Cracked concrete ramps led up to heavy steel vehicle doors at the front of each, and the occasional passageway door had been cut into these.

McNulty directed Bea along a track on the far north edge of the airfield. After a spine-damaging jounce for some three hundred yards, he mercifully said, 'Here you go, guv,' and indicated one hut of three that he claimed had once been housing for Wrens. She found that difficult enough to believe, but times had been tough. Compared to eking out an existence on a bombsite in London or Coventry, this had probably seemed like paradise.

When they alighted and did a little chiropractic manoeuvring of their spinal cords, McNulty pointed out how much closer they were at this point to the habitation of the surfers. He called it Binner Down House, and it stood in the distance directly across the down from them. Convenient for the surfers when you thought about it, he noted. If their boards needed repairing they could just nip across the down and leave them here with Lew Angarrack.

They entered LiquidEarth by means of a door fortified with no fewer than four locks. Immediately, they were within a small show-room where in racks along two walls long boards and short boards leaned nose up and finless. On a third wall surfing posters hung, featuring waves the size of ocean liners, while along the fourth wall stood a business counter. Within and behind this a display of surfing accoutrements were laid out: board bags, leashes, fins. There were no wetsuits. Nor were there any T-shirts designed by Santo Kerne.

The place had an eye-stinging smell about it. This turned out to be coming from a dusty room beyond the showroom where a boiler-suited man with a long grey ponytail and large-framed spectacles was carefully pouring a substance from a plastic bucket onto the top of a surfboard. This lay across two sawhorses.

The gent was slow about what he was doing, perhaps because of the nature of the work, perhaps because of the nature of his disability, his habits, or his age. He was a shaker, Bea saw. Parkinson's, the drink, whatever.

She said, 'Excuse me. Mr Angarrack?' just as the sound of an electrical tool powered up from behind a closed door to the side.

'Not him,' McNulty said *sotto voce* behind her. 'That'll be Lew shaping a board in the other room.'

By this, Bea took it to mean that Angarrack was operating whatever tool was making the noise. As she reached her conclusion, the older man turned. He had an antique face, and his specs were held together with wire.

He said, 'Sorry. Can't stop just now,' with a nod at what he was doing. 'Come in, though. You the cops?'

That was obvious enough, as McNulty was in uniform. But Bea stepped forward, leaving tracks along a floor powdered with polystyrene dust, and offered her identification. He gave it a cursory glance and a nod and said he was Jago Reeth. The glasser, he added. He was putting the final coat of resin on a board, and he had to smooth it before it began to set or he'd have a sanding problem on his hands. But he'd be free to talk to them when he was finished if they wanted him. If they wanted Lew, he was doing the initial shaping of the rails on a board and he wouldn't want to be disturbed as he liked to do it in one go.

'We'll be sure to make our apologies,' Bea told Jago Reeth. 'Can you fetch him for us. Or shall we . . . ?' She indicated the door behind which the shrieking of a tool told the tale of some serious rail shaping.

'Hang on, then,' Jago said. 'Let me get this on. Won't take five minutes and it's got to be done all at once.'

They watched as he finished with the plastic bucket. The resin formed a shallow pool defined by the curve of the surfboard, and he used a paint brush to spread it evenly. Once again Bea noted the degree to which his hand shook as he wielded the paintbrush. He seemed to read her mind in her glance.

He said, 'Not too many good years left. Should have taken on the big waves when I had the chance.'

'You surf yourself?' Bea asked Jago Reeth.

'Not these days. Not if I want to see tomorrow.' He peered up at her from his position bent over the board. His eyes behind his spectacles – the glass of which was flecked with white residue – were clear and sharp despite his age. 'You're here about Santo Kerne, I expect. Was a murder, eh?'

'You know that, do you?'

'Didn't know,' he said. 'Just reckoned.'

'Why?'

'You're here. Why else if not murder? Or are you lot going round offering condolences to everyone who knew the lad?'

'You're among those?'

'Am,' he said. 'Not long, but I knew him. Six months or so, since I worked for Lew.'

'So you're not long here in town?'

He made a long sweep with his paintbrush, the length of the board. 'Me? No. I come up from Australia this time round. Been following the season long as I can tell you.'

'Summer or surfing?'

'Same thing in some places. Others, it's winter. They always need blokes who can do boards. I'm their man.'

'Isn't it a bit early for the season here?'

'Not hardly, eh? Just a few more weeks. And now's when I'm needed most cos before the season starts is when the orders come in. Then *in* the season boards get dinged and repairs are needed. Newquay, North Shore, Queensland, California. I'm there to do them. Used to work first and surf later. Sometimes the reverse.'

'But not now.'

'Hell no. It'd kill me for sure. His dad thought it'd kill Santo, you know. Idjit, he was. Safer than crossing the street. *And* it gets a lad out in the air and sunlight.'

'So does seacliff climbing,' Bea pointed out.

Jago eyed her. 'And look what happened there.'

'D'you know the Kernes, then?'

'Santo. Like I said. And the rest of them from what Santo said. And that would be the limit of what I know.' He set his paintbrush in the bucket, which he'd put on the floor beneath the board, and he scrutinised his work, squatting at the end of the board to study it from tail to nose. Then he rose and went to the door behind which the rails of a board were being shaped. He closed it behind him. In a moment, the tool was shut off.

Constable McNulty, Bea saw, was looking about, a line forming between his eyebrows, as if he was considering what he was observing. She knew nothing about the making of surfboards, so she said, 'What?' and he roused himself from his thoughts.

'Something,' he said. 'Don't quite know yet.'

'About the place? About Reeth? About Santo? His family? What?'

'Not sure.'

She blew out a breath. The man would probably need a bloody ouija board.

Lew Angarrack joined them. He was outfitted like Jago Reeth, in a white boiler suit fashioned from heavy paper, the perfect accompaniment to the rest of him which was also white. His thick hair could have been any colour – probably salt and pepper, considering his age, which appeared to be somewhere past forty-five – but now it looked like a barrister's wig, so thoroughly covered as it was by polystyrene dust. This same dust formed a fine patina on his forehead and cheeks. Round his mouth and eyes there was none, its absence explained by the air filter that dangled round his neck along with a pair of protective glasses.

Behind him, Bea could see the board he was working on. Like the board being finished by the glasser, it lay on two tall sawhorses: shaped from its earlier form of a blank oblong of polystyrene that was marked in halves by a wooden stringer. Other of these blanks lined a wall to one side of the shaping room. The other side, Bea saw, bore a rack of tools: planers, sanders, and Surforms, by the look of them.

Angarrack wasn't a big man, not much taller than Bea herself. But he appeared quite powerful in the upper body, and Bea reckoned he had a great deal of strength. Jago Reeth had apparently put him in the picture about the facts of Santo's death, but he didn't seem wary to see the police. Nor did he seem surprised. Or shocked or sorrowful, for that matter.

Bea introduced herself and Constable McNulty. Could they speak with Mr Angarrack?

'That bit's a formality, isn't it?' he replied shortly. 'You're here, and I assume that means we're going to be speaking.'

'Perhaps you can show us round as we do so,' Bea said. 'I know nothing about making surfboards.'

'Called shaping,' Jago Reeth told her. He stood nearby.

'Little enough to see,' Angarrack said. 'Shaping, spraying, glassing, finishing. There's a room for each.' He used his thumb to indicate them as he spoke. The door to the spraying room was open but unlit, and he flipped a switch on the wall. Bright colours leapt out at them, sprayed onto the walls, the floors, and the ceiling. Another sawhorse stood in the middle of the room, but no board waited upon it, although five stood against the wall, shaped and ready for someone's artistry.

'You decorate them as well?' Bea asked.

'Not me. An old-timer did the designs for a time till he moved on. Then Santo did them, as a way of paying for a board he wanted. I'm looking for someone else now.'

'Because of Santo's death?'

'No. I'd already sacked him.'

'Why?'

'I'd guess you say loyalty.'

'To?'

'My daughter.'

'Santo's girlfriend.'

'For a time, but that time was past.' He moved by them and out into the show room, where an electric kettle stood – along with brochures, a clipboard thick with paperwork, and board designs – on a card table behind the counter. He plugged this in and said, 'You want something?' and when they demurred, he called out, 'Jago?'

'Black and nasty,' Jago returned.

'Tell us about Santo Kerne,' Bea said as Lew went about his business with coffee granules which he loaded up into one mug and used more sparingly in another.

'He bought a board from me. Couple years ago. He'd been watching the surfers round the Promontory and said he wanted to learn. He'd started out down at Clean Barrel—'

'Surf shop,' McNulty murmured, as if believing Bea would need a translator.

'—and Will Mendick, bloke who used to work there, recommended he get a board from me. I place some boards in Clean Barrel, but not a lot.'

'No money in retail,' Jago called from the other room.

'Too right, that,' Angarrack said. 'Santo had liked the look of one at Clean Barrel, but it was too advanced for him, although he wouldn't have known that at the time. It was a short board. A three-fin thruster. He asked about it, but Will knew he'd not learn well with that – if he learned at all – so he sent him to me. I made him a board he could learn on, something wider, longer, with a single fin. And Madlyn – that's my daughter – gave him lessons.'

'That's how they became involved, then.'

'Essentially.'

The kettle clicked off. Angarrack poured the water into the mugs, stirred the liquid and said, 'Here it is, mate,' which brought Jago Reeth to join them. He drank noisily.

'How did you feel about that?' Bea asked Angarrack. 'About their involvement.' She noted that Jago was watching Lew intently. Interesting, she thought, and she made a mental tick against both of their names.

'Truth? I didn't like it. She lost her focus. Before, she had a goal. The Nationals. International competitions. After she met Santo, all of that was gone. She could still see beyond the nose on her face but she couldn't see an inch beyond Santo Kerne.'

'First love,' Jago commented. 'It's brutal.'

'They were both too young,' Angarrack said. 'Not even seventeen when they met, and I don't know how old when they began . . .' He made a gesture with his hand to indicate they were to complete the sentence.

'Became lovers,' Bea said.

'It's not love at that age,' Angarrack told her. 'Not for boys. But for her? Stars in the eyes and cotton wool in the head. Santo this and Santo that. I wish I could have done something to prevent it.'

'Way of the world, Lew.' Jago leaned against the doorway to the glassing room, mug in his hand.

'I didn't forbid her from seeing him,' Angarrack went on. 'What would have been the point? But I told her to have a care.'

'As to what?'

'The obvious. Bad enough she wasn't competing any longer. Even worse if she came up pregnant. Or worse than that.'

'Worse?'

'Diseased.'

'Ah. Sounds as if you thought the boy was promiscuous.'

'I didn't know what the hell he was. And I didn't want to find out by means of Madlyn being in some sort of trouble. *Any* sort of trouble. So I warned her and then I let it be.' Angarrack had not yet taken up his mug, but he did so now and took a gulp. 'That was probably my mistake,' he said.

'Why? Did she—'

'She would've got over him faster when things ended. As it is, she hasn't.'

'I dare say she will now,' Bea said.

The two men exchanged looks. Quick, nearly furtive. Bea noted this and made two more mental ticks against them. She said, 'We found a T-shirt design for LiquidEarth on Santo's computer.' Constable McNulty brought the drawing forth and passed it over to the surf-board shaper. 'Was that at your request?'

Angarrack shook his head. 'When Madlyn finished with Santo, I finished with Santo as well. He might have been doing a design to pay for the new board—'

'Another board?'

'He'd got way beyond the first. He needed another, beyond the learning board, if he was going to improve. But once I sacked him, he had no way to pay me back. This might have been it.' He handed the design back to McNulty.

Bea said to the constable, 'Show him the other,' and McNulty brought forth the design for *Commit an Act of Subversion* and handed it over. Lew looked at it and shook his head. He passed it on to Jago who knuckled his spectacles into place, read the logo, and said, 'Will Mendick. This was for him.'

'The bloke from Clean Barrel Surfing?' Bea said.

'Used to be. He works at Blue Star Grocery now.'

'What's the significance of the design?'

'He's freegan. Least that's what Santo said he calls himself.'

'Freegan? I've not heard that term.'

'Only eats what's free. Clobber he grows 's well as muck from wheelie bins behind the market and at the back of restaurants.'

'How appealing. Is this a movement or something like?'

Jago shrugged. 'Don't know, do I. But he and Santo were mates, more or less, so it might've been a favour. The T-shirt that is.'

Bea was gratified to hear the sound of Constable McNulty jotting all of this down instead of studying the nearby surfing posters. She was less gratified when he suddenly said to Jago, 'Ever see the big waves?' He'd coloured as he spoke, as if he knew he was out of order but could no longer contain himself.

'Oh, aye. Ke Iki. Waimea. Jaws. Teahupoo.'

'Big as they say?'

'Depends on the weather,' Jago said. 'Big as office blocks some-times. Bigger.'

'Where? When?' And then apologetically to Bea, 'I mean to go, you see. The wife and I and the kids . . . It's a dream . . . And when we go, I want to be sure of the place and the waves . . . you know.'

'Surf then, do you?' Jago asked.

'Bit. Not like you lot. But I—'

'That'll do, Constable,' Bea told McNulty.

He looked anguished, an opportunity ripped from his hands. 'I just wanted to know—'

'Where might we find your daughter?' she asked Lew Angarrack, waving McNulty impatiently to silence.

Lew finished his coffee and placed his mug on the card table. 'Why do you want Madlyn?'

'I should think that's rather obvious.'

'As it happens, it's not.'

'Former and potentially discarded lover of Santo Kerne, Mr Angarrack? She's got to be interviewed like everyone else.'

It was clear that Angarrack didn't like the direction in which Bea intended to head, but he told her where she could find his daughter at her place of employment. Bea gave him her card, circling her mobile number. If he thought of anything else . . .

He nodded and returned to his work, shutting the door to the shaping room behind him. A moment later, the sound of an electric tool shrieked in the building again.

Jago Reeth remained with Bea and the constable. He said, casting a look over his shoulder, 'One more thing . . . I got a conscience on this, so if you have a moment for 'nother word . . .' And when Bea nodded, he said, 'I'd be chuffed if Lew didn't know this, got me? The way things turned out, he'll be dead cheesed off if he knows.'

'What?'

Jago shifted his weight. 'Was me giving them the place. I know I prob'ly shouldn't've. I saw that afterwards but by then the bloody milk was spilt. Couldn't exactly pour it back into the bottle when it was spread all over the floor, could I?'

'While I admire your adherence to your metaphor,' Bea told him, 'perhaps you could make it more clear?'

'Santo and Madlyn. I go to the Salthouse Inn regular, in the afternoons. Have a mate I meet over there most days. Santo and Madlyn, they used my place then.'

'For sex?'

He didn't look happy about making the admission. 'Could have left them to sort things out on their own but it seemed . . . I wanted them to be *safe*, see. Not in the backseat of a car somewhere. Not in . . . I don't know.'

'Yet as his father owns a hotel . . .' Bea pointed out.

Jago wiped his mouth on the back of his wrist. 'All right. Yeah. There's the rooms at the old Promontory King George for what they're worth. But that didn't mean . . . the two of them there . . . I just . . . Oh hell. I couldn't be sure he'd use what he needed to keep her safe, so I left them for him. Right by the bed.'

'Condoms.'

He looked moderately embarrassed, an old bloke unused to having such a frank conversation with someone he might otherwise have deemed a lady. One of the fairer sex. Bea could see this thought playing across his face. 'He used 'em, but not every time, see.'

'And you know he used them because . . . ?' Bea prompted.

He looked horrified. 'Good God, woman.'

'I'm not sure God had much to do with this, Mr Reeth. If you'd answer the question. Did you count them up before and after? Search them out in the rubbish? What?'

He looked miserable. 'Both,' he said. 'Bloody hell. I *care* about that girl. She's got a good heart. Bit of a temper but a good heart. Way I saw it, it was going to happen between them anyways, so I might as well make certain it happened right.'

'Where would this be? Your house, I mean.'

'I've a caravan over in Sea Dreams.'

Bea glanced at Constable McNulty and he nodded. He knew the place. That was good. She said, 'We may want to see it.'

'Reckoned as much.' He shook his head. 'Young people. What's consequences to them when they're young?'

'Yes. Well. In the heat of the moment, who thinks of consequences?' Bea asked.

'But it's more than consequences, isn't it?' Jago said. 'Just like this.' He was now, apparently, referring to one of the posters on the wall. It depicted a surfboard shooting into the air, its rider in the middle of a massive and memorable wipeout that had him looking crucified against a monstrous wave. 'They don't think of the moment *itself*, let alone beyond the moment. And look what happens.'

'Who's that?' McNulty asked, approaching the poster.

'Bloke called Mark Foo. Minute or two before the poor bastard died.'

McNulty's mouth formed a respectful *o* and he began to respond. Bea saw him settling in for a proper surfing natter and she could only imagine where a trip down this watery and mournful memory lane was going to lead them.

She said, 'That looks a bit more dangerous than seacliff climbing, doesn't it? Perhaps Santo's father had the right idea, discouraging surfing.'

'Trying to keep the boy from what he loved? What kind of idea's that?'

'Perhaps one that was intended to keep him alive.'

'But it *didn't* keep him alive, did it?' Jago Reeth said. 'End of the day, that's not always something we can do for others.'

Daidre Trahair used the internet once again in Max Priestley's office in the *Watchman*, but she had to pay this time round. Max didn't ask for money, however. The price was an interview with his sole reporter. Steve Teller, he said, just happened to be in the office working on the story of the murder of Santo Kerne. She was the missing piece. The crime asked for an eyewitness account.

Daidre said, 'Murder?' because, she decided, the response was expected. She'd seen the body and she'd seen the sling, but Max didn't know that although he might suppose it.

'Cops gave us the word this morning,' Max told her. 'Steve's working in the layout room. As I'm using the computer just now, you'll have time to have a word with him.'

Daidre didn't believe that Max was using the computer, but she didn't argue. She didn't want to be involved, didn't want her name, her photo, the location of her cottage or anything else related to her put into the paper, but she saw no way to avoid it that wouldn't arouse the newsman's suspicion. So she agreed. She needed the computer and this spot afforded her more time and privacy than the sole computer in the library did. She was being paranoid but embracing paranoia seemed the course of wisdom.

So she went with Max to the layout room, taking a moment to cast a surreptitious look at him in order to ascertain whatever might lie beneath the surface of his composure. Like her, he walked the coastal path. She'd come across him more than once at the top of one sea cliff or another, his dog his only companion. The fourth or fifth time, they'd joked with each other, saying, 'We've got to stop meeting like this,' and she'd asked him why he walked the path so much. He'd said Lily liked it and, as for him, he liked to be alone. 'An only child,' he'd said. 'I'm used to solitude.' But she'd never thought that was the truth of the matter.

He wasn't readable on this day. Not that he ever was, particularly. He was, as ever, put together like a man stepping out of a *Country Life* fantasy pictorial on daily doings in Cornwall: The collar of a crisp blue shirt rose above a cream fisherman's sweater; he was cleanly shaven and his spectacles glinted in the overhead lights, as spotless as the rest of him. A fortysomething man without sin.

'Here's our quarry, Steve,' he said to the reporter working at a PC in the corner. 'She's agreed to an interview. Show her no mercy.'

Daidre cast him a look. 'You make it sound as if I'm involved somehow.'

'You didn't appear surprised, not to mentioned horrified, to hear it was murder,' Max said.

They locked eyes. She weighed potential answers and settled on, 'I'd seen the body. You forget.'

'That obvious, was it? Initial knowledge given out was that he'd fallen.'

'I think it was meant to look that way.' She heard Teller typing away at his PC, and she said rather too sharply, 'I hadn't indicated that the interview was beginning.'

Max chuckled. 'You're with a journalist, my dear. Everything is meat, with due respect. Forewarned, et cetera.'

'I see.' She sat and knew she did so primly, perched on the edge of a ladder back chair that would have had to work hard to be more uncomfortable. She kept her shoulder bag on her knees, her hands folded over the top of it. She knew she looked like a schoolmarm or a hopeful interviewee. That couldn't be helped and she didn't try to help it. She said, 'I'm not entirely happy about this.'

'No one ever is, save B-list celebrities.' Max left them, then, calling out, 'Janna, have we heard about the inquest time, yet?'

Janna made some reply as Steve Teller asked Daidre his first question. He wanted the facts first and then her impressions second, he told her. The latter, she decided, was the last thing she'd give anyone, least of all a journalist. But like a policeman, he was doubtless trained to sniff out falsehoods and note diversions. So she would have a care with how she said what she said. She didn't like leaving things to chance.

The entire *Watchman* experience ate up two hours and was evenly divided between the conversation with Teller and her investigation on the internet. When she had what she needed in print for her later perusal, she concluded her research with the words *Adventures*

Unlimited. She paused before she clicked the search engine into action. Was it better to know or not to know and if she knew could she keep the knowledge from her face? She wasn't sure.

The list of references to the neophyte business wasn't long. The *Mail on Sunday* had featured it in a lengthy piece, she saw, as had several small journals in Cornwall. The *Watchman* was among them.

And why not? she asked herself. Adventures Unlimited was a Casvelyn story. The *Watchman* was the Casvelyn newspaper. The Promontory King George Hotel had been saved from destruction – well, come along, Daidre, it's a listed building so it was hardly going under the wrecking ball, was it – so there was that as well.

She read the story and looked at the photos. It was all standard stuff: the architectural interest, the plan, the family. And there they were in pictures, Santo among them. There was background on them all, with no one emphasised in particular because it was, of course, a family affair. Last of all she looked at the by-line. She saw that Max had done the story himself. This was not unusual because the newspaper was tiny and, consequently, work was shared. But it was potentially damning all the same.

She asked herself what this was to her: Max, Santo Kerne, the sea cliffs, and Adventures Unlimited. She thought of Donne and then dismissed the thought of Donne. Unlike the poet, there were too many times when she didn't feel part of mankind at all.

She left the newspaper office. She was thinking about Max Priestley and about what she'd read, when she heard her name called. She turned round to see Thomas Lynley coming along Princes Street, a large piece of cardboard under his arm and a small bag dangling from his fingers.

Once again she thought how different he looked without the growth of beard, newly dressed, and at least partially refreshed. She said, 'You're not looking too chastened by the trouncing you took at the dart board last night. May I assume your ego's intact, Thomas?'

'Marginally,' he said. 'I was up all night practising in the bar at the inn. Where, by the way, I learned that you regularly thrash all comers. Practically blindfolded, the way they tell it.'

'They exaggerate, I'm afraid.'

'Do they? What other secrets are you keeping?'

'Roller derby,' she told him. 'Are you familiar with that? It's an American sport featuring frightening women bashing one another about on inline skates.'

'Good Lord.'

'We've a fledging team in Bristol and I'm absolute hell on wheels as a jammer. Far more ruthless on my blades than I am with my darts. We're Boudica's Broads, by the way, and I'm Kickarse Electra. We all have suitably threatening monikers.'

'You never cease to surprise, Ms Trahair.'

'I like to consider that part of my charm. What have you got, then?' with a nod at his package.

'Ah. You're very well met as things turn out. May I stow this in your car? It's the replacement glass for the window I broke at your cottage. And the tools to fix it as well.'

'However did you know the size?'

'I've been out there to measure.' He cocked his head in the vague direction of her cottage, far north of the town. 'I had to go inside again, finding you gone,' he admitted. 'I hope you don't mind.'

'I trust you didn't break another window to do so.'

'Didn't have to with the first one broken. Best to get it repaired before someone else discovers the damage and avails himself of . . . whatever you've got cached away within.'

'Little enough,' she said, 'unless someone wants to nick my dartboard.'

'Would they only,' he replied, fervently, at which she chuckled. He said, 'So now that we've met, may I put this in your car?'

She led him to it. She'd left the Vauxhall in the same spot where she'd left it on the previous day, in the car park across from Toes on the Nose, which was hosting another gathering of surfers although this time they stood about outside, gazing vaguely towards St Mevan Beach. From the vantage point of the car park, the Promontory King George Hotel squared off some three hundred yards away. She pointed the structure out to Lynley. That was where Santo Kerne came from, she told him. Then she said, 'You didn't mention murder, Thomas. You must have known last night, but you said nothing.'

'Why do you assume I knew?'

'You went off with that detective in the afternoon. You're one yourself. A detective that is. I can't think she didn't tell you. Brotherhood of police and all that.'

'She told me,' he admitted.

'Am I a suspect?'

'We all are, myself included.'

'And did you tell her . . . ?'

'What?'

'That I knew – or at least recognised – Santo Kerne?'

He took his time about answering and she wondered why. 'No,' he said at last. 'I didn't tell her.'

'Why?'

He didn't reply to this. Instead he said, 'Ah. Your car,' as they reached it.

She wanted to press him for an answer but wasn't sure what she'd do with it when she got it. She fumbled in her bag for her keys. The paperwork she was carrying from the *Watchman* slipped from her grasp and slid onto the tarmac. She said, 'Damn,' as it soaked up rainwater. She started to squat to gather it up.

Lynley said, 'Let me,' and ever the gentleman, he set down his package and bent to retrieve it.

Ever the cop as well, he glanced at it and then at her. She felt herself colouring.

'Hoping for a miracle, are you?'

'My social life has been rather bleak for the past few years. Everything helps, I find. May I ask why you didn't tell me, Thomas?'

'Tell you what?'

'That Santo Kerne had been murdered. It can't have been privileged information. Max Priestley knew it.'

He handed her the printouts she'd made from the internet and picked up his own package as she unlocked the Vauxhall's boot. 'And Max Priestley is?'

'The publisher and editor of the *Watchman*. I spoke to him earlier.'

'As a journalist, he would have been given the word by DI Hannaford, I expect. She'd be the officer determining when information gets disseminated as I doubt there's a press officer here in town unless she's directed someone to act as one. It wouldn't be up to me to tell anyone until Hannaford was ready for the word to go out.'

'I see.' She couldn't say to him, 'But I thought we were friends' because that was hardly the case. There seemed no point carrying the matter further, so she said, 'Are you coming out to the cottage now, then? To repair the window?'

He told her he had a few things more to do in town but that afterwards, if she didn't mind, he would drive out to Polcare Cove and make the repair. She asked him if he actually knew how to repair a window. Somehow one didn't expect an earl – gainfully employed as a cop or not – to know what to do with glass and putty. He told her he was certain he could muddle through it somewhat proficiently.

Then he said, for reasons she couldn't sort out, 'D'you generally do your research at the newspaper office?'

'I generally don't do research at all,' she told him. 'Especially when I'm in Cornwall. But if there's something I need to look up, yes. I use the *Watchman*. Max Priestley's got a retriever I've treated so he gives me access.'

'That can't be the only internet site.'

'Consider where we are, Thomas. I'm lucky there's access in Casvelyn at all.' She gestured south, in the direction of the wharf. 'I could use the library's access, I suppose, but they ration time. Fifteen minutes and the next person gets a whack. It's maddening if you're trying to do something more meaningful than answering your email.'

'More private, as well, I suppose,' Lynley said.

'There's that,' she admitted.

'And we know you like privacy.'

She smiled, but she knew the effort showed. It was time for an exit, graceful or otherwise. She told him she would, perhaps, see him when he came to repair her window. Then she took herself off.

She could feel his steady gaze on her as she left the car park.

Lynley watched her go. She was a cipher in more ways than one, holding much to herself. Some of it had to do with Santo Kerne, he reckoned. He wanted to believe that not all of it did. He wasn't sure why this was the case but he did admit to himself that he liked the woman. He admired her independence and what appeared to be a lifestyle of going against the common grain. She was unlike anyone he knew.

But that in itself raised questions. Who was she, exactly, and why did she seem to have sprung into existence as an adolescent, fully formed like Athena from the head of Zeus? The questions about her were disturbing. He had to acknowledge the fact that a hundred red flags surrounded this woman, only some of them having to do with a dead boy at the foot of a cliff nearby her cottage.

He walked from the car park to the police station at the end of Lansdown Road. This was a narrow cobbled lane of white terraced houses, ill-roofed and largely stained by rainwater from rusty gutters. Most of them had fallen into the disrepair prevalent in the poorer sections of Cornwall, where gentrification had not yet extended its greedy fingers. One of them was undergoing refurbishment, however, its scaffolding suggesting that better times for someone had come to the neighbourhood.

The police station was an eyesore, even here, a grey stucco building with nothing of architectural interest to recommend itself. It was flat in front and flat on top, a shoebox with occasional windows and a notice board near its door.

Inside, a small vestibule offered a line of three institutional plastic chairs and a reception counter. Bea Hannaford sat behind this, the telephone receiver pressed to her ear. She raised a finger in greeting to Lynley and said to whoever was on the other end of the line, 'Got it. Well, there's no surprise in that, is there? We'll want to have another little chat with her, won't we, then.'

She rang off and took Lynley up to the incident room, which was set up on the first floor of the building in what seemed to be otherwise a conference room, coffee room, locker room, and meal room. Up here they were making do with a few china boards and computers set up with HOLMES but clearly an insufficiency of manpower. The constable and the sergeant were hard at it, Lynley saw, and two other officers were huddled together exchanging either information on the case or background on the horses currently running at Newmarket. It was difficult to tell. Actions were listed on the china board, some completed and others pending.

DI Hannaford said to Sergeant Collins, 'Man reception, Sergeant,' and then to Lynley when Collins left the room to do so, 'She was lying, as it turns out.'

He said, 'Who?' although there was only one *she* they'd been looking at, as far as he knew.

'Pro forma question, isn't that?' the DI said meaningfully. 'Our Ms Trahair, that's who. Not a pub remembers her on the route she claimed she took from Bristol. And she'd be remembered this time of year, considering how few people are out and about in this part of the country.'

'Perhaps,' he said. 'But there must be a hundred pubs involved.'

'Not the way she came. Claiming that was the route may have been her first mistake. And where there's one, there are others, trust me. What've you got on her?'

Lynley related what he'd gleaned from Falmouth about Daidre Trahair. He added what he knew about her brother, her work, and her education. Everything she'd said about herself checked out. So far, so good.

'Why is it I think you're not telling me everything there is to tell?'

was Bea Hannaford's reply after a moment of observing him. 'Are you holding back something, Superintendent Lynley?'

He wanted to say that he wasn't Superintendent Lynley any longer. He wasn't anything related to police work, which was why he also wasn't required to tell her every fact he had acquired. But he said, 'She's doing some curious research on the internet just now. There's that, although I can't see how it relates to murder.'

'What sort of research?'

'Miracles,' he said. 'Or rather, places associated with miracles. Lourdes, for one. A church in New Mexico. There were others as well, but I didn't have time to look through all the paperwork and I wasn't wearing my reading glasses anyway. She's been on the internet at the *Watchman*. That's the local paper. She knows the publisher, evidently.'

'That'd be Max Priestley.' It was Constable McNulty speaking up from a computer in one corner of the room. 'He's had some contact with the dead boy, by the way.'

'Has he indeed?' Bea Hannaford said. 'Now that's an interesting twist.' She told Lynley that the constable was digging through Santo Kerne's old emails, looking for nuggets of information. 'What was he saying?'

'"No skin off my back. Just watch your own." I reckon it's Priestley 'cause it's come from MEP at *Watchman dot co* et cetera. Although it could have come from anyone who knows his password and has access to a computer at the paper, I s'pose.'

'That's it?' Hannaford asked the constable.

'That's it from Priestley. But there's a whole collection from the Angarrack girl, coming straight out of LiquidEarth. The course of most of the relationship being charted. Casual, closer, intimate, hot, graphic, and then nothing else. Like once they started doing the nasty, she didn't want to commit to writing.'

'Interesting, that.'

'S'what I thought as well. But "wild for him" doesn't even touch how she felt about the boy. You ask me, I'll wager she wouldn't've said no to the idea of someone chopping off his bollocks when they got to the end game, her and Santo. What d'they say about a woman's scorn?'

'"A woman scorned,"' Lynley murmured.

'Right. Well. I'd say we give her a closer look. She'd've likely had access to his climbing kit at some point. Or she'd've known where he kept it.'

'She's on our list,' Hannaford said. 'Is that it, then?'

'I've got emails from someone calling himself Freeganman as well, and I'd say that's Mendick 'cause I doubt the town's crawling with people of his ilk.'

Hannaford explained the moniker to Lynley. 'And what's Mr Mendick got to say for himself?'

'"Can we keep it between us?" Not exactly illuminating, I'll give you that, but still . . .'

'A reason to talk to him, then. Let's put Blue Star Grocery on the schedule.'

'Right.' McNulty went back to the computer.

Hannaford strode over to a desk where she dug in a heavy-looking shoulder bag. She brought forth a mobile phone. This she tossed to Lynley. She said, 'Reception's the devil round here, I've found, but I want you carrying this and I want it turned on.'

'Your reason?' Lynley asked.

'I need a stated reason, do I, Superintendent?'

'If nothing else, because I outrank you' would have been his answer in other circumstances, but not in these. He said, 'I'm curious. It suggests my usefulness to you hasn't come to an end.'

'That would be correct. I'm undermanned and I want you available to me.'

'I'm not—'

'Bollocks. Once a cop, always a cop. There's a need here, and you and I know you're not about to walk away from a situation where your help is required. Beyond that, you're a principal figure and you're not going anywhere without me coming after you until you have my blessing to leave, so you may as well make yourself useful.'

'You've something in mind?'

'Ms Trahair. Details. Everything. From her shoe size to her blood type and all points in between.'

'How am I supposed to—'

'Oh please, Detective. Don't take me for a fool. You've sources and you've charm. Use them both. Dig into her background. Take her on a picnic. Wine her. Dine her. Read her poetry. Caress her palm. Gain her trust. I don't bloody care *how* you do it. Just do it. And *when* you've done it, I want it all. Are we clear on that?'

Sergeant Collins had appeared in the doorway as Hannaford was speaking. He said, 'Guv? Someone to see you. Queer bird called Tammy Penrule down below. Says she's got information for you.'

The DI said to Lynley, 'Keep that phone charged. Take your spade and use it. Do whatever you have to do.'

'I'm not comfortable with—'

'That's not my concern. Murder's not comfortable either.'

13

Downstairs, Bea found the aforementioned Tammy Penrule sitting in one of the plastic reception chairs, her feet flat on the floor, her hands clasped in her lap, her back a plane perpendicular to the seat. She was dressed in black, but she wasn't a goth, as Bea first suspected when she caught sight of her. She wore no makeup, no hideous black nail vanish, and she had no silver protrusions erupting from various points on her head. She also wore no jewellery, and nothing else relieved the midnight of her clothes. She looked like mourning made flesh.

'Tammy Penrule?' Bea said to her, unnecessarily.

The girl jumped to her feet. She was thin as a miser's good wishes. One couldn't look at her without considering eating disorders.

'You've got information for me?' When the girl nodded, Bea said, 'Come with me, then,' before she realised she had not yet located the interview rooms at the station. Stumbling about wasn't going to inspire confidence in anyone, so she reversed herself, said, 'Hang on a moment,' and found a cubbyhole next to a broom cupboard that would do until further exploration of the station might provide its secret as to the site of interrogations.

When she had Tammy Penrule situated in this spot, she said to her, 'What've you got to tell me?'

Tammy licked her lips. She needed balm for them. They were badly chapped and a thin line of scabbing marked a spot where her lower lip had cracked seriously enough to bleed. 'It's about Santo Kerne,' she said.

'I've got that much.' Bea crossed her arms beneath her breasts. Unconsciously, it seemed, Tammy did the same, although she had no breasts to speak of, and Bea wondered if Santo Kerne's relationship with Madlyn Angarrack had ended because of this girl. She hadn't yet met Madlyn, but the fact that the girl had been a competitive surfer suggested someone . . . perhaps 'more physically defined' was the term she wanted. This teenager seemed more like an evanescent being, corporeal only as long as she had the strength to manifest in human form. Bea couldn't picture her spread-eagled beneath a hot-blooded adolescent boy.

Tammy said, 'Santo talked to me.'

'Ah.'

The girl seemed to be waiting for more of a response, so Bea said cooperatively, 'How did you know him?'

'From Clean Barrel Surf Shop,' Tammy said. 'It's where I work. He comes there for wax and the like. And to look at the isobar chart except I think that may have been just an excuse to hang about with the other surfers. You c'n look up the isobar chart on the internet, and I expect they've got internet over at the hotel.'

'Adventures Unlimited?'

Tammy nodded. The hollow of her throat was deep and shadowed. Above the neck of her jersey, the points of her collarbone protruded like the excrescent evidence of dutch elm disease on the bark of a tree. 'So that's how I know him. That and Sea Dreams.'

Bea recognised the name of the caravan park and she cocked her head. Perhaps she'd been wrong about this girl and Santo. She said, 'Did you meet him there?'

'No. Like I said, I met him at Clean Barrel.'

'Sorry. I don't mean met him as in *met* him,' Bea clarified. 'I mean met him as in having assignations with him.'

Tammy flushed. There was so little substance between her skin and her blood vessels that she coloured nearly to purple and she did so quickly. 'You mean . . . Santo and me . . . *for sex*? Oh no. I live there. At Sea Dreams. My granddad owns the caravan park. I knew Santo from Clean Barrel like I said, but he came to Sea Dreams with Madlyn. And he came on his own as well because there's a cliff he used to practise on sometimes and granddad said he could get to it across our land if he wanted to abseil. Or to surf. Anyway, I saw him there and we talked sometimes.'

'On his own?' Bea asked. This was something new.

'Like I said. He climbed. Down and up but sometimes just up so he'd come from below . . . or I suppose he just went down and then up all the time because I can't quite remember. He also visited Mr Reeth. So did she. Madlyn. Mr Reeth, he works for Madlyn's dad at—'

'Yes. I know. We've spoken to him.' But what she didn't know was that Santo had been there to Sea Dreams on his own. This was a new wrinkle.

'He was nice, Santo.'

'He was especially nice to girls, I gather.'

Tammy's flush had receded, and she didn't flush again. 'Yes, I suppose he was. But it wasn't like that for me because . . . Well, that's not important. What *is* important is that we talked from time to time. When he was finished with his climbing or when he was leaving Mr Reeth's. Or sometimes when he was waiting for Madlyn to get there from work.'

'They didn't come together?'

'Not always. Madlyn works in town now, but she didn't earlier. She had to come a greater distance than Santo, from out by Brandis Corner. She worked on a farm, making jam.'

'I expect she preferred teaching surfing.'

'Oh yes, she did. She does. But that's in the season, when she teaches surfing. She's got to do something else the rest of the year. She works in the bakery now. In town. They make pasties. Mostly for wholesale, but they sell some of them out of the shop as well.'

'And where does Santo fit in with all this?'

'Santo. Of course.' She'd been using her hands to gesture with as she talked, but now she clasped them again in her lap. She said, 'We talked now and again. I liked him but I didn't *like* him in the way most girls probably would, if you know what I mean, so I think that made me different and maybe safer or something. For advice or whatever because he couldn't go to his dad or his mum—'

'Why not?'

'His dad, he said, would've got the wrong impression and his mum . . . I don't know his mum, but I get the idea she's . . . well, she's not very mummish, apparently.' She smoothed her skirt. It looked like something that would be scratchy against the skin and it was virtually shapeless, a fashion penance. 'Anyway, Santo asked me for advice about something and that's what I thought you ought to know.'

'Advice of what kind?'

She seemed to look for a gentle way to say what came next and, not finding a euphemism, went for a circuitous route to the truth. 'He'd got someone new, you see, and the situation was irregular – that's the word he used when he talked to me, he said it was *irregular* – and he wanted to ask me what I thought he should do about that.'

'Irregular. That was his word? You're sure?'

Tammy nodded. 'He said he thought he loved her – this is Madlyn – but he wanted this other thing as well. He said he wanted it very badly and did that mean he didn't actually love Madlyn?'

'He talked to you about love, then?'

'No, that part was more like Santo talking to Santo. He wanted to know what I thought he should do about the whole situation. Should he be honest with everyone about it, he wanted to know? Should he tell the truth start to finish? he asked.'

'And what did you tell him?'

'I said he should be honest. I said he should *always* be honest because when people are honest about who they are, what they want, and what they do, it gives *other* people – this is the people they're involved with, I mean – the chance to decide if they really want to be with them.' She looked at Bea and her expression was earnest. 'So I suppose he was, you see,' she said. 'Honest, I mean. And that's why I've come. I think that maybe he's dead because of it.'

'More than anything else, it's a question of balance,' was the declaration that Alan used to conclude. 'You see that, don't you, darling?'

Kerra's hackles stood stiffly. *Darling* was too much. There was no darling. *She* was no darling. She thought she'd made that clear to Alan, but the bloody man refused to believe it.

They stood before the glass-fronted notice board in the entry area of the former hotel. *Your Instructors* was the purpose of their discussion. The imbalance between male and female instructors was Alan's point. In charge of hiring all of the instructors, Kerra had allowed the balance to swing to females. This was not good for several reasons, according to Alan. For marketing purposes, they needed an equal number of men and women offering instruction in the various activities and, if possible and what was highly desirable, they needed *more* male than female. They needed the males to be nicely built and good-looking because, first of all, such men could serve as a feature to bring unmarried females to Adventures Unlimited and, second of all, Alan intended to use them in a video. He'd lined up a crew from Plymouth to take video footage, by the way, so whatever instructors Kerra came up with also needed to be on board within three weeks. Or, he supposed – thinking aloud – perhaps they could actually use actors . . . no, stunt men . . . yes, stunt men could be very good in making the video, actually. The initial outlay would be higher because stunt men no doubt had some sort of scale on which they were paid, but it wouldn't take as long to film them because they'd be professionals so the final cost would likely not be as high. So . . .

He was absolutely maddening. Kerra wanted to argue with him and she had been arguing, but he'd matched her point for point.

He said, 'The publicity from that *Mail on Sunday* article helped us enormously, but that was seven months back, and we're going to need to do more if we're to begin heading in the direction of the black. We won't be *in* the black of course, not this year and probably not next, but the point is we have to chip away at debt. So everyone has to consider how best to get us out of the red.'

Red did it for her. *Red* held her between wanting to run and wanting to argue. She said, 'I'm not *refusing* to hire men, Alan, if that's what you're implying. I can hardly be blamed if they're not applying in droves to work here.'

'It's not a question of blame,' he reassured her. 'But, to be honest, I do wonder how aggressive you're being in trying to recruit them.'

Not aggressive at all. She couldn't be. But what was the point of telling him that?

She said with the greatest courtesy she could manage, 'Very well. I'll start with the *Watchman*. How much can we spend on an advertisement for instructors?'

'Oh, we'll need a much wider net than that,' Alan said, affably. 'I doubt an ad in the *Watchman* would do us much good at all. We need to go national: advertisements placed in specialised magazines, at least one for each sport.' He studied the notice board where the pictures of the instructors were posted. Then he looked at Kerra. 'You do see my point, don't you, Kerra? We must consider them as an attraction. They're more than merely instructors. They're a *reason* to come to Adventures Unlimited. Like social directors on a cruise line.'

'Come to Adventures Unlimited for a Shag,' Kerra said. 'Yes. I've got the point well enough.'

'That's the implication, naturally,' Alan said. 'Sex sells. You know that.'

'It all gets reduced to sex in the end, doesn't it?' Kerra said bitterly.

He gazed at the pictures again. He was either evaluating them or avoiding her. He said, 'Well, yes. I suppose it does. That's life.'

She left him without replying. She said abruptly that she was going to the *Watchman* if anyone wanted her, daring him to make his point again about the futility of placing an advertisement in that paper, and she set out on her bicycle.

This time, however, she had no intention of riding until the sweat of her efforts bled the anxiety from her muscles. She also had no intention of going to the *Watchman* to place an advertisement for randy males willing to instruct equally randy females during daylight hours and fulfil their sexual fantasies at night. That was *all* they needed at Adventures Unlimited: an excess of testosterone oozing down the corridors.

Kerra pedalled off the promontory in the direction of Toes on the Nose, where she was forced to follow the one-way system through town. She climbed to the crest of the hill where St Mevan Down rolled inland from the sea and made her way to Queen Street with its clutter of cars. Ultimately she coursed downward towards the Casvelyn Canal, where just beyond the wharf that edged it, a bridge arched to a *Y* in the road. Go left and one ultimately headed to Widemouth Bay. Go right and you found yourself out on the Breakwater.

This formed the southwest side of the canal, just as the wharf served as its northeastern edge. Cottages lined it, sitting some fifteen feet above the tarmac, and at their far end was the largest of them, one that only a blind man could miss seeing. It was trimmed in fuchsia and painted the pink of flamingos. Unimaginatively, it was called Pink Cottage, and its owner was a maiden lady long referred to by townspeople as Busy Lizzie and only in part as a reference to the flowers she planted in enormous banks with riotous abandon every late spring in her front garden.

Kerra was known to Busy Lizzie as a regular visitor, so when she knocked on the door, the woman admitted her without question, saying, 'Why, isn't this the nicest surprise, Kerra! Alan's not here at the moment, but I expect you know that. Come in, my dear.'

She was not even five feet tall, and she'd long reminded Kerra of a chess piece. Specifically, she looked very much like a pawn. She wore her white hair in an impressively constructed Edwardian pouf and she favoured high-necked ivory blouses and bell-shaped flannel skirts of navy or grey that fell to the floor. She always looked like someone on the verge of being discovered for a part in a Henry James novel brought to life, but as far as Kerra had ever been able to learn – which admittedly wasn't very far – Busy Lizzie had no inclination for either screen or stage.

She let one of the bedrooms in her house, the rest being filled with her vast collection of Carltonware from the 1930s. She was liberal in her thinking, and, preferring young men to young women as her lodgers – 'Somehow one always feels *safer* with a man in the house' was her way of putting it – she recognised that her lodgers had appetites whose fulfilment she oughtn't to deny. So each successive lodger had kitchen privileges, and if a sleepover occurred in which a young lady might put in an appearance at the breakfast table, Busy Lizzie did not complain. Indeed, she provided either tea or coffee and she asked, 'Sleep well, dear?' quite as if the young lady belonged there.

While his house in Lansdown Road was undergoing work, Alan had his temporary lodging here in Pink Cottage. He could have moved in with his parents – it would have saved him money – but he'd explained to Kerra that, while he loved his mum and dad devotedly, he liked to have a degree of freedom that his parents' blind adoration of him sometimes precluded. Besides, he'd delicately said to her, they had a certain *image* of him that he didn't want to mess about with.

Kerra read this as he intended. She said, 'God, they can't think you're a *virgin*, Alan.' And when he didn't answer, '*Do* they, Alan?'

'No, no. Of course not. Of course they don't. What a ridiculous . . . They know I'm *normal*. But they're older people, aren't they, and it's a sign of respect that I don't take a woman to bed while I'm unmarried and under their roof. They'd feel very . . . well, *odd* about it.'

Kerra understood, at least at first. But in the end, the whole question of Alan having this lodging separate from his parents began to have a different resonance.

So she had to know. She had to be certain. She said to Busy Lizzie, 'I've left a rather personal item in Alan's room, Miss Carey, and I wonder if I might dash in and have a look for it? Alan's forgotten to give me his key, but if you'd like to phone him at work . . . ?'

'Oh my dear, no need for that. The room's unlocked anyway as this is bed linen day. You know the way. I was just watching my telly. Would you like a cup of tea? Do you need my help?'

Kerra refused: both the offer of tea and the offer of help. She shouldn't be long, she said. She'd let herself out when she had what she'd come for.

'And are you riding about in the rain, my dear? On your bicycle? Why, you'll catch your death, Kerra. Are you sure you wouldn't care for a nice cup of P.G. Tips?'

No, no. She was fine, Kerra assured Miss Carey. She was right as rain. They both chuckled at her lame remark and parted at the far end of the sitting room. Busy Lizzie went back to her telly as Kerra ducked into the corridor that led along to the far end of the house. There, Alan's room overlooked the southwest section of St Mevan Beach. From the window, Kerra could see that the tide was in. The waves were breaking from three foot swells, and at least a dozen surfers bobbed in the distance.

Kerra turned from the sight of them. The thought came to her of her father last night, and of what it meant that part of his life had been hidden from her. But she dismissed this consideration because now was not the time and, anyway, she had to work quickly.

She was looking for signs without actually knowing what the signs would be. She needed to understand why the Alan Cheston of the last few days was not the Alan Cheston she had known and involved herself with. She reckoned she *knew* the explanation, but still she wanted hard evidence although what she would do with it was something she hadn't yet considered.

She'd also never done a search before. The whole enterprise made her feel unclean, but there was no alternative besides hurling accusations at him, and going that route was something she couldn't afford to do.

She girded herself mentally and began to look about. It was, she saw, all so vintage Alan, with every item in its place. His Djembe drum stood in its stand in the corner of the room, in front of a stool upon which Alan sat when he played it during his daily meditation. A tambourine – something of a joke gift which Kerra had given him before she'd understood how significant the drum actually was to Alan's spiritual regimen – leaned nearby, against a bookcase where he kept his Yoga books. On top of this bookcase were his photos: Alan, wearing the cap and gown of the university graduate, flanked by his beaming parents; Alan and Kerra on holiday in Portsmouth, his arm round her shoulders on the deck of *Victory*; Kerra by herself, perched on the flat stone top of Lanyon Quoit; a younger Alan with his childhood dog, a mixed breed terrier with a coat the colour of rusty bedsprings.

The trouble was that Kerra had no idea what she was looking for. She wanted a sign, but she didn't know if she'd recognise anything that wasn't written out for her by means of flashing neon lights. She prowled the room, opening and closing drawers in the chest and then in the desk. Aside from neatly folded clothes in conservative hues, the only items of interest she came up with were a collection of birthday cards given or sent to him through the years and a list entitled Five Year Objectives upon which she read that he intended to learn Italian, take xylophone lessons, and visit Patagonia, in addition to 'marry Kerra,' which came before Patagonia but after Italian.

And then in a tarnished silver toast rack where Alan kept his post she found it: the item without a purpose in the bedroom of a man for whom every item had a purpose, either in the present, the past, or the future. This was a post card, tucked at the back of correspondence from Alan's bank, his dentist, and the London School of Economics. The picture on the card was taken from the sea, into the shore, and the view presented was of two deep sea caves, one on either side of a cove. Above the cove was a Cornish village well known to Kerra, as it was the place she'd been sent with her brother throughout their child-hood, to stay with their grandparents while their mother was going through one of her spells.

Pengelly Cove. They were not allowed to go to the beach there, no matter the weather. The reason given was the tide and the sea caves. The tide came in fast, the way it came in at Morecambe Bay. Deep in a sea cave where you thought you were safe with your exploration – or whatever else you were doing – the water swept in and the walls marked its depth, which was higher than the top of the tallest man's head, as relentless as it was unforgiving.

Kids just like you lot've died in those caves, Granddad would thunder, so there'll be no beach going while you're stopping here. 'Sides, there's work enough round this place to keep you busy, and if I see you're bored, I'll give you more.

But all of that was an excuse, and they knew it, Kerra and Santo. Beach-going meant village-going, and in the village they were known as the children of Dellen Kerne, or Dellen Nankervis as she'd been then. Long, loose, wide-spreading Dellen, the village tart. Dellen whose unmistakable handwriting formed the sentence 'This is it', which was scripted in red on the face of the postcard in Alan's old toast rack. From the *it* an arrow extended down to the sea cave on the south side of the cove.

Kerra pocketed the post card and looked about for something more. But nothing else was actually needed.

Cadan had spent the morning with a mouth that felt like a wrestler's jock strap and a stomach doing a shimmy to his throat. More hair of the dog that had bitten him was what he'd needed, but an unexpected pre-Adventures Unlimited conversation with his sister had prevented him from doing a recce for his father's booze. Not that Madlyn would have reported Cadan to Lew had she caught him in the act of going through cupboards – despite her general weirdness, Cadan's sister had never been a sneak – but she would have known what he was doing and she would have ragged on him about it. He couldn't handle that. As it was, he'd had enough trouble merely responding to what she had to say when the subject wasn't him at all. It was, instead, Ione Soutar, who'd phoned three times in the last thirty-six hours, on one spurious excuse after another.

'Well, she was stupid if she ever thought it was going to go somewhere,' Madlyn had said. 'I mean, did they ever have anything between them besides sex and dating, *if* you can call what they did dating because judging surfing competitions in Newquay and having pizza nights and takeaway curry nights with those two obnoxious girls of hers . . . Not exactly what *I'd* call a promising relationship, would you? So what was she thinking?'

Cadan was the last person capable of answering these questions, and he wondered if Madlyn herself ought to be holding forth on what comprised a promising relationship. But he reckoned her final query was rhetorical, and he was happy enough that he didn't have to reply.

Madlyn went on. 'All she had to do was look at his history. But could she do that. *Would* she do that? No. And why? Because she saw him as father material, and that's what she wanted, for Leigh and Jennie. Well, God knows they need that. Especially Leigh.'

Cadan managed an answer to this. 'Jennie's all right.' He hoped that would put an end to the matter, leaving him to his headache and general queasiness in peace.

Madlyn said, 'Oh, I suppose, if you like them that age, she's all right. The other one, though . . . Leigh's a real piece of work.' She said nothing for a moment, and Cadan saw that she was watching him watching Pooh. He was waiting for the parrot to finish a breakfast of sunflower seeds and apples. Pooh preferred English apples – Cox, if he could get them – but at a pinch and in the off-season, he enjoyed an imported Fuji, which he was doing now.

Madlyn continued. 'But for God's sake, he's *had* his kids. Why would he want to go through all that again? And why didn't she see that? *I* can see it. Can't you?'

Cadan mumbled noncommittally. Even if he hadn't felt like worshipping the porcelain god, he knew better than to engage his sister lengthily or otherwise on the topic of their dad. So he said, 'Come on, Pooh. We got work to go to,' and he offered the last sixteenth of apple. Pooh ignored it, and instead wiped his beak on his right claw. Then he set about investigating the feathers under his left wing, looking like an avian miner with all the digging he was doing there. Cadan frowned and thought about mites. In the meantime, Madlyn went on.

She was turning to use the mirror over the tiny coal fireplace in order to see to her hair. In the past, she'd never given much attention to her hair, but she hadn't needed to. Like Cadan's and like their father's, it was dark and curly. Kept short enough, it was low maintenance: A good shaking sorted it out in the morning. But she'd grown it because Santo Kerne had liked it longer. Once their whatever-it-was-because-Cadan-didn't-want-to-call-it-a-relationship ended, he'd thought she would cut it – to get even with Santo if for no other reason – but so far she hadn't done so. She hadn't got back to surfing yet, either.

She said, 'Well, he'll move on to someone else now, if he hasn't already. And so will she. And that will be an end to the whole thing. Oh, I expect there may be a few more weeks of tearful phone calls, but he'll do his pained silence thing, and after a time, she'll get sick of that and realise she's thrown away three years of her life or however long it's been because I can't remember and as the clock is ticking, she'll move on. She'll want a man before her sell-by date comes along. And, believe me, she knows it's out there.'

Madlyn was pleased. Cadan could hear it in her voice. The longer their father had seen Ione Soutar, the more anxiety ridden Madlyn had become. She'd been household goddess for most of her life – thanks to the Bounder's final bounding shortly before Madlyn's fifth birthday – and the last thing she had ever wanted was another woman usurping her position of Sole Female. She'd wielded considerable power from that position, and no one with power ever wanted to let it go.

Cadan scooped up the newspapers from beneath Pooh's perch, balling them up against the detritus of his meal and the copious morning excretions of his body. He spread out a fresh old edition of the *Watchman*, and said, 'Whatever. We're off, then.'

'Off? Where?' Madlyn frowned.

'To work.'

'Work?'

She didn't, Cadan thought, need to sound so amazed. 'Adventures Unlimited,' he told her. 'I got hired there.'

Her face altered. Cadan could see how she would take the information: as a fraternal betrayal, no matter his need for gainful employment. Well, she was going to have to take it whatever way she wanted. He required a source of income and jobs were practically nonexistent. Still, he didn't want to engage her on the topic of Adventures Unlimited any more than he'd wanted to engage her on the topic of Ione Soutar and the end of her affair with their father. So he set Pooh on his shoulder and said by way of diversion, 'Talking of sell-by dates, Mad, what the hell were you doing with Jago night before last? His went by round forty years ago, didn't it?'

'Jago,' she said, 'is a friend.'

'I got that much. I like the bloke myself. But you won't catch me spending the night out there.'

'Are you actually suggesting . . . You know, you're quite nasty, Cade. If you need the information, he came to tell me about Santo but he didn't want to tell me at the bakery, so he took me home because he cared about how I was going to react to the news. He actually *cares* about me, Cadan.'

'And we don't?'

'You didn't like Santo. Don't pretend you did.'

'Hey. At the end, neither did you. Or did something change? Did he come crawling back to you, begging forgiveness and declaring love?' Cadan hooted. Pooh duplicated the sound exactly. 'Not bloody likely,' Cadan said.

'Blow holes in the attic,' Pooh remarked shrilly.

Cadan winced at the sound so near his ear. Madlyn saw this. She said, 'You got drunk last night. That's what you were doing in your room, isn't it? What's the matter with you, Cade?'

He wished he could have answered that question. But the fact was he'd headed for the off-licence without thinking, and in the same manner he'd purchased the Beefeater's and in the same manner he'd drunk it. He'd told himself that the fact he was doing his drinking at home was admirable when one considered he could be out at a pub or sitting on a street corner or – worse – driving round in a car while pouring gin down his throat. But instead, he was being *responsible*: getting obliterated in silence within the four walls of his room, where he would hurt no one but himself.

What this was related to, he'd not questioned. But as his hangover subsided – a blessed event that did not occur till the middle of the afternoon – he realised he was perilously close to having to think.

What he ended up thinking about was his father, as well as Madlyn and Santo Kerne. But he didn't like where his thoughts headed when he bunched those three individuals together in his mind because when he did that, the fourth thought that popped up like an unwanted uncle at Christmas lunch was the thought of murder.

It went like this: Madlyn in love. Madlyn heartbroken. Santo dead. Lew Angarrack . . . what? Out with his surfboard on a day when not a *single* wave was worthy of a ride. Missing in action and determinedly mum on the subject of his whereabouts. And what did those two considerations add up to? A daughter scorned? A father enraged? Cadan didn't want to begin an extended consideration of that topic.

So he considered Will Mendick instead. Torch-bearer for Madlyn. Unrequited love for Madlyn. Waiting to step in as chief comforter once Santo Kerne was finally dispatched.

But would Will have had access to Santo's climbing equipment? And was Will the sort to go for such a crafty way to dispose of someone? And even if the answer to both of those questions was yes, wasn't the *real* question whether Will was actually so hot for Madlyn's knickers that he'd get rid of Santo in the hope of closing the deal with Madlyn? Did that even make sense? *Why* rid Madlyn's life of Santo when Santo himself had already rid her life of Santo? Unless Santo's death had nothing to do with Madlyn at all. And wouldn't *that* be a bloody relief?

But if it *did* have to do with Madlyn, what about Jago, then? Jago in the role of elderly Avenger. Who'd suspect an old bloke with shakes like a barman making martinis? He was hardly fit enough to sit on the loo unassisted, let alone in the shape one considered necessary to do away with another human being. Except, it had been a hands off murder, hadn't it? Santo's equipment had been messed about with, if Kerra Kerne was to be believed. Surely Jago could have managed that. But then, so could any of them. So could Madlyn, for instance. So could Lew. So could Will. So could Kerra Kerne or Alan Cheston or Father Christmas or the Easter Bunny.

Cadan's head felt stuffed with cotton wool. It was too soon after the hangover to be doing any serious thinking. He hadn't taken a break since his arrival at Adventures Unlimited that morning, and he was owed one at this point. Perhaps some fresh air – and even a sandwich – would allow him to dwell on these thoughts more clearly.

Pooh had been patient. Without doing the slightest bit of damage and only once letting his bird bowels loose, he'd spent hours watching Cadan paint radiators from his perch on a series of shower curtain rods. He too was owed some R & R, and he probably wouldn't say no to a bite of sandwich.

Cadan hadn't brought one from home, so that was a bit of a problem.

But he could solve it with a quick trip to Toes on the Nose. Now that his stomach had returned to its normal condition, tuna and sweetcorn on brown bread sounded good to him, with crisps on the side and a Coke.

First, he needed to move his painting supplies to the next room up for radiator refreshment, something he accomplished quickly. He headed for the stairs – forgoing the groaning old lift that, frankly, gave him the willies – and shared with Pooh what was coming next.

He said, 'Toes on the Nose, and behave yourself. No swearing in front of the ladies.'

'Which ladies are you talking about?'

The question came from behind him. Cadan swung about. Santo Kerne's mother had appeared out of nowhere, like a spirit material-ising directly through the wainscoting. She was coming towards him soundlessly on the new carpet runner. She wore black once again but now it was relieved at her throat by a billowy red scarf that exactly matched the red of her shoes.

Those shoes reminded Cadan, ridiculously, of a description he'd heard once of *The Wizard of Oz*: the story of two old birds fighting over a pair of red shoes. He smiled unconsciously at the thought. Dellen returned the smile.

'You didn't ask him not to swear in front of me.' She had a throaty voice, like a blues singer.

He said stupidly, 'What?'

'Your bird. When we were first introduced. You didn't tell him not to swear in my presence. I wonder how I'm to take that, Cadan. Am I not a lady?'

He hadn't the first clue how to reply, so he chuckled lamely. He waited for her to pass him in the corridor. She didn't do so. He said, 'Going to lunch.'

She looked at her watch. 'Rather late for that, isn't it?'

'I wasn't hungry earlier.'

'And are you now? Hungry, that is?'

'Bit. Yeah.'

'Good. Come with me.'

She went towards the stairs but she didn't descend. Instead she headed upwards and when he didn't follow at once, she turned. 'Come with me, Cadan,' she told him. 'I don't bite. There's a kitchen above and I'll sort something out for you up there.'

'Oh. S'okay,' he said. 'I was going to walk over to Toes—'

'Don't be silly. This will be quicker and you won't have to pay for it.' She smiled wistfully. 'Not in money, that is. In companionship. I'd like someone to talk to.'

'P'rhaps Kerra—'

'She's out. My husband's disappeared. Alan is closeted with his telephone. Come with me, Cadan.' Her eyes clouded when he didn't move. 'You need to eat and I need to talk. We can be of service to each other.' When he still didn't move because he couldn't come up with a way to get himself out of the situation, she added, 'I'm the boss's wife. I think you've no choice but to humour me.'

He gave a two-chuckle laugh, feeling no amusement. There seemed nothing for it but to follow her.

They went up to what seemed to be the family's flat. It was a good size space that was modestly furnished in what had once been Danish modern but now was Danish retro. She led him through a sitting room and into a kitchen, where she pointed to the table and told him to sit. She turned on a radio that sat on the spotless white work top, and she fiddled with the knob till she had a station that she seemed to prefer. It featured dance music of the ballroom type. She said, 'That's nice, isn't it?' and kept the volume low. 'Now,' she put her hands on her hips. 'What do you fancy, Cadan?'

It was just the sort of question one saw in films: a Mrs Robinson question while poor Benjamin was caught up still thinking about plastics. And Dellen Kerne was a Mrs Robinson type, no doubt about that. She was, admittedly, a bit gone to seed but it was a *voluptuous* gone to seed. She had the kind of curves one didn't see in younger women obsessed with looking like catwalk models and if her skin was grooved from years of sun and cigarettes, her masses of blonde hair made up for that. As did her mouth, which had what they called beestung lips.

Cadan reacted to her. It was automatic: too long a period of celibacy and now too much blood heading in the wrong direction. He stammered, 'I was . . . that is . . . going to . . . tuna and sweetcorn.'

Her full lips curved. 'I think we can manage that.'

He was vaguely aware of Pooh moving restlessly on his shoulder, claws digging a little too deeply into his flesh. He needed to remove the bird but he didn't like to put the parrot onto the back of a chair since often Pooh took a removal from Cadan's shoulder to a perch as a sign he was meant to drop his load. Cadan looked about for a newspaper that he could use beneath a chair, just in case. He spied one sitting on the worktop, and he went to fetch it. Last week's edition of the *Watchman*, he saw. He picked it up and said, 'Mind?' to Dellen. 'Pooh needs to perch and if I could put this on the floor . . . ?'

She was opening a tin. She said, 'For the bird? Of course,' and when he had the paper spread and Pooh on the back of the chair, she went on to say, 'An unusual choice of pet, isn't he?'

Cadan didn't think he was meant to answer, but he did so anyway. 'Parrots c'n live to be eighty.' The answer seemed to be sufficient unto itself: A pet who could live eighty years wasn't likely to be going anywhere, and it didn't take a degree in psychology to sort *that* one out.

'Yes,' Dellen said. 'Eighty. I do understand.' She cast him a look and her smile was tremulous. 'I hope he makes it. But they don't always, do they.'

He dropped his gaze. 'I'm sorry about Santo.'

'Thank you.' She paused. 'I can't talk about him yet. I keep thinking that if I just move forward a bit, even try to distract myself, I won't have to face he's dead. I know that's not true, but I'm not . . . How can one ever be ready to look squarely at the death of one's child?' She reached hastily for the knob of the radio and raised the volume. She began to move with the music. She said, 'Let's dance, Cadan.'

It was a vaguely South American rhythm. A tango, a rumba. Something like that. It called for bodies moving together sinuously, and no way did Cadan want to be one of them. But she moved across the kitchen towards him, each step a swaying of the hips, a rolling of one shoulder then the other, hands extended.

Cadan saw she was crying in the way that actresses cried in films: no redness of face, no screwing up of features, just tears marking a forking path downward from her remarkable eyes. She danced and she wept simultaneously. His heart went out to her. Mother of a son who'd been murdered . . . Who was to say *how* the woman was meant to act? If she wanted to talk, if she wanted to dance, what did it matter? She was coping as best she could.

She said, 'Dance with me, Cadan. Please dance with me.'

He rose and took her into his arms.

She pressed against him at once, each movement its own form of caress. He didn't know the dance, but that didn't appear to matter. She raised both arms to his neck and held him close, one hand on the back of his head. When she lifted her face to his, the rest was natural.

His mouth lowered to hers, his hands moved from her waist to her bum, and he drew her tightly against him.

She did not protest.

14

The identification of Santo's body was pro forma. While Ben Kerne knew this, he still experienced a moment of ludicrous hope that a terrible mistake had occurred, that despite the car later found by the police and the identification within the car, the dead boy at the bottom of the cliff in Polcare Cove was someone other than Alexander Kerne. All fancy of this died, however, when he gazed at Santo's face.

Ben had gone to Truro alone. He'd taken the decision that there was no point to exposing Dellen to Santo's autopsied body, especially when he himself had no idea what condition the corpse would be in. That Santo was dead was terrible enough. That Dellen might have to *see* anything that had reduced him to death was unthinkable.

When he looked upon Santo, though, Ben also saw that his protection of Dellen had been largely unnecessary. Santo's face had been seen to with makeup. The rest of him, which undoubtedly had been most thoroughly dissected and explored, remained beneath an institutional bed sheet. Ben could have asked to see more, to see it all, to know every inch of Santo as he had not known him since early childhood, but he had not. It seemed an invasion, somehow.

Ben had given a nod in answer to the formal question, 'Is this Alexander Kerne?' and then he'd signed the documents placed before him and listened to what various individuals had to say about police, inquests, funeral homes, burials, and the like. He was numb to everything during these proceedings, especially to expressions of sympathy. For they *were* sympathetic, all the people he had to deal with at the Royal Cornwall Hospital's mortuary. They'd gone this route a thousand times before – more than that, probably – but the fact had not robbed them of their ability to express fellow feeling for someone's grief.

When he got outside, Ben began to feel in earnest. Perhaps it was the light rain that melted away his meagre protection, because as he walked to his Austin in the car park, he was struck by sorrow at the thought of the immensity of their loss and he was ravaged by guilt at his part in having brought it about. And then there was the knowledge that he would live with forever: that his last words to Santo had been spoken in a disgust born of his own inability to accept the boy for who he was. And that inability came from suspicion, one that he would never voice.

Why can't you see how others feel about what you do? Ben would say to him, the constant refrain of a song of relationship they'd sung with each other for years. For Christ's sake, Santo, people are *real*.

You act like I'm a user or something. You act like I force my will on everyone, and that's *not* how it is. Besides, you never say a word when—

Do *not* bloody try that with me, all right?

Look, Dad, if I could—

Yes, that's it, isn't it? I, I, and me, me. Well let's get something straight. Life is not all about you. What we're doing here, for example, is not about you. What you think and want does not concern me. What you *do* does. Here and elsewhere. Are we clear on that?

So much had gone unspoken. Especially unsaid were Ben's fears. Yet how could those fears be brought into the open, when everything that related to them was swept under the carpet?

Not today, though. Today the present moment demanded an acknowledgment of the past that had brought him here. Thus, when Ben climbed into his car and began the drive out of Truro, meaning to head north in the direction of Casvelyn, he braked at the signpost indicating the route to St Ives and while he waited for the shimmering in his vision to clear, he made his decision and turned for the west.

Ultimately, he coursed south on the A30, the north coast's main artery. He had no clear intention in his mind, but as the signposts grew more and more familiar to him, he made the proper turns by rote, working his way over to the sea through an uneven landscape made externally inhospitable by granite intrusions but internally rich with mineral ore. In this part of the countryside, ruined engine houses stood in mute testimony to generations of Cornishmen working beneath the ground, digging tin and copper till the lodes gave out and the mines were abandoned to weather and time.

These mines had long been served by remote stone villages which were forced to redefine themselves or die altogether when mining failed. The land was too stony and barren for farming, and so constantly windswept that only thickets of gorse and the hardiest, low-growing weeds and wildflowers managed to gain a foothold. So people turned to cattle and sheep where they could afford a herd, and they turned to smuggling when times were tough.

Cornwall's myriad coves were the provenance of smuggling. Those who were successful in this line of work were those who knew the ways of the sea and the tide. But over time this, too, gave way to other means of support. Transport to the southwest improved, and transport brought tourists. Among them were summer people who sunned themselves on the beaches and crisscrossed the countryside on walking paths. Among them, ultimately, came the surfers.

In Pengelly Cove, Ben saw them from above, where the main part of the village stood, unpainted granite that was roofed in slate, looking bleak and deserted in the wet spring weather. Three streets only defined the place: two that were lined with shops, houses, two pubs, and an inn called The Curlew and a third marking a steep and twisting route down to a small carpark, a life boat station, the cove, and the sea.

Out among the waves, lifelong surfers braved the weather. For the swells were from the northwest, coming in even sets and the grey faces of the waves were building to the barrels for which Pengelly Cove was known. Into these, the surfers dropped, carving across the face of a wave, rising to its shoulder, fading over the top to paddle out to the swell line and wait for another. No one wasted the energy riding a wave to shore, not in this weather and not with the waves breaking in mirror images of one another, over the reefs some one hundred yards out. The shore break was for rank beginners, a low wall of white water that gave the neophyte a semblance of success but no respectability.

Ben descended to the cove. He did so on foot rather than by car, leaving his vehicle in front of The Curlew and walking back along the street to the junction. He wasn't bothered by the weather. He was dressed for it, and he wanted to experience the cove as he'd experienced it in his youth: hiking down what had been only a path then, with no carpark below and nothing else save the water, the sand, and the deep sea caves to greet him when he reached the bottom, his surfboard tucked under his arm.

He'd hoped to go to the sea caves now, but the tide was too high and he knew better than to risk it. Instead he considered all the ways that the place had altered in the years since he'd been here.

Money had come to the area. He could see that in the summer houses and the holiday cottages that overlooked the cove. Long ago there had been only one of them – far out on the end of the cliff, an impressive granite structure whose proud white paint and gleaming black gutters and trim spoke of more money than any local family had – but now there were at least a dozen although Cliff House still stood as proudly as ever. He'd been inside only once, at teenage party orchestrated by a family called Parsons who took up residence for five summers in a row. A celebration before our Jamie heads off to university, they'd called the gathering.

None of the locals had liked Jamie Parsons, who'd spent his gap year travelling the globe and who hadn't possessed the common sense to keep quiet about it. But all of them had been willing to pretend the kid was everything from best mate to the Second Coming for a night of carousing inside his home.

They'd had to look cool, though. Ben remembered that. They had to look like kids who experienced this sort of revelry all the time: end of summer, an invitation that had arrived for God's sake by *post*, a rock band come down from Newquay to play, tables of food, a strobe above the dance area, and nighttime bolt holes all over the house where mischief of every imaginable kind could be got up to with no one the wiser. At least two of the Parsons kids were there – had there been four of them in all? Perhaps five? – but no parents. Beer of every imaginable kind, as well as the contraband: whisky, vodka, rum mixed with cola, tabs of something no one would identify, and cannabis. Cannabis by the crateful, it seemed. Cocaine as well? Ben couldn't remember.

What he did remember was the talk, and he remembered that because of surfing that summer and what had come of surfing that summer.

The great divide: It existed in any place invaded seasonally by people not born and bred to a spot. There were always the townies and the interlopers. In Cornwall especially, there were those who toiled and scrabbled to make a modest living, and there was everyone who arrived to spend their holiday time and money enjoying the pleasures of the southwest. The main pleasure was the coast with its brilliant weather, crystalline sea, pristine coves, and soaring cliffs. The lure, however, was the water.

Longtime residents knew the rules. Anyone who surfed regularly knew the rules, for they were easy and basic. Take your turn, do not snake, do not drop in when someone else calls a wave, give way to the more experienced, respect the hierarchy. The shorebreak belongs to beginners with wide boards, to kids playing in the water, and sometimes to knee boarders and body boarders wanting a quick return for their efforts. Anyone surfing beyond the shore break rode in at the end of a session but otherwise remained outside, dropping off the board or cutting over the shoulder of the wave and down the backside of it to paddle out again long before reaching the area where the beginners were. It was simple. It was also unwritten, but ignorance was never an acceptable excuse.

No one knew whether Jamie Parsons operated in ignorance or indifference. What everyone *did* know was that Jamie Parsons somehow felt that he had certain rights, which he *saw* as rights and not as what they actually were: inexcusable blunders.

'This stuff's total shit compared to the North Shore, you know' might have been bearable, but declared after a shout of 'Give way, mate' had acted as the harbinger of snaking one of the locals, it was not destined to impress. The line up meant nothing to Jamie Parsons. 'Hey. Cope with it' was his answer to being informed that he was out of order among the surfers. Those things didn't matter to him because he wasn't one of them. He was better than they because of money, life, circumstances, education, potential, or whatever you wanted to call it. He knew this, and they knew this. He just lacked the common sense to keep the fact to himself.

So a party at the Parsons'? Of course they would go. They would dance to his music, eat his food, drink his drink, and smoke his weed. They were owed because they'd put up with the sod. They'd had him round for five summers in a row, but this last one had been the worst.

Jamie Parsons. Ben hadn't considered the bloke in years. He'd been too consumed with Dellen Nankervis even though, as things turned out, it was Jamie Parsons and not Dellen Nankervis who had actually determined the course of his life.

It came to Ben as he stood at the edge of the carpark and looked out at the surfers that everything he'd become was the result of decisions he'd made right here in Pengelly Cove. Not in Pengelly Cove the village, but in Pengelly Cove the geographical location: at high tide a horseshoe of water beating against slate and granite boulders; at low tide a vast sandy beach far beyond the cove itself, a beach that stretched in two directions, intruded upon by reefs and lava dykes and backed by sea caves that twisted into cliffs in which rich mineral veins could still be seen. Maws in the rock created by eons of geological cataclysms and oceanic erosion, the sea caves had served as Ben Kerne's destiny from the moment he'd seen them as a very young child. The dangers they presented made them utterly compelling. The privacy they offered made them utterly necessary.

His history was inextricably tied to Pengelly Cove's two largest sea caves. They represented all the firsts he'd experienced: his first cigarette, his first spliff, his first drink, his first kiss, his first sex. They also charted the storms that patterned the trajectory of his relationship with Dellen. For if his first kiss and first sex had been shared with Dellen Nankervis in one of the cove's two great brooding sea caves, so also had those two caves borne witness to every betrayal they'd committed against each other.

Christ, can't you escape the bloody cow? his father had demanded. She's making you into a madman, boy. Cut her loose, God damn it, before she chews you up and spits you into the dirt.

He'd wanted to, but he couldn't. The hold she had on him had been too profound. There were other girls, but they were simple creatures compared to Dellen: gigglers, teasers, superficial natterers, endlessly combing their sun-streaked hair and asking a bloke did he think they looked fat. They had no mystery, no complexity of character. Most important, not a single one of them needed Ben as Dellen did. She always came back to him, and he was always ready. And if two other blokes made her pregnant during those frenzied years of their adolescence, he'd done no worse to her by the time he was twenty, and he'd even managed to equal their score.

The third time it happened, he asked to marry her, for she'd proved the very nature of her love: She'd followed him to Truro with no money to speak of and only what she'd been able to fit in a canvas holdall. She'd said, It's yours, Ben, and so am I, with the inchoate curve of her belly telling the tale.

It would be better now, he'd thought. They would marry, and marriage would put an end forever to the cycles of connection, betrayal, breakup, longing, and reconnection.

So the story was that he'd moved from Pengelly Cove to Truro for a fresh start that had not come about. He'd moved from Truro to Casvelyn for the very same reason with much the same result. Indeed, with a far worse result this time. For Santo was dead, and the insubstantial fabric of Ben's own life was torn asunder.

It seemed to Ben now that the idea of lessons needing to be taught had started everything. What an excruciating realisation it was that lessons needing to be taught had ended everything as well. Only the student and the teacher were different. The crucial fact of acceptance remained the same.

Lynley settled on the idea of a drive down the coast to Pengelly Cove once DI Hannaford had identified it as the village from which the Kerne family had originated. 'It's a two birds and one stone situation,' he explained, to which Hannaford had shrewdly replied, 'You're avoiding a bit of responsibility here, aren't you? What is it about Ms Trahair that you don't want me to know, Detective Superintendent?'

He wasn't avoiding it at all, he told her blithely. But as the Kernes needed looking into and as he was intended to garner Daidre Trahair's trust at DI Hannaford's own instructions to him, it seemed that having a rational reason for suggesting a drive to Daidre—

'It doesn't *have* to be a drive,' Hannaford protested. 'It doesn't *have* to be anything. You don't even *have* to see her to sift through her details, and I expect you know that.'

Yes, of course, he said. But here was an opportunity—

'All right, all right. Just mind you bloody well stay in touch.'

So he took Daidre Trahair with him, an arrangement which was easy enough to effect because he began by keeping his word and going to her cottage to repair the window he'd broken. He'd decided that the replacement of such could hardly involve a serious mental workout and as an Oxford graduate – albeit with a degree in history, which hardly applied to matters vitric – he certainly had the brainpower to sort out how the repair needed to be made. The fact that he'd never in his life engaged in a single instance of home improvement did not dissuade him. Surely he was a man to match the mountain of the job. There would be no problem involved.

'This is so good of you, Thomas, but perhaps I ought to arrange for a glazier?' Daidre had said. She sounded doubtful about his intentions to wield glass and putty.

'Nonsense. It's all very straightforward,' he told her.

'Have you . . . I mean, before this?'

'Many times. Other projects, I mean. As far as windows are concerned, I admit to being something of a virgin. Now, let's see what we have.'

What they had was a cottage two hundred years old, possibly older, Daidre wasn't sure. She kept meaning to do a history of the place, she told him, but so far she'd not got round to it. She did know it had begun its life as a fishing hut used by a great house near Alsperyl. That house was vanished, its interior long ago destroyed by fire and its stones eventually carted away by locals for building cottages or defining property lines, but as it had dated to 1723, there was every chance that this little building was of similar age.

This meant, of course, that nothing was straight, including the windows whose frames had been precisely constructed to fit apertures that were themselves without precision. Lynley discovered this to his dismay when he held the glass up to the frame once the debris of the broken window was cleared away. A slight horizontal drop existed, he saw, just enough to make the placement of the glass . . . something of a challenge.

He should have measured both ends, he realised. He felt his neck grow hot with embarrassment.

'Oh dear,' Daidre said. And then quickly, as if her remark spoke of a lack of confidence, 'Well, I'm sure it's only a matter of—'

'Putty,' he said.

'I beg your pardon?'

'This merely calls for a greater amount of putty at one end. There's no real problem.'

'Oh that's good. That's excellent.' She took herself off to the kitchen at once, murmuring obscurely about brewing tea.

He struggled with the project: the putty, the putty knife, the glass, the placement of the glass, the falling rain which he should have damn well known was going to make the entire enterprise impossible. She stayed in the kitchen. She remained there so long that he drew the conclusion she was not only laughing at his ineptitude but also hiding the fact that she herself could have repaired the window with one hand tied behind her back. After all, she was the woman who'd used him as a mop when it came to darts.

When at last she emerged, he'd managed to get the glass in, but it was obvious that someone with more skill than he had was going to have to repair his repair. He admitted as much and apologised. He had to go down to Pengelly Cove, he told her, and if she had the time to accompany him there, he'd make everything up to her with dinner.

'Pengelly Cove? Why?' she asked.

'Police business,' he replied.

'Does DI Hannaford think there are answers in Pengelly Cove? And she's setting you after them? Why not one of her own policemen?' Daidre asked. When he hesitated about giving her an answer, it took her only a moment to understand. 'Ah. So you're not a suspect any longer. Is that wise of DI Hannaford?'

'What?'

'To dismiss you from suspicion because you're a cop? Fairly short-sighted, isn't it?'

'I think she's had trouble coming up with a motive.'

'I see.' Her voice had altered, and he knew she'd put the rest of it together. If he was no longer a suspect, she still was.

He thought she might refuse to go with him, but she didn't, and he was glad. He was seeking a way to get to the truth of who she was and what she was hiding, and with no easy resources at hand to do this, gaining her trust through companionship seemed the best way.

Miracles proved to be his means of access. They'd driven up from the cove and they'd wound through Stowe Wood on their way to the A39 when he asked her if she believed in miracles. At first she frowned at the question. Then she said, 'Oh. The internet printouts you saw. No, I don't, actually. But a friend of mine – a colleague at the zoo, the primate keeper, as a matter of fact – is planning a trip for his parents because *they* believe in miracles and they're in rather bad need of one at the moment. A miracle, that is, not a trip.'

'That's very good of you to help him out.' He glanced over at her. Her skin was blotchy. What was the colleague to her? he wondered. Your lover, your boyfriend, your erstwhile partner? Why this reaction?

'It's an act of friendship,' she said, as if he'd asked those questions. 'Pancreatic cancer. There's no real coming back from that diagnosis, but he's not an old man – Paul says his dad's only fifty-four – and they want to try everything. I think it's futile, but who am I to say? So I told him I'd look for the place with the best statistics. Silly, isn't it?'

'Not necessarily.'

'Well, of course it is, Thomas. How does one apply statistics to a place dominated by mysticism and misplaced belief? If I bathe in these waters, are my chances for a cure better than if I scribbled my request on a scrap of paper and left it at the foot of a marble statue of a saint? What if I kiss the ground in Medjugorje? Or is the best course to stay at home and pray to someone on the fast track for a halo? *They* need miracles to get their sainthood, don't they? What about that route? It would at least save money that we can't afford to spend anyway.' She drew a breath and he glanced her way again. She was leaning against the car door, and her face looked rather pinched. 'Sorry,' she said. 'I do go on. But one so *hates* to see people divorce themselves from their own common sense because a crisis has arisen. If you know what I mean.'

'Yes,' he said evenly. 'As it happens, I do know what you mean.'

She raised her hand to her lips. She had strong-looking hands, sensible hands, a doctor's hands with clipped, clean nails. 'Oh my God. I am *so* bloody sorry. I've done it again. Sometimes, my mouth goes off.'

'It's all right.'

'It *isn't*. You would have done anything to save her. I'm terribly sorry.'

'No. What you said is perfectly true. In a crisis people thrash about, looking for answers, trying to get to a solution. And to them the solution is always what *they* want and not necessarily what's actually best for anyone else.'

'Still, I didn't mean to cause you pain. I don't ever mean that for anyone, for that matter.'

'Thank you.'

From there he couldn't see how to get to her lies except to tell a few of his own, which he preferred not to do. Surely, it was up to Bea Hannaford to question Daidre Trahair about her alleged route from Bristol to Polcare Cove. It was up to Bea Hannaford to reveal to Daidre exactly what the police knew about her putative lunch at a pub, and it was up to Bea Hannaford to decide how to utilise that knowledge to force the vet into an admission of whatever it was that she needed to admit.

He used the pause in their conversation to head in another direction. He said lightly, 'We started with a governess. Have I told you that? Completely nineteenth century. It only lasted till my sister and I rebelled and put frogs into her bed on Guy Fawkes night. And at that time of year, believe me, frogs weren't easy to find.'

'Are you saying you actually *had* a governess as child? Poor Jane Eyre with no Mr Rochester to rescue her from a life of servitude, dining in her bedroom alone because she wasn't upstairs or downstairs either?'

'It wasn't as bad as that. She dined with us. With the family. We'd begun with a nanny but when it was time for school, the governess came on board. This was for my older sister and me. By the time my brother was born – he's ten years younger than I, have I told you? – that had all been put to rest.'

'But it's so charmingly antique.' Lynley could hear the laughter in Daidre's voice.

'Yes, isn't it? But it was that, boarding school, or the village school where we would mix with the local children.'

'With their ghastly Cornish accents,' Daidre noted.

'The very thing. My father was determined that we would follow in his educational footsteps which did not lead to the village school. My mother was equally determined we wouldn't be packed off to boarding school at seven years old—'

'Wise woman.'

'—so their compromise was a governess until we drove her off with her sanity barely intact. At which point, we did go to the local school, which was what we both wanted anyway. My father must have tested our accents every day, however. It seemed so. God forbid that we should ever sound common.'

'He's dead now?'

'Years and years.' Lynley ventured a look. She was studying him and he wondered if she was considering the topic of schooling and wondering why they were talking about it. He said, 'What about you?' and tried to make it casual, noting his discomfort as he did so. In the past, attempting to work a suspect round to a trap had presented no problem for him.

'Both of my parents are hale and hearty.'

'I meant school,' he said.

'Oh. It was all tediously normal, I'm afraid.'

'In Falmouth, then?'

'Yes. Ours wasn't the sort of family that packs its children off to boarding school. I went to school in town, with all the riffraff.'

She was caught. It was the moment at which Lynley would have ordinarily sprung the trap, but he knew he could have missed a school somewhere. She *could* have attended an institution now closed. He found that he wanted to give her the benefit of the doubt. He let matters go. They made the rest of the journey to Pengelly Cove in a companionable fashion. He spoke of how a privileged life had led to police work; she spoke of a passion for animals and how that passion had taken her from rescuing hedgehogs, seabirds, songbirds, and ducks to veterinary school and ultimately to the zoo. The only creature from the animal world that she didn't like, she confessed, was the Canada goose. 'They're taking over the planet,' she declared. 'Well, at least they seem to be taking over England.' Her favourite animal she declared to be the otter: freshwater or sea. She wasn't particular when it came to otters.

In the village of Pengelly Cove, it was a matter of a few minutes in the post office – a single counter in the village's all-purpose shop – to discover that more than one Kerne lived in the vicinity. They were all the progeny of one Eddie Kerne and his wife Ann. Kerne maintained a curiosity that he called Eco-House some five miles out of town. Ann worked at the Curlew Inn although the job appeared to be a sinecure at this point since she was aging badly after a stroke some years ago.

'There's Kernes crawling all over the landscape,' the postmistress told them. She was the lone labourer in the shop, a grey-haired woman of uncertain but clearly advanced years whom they'd come upon in the midst of sewing a tiny button onto a child-size white shirt. She poked her finger with the needle as she worked. She said *bloody hell, damn* and *pardon* and then wiped a spot of blood onto her navy cardigan before going on with, 'You go outside and shout the name Kerne, ten people on the street'll look up and say "What?"' She examined the strength of her repair and bit off the thread.

'I'd no idea,' Lynley said. While Daidre looked at a dismal arrangement of fruit just inside the shop door, he was making a purchase of postcards that he would never use, along with stamps, a local newspaper, and roll of breath mints, which he would. 'The original Kernes had quite a brood, then?'

The postmistress rang up his selections. 'Seven in all, Ann and Eddie produced. And all of them still around save the oldest. That would be Benesek. He's been gone for donkey's years. Are you friends of the Kernes?' The woman looked from Lynley to Daidre. She sounded doubtful.

Lynley produced his police identification. The postmistress's expression altered. *Cops* and *Caution* could not have been written more plainly on her face.

'Ben Kerne's son has been killed,' Lynley told her.

'*Has* he?' she said, a hand moving to her heart. Unconsciously, she cupped her left breast. 'Oh Lord, Now *that's* a very sad bit of news. What happened to him?'

'Did you know Santo Kerne?'

'Wouldn't be anyone round here who doesn't know Santo. They stayed with Eddie and Ann on occasion when he and his sister, that would be Kerra, were little 'uns. Ann'd bring 'em in for sweets or ices. Not Eddie, though. Never Eddie. He doesn't come to the village if he can help it. Hasn't for years.'

'Why?'

'Some'd say too proud. Some'd say too shamed. But not his Ann. Besides, she had to work, hadn't she, so Eddie could have his dream of living green.'

'Shamed about what?' Lynley asked.

She gave a brief smile, but Lynley knew it had nothing to do with friendliness or humour. Rather, it had to do with acknowledging the position each of them was in at the moment: he the professional interlocutor and she the source of information. 'Small village,' she said. 'When things go bad for someone, they c'n stay bad. If you know what I mean.'

It might have been a statement about the Kernes, but it also could have been a statement about her own position, and Lynley understood this. Postmistress and shopkeeper, she'd know a great deal about what was going on in Pengelly Cove. Citizen of the village, she would also know the course of wisdom was to keep her mouth closed about things that did not matter to an outsider.

'You'll have to speak to Ann or Eddie,' she said. 'Ann's got a bit of a speech problem from the stroke she had, but Eddie'll bend your ear, I expect. You speak to Eddie. He'll be at home.'

She gave them directions to the Kerne property, which proved to be a number of acres northeast of Pengelly Cove, a former sheep farm that had been transformed by one family's attempt to live green.

Lynley accessed the land alone, Daidre having decided to remain in the village until his business with the Kernes was completed. He entered the property by means of a disintegrating rusty gate, which stretched across a stony lane but was unlocked. He rattled along for three-quarters of a mile before seeing a dwelling, midway down the hillside. It was a mishmash of architecture characterised by wattle and daub, stone, tiles, timbers, scaffolding, and sheets of heavy plastic. The house could have been from any century. The fact that it was standing at all made it something of a marvel.

Not far beyond it, a waterwheel turned at the base of a sluice, both of them roughly constructed. The former appeared to be a source of electricity, if its connection to a hulking rusty generator was any indication. The latter appeared to be redirecting a woodland stream, so that it provided water to the wheel, to a pond, and then to a series of channels, which served an enormous garden. This was newly planted by the look of it, waiting for the sun of late spring and summer. A huge compost heap made an amorphous lump nearby.

Lynley parked near a stand of old bicycles. Only one of them had inflated tyres, and all of them were rusting to the point of disintegration. There appeared to be no direct route to the front or back door of the house. A path meandered from the bicycles in the vague direction of the scaffolding, but once in its near presence, it transformed to the occasional brick or two lying together amidst trampled weeds. By stepping from one set of bricks to the other, Lynley finally reached what seemed to be the entrance to the house: a door so pitted by weather, rot, and insect life that it seemed hardly credible to assume it was in working order.

It was, however. A few knocks forcefully applied to wood brought him face to face with an old and badly shaven man, one eye clouded by a cataract. He was roughly and somewhat colourfully dressed in old khaki trousers and a lime green cardigan that was buttoned to the throat and drooping round the elbows. He had sandals and orange and brown Argyll socks on his feet. Lynley decided he had to be Eddie Kerne. He produced his identification for the man as he introduced himself.

Kerne looked from it to him. He turned and walked away from the door, heading wordlessly back into the bowels of the house. The door hung open, so Lynley assumed he was meant to follow.

The interior of the house wasn't a great improvement over the exterior. It appeared to be a work long in progress, if the age of the exposed timbers was anything to go by. Walls along the central passage into the place had been taken down to their frames, but there was no scent of freshly replaced wood here. Instead there was a fur of dust upon the timbers, suggesting that a job had been begun years in the past without ever reaching completion.

A workshop was Kerne's destination, and to get to it he led Lynley through a kitchen and a laundry room that featured a washing machine with an old-fashioned wringer and thick cords crisscrossing the ceiling where clothing was hung to dry in inclement weather. A room that had been fashioned more recently than the rest of the house, the workshop was made of unadorned concrete blocks. It was frigid within, like an old-time larder without the marble shelves.

Lynley thought of the term *man-cave*. A workbench, haphazardly hung cupboards, one tall stool, and myriad tools were crammed within the work space, and the overall impression was one of sawdust, oil leakage, paint spills, and general filth. It comprised a somewhat dubious excuse for a bloke to escape the wife and children to tinker on this or that project.

There appeared to be plenty of them on Eddie Kerne's workbench: part of a hoover, two broken lamps, a hairdryer missing its flex, five tea cups wanting handles, a small footstool belching its stuffing. Kerne seemed to be at work on the teacups, for an uncapped tube of glue was adding to the other scents in the room, most of which were associated with the damp. Tuberculosis seemed the likely outcome of an extended stay in such a place, and Kerne had a heavy cough that made Lynley think of poor Keats writing anguished letters to his beloved Fanny.

'Can't tell you nothing,' was Kerne's opening remark. He made it over his shoulder as he picked up one of the teacups and squinted at it, comparing a dismembered handle to the spot at which one had been shattered from the cup. 'Know why you're here, don't I, but I can't tell you nothing.'

'You've been informed about your grandson's death.'

'Phoned, didn't he.' Kerne hawked but mercifully did not spit. 'Gave me the word. That's it.'

'Your son? Ben Kerne? He phoned?'

'The same. Good for that, he was.' The emphasis on *that* indicated what else Kerne deemed his son good for, which was nothing.

'I understand Ben hasn't lived in Pengelly Cove for a number of years,' Lynley said.

'Wouldn't have him round.' Kerne grabbed the tube of glue and applied a good size dollop to both ends of the handle he'd chosen for the teacup. He had a steady hand, which was good for such employment. He had an unfortunate eye, which was bad. The handle clearly belonged to a different cup: the colour wasn't right and the shape even less so. Nonetheless, Kerne held it in place, waiting for some acceptable form of agglutination to occur. 'Sent him off to his uncle in Truro and there he stayed. Had to, didn't he, once she followed him there.'

'She?'

Kerne shot him a look, one eyebrow raised. It was the sort of look that said *You don't know yet?* 'The wife,' he said shortly.

'Ben's wife. The present Mrs Kerne?'

'That'd be her. He went off to escape, and she was hot on his tail. Just like he was hot on hers and into hers, if you'll pardon the expression. She's a piece of work and I want no part of her and no part of him whilst he stays with the scrubber. Source of everything went wrong with him from day one till now, that Dellen Nankervis. And you c'n note that down in your whatever if you want. And note who said it. I'm not shamed of my feelings as every one of them's proved right over the years.' He sounded angry, but the anger seemed to be hiding what had been broken within him.

'They've been together a long time.'

'And now Santo.' Kerne grabbed another teacup and handle. 'You don't think she's at bottom of *that*? You do some sniffing. Sniff here, sniff Truro, sniff there. You'll catch the smell of something nasty and the trail of it's leading directly to her.' He used the glue again, with much the same result: a teacup and handle like distant relatives unacquainted with each other. 'You tell me how,' he said.

'He was abseiling, Mr Kerne. There's a cliff in Polcare Cove—'

'Don't know the spot.'

'—north of Casvelyn, where the family live. It's perhaps a two hundred foot drop. He had a sling fixed on the top of the cliff – we think it was attached to the pillar of a drystone wall – and the sling failed when he began his descent. But it had been tampered with.'

Kerne didn't look at Lynley, but he stopped his work for a moment. His shoulders heaved, then he shook his head forcefully.

'I'm sorry,' Lynley said. 'I understand Santo and his sister spent a great deal of time with you when they were younger.'

'Cos of her.' He spat the words. 'She'd get a new man and bring him home and have him there in her husband's own bed. D'he tell you that? *Anyone* tell you that? No, I expect not. Did that to him when she was a girl and did that to him when she was a woman grown. Up the shoot, as well. More 'n once, she was.'

'Made pregnant by someone else?'

'Doesn't know that I know, does he,' Kerne said. 'But Kerra told me, Mum's got pregnant off someone and she's got to get rid of it, she tells us. Matter of *fact*, she tells me, just like that, and her nothing but ten years old. Ten bloody years and what sort of woman lets her little girl know the filthy business she's making of her life? Dad says she's having a bad patch, she tells us, but I saw her with the estate agent, Grandpa. Or the dance instructor, or the science teacher from the secondary school. What did it matter to her? When she got the itch, it had to be scratched and if Ben didn't scratch it the way she liked and when she wanted, she'd damn well see to it someone else would. So don't tell me she's not the bottom of this when she's the bottom of everything *ever* happened to that boy.'

Not to Santo, Lynley thought. Kerne was speaking of his own son, from a well of bitterness and regret and a father's knowledge that nothing he says or does can change the life-course of a son who's made the wrong decision. In this, Kerne reminded Lynley of his own father and the admonitions he'd given throughout Lynley's childhood about mixing too closely with anyone the older man deemed common. It had done no good, and Lynley had always considered himself richer for the experience.

'I'd no idea,' he said.

'Well, you wouldn't, would you, cos he's not likely to tell anyone. But she gets her claws into him when he's a lad, and from that point on, he doesn't see straight. It's off and on with them for years, and every time me and his mum start thinking he's rid himself of the cow at last and he sees the light and she's out of his hair and out of our hair and he can start to live normal like the rest of us, there she is again, filling his head with rubbish 'bout how she *needs* him and he's the *only* one for her and she's sorry so sorry that she had a shag with someone else but it wasn't her fault cos he wasn't there to take care of her, he wasn't paying her proper attention. And there she is flashing her knickers at him and he can't see what she's like or what she's doing or how he's caught. It leads to ruin, so we send him off. And doesn't she follow? Doesn't the trollop just pack her bags and follow our Ben?' He set the second badly repaired cup to one side. He was breathing jerkily, a liquid sound in his chest. Lynley wondered if the man ever saw a doctor. 'So what we think, me and his mum, is if we say to him You're no son of ours if you don't rid yourself of this bloody cow, he'll do it. He's our boy, he's our oldest, and he's got his brothers and sisters to think about and they love him, they do, and they all get on. We reckon he only needs to be gone a few years anyway, till it all blows over, and then he c'n return to where he belongs, which is with us. Only it doesn't work, does it, because he will *not* shake himself of her. She's under his skin and in his blood and there's an end to the matter.'

'Until what blows over?' Lynley asked.

'Eh?' Kerne turned his head from the workbench to look at Lynley.

'You said your son needed to be gone a few years only, "till it all blows over." I was wondering what.'

Kerne's good eye narrowed. He said, 'You don't talk like a cop. Cops talk like the rest of us, but you got a voice that . . . Where you from?'

Lynley wasn't about to be diverted with a discussion of his roots. 'Mr Kerne, if you know something, and you obviously do, that might be related to the death of your grandson, I need to know what it is.'

He turned back to his bench. 'What happened happened years ago. It's nothing to do with Santo.'

'Please let me decide that.'

Lynley waited. He hoped the old man's sorrow, suppressed but so alive in him, would force him to speak.

Kerne finally did so, although it sounded as if he talked more to himself than to Lynley. 'They're all surfing, and someone gets hurt. Everyone points fingers at everyone else and no one takes the blame. But things get nasty so me and his mum send him off to Truro till he isn't likely to get no more squinty-eyed looks from people.'

'Who got hurt? How?'

Kerne slapped his palm on the bench. 'I'm telling you it's of *no* account. What's it got to do with Santo? It's Santo who's dead, not his dad. Some bloody kid gets himself drunk one night and ends up sleeping it off in one of the sea caves down the cove. So what's that got to do with Santo?'

'Were they surfing at night?' Lynley asked insistently. 'What happened?'

'What d'you *think* bloody happened? They're not surfing, they're partying. And he's partying like the rest of them. He mixes drugs of some sort with whatever else he's swallowed and when the tide comes in, he's done for. Tide sweeps into those caves more fast 'n a man can move cos they're *deep*, aren't they, and everyone knows if you go in, you best know where the sea is and what it's doing cos if you don't, you aren't coming out. Oh you might think you are. You might think what the bloody hell does it matter cos I c'n swim, can't I? But you get battered and turned about and it's *no* one's fault if you're too bloody stupid to listen when you're told not to go down to the cove when conditions are dicey.'

'But that's what happened,' Lynley said.

'That's what happened.'

'To whom?'

'Lad come here for his summers. His family has money and they take the big cliff house. I don't know them but Benesek does. All the young ones do cos they're all down the beach in summers, aren't they? This lad John or James . . . Yes, James, he's the one.'

'The one who drowned?'

'Only his family don't see it that way. They don't want to see it's his own damn fault. They want to blame and they choose our Benesek. Others as well but Benesek's at the bottom of what happened, so they say. They bring the cops from Newquay and they *don't* let up, not the family and not the cops. You know something and you damn well *will* tell us, they say. But he don't know a bleeding *thing*, does he, which is what he says over and over and the cops finally have to believe him, but at that point kid's dad's built a bloody great stupid memorial to the boy and everyone's looking at our Ben dead funny, so we send him to his uncle cos he's got to have a *chance* in life, and he's not bloody likely to have one here.'

'A memorial? Where?'

'Out on the coast somewheres. Up on the cliff. Likely they thought a memorial 'd make people never forget what happened. I don't walk the coast path, so I never saw it, but it'd be what they wanted so it'd stay fresh for people.' He laughed bleakly. 'They'd spend a good sum, prob'ly hoping it'd haunt our Ben till the day he died only they di'n't know he'd never come home so it went for nought.' He picked up another teacup, this one far more broken than its companions, with a large crack running from rim to bottom and a significant chip on each side, right where the drinker would place his lips. It seemed foolish to repair it, but it also seemed clear that Eddie Kerne was going to make the attempt anyway. He said quietly, 'He was a good lad. I wanted the best for him. I *tried* to get the best for him. What dad doesn't want the best for his lad?'

'No dad at all,' Lynley acknowledged.

An exploration of Pengelly Cove didn't take a great deal of time. After the shop and the two main streets, there was either the cove itself, an old church sitting just outside of town, or the Curlew Inn to occupy one's time. Once she was left alone in the village, Daidre began with the church. She reckoned it might be locked as so many country churches were in these days of religious indifference and vandalism, but she was wrong. The place was called St Sithy's, and it was open, sitting in the middle of a graveyard where the remains of this year's daffodils still lined the paths, giving way to columbine.

Within, the church smelled of stones and dust, and the air was cold. There was a light switch just inside the door, and Daidre used this to illuminate a single aisle, a nave, and a collection of multi-coloured ropes that looped down from the bell tower. A roughly hewn granite baptismal font stood to her left, while to her right, an unevenly placed stone aisle led to pulpit and altar. It could have been any church in Cornwall save for one difference: an honesty stall. This comprised a table and shelves just beyond the baptismal font, and upon it used goods were for sale, with a locked wooden box serving as the till.

Daidre went to inspect all this and found no organisation to it but rather a quirky charm. Old lace mats mingled with the odd bit of porcelain; glass beads hung from the necks of well-used stuffed animals. Books eased away from their spines; cake plates and pie tins offered garden tools instead of sweets. There was even a shoebox of historic post cards, which she flipped through to see that most of them were already written upon, stamped, and received long ago. Among them was a depiction of a gipsy caravan, of the sort she hadn't seen in years: rounded on the top and gaily painted, celebrating a peripatetic life. Unexpectedly, her vision blurred when she picked up this card. Unlike so many of the others, nothing had been written upon it.

She wouldn't have done so at another time, but she bought the card. Then she bought two others with messages on them: one from an Auntie Hazel and Uncle Dan that depicted fishing boats in Padstow harbour and another from Binkie and Earl showing a line of surfers standing in front of long Malibu boards that were upright in the Newquay sand. *Fistral Beach* scrolled across their feet, and this was apparently the location where – according to either Binkie or Earl – *It happened here!!!! Wedding's next December!*

With these in her possession, Daidre left the church. But not before she looked at the prayer board, where members of the congregation posted their requests for collective appeals to their mutual deity. Most of these had to do with health, and it came to Daidre how seldom people seemed to consider their God unless physical illness descended upon them or upon someone they loved.

She was not religious but here was an opportunity, she realised, to step up to the spiritual cricket pitch. The God of chance was bowling and she stood in front of the wicket with the bat in her hands. To swing or not and what did it matter? were the issues before her. She'd been searching the internet for miracles, hadn't she? What was this but another arena in which a miracle might be found?

She picked up the biro provided and a slip of paper, which turned out to be part of the back of an old hand-out on which a cake sale was being advertised. She flipped this to the blank side and started to write. She got as far as *Please pray for,* but she found that she could advance no further. She couldn't find the words to shape her request because she wasn't even sure it *was* her request. So to write it and then to post it on a board for prayers proved too monumental a task, one that was coloured by a hypocrisy that she could not bear to live with. She replaced the pen, balled up the slip of paper and shoved it into her pocket. She left the church.

She refused to feel guilt. Anger was easier. It might have been the last refuge of the fearful, but she didn't care. She used terms like *I don't need, I don't care,* and *I certainly don't owe* and these carried her from the church through the graveyard, from the graveyard to the road, and from there along Pengelly Cove's main street. By the time she reached the Curlew Inn, she'd dismissed all matters relating to prayer boards, and she was helped in her efforts by the sight of Ben Kerne entering the Curlew Inn before her.

She'd never met him. She knew of him, of course, and she'd heard him mentioned in the midst of more than one conversation in the last two years. But she might not have recognised him so readily had she not just that morning been looking at his picture in the *Watchman's* article about his enterprise involving the Promontory King George Hotel.

She'd been heading for the Curlew Inn anyway, so she followed Ben Kerne inside. She had the advantage, as they'd never been introduced. Consequently, it was an easy matter to be his distant shadow. She reckoned he was seeking his mother, as she'd overheard the postmistress's conversation with Thomas Lynley about Ann Kerne's employment. It was either that or he wanted a meal, but she thought that was unlikely although it was indeed nearing time for dinner.

Once within, Ben Kerne didn't walk in the direction of the inn's restaurant and it was obvious to Daidre that he was quite familiar with this place. He bypassed a reception desk, and he walked down a gloomy corridor towards a square of light that fell from the window of what seemed to be an illuminated office at the back of the building. He entered without knocking, which suggested that either he was expected or he wished his appearance to come as a surprise and hence to disarm whoever was inside.

Daidre moved quickly to observe, and she was in time to see an older woman rising awkwardly from behind a desk. She was grey of hair and colourless of face, and part of her dragged a bit, and Daidre recalled she'd suffered a stroke. But she'd recovered well enough to be able to hold out one arm to her son. When he strode to her, she embraced him in a grip so fierce that Daidre could see its power to crush his body to hers. They said nothing to each other. Instead they merely expressed and rested within the bond of mother and child.

The sheer force of the moment reached through the office window to Daidre and embraced her as well. But she felt no succour rushing through her. Instead, she felt a grief she could not bear to experience. She turned away.

15

D I Bea Hannaford interrupted her work day because of the dogs. She knew this was a feeble excuse that would have proved embarrassing had someone pointed it out to her, but that fact did not lessen its efficacy. Dogs One, Two and Three needed to be fed, walked, and otherwise attended to, and Bea told herself that only an inexperienced companion to canines actually believed that dogs were sufficient company for each other during the long hours when their humans had to be away. So not too long after her conversation with Tammy Penrule, she checked on the progress among the officers in the incident room – there was little enough of this and damn if Constable McNulty wasn't studying large surfing waves on the screen of Santo Kerne's computer monitor and doing everything but drooling over them – and afterwards she climbed into her car and drove to Holsworthy.

As she suspected would be the case, Dogs One, Two and Three were delighted to see her, and they expressed their enthusiasm with a series of leaps and yelps as they dashed about the back garden seeking something with which they might present her: a plastic garden troll from One, a half-masticated rawhide bone from Two, the tooth-marked handle of a trowel from Three. Bea accepted these offerings with suitable oohs and ahhs, unearthed the dogs' leads from within a pile of boots, gloves, anoraks, and pullovers on a stool just inside the kitchen door, and hooked up the Labradors without further ado. Rather than take them on walkies, however, she led them to the Land Rover. She said, 'In you go,' as she opened the rear of it and when they cooperatively leapt inside, she knew they thought it was – oh frabjous day! – countryside time.

Unfortunately, they were mistaken. It was Raytime. If he wanted Pete, Bea reckoned, Ray should also be willing to take on Pete's animals. True, they were equally her dogs. They were, actually, even *more* her dogs than they were Pete's, but her hours on this case were going to be long, as Ray himself had pointed out, and the dogs needed watching over as much as did Pete. She grabbed the animals' enormous bag of food along with their dishes and other items guaranteed to lead to doggie pleasure, and off they went, with dog tails wagging and dog noses pressed messily to the windows.

When she arrived at Ray's house, Bea had two intentions. The first was to deliver One, Two and Three into the back garden, where Ray's limited time, lack of skill, and general indifference had never produced anything more than a square of cement for a patio and a rectangle of lawn for visual relief. There were no herbaceous borders for the dogs to rip into and nothing else for them to chew up. It was perfect for housing three rambunctious black Labs, and she'd brought fresh rawhide bones, a bag of toys, and an old football to make sure the hours spent here did not result in canine boredom. This left her free to pursue her second intention, which was to get inside Ray's house. She had to deliver the dog food and the dishes, and she would just check Ray was caring for Pete properly. Ray was a man, after all, and what did a man know about nurturing a fourteen-year-old boy? Only a mother knew what was best for her son.

All of this was part of the general excuse, but Bea didn't allow her thoughts to travel there. She told herself she was acting in Pete's best interests, and since she had a key to Ray's house, as he had a key to hers, it was a small matter to insert it in the lock once she had the dogs happily snuffling the lawn in the garden. No one would be any the wiser, she told herself. Ray was at work; Pete was at school. She'd leave the food, the dishes, and a note about the dogs, and she'd be gone after a quick peek in the fridge and through the rubbish to make sure there were no takeaway pizza boxes or Chinese or curry containers among the other debris. And while she was there, she'd have a quick look through Ray's videos to make certain he had nothing questionable that Pete might get into, and if evidence of what she knew was Ray's predilection for curvy blonde females under thirty was anywhere about, she'd get rid of that as well.

She got only a step inside the door when it became clear that her plan was not going to be carried out without some fancy footwork, however. For someone came clattering down the stairs, undoubtedly alerted by the happy barking of dogs in the garden, and in a moment she was face to face with her son.

He said, 'Mum! What're you doing here? Those the Labs?' with an inclination of his head in the general direction of the garden.

Bea saw he was eating, which would have been a mark against his father had Pete's snack consisted of crisps or chips. But he was munching from a plastic bag of apple slices and almonds, of all things, and the bloody child appeared to be actually enjoying them. So she couldn't get riled at that, but she *could* get riled at the fact that he was home at all.

She said, 'Never mind about me. What're *you* doing here? Did your father allow you to stay home from school? Or have you done a bunk? What's going on? Are you alone? Who's upstairs? What the *hell* are you doing?' Bea knew the game: it started with truancy and went on to drugs. Drugs led to breaking and entering. That led to gaol. Thank you so very *much*, Ray Hannaford. Wonderful job. Father of the Year.

Pete took a step backwards. He chewed thoughtfully and watched her.

She said, 'Answer me at once. Why aren't you at school?'

'Half-day,' he said.

'What?'

'Half-day today, Mum. There's a conference or something. I don't know. I mean, I knew but I forgot. Teachers're doing something. I told you about it. I brought home the letter.'

She remembered. He had done, several weeks ago. It was on the calendar. She and Ray had even discussed who'd fetch Pete when the shortened day ended. Still, she wasn't ready to apologise for the suspicious leap she'd made. There remained fertile ground here, and she intended to till it. 'So. How'd you get home?'

'Dad.'

'And where is he now? What're you doing here alone?' She was quite determined. There *had* to be something.

Pete was too astute for her, his parents' own son, possessing their ability to cut to the quick. 'Why're you always so mad at him?'

That wasn't a question Bea was ready to answer. She said, 'Go and say hello to your animals. We'll talk afterwards.'

'Mum . . .'

'You heard me.'

He shook his head: a teenager's black movement that signalled his disgust. But he did as she said although the fact that he went outside without a jacket telegraphed his intention of not remaining long with the Labradors. She had little enough time, so she ran up the stairs.

The house had two bedrooms only. She made for Ray's. She did *not* want her son exposed to photos of Ray's lovers posed suggestively, with backs arched and pert breasts thrust skyward. Nor did she want him looking at their discarded bras and flimsy knickers. If there were coy notes and gushing letters lying about, she intended to find them. If they'd left smears of lipstick playfully on mirrors, she would wipe them off. She intended to absent the premises of *whatever* souvenirs his father kept of his conquests, and she told herself it was in Pete's best interests that she do so.

But there was nothing. Ray had swept the place clean in advance of Pete's arrival. The only evidence of anything was evidence of his fatherhood: on the chest of drawers Pete's most recent school photo in a wooden frame, next to it their daughter Ginny and *her* daughter Audra, and next to that a photo from Christmas: Ray, Bea, their two children, Ginny's husband with Audra in his arms. Playing happy extended family, which they were not. Ray's left arm around her, his right arm around Pete.

She told herself it was better than displaying a photo of Brittany or Courtney or Stacy or Katie or *whoever* she was, coyly smiling on a summer holiday, bikini clad and tan of skin. She checked the wardrobe but found nothing there either and she went on to slide her hands under the pillows in a search for a few bits of lace that would pass for night clothes. Nothing. All to the good. At least the man was being discreet. She turned to the bathroom. Pete was watching from the doorway.

He was no longer chewing. The bag of his carefully prepared guaranteed-to-be-nutritious snack dangled from his fingers. His jaw looked slack.

She said hastily, '*Why* aren't you with the dogs? I swear to you, Pete, if you insist on having pets and you don't take care of them—'

'Why d'you hate him so much?'

The question stopped her dead this time. As did his face, which bore an expression of pained knowledge that no fourteen-year-old boy should carry round on his shoulders. She felt deflated. 'I don't hate him, Pete.'

'Yeah, you do. You always have And see, I don't get it, Mum, 'cause he's a decent bloke, seems to me. He loves you, as well. I can see that, and I don't get why you can't love him back.'

'It isn't as easy as that. There are things . . .' She didn't want to hurt him, and the truth would do that. It would come at this point of his delicate dawning manhood and it would tear it to pieces. She began to move to the bathroom, to complete her futile investigation, but he was in the doorway and he didn't move. She realised how much he'd grown over the last year. He was taller than she now although still not as strong.

'What'd he do?' Pete asked. 'He must've done something 'cause that's why people get divorced, eh?'

'People get divorced for lots of reasons.'

'Did he have a girlfriend or something?'

'Pete, that's really none—'

''Cause he doesn't have one now, if that's what you're looking for. And it can't be drugs or something like that 'cause you know he doesn't take drugs. But is that it? Did he? Or drink or something 'cause there's this bloke at school called Barry and his parents are splitting up 'cause his dad broke the front window in a rage when he was drunk.' Pete seemed to be trying to read her face. 'It was double glazed,' he added.

She smiled in spite of herself. She put her arms around him and pulled him to her. 'Double glazed,' she said. 'Now that's a reason to throw a husband out.' But he jerked away from her.

'Don't make fun.' He went to his room.

'Pete, come on . . .'

He didn't reply. He shut the door instead, leaving her looking at its blank panels. She could have followed, but she went to the bathroom. She couldn't stop herself from a final check even though she knew how ridiculous she was being. Here, like everywhere else, there was nothing. Just Ray's shaving gear, damp towels hanging lopsided from a towel rail, across the tub a sky blue shower curtain drawn to dry. And in the tub, nothing other than a soap tray.

A clothes hamper stood beneath the bathroom window, but she didn't go through this. Instead, she sat on the toilet seat and looked down at the floor. This was not to study the tiles for evidence of sexual malefaction, but to force herself to stop and consider all the ramifications.

She'd done that more than fourteen years ago. What it would mean to stay with a man and have his child when day after day what he so plainly told her he wanted was a termination to the pregnancy. *An abortion, Beatrice. Do it now. We've raised our child. Ginny's left the nest and this is* our *time now. We don't want this pregnancy. It was a stupid miscalculation and we don't have to pay for it the rest of our lives.*

They had plans, he'd told her. They had great and wonderful things to do now Ginny was grown up. Places to go, sights to see. *I don't want this kid. Neither do you. One visit to the clinic and it's behind us.*

It was odd to think now how one's perception of a person could change in an instant. But that was what had happened. She'd looked at Ray with eyes newly born. The passion of the man, and all of it about killing off their own child. She'd just gone cold, right to her core.

While he'd spoken the truth – she *had* given up on the idea of a second pregnancy when it hadn't happened within a reasonable period after Ginny's birth and with Ginny at university and engaged to be married, she and Ray *were* free to plan a future – it wasn't a truth carved in stone for her. It never had been. It had, instead, been a quiet acceptance that had bloomed from initial disappointment. But it wasn't meant to be interpreted as the end all and be all of her life. She couldn't come to terms with how Ray had arrived at the belief that it was.

So she'd told him to leave. She'd done it not to shake him and not to make him see things her way. She'd done it because she'd believed she'd never really known him at all. How *could* she have known him if what he wanted was to end a life they had created from their love for each other?

But to tell Pete all this? To let him know his father had wished to deny him his place on earth? She couldn't do that. Let Ray tell him if he wished.

She went to Pete's room and knocked on the door. He said nothing, but she entered anyway. He was at his computer, on Arsenal's website, surfing through pictures of his idols in a desultory way completely unlike him.

She said, 'Homework, love?'

'Did it already.' And then after a moment, he added, 'I got a hundred per cent mark on the maths exam.'

She went to kiss the top of his head. 'I am so proud of you.'

'That's what Dad says.'

'Because he is. We both are. You're our shining star, Pete.'

'He asked me about those internet blokes you date.'

'That must have made for some good stories,' she said. 'Did you tell him about the bloke Dog Two lifted a leg on?'

Pete snuffled, his form of a forgiving laugh. 'That bloke was a real wanker. Two knew that.'

'Language, Pete,' she murmured. She stood for a moment, looking at the pictures of Arsenal that he continued to click through. 'World Cup soon,' she said unnecessarily. The last thing Pete would be likely to forget was their plans for a World Cup match.

'Yeah,' he breathed. 'C'n we ask Dad if he wants to go with us? He'd like us to ask him.'

It was a simple thing, really. They'd not likely be able to get an extra ticket, so what did it matter if she agreed? 'All right, We'll ask Dad. You can ask him tonight when he gets home.' She smoothed his hair and kissed his head again. 'Are you going to be okay on your own till he gets here, Pete?'

'Mum.' He made it a drawn out and patient multi-syllable word. *I'm not a baby* was the implication.

'Okay, okay. I'm off,' she said.

'See you later. Love you, Mum.'

She went back to Casvelyn. The bakery where Madlyn Angarrack worked was not any great distance from the police station, so she parked in front of that grey squat building and walked to find it. The wind had picked up, blowing in from the northwest and carrying with it a chill reminder of winter. It would be this way until very late spring. That season came slowly, in fits and starts.

A pleasant-looking white building on the corner of Burn View Lane, Casvelyn of Cornwall was opposite St Mevan Down. Bea reached it after a hike up Queen Street, where the pavements still held shoppers and cars still lined the kerb despite the growing lateness of the after-noon. It might have been any shopping precinct in any town in the country, Bea thought as she hurried along it. Here, identifying the shops by name, were the ubiquitous dismal plastic signs above doors and windows. Here, beneath them, were the tired-looking mothers pushing their babies in pushchairs and the uniformed schoolchildren smoking in front of a video arcade.

The bakery was only slightly different from the other shops in that its signage was faux Victorian, fabricated from wood. In its bow-front window, trays held row upon row of the golden pasties for which the bakery was known. Within, two girls were boxing these up for a rangy young man wearing a hoodie with *Outer Bombora, Outa Sight* printed on the back.

One of these girls would be Madlyn Angarrack, Bea reckoned. She decided it had to be the slim, dark-haired one. The other, enormously overweight and spotty faced, did not appear to be someone who might have been the object of an attractive eighteen-year-old boy's lust.

Bea entered and waited till they had served the customer, who relieved them of the last of the day's pasties. Then she asked for Madlyn Angarrack and the dark-haired girl, as Bea had suspected, identified herself. Bea showed her warrant card and asked for a word. Madlyn wiped her hands down the front of her striped pinny, glanced at her companion who looked a bit too interested in the proceedings, and said she'd talk to Bea outside. She fetched an anorak. She didn't, Bea noted, look surprised to have a detective come calling.

When they were out on the pavement, Madlyn said, 'I know that Santo was murdered. Kerra told me. Kerra's his sister.'

'You won't be surprised that we'd want to speak with you, then.'

'I'm not surprised.' Madlyn gave no other information and she waited, as if fully informed of her rights and wanting to see how much Bea knew and what, if anything, Bea suspected.

'You and Santo were involved.'

'Santo,' Madlyn said, 'was my lover.'

'You don't call him your boyfriend?'

Madlyn glanced at the down across the street from them. Marram and sea lime grasses at its edge were being tossed by the growing wind. 'He started out my boyfriend,' she said. 'Boyfriend and girlfriend, that's what we were. Going on dates, hanging about, surfing. That's how I met him. I taught him surfing. But then we became lovers and I call it lovers because that's what we were. Two people in love who expressed their love through sexual intercourse.'

'Baldly stated.' Most girls her age wouldn't have been so direct. Bea wondered why she was.

'Well, that's what it is, isn't it?' Madlyn's words sounded brittle. 'A man's penis entering a woman's vagina. All the befores and all the afters as well, but it really comes down to a penis entering a vagina. So the truth is that Santo put his penis into my vagina and I let him do it. He was my first. I wasn't his. I heard he was dead, I can't say I'm sorry, but I didn't know he'd been murdered. That's actually all I have to tell you.'

'It's not all I need to know, I'm afraid. Look. Would you like to go for a coffee?'

'I'm not off work yet. I shouldn't even be out here talking to you.'

'If you'd like to meet later?'

'I don't know anything. I have nothing to tell you other than what I've already said. And this: Santo broke up with me nearly eight weeks ago and that was that. I don't know why.'

'He gave you no reason?'

'It was time, he said.' She still sounded hard, but for the first time, her composure seemed slightly shaken. 'There was probably someone else that he'd found, but he wouldn't say. Just that it'd been good between us but it was time for it to end. One day things're fine and the next day they're over. That was probably the way he was with everyone but I didn't know it, because I didn't know *him* before he came to my father's shop for a surfboard and wanted lessons.' She turned her gaze to Bea. 'Is that all? I don't know anything else.'

'I've been told that Santo was embarking on something irregular,' Bea said. 'That was the word used. Irregular. I'm wondering if you know what that was.'

She frowned. 'What do you mean, "irregular"?'

'He told a friend of his, a girl here in town—'

'That would be Tammy Penrule, I expect. She didn't interest him in the other way girls interested him. If you've seen her, you'll know why.'

'—that he'd met someone, but that the situation was irregular. That was his word. Perhaps he meant unusual or abnormal? We don't know. But he asked her for advice. Should he tell everyone involved? he asked her.'

Madlyn gave a harsh laugh. 'Well, whatever it was, he didn't tell me. But he was . . .' She stopped. Her eyes were unnaturally bright. She coughed and gave a little stamp with one foot. 'Santo was Santo. I loved him then I hated him. I expect he just met someone else he wanted to fuck. He liked to fuck, you see. He definitely liked to fuck.'

'But if it was "irregular", why would that be?'

'I don't bloody know and I don't bloody care. Maybe he had two girls at once. Maybe he had a girl and another bloke. Maybe he'd decided to fuck his own mum. I don't *know.*'

With that, she was gone, inside the shop and shedding her anorak. Her face was hard, but Bea had a feeling the girl knew far more than she was saying.

For the moment, however, there was nothing else to gain by standing there on the pavement, other than giving in to the temptation to purchase a croissant, which would certainly do her no good. So she went back to the police station, where she found the TAG officers – those thorns in her side – reporting their actions to Sergeant Collins who was dutifully noting their completion on the china board.

'Where are we?' Bea asked him.

'We've got two cars noticed in the area,' Collins said. 'A Defender and a RAV4.'

'In the vicinity of the cliff? Near Santo's car? Where?'

'One of them was in Alsperyl, this is to the north of Polcare Cove, but there's access to the cliff. It's a bit of a walk across a paddock, but easy enough to get to the cove once you reach the coastal path. That vehicle would be the Defender. The RAV4 was just south of Polcare, up above Buck's Haven.'

'Which is?'

'Surfing spot. So that *might* have been why the car was there.'

'Why "might"?'

'Wasn't a good day for surfing in that spot—'

'Waves were better at Widemouth Bay.' Constable McNulty put this in from Santo's computer. Bea made a mental note to see what he'd been up to in the past few hours.

'Whatever,' Collins said. 'We've got the DVLA running all the Defenders and all the RAV4s from the area.'

'You have number plates?' Bea asked, feeling a frisson of excitement that was soon enough squashed.

'No luck on that,' Collins said. 'But I reckon there are few enough Defenders down here, so we might have some joy seeing a familiar name on the list of owners. Same for the RAV4, although we can expect quite a number of them. We'll have to go through the list and look for a name.'

All fingerprints from all relevant parties had been taken at this point, Collins continued, and all of them were being run through the PNC and being compared to the prints from Santo Kerne's vehicle as well. Background checks were continuing. So far the only person of interest was one William Mendick, the bloke mentioned by Jago Reeth. He had a record, Collins informed her.

'Nice one,' Bea said. 'What sort of record?'

'Went down for assault with intent in Plymouth, and he did time for it. He's only just got out of open prison.'

'His victim?'

'Some young hooligan called Conrad Nelson he got into a brawl with. Ended up paralysed, he did, and Mendick denied the whole thing . . . or at least he put it down to drink and asked for mercy. Both of them were drunk, he claimed. But Mendick's got a real problem with it. *His* booze-ups led to regular fights in Plymouth, and part of his parole is attendance at AA meetings.'

'Can we check on that?'

'Don't see how. Unless he's turning in some sort of document to his parole officer, proving he was there. But what would that mean, anyway? He could be going to meetings regular as a saint and bluffing his way through the whole programme, if you know what I mean.'

She did. But Will Mendick with a drinking problem and Will Mendick with an assault conviction put a useful wrinkle in the blanket. She thought about Santo Kerne's black eye. She wandered over to Constable McNulty's station. She saw on the monitor of Santo Kerne's computer exactly what she thought she'd see: an enormous wave and a surfer riding it.

Damn the man. 'Constable, *what* the bloody hell are you doing?'

'Jay Moriarty,' McNulty said obscurely.

'What?'

'That's Jay Moriarty,' with a nod at the screen. 'He was sixteen years old at the time, guv. Can you credit that? They said that wave measured fifty feet.'

'Constable.' Bea did her best to restrain herself. 'Does the term "living on borrowed time" meaning anything to you?'

'It was Maverick's. Northern California.'

'Your knowledge astounds me.'

Her sarcasm went unnoticed. 'Oh, I don't know much. I try to follow it, but who really has time, what with the little one at home? But see, the thing is, guv, this picture of Jay Moriarty was taken the same week that—'

'Constable!'

He blinked. 'Guv?'

'Get off that site and get back to work. And if I see you looking at one more wave on that monitor, I'll boot you from here to next week. You are supposed to be looking for information relevant to Santo Kerne's death. You are not supposed to be using your time to channel his interests. Is that clear?'

'But the thing is that that bloke Mark Foo—'

'*Do* you understand me, Constable?' She wanted to grab him by the ears.

'Yes. But there's more to this than his email, guv. Santo Kerne went to these sites and I've gone to these sites, so it stands to reason that anyone—'

'Yes. I see. Anyone *else* could go to these sites. Thank you very much. I'll go to them myself on my *own* time and read up all about Jay Moriarty, Mark Boo, and everyone else.'

'Mark Foo,' he said. 'Not Mark Boo.'

'God *damn* it, McNulty.'

'Guv?' From the doorway, Collins spoke. He nodded towards the corridor.

She said, 'What? *What*, Sergeant?'

'Someone to see you below. A . . . lady?' He seemed doubtful of the term.

Bea swore beneath her breath. She said to McNulty, 'Get back to work and *stay* back at work,' before pushing past Collins and clattering down the stairs.

The lady in question was in reception, and when she saw her, Bea assumed it was the woman's appearance that had made Collins sound hesitant. She was in the process of reading the notice board, which gave Bea a moment to assess her. A yellow fisherman's hat sat on her head although it wasn't raining any longer, and she wore a lint-speckled donkey jacket over mud-coloured corduroy trousers. She had bright red trainers – they appeared to be high-tops – on her feet. She didn't look like anyone who would have information. Instead, she looked like an orphan of the storm.

'Yes?' Bea was in a hurry and she made no attempt to sound otherwise. 'I'm DI Hannaford. How may I help you?'

The woman turned and extended her hand. When she spoke, she showed a chipped front tooth. 'DS Barbara Havers,' she said. 'New Scotland Yard.'

Cadan pumped his bicycle like a lost soul fleeing from Lucifer, which was no mean feat considering it was a trick bike not meant for maniacal street riding. Pooh clung to his shoulder and squawked in protest, occasionally shrieking, 'Hang bells from the lamppost!', a non sequitur he used only on occasions when wishing to indicate the level of his concern. The bird had good reason for voicing his trepidation, for it was the time of day when people were returning from some of the more distant places of employment, so the streets were crowded. This was particularly true of Belle Vue, which was part of the main route through town. It was a one-way thoroughfare, and Cadan knew he ought to have gone with the flow of traffic round the circular route long ago laid out to relieve congestion. But that would have meant riding out of his way for part of the journey, and he was in too much of a hurry to do that.

So he went against the flow of traffic, enduring horns honking and a few shouts of protest. They were small enough concerns to him, in comparison with his need for escape.

The truth of the matter was that Dellen Kerne – despite her age, which wasn't really all *that* old, was it? – represented exactly the kind of sexual encounter that Cadan always looked for: hot, brief, urgent and done with, with no regrets and no expectations. But the truth of the matter *also* was that Cadan was not an idiot. Bonking the wife of the boss? In the family kitchen? Nothing like putting a tombstone on one's grave.

Not that bonking in the kitchen per se was what Dellen Kerne had had in mind, as things developed. She'd released herself from their embrace, one that had left Cadan's head swimming and all the important parts of his body rushing with blood, and continued the sensuous dance she'd begun as the Latin music from the radio played on. Within a moment, though, she was back at him. She shimmied against him and walked her fingers up his chest. From there, it required no complicated set of dance steps for them to be hip to hip and groin to groin, and the rhythm of the music provided a primal beat whose intentions were impossible to ignore.

It was the sort of moment when conscious thought absents itself. The big brain stops functioning and the little brain, knowing only the most atavistic of motives, takes over until satisfaction is achieved. So when Dellen's hand slithered down his chest and her fingers found the most sensitive part of him, he was ready to take her on the kitchen floor if she was ready to allow him the pleasure.

He grabbed her arse with one hand, her breast with the other, caught a nipple tightly between his fingers, and hungrily shoved his tongue into her mouth. This, it seemed, was the signal she needed. She backed away with a breathless laugh and said, 'Not *here*, silly boy. You know where the beach huts are, don't you?'

He said stupidly, 'Beach huts?' because, of course, the big brain was not functioning at all at this point and the little brain knew and cared nothing of huts, beach or otherwise.

'Darling, the *beach* huts,' Dellen said. 'Down below. Just above the beach. Here. Here's a key,' which she took from a chain she wore deep between her sumptuous breasts. Had she had it on yesterday? Cadan hadn't noticed, and he didn't want to think of the implications behind this being a new piece of wearing apparel. 'I can be there in ten minutes,' she said. 'Can you?' She kissed him as she pressed the key into his palm. In case he'd forgotten what they were about, she reminded him with her fingers.

When she released him, he looked at the key he was holding. He tried to clear his head. He looked at her. Then he looked at the doorway. Kerra was standing there, watching them.

'Disturbing you, am I?' Kerra's face was a sheet. Two spots of colour appeared on her cheeks.

Dellen trilled a laugh. 'Oh my God,' she said. 'It's that damn music. It *always* gets into a young man's blood. Cadan, you *naughty* boy. Getting me all silly like that. Goodness I'm old enough to be your mum.' She turned the radio off. The silence that followed was like an explosion.

Cadan was mute. There was simply nothing in his brain, at least not in the big brain. The little brain hadn't yet caught up to what was happening, and between big and little existed a maw the size of the English Channel, into which he wished he could fall and drown. He stared at Kerra, knowing if he turned his body her way she would see the huge betraying bulge in his trousers and, what was worse, the damp spot he could feel himself. Beyond that, he was struck dumb by the horror of what she might say to her father about all this. Beyond that, there was the need to escape.

He did so. Later, he would not be able to say how he managed it, but he grabbed Pooh from the back of the chair he'd been perched upon and he tore out of the kitchen like Mercury on meth, leaving behind their voices – Kerra's mostly, and her tone was not pleasant – and hauling his arse down three flights of stairs and into the afternoon. He made for his bicycle and he took off at a gallop, pushing it till he reached the speed he wanted. Then he mounted and away they went, with him pumping like a bloke who'd recently seen the headless horseman and Pooh just trying to stay on his shoulder.

He thought little else than *oh no oh no bloody hell damn fuck wanking idiot.* He wasn't sure what to do or where to go, and by rote, it seemed, his furiously working legs and arms guided the bike towards Binner Down. He needed advice and he needed it quickly. LiquidEarth was the place where he could get it.

He made the turn into Vicarage Road and from there he trundled onto Arundel Lane. It was smooth going and he made good time, but Pooh protested mightily when they got to the erstwhile air field with its ruts and potholes. It couldn't be helped. Cadan told the parrot to hold on tight and in less than two minutes, he was dumping the bike on the old concrete ramp just outside the hut where his father made surfboards.

Inside the door, he set Pooh on top of the till behind the counter. He said, 'Do *not* dump, mate,' and he went inside the workshop. There, he found the one person he was looking for. Not his father, who would have undoubtedly greeted Cadan's forthcoming tale with a lecture about his lifelong stupidity. Instead, he found Jago, who was engaged in the delicate final process of sanding the rough edges of fibreglass and resin from the rails of a swallowtail board.

Jago looked up as Cadan stumbled into the finishing room. He seemed to take a reading of Cadan's state at once because there was music coming from the dusty radio that sat on an equally dusty shelf just beyond the sawhorses holding the board, and Jago went to turn this off. He removed his glasses and wiped them on the thigh of his white boiler suit to little effect.

'What's happened, Cade? Where's your dad? He's all right? Where's Madlyn?' His left hand moved spasmodically.

Cadan said, 'No. No. I don't know.' What he meant was that he assumed everything was fine with his father and with his sister, but the truth was that he had no clue. He hadn't seen Madlyn since that morning, and he hadn't seen his father at all. He didn't *want* to consider what that latter detail might mean because his head was already bursting. He finally said, 'Okay, I s'pose. I expect Madlyn went to work.'

'Good.' Jago gave a sharp nod. He went back to the surfboard. He picked up the sandpaper, but before he applied it, he ran his fingertips along the rails. He said, 'You come in here like the devil's chasing you.'

'Not far from the truth. You got a minute?'

Jago nodded. 'Always. Hope you know that.'

Cadan felt as if someone had kindly withdrawn his thumb from the dyke, offering to take over the rescue of the lowlands in his stead. The story spilled out. His father's disgust, Cadan's dreams of the X Games, Adventures Unlimited, Kerra Kerne, Ben Kerne, Alan Cheston, and Dellen. Last of all, Dellen. It was all a jumble to which Jago listened patiently. He sanded the surfboard's rails slowly, nodding as Cadan went from point to point.

At the end he homed in on what they both knew was the salient detail: Cadan Angarrack caught in a delicto that was just about as flagrante as it could have been, short of the two of them – himself and Dellen Kerne – having been caught writing and moaning on the kitchen floor. Jago said, 'Sounds like mother, like son to me. Didn't think of that when she played with you, Cade?'

'I didn't *know* her, see. I thought something was a bit off when she came upon me yesterday, but I didn't think . . . Jago, she could be my *mum.*'

'Not bloody likely. For her faults, your mum stuck to her own kind, yes?'

'What d' you mean?'

'Way Madlyn tells it – and, mind, she doesn't think much of your mum – Wenna Angarrack with her list of surnames always sticks to her own age group. From what you say, this one doesn't appear to mind what age she's doing it with. 'Spect you had signs when you met her.'

'She did ask me what I did for sex,' Cadan admitted.

'And you didn't think that was a bit off, Cade? Woman her age making enquiries like that? She was readying you.'

Cadan shifted his uneasy gaze off Jago's shrewd one. Above the radio hung a poster, a Hawaiian girl inexplicably wearing nothing but a lei round her neck and a wreath of palm leaves on her head as she surfed a good size wave with casual skill. It came to Cadan as he looked upon her that some people were born with amazing confidence, and he was not one of those people.

'You knew what was going on,' Jago said. ''S'pose you thought you got yourself a three-way girl with no asking, eh? Or, worst case, a bit of how's yer father. Either way, you're happy.' He shook his head. 'Blokes your age never can think outside of the envelope, and we both know what that envelope is.'

'She offered me lunch,' Cadan said in his own defence.

Jago laughed. 'Bet she did. And she was planning to be your pudding.' He set down his sandpaper and leaned against the board. 'Girl like that's trouble, Cade. You got to know how to read her from the start. She gets a boy by the short ones by giving him a taste, eh? A little bit now, and a little bit then till he's got the whole. Then it's on again, off again till he don't know which part of her's the part to believe in so he believes in it all. She makes him feel ways he's never felt, and he thinks no one can make him feel the same. That's how it works. Best learn from this and let it go.'

'But I need the *job*, Jago.'

Jago pointed at him with his trembling hand. 'What you don't need is that family. Look what hooking into the Kernes did to Madlyn. She better off for spreading her legs for that boy of theirs?'

'But you let them use your—'

'Course I did. When I saw I couldn't talk her out of letting Santo in her knickers, least I could do was my best to make certain they were safe about it, so I said for them to go to Sea Dreams. But did that help matters? Made them worse. Santo used her up and spat her out. Only good was that at least the girl had someone to talk to who didn't shout the I-told-you-so's at her.'

'Reckon you wanted to, though.'

'Bloody right I wanted to. But what was done was done, so what was the point? Question is, Cade, are you going to go the way of Madlyn?'

'There're obvious differences. And anyway, the job—'

'Sod the job! Make peace with your dad. Come back here. We got the work. We got too much work, with the season nearly here. You can do it well enough if you've a mind to.' Jago returned to his own employment but before he began, he made a final comment. 'One of you two's going to have to swallow pride, Cade. He took your car keys and your driving licence cos he had a reason. To keep you alive. Not every father makes that kind of effort. Not every father makes it and succeeds. Best you start thinking of that, my boy.'

'You're disgusting,' Kerra said to her mother. Her voice was trembling. This somehow made things seem even worse to her. Trembling might suggest to Dellen that her daughter was feeling fear, embarrassment, or, what was truly pathetic, a form of dismay when all the time what Kerra was feeling was rage. Seething, white hot, utterly pure and all of it directed towards the woman before her. She was feeling far more of it than she'd felt towards Dellen in years, and she wouldn't have believed that possible. 'You're disgusting,' she repeated. 'Do you hear me, Mum?'

Dellen said in turn, 'And what the hell do you think you are, coming upon me like a little spy? Are you proud of yourself?'

'You can turn this on *me*?'

'Yes, I can. You sneak round here like a copper's nark and don't think I don't know it. You've been watching me for years and reporting back to your father and *anyone* else who'd listen.'

'You absolute bitch,' Kerra said, more in wonder than in anger. 'You absolute, *unbelievable* bitch.'

'Hurts a bit to hear the truth, doesn't it? So hear some more. You caught your mum off guard and now you've got the chance you've waited for to do her in. You see what you want to see, Kerra, instead of what's right in front of your nose.'

'Which is?'

'The truth. He got carried away by the music. You saw for yourself I was pushing him away. He's a randy little worm and he saw an opportunity. And *that's* what happened. So get out of here with your nasty speculation and find something useful to do with your time.' Dellen moved her head in a way that tossed her hair at the same time as it dismissed whatever conclusions her daughter may have drawn. Then, despite her previous words, she apparently decided she'd not said enough, for she went on with, 'I offered him *lunch*. There can't be a problem with that, can there? Surely that can't *possibly* meet with your disapproval. I turned on the radio. Well, what else was I supposed to do? It was easier than making conversation with a boy that I barely know. He took the music as some sort of sign. It was sexy, the way Latin music always is, and he got caught up in—'

'Shut *up*,' Kerra said. 'We both know what you had in mind, so don't make it worse by pretending poor little Cadan tried to seduce you.'

'Is that his name? Cadan?'

'Stop it!' Kerra entered the kitchen. She advanced on her mother. Dellen, she saw, had taken care with her make-up in that way she had: her lips looking fuller, her violet eyes large, everything highlighted like a catwalk model, which was idiotic because the last thing Dellen Kerne had was a catwalk body. But even that she'd managed to make look seductive because what she had always known was that men of every age respond to the voluptuous. Today she was red of scarf, red of shoes, and red of belt, which was little enough colour from which to make a judgement, but her jersey was unseasonably thin and its neck plunged downward displaying inches of cleavage and her trousers hugged her hips tightly. And from all of that, Kerra could judge and conclude, which she did with an alacrity born of years of experience. 'I saw everything, Mum. And you're a pig. You're a cow. You're a fucking minge bag. You're even *worse*. Santo's dead and even *that* doesn't stop you. It gives you an excuse. Poor little me . . . I'm suffering so . . . But a nice fuck'll take my mind off it all. Is that what you're telling yourself, Mum?'

Dellen had backed away as Kerra advanced. She stood butted up against the worktop. Then, on a hair, her mood altered. Tears rushed to her eyes. 'Please,' she said. 'Kerra. You can see . . . Obviously, I'm not myself. You *know* there're times . . . You know, Kerra. And it doesn't mean—'

'Don't you bloody say it!' Kerra cried. 'You've made excuses for years, and I'm finished with hearing "Your mum's got problems" because you know what, Mum? We all have problems. And mine is standing here in this kitchen, looking at me like a lamb that's heading for the axe. All innocence and pain and "Look at what I've had to suffer" when all she's done is make *us* suffer. Dad, me, Santo. All of us. And now Santo's dead, which is probably down to you as well. You make me sick.'

'How can you say . . . ? He was my son.' Dellen began to weep. No crocodile tears, these, but the real thing. 'Santo,' she cried. 'My precious.'

'Your *precious*? Don't even start. Alive, he was nothing to you and neither was I. We got in your way. But dead, Santo has real value. Because now you can point to his death and say exactly what you've just been saying. "It's because of Santo. It's because of this tragedy that's befallen our family." But it's *not* the reason and it never will be although it's perfect for an excuse.'

'Don't talk to me like that! You don't know what I—'

'What? I don't know what you suffer? I don't know what you've suffered for years? Is that it? Because all of this has been about your suffering? Is that what Stuart Mahler was about? About your terrible, horrible agonising suffering that no one can ever understand but you?'

'Stop this, Kerra. Please. You must stop.'

'I saw it. You didn't know that, did you? My first boyfriend and I was thirteen years old and there you were, standing in front of him, with your top lowered and your bra removed and—'

'No! No! That *never* happened!'

'In the garden, Mum. Faded from your memory, has it, with all the current *tragedy* you're living through?' Kerra felt on fire. So much energy was rushing through her limbs that she didn't know if she could contain it all. She wanted to scream and kick holes in the walls. 'Let me bloody refresh you, all right?'

'I don't want to hear!'

'Stuart Mahler, Mum. He was fourteen. He came round. It was summer and we listened to music in the gazebo. We kissed a bit. We didn't even use our tongues because we were so bleeding innocent we didn't know what we were doing. I went into the house for drinks and biscuits because the day was hot and we were sweaty and that was all the time you needed. Does this sound at *all* familiar to you?'

'Please. Kerra.'

'No. Please Dellen. That was the game. Dellen did as she pleased, and she still does. And the rest of us pussyfoot all round her because we're so afraid we'll set her off again.'

'I'm not responsible. You *know* that. There are things I can't . . .'

Dellen turned away, sobbing. She bent across the work top, her arms extended. Her posture suggested submission and penitence. Her daughter could do what she would with her. Buckle of belt, cat o' nine tails, scourge, whip. What did it matter? Punish me, punish me, make me suffer for my sins.

But Kerra knew better than to believe at this point. Too much water had flowed beneath the arc of this endless bridge, and all of it had always gone in the same direction.

'Don't even try that,' she told her mother.

'I am who I am,' Dellen said, weeping.

'So try being someone else.'

Daidre tried to pick up the bill for dinner, but this was something Lynley wouldn't allow. It was not only that a gentleman never let a lady pay for a meal that they had enjoyed together, he told her. It was also that he'd dined at her home on the previous night and if they wanted to keep matters on an even keel, then it was his turn to provide a meal for her. And even if she felt otherwise, he could hardly ask her to pay for what she'd barely consumed at the Curlew Inn.

'I *am* sorry about the meal,' he told her.

'You can hardly be blamed for my choice, Thomas. I should have known better than to order something referred to as "the Vegetarian Surprise".'

She'd wrinkled her nose and chuckled when she'd seen it, and he could hardly blame her. What had arrived for her consumption was something green baked into a loaf, with a side dish of rice and vegetables boiled so thoroughly that they were nearly drained of colour. She'd gamely washed down the rice and the medley of veg with the Curlew Inn's best wine – an indifferent Chablis insufficiently cooled – but she'd given up after a few bites of the loaf. She'd cheerfully pronounced herself 'Quite full. It's amazingly rich, a bit like cheesecake,' and she'd looked astonished that he hadn't believed her. When he'd declared he intended to take her out for a proper dinner, she told him it would probably have to be in Bristol because there wasn't likely to be a place in Cornwall that would meet with her gastronomic standards. 'I'm a troublesome wretch when it comes to food. I should broaden my horizons to fish, but somehow I can't get my mind round it.'

They left the Curlew Inn and went out into the evening, where darkness was falling. She remarked upon the change in seasons, the subtle manner in which daylight began extending itself from winter solstice onward. She said she never really understood why people hated winter so much as she herself found it a most comforting season. 'It leads directly to renewal,' she said. 'I like that about it. It always suggests forgiveness to me.'

'Are you in need of forgiveness?' They were walking in the direction of Lynley's hired car, which he'd left at the junction of the high street and the lane leading down to the beach. He watched her in the fading light, waiting to read something revealing in her answer.

'We all are in some way or another, aren't we?' Using this as a logical segue, she told him then of what she'd seen: Ben Kerne in the arms of a woman whom she'd assumed to be his mother. She confessed that she'd inquired on the matter: It was indeed Ann Kerne he'd visited. 'I don't know if it was forgiveness, of course,' she concluded. 'But it was definitely emotional and they shared the feeling.'

In exchange and because it seemed only fair, Lynley told her a bit about his visit to Ben Kerne's father. Not everything because she was, after all, not above suspicion and despite his liking for the woman he knew better than to forget that fact. So what he told her was limited to Eddie Kerne's aversion for his son's wife. 'It seems he sees Mrs Kerne as the root of what's gone wrong in Ben's life.'

'Including Santo's death?'

'I expect he'd have it that way as well.'

Because of his conversation with the older Kerne, Lynley wanted to explore the sea caves. So when they were in the car and he'd started the engine, he drove not out of town as logic would dictate, but rather down the steep lane in the direction of the cove below them. He said, 'There's something I want to see. If you prefer to wait in the car . . . ?'

'No. I'd like to come.' She smiled and added, 'I've never actually observed a detective at work.'

'This will be less detecting than satisfying my curiosity.'

'Most of the time, I suspect it's the same thing.'

Lynley couldn't disagree. In the carpark, he pulled parallel to a low sea wall that looked to be of recent construction. As did the granite lifeboat shed, which sat nearby with a rescue torpedo buoy available next to it. He got out and looked at the cliffs that formed a horseshoe round the cove. They were high, with outcroppings like broken teeth, and a fall from them would likely prove fatal. Atop them sat houses and cottages, beaming lights in the gloom. At the far end of the southernmost cliff, the largest house of all sprawled in an impressive declaration of someone's wealth.

Daidre came round the car to join him. 'What are we here to see?' She drew her coat more closely round her body. A brisk wind blew.

'Caves,' he said.

'Are there caves here? Where?'

'On the water side of the cliffs. You can access them at low tide but when the water's in, they're at least partially submerged.'

She mounted the wall and gave a look towards the sea. 'I'm hopeless at this, which is pathetic for someone who spends part of her time on the coast. I'd say it's either going out or coming in, but in either case, it doesn't make a lot of difference because it's a fairly good distance from shore.' Then with a look at him, 'Is that at all helpful?'

'Barely,' he said.

'That's what I reckoned.' She hopped down on the sea side of the wall. He followed her.

Like so many beaches in Cornwall, this one began with boulders tumbled one upon the other near to the carpark. These were mostly granite, with lava mixed in, and the light streaks upon them gave mute testimony to the unimaginable former liquid nature of something now solid. Lynley extended his hand to help Daidre over them. Together they clambered carefully till they reached the sand.

'On its way out,' he told her. 'That would be my first piece of detection.'

She looked round as if to understand how he'd reached this conclusion. 'Oh yes, I see,' she finally said. 'No footprints, but that could be because of the weather, couldn't it? A bad time of year for the beach.'

'Yes. But look at the pools of water at the base of the cliffs.'

'Wouldn't they always be there?'

'I daresay. Especially this time of year. But the rocks that back them wouldn't be wet, and they are. The lights from the houses are glittering off them.'

'Very impressive,' she said.

'Elementary,' was his rejoinder.

They made their way across the sand. It was quite soft, telling Lynley they would need to take care. Quicksand wasn't unheard of on the coast, especially in locations like this one, where the sea ebbed a considerable distance.

The cove broadened some one hundred yards from the boulders.

At this point, when the tide was out, a grand beach stretched in both directions. They turned landward when the cliffs were entirely behind them. It was an easy matter, then, to see the caves.

The cliffs facing the water were cratered with them, darker cavities against dark stone, like dusted fingerprints, and two of them of enormous size. Lynley said, 'Ah,' and Daidre said, 'I'd no idea,' and together they approached the largest, a cavern at the base of the cliff upon which the biggest house was built.

The cave's opening looked to be some thirty feet high, narrow and roughly shaped like a keyhole turned on its head, with a threshold of slate that was streaked with quartz. It was gloomy within, but not altogether dark, for some distance at the rear of the cave dim light filtered from a roughly formed chimney that geological action had aeons ago produced in the cliff. Still, it was difficult to make out the walls until Daidre produced a book of matches from her shoulder bag and said to Lynley with an embarrassed shrug, 'Sorry. Girl guides. I've a Swiss army knife as well, if you need it. Plasters, too.'

'That's comforting,' he told her. 'At least one of us has come prepared.'

A match's light showed them at first how deeply the cave was affected at high water, for hundreds of thousands of molluscs the size of drawing pins clung to the rough, richly veined stone walls, making them rougher still to a height of at least eight feet. Mussels formed black bouquets beneath them, and interspersed between these bouquets, multicoloured shellfish scalloped against the walls.

When the match burned low, Lynley lit another. He and Daidre worked their way farther in, picking through stones as the cave's floor gained slightly in elevation, a feature that would have allowed the water to recede with the ebbing tide. They came upon one shallow alcove, then another, where the sound of dripping water was rhythmic and incessant. The scent within was utterly primeval. Here, one could easily imagine how all life had actually come from the sea.

'It's rather wonderful, isn't it?' Daidre spoke in a hushed voice.

Lynley didn't reply. He'd been thinking of the myriad uses a spot like this had seen over the centuries. Everything from smugglers' cache to lovers' place of assignation. From children's games of marauding pirates to shelter from sudden rainfall. But to use the cave for anything at all, one had to understand the tide because to remain in ignorance of the sea's acts of governance was to court certain death.

He imagined a boy being caught in here, in this cave or in another just like it. Drunk, drugged, possibly unconscious, and if not unconscious, then sleeping it off. It didn't matter at the end of the day. If he'd been in darkness and deep within this place when the tide swept in, he would likely not have known which way to go to attempt an escape.

'Thomas?'

The match flickered as he turned to Daidre Trahair. The light cast a glow against her skin. A piece of her hair had come loose from the slide she used to hold it back, and this fell to her cheek, curving into her lips. Without thinking, he brushed it away from her mouth. Her eyes, unusually brown like his own, seemed to darken.

It came to him suddenly what a moment such as this one meant. The cave, the weak light, the man and the woman in close proximity. Not a betrayal, but an affirmation. The knowledge that somehow life had to go on.

The match burnt to his fingers. He dropped it hastily. The instant passed and he thought of Helen. He felt a searing within him because he couldn't remember what this moment clearly demanded that he remember: when had he first kissed Helen?

He couldn't recall and, worse, he didn't know *why* he couldn't recall. They'd known each other for years before their marriage, for he'd met her when she'd come to Cornwall in the company of his closest friend during one holiday or another from university. He may have kissed her then, a light touch on the lips in farewell at the end of that visit, a lovely-to-have-met-you gesture that meant nothing at the time but now might mean everything. For it came to him suddenly that it was essential he recall every instance of Helen in his life. It was the only way he could keep her with him and fight the void. And that was the point: to fight the void. If he floated into it, he knew he'd be lost.

He said to Daidre Trahair, who was only a silhouette in the gloom, 'We should go. Can you lead us out?'

'Of course, it shouldn't be difficult.'

She found her way with assurance, one hand moving lightly along the tops of the molluscs on the wall. He followed her, his heart pulsing behind his eyes. He believed he ought to say something about the moment that had passed between them, to explain himself in some way to Daidre. But he had no words and even if he had possessed the language necessary to communicate the extent of his grief and his loss, they were not necessary. For she was the one to break the silence, and she did so when they emerged from the cave and began to make their way back to the car.

'Thomas, tell me about your wife,' she said.

'What would you like to know?'

A kind smile touched her lips. 'Whatever you wish to tell me,' she said.

16

Lynley found himself humming in the shower the next morning. The water coursed through his hair and down his back, and he was in the middle of the waltz from Tchaikovsky's *The Sleeping Beauty* before he stopped abruptly and realised what he was doing. He felt swept up in guilt, but it only lasted a moment. What came on its heels was a memory of Helen, the first one he'd had since her death that made him smile. She'd been completely hopeless about music, aside from a single Mozart piece that she regularly and proudly recognised. When she'd heard the *The Sleeping Beauty* in his company for the first time, she'd said, 'Walt Disney! Tommy, darling, when on *earth* did you start listening to Walt Disney? That seems entirely unlike you.'

He'd looked at her blankly till he'd made the connection to the old cartoon, which he realised she must have seen while visiting her niece and nephew recently. He said solemnly, 'Walt Disney stole it from Tchaikovsky, darling,' to which she replied, 'He didn't! Did Tchaikovsky write the words as well?' To which he had raised his head ceilingward and laughed.

She hadn't been offended. That had never been Helen's way. Instead, she'd lifted a hand to her lips and said, 'I've done it again, haven't I? You see, this is the reason I need to keep buying shoes. So many pairs end up in my mouth and my saliva ruins them.'

She was completely impossible, he thought. Engaging, lovely, maddening, hilarious. And wise. Always, at heart, wise in ways he would not have thought possible. Wise about him and wise about what was essential and important between them. He missed her in this moment, yet he celebrated her as well. In that, he felt a slight shift within him, the first that had occurred since her murder.

He returned to his humming as he towelled himself off. He was still humming, towel wrapped round his waist, when he opened the door.

And came face to face with DS Barbara Havers.

He said, 'My God.'

Havers said, 'I've been called worse.' She scratched her mop of badly cut and currently uncombed hair. 'Are you always so chipper before breakfast, sir? Because if you are, this is the last time I'm sharing a bathroom with you.'

He could, for the moment, do nothing but stare, so unprepared was he for the sight of his former partner. She was wearing floppy sky blue socks in lieu of slippers and she had on pink flannel pyjamas printed everywhere with the image of vinyl records, musical notes, and the phrase 'Love like yours is sure to come my way.' She seemed to realise he was examining her getup because she said, 'Oh. A gift from Winston,' in apparent reference to it.

'Would that be the socks or the rest of it?'

'The rest. He saw them in a catalogue. He said he couldn't resist.'

'I'll need to speak to Sergeant Nkata about his impulse control.'

She chuckled. 'I knew you'd love them if you ever saw them.'

'Havers, the word *love* does not do justice to my feelings.'

She nodded at the bathroom. 'You finished your morning whatevers in there?'

He stepped aside. 'It's all yours.'

She passed him but paused before closing the door. 'Tea?' she said. 'Coffee?'

'Come to my room.'

He was ready for her when she arrived, dressed for her day. He himself was clothed and he'd made tea – he wasn't desperate enough to face the provided coffee granules – when she knocked on his door and said unnecessarily, 'It's me.'

He opened it to her. She looked round and said, 'You demanded the more elegant accommodation, I see. I've got something that used to be the garret. I feel like Cinderella before the glass boot.'

He held up the tin teapot. She nodded and plopped herself onto his bed, which he'd made. She lifted the old chenille counterpane and inspected the job he'd done. 'Hospital corners,' she noted. 'Very nice, sir. Is that from Eton or somewhere else in your chequered past?'

'My mother,' he said. 'Proper bed-making and the correct use of table linens were at the heart of her childrearing. Should I add milk and sugar or do you want to do your own honours?'

'You can do it,' she said. 'I like the idea of you waiting on me. This is a first, and it may be a last so I think I'll enjoy it.'

He handed her the doctored tea, poured his own, and joined her on the bed as there was no chair. 'What are you doing here, Havers?'

She gestured at the room with her teacup. 'You invited me, didn't you?'

'You know what I mean.'

She took a sip of tea. 'You wanted information about Daidre Trahair.'

'Which you could easily have provided on the phone.' He thought about this and recalled their conversation. 'You were in your car when I phoned you on your mobile. Were you on your way down here?'

'I was.'

'Barbara . . .' He spoke in a fashion to warn her off: Stay out of my life.

She said, 'Don't flatter yourself, Superintendent.'

'Tommy. Or Thomas. Or whatever. But not superintendent.'

'"Tommy"? "Thomas"? Not bloody likely. Are we fine with "sir"?' And when he shrugged, 'Good. DI Hannaford has no MCIT blokes working the case for her. When she phoned the Met for your identification, she explained the situation. I got sent on loan.'

'And that's it?'

'That's it.'

Lynley looked at her evenly. Her face was a blank, an admirable poker face that might have duped someone who knew her less well than he did. 'Am I actually meant to believe that, Barbara?'

'Sir, there's nothing else *to* believe.'

They tried to stare each other down. But ultimately there was nothing to be gained. She'd worked with him too long to be intimidated by any implications that might hang upon silence. She said, 'By the way, no one ever put your resignation through channels. As far as anyone's concerned, you're on compassionate leave. Indefinitely if that's what it takes.' She sipped her tea again. '*Is* that what it takes?'

Lynley looked away from her. Outside, a grey day was framed by the window, and a sprig of the ivy that climbed on this side of the building was blowing against the glass. 'I don't know,' he said. 'I think I'm finished with it, Barbara.'

'They've advertised the job. Not your old one but the one you were in when . . . You know. Webberly's job: the detective superintendent's position. John Stewart's applying. Others as well. Some from outside and some from within. Stewart's obviously got the inside track on it, and between you and me, it would be a disaster for everyone if he gets it.'

'It could be worse.'

'No, it couldn't.' She put her hand on his arm. So rare a gesture it was that he had to look at her. 'Come back, sir.'

'I don't think I can.' He rose then, to distance himself not from her but from the idea of returning to New Scotland Yard. He said, 'But why here, in the middle of nowhere? You could be staying in town, which makes far more sense if you're working with Bea Hannaford.'

'I could ask the same of you, sir.'

'I was brought here the first night. It seemed easiest to stay. It was the closest place to where the body was found. And why are we turning this into an examination of me? What's going on?'

'I've told you.'

'Not everything.' He studied her evenly. If she'd come to keep a watch over him, which was likely the case, Havers being Havers, there could be only one reason. 'What did you learn about Daidre Trahair?' he asked her.

She nodded. 'You see? You haven't lost your touch.' She downed the rest of her tea and held out her cup. He poured her another and put in a packet of sugar and two of the thimbles of milk. She said nothing else until he'd handed the cup back and she'd taken a swig. 'A family called Trahair are longtime residents of Falmouth, so that part of her story's on the up-and-up. The dad sells tyres; he's got his own company. The mum does mortgages for homes. No primary school records for a kid called Daidre, though. You were right about that. In some cases that might suggest she was sent off to school in the old way: booted out the door when she was five or whatever, home for half-terms and the holidays but otherwise unseen and unheard till emerging from the great machine of proper—' She rolled the final *r* to indicate her scorn – 'education at eighteen or whatever.'

'Spare me the social commentary.'

'I speak purely from jealous rage, of course,' Havers said. 'Nothing I would have liked better than to be packed off to boarding school as soon as I learned to blow my nose.'

'Havers . . .'

'You haven't lost that tone of martyred patience,' she noted. 'C'n I smoke in here, by the way?'

'Are you out of your mind?'

'Just enquiring, sir.' She curved her palm around her teacup. 'So while I reckon she could have gone away to primary school, it doesn't seem likely to me because there she is at the local comprehensive from the time she's thirteen. Playing hockey. Singing in the school choir. Mezzo-soprano if that's of interest.'

'And you're rejecting the idea of earlier boarding school for what reason?'

'First of all, because it doesn't make sense. I can see it done the reverse way: primary day school and *then* boarding school when she was twelve or thirteen. But boarding out through primary school and then returning home for secondary? This is a middle-class family. What middle-class family sends its kids off at that age and then has them back home when they're thirteen?'

'It's been known to happen. What's the second of all?'

'The second of . . . ? Oh. Second of all, there's no record of her birth. Not a cracker, not a hint. Not in Falmouth, that is.'

Lynley considered the implications of this. He said, 'She told me she was born at home.'

'The birth would still have to be registered within forty-two days. And if she *was* born at home, the midwife would have been there, yes?'

'What if her father delivered her?'

'Did she tell you that? If you and she were exchanging intimate details—'

He glanced at her sharply, but her face betrayed nothing.

'—then wouldn't that have been an intriguing one to share? Mum doesn't make it to the hospital for some reason: like it's a dark and stormy night. Or the car breaks down. The electricity goes out. There's a maniac loose in the streets. There's been a military coup that history failed to record. There's a curfew due to racial rioting. The Vikings, having missed the east coast entirely because you know how Vikings are when it comes to having a decent sense of direction, have emerged from a time warp to invade the south coast of England. Or maybe aliens. They might have landed. But whatever the reason, there they are at home with Mum in labour and Dad boiling water without knowing what he's supposed to do with it but nature takes its course anyway and out pops a baby girl they call Daidre.' She placed her teacup on the narrow nightstand next to the bed. 'Which still doesn't explain why they wouldn't have registered the birth.'

He said nothing.

'So there's something she's not telling you, sir. I'm wondering why.'

'Her story about the zoo checks out. She *is* a large animal veterinarian. She does work for Bristol Zoo.'

'I'll give you that,' Havers said. 'I went to the Trahairs' house once I'd had a look through the birth registry. No one was at home, so I spoke to a neighbour. There's a Daidre Trahair, definitely. She lives in

Bristol and works at the zoo. But when I pressed a bit further for more information, the woman dummied up. It was just, "Ms Trahair is a credit to her parents and a credit to herself and you write that down in that notebook of yours. *And* if you want to know more, I'll need to speak to my solicitor first," before the door was shut in my face. Too many sodding cop dramas on telly,' she concluded darkly. 'It's killing our ability to intimidate.'

Lynley found he was struggling with a fact that disturbed him, and it was not a fact about Daidre Trahair. He said, 'You went to the house? You spoke to a neighbour? Havers, this was supposed to be confidential. Did you not understand that?'

She frowned, drawing her eyebrows together. She used her teeth to pull on the inside of her lip and she observed him. From below them came the distant sound of pots and pans clanging as breakfast began to be sorted out at the Salthouse Inn.

Havers finally said with some evident care, 'These are background checks, sir. When it comes to murder, everyone involved has a background check. There's nothing secret about that.'

'But not every background check is done by New Scotland Yard. And you identified yourself when you spoke to the neighbour. You showed your warrant card. You told her where you were from. Yes?'

"Course.' Havers spoke carefully and this agitated Lynley: the idea that his former partner would use care with him, whatever her reason. 'But I don't see what that has to do with anything, sir. If you hadn't come upon the body the way you did, have you thought of—'

Lynley cut in with, 'It has everything to do with everything. She knows I work – once worked – for the Met. If the Met's now investigating her, the Met and not the local police, don't you see what that will mean to her?'

'That p'rhaps you're behind the investigation,' Havers said. 'Well, you *are* behind it and with damn good reason. Sir, let me finish what I was saying. You know how this works. If you hadn't come upon Santo Kerne's body, the first person at the scene would have been Daidre Trahair. And I don't have to tell you the game on that one.'

'For God's sake, she didn't kill Santo Kerne. She didn't show up to pretend she found the body. She came into her cottage and discovered me there and I took her to the body because she asked to see it. She said she was a doctor. She wanted to see if she could help him.'

'She could have done that for a dozen reasons and heading the list is the fact that it might have looked damn odd if she hadn't done it.'

'She has absolutely no motive.'

'Okay. What if everything you're claiming is true? What if she is who she says she is and it all checks out? What does it matter that she knows we're looking into her story? That I'm looking into it? That you're looking into it? That Father effing Christmas is looking into it? What does it matter?'

He blew out a breath. He knew part of the answer, but only part. He wasn't willing to give it.

He drank down his tea. He longed for simplicity where there was none. He longed for answers that were *yes* or *no* instead of an infinite string of *maybe*.

The bed creaked as Havers rose. The floor creaked as she walked across it to stand behind him. She said, 'If she knows we're investigating her, she's going to get nervous and that's where we want her. That's where we want them all, isn't it? Nervous people betray themselves. Betrayal like that works in our favour.'

'I can't see how openly investigating this woman—'

'Yes, you can. I know you can. You can and you do.' She touched him lightly, briefly on the shoulder. Her voice was cautious but it was also gentle. 'You're, you're in something of a state, sir, and that's normal after what you've been through. Now, I wish this wasn't a world where people took advantage of others when they're susceptible, but you and I know what kind of world this is.'

The kindness in her voice shook him. It was the primary reason he'd avoided everyone since Helen's burial. His friends, his associates, his colleagues, and finally his very family. He couldn't bear their kindness and their unbounded compassion because it kept reminding him endlessly of the very thing he so desperately wanted to forget.

'You've got to have a care. That's all I'm saying. That and this: we have to look at her exactly like we're looking at everyone else.'

'I know that,' he said.

'Knowing is one thing, Superintendent. Believing will always be something else.'

Daidre sat on a stool at the corner of the kitchen work top. Against a tin canister of lentils, she propped the postcard she'd bought in the honesty stall of St Sithy's Church on the previous afternoon. She studied the gipsy caravan and the countryside in which it sat, with a tired-looking horse munching grass nearby. Picturesque, she thought, a charming image of a time long gone. On occasion, one still saw these sorts of conveyances on a country lane in this part of the world. But now, with their pleasing curved roofs and gaily painted exteriors, they mainly served tourists who wanted to play briefly at being Romany travellers.

When she'd gazed upon the postcard as long as she could without taking action, she left the house. She got into her car, reversed it onto the narrow lane to Polcare Cove, and drove forward down to the beach itself. Proximity to the beach reminded her of the previous night, which she would have preferred not to think about but which she ended up thinking about anyway: her slow walk back to the car with Thomas Lynley; his quiet voice talking about his dead wife; the darkness nearly complete so that, aside from distant lights coming from the houses and cottages above them on the cliff, she could barely see anything save his rather disturbing patrician profile.

Helen was her name and she'd come from a family not unlike his own. Daughter of an earl who had married an earl, moving easily in the world into which she'd been born. Filled with self-doubts, evidently, although Daidre found this piece of information about Helen Lynley difficult to believe, because of how she'd been educated. But at the same time extraordinarily kind, witty, amusing, companionable, fun-loving. Gifted with the most admirable and desirable of human qualities.

Daidre couldn't imagine his surviving the loss of such a woman and she couldn't see how anyone could ever come to terms with this loss being precipitated by murder. 'Twelve years old,' he'd said. 'No one knows why he shot her.'

'I'm so sorry,' she'd said. 'She sounds perfectly lovely.'

'She was.'

Now, Daidre made the turn she always made, using Polcare Cove's small carpark to point her car in the direction that would take her out of the area. Behind her, she heard the breakers collapsing onto the toothy slate reef. Before her, she saw the sweep of the ancient valley and Stowe Wood above it, where the trees were coming into leaf. Very soon beneath them, bluebells would bloom, carpeting the woods with a colour that tossed in rhythmic undulations in the springtime breeze, like sapphire linen.

She made her way up and out of the cove. She followed the lanes in the crisscrossing pattern dictated by the lay of land and its ownership. In this way, she came to the A39 and there she headed south.

The drive she intended was an extended one. At St Columb Road, she stopped for a coffee and decided to have a *pain au chocolat* at a bakery café. She spoke at length about guiltless chocolate consumption to the young man behind the till, and she went so far as to ask that he give her a receipt for her food and her drink, which she tucked into her wallet. One never knew when the police were going to require an alibi of one, she decided wryly. Best to keep records of one's every movement. Best to make certain people along the way have a vivid memory of one's visit to their establishment. As far as the *pain au chocolat* was concerned, what were a few unnecessary calories in the cause of substantiating a claim of innocence?

When she set off again, she gained the roundabout that took her onto the A30. From there, the distance wasn't great, and the route was familiar. She skirted Redruth, recovered quickly from one wrong turn, and at last ended up at the junction of the B3297 and a numberless lane that was signposted for the village of Carnkie.

This part of Cornwall was completely unlike the vicinity of Casvelyn. Here, Daidre parked her Vauxhall in the triangle of pebble-strewn weeds that served as a meeting point of the two roads, and she sat with her chin on her hands and her hands on the top of the steering wheel. She looked out at a landscape green with spring, rippling into the distance towards the sea, penetrated periodically by derelict towers similar to those one found in the Irish countryside, the domiciles of poets, hermits, and mystics. Here, however, the old towers represented what remained of Cornwall's great mining industry: each of them an enormous engine house that sat atop a network of tunnels, pits, and caverns beneath the earth. These were the mines that once had produced tin and silver, copper and lead, arsenic and wolfram. Their engine houses had contained the machinery that kept the mine operational: pumping engines that rid the mines of water, and whims that hauled both the ore and the waste rock in bucket-like kibbles up to the surface.

Like gipsy caravans, the engine houses were the stuff of picture postcards now. But once they'd been the mainstay of people's lives, as well as the symbol of so many people's destruction. They stood all over the western part of Cornwall, and they existed in inordinate numbers particularly along much of the coast. Generally, they came in pairs: the tower of the mighty stone engine house rising three or four floors and roofless now, with narrow arched windows as small as possible to avoid weakening the overall structure, and next to it – often soaring above it – the smokestack, which had once belched grim clouds into the sky.

Now both the engine house and the smoke stack provided a nesting place for birds above and a hiding place for dormice below and, in the crannies and crevices of the structures, a growing place for herb Robert's pert magenta flowers that tangled with yellow bursts of ragwort as red valerian rose above them.

Daidre saw all this at the same time as she did not see it. She found herself thinking of another place entirely, on the coast opposite the one towards which she now gazed.

It was near Lamorna Cove, he'd said. The house and the estate upon which the house sat were together called Howenstow. He'd said, with some evident embarrassment, that he had no idea where the name of the place had come from, and from this admission she'd concluded, incorrectly or not, his ease with the life into which he'd been born. For over two hundred and fifty years his family had occupied both the house and the land, and apparently there had never been a need for them to know anything more than the fact of it being theirs: a sprawling Jacobean structure into which some long-ago ancestor had married, the youngest son of a baron making a match with the only child, the daughter, of an earl.

'My mother could probably tell you everything about the old pile,' he'd said. 'My sister as well. I'm afraid my brother and I both rather let down the side when it comes to family history. Without Judith I'd likely not know the names of my own great-grandparents. And you?'

'I suppose I did have great-grandparents somewhere along the line,' she'd replied. 'Unless, of course, I came like Venus via the half-shell. But that's not very likely, is it? I think I'd have remembered such a spectacular entry.'

So what was it like? she wondered. What *was* it like? She pictured his mother in a great gilded bed, servants on either side of her gently dabbing her face with handkerchiefs soaked in rosewater as she laboured to bring forth a beloved son. Fireworks upon the announcement of an heir and tenant farmers tugging their forelocks and hoisting jugs of homebrew as the news went round. She knew the image was completely absurd, like Thomas Hardy meeting Monty Python, but stupidly, foolishly she could not let it go. So she finally cursed herself, and she scooped up the postcard she'd brought from her cottage. She got out of the car into the chilly breeze.

She found a suitable stone just on the verge of the B3297. The rock was light enough and not half-buried, which made its removal easy.

She carried it back to the triangular juncture of the road and the lane, and at the apex of this triangle she set the stone down. Then she tilted it and placed the postcard of the gipsy wagon beneath it. That done, she was ready to resume her journey.

17

The final remark Tammy had hurled at him before getting out of the car in Casvelyn was 'You don't understand anything, Grandie. No wonder everyone left you like they did.' She hadn't sounded angry as much as sad, which had made it difficult for Selevan Penrule to counter with anything abusive. He'd have *liked* to fire a verbal missile in her direction and, with the satisfaction that comes with long experience in the field of vocal warfare, to watch it hit its mark, but there was something in her eyes that prevented him, despite the pain that her parting shot caused him. Perhaps, he thought, he was losing his touch. Either that or the girl was getting under his skin. He hated to think that might be the case.

He'd confronted her when they were on the road to Clean Barrel Surf Shop and he was quite proud that he'd mastered in himself the compulsion to tackle her on the previous afternoon. He didn't like secrets, and he *hated* lies. That Tammy possessed the first and acted on the second disturbed him more than he wanted to admit. For despite her oddities of dress, behaviour, nutrition, and intention, he liked the girl, and he wanted to think her different from the rest of the world's furtive adolescents, who had clandestine secondary lives that appeared to be defined by sex, drugs and bodily mutilation.

He'd *believed* this to be the case about her: her essential difference from others of her age. But then he'd found the envelope under her mattress when he'd changed the sheets, and he knew from reading its contents that she was, indeed, very like her contemporaries. Whatever progress he thought he'd made was nothing but a sham.

In some situations, that knowledge wouldn't have bothered him. Nothing was going to happen immediately, so he could redouble his efforts and eventually bend her will to his, and to her parents' as well. But the problem with that belief was that Tammy's mum was a woman not known for her patience. She wanted results and if she didn't get them, Selevan knew that Tammy's time in Cornwall would be terminated.

So he'd brought out the envelope he'd found beneath her mattress and he'd placed it on the dashboard as they drove into town. She'd looked at it. She'd looked at him. And damn the girl, she'd taken the offensive. 'You're going through my personal things when I'm not home,' she'd said, sounding for all the world like a fatally wounded spirit. 'That's what you did to Auntie Nan, didn't you?'

He wasn't about to get into a discussion of his daughter and the worthless hooligan to whom she'd been married in *alleged* bliss for twenty-two years. He said, 'Don't make this about your aunt, girl. Tell me what you're about with this nonsense.'

'You can't tolerate anyone who disagrees with you, Grandie, and Dad's just like you. If something's not part of your experience, it's not to be bothered with. Or it's bad. Or evil, even. Well, this isn't evil. It's what I want and if you and Dad and Mum can't see that it's the sort of answer the whole bloody *world* needs just now in order to stop *being* the whole bloody world . . .' She'd grabbed the envelope and shoved it into her ruck-sack. He thought to snatch it from her and toss it from the window, but what would have been the point? Where that one came from, another could be got.

Her voice was different when she spoke again. She sounded shaken, the victim of betrayal. 'I thought you understood. And, anyway, I didn't think you were the sort of person who snoops in other people's belongings.'

That was rather maddening to Selevan. *He* was the one betrayed by *her*, wasn't he? *She* was hiding correspondence from *him*, not the other way round. When her mum phoned from Africa and Tammy was the object of discussion, *he* didn't hide that from her and they didn't speak in code. So *her* umbrage was completely out of order.

'Now you listen to me,' he'd begun.

'Not till you start listening to me as well,' she said quietly.

That had been that until she'd opened the car door in Casvelyn. She'd made her final statement and trudged to the shop. At another time he would have followed her. No child of his had *ever* spoken to him in such a way without feeling the strap. Problem was, Tammy was not his child. An injured generation stood between them, and both of them knew who'd caused the wounds.

So he'd let her go, and he'd driven back to Sea Dreams with a very heavy heart. He did some cleaning and cooked himself a second break-fast of beans on toast, hoping that putting something more in his stomach would cure its roiling. He took this to the table and he ate it, but the food didn't stop him from feeling sick.

A car door slamming outside diverted Selevan from his misery. He glanced out of the window and saw Jago Reeth opening the door of his caravan as Madlyn Angarrack approached him. Jago came down the steps and held out his arms. Madlyn walked into them and Jago patted first her back and then her head. They went inside the caravan together, with Madlyn wiping her eyes on the sleeve of Jago's flannel shirt.

The sight pierced Selevan. He couldn't work out how Jago Reeth managed what was so bloody impossible for himself: being a man to whom young people actually wished to talk. Obviously, there was something to the way Jago listened and responded to youngsters that Selevan had failed to learn.

Except it was so *easy* when they weren't your relations, wasn't it? And wasn't that something that Jago himself had already said?

It didn't matter. All Selevan knew was that Jago Reeth might possess the key to a grandfather's having one single reasonable conversation with his own granddaughter. He needed to find out what that key was, before Tammy's mother pulled the plug and sent the girl elsewhere to take the mental cure.

He waited till Madlyn Angarrack had left, exactly forty-three minutes after she'd arrived. Then he crossed over to Jago's caravan and rapped upon the door. When Jago opened it, Selevan saw that his friend was about to head off somewhere, as he'd put on his jacket, the half-broken specs which he wore only at LiquidEarth, and a headband to keep his long hair away from his face. Selevan was about to offer an apology for the disruption to Jago's plans, but the other man stopped him and told him to come inside.

'You got something eating at you,' he said. 'I c'n see that without you telling me, mate. Just let me . . .' Jago went to a phone and punched in a few numbers. He reached an answer machine, it seemed, because he said, 'Lew, me. Going to be late. Got a bit of 'mergency here at home. Madlyn stopped in, by the way. Bit upset again, but I think she's sorted. There's a board needs checking in the hot cupboard, eh?' He rang off, replacing the receiver.

Selevan watched his movements. The Parkinson's looked bad this morning. Either that, or Jago's medication hadn't kicked in. Old age was a bugger, no doubt of that. But old age and disease together were the devil.

As a means of introducing the subject for discussion, he took from his pocket the necklace he'd removed from Tammy on the previous day.

He laid it on the table and when Jago joined him at the banquette that served as a seat, he gestured to it.

'Found this on the girl,' Selevan told him. 'She was wearing it round her neck. Said the *M* means *Mary*. Do you credit that? Came right out and said it, didn't she, bland as could be, like it was the most natural thing in the world.'

Jago picked the necklace up and examined it. 'Scapular,' he said.

'That's it. That's what she called it. Scapular. But the *M*'s for *Mary*. That's the concern. The Mary bit.'

Jago nodded, but Selevan could see that a smile was playing round the corners of his mouth. This was a bit of an irritant to Selevan. Easy for Jago to have a bleeding laugh at the situation. Wasn't *his* grand-daughter wearing *M* for *Mary* round her neck.

'Something's happened to the girl somewhere 'long the line. That's all I can reckon from the mess she is now. I put it down to Africa. Being exposed to all those native women in the raw. Walking round the streets of wherever with their privates hanging out. 'S no wonder to me she's got herself confused.'

'Mother of Jesus,' Jago said.

'That and then some.'

Jago laughed then, and he did so heartily. Selevan reared up. Jago said, 'Don't get yourself twisted, mate. You said yourself it's *M* for *Mary*. On a scapular, that would mean *M* for *Mary* the mother of Jesus. It's a devotional thing, this is. Catholics wear them. You might see a picture of Jesus on one. A saint on another: St Whoever of Whatever. It's a mark of devotion.'

'Damn,' Selevan muttered. 'No bloody end to this mess.' Tammy's mum would have a seizure, no doubt about that. One more reason to pack Tammy up and send her on her way. In Sally Joy's mind the only thing worse than being a Catholic was being a terrorist. 'St George and the Dragon would've been better,' Selevan said. That image, at least, could have been seen as patriotic.

'Not likely to find St George on one of these,' Jago said, allowing the scapular to dangle from his fingers, 'dragons being the work of imagination which makes St George himself something of a question mark, eh? But that's the general idea of 'em. A believer in this or that holy person puts this thing round his neck – or her neck in the case of your Tammy – and I s'pose she ends up feeling holy herself.'

'I blame the effing politicians,' Selevan said darkly. 'They made the world in the state it's in today and that's why the girl's working to get herself holy. Trying to prepare for the end of days, she is. And, there's no one been able to talk her out of it.'

'That what she says?'

'Eh?' Selevan took the scapular and shoved it into the breast pocket of his shirt. 'She *says* she wants a prayerful life. That's her very words. "I want a prayerful life, Grandie. I believe it's what everyone should aspire to." As if sitting alone in a cave somewhere and eating grass for your meals and drinking your own piss once a week is going to do *one* bleeding thing to solve the world's problems.'

'That's the plan, is it?'

'Oh I don't *know* what the effing plan is. No one knows, and that *includes* the girl. You see how it is? She hears about a cult she can join and she means to join it because *this* cult, unlike the *rest* of the God damn cults out there, is the one that's going to save the world.'

Jago looked thoughtful. Selevan hoped the other man was coming up with a solution to the problem of Tammy. But Jago said nothing, so Selevan had to speak again. He said, 'I can't get through to the girl. Can't even begin to. Found a letter under her bed and they were telling her to come on by and check things out, have an interview here so's we c'n take the measure of you and see if you're suitable and if we like you and whatever else. I show her I found it and *she* goes off her chump 'cause *I'm* doing the snoop through her things.'

Jago looked thoughtful. He scratched his head. 'Were, eh?' he said.

'What's that?'

'You *were* doing the snoop. I'n't that the case?'

'I got to. If I don't, her mum's all over me like melted cheese on the radiator. She says, "We need you to make her see the light. Someone's got to make her see the light before it's too late."'

'That's just the problem,' Jago pointed out. 'That's where the lot of you're going wrong.'

'Which's where?' Selevan spoke to his friend without defence. If he was going at this problem of Tammy in the wrong way, he meant to learn the right way at once, and he'd come to Jago to do so.

'The devil of young people,' Jago said, 'is that they got to be allowed to take their own decisions, mate.'

'But—'

'Hear me out. It's part of making their way to being grown. They take a decision, they make a mistake, and if no one rushes like the fire brigade to save them from the outcome, they learn from the whole experience. 'Tisn't the job of the dad, or the granddad or the mum or the gran, to keep them from learning what they got to learn, mate. What *they* got to do is help work out the end of the story.'

Selevan could see this. He could even run it through his mind and largely agree with it. But agreement was a process of intellect. It had nothing to do with the heart. Jago's position in life, having no children or grandkids of his own, made it simple for him to adhere to this admirable philosophy. It also explained why young people felt able to talk to him. They talked; he listened. Likely, it was similar to sharing one's secrets with a wall. But what was the point if the wall didn't say, 'Hang on a minute. You're making a bloody fool of yourself'? Or 'You're choosing wrong, damn it'? Or 'Listen to me cos I been alive about sixty years longer'n you and those years damn well ought to count for something or what's the point in having lived them'? Beyond that, didn't parents and grandparents have some right to sort out their offspring, not to mention to determine what the offspring would be doing with the rest of their lives? That was what had happened to him, wasn't it? He may not have liked it, he may not have wanted it, he may not in a hundred years have chosen it for himself, but wasn't he a better and stronger person for having rubbished his dreams of the Royal Navy in favour of a dutiful life on the farm?

Jago was watching him, one bushy eyebrow raised above the frame of his worn-out specs. His expression said that he knew what Selevan was thinking and didn't disagree with Selevan's assessment. He said, 'There's more to it than that, mate, despite what you're thinking. If you get to know 'em, you end up caring and you end up hating to see 'em decide something that you *know's* for the bad. But no one listens when they're young. Did you?'

Selevan dropped his gaze. For that was the fly in the ointment of his life, when everything was laid out in front of him. He *had* listened. He had chosen as he'd been told to choose. And doing that hadn't spared him a lifetime of regret. Indeed, it was the single cause of it.

'Bloody hell,' he sighed. He put his head in his hands.

'The very thing,' his friend agreed.

Bea Hannaford hadn't started her day in the best of moods, and her outlook wasn't improving during her meeting with New Scotland Yard's Detective Sergeant Barbara Havers. Upon the sergeant's arrival in Casvelyn, Bea had instructed her to check into the Salthouse Inn and to do some serious trolling through what Thomas Lynley had so far managed to discover about Daidre Trahair. She knew DS Havers had long worked with Lynley in London and if anyone was going to be able to wring something out of the man, it was going to be Barbara Havers. But 'apparently clean so far' was the extent of what Havers had to report about Lynley's excursions into the mysterious Ms Trahair's background, which made Hannaford wonder about her own wisdom in accepting the offer of the Met's Assistant Commissioner Sir David Hillier to send Lynley's former partner on loan to work the murder inquiry. The response of 'He says she's clean so far but he's carrying on' in answer to 'What do we know from Superintendent Lynley about Ms Trahair?' had not been what Hannaford wished to hear. It had made her wonder about loyalties and where they ought to be lying.

She herself had spoken to Lynley. He'd reported on his excursion to Pengelly Cove on the previous afternoon, and she could tell his interest was now decidedly caught up in the Kernes. This was all well and good since everything had to be looked into eventually, but digging into the Kernes' background was not going to keep Lynley interested in Daidre Trahair, which was where Bea Hannaford wanted him to be. The vet was a liar, no question about it. Based upon the way she had looked at Lynley when Bea had seen them together – a bit of a mix among compassion, admiration, and lust – Lynley had appeared to be the best road to drive along if the destination was sorting the doctor's truths from the doctor's lies. Now Bea wasn't so sure.

So in speaking to Barbara Havers, Bea's mood was blacker than it had been upon waking, and she wouldn't have thought that possible. For she'd awakened with Pete's questions and Pete's comments of the previous day on her mind, which meant she'd awakened in exactly the same manner as she'd fallen asleep. *Why do you hate Dad? Dad loves you, Mum.*

Clearly, it was time for another round of internet dating, if only she could have spared the hours it would take to troll, to select, to contact, to try to discern if the individual was worth an evening, and then somehow to find that evening. And then . . . what would be the point, really? How many more toads was she going to have to dine with, drink with, or coffee with before one of them showed colours more princely than amphibious? Hundreds, it seemed. Thousands. All that and she wasn't even sure she *wanted* another relationship anyway. She, Pete, and the dogs were doing fine on their own.

Thus, when Bea faced Barbara Havers in the vicinity of the china board as they looked over the day's activities, she examined the Met sergeant with a critical eye that had more to do with an assessment of her professional commitment than it had to do with an evaluation of her fashion sense, which was more deplorable than Bea would have thought possible in a female adult. Today DS Havers was wearing a lumpy fisherman's sweater over a high-necked T-shirt with what looked like a coffee stain on its collar. She had on figure-reducing olive tweed trousers, easily an inch too short and possibly twelve years too old, and yesterday's red high top trainers on her feet. She looked like a cross between a street vagrant and a refugee fleeing from a war zone, with clothing provided from castoffs of Oxfam castoffs.

Bea tried to ignore all this. She said, 'I've got the distinct impression Superintendent Lynley's dragging his feet on the issue of Ms Trahair. What do you think, Sergeant?' She then watched to gauge Havers' answer.

'He might well be,' Havers replied easily enough. 'Considering all that's happened to him, he's not exactly one hundred per cent. But if she's at the bottom of what happened to this kid and he susses it out, he'll move on her. You can depend on him.'

'Are you saying I ought to allow him to pursue this in whatever way he sees fit?'

Havers didn't reply at once. She looked at the china board. Careful thought could indicate her priorities, and Bea made this a mark in her favour.

'I think he'll be okay,' Havers said. 'The last thing he's about to do is let anyone get away with murder, all things considered. If you know what I mean.'

Of course. There was that. What made him susceptible also made him a man who would never want another person to go through what he himself had gone through. Besides that, his very susceptibility could work in their favour since a vulnerable person was one in whose presence essential mistakes might be made by another person. These would be Ms Trahair's mistakes, naturally. Where she'd made one, she'd eventually make others.

'All right. Come with me, then. We've a bloke in town who did a turn inside for doing the job on someone, down the south coast. This was a few years ago. He ended up crying "It's the drink" to the judge, but as the bloke on the receiving end of his attention came up a paraplegic—'

'Bloody hell,' DS Havers said.

'—the judge sent him away. He's out now, but so's his temper and his proclivity for the drink. He knew Santo Kerne, and someone blackened Santo Kerne's eye shortly before his death. Granted, it's not the sort of beating put this bloke away, but he wants a thorough talking to.'

Will Mendick was at his place of employment, a modern brick supermarket looking wildly out of place as it stood at the junction of the top of Belle Vue and St Mevan Crescent which Bea pointed out to Havers as the route to Adventures Unlimited, a visible hulk out on the promontory. The shop was also a very short distance from the baked delights of Casvelyn of Cornwall, and when they alighted from Bea's Land Rover in the carpark at the back of the grocery, the morning breeze was sending the fragrance of fresh pasties in their direction. Barbara Havers cut into this perfume by lighting a cigarette. She pulled at it hungrily as they walked along the side of the building to its front door, managing to smoke half of it before they entered.

In an extremely optimistic embracing of spring, the supermarket's management had turned off the heating, so it was frigid within. Custom was sparse at this time of day, and only one of the six tills was open. A question at it led Bea and Sergeant Havers towards the back of the premises. There, two swinging doors closed off the warehouse where goods were stored. **No Admittance** and **Staff Only** were posted upon them.

Bea shouldered through, her identification ready. They encountered an unshaven man ducking into the employees' loo and stopped him with the word, 'Police.' He didn't snap to as Bea would have liked, but at least he appeared cooperative. She asked for Will Mendick. At his response of 'Outside, I expect,' they found themselves heading in the direction from which they'd originally come: working their way along the side of the building but within it this time, along a gloomy aisle, and beneath towering shelves of paper products, boxed-up tins of this and that, and huge cartons printed with enough brands of junk food to keep morbid obesity going for several generations.

On the south side of the building, a loading dock bore pallets of goods in the process of being removed from an enormous articulated lorry. Bea expected to find Will Mendick here, but the answer to another question pointed her over to a collection of wheelie bins at the far end of the dock. There, she saw a young man stowing discarded vegetables and other items into a black rubbish bag. This, apparently, was Will Mendick, committing the act of subversion for which Santo Kerne had created his T-shirt. He was fighting off the gulls to do it, though. Above and around him, they flapped their wings. They soared near to him occasionally, apparently trying to frighten him off their patch like extras in Hitchcock's film.

Mendick looked at Bea's identification carefully when she produced it. He was tall and ruddy, and he grew immediately ruddier when he saw the cops had come to call. Definitely the skin of a guilty man, Bea thought.

The young man glanced from Bea to Havers and back to Bea, and his expression suggested that neither woman fitted his notion of what a cop should look like. 'I'm on my break,' he told them, as if concerned that they were there to monitor his employment hours.

'That's fine with us,' Bea informed him. 'We can talk while you do whatever it is you're doing.'

'D'you know how much food is wasted in this country?' he asked her sharply.

'Rather a lot, I expect.'

'That's an understatement. Try tonnes of it. *Tonnes*. A sell-by date passes and out it's chucked. It's a crime, it is.'

'Good of you, then, to put it to use.'

'I *eat* it.' He sounded defensive.

'I gathered that,' Bea told him.

'You have to, I wager,' Barbara Havers noted pleasantly. 'Bit tough for it to make it all the way to the Sudan before it rots, moulds, hardens, or whatevers. Costs you next to nothing as well, so it has that in its favour, too.'

Mendick eyed her as if evaluating her level of disrespect. Her face showed nothing. He appeared to take the decision to ignore any judgement they might make about his activity. He said, 'You want to talk to me. So talk to me.'

'You knew Santo Kerne. Well enough for him to design a T-shirt for you, from what we've learned.'

'If you know that, then you'll also know that this is a small town and most people here knew Santo Kerne. I hope you're talking to them as well.'

'We'll get to the rest of his associates eventually,' Bea replied. 'Just now it's you we're interested in. Tell us about Conrad Nelson. He's operating from a wheelchair these days, the way I hear it.'

Mendick had a few spots on his face, near his mouth, and these turned the colour of raspberries. He went back to sorting through the supermarket's discards. He chose some bruised apples and followed them with a collection of limp courgettes. He said, 'I did my time for that.'

'Which we know,' Bea assured him. 'But what we don't know is how it happened and why.'

'It's nothing to do with your investigation.'

'It's assault with intent,' Bea told him. 'It's grave bodily injury. It's a stretch inside at the pleasure of you-know-who. When someone's got details like that in his background, Mr Mendick, we like to know about them. Especially if he's an associate, close or otherwise, of someone who ends up murdered.'

'Where there's smoke there's fire.' Havers lit up another cigarette as if to emphasise her point.

'You're destroying your lungs and everyone else's,' Mendick told her. 'That's a disgusting habit.'

'While wheelie bin diving is what?' Havers asked.

'Not letting something go to waste.'

'Damn. I *wish* I shared your nobility of character. Reckon you lost sight of it – that noble part of you – when you bashed that bloke in Plymouth, eh?'

'I said I did my stretch.'

'We understand you told the judge it had to do with drink,' Bea said. 'D'you still have a problem with that? Is it still leading you to go off your nut? That was your claim, I've been told.'

'I don't drink any longer so it's not leading me anywhere.' He looked into the wheelie bin, spied something he apparently wanted, and dug down to bring out a packet of fig bars. He stowed this in his bag and went on with his search. He ripped open and tossed a loaf of apparently stale bread onto the tarmac for the gulls. They went after it greedily. 'I do AA if it's any of your business,' he added. 'And I haven't had a drink since I came out.'

'I do hope that's the case, Mr Mendick. How did that altercation in Plymouth begin?'

'I *told* you it's got nothing to do . . .' He seemed to rethink his angry tone – as well as the direction of conversation – because he sighed and said, 'I used to get blind drunk. I had a dust-up with this yob, and I *don't* know what it was about because when I drank like that I couldn't remember what set me off or even *if* something set me off at all. I didn't remember the fight the next day and I'm *damn* sorry that bloke ended up like he did because it wasn't my intention. I probably just wanted to sort him.'

'Is that your general method of sorting people?'

'When I drank, it was. It's not something I'm proud of. It's also in the past. I did my time. I made amends. I try to stay clean.'

'Try?'

'Bloody *hell*.' He climbed up into the wheelie bin. He began a more furious rooting through its contents.

'Santo Kerne took a fairly serious punch sometime before he died,' Bea said. 'I wonder if you can tell us anything about that.'

'I can't,' he said.

'You can't or you won't?'

'*Why* d'you want to pin this on me?'

Because you look so damn guilty, Bea thought. Because you're lying about something and I can read it in the colour of your skin which is flaming now, from your cheeks to your ears and even to your scalp. 'That's my job,' Bea told him, 'to pin this on someone. If that someone's not you, I'd like to know why.'

'I had no reason to hurt him. Or to kill him. Or to anything.'

'How'd you come to know him?'

'I worked at Clean Barrel, that surf shop on the corner of the Strand.' Mendick nodded in the general direction. 'He came in because he wanted a board. That's how we met. Few months after he moved to town.'

'But you no longer work at Clean Barrel Surf Shop. Has that something to do with Santo Kerne as well?'

'I sent him to LiquidEarth for a board, and I got found out. I lost my job. I wasn't supposed to be sending anyone to the competition. Not that LiquidEarth *is* the competition but there was no telling the boss-man that, was there? So I got the sack.'

'Blamed Santo for that, did you?'

'Sorry to disappoint you, but no. It was the right thing to do, sending him to LiquidEarth. He was a beginner. He'd never even been out. He needed a beginner's board. We didn't have any decent ones at the time – just shit from China, if you want to know, and we sold that clobber mostly to tourists – so I told him to go see Lew Angarrack, who'd make him a good one that he could learn on. It would cost more but it would be right for him. That's what I did. That's all I did. Jesus. From Nigel Coyle's reaction, you would've thought I'd shot someone. Santo brought the board by to show me, Coyle happened to be there, and the rest is history.'

'Santo did you a bad turn, then.'

'So I killed him? Waited two *years* to kill him? Not likely. He felt bad enough about what happened. He apologised maybe six dozen times.'

'Where?'

'Where what?'

'Where did he apologise? Where did you see him?'

'Wherever,' he said. 'The town's small, like I said.'

'On the beach?'

'I don't go to the beach.'

'In a surfing town like Casvelyn you don't go to the beach?'

'I don't surf.'

'You were selling surf boards but you yourself don't surf? Why's that, Mr Mendick?'

'God damn it!' Mendick rose up. He towered above them in the wheelie bin, but he would have towered above them anyway, for he was tall, albeit gangly.

Bea could see the veins throbbing in his temples. She wondered what it took for him to control that nasty temper of his and she also wondered what it took for him to unleash it on someone.

She felt Sergeant Havers tense next to her, and she glanced her way. The DS had a hard expression on her face, and Bea liked her for this, for it told her Havers wasn't the sort of woman who backed down easily in a confrontation.

'Did you compete with other surfers?' Bea asked. 'Did you compete with Santo? Did he compete with you? Did you give it up? What?'

'I don't like the sea.' He spoke through his teeth. 'I don't like not knowing what's beneath me in the water because there's sharks in every part of the world and I don't care to become acquainted with one. I know about boards and I know about surfing but I don't surf. All right?'

'I suppose so. Do you climb, Mr Mendick?'

'Climb what? No, I don't climb.'

'What do you do, then?'

'I hang out with my friends.'

'Santo Kerne among them?'

'He wasn't . . .' Mendick backed off from the rapidity of their conversation, as if he recognised how easily he could become trapped if he continued the pace. He packed more items into his rubbish bag: a few seriously dented tins, some bags of spinach and other greens, a handful of packaged herbs, a packet of tea cakes. Then he climbed out of the bin and made his reply. 'Santo didn't have friends, not in the normal sense. Not like other people do. He had people he associated with when he wanted them for something.'

'Such as?'

'Such as having experiences with them. That's how he put it. He was all about having experiences . . .'

'What sort of experiences?'

Mendick hesitated, which told Bea they'd come to the crux of the matter. It had taken her longer than she liked to get him to this point, and she briefly considered that she might be losing her touch. But at least she'd got him there, so there was life in her yet. 'Mr Mendick?' she said.

'Sex,' he replied. 'Santo was dead mad about sex.'

'He was eighteen,' Havers noted. 'Is there an eighteen-year-old boy alive who isn't dead mad about sex?'

'The way he was? What he was into? Yeah, I'd say there's eighteen year olds who aren't a bit like him.'

'What was he into?'

'I don't know. Just that it was off. That's all she'd say. That and the fact he was cheating on her.'

'She?' Bea asked. 'Would that be Madlyn Angarrack? What did she tell you?'

'Nothing. Just that what he was into made her sick.'

'Ah.' That brought them nearly full circle, Bea thought. And in this investigation full circle seemed to mean continually that yet another liar had been revealed.

'Close to Madlyn, are you?' Havers was asking.

'Not particularly. I know her brother, Cadan. So I know her as well. Like I said, Casvelyn's small enough. Given time, everyone ends up knowing everyone.'

'In what sense would that be?' Bea asked Will Mendick.

He looked confused. 'What?'

'The knowing bit,' she said. 'Everyone ends up knowing everyone, you said. I was wondering in what sense you meant that?'

It was clear from Mendick's expression that the allusion was lost upon him. But that was no matter. They had Madlyn Angarrack where they wanted her.

18

Had it not been for the rain on the previous afternoon, Ben Kerne would likely not have seen his father when he went to Pengelly Cove. But because of the rain, he'd insisted upon driving his mother back to Eco House from the Curlew Inn at the end of her workday. She'd had her large three-wheeler with her, upon which she daily pedalled to and from work without too much difficulty despite her stroke in earlier years, but he'd insisted. The tricycle would fit into the back of the Austin without too much trouble, he told her. He didn't want her on the narrow lanes in bad weather. She shouldn't be on them in good weather either, if it came down to it. She wasn't of an age, let alone in the physical condition, where she should be out on a tricycle anyway. To her carefully enunciated, post-stroke words, 'Got three wheels, Ben,' he said it didn't matter. His father should have the common sense to purchase a proper vehicle now that he and his wife were old.

Even as he said this, he wondered at the evolution of parent-child relationships in which the parent ultimately becomes the child. And he wondered without wanting to wonder if his own fragile connection with Santo would have mutated in a similar fashion. He doubted it. Santo seemed at the moment as he would now be forever: frozen in an eternal youth with no chance to move on to things more important than the concerns of randy adolescence.

It was the thought of randy adolescence that plagued him throughout the long night that followed his visit to Eco House. Yet when he drove down the deeply rutted lane towards the old farmhouse, that was the last subject upon which he would have thought his mind would lock. Instead, he followed the rises, falls, and curves of that unsurfaced lane, and he marvelled that the passage of years had done nothing to release him from the fear he'd always harboured of his father. Apart from Eddie Kerne, he did not have to consider fear. Nearing him, it was as if he'd never left Pengelly Cove.

His mother had sensed this. She'd said in that altered voice – God, did she actually sound *Portuguese*? he'd wondered – that he'd find his father very much changed in the years he'd been gone. To which he'd replied, 'He didn't sound any different on the phone, Mum.'

Physically, she'd said. Now there was a frailty about him. He tried to hide it but he was feeling his age. She didn't add that he was feeling his failure as well. Eco House had been the dream of his life: living off the land, in harmony with the elements. Indeed, he'd planned to master those elements so that they worked for him. It had been an admirable attempt at living green, but he'd bitten off too much and he hadn't possessed the jaws to chew it all.

If Eddie Kerne heard the Austin drive up to Eco House, he didn't emerge. Nor did he emerge as Ben wrestled his mother's tricycle from the back of the car. When they approached the wreck of the old front door, however, Eddie was waiting for them. He swung it open before they reached it, as if he'd been watching from one of the filthy and ill-hung windows.

Despite his mother's warning, Ben felt the shock when he saw his father. Old, he thought, and looking older than he actually was. Eddie Kerne wore old man's spectacles, with thick, black frames and thick, smeared lenses, and behind them his eyes had lost much of their colour. One of them was clouded by a cataract, which Ben knew he'd never have removed. The rest of him was old as well: from his badly matched and badly patched clothing, to the places on his face that his razor had missed, to the corkscrew of hairs springing out of his ears and his nose. His gait was slow, and his shoulders were round. He was the personification of End of Days.

Ben felt a sudden rush of dizziness when he saw him. He said, 'Dad.'

Eddie Kerne looked him over, one of those abrupt head-to-toe movements that – to an offspring of the adult performing them – tend to signify assessment and judgement simultaneously. He stepped away from the door without comment, and disappeared into the bowels of the house.

Under other circumstances Ben would have departed then. But his mother murmured, 'Shush, shush,' from which he took comfort, no matter where she was directing the sound. It came straight from his childhood, and he embraced its meaning. *Mummy's here, darling. No need to cry.* He felt her hand on the small of his back, urging him forward.

Eddie was waiting for them in the kitchen, which seemed to be the only remaining habitable room in the downstairs of the house. It was well lit and warm, while the rest of the place was shrouded in shadows, packed with bits and bobs and clobber, smelling of mildew, filled with the skittering of rodents in the walls.

He'd put on the kettle. Ann Kerne nodded towards this meaning-fully, as if it gave evidence of something within Eddie that had altered along with his physical decay. He shuffled to the cupboard and brought out three mugs, a jar of coffee granules and a raggedy box of sugar cubes. When he had this on the chipped yellow table beside a plastic jug of milk, a loaf of bread, and an unwrapped cube of margarine, he said to Ben, 'Scotland Yard. Not the locals, mind you, but Scotland Yard. Not like you thought, eh? It's bigger'n the locals. Didn't 'spect that, did you? Question is, does she?'

Ben knew who *she* was. *She* was who *she* had always been.

Eddie went on. 'Other question is, who phoned 'em. Who wants Scotland Yard on the case and why'd they come running like a fire's lit under 'em?'

'I don't know.'

'Wager you don't. If it's bigger 'n the locals, it's bad. If it's bad, it's her. Things is home to roost now, Benesek. Knew this would happen, didn't I?'

'Dellen's nothing to do with this, Dad.'

'Don't say her name round me. It's a curse, it is.'

His wife said, 'Eddie,' in a conciliatory tone, and she put her hand on Ben's arm as if afraid he would bolt.

But the sight of his father had abruptly changed things for Ben. So old, he thought. So terribly old. Broken as well. He wondered how he had failed to understand till now that life had long ago defeated his father. He'd beaten his fists against it, had Eddie Kerne, and refused to submit to its demands for compromise and change: to take life on life's terms, which required the ability to switch courses when neces-sary, to modify behaviour, and to alter dreams so that they could meet the realities that they came up against. But he'd never been able to do any of that, so he'd been crushed, and life had rolled over his shattered body.

The kettle clicked off as the water came to a boil. When Eddie turned to fetch it to the table, Ben went to him. He heard his mother murmur *shush* and *shush* another time, but he found that comfort unnecessary now. He approached his father, one man to another. He said, 'I wish things could have been different for all of us. I love you, Dad.'

Eddie's shoulders bowed further. 'Why couldn't you shake her *off*?' His voice sounded as broken as his spirit.

'I don't know,' Ben said. 'I just couldn't. But that's down to me, not to Dellen. She can't bear the blame for my weakness.'

'You wouldn't *see*.'

'You're right.'

'And now?'

'I don't know.'

'Still?'

'Yes. That's my personal hell. Do you understand? In all these years, never once did you have to make it yours.'

Eddie's shoulders shook. He tried and failed to lift the kettle. Ben carried it for him to the table, where he poured the water into their mugs. He didn't want the coffee; it would keep him awake that night when all he wanted was indefinite sleep. But he would drink it if that was what was required, if that was the communion his father wanted.

All of them sat, Eddie last. His head looked too heavy for his neck to bear, and it fell forward, his chin nearing his chest.

'What is it, then, Eddie?' Ann Kerne asked her husband.

'I told the cop,' he said. 'I could've tossed him from the property, but I didn't do that. I wanted . . . I don't know what I wanted. Benesek, I told him everything I knew.'

The restless night that followed thus had a twofold source: the coffee he'd drunk and the knowledge he'd gained. For if his conversation with Eddie Kerne had at least gone some way towards burying some of the excruciating past between them, that same conversation had resurrected another part of it. For the remainder of the day and into the night, he'd had to look at that part squarely. He'd had to wonder about it. Neither was an activity in which he particularly wished to engage.

Set against the rest of his life, one night should have been insignificant. A party with his mates, and that was all. A gathering he wouldn't even have gone to had he not just two days earlier had the courage to break off with Dellen Nankervis yet again. He was thus morose, his life in tatters. 'You want cheering up,' was his mates' recommendation. 'That wanker Parsons is having a party. Everyone's invited, so come with us. Get your mind *off* the bloody cow for once.'

That had proved impossible, for Dellen had been there: in a crimson sundress and spiky sandals, smooth of leg and tan of shoulder, blonde hair soft and long and thick, eyes like bluebells. Seventeen years old with the heart of a siren, she'd come alone but she hadn't remained so. For she was dressed like a flame, and like a flame she drew them. His mates were not among them, for they knew the trap Dellen Nankervis presented: how she baited it, how she sprang it and, in the end, what she did with her prey. So they kept their distance, but the others didn't. Ben watched until he could bear no more.

Palm curved round a glass and he drank it. Pill pressed into his hand and he took it. Spliff placed between his fingers and he smoked it. The miracle was that he hadn't died from everything he'd ingested that night. What he *had* done was welcome the ministrations of any girl willing to vanish into a darkened corner with him. He knew there had been three; there may have been more. It hadn't mattered. What counted was only that Dellen *see*.

Take your fucking hands off my sister had brought a sudden end to the game. Jamie Parsons was the hot-voiced speaker, acting the part of outraged brother – not to mention gap-year brother, wealthy brother, travelling-the-earth-to-the-hot-spots-of-surfing-and-making-sure-everyone-knew-about-it brother – discovering a lowlife nonce with his fingers in his sister's knickers and his sister shoved up against the wall with one leg lifted and loving it *loving* it, which Ben had foolishly, loudly and in the presence of everyone in hearing distance declared to be his real crime once Jamie Parsons had separated them.

He'd been summarily and with no delicacy thrown out, and his mates had followed, and as far as he had ever known or dared to ask, Dellen had remained behind.

'Christ, that bloody wanker needs sorting,' they all agreed, up to their eyeballs with drink, with drugs, and with resentment towards Jamie Parsons.

And after that? Ben simply didn't know.

He ran the story through his head all night, after returning to Casvelyn from Eco House and Pengelly Cove. He'd got back around ten, and he'd not done more than pace the hotel, pausing at windows to look out at the restless bay. The hotel was quiet, Kerra not there, Alan gone for the day, and Dellen . . . She was not in the sitting room or the kitchen of the family quarters and he looked no further. For he needed time to sift through what he remembered and to differentiate it from what he imagined.

He finally entered their bedroom at mid-morning. Dellen lay diag-onally across the bed. She breathed a heavy, drug-induced sleep, and the bottle of pills that had sent her there was uncapped on the bedside table, where the light still burned as it had likely done all night, Dellen too incapacitated to turn it off.

He sat on the edge of the bed. She did not awaken. She hadn't changed out of her clothing on the previous night, and her red scarf formed a pool beneath her head, its fringe fanning out like petals with Dellen its centre, heart of the flower.

His curse was that he still could love her. His curse was that he could look at her now and, despite everything and especially despite Santo's murder, he could still want to claim her because she possessed and, he feared, would forever possess the ability to wipe from his heart and his mind everything else that was not Dellen. And he did not understand how this could be or what terrible twist of his psyche made it so.

Her eyes opened. In them and just for an instant, before awareness came to her completely, he saw the truth in the dullness of her expression: that what he needed from his wife she could not give him, though he would continue to try to take it from her again and again.

She turned her head away.

'Leave me,' she said. 'Or kill me. Because I can't—'

'I saw his body,' Ben told her. 'Or rather, his face. They'd dissected him – that's what they do except they use a different word for it – so they kept him covered up to his chin. I could have seen the rest but I didn't want to. It was enough to see his face.'

'Oh God.'

'It was just a formality. They knew it was Santo. They have his car. They have his driving licence. So they didn't need me to look at him. I expect I could have closed my eyes at the last moment and just said yes, that's Santo, and not have looked at all.'

She raised her arm and pressed her fist against her mouth. He didn't want to evaluate all the reasons why he was compelled to speak at this point. All he accepted was that he felt it necessary to do more than relay antiseptic information to his wife. He felt it necessary to move her out of herself and into the core of her motherhood, even if that meant she would blame him as he deserved. It would be better, he thought, than watching her go elsewhere.

She can't help it. He'd reminded himself of that fact endlessly throughout the years. *She is not responsible. She needs me to help her.* He didn't know if this was the truth any longer. But to believe something else at this late hour would make more than a quarter century of his life a lie.

'I bear the fault for everything that happened,' he went on. 'I couldn't cope. I needed more than anyone could ever give me and when they couldn't give it, I tried to wring it from them. That's how it was with you and me. That's how it was with Santo.'

'You should have divorced me. Why in God's name did you never divorce me?' She began to weep. She turned to lie on her side, facing the bedside table where her bottle of pills stood. She reached for them as if intending another dose. He took the bottle and said, 'Not now.'

'I need—'

'You need to stay here.'

'I can't. Give them to me. Don't leave me like this.'

It was the cause, the very root of the tree. *Don't leave me like this. I love you, I love you . . . I don't know why . . . My head feels like something about to blow up, and I can't help . . . Come here, my darling. Come here, come here.*

'They've sent someone down from London.' He could see from her expression that she did not understand. She'd strayed from Santo's death at this point, and she wanted to stray farther, but he would not let her. 'A detective,' he said. 'Someone from Scotland Yard. He spoke to my father.'

'Why?'

'They check everything when someone's been murdered. They look into every nook and cranny of everyone's life. Do you understand what that means? He spoke to Dad and Dad told him everything he knew.'

'About what?'

'About why I left Pengelly Cove.'

'But that has nothing to do with—'

'It's something to look at and that's what they do. They look.'

'Give me the pills.'

'No.'

She made a grab for them anyway. He held the bottle out of her reach. He said, 'I didn't sleep last night. Being in Pengelly Cove, talking to Dad. It brought everything back. That party at Cliff House, the drink, the drugs, groping in the shadows and who the hell cared who saw if things went further? And things did go further. Didn't they?'

'I don't remember. It was a long time ago. Ben, please. Give me the pills.'

'You'll go away if I do, but I want you here. You need to feel something of what I feel. I want that from you because if I don't have that much . . .' What? he wondered. If she couldn't give him what he asked of her now, what would he do that he hadn't already tried and failed to do in the past? His threats were empty, and both of them knew it.

'Death asks for death in the end, no matter what we do,' he told her. 'I didn't like Santo surfing. I believed that surfing could lead him to where surfing had led me. But the truth was that I wanted to take from him the core of who he was because *I* was afraid. It all came down to believing he had to live the way I live. I as much as said, Live like a dead man and I'll love you for it. And these—' He gestured with the pills and rose from the bed. 'These make you dead as well, dead to the world. But *in* the world is where I want you to be.'

'You know what'll happen. I can't stop myself. I *try* and I feel like my skull is pounding.'

'And it's always been that way.'

'You *know* that.'

'So you get relief. From pills and from drink. And if there are no pills and if drink doesn't work—'

'Give them to me!' She too rose from the bed.

He was near the window, so it took no effort. He opened it and spilled sedatives down the side of the building, into the muddy border where springtime plants languished, waiting for sun that was long in coming.

Dellen wailed. She ran to Ben. She beat her fists against him. He caught them and held them.

'I want you seeing,' he said. 'And hearing and feeling. And remembering. If I have to cope with all of this alone—'

'I hate you!' she screamed. 'You want and you *want*. But you *won't* find someone who'll give you what you want. That person's not me. It never has been and you won't let me go. And I hate you. God, *God* how I hate you!'

She tore herself from him and for a moment he thought she meant to dash from the room and scrabble in the mud below in order to rescue her fast dissolving pills. But instead she went to the cupboard, where she began yanking clothing from within. It was red upon red, crimson, magenta and every point in between, and all of it she threw in a heap on the floor. She was looking for the one that said the most, he thought, like the crimson sun dress on that long ago evening.

He said, 'Tell me what happened. I was with Parsons' sister. I was doing what I could do to her, what she'd let me get away with and that was a lot. He found us together and he threw me out. Not because he cared that his sister was about to get stuffed in the corridor of her parents' house in the midst of a party but because he liked feeling superior to everyone, and this was another way to do it. It wasn't a class thing. Or even a money thing. It was a Jamie thing. Tell me what happened once I left.'

She continued throwing her clothes on the floor. When she'd finished with the cupboard, she went to the chest. Here she did the same. Knickers and bras, petticoats, jerseys, scarves. Just the red of it all until the clothing was pooled round her feet like the pulp of fruit.

'Did you fuck him, Dellen? I've never asked about any of them specifically, but this is the one I want to know. Did you say to him, "There's a sea cave on the beach where Ben and I go for sex and I'll meet you there." And he wouldn't have known we were finished, you and I. He would have thought it a good way to get his own back. So he'd meet you there and—'

'No!'

'—he'd fuck you like you wanted. But he'd taken some of the drugs on offer, weed, coke, whatever else was there . . . LSD . . . Ecstasy, and he'd mixed them with whatever he was drinking and once he'd done what you wanted him to do, you just left him, passed out cold, and deep in the cave, and when the tide came in the way it always comes in—'

'No!'

'—you were long gone. You'd got what you wanted, and that was nothing to do with getting stuffed and everything to do with getting revenge. And what you reckoned was that, Jamie being Jamie, he'd make certain I knew he'd had you the very next time he saw me. But what you *hadn't* reckoned was the tide would get the better of your plan and—'

'I told!' she screamed. She had no more clothes to throw onto the floor, so she reached for the bedside lamp and she brandished it. 'I talked and I told *everything* I knew. Are you happy now? Is that what you've wanted to hear from me?'

Ben was rendered speechless. He wouldn't have thought anything could have robbed him of words at this point, but he had none. He wouldn't have thought there wcre any surprises left from his past, but that was clearly not the case.

Bea and DS Havers walked from the Blue Star Grocery to Casvelyn of Cornwall. The bakery was in full production, preparing for the delivery of goods to the area's pubs, hotels, cafés, and restaurants. Hence, the heady fragrance of flaky, succulent pastry formed a hypnotic miasma in the air. It became more powerful as they drew closer to the shop, and Bea heard Barbara Havers murmur fervently, 'Bloody blooming *hell.*'

The sergeant was gazing longingly in the direction of Casvelyn of Cornwall's front window, where the trays of newly baked pasties lay in seductive, eye-popping, and utterly diet-busting ranks of cholesterol, carbohydrates, and calories. 'Tempting, isn't it?' Bea said to the sergeant.

'It's got Pop Tarts beat. I'll give you that.'

'You must have a pasty while you're in Cornwall. And if you're going to do so, these are the best.'

'I'll make a note of it.' Havers gave a lingering look to them as she followed Bea into the shop.

Madlyn Angarrack was serving a queue of customers while Shar heaved trays of the bakery's products out of the enormous kitchen and into the display cases. It seemed they had more than pasties going on this day, since Shar was currently bringing out loaves of artisan bread, thick of crust and topped with rosemary.

Although Madlyn was busy, Bea had no intention of standing at the end of a queue. She excused herself to the waiting customers by ostentatiously showing her identification and murmuring, 'Excuse me. Police business,' as she passed them by. At the till, she said at some considerable volume, 'A word, Miss Angarrack. Here or in the station but in either case, now.'

Madlyn didn't attempt to temporise. She said to her co-worker, 'Shar, will you take the till?' although she did add meaningfully, 'I won't be a moment,' to indicate either her cooperation with the police or her intention of immediately demanding a solicitor. She then fetched a jacket and went outside.

'This is DS Havers,' Bea said by way of introduction. 'She's come down from New Scotland Yard to assist in the investigation.'

Madlyn's eyes flicked to Havers and then back to Bea. In a voice that sounded something between wary and confused she said, 'Why's Scotland Yard—'

'Think about it.' Bea saw that being able to bandy about the term *New Scotland Yard* was going to have one or two unanticipated uses. It consisted of three words that asked people to sit up and take notice, no matter what they knew or did not know about the Metropolitan police.

Madlyn was silent. She regarded Havers, and if she wondered what a representative from New Scotland Yard was doing dressed like a survivor of Hurricane Katrina, she did not say it. Havers took out a tattered notebook and jotted down a note. It was likely a reminder to buy a pasty before leaving Casvelyn for the Salthouse Inn that evening, but that didn't matter to Bea. It looked official and that was what counted.

'I don't appreciate being lied to,' Bea told Madlyn. 'It wastes my time, it forces me to go over old ground, and it throws me off my stride.'

'I didn't—'

'Save us all some time during this second round of the boxing match, all right?'

'I don't see why you think—'

'Need a refresher? Seven and a half weeks ago, Santo Kerne ended your relationship and, according to you, that was that: It was all you knew, full stop, no window dressing included. But as it turns out, you knew a bit more than that, didn't you? You knew he was seeing someone else and something about that made you sick. Does any of this sound familiar to you, Miss Angarrack?'

Madlyn's gaze shifted. Her brain was clearly engaged in calculations, and her expression said that the calculations were of the *who's the bloody grass?* variety. The suspects were probably not innumerable, and when Madlyn's glance took in the Blue Star Grocery, satisfaction played her face like a keyboard. Resolution followed. Will Mendick, Bea Hannaford reckoned, was likely burnt toast.

'What would you like to tell us?' Bea asked. Sergeant Havers tapped her pencil against her notebook with great meaning. It was a chewed-up pencil, but that was no surprise, as possessing a writing utensil in any other condition would have been wildly out of character in the woman.

Madlyn's gaze came back to Bea. She didn't look resigned. She looked avenged, which to Bea's way of thinking, was *not* the way a suspect ought to look when it came to murder.

'He broke up with me. I told you that and it was the truth. I didn't lie, and you can't make out that I did. *And* I wasn't under oath anyway.'

'Save the legal wrangling,' Havers spoke up. 'Far as I know, this isn't an episode of *The Bill*. You lied, you cheated, or you danced the polka. We don't much care. Let's get to the facts. I'll be happy, the DI'll be happy, and, trust me, you'll be happy as well.'

Madlyn didn't look appreciative of this advice. She made a moue of distaste, but it seemed to be an expression that served the purpose of jockeying for position because when she next spoke, she told a completely different tale from the one she'd told earlier. She said, 'All right. I broke up with him. I thought he was cheating, so I followed him. It's not something I'm proud of, but I had to know. When I knew, I ended it. It hurt to do it because I was stupid and I still loved him, but I ended it anyway. That's the story. And it's the truth.'

'So far,' Bea said.

'I just *told* you—'

'Followed him where?' Havers asked, her pencil poised. 'Followed him when? And how? On foot, by car, on bicycle, on a pogo stick?'

'What about his cheating on you made you sick?' Bea asked. 'Just the fact of it, or was there something else? I think "off" was your description.'

'I *never* said—'

'Not to us, no. That's part of the current problem. *Your* problem, that is. When you say one thing to one person and another thing to the coppers, it all comes back to bite you in the end. So I suggest you consider yourself bitten and do something to get the teeth out of your bum, in a matter of speaking.'

'Rabies being rabies and all,' DS Havers murmured. Bea stifled a smile. She was starting to like the dishevelled woman.

Madlyn's jaw tightened. It seemed that the full reality of her situation was beginning to dawn upon her. She could remain obdurate and accept the threats and the ridicule of the other two women, or she could talk. She chose the option that seemed likeliest to effect their imminent departure.

'I think people should stick to their own,' she said.

'And Santo didn't stick to his own?' Bea asked. 'What's that mean, exactly?'

'Just what I said.'

'What?' Havers asked impatiently. 'He was doing altar boys on the side? Goats? Sheep? The occasional vegetable marrow? *What?*'

'Stop it!' Madlyn cried. 'He was doing other women, all right? *Older* women. I confronted him when I knew about it. And I knew because I followed him.'

'We're back to that,' Bea said. 'You followed him where?'

'To Polcare Cottage.' Her eyes were bright. 'He went to Polcare Cove and I followed him. He went inside and I waited and waited because I was stupid and I wanted to think that . . . But no. No. So I went to the door after a bit and I banged upon it and you can work out the bloody rest, can't you? And that's all I have to say to you two, so leave me alone. Leave me bloody well *alone*.'

She pushed between them and stalked back towards the bakery door, rubbing at her cheeks furiously.

'What's Polcare Cottage?' DS Havers asked.

'A *very* nice place to pay a call on,' Bea said.

Lynley didn't approach the cottage at once because he saw immediately that there was probably going to be no point. She didn't appear to be at home. Either that or she'd parked her Vauxhall in the larger of the two outbuildings that stood on her property in Polcare Cove. He tapped his fingers against the steering wheel of his hired Ford, and considered what his next move ought to be. Reporting what he knew to DI Hannaford seemed to top the list, but he didn't feel settled with that decision; he wanted to give Daidre Trahair an opportunity to explain herself.

Despite what Barbara Havers might have thought once they parted at the Salthouse Inn, Lynley had taken her comments to heart. He *was* in a precarious position, and he knew it, although he hated to admit or even think about it. He wanted desperately to escape the black pit in which he'd been floundering for weeks upon weeks, and he felt inclined to clutch just about any life rope that would get him out of there. The long walk along the South-West Coast Path hadn't provided that escape as he'd hoped it would. So he had to admit that perhaps Daidre Trahair's company in conjunction with the kindness in her eyes had beguiled him into overlooking details that would otherwise have demanded acknowledgement.

He'd come upon another of those details on Havers' departure earlier that morning. Neither pigheaded nor blind when it came down to it, he'd placed another phone call to the zoo in Bristol. This time, however, instead of enquiring about Ms Trahair, he inquired about the primate keepers. By the time he wended his way through what seemed like half a dozen employees and departments, he was fairly certain what the news would be. There was no Paul the primate keeper at the zoo. Indeed, the primates were kept by a team of women, headed by someone called Mimsie Vance, to whom Lynley did not need to speak.

Another lie chalked up against her, another black mark that needed confrontation.

What he reckoned he ought to do was lay his cards on the table for the vet. He, after all, was the person to whom Daidre Trahair had spoken about Paul the primate keeper and his terminally ill father. Perhaps, he thought, he had misinterpreted or misunderstood what Daidre had said. Certainly, she deserved the chance to clarify. Didn't anyone in her position deserve as much?

He got out of the Ford and knocked on the blue front door. As he expected, the vet was not at home. But he went to the outbuildings just to make sure.

The larger one was empty of everything, as it would have to be for a car to be accommodated within its narrow confines. It was also largely unfinished inside and the presence of cobwebs and a thick coating of dust indicated that no one used it often. There were tyre tracks across the floor of the building, though. Lynley squatted and examined these. Several cars, he saw, had parked here. It was something to note, although he wasn't sure what to make of the information.

The smaller building was a garden shed. There were tools inside, all of them well used, testifying to Daidre's attempts to create something gardenlike out of her little plot of land, no matter its proximity to the sea.

He was studying these for want of studying something when he heard the sound of a car driving up, its tyres crunching on the pebbles along the verge. He was blocking her driveway, so he left the garden shed to move his vehicle out of her way. But it wasn't Daidre Trahair who'd arrived. Rather it was DI Hannaford. Barbara Havers was with her.

Lynley felt dispirited at the sight of them. He had rather hoped Havers would have said nothing to Bea Hannaford about what she'd uncovered in Falmouth although he'd known how unlikely that was. Barbara was a pit bull when it came to an investigation. She'd run over her grandmother with an articulated lorry if she was on the trail of something relevant. The fact that Daidre Trahair's past *wasn't* relevant would not occur to her because anything odd, contradictory, quirky, or suspicious needed to be tracked down and examined from every angle, and Barbara Havers was just the cop to do it.

Their eyes met as she got out of the car, and he tried to keep the disappointment from his face. She paused to shake a cigarette out of a packet of Players. She turned her back to the breeze, sheltering a plastic lighter from the wind.

Bea Hannaford approached him. 'She's not here?'

He shook his head.

'Sure about that, are you?' Hannaford peered at him intently.

'I didn't look in through the windows,' he replied. 'But I can't imagine why she wouldn't answer the door if she were at home.'

'I can. And how're we coming along with our investigation into the good doctor? You've spent enough time with her so far. I expect you've something to report.'

Lynley looked to Havers, feeling a curious rush of gratitude towards his former partner. He also felt the shame of having misjudged her, and he saw how much the last months had altered him. Havers remained largely expressionless, but she lifted one eyebrow. She was, he saw, putting the ball squarely into his court. For now.

'I don't know why she lied to you about the route she took from Bristol,' he told Hannaford. 'I've not got much further than that. She's very careful with what she reveals about herself.'

'Not careful enough,' the DI said. 'She lied about knowing Santo Kerne, as things turn out. The kid was her lover. She was sharing him with his girlfriend without his girlfriend knowing. At first, that is. The girlfriend had some suspicions on that front so she followed Santo and he led her straight here. He seems to have been a bloke who liked them any way he could get them. Older, younger, and in between.'

Although he found that his heart had begun beating quickly as the DI was speaking, Lynley said in an even tone, 'I'm not quite tracking this.'

'Not tracking what?'

'His girlfriend following him and the conclusion you've drawn: that he and Ms Trahair were lovers.'

'Sir.' It was Havers' monitory tone.

'Are you mad?' Hannaford said to Lynley. 'The girlfriend confronted him, Thomas.'

'Confronted him or confronted them?'

'Him or them? What difference does it make?'

'All the difference in the world if she didn't actually see anything.'

'Really? And what'd you expect the girl to do? Jump through the window with a camera while they were doing the deed? She saw enough to have words with him and he told her what was going on.'

'He said that Ms Trahair was his lover?'

'What the hell do you think—'

'It just seems to me that if he had a taste for older women, he'd want to go after one more readily available to him. Ms Trahair, according to what she's said, comes here only for holidays and occasional weekend breaks.'

'According to what she bloody says. My good man, she's lied about nearly everything so far, so I think we're God damn safe to assume that if Santo Kerne came to this cottage—'

'Could I have a word, Inspector Hannaford?' Havers broke in. 'With the superintendent, I mean.'

Firmly Lynley said, 'Barbara, I'm no longer—'

'With his lordship,' Havers corrected herself acidly. 'With his earlishness, with *Mister* Lynley, with *whatever* he wishes to be called at this point. If you don't mind, guv.'

Hannaford threw up her hands. 'Take him.' She began to walk towards the cottage, but she paused and pointed her finger at Lynley. 'Detective, if I find you're obstructing this investigation in *any* way . . .'

'You'll have my job,' Lynley said wryly. 'I know.'

He watched her stalk towards the cottage and knock on the door. When no one answered, she went round the side of the building, clearly intending to do what she thought Santo's girlfriend ought to have done: peer through the windows. He turned to Havers.

'Thank you,' he said.

'I wasn't rescuing you.'

'Not for that.' He indicated Hannaford with a nod towards the cottage. 'For not giving her the information from Falmouth. You could have done. You ought to have done. Both of us know that. Thank you.'

'I like to stay consistent.' She drew in deeply on her cigarette before she tossed it to the ground. She removed a bit of tobacco from her tongue. 'Why develop a respect for authority at the eleventh hour, if you know what I mean?'

He smiled. 'So you see—'

'No,' she said. 'I don't see. At least I don't see what you want me to see. She's a liar, sir. That makes her dirty. We came here to take her in for questioning. More, if we need to.'

'More? An arrest? For what? It seems to me that if she *was* having an affair with this boy, the motive to kill him sits squarely on someone else.'

'Not necessarily. And please don't tell me you don't know that.' She glanced at the cottage. Hannaford was gone from view, now at the seaside windows on the west end of the building. Havers drew a deep breath. She coughed a smoker's cough.

'You've got to give up tobacco,' he told her.

'Right. Tomorrow. In the meantime, we have a bit of a problem.'

'Come with me to Newquay.'

'What? Why?'

'Because I've got a lead on this case and that's where it is. Santo Kerne's father was involved in a death some thirty years ago. I think it needs to be checked into.'

'Santo Kerne's father? Sir you're avoiding the issue.'

'What issue?'

'You *know*.' She cocked her head at the cottage.

'Havers, I'm not. Come with me to Newquay.' The plan sounded so sensible to him. It even had the flavour of old times: the two of them doing some digging around, talking about leads, tossing round possibilities. Suddenly, he *wanted* the sergeant with him.

'I can't do that, sir,' Havers said.

'Why not?'

'First of all, because I'm here on loan to DI Hannaford. And second—' She drove her hand through her sandy hair, badly cut as always, and straight as the route of a martyr's path to heaven. It was filled, as usual, with static electricity. Much of it stood on end. 'Sir, how do I say this to you?'

'What?'

'This. You've been through the worst.'

'Barbara—'

'No. You've *bloody* well got to listen to me. You lost your wife to murder. You lost your child. For God's sake, you had to shut off their *life* support.'

He closed his eyes. Her hand grabbed his arm and held it firmly.

'I know this is hard. I *know* it's horrible.'

'No,' he murmured, 'You don't. You can't.'

'All right. I don't, and I can't. But what happened to Helen ripped your world apart and no one, bloody *no one*, sir, walks away from something like that with his head on straight.'

He looked at her, then. 'You're saying I'm mad? Have we come to that?'

She released his arm. 'I'm saying you're badly wounded. You're not coming at this from a position of strength because you *can't* and to expect anything else of yourself is just bloody wrong. I don't know who this woman is or why she's here or *if* she's Daidre Trahair or someone who's claiming to be Daidre Trahair. But the fact remains that when someone lies in the middle of a murder investigation, *that's* what the cops look at. So the question is, Why don't you want to? I think we both know the answer to that.'

'What would that be?'

'You're using your lordship voice. I know what that means: You want distance, and you usually get it. Well, I'm not giving it to you, sir. I'm here, standing in your face, and you have to look at what you're doing and why. And if you can't cope with the thought of doing it, you have to look at *that* as well.'

He felt as if a wave were washing over him, breaking through everything he'd built to hold it temporarily at bay. He finally said, 'Oh God,' but that was all he could say. He lifted his head and looked at the sky, where grey clouds were promising to transform the day.

When Havers spoke again, her voice was altered, from hard to soft. The change cut into him as much as her declarations had done. 'Why did you come here? To her cottage? Have you found out anything else about her?'

He cleared his throat and looked from the sky to her. She was so solid and so unutterably real and he *knew* that she was on his side. But he couldn't make that matter at the moment. If he told Havers the truth, she'd move upon it. The very fact of yet another lie from Daidre Trahair would tip the balance. 'I thought she might want to go to Newquay with me,' he said. 'It would give me a chance to talk to her another time, to try to sort out . . .' He didn't complete the thought. It sounded now, even to his ears, so pathetically desperate. Which is what I am, he thought.

Havers nodded. Hannaford came round the far side of the cottage. She was tramping through the heavy growth of marram grass and cowslip beneath the windows. It was more than obvious that she fully intended Daidre Trahair to know that someone had been there.

Lynley told her his intention: Newquay, the police, the story of Ben Kerne and the death of a boy called Jamie Parsons.

Hannaford was not impressed. 'Fool's errand,' she declared. 'What're we supposed to make of all that?'

'I don't know yet.'

'I want you on *her*, Superintendent. Is she somehow involved in what happened during the Ice Age? She would have been, what? Four years old? Five?'

'I admit that there may be issues about her that need exploring.'

'Do you indeed? How good to hear. So explore them. Got that mobile with you? Yes? Keep it on, then.' She jerked her fuchsia-coloured head towards her car. 'We'll be off. Once you locate our Ms Trahair, escort her to the station. Do I make myself clear?'

'Completely clear,' Lynley said.

He watched as Hannaford headed to her car. He and Havers exchanged a look before she followed.

He decided on Newquay anyway, that being the beauty of his role in the investigation. And damn the consequences if he and Hannaford disagreed, he wasn't obliged to discount his own inclinations in favour of hers.

He took the most direct route once he'd made his way through the tangled skein of lanes that separated Polcare Cove from the A39. He hit a tailback caused by an overturned lorry some five miles out of Wadebridge, which slowed him considerably, and he ended up in Cornwall's surfing capital shortly after two in the afternoon. He became immediately lost and cursed the obedient, parent-pleasing young adolescent he had been prior to his father's death. Newquay, his father had more than once intoned, was a vulgar town, not the sort of place a 'true' Lynley frequented. Consequently, he knew nothing of the town while his younger brother, never burdened with the need to please, could probably have found his way round blindfolded.

Having suffered the frustrating one-way system twice and having nearly driven into the pedestrian precinct once, Lynley gave up the effort and followed the signs to the information office, where a kindly woman asked him if he was 'looking for Fistral, love?' by which he took it that he was being mistaken for an ageing surfer. She was happy enough to give him directions to the police station, however, and they were of a detailed nature, so he managed to get there without further difficulty.

His police identification worked as he'd hoped it would, although it didn't take him as far as he'd planned. The special constable in reception handed him over to the head of the MCIT squad, a detective sergeant called Ferrell with a globelike head and eyebrows so thick and black that they looked artificial. He was aware of the investigation on-going in the Casvelyn area. He wasn't, however, aware that the Met had become involved. He said this last bit meaningfully. The Met presence suggested an investigation into the investigation, which in itself suggested gross incompetence on the part of the officer in charge.

In fairness to Hannaford, Lynley disabused DS Ferrell of whatever notion he was brewing about her capabilities. He'd been in the area on holiday, he explained. He'd been present when the body was found. The boy, he explained, was the son of a man who had himself been at least tangentially involved in a death a number of years ago, one that had been investigated by the Newquay police, and that was why Lynley had come to Newquay: for information relating to that situation.

Thirty years ago had obviously seen Ferrell not long out of nappies, so the DS knew nothing about anyone called Parsons, about Benesek Kerne, or about a sea cave mishap in Pengelly Cove. On the other hand, it wouldn't be tough for him to suss out who did know what in relation to that death. If the Superintendent didn't mind a bit of a wait?

Lynley chose to do his waiting in the canteen, the better to be a hovering presence that might spur things on. He bought himself an apple because he knew he ought to eat, despite not having felt hungry since his conversation with Havers that morning. He bit into it, was gratified to find it woolly, and tossed it into the rubbish bin. He followed up with a cup of coffee and wished vaguely that he was still a smoker. There was, of course, no smoking in the canteen these days, but having something to do with his hands would have been gratifying, even if it was only rolling an unsmoked cigarette in his fingers. At least he wouldn't feel as if he needed to tear packets of sugar into shreds, which was what he did as he waited for DS Ferrell to return. He opened one and dumped it into his coffee. The others he dumped into a neat pile onto the table, where he then ran a plastic stir stick through the mess, creating designs as he tried not to think.

There was no Paul the primate keeper, but what did that mean, really? A private person who'd been caught looking at sites for miracles, she'd want to make an excuse for that. It was human nature. Embarrassment led to prevarication. This was not a crime. But that, of course, was not the only instance of prevarication on the vet's part, and this was the problem he faced: what to do about Daidre Trahair's lies and, even more, what to think about them.

DS Ferrell did not return for a very long twenty-six minutes. When he did come into the canteen, however, he had nothing with him but a slip of paper. Lynley had been hoping for boxes of files he might look through, so he felt deflated. But there was moderate cheer in what Ferrell had to say.

'DI running that case retired long before my time,' he told Lynley. 'Must be over eighty by now. He lives in Zennor. Across from the church and next to the pub. He says he'll meet you by the mermaid's chair if you want to talk.'

'The mermaid's chair?'

'That's what he said. Said if you're a proper detective, you should be able to find it.' Ferrell shrugged and looked a bit embarrassed. 'Funny bloke, you ask me. Fair warning and all that. I think he may be a bit gaga.'

19

Daidre Trahair not being at home, there was nothing for it but to return to the police station in Casvelyn, which was what Bea and DS Havers did. Bea wedged her card into the cottage doorway in Polcare Cove before they left, with a note scribbled upon it, asking the vet to phone or to come to the station, but she didn't have much faith in that producing any positive results. Ms Trahair was, after all, without a telephone or a mobile and, considering her dealings with the truth so far, which could best be described as either fast and loose or non-existent, she wouldn't be entirely motivated to get in touch with them anyway. She was a liar. They knew she was a liar. She knew they knew she was a liar. With that combination of rather compelling details as the background of Bea's request that she get in touch, why would Daidre Trahair want to place herself in a position where a nasty confrontation with the cops was likely?

'He's not looking at things the way he ought,' Bea said to DS Havers abruptly as they headed upwards and out of Polcare Cove. Her thoughts had made a natural segue. Daidre Trahair and Polcare Cottage led inevitably to Thomas Lynley and Daidre Trahair and Polcare Cottage. Bea didn't like the fact that Lynley had been there, acting the part of informal welcome to her and DS Havers. Even less did she like the fact that Lynley had protested a bit too much when it came to Daidre Trahair's innocence in all matters pertaining to Santo Kerne.

'He's got a thing about keeping all the possible options in place,' Havers said. She sounded cautiously casual, and Bea narrowed her eyes suspiciously. The sergeant, she saw, was looking steadily forward as if a study of the lane were imperative for some reason. 'That's all that was, that business at the cottage. He looks at situations and sees them the way the CPS would see them. Forget an arrest for the moment, he thinks. The real question is: Is this good enough to take to court? Yes or no? If it's a *no*, he makes everyone keep digging. Gives you aggro-and-a-half sometimes, but it all comes right in the end.'

'That being the case, we might ask ourselves why he's reluctant to dig into Ms Trahair's story, mightn't we?'

'I think he reckons the Newquay angle is stronger. But no matter, really. He'll pick up where he left off on her.'

Bea eyed Havers again. The DS's body language didn't match her tone, one tense and the other too easy. There was far more here than met the eye, and Bea reckoned she knew what it was. 'Rock and a hard place,' she said to Havers.

'What?' Havers glanced at her.

'You, Sergeant Havers. That's where you are, isn't it? Loyalty to him versus loyalty to the job. Question is, How will you make the choice if you have to?'

Havers smiled thinly, clearly without humour. 'Oh, I know how to choose when it comes to it, guv. I didn't get where I am by choosing like a fool.'

'All of which is defined by the individual, isn't it?' Bea noted. 'The choosing-like-a-fool-bit. I'm not an idiot, Sergeant. Don't play me for one.'

'I hope I wouldn't be that stupid.'

'Are you in love with that man?'

'Who?' Havers' eyes widened. She had unappealingly small eyes, but when she opened them wide, Bea saw their attractive colour, which was highland sky blue. 'D'you mean the super?' Havers used her thumb to point in the direction Lynley had taken ahead of them. 'We'd make quite the couple, wouldn't we?' She barked a laugh. 'Like I said, guv, I bloody well hope I wouldn't be that stupid.'

Bea saw that, in this, she was telling the truth. Or at least a partial truth. And because it was partial, Bea knew she would have to watch Havers closely and monitor her work. She didn't like the idea – damn, was there *no* one on this case upon whom she was going to be able to rely? – but she couldn't see she had a choice.

Back in Casvelyn, the incident room displayed a gratifying scene of business in motion. Sergeant Collins was making notations on the china board; Constable McNulty was beavering away at Santo Kerne's computer; in the absence of a civilian typist one of the TAG team officers was transcribing a stack of notes into HOLMES. In the meantime, the DVLA had weighed in with a list of owners of cars like the two seen in the vicinity of Santo Kerne's cliff fall. The Defender, as Bea had assumed, had been the easier one when it came to comparing listed owners of such vehicles with all the principals in the case. Jago Reeth owned a Defender very similar to the car seen in Alsperyl approximately one mile to the north of the cliff where Santo Kerne was doing his abseiling. As to the RAV4, the vehicle seen to the south of that same cliff likely belonged to one Lewis Angarrack.

'Madlyn's stand-in granddad and Madlyn's father,' Bea told Havers. 'Isn't that a lovely detail?'

'As to that?' It was Constable McNulty speaking, half-risen from behind Santo Kerne's computer. He sounded something between hopeful and excited, 'Guv, there's—'

'Vengeance,' Havers agreed. 'He takes the girl's virtue and cheats on her. They take care of him. Or at least one of them does. Or they plan it together. That sort of thing plays strong when it comes to murder.'

'Guv?' McNulty again, fully upright now.

'And both Reeth and Angarrack would've had access to the boy's equipment,' Bea said. 'In the boot of his car? They would've likely known it was there.'

'Madlyn telling them?'

'Perhaps. But either one of them just could have seen it at one time or another.'

'Guv, I know you wanted me off the big wave thing,' McNulty broke in. 'But you need to have a look at this.'

'In a minute, Constable. Let me follow one thought at a time.'

'But this one part of the picture.'

'Damn it, McNulty!'

He exchanged a black look with Sergeant Collins. *Bloody cow* was its message. Bea saw this and said sharply, 'That'll do, Constable. All right, all right. *What*?' She approached the computer. He sat and tapped frantically at the keyboard. A website appeared, featuring an enormous wave with a flea-size surfer upon it. Bea saw this and prayed for patience although she wanted to drag McNulty from the computer by his ears.

'It's what he said about that poster,' McNulty told her. 'That old bloke over at LiquidEarth. See, first of all that kid on the wave – riding Maverick's, he said, remember? – couldn't've have been Mark Foo. That's a picture of Jay Moriarty.'

'Constable, this is all sounding rather too familiar,' Bea cut in.

'But wait. Like I said, it's a picture of Jay Moriarty and it's famous, least among surfers who ride big waves. Not only was the kid sixteen, but he was the youngest surfer ever to ride Maverick's at the time. And that picture of him was taken during the same swell that killed Mark Foo.'

'And this is critically important because?'

'Because surfers *know*. At least surfers who've been to Maverick's know.'

'Know what, exactly?'

'The difference between them. Between Jay Moriarty and Mark Foo.' McNulty's face was alight, as if he'd cracked the case on his own and was waiting for Bea to say 'Just call me Lestrade.' When she did not, he continued, perhaps less enthusiastically but certainly no less doggedly. 'Don't you see? That bloke with the Defender, Jago Reeth, said the poster at LiquidEarth was Mark Foo. Mark Foo on the wave that killed him. But here, right here,' McNulty tapped a few keys, and a photo identical to the poster appeared. '*This* is the same picture, guv. And it's Jay Moriarty, not Mark Foo at all.'

Bea thought about this. She didn't like to dismiss anything out of hand, but McNulty's enthusiasm for surfing appeared to be taking him into an area that bore no relevance to the case in hand. 'All right. So. The poster at LiquidEarth was misidentified by Jago Reeth. Where do we go with that?'

'To the fact that he doesn't know what he's talking about,' McNulty proclaimed.

'Just because he's misidentified a poster he likely didn't put up in the first place?'

'He's blowing smoke,' McNulty said. 'Mark Foo's last ride is part of surfing history. Jay Moriarty's wipe-out is the same. Someone green to the sport might not know who he was and what happened to him. But a longtime surfer? Someone who *says* he's hung round the scene for decades? Someone who says he's been all over the *world* following waves? He's going to know. And this bloke Reeth didn't. And *now* we've got his car near the spot where Santo Kerne fell. I say he's our man.'

Bea thought about this. McNulty was borderline incompetent as a detective, it was true. He would spend his life at the Casvelyn police station, never rising above the level of sergeant and even *that* advancement would come only if he was extremely lucky and Collins died with his boots on. But there were times when out of the mouths of babes and just as much out of the mouths of the bungling dribbled the truth. She didn't want to overlook that possibility just because most of the time she wanted to smack the constable on the side of his head.

She said to Sergeant Collins, 'What've we got on the prints from the Kerne boy's car? Are Jago Reeth's among them?'

Collins consulted a document, which he unearthed from a pile on

Bea's desk. The boy's prints were everywhere on the car, as one would expect, he said. William Mendick's were on the exterior: on the driver's side. Madlyn Angarrack's were nearly everywhere Santo's were: interior, exterior, inside the glove compartment, on the CDs. Others belonged to Dellen and Ben Kerne, and still others remained to be identified: from the CDs and the boot of the car.

'On the climbing equipment?'

Collins shook his head. 'Most of those aren't any good. Smears, largely. We've got a clear one of Santo's and a partial that hasn't been identified. But that's the limit.'

'Mush,' she said. 'Cold porridge. Nothing.' They were back to those cars from the vicinity of the fall. She spoke more meditatively than directly to anyone present, saying, 'We know the boy met Madlyn Angarrack for sex at Sea Dreams, so that takes care of Jago Reeth's access to his car, prints or not. I'll give you that, Constable. We know the boy got his surfboard from LiquidEarth, so there you've got Lewis Angarrack. For that matter, as he was dating Madlyn Angarrack, he would've been at her home one time or another. So Dad could've picked up the knowledge of the climbing kit there as well.'

'There'd be others, though, wouldn't there?' Havers asked. She was looking at the china board where DS Collins was listing activities. 'Anyone who knew the kid – his mates and even his own family, yes? – probably knew where he kept his kit. And wouldn't they have easier access?'

'Easier access but perhaps less motive.'

'No one stands to gain from his death? The sister? Her boyfriend?' Havers turned from the china board and seemed to read something on Bea's face because she added deferentially, 'Devil's advocate, guv. Seems like we don't want to slam any doors.'

'There's Adventures Unlimited,' Bea noted.

'Family business,' Havers pointed out. 'Always a nice motive.'

'Except they haven't opened yet.'

'Someone wanting to throw a spanner in, then? Stop them from opening? A rival?'

Bea shook her head. 'Nothing's as strong as the sex angle, Barbara.'

'So far,' Havers noted.

The village of Zennor was bleak at best of times, a situation arising from its location, tucked into a protective fold of otherwise windswept land perhaps one half mile from the sea, and from its monochromatic appearance, which was unadorned granite occasionally graced by the oddity of a desiccated palm tree. At the worst of times, defined by foul weather, gloom, or the dead of night, it was sinister, surrounded by fields from which boulders erupted like curses rained down by an angry god. It hadn't changed in a hundred years and likely wouldn't change in another hundred. Its past sprang from mining and its present relied on tourism, but there was little enough of that even at the height of summer as no beach close by was easy to get to and the only attraction even remotely likely to draw the curious into the village was the church. Unless one counted the Tinner's Arms, of course, and what that pub could provide in the way of food and drink.

The size of the carpark of this establishment did suggest that, in the summer at least, a fair amount of business occurred. Lynley parked there and went inside to inquire about the mermaid's chair. When he approached the publican, Lynley found him working a Sudoku puzzle. He held up a hand in that universal give-me-a-moment gesture, jotted a number in one of the puzzle's boxes, frowned, and rubbed it out. When he finally allowed himself to be questioned, he removed the possessive from the chair Lynley was seeking.

'Mermaids not being much inclined to sit, if you think about it,' the publican said.

Thus Lynley learned it was the *Mermaid* Chair he was looking for, and he would find it in Zennor Church. This structure sat not far from the pub as indeed, nothing in Zennor sat far from the pub since the village consisted of two streets, a lane, and a path winding past an odoriferous dairy farm and leading to the cliffs above the sea. The church had been built some centuries earlier on a modest hillock overlooking most of this.

It was unlocked, as most churches tended to be in the Cornish countryside. Within, silence defined the place, as did the scent of musty stones. Colour came from the kneeling cushions, which lined up precisely at the base of the pews, and from the stained glass window of the crucifixion above the altar.

The Mermaid Chair was apparently the church's main feature, for it had been established in a special spot in the side chapel, and above it hung a sign of explanation, which gave an account of how a symbol of Aphrodite had been appropriated by the Christians of the Middle Ages to symbolise the two natures of Christ as man and God. It was a stretch as far as Lynley was concerned, but he reckoned the

Christians of the Middle Ages had had their work cut out for them in this part of the world.

The chair was simple and looked more like a one-person pew than an actual chair. It was formed from ancient oak and it featured carvings of the eponymous sea creature holding a quince in one hand and a comb in the other. No one, however, was sitting upon it waiting for Lynley.

There was nothing for it but to wait himself, so Lynley took a place in the pew closest to the chair. It was frigid in the building and completely silent.

At this point in his life, Lynley didn't like churches. He didn't like the intimations of mortality suggested by their graveyards, and he desired more than anything not to be reminded of mortality at all. Beyond that, he didn't count himself a believer in anything other than chance and man's regular inhumanity to man. To him, churches and the religions they represented made promises they failed to keep. It was easy to guarantee eternal bliss after death since no one came back to report on the outcome of life lived in rigorous acceptance not only of the moral strictures devised by man but also of the horrors man wrought upon his fellows.

He hadn't been waiting long when he heard the clank of the church door opening and slamming shut with a disregard for things prayerful. He rose at this and left the pew. A tall figure was striding purposefully forward in the dim light. He walked with vigour and only when he came into the side chapel did Lynley see him clearly, in a broad shaft of illumination that fell from one of the church's windows.

His face alone betrayed his age, for his posture was upright and his body was sturdy. His face, however, was deeply lined, his nose misshapen by rhinophyma, its appearance akin to a floret of cauliflower dipped in beetroot juice. Ferrell had told Lynley the name of this potential source of information on the Kerne family: David Wilkie, retired Detective Chief Inspector from the Devon and Cornwall Constabulary, once the DI at the head of the investigation into the untimely death of Jamie Parsons.

'Mr Wilkie?' Lynley introduced himself. He produced his warrant card, and Wilkie put on a pair of spectacles to examine it.

'Off your patch, aren't you?' Wilkie didn't sound particularly friendly. 'Why're you nosing around the Parsons death?'

'Was it murder?' Lynley asked.

'Never proved as much. Death by Misadventure at the inquest, but you and I both know what that means. Could be anything with proof of nothing, so you got to rely on what people say.'

'That's why I've come to talk to you. I've spoken to Eddie Kerne. His son Ben—'

'Don't need memory jogging, lad. I'd still be working the job if regulations let me.'

'May we go somewhere to talk, then?'

'Not much for the house of God, are you?'

'Not at present, I'm afraid.'

'What are you, then? Fair-weather Christian? Lord doesn't come through for you the way you want so you slam the door in His face. That it? Young people. Bah. You're all alike.' Wilkie dug deeply into his waxed jacket's pocket and brought out a handkerchief that he wiped with surprising delicacy beneath his terrible nose. He gestured with it to Lynley and for a moment Lynley thought he was meant to use it as well, a form of bizarre communion with the older man. But Wilkie went on, saying, 'Look at that. White as the day I bought it and I do my own laundry. What d'you think of that?'

'Impressive,' Lynley said. 'I couldn't match you there.'

'You young cocks, you couldn't match me anywhere.' Wilkie shoved the handkerchief back to its home. 'It'll be here in God's house or not at all. 'Sides, I've got to dust the pews. You wait here. I've got supplies.'

Wilkie, Lynley thought, was definitely not gaga. He could probably have run circles round DS Ferrell in Newquay. On his hands, at that.

When the old man returned, he had a basket from which he took a broom, several rags, and a tin of polish, which he prised open with a house key and roughly swished a rag through. 'I can't sort out what's happened to churchgoing,' he revealed. He handed over the broom and gave Lynley detailed instructions as to its use upon and beneath the pews. He'd be following Lynley with the polish rag, so don't be leaving any spots unseen to, he said. There weren't enough rags if this lot – here he indicated the basket – got filthy. Did Lynley understand? Lynley did, which apparently gave Wilkie licence to return to his previous line of thought. 'My day, the church was filled to capacity. Two, maybe three times on Sunday and then for evensong on Wednesday night. Now between one Christmas and the next, you won't see twenty regular goers. Some extras on Easter, but only if the weather is good. I put this down to those Beatles, I do. I remember that one saying he was Jesus way back when. He should've been sorted straightaway, you ask me.'

'Long time ago, though, wasn't it?' Lynley murmured.

'Church's *never* been the same after that heathen spoke. Never. All those wankers with hair growing down to their arses singing 'bout getting their satisfactions met. *And* smashing their instruments to nothing. Those things cost money, but do they care? No. It's all ungodly. No wonder everyone stopped coming to pay the Lord His due respect.'

Lynley was considering a reassessment of the gaga bit. He also needed Havers with him to sort out the old man when it came to his rock 'n' roll history. He himself had been a late bloomer when it came to just about everything, and rock 'n' roll was among the many areas of pop culture from the past upon which he could not wax, eloquently or otherwise. So he waited until Wilkie had run out of steam on the topic, and in the meantime he became as admirably industrious with the broom as he could manage within the confines of the pews and in the church's inadequate lighting.

Presently, as he'd hoped, Wilkie concluded with 'World's going to hell in a shopping trolley, you ask me,' an assessment with which Lynley did not disagree.

'Was the parents wanted to see that lad go down for the death.' The old man spoke suddenly, some minutes later as they worked their way along another row of pews. 'Benesek Kerne. Parents got their jaws round him and they wouldn't let go.'

'That would be the parents of the dead boy?'

'Dad especially went off his nut when that lad died. Was the apple of his eye, was Jamie, and Jon Parsons, that's the dad, he never made bones about it to me. Man's *s'posed* to have a favourite child, he said, and the others're supposed to em'late *him* to get into the dad's good graces.'

'There were other children in the family, then?'

'Four in all. Three young girls, one just a wee toddler, and that boy which died. Parents waited for the verdict from the inquest and when the verdict was death by misadventure, Dad came to me. Few weeks later, this was. Dead crazed, poor bloke. Told me he knew for *certain* the Kerne boy was responsible. I ask him why he waits to tell me this – 'cause I'm discounting what he's saying as the ravings of a man mad with grief, and he tells me someone grassed. After the fact of the inquest, this was. He's been doing his *own* nosing round, he tells me. He's brought in his own investigator. And what they came up with was the grass.'

'Did you think he was telling you the truth?'

'Isn't *that* the question? Who bloody knows?'

'This person, the grass, never spoke to you?'

'Just to Parsons. So he claimed. Which as you and I know is damn meaningless since what he wants more'n anything is an arrest of someone. He needs someone to blame. So does the wife. They need *anyone* to blame because they think that accusing, arresting, putting on trial, and imprisoning is going to make them feel better, which of course it isn't. But Dad doesn't want to hear that. What dad would? Running his own investigation is the only thing keeping *him* from sliding over the edge. So I'm willing to cooperate with him, help him out, help him through the bloody mess his life's become. And I ask him to tell me who the grass is. I can't ecksackly make an arrest on some tittle tattle I didn't even hear first hand.'

'Of course,' Lynley noted.

'But he won't tell me, so what can I do that I hadn't already done, eh? We'd investigated the death of that lad left, right, and centre, and believe me, there was sod all to go on. The Kerne boy didn't have an alibi, aside from "walking the long way home to clear my head," but you don't hang a man for that, do you? Still, I wanted to help. So we had the Kerne boy into the station one more time, four more times, eighteen more times . . . Who the bloody hell remembers. We nosed round every aspect of his life and all of his friends' lives as well. Benesek didn't like the Parsons boy, we uncovered that much straightaway, but as things turned out, no one else liked the blighter neither.'

'Did they have alibis? His friends?'

'All told the same story. Home and to bed. Those stories stayed the same and no one broke ranks. Couldn't get a drop of blood out of them even by using a leech. They were either sworn to each other or they were telling the truth. Now, in my experience, when a group of lads gets up to no good, one of them breaks eventually if you keep pressing. But no one ever did.'

'Which led you to conclude they were telling the truth?'

'Nothing else *to* conclude.'

'What did they tell you about their relationship with the dead boy? What was their story?'

'Simple. Kerne boy and Parsons had words that night, a bit of a dust-up about something during a party at the Parsons' home. Kerne left the scene and his mates did the same. And, 'cording to them all, no one went back later to coax the Parsons boy to his end. He must've gone to the beach on his own, they said. End of story.'

'I've learned he died in a sea cave.'

'Went down there at night, the tide came in, he got caught up in it, and he couldn't get out. Toxicology showed he was pissed to oblivion and he'd done some doping on top of that. Common thought at first was that he'd met a girl in the cave for a poke and passed out either before or after.'

'"Common thought at first?"'

'The body was well banged up from the cave, see, being slung round for six hours while the tide came in and went out, but pathologist pointed out marks that couldn't be accounted for and these happened to be round the wrists and ankles.'

'Tied up, then. But no other evidence?'

'Faeces in the ears and wasn't *that* a bit peculiar, eh? But that was it. And there wasn't a witness to anything. Start to finish, it was a case of he said, she said, we said, they said. Finger pointing, gossiping, and that was that. Without hard evidence, without a witness to a thing, without even a scrap of *circumstantial* evidence, all we could hope for was someone to break and that might've happened had the Parsons kid not been the Parsons kid.'

'Which means?'

'Bit of a wanker, sad to say. Family had money so he thought he was better'n the rest of 'em and he liked to show it. Not the sort of thing going to make him popular with the local youngsters, you know what I mean.'

'But they went to his party?'

'Free booze, free dope, no parents at home, a chance to snog with the girl of your choice. Not a lot to do in Pengelly Cove at the best of times. They wouldn't've turned down a chance for some fun.'

'What happened to them, then?'

'The other boys? The Kerne boy's mates? They're still round Pengelly Cove, for all I know.'

'And the Parsons family?'

'Never went back to Pengelly Cove as such. They were from Exeter, and they went back there and there they stayed. Dad had a property management business in town. Called Parsons and . . . someone else. Can't recall. He himself went back to Pengelly regular for a bit, weekends and holidays, trying to get some full stop put to the case, but it never happened. He hired more 'n one investigator to take up the pieces as well. Spent a fortune on the whole situation. But if Benesek Kerne and those boys were behind what happened to Jamie Parsons, they'd learned from the first investigation into his death: If there's no hard evidence, and no witness to anything, keep the mug plugged and no one can touch you.'

'I understand he built something of a monument to him,' Lynley noted.

'Who? Parsons? Well, the family had the funds to do it and if it gave them some peace, more power to the whole idea.' Wilkie had been working his way along the pews, and now he straightened and stretched his back. Lynley did likewise. For a moment, they stood there in silence in the centre of the church, studying the stained glass window above the altar. Wilkie sounded meditative when he next spoke, as if he'd given the matter considerable thought over the years. 'I didn't like to leave things unsettled,' he said. 'I had a feeling that the dead boy's dad wouldn't be able to get a moment's peace if we didn't have someone called to account for what happened. But I think . . .' He paused and scratched the back of his neck. His expression said that his body was present but his mind had gone to another time and place. 'I think those boys, if they *were* involved, didn't mean the Parsons lad to die. They weren't that sort. Not a one of them.'

'Then what did they intend?'

He rubbed his face. The sound of rough skin on rough whiskers sandpapered at the air. 'Sort him out. Give him a bit of a scare. Like I said, from what I learned, the boy was full of himself and he didn't mind making clear what he did and what he had that they didn't.'

'But to tie him up. To leave him . . .'

'Drunk, the lot of them. Doped up as well. They get him down there to the cave, p'rhaps they tell him they've more dope to sell, and they jump him. They tie him at the wrists and ankles and give him some discipline. A talking to. A bit of a roughing up. Smear some shit on him for good measure. Then they untie him and leave him there and they think he'll make his own way home. Only they don't account for how drunk he is and how doped up he is and he passes out and that's the end of it. See, thing is, like I said, there really wasn't a truly bad one 'mongst those boys. Not one of 'em ever been in a spot of trouble. And I told the parents that. But it wasn't something they wanted to hear.'

'Who found the body?'

'That was the worst bit,' Wilkie said. 'Parsons phoned up the cops morning after the party to say his boy'd gone missing. Cops said the usual: He probably got into a local girl's knickers and he's sleeping off the aftermath in her bed or under it, so phone us again if he doesn't turn up in a day or two because otherwise we can't be bothered. Meantime, one of the boy's sisters tells him about the scuffle Jamie'd had with the Kerne lad, and Parsons thinks there's more here than meets the eye. So he sets off to have a look round for the boy. And he's the one who finds him.' Wilkie shook his head. 'Can't imagine what that would be like, but I expect it could drive a man to madness. Favourite child. Only son. No one ever called to answer for what happened. And the one name associated with the hours leading up to the death: Benesek Kerne. You can see how he fixed on him.'

'D'you know Benesek Kerne's own son has died?' Lynley asked. 'He was killed in a fall from one of the sea cliffs. His equipment had been tampered with. It's murder.'

Wilkie shook his head. 'Didn't know,' he said. 'That's bloody unfortunate. How old's the boy?'

'Eighteen.'

'Same as the Parsons lad. Now, that's a bloody shame.'

Daidre was shaken. What she wanted was the peace she'd had a week earlier, when all that her life had asked of her was that she look after herself and meet the obligations of her career. She might have been alone as a result of this, but that was her preference. Her small existence was safer that way, and safety was paramount.

Now, however, the smooth moving vehicle that had been her life had developed serious engine troubles. What to do about them was the issue that intruded upon her serenity.

So on her return to Polcare Cove, she'd left her car at the cottage and walked the remainder of the distance down the lane to the sea. There, she'd made for the path and picked her way along its stony ascent.

It was windy there and windier still on the cliff top. Daidre's hair whipped round her face and flicked its ends into her eyes, which smarted. When going out onto the cliffs, she usually removed her contact lenses and wore her glasses instead. But she hadn't taken her glasses when she'd left that morning, which had been a matter of vanity. She should have stopped into the cottage to get her glasses, but at the end of her day's journey, it had seemed that only a vigorous climb to the cliff top could keep her fixed in present time.

Some situations one came across required a person's intervention, she thought. But surely this wasn't one of them. She didn't *want* to do what was being asked of her, but she was wise enough to know that wanting was not what this was about.

The sound of an unmuffled engine came to her not long after she reached the top of the cliff. She'd been sitting upon an outcrop of lime-stone, watching the kittiwakes, and following the majestic arcs the birds made in the air as they sought shelter in niches in the cliff. But now she stood and walked back to the path. A motorcycle, she saw, was coming down the lane. It reached her cottage and veered into the pebbly driveway, where it stopped. The rider removed his helmet and approached the front door.

Daidre thought of couriers and messengers when she saw him knock: someone carrying a package for her, perhaps a message from Bristol? But she was expecting nothing and from what she could tell, the rider had nothing with him. He went round her cottage to seek another door or to look into a window. Or worse, she thought.

She made for the path and began to descend. There was no point shouting because she couldn't have been heard from this distance. Indeed, there was also little point in hurrying. The cottage was some way from the sea and she was some way above the lane. By the time she got back, the rider would have left.

But the thought that someone might be breaking into her cottage spurred her downward. She kept her glance going between her feet and her cottage as she went, and the fact that the motorcycle remained in place in her driveway kept her speed up and her curiosity piqued.

She arrived breathless and dashed in through the gate. Instead of a housebreaker half in and half out of a window, though, she found a girl clad in leathers lounging on her front step. She was sitting with her back against the bright blue door and her legs stretched out in front of her. She had a hideous silver ring through her septum and a turquoise coloured choker tattooed brightly round her neck.

Daidre recognised Cilla Cormack, the bane of her own mother's life. Her gran lived next door to Daidre's family in Falmouth. What on *earth*, Daidre thought, was the girl doing here?

Cilla looked up as Daidre approached. The dull sun glinted off her septum ring, giving it the unappealing look of those rings once used on cows to urge their cooperation when they were attached to a lead. She said, 'Hey,' and gave Daidre a nod. She rose and stamped her feet as if with the need to get the circulation going.

'This is a surprise,' Daidre said. 'How are you, Cilla? How's your mum?'

'Cow,' Cilla said, by which Daidre assumed she meant her mother, Cilla's disputes with that woman being something of a neighbourhood legend. 'C'n I use your toilet or summick?'

'Of course.' Daidre unlocked the front door and ushered the girl inside. 'Through there.' She waited to see what would happen next because surely Cilla hadn't come all the way from Falmouth just to use the loo.

Some minutes later, during which time water ran enthusiastically and Daidre began to wonder if the girl had decided to have a bath, Cilla returned. Her hair was wet and slicked back and she smelled as if she'd decided to help herself to Daidre's perfume as well. 'That's better,' she said. 'Felt like bloody hell, I did. Roads're bad this time of year.'

'Ah,' Daidre said. 'Would you like something? Tea? Coffee?'

'Fag?'

'I don't smoke. I'm sorry.'

'Figgers, that.' Cilla looked round and nodded. 'This's nice, innit. But you don't live here reg'lar, right?'

'No. Cilla, is there something . . . ?' Daidre felt stymied by her upbringing. One didn't come out and ask a visitor what on earth she was doing visiting. On the other hand, it was impossible that the girl had just been passing by. Daidre smiled and tried to look encouraging.

Cilla wasn't the brightest bulb in the chandelier, but she did manage to get the point. She said, 'My gran asked me would I come. Said you di'n't have a mobile.'

Daidre felt alarmed. 'What's going on? Is someone ill?'

'Gran says Scotland Yard came by. She says you'd best know straight-away cos they were asking about you. She says they went to your house first but when no one was home, they started banging doors up an' down the street. She phoned up Bristol to tell you. You wa'n't there, so she reckoned you might be here and she aksed would I come here to let you know. Whyn't you get yourself a mobile, eh? Or even a phone here? That'd make sense, you know. I mean just like in a 'mergency. Cos it's one hell of a way to get here from Falmouth. And d'you know how much petrol costs these days?'

The girl sounded aggrieved. Daidre went to the sideboard in the dining room and fetched twenty pounds. She handed it over. She said, 'Thank you for coming. It can't have been easy, all this way.'

Cilla relented. 'Well, Gran aksed. And she's a good old girl, innit. She always lets me stop there when Mum throws me out, which's about once a week, eh? So when she aksed me and said it was important . . .' She shrugged. 'Anyways. Here I am. She said you should know. She also said—' Here Cilla frowned as if trying to remember the rest of the message. 'Oh. Yeah. She also said not to worry because she di'n't tell them nuffink.' Cilla touched her septum ring as if to make sure it was still in place. 'So why's Scotland Yard nosing round you?' she asked, grinning. 'What you done? You got bodies buried in the garden or summick?'

Daidre smiled faintly. 'Six or seven.'

'Thought as much.' Cilla cocked her head. 'You've gone dead white. You best sit down. Put your head . . .' She seemed to lose the thread of where one's head was supposed to go. 'You want a glass of water, eh?'

'No, no. I'm fine. Haven't eaten much today. Are you sure you don't want something?'

'Gotta get back,' she said. 'I've a date tonight. M'boyfriend's taking me dancing.'

'Is he?'

'Yeah. We're taking lessons. Bit daft, that, but it's summick to do, innit. We're at that one where the girl gets thrown around a bit and you got to keep your back real stiff otherwise. Stick your nose in the air. That sorta thing. I got to wear high heels for it, which I don't like much, but the teacher says we're getting quite good. She wants us to be in a competition, she says. Bruce, that's m' boyfriend, he's dead chuffed 'bout it and he says we got to practise every day. So that's why we're going dancing tonight. Mostly we practise in his mum's sitting room, but *he* says we're ready to go out in public.'

'How lovely,' Daidre said. She waited for more. More, she hoped, would consist of Cilla's leaving the premises so that Daidre could come to terms with the message the girl had brought. Scotland Yard in Falmouth. Asking questions. She felt anxiety climbing up her arms.

'Anyway, got to dash,' Cilla said, as if reading Daidre's mind. 'Look, you best think about having a phone put in, eh? You could keep it in a cupboard or summick. Plug it in when you want it. That sort of thing.'

'Yes. Yes, I will,' Daidre told her. 'Thanks so much, Cilla, for coming all this way.'

The girl left her then, and Daidre stood on the front step, watching her expertly kick-start the motorcycle – no electronic ignition for *this* rider – and turn it on the drive. In a few more moments and with a wave, the girl was gone. She zoomed up the narrow lane, curved out of sight, and left Daidre to deal with the aftermath of her visit.

Scotland Yard, she thought. Questions being asked. There could be only one reason, only one person, behind this.

20

Kerra's night had been sleepless and much of her following day had been useless. She'd attempted to carry on as well as possible, keeping to a schedule of interviews that she'd set up in the preceding weeks: the search for potential instructors. She'd thought she could, at least, divert herself with the hopeful if unlikely pretence that Adventures Unlimited was actually going to open in the near future. The plan hadn't worked.

This is it. That simple declaration, that coy little arrow from *This is it* to the great sea cave depicted on the postcard, the implication that conversations of a nature having nothing to do with business had passed between the writer of those words and the reader of those words, what lay behind, beneath, and beyond those conversations . . . These disquieting and turbulent thoughts had been the stuff of Kerra's day and the sleepless night that had preceded it.

The postcard had now for some hours been burning a small rectangular patch against her skin from within the pocket where she'd stowed it. Each time she'd moved, she'd been aware of it, taunting her. She was going to have to do something about it, eventually. That dull burning told her as much.

Kerra hadn't been able to avoid Alan as she would have liked to do that day. The marketing office was not far from her own cubbyhole, and while she'd routinely taken prospective instructors to the first floor lounge for their interviews rather than to her cubbyhole, she'd greeted them in the vicinity of the marketing office. Alan had popped out more than once to observe her, and she wasn't long in working out what his silent observation meant.

It was more than disapproval of her choice of candidates, all of them female. He'd made himself clear on that topic earlier, and Alan wasn't the sort to keep pressing a point when someone was being bloody-minded. Rather, his mute scrutiny told her that Busy Lizzie had mentioned Kerra's visit to Pink Cottage. She'd likely told Alan about Kerra's putative need to find a personal possession in Alan's room, and he'd be wondering why Kerra herself hadn't mentioned it. She had her answer ready, but he hadn't asked.

She didn't know where her father was. She'd seen him go out in the direction of St Mevan Beach some hours ago, and as far as she knew he'd not returned. She'd reckoned at first he'd gone to watch the surfers, for the swells were good and the wind was off-shore and she herself had seen a ragtag line of them working their way across the Promontory. Had things been wildly different, Santo might have been among them, lining up out there in the water to get into position. Her father might have been there as well. Her father *and* her brother together, as a matter of fact. But things were not different, and they never would be. That appeared to be the family's curse.

And at the root of that curse: Dellen. It was as if all of them were wandering in a maze, trying to get to its mysterious centre, where Dellen waited, black widow-like. The only way to elude her was to purge her, but it was far too late for that.

'Want anything?'

Alan spoke. Kerra was in her office, where looking through a meagre stack of applicants was proving to be a dispiriting activity. She'd been working on sea kayaking, and she'd spoken to five possible instructors that day. Only two had the background she was looking for and, of those, only one had a physique suggestive of experience in the sea. The other looked like someone who kayaked on the River Avon, where the biggest challenge she faced would be taking care not to brain a cygnet with her paddle.

Kerra closed the last of the manila folders with their paltry bits of information. She wondered how best to answer Alan's question. She was working on whether irony, sarcasm, or a display of wit was in her best interests when he spoke again.

'Kerra? Want anything? Cup of tea? Coffee? Something to eat? I'm going out for a bit, and I can stop—'

'No. Thanks.' She didn't want to be beholden to him, even in so small a matter as this.

Instead, she examined him and he examined her. It was one of those moments when two individuals who have been lovers scrutinise each other like cultural anthropologists studying a tract of land for the remains of an ancient civilisation long believed to have dwelt there. There should be marks, signs, indications of a passage . . .

'How is it going?' he asked.

She knew that he was well aware of how it was going, but she played the game. 'I've come up with several strong possibilities. I'm doing additional interviews tomorrow. But the real question is whether we're actually going to open, isn't it? We seem rather without direction, especially today. Have you seen my father?'

'Not for hours.'

'What about Cadan? Did he show up to work on the radiators?'

'He may have done, but I haven't seen him. It's been rather quiet all the way round.'

He didn't mention Dellen. On this day, she was as she had always been when things went bad: the great unmentionable. Just the thought of her, of Dellen the malodorous dead elephant in the room, reduced everyone to mute trepidation.

'What've you been doing?' Kerra inclined her head towards his office. He seemed to take this as welcome, for he entered hers although this wasn't what she'd intended. She wanted him at a distance. Things were, she'd decided, finished between them now.

'I've been trying to get everyone in place for the video. Despite what's happened, I do still think . . .' He pulled out a chair from its position between the office wall and the open door. When he sat, they were virtually knee-to-knee. Kerra didn't like this. 'This is important,' Alan said. 'I want your dad to see that. I know the timing couldn't be worse, but—'

'Not my mother?' Kerra inquired.

Alan looked momentarily puzzled, perhaps by her tone. He said, 'Your mum as well but she's already on board, so your dad—'

'Oh, is she?' Kerra said. 'But then, I suppose she would be.' His embracing of her mother as a topic was surprising. Dellen's opinion on anything had hardly ever counted since she was incapable of consistency, so to hear someone counting it now came as something of a shock. Yet on the other hand, it did make sense. Alan worked with Dellen in marketing, on the rare occasions when Dellen actually worked at all, so they would have talked the video project through before he presented it to Kerra's father. Alan would have wanted Dellen on his side: It meant one vote in the bag and a vote from someone who might have considerable influence with Ben Kerne.

Kerra wondered if Alan had talked to Santo as well, and what Santo had made of Alan's ideas for Adventures Unlimited.

'I'd like to talk to him again, but I haven't actually seen . . .' Alan hesitated. Then he finally appeared to give in to his curiosity. He asked, 'What's going on? Do you know?'

'About what, exactly?' Kerra kept her voice polite.

'I heard them, earlier in the day. I'd gone upstairs to look for . . .' His face was colouring.

Ah, she thought, were they there at last? 'To look for?' Now she sounded arch, and she wouldn't have thought it was possible to manage *arch* when what she felt was anything but.

'I heard your mum and dad. Or rather your mum. She was . . .' He lowered his head. He appeared to be examining his shoes. These were two-tone, saddle shoes. What other man would wear saddle shoes? Kerra wondered. And what on earth did it mean that he somehow managed to carry off wearing them without looking like Bertie Wooster? 'I know things are bad,' he said. 'I'm just not sure what I'm meant to be doing. At first I thought soldiering on was the ticket, but now it's begun to seem inhuman. Your mum's clearly in pieces, your dad's—'

'How would you know that?' The question came out precipitately. Kerra regretted it the moment she spoke.

'What?' He'd been speaking meditatively, and her question appeared to have disrupted his chain of thought.

'About the pieces my mother is in?'

'As I said, I heard her. I'd gone up because no one was about and we're at the point when we have to decide whether we're still taking bookings or throwing the whole thing into the rubbish.'

'Concerned about that, are you?'

'Shouldn't we all be?' He leaned back in his chair, looked at her squarely, and folded his hands over his stomach. 'Why don't you tell me, Kerra?'

'What?'

'I think you know.'

'And *I* think that's a trap.'

'You were at Pink Cottage. You went through my room.'

'You've got a good landlady.'

'What else would you expect?'

'So I suppose you're asking me what I was looking for?'

'You told her you'd left something; I assume you'd left something. But I can't work out why you didn't ask me to bring it here for you.'

'I didn't want to bother you.'

'Kerra.' Huge breath drawn in, huge breath expelled. He slapped his hands onto his knees. 'What in God's name is going *on*?'

'Excuse me?' She managed arch again. 'My brother's been murdered. Does something else need to be "going on"?'

'You know what I mean. God knows what's happened is a nightmare. And a gut-ripping tragedy.'

'Nice of you to add that last bit.'

'*But* there's also what's been going on between you and me and *that*, whether you want to admit it or not, began the same day as what happened to Santo.'

'Murder happened to Santo. Why can't you say that, Alan? Why can't you say *murder?*'

'For the obvious reason. I don't want you to feel worse than you already feel. I don't want *anyone* to feel worse than they already feel.'

'Anyone?'

'Everyone. You. Your dad. Your mum. Kerra—'

She got to her feet. The postcard was singeing her skin. It begged to be withdrawn from her pocket and flung at him. *This is it* demanded an explanation. But the explanation already existed. Only the confrontation remained.

Kerra knew who needed to be on the other side of that confrontation, and it wasn't Alan. She excused herself and she left her office. She used the stairs rather than the lift.

She entered her parents' room without knocking, the postcard in her hand. At some point in the day the curtains had been opened, so dust motes swam in an oblong of weak spring sunlight. But no one had thought to open the window to refresh the rank air. It smelled of perspiration and sex.

Kerra hated the smell, for what it stated about her parents and the stranglehold one had upon the other. She walked across the room and shoved the window open as wide as she could get it. Cold air swept in.

When she turned, she saw that her parents' bed was lumpy and the sheets were stained. A pile of her father's clothes lay on the floor as if his body had dissolved and left this trace of him behind. Dellen herself was not immediately evident, until Kerra walked round the bed and found her lying on the floor, atop a considerable pile of her own clothing. Red, this was, and it seemed to be every article of crimson that she possessed.

For an instant as she gazed down upon her, Kerra felt renewed: a bulb's single flower finally being released from both the soil and the stalk. But then her mother's lips worked and her tongue appeared between them, French kissing the air. Her hand opened and closed. Her hips moved then rested. Her eyelids twitched. She sighed.

Kerra wondered for the first time what it was actually like to *be* this woman. But she didn't want to entertain that thought, so she used her foot to flip her mother's right leg roughly off her left leg. 'Wake up,' she told her. 'It's time to talk.' She gazed at the postcard to gain the strength she needed. *This is it* her mother's red writing said. Yes, Kerra thought. This was definitely it. 'Wake up,' she said again, more loudly. 'Get up from the floor.'

Dellen opened her eyes. She looked confused until she saw Kerra, and then she pulled to her the garments nearest to her right hand. She clutched these to her breasts and in doing so, she uncovered a pair of shears and a carving knife. Kerra looked from these to her mother to the clothes. She saw that every item on the floor had been rendered useless through slashing, slicing, hacking, and cutting.

'I should have used them on myself,' Dellen said dully. 'But I couldn't. Still, wouldn't you have been happy had I done it? You and your father? Happy? Oh God, I want to die. Why won't anyone help me die?' She began to weep, tearlessly, and drew more and more of the clothing to her until she'd formed an enormous pillow of ruined clothes.

Kerra knew she was meant to feel guilt. She also knew she was meant to forgive. Forgive and forgive until you were the incarnation of forgiveness. Understand until there was nothing left of you except that effort to understand.

'Help me.' Dellen extended her hand, then dropped it to the floor. The gesture was useless, virtually noiseless.

Kerra shoved the damning postcard back into her pocket. She grabbed her mother's arm and hauled her upwards. She said, 'Get up. You need a bath.'

'I can't,' Dellen said. 'I'm sinking. I'll be gone soon enough and long before I can . . .' And then a wily shift, perhaps reading in Kerra's face a brittleness of which she needed to be wary. 'He threw out my pills. He had me this morning. Kerra, he as good as raped me. And then he threw out my pills.'

Kerra shut her eyes tight. She didn't want to think about her parents' marriage. She merely wanted to force the truth from her mother, but she needed to direct the course of that truth. 'Up,' she said. 'Come on. Come *on*. You've got to get up.'

'Why will no one listen to me? I can't go on like this. Inside my mind is a pit so deep. Why won't anyone help me? You? Your father? I want to die.'

Her mother was like a sack of sand and Kerra heaved her onto the bed. There Dellen lay. 'I've lost my *child.*' Her voice was broken. 'Why does no one begin to understand?'

'Everyone understands.' Kerra felt as if something were simultaneously squeezing her down and burning her up. Soon there would be nothing of her left. Only speaking would save her. 'Everyone knows you've lost a child, because *everyone* else has lost Santo too.'

'But his mother, only his mother, Kerra—'

Something snapped within Kerra. She pulled Dellen upright, forcing her to sit at the edge of the bed. 'Stop the drama.'

'Drama?' As so often in the past, Dellen's mood shifted, like an unanticipated seismic event. 'You call this drama?' she demanded. 'Is that how you react to your own brother's murder? What's the matter with you? Have you no feelings? My God, Kerra. Whose daughter *are* you?'

'Yes, I expect you've asked yourself *that* question a number of times, haven't you. Counting back the weeks and the months and wondering. Who does she look like? Who does she belong to? Who can I say fathered her and – this would be critical, wouldn't it, Dellen? – will *he* believe me? Oh, p'rhaps if I look pathetic enough. Or pleased enough. Or happy enough. Or *whatever* it is that you look when you know you've got to explain some mess you've made.'

Dellen's eyes had grown dark. She'd shrunk away from Kerra. She said, 'How can you possibly say . . . ?' and her hands rose to cover her face in a gesture that Kerra assumed was meant to be read as horror.

It was time. Kerra pulled the postcard from her pocket. She said, 'Oh, stop it,' and knocked her mother's hands to one side and held the postcard to Dellen's face. She put a hand on the back of her neck so Dellen could not remove herself from their conversation. 'Look what I found. "This is it", Mum? "This is *it*"? What, exactly? What is "it"?'

'What are you talking about? Kerra, I don't—'

'You don't *what*? You don't know what I've got in my hand? You don't recognise the picture on this card? You don't recognise your own bloody writing? Which is it, Mum? Answer me. Which?'

'It's *nothing*. It's just a postcard, for heaven's sake. You're behaving like—'

'Like someone whose mother fucked the man she thought she was going to marry,' Kerra cried. 'In this cave where you fucked the rest of them.'

'How can you—'

'Because I know you. Because I've watched you. Because I've seen the story played out over and over. Dellen in need and who's there to help her but a willing male of *whatever* age because it never bloody mattered to you, did it? Just that you had him, whoever he was and whoever he belonged to. Because what you wanted and *when* you wanted it was more important than . . .' Kerra felt her hands begin shaking. She pressed the card to her mother's face. 'I should make you . . . God. God, I should make you . . .'

'No!' Dellen squirmed beneath her. 'You're mad.'

'Even Santo can't stop you. Santo dead can't stop you. I thought "*This* will get through to her" but it didn't, did it? Santo dead – my God, Santo *murdered* – didn't make a ripple. Not the slightest diversion in what you planned.'

Dellen began to fight her, clawing at her hands and her fingers now. She kicked and rolled to get away, but Kerra was too strong. So she began to scream.

'*You* did this! You! *You!*' Dellen grabbed at her daughter's hair and eyes. She pulled Kerra down. They rolled on the bed, seeking purchase among the mass of sheets and covers. Their voices shrieked. Their arms flailed. Their legs kicked. Their hands grasped. They found. They lost. They grasped again, punching and pulling as Dellen shrieked, 'You. You. You did it.'

The bedroom door crashed open. Footsteps hurried across the room. Kerra felt herself lifted and heard Alan's voice in her ear.

'Easy,' he said. 'Easy, *easy*. Jesus. Kerra, what're you *doing*?'

'Make her tell you,' Dellen cried. She had fallen to her side on the bed. 'Make her tell you everything. Make her tell you what she's done to Santo. Make her tell you about him. Santo!'

One arm holding Kerra, Alan began moving towards the door.

'Let me go!' Kerra cried. 'Make *her* tell the truth.'

'You come with me,' Alan told her instead. 'It's time that you and I had a proper talk.'

Both of the cars, similar to those that had been reported in the general area on the day of Santo Kerne's death, stood at one side of LiquidEarth when Bea and DS Havers pulled up at the erstwhile Royal Air Force station. A quick glance through the window showed that Lew Angarrack's RAV4 held a surfing kit along with a short board. Jago Reeth's Defender held nothing as far as they could see. It was pitted with rust on the outside – the salt air was murder on any car in this part of the country – but otherwise it was as clean as was possible, which wasn't very clean at all, considering the weather and the likelihood that he had to keep it parked outside. It did have floor mats and on both driver's side and passenger's side there was plenty of dried mud for their consideration. But mud was a hazard of life on the coast from late autumn through to the end of spring, so its presence in the Defender didn't count for as much as Bea would have liked.

Daidre Trahair being God-only-knew-where at this point, taking another jaunt over to the surfboard maker's establishment had seemed the logical next move. Every lead needed to be followed up, and both Jago Reeth and Lewis Angarrack were eventually going to have to explain what they were doing in the general vicinity of Santo Kerne's fall, no matter that Bea would have vastly preferred to have Daidre Trahair to the station for the thorough grilling she so richly deserved.

Bea had taken a call from Thomas Lynley on their way out to the old air station. He'd gone from Newquay to Zennor, and he was on his way to Pengelly Cove again. He might have something for her, he said. But that something required additional nosing round the area from which the Kerne family had sprung. He sounded unduly excited.

'And what about Ms Trahair?' she had asked him sharply.

He hadn't yet seen her, he said. But then, he hadn't expected to. He hadn't actually been keeping an eye open for her, as a matter of fact. If he was being honest, his mind had been on other things. This new situation with the Kernes—

Bea hadn't wanted to hear about the Kernes, this new situation or otherwise. She didn't trust Thomas Lynley and this fact cheesed her off because she *wanted* to trust him. She needed to trust everyone involved in looking into the death of Santo Kerne, and the fact that she couldn't made her cut him off abruptly. 'Should you see our fair and gambolling Ms Trahair along the way, you bring her to me,' she said. 'Are we clear on that?'

They were clear on that, Lynley assured her.

'And if you're intent on following up on the Kernes, then do keep in mind she's part of Santo Kerne's story as well.'

If the Angarrack girl was to be believed, he noted. Because a woman scorned . . .

'Oh yes. How true,' she'd declared impatiently, but Bea knew there was some truth in what he was saying: Madlyn Angarrack wasn't looking any more unsoiled than the rest of them.

Inside LiquidEarth, Bea introduced DS Havers to Jago Reeth, who was sanding the rough edge of fibreglass and resin on one rail of a swallowtail board, which he'd stretched between two sawhorses. These were thickly padded to protect the board's finish, and Jago was taking care to be gentle with his sanding. An enormous cupboard emanating warmth stood open at one side of the room with additional boards loaded within it, apparently awaiting his attention. LiquidEarth seemed to be having a profitable preseason, and business was continuing to boom, if the noise from the shaping room was anything to go by.

As before, Jago wore a disposable white boiler suit. It masked a lot of the dust that covered his body but none of the dust that covered his hair and his face. Any exposed part of him was white, even his fingers, and his cuticles formed ten Cheshire cat smiles at the base of his nails.

Jago Reeth asked Bea if she wanted Lew or himself this time round. She said she wanted them both but her conversation with Mr Angarrack could wait a bit, so as to allow her to talk to Jago alone.

The old bloke didn't appear disconcerted by the idea of the police wanting to talk to him, alone or otherwise. He did say he thought he'd told them all he knew about the Santo-and-Madlyn affair, but Bea informed him pleasantly that she generally liked to make that determination herself. He gave her a look, but he made no comment other than to tell her he would go on with his sanding if that wasn't a problem.

It wasn't, Bea assured him. She asked Jago Reeth what he could tell her about his Defender being in the vicinity of Santo Kerne's fall on the day of his death. DS Havers did her bit with notebook and pencil.

Jago stopped sanding, glanced at Havers, then cocked his head as if he was evaluating Bea's question. 'Vicinity?' he asked. 'Of Polcare Cove? Not hardly, I don't reckon.'

'You car was seen in Alsperyl.'

'You count that as *near*? Alsperyl might be near like the crow flies, but it's miles and miles by car.'

'A walk along the cliffs would take you from Alsperyl to Polcare Cove easily enough, Mr Reeth. Even at your age.'

'Seen on the cliff top, was I?'

'I'm not saying you were. But the fact of your Defender being even remotely in the area where Santo Kerne met his death . . . You can understand my curiosity, I hope.'

'Hedra's Hut,' he said.

'Who's what?' Sergeant Havers asked the question. Her expression said she thought the term was some sort of expletive peculiar to Cornwall.

'Old wooden shack built into the cliffs,' Jago explained to her. 'That's where I was.'

'May I ask what you were doing there?' Bea said.

Jago seemed to consider the propriety either of her questions or of giving an answer. 'Private matter,' he finally said. He applied himself to his sanding again.

'I'll decide that,' Bea told him.

The noise from the shaping room ceased and Lew Angarrack came out. As before, he was attired as Jago was, and he had a breathing mask and eye-wear slung round his neck. A circular section of skin round his eyes, mouth and nose looked oddly pink against the white of the rest of him. He and Jago Reeth exchanged an unreadable look.

'Ah. You were in the vicinity of Polcare Cove as well, Mr Angarrack,' Bea noted in a welcoming manner. She clocked the surprise on Jago Reeth's face.

'When was this?' Angarrack removed the breathing mask and goggles from round his neck and set them on top of the surfboard that Jago was sanding.

'On the day of Santo Kerne's fall. Or perhaps better stated, on the day of Santo Kerne's murder. What were you doing there?'

'I wasn't there,' he said. 'Not in Polcare Cove.'

'I said in the vicinity.'

'Then you're speaking of Buck's Haven, which I suppose is arguably in the vicinity. I was surfing.'

A quick look went from Jago to Lew Angarrack. The latter didn't seem to notice it.

Bea said, 'Surfing? And if I go back to have a look at those charts you lot use . . . What do you call them?'

'Isobar. And yes, if you go back and have a look you'll see the swells were rubbish, the wind was wrong, and there was no point at all in going out.'

'So why did you?' DS Havers asked.

'I wanted to think. The sea's always been the best place for me to do that. If I caught a few waves as well, that'd be a bonus. But catching waves wasn't why I was there.'

'You were thinking about what?'

'Marriage,' he said.

'Yours?'

'I'm divorced. Years ago. The woman I've been seeing . . .' He looked like a man who'd had any number of sleepless nights, and Bea wondered how many she could realistically ascribe to a gentleman's quandary about his marital state. 'We've been together a few years.

She wants to get married. I prefer things as they are. Or with a few changes.'

'What sort of changes?'

'What the hell difference does that make to you? It's a case of been there, done that for both of us, but she won't see it that way.'

Jago Reeth made a noise, cousin to a snort. It seemed to indicate that he and Lew Angarrack were at one on this topic. He went on with his sanding, and Lew gave a look to what he was doing. He nodded as he ran his fingers along the part of the rail that Jago had already seen to.

'So you were bobbing in the waves, trying to decide whether to marry her or not?'

'No. I'd already decided that.'

'And your decision was?'

He stepped away from the sawhorses and the board that Jago was working on. 'I don't see what that question has to do with anything. So let me get us to the point. If Santo Kerne fell from the cliff, he was either pushed or his climbing gear failed. Since my car was some distance away from Polcare Cove and since I was on the water, I couldn't have pushed him, which leaves his equipment failing in some way. So I expect what you really want to know is who had access to his equipment. Have I got us there a bit quicker by using the direct route, Inspector Hannaford?'

'I find there's usually half a dozen routes to the truth,' Bea told him. 'But you can travel this one, if you've a mind to.'

'I had no idea where he kept his equipment,' Angarrack told her. 'I still don't know. I'd assume he kept his climbing kit at home.'

'It was in his car.'

'Well, of course it would have been on that day, wouldn't it? He'd gone for a bloody climb, woman.'

'Lew, just doing her job.' Jago spoke soothingly before he said to Bea, 'I had access, if it comes down to it. Knowledge as well. The boy and his father had one run-in too many—'

'Over what?' Bea interrupted.

Jago Reeth and Angarrack exchanged a look. Bea saw this and repeated her question.

'Over anything,' was Jago's reply. 'They didn't see eye to eye on much, and Santo removed his kit from the premises. Bit of an I'll-show-you gesture, if you know what I mean.'

'"I'll show you" what, exactly Mr Reeth?'

'I'll show you . . . whatever boys think they got to show their dads.'

This answer hardly satisfied. Bea said, 'If you know something pertinent, either of you, I'll have it, please.'

Another look between them, this one longer. Jago said to Lew, 'Mate, you know it's not my place.'

'He made Madlyn pregnant,' Lew said abruptly. 'And he had no intention of doing anything at all about it.'

Bea felt DS Havers stir, itching to get involved but restraining herself. For her part, Bea had to wonder at the information's being delivered so perfunctorily by the man who'd have had the most reason to do something about it.

''Cording to Santo, his dad wanted him to do right by Madlyn,' Jago said. Then he added, 'Sorry, Lew. I did still talk to the boy. Seemed the best, what with the baby coming.'

'Your daughter didn't terminate the pregnancy, then?' Bea asked Angarrack.

'She intended to keep the child.'

'Intended?' DS Havers asked. 'Past tense meaning?'

'Miscarriage.'

'When did all this happen?' Bea asked.

'Miscarriage? At the beginning of April.'

'According to her. And she'd already ended their relationship by then? So she'd done that in the midst of her pregnancy?'

'That would be correct.'

Bea glanced at Havers. The sergeant's lips were rounded to an *oh*, which was likely short for *oh boy*. They were on a most interesting track.

'How did you feel about this, Mr Angarrack? And you as well, Mr Reeth, since you'd taken such care to see the boy was supplied with condoms.'

'I didn't feel good,' Angarrack said. 'But if doing right by Madlyn was going to mean they'd *marry*, I was happier they were apart, believe me. I didn't want her marrying him. They were only eighteen and besides.' He gestured away the rest of what he was going to say.

'Besides?' Havers prompted him.

'He'd shown his colours. He was a little sod. I didn't want the girl involved with him any longer.'

'D'you mean he wanted her to abort?'

'I mean he didn't care one way or another what she did, according to Madlyn. Which, apparently, was his style. Only she didn't know that at first. Well, none of us did.'

'Must have made you frantic when you found out.'

'So did I kill him in my frantic state?' Lew asked. 'Hardly. I had no reason to kill him.'

'Ill use of your daughter being insufficient reason?'

'It was over and done with. She was . . . She *is* recovering.' And he added, with a look at Jago, 'Wouldn't you agree?'

'Slow process.'

'Made easier if Santo was dead, I dare say,' Bea pointed out.

'I've told you. I didn't know where he kept his equipment, and *had* I known—'

'I knew,' Jago Reeth cut in. 'Santo's dad kept trying to sort him, see, after Madlyn came up pregnant. Like I said before, they rowed. Part of the row was that act-like-a-man-for-once challenge dads give their sons sometimes, and for Santo, it's easier to apply acting like a man to something *other* than act-like-the-proper-father-of-a-baby-that's-coming. So he takes his climbing kit to do just that. 'Nstead of "You want me to stand by Madlyn, I'll stand by Madlyn," it was easier to have it, "You'd rather I climb cliffs than surf? Then I'll climb. I'll show you a *real* cliff climber, come down to it." Then off he went to climb. Now. Then. Whenever. He kept his kit in the boot of his car. I knew it was there.'

'May I assume that Madlyn knew as well?'

'She was with me,' Jago said. 'The two of us had gone to Asperyl. We made the walk out to Hedra's Hut. There was something inside she wanted to be rid of. It was the last thing that tied her to Santo Kerne.'

Aside from Santo himself, Bea thought. She said, 'And what would this be?'

Jago set his sanding block gently on the deck of the surfboard. He said, 'Look, she fell dead hard for Santo. He was – sorry, Lew, no dad likes to hear this – he was her first in bed. When things ended with them, she was in a bad way about it. And then came the matter of losing that baby. She was having trouble getting past it all, and who wouldn't? So I told her to get rid of everything Santo, start to finish. She'd done that but there was this one last bit, so that's what we were doing there. They'd carved their initials in the hut. Stupid kid stuff, with a heart and everything, if you c'n believe it. We went there to destroy it. Not the hut, mind you. We didn't want to hurt the hut. Just the initials. We left the heart as it was.'

'Why not carry all this to the logical end?' Bea asked him.

'Which would be what?'

'The obvious, Mr Reeth,' Havers put in. 'Why not give Santo Kerne the chop as well?'

Lew Angarrack said hotly, 'You hang on just a God damn minute—'

Bea cut him off. 'Is she a jealous girl? Has she a history of striking back when she's hurt? Either of you can answer, by the way.'

'If you're trying to say—'

'I'm trying to get to the truth, Mr Angarrack. Did Madlyn tell you, or you, Mr Reeth, that Santo was seeing someone else in the midst of all this? And I do use *seeing* as a euphemism, by the way. He was shagging one of the older women hereabouts at the same time as he was shagging and impregnating your daughter. She's told us as much, at least the shagging part. Well, she had to as we've caught her in more than one lie so far and I'm afraid she'd lied herself into a brick wall. As things turn out, she'd followed the boy and there they were in this woman's home, the virile, energetic, and young white ram enthusiastically tupping the ageing ewe. Did you know about this? Did you, Mr Reeth?'

Lew Angarrack said, 'No. No.' His drove his hand through his greying hair, dislodging a sand-fall of polystyrene dust. 'I've been caught up in my own affair. I *knew* she and the boy were done for, and I thought that with time . . . Madlyn's always been edgy. I've long thought it was due to her mum and the fact she left us and the fact that Madlyn doesn't cope well with being left. Well, that seemed natural enough to me, and she always got past it in the end if something died between herself and someone else. I believed she'd get past this as well, even past the loss of the baby. So when she was as disturbed as she was, I did what I could, or what I *thought* I could to help her through it.'

'Which was?'

'I sacked the boy, and I encouraged her to get back to her surfing. Get back in shape. Get back on the circuit. I told her no one goes through life without getting their heart broken, but people recover.'

'Like you had?' Havers asked.

'If it comes to it, yes.'

'And what did you know of this other woman?' Bea asked him.

'Nothing. Madlyn never said.'

'You, Mr Reeth?'

Jago picked up his block and examined it. He nodded slowly. 'She told me. She wanted me to have a word with the boy. I s'pose it was to try to set him straight. But I told her it wouldn't do much good. That age? A boy i'n't thinking with his brain, and didn't she *see* that? I tell her there's lots of fish in the sea, like they say. I said, Let's be rid of this sorry piece of business, girl, and get on with our lives. It's the only way.'

He didn't seem to realise what he had just said. Bea eyed him carefully. She could tell that Havers was doing the same. Bea said, '*Irregular* is the term that's been used for what Santo was up to on the side while he was seeing Madlyn, and Santo himself was the one to use it. He was advised to be honest about it, about the irregular bit. He may have been, but apparently not with Madlyn. Was he honest with you, Mr Reeth? You appear to have something of a touch with young people.'

'I only knew what our Madlyn knew,' Jago Reeth said. 'Irregular, you say?'

'Irregular, yes that's what he said. Irregular enough for him to ask advice about it.'

'Having it off with an older woman might've been irregular enough,' Lew noted.

'But enough to seek advice about it?' Bea asked, more to herself than to them.

'S'pose,' Jago said, 'it depends on who the woman was, eh? It always comes down to that in the end.'

21

Despite Jago's warning, Cadan couldn't help himself. It was complete insanity and he damn well knew it, but he engaged in it anyway: the soft silken feel of her thighs tightening round him; the sound of her moaning and then the heightened growing rapturous *yes* of her response, and this set against a backdrop of waves crashing against the nearby shore; the mixed scents of the sea, of her female smells, and of wood rot from the tiny beach hut; the eternal female salt of her where he licked as she shrieked and *yes yes* as her fingers dug into his hair; the dim light from the cracks round the door casting a nearly ethereal glow on skin that was slick but lithe and firm and willing God so eager and ever so willing . . .

It *could* have been like that, Cadan thought, and despite the growing lateness of the day he wasn't all that far from establishing Pooh in the sitting room, hauling his bicycle out of the garage, and pedalling frantically to Adventures Unlimited to take Dellen Kerne up on her offer to meet at the beach huts. He'd seen just enough films in the cinema to know that the older woman-younger man bit was never perfect, let alone permanent, but that was a plus as far as he was concerned. The very idea of having it off with Dellen Kerne was all so right in Cadan's mind that it had moved quite beyond rightness into another realm altogether: into the sublime, the mystical, the metaphysical. The only metaphorical monkey in the barrel was, alas, Dellen herself.

The woman was a nutter, no question about it. Despite his longing to press his lips to various parts of her body, Cadan knew barm when he saw barm, providing barm was actually a word, which he seriously doubted. But if it wasn't a word, it needed to be one, and she was barm in spades. She was the walking, talking, breathing, eating, sleeping personification of barm, and the one thing Cadan Angarrack was besides randy enough to take on a herd of sheep was clever enough to give barm a wide berth.

He hadn't gone to work that day, but he hadn't been able to face any questions from his father about why he was hanging about the

house. So to keep Lew from venturing into that conversational territory, Cadan had risen as usual, had dressed as usual – going so far as
to don his paint-spattered jeans, which he considered a *very* nice touch
indeed – and had shown up as usual at the breakfast table where Madlyn
was eating a virtuous half-grapefruit, and Lew was sliding a decent fry-
up from the pan onto his plate.

Seeing Cadan, Lew had gestured towards the food in a surprisingly
affable fashion. Cadan took this as a peace offering and as acknowledgement of his efforts at self-rehabilitation through gainful employment,
so he accepted the food with a 'Fantastic, Dad. Ta,' and tucked right in,
asking his sister how she was coping.

Madlyn cast him a baleful glance that recommended a change in
conversational direction, so Cadan gave his father a moment's study
and realised Lew had about him the ease of movement that had in the
past signified recent sexual release. He decided that his father was
unlikely to be wanking in the midst of his morning shower, so he said,
'Get back with Ione, Dad?' in a man-to-man tone whose implication
could not be misconstrued.

And Lew definitely did not misconstrue, Cadan could tell that much.
His father's swarthy skin darkened ever so slightly before he went back
to the cooker to prepare a second fry-up. This he did in silence.

So much for the warm, familial colloquy. But, no worries. Since there
was to be no additional sound beyond that which was made by masti-
cation and swallowing, the entire issue of Cadan's employment did not
come up. On the other hand, Cadan was burning to ask what the big
deal *actually* was if they exchanged a few bawdy words about Lew
successfully talking Ione out of her pique long enough to pin her manfully
to the mattress. All right, Madlyn *was* there and perhaps one ought to
show deference to her femininity – not to mention everything that had
gone wrong for her recently – by not bringing up the coarser aspects
of male-female relationships. On the other hand, a wink between men
wouldn't have gone amiss, and in finer days Lew had not been averse
to allowing his son a wee bit of knowledge in the area of triumphant
conquests.

Which made Cadan wonder what was going on.

Had Lew moved on to another woman? It was definitely in his nature.
A succession of women had come into the lives of the small Angarrack
clan, women who had generally ended up weeping, ranting, or trying
to be reasonable with conversation at the kitchen table or the front door
or in the garden or *wherever* because Lew Angarrack would not commit

to her. But *when* another woman was being worked into the picture, Lew generally brought her home to meet the kids prior to sex because bringing her home to meet the kids always gave the impression that something was possible between them, like a future. So what did it mean that here Lew was in the kitchen loose of limb and looking like a man who's properly oiled a woman's hinges, when no one had been brought by at all? The kids were older, true enough, but some things were written in concrete round here and one of them had long been Lew's behaviour.

Which brought to mind Dellen Kerne. Not that she was far from Cadan's mind at any one moment, but it seemed to him that Lew's secrecy meant there was a *reason* for secrecy, and a reason for secrecy implied the illicit, and illicit definitely led one down the mental garden path to adultery. A married woman. Christ, he concluded. His father had got to Dellen first. He didn't know how, but he reckoned it had happened. He felt a stab of real jealousy.

So he had plenty of time during the day to dwell on the what-could-still-bes of a run-in with Dellen. He had the feeling she wouldn't take it amiss to be doing a father-and-son shag, but the truth was that he didn't want to make things with his father worse than they'd already been, so he ended up trying to occupy himself with other thoughts.

The trouble here was that he was a doer, not a thinker. Heavy thinking bound him up in anxiety, the cure for which lay in two directions. One of them was action and the other was drink. Cadan knew which of the two he *ought* to choose, with respect to his history, but he damn well wanted to choose the other, and as the hours wore on, the wanting increased. When the wanting pressed him to the point at which rational thought was no longer possible, he gave Pooh a plate of fruit to keep him occupied – among other edibles, the parrot was particularly partial to Spanish oranges – and he fetched his bicycle. Binner Down House was his destination.

Cadan's purpose was to acquire a boozing companion. Drinking alone more than once in a week suggested that a man might have something of a problem with mood altering substances of the liquid variety, and Cadan didn't wish to be labelled as anything other than a bon vivant. So he settled on Will Mendick as a likely partner in drink.

Nothing having progressed for Will in the Madlyn arena, it stood to reason he might well want to get soused. Once that was accomplished, they could both sleep it off at Binner Down House with no one the wiser. It seemed like a grand idea.

Will lived at Binner Down House with nine surfers, male and female. He was the odd man out. He didn't ride the waves because he didn't like sharks and he wasn't overly fond of weever fish either. Cadan found him on the south side of the property, which was an ancient place in the sort of condition a property gets into when it's near the sea and no one takes proper care of it. So the land surrounding it was overgrown with gorse, bracken, and a tangle of sea grasses. A single gnarled cypress in what passed for a front garden needed trimming, and weeds took the place of a lawn that had too long fought the good fight against them. The building itself was in sore need of repair, especially with regard to roof tiles and wood surrounds of windows and doors. But the occupants had more important concerns than property maintenance, and a disreputable shed in which their surfboards lined up like colourful book marks served as ample evidence of this. As did their wet suits, which generally hung to dry from the lower branches of the cypress.

The south side of the house faced onto Binner Down from whose environs floated the lowing of cows. Along the wall of the building, a triangular sort of greenhouse had been fashioned. Its glass roof tilted into the house, with one side of it also glass and the other comprising the existing granite of the old building, but painted white to reflect the sun. This was a vinery, Cadan had learned, its purpose being to grow grapes.

Cadan found Will inside. He was bent to accommodate the sloping glass of the ceiling, digging round the base of an infant grapevine. When Cadan entered, Will straightened and said, 'Fuck, it's about bloody time,' before he saw who it was coming through the door. 'Sorry,' he then said. 'I thought it was one of them.' He was, Cadan knew, referring to his surfing housemates.

'Still not helping round here?'

'Hell no. They might actually have to get off their bums.' Will had been using a pitchfork to work the soil – which didn't look to Cadan the best way to go about it, considering the size of the plants, but he said nothing – and Will tossed the tool aside. He took up a cup of something sitting on a ledge, and he quaffed the rest of whatever was in it. It was warm in the greenhouse, as it was supposed to be despite the hour of the day, and he was sweating, which made his wispy hair cling to his skull. He was going to be bald by the time he was thirty, Cadan decided, and he gave silent thanks for his own thick locks.

'I owe you,' Cadan told Will by way of prefatory remarks. 'I came to tell you that.'

Will looked confused. He reached for his pitchfork and resumed his digging. 'You owe me what, exactly?'

'An apology. For what I said.'

Will straightened again. He wiped his arm across his forehead. He was wearing a flannel shirt, partially unbuttoned. He had on his usual black T-shirt beneath it. 'What did you say?'

'That bit about Madlyn. The other day. You know. When you stopped by.' Cadan thought that the less said about Madlyn the better life would be for them both, but he wanted to make sure Will knew what he was talking about. 'Thing is, man, how the hell do I know who has a chance with my sister and who doesn't?'

'Oh, I expect you'd know well enough.'

'Not as things turn out. She was talking about you this morning at breakfast, as it happens. I heard that and I realised I was dead wrong.' He was lying, of course, but he reckoned he could be forgiven for that. A greater good was involved here: He *didn't* actually know his sister's mind on the subject of romantic entanglements, did he? Aside from how she felt about Santo Kerne at the moment and he wasn't altogether sure of that, either. Besides, he needed Will Mendick just now. So if a small prevarication was going to get Will to open a bottle with him, that certainly could be forgiven. 'What I'm saying's that you shouldn't write her off. She's been in a bad way for a bit, and I reckon she needs you, even if she doesn't know that yet.'

Will went to the far end of the greenhouse and fetched down a box of fertiliser from a shelf. Cadan followed him.

'So I reckoned we could hoist a brew—' Cadan cringed internally at the bizarre expression; he sounded like someone on American telly – 'and let bygones be bygones. What d'you say?'

'I can't leave at the moment.'

'That's where you're lucky. I wasn't actually talking about leaving,' Cadan told him frankly. 'I reckoned we could booze up here.'

Will shook his head. He returned to his vines and his pitchfork. Cadan had the distinct impression that something was eating at his friend's peace of mind.

'Can't. Sorry.' Will picked up the pace of his work and clarified his situation by adding tersely, 'Cops were at the grocery, Cade. They gave me a grilling.'

'What about?'

'What the hell d'you think it was about?'

'Santo Kerne?'

'Yeah, Santo Kerne. Is there another subject?'

'Why you, for God's sake?'

'The hell I know. They've been talking to everyone. How'd *you* escape?' Will dug furiously once again.

Cadan felt ill at ease. Speculatively, he looked at Will. The fact that the cops had sought him out suggested things Cadan didn't want to begin to consider.

'Well,' he said in the expansive tone that always indicates an end to a conversation.

'Yeah,' Will said grimly. 'Well.'

Cadan made his farewell soon after this and was thus at a loose end once again. Will and Will's troubles aside, fate seemed to be telling him that action was called for. And action meant the single deed – aside from drinking – that Cadan had not been able to get out of his brain.

Christ, but his mind seemed *fixed* on her. She might as well have been a deadly infection eating away at his brain. Cadan knew that his choices were simple: he had to get rid of her or he had to have her. Yet having her was not unlike committing ritual suicide, so he rode from Binner Down House to the only place left in his limited list of escape hatches from the self: the Royal Air Force station. He couldn't come up with any other alternative. He'd lie to his father about having gone to work, if it came to that. He just needed to be somewhere that wasn't at home alone or at Adventures Unlimited in the vicinity of that woman.

As luck had it, his father's car wasn't there. But Jago's was, which seemed a godsend. If anyone could act the part of confidant, it was Jago Reeth.

Unfortunately, someone else had the same idea. Cadan walked in to find the two daughters of Ione Soutar in the reception area and the door to the inner workshops closed. Jennie was scrupulously attending to her school prep at the card table that served as his father's desk while the redoubtable Leigh was pressing one finger to the side of her nostril, a tube of Superglu on the counter in front of her along with a compact mirror into which she gazed.

'Mum's in*side*, Cadan?' Leigh told him with that perpetual, maddening interrogatory inflection of hers, which always suggested she was speaking to a fool. 'She's said it's *personal*, so you're not to go in?'

'I expect she's talking to Jago 'bout your dad,' Jennie added frankly. She was sucking on her lower lip as she rubbed out pencil marks on her paper. 'She said it's over, but she keeps crying at night in the bath when she thinks we can't hear, so I reckon it's not as over as she wants it to be.'

'She needs to give him the permanent heave-*ho*?' Leigh said. 'I mean, no offence, Cadan, but your father's a *dick*head? Women need to stand *up* for themselves and they need to stand firm and they *especially* need to kick arse when they're not being treated the way they deserve to be treated. I mean, like, what sort of example is she setting for the two of *us*?'

'What the hell're you doing to your face?' Cadan asked.

'Mummy wouldn't let her get her nose pierced, so she's gluing a stone on,' Jennie informed Cadan in the friendly fashion that was her nature. 'C'n you do long division, Cade?'

'God, don't ask *him*,' Leigh said to her sister. 'He didn't even pass one *GSCE*? You *know* that, Jennie.'

Cadan ignored her. 'You want a calculator?' he asked Jennie.

'She's supposed to show her *work*?' Leigh told him. She inspected her nose stud and said to the mirror, 'I'm not *stu*pid. I'm not going to rubbish up my *face*. Like I'd ackshully *do* that?' She rolled her eyes. 'What d'you think, Jennie?'

Jennie said without looking, 'I think you're going to have a real row with her now.'

Cadan couldn't disagree. Leigh looked like someone with a large spot of blood on the side of her nose. She should have chosen a different coloured stone.

'Mum's going to make her take it off,' Jennie went on. 'It'll hurt when she does, as well, cos the Superglu holds it real good. You'll be sorry, Leigh.'

'Shut *up*?' Leigh said.

'I only said—'

'Shut *up*? Put a *sock* in it? Cram your *fist* down your throat? Gag yourself with a *shovel*?'

'You aren't s'posed to talk to me like—'

The inner door swung open. Ione stood there. She'd been crying. Massively, by the look of her. Damn, but she actually must love his father, Cadan thought.

He wanted to tell her to let his dad go and to get *on* with her life. Lew Angarrack wasn't available, and he probably wouldn't ever be. He'd been dumped by the Bounder – his one, true, eternal childhood love – and he'd not got over it. None of them had. That was their curse.

But how could one explain that to a woman who'd managed to carry on with her life when *her* marriage had ended? There was no way.

It looked, however, as if Jago had made a heroic effort in that direction. He stood behind Ione with a handkerchief in his hand. He was folding this and returning it to the pocket of his boiler suit.

Leigh took one look at her mother and rolled her eyes. She said, 'I suppose this means we won't be *surfing* any longer?'

Jennie added loyally, '*I* didn't like it anyway,' as she gathered up her schoolbooks.

'Let's go, girls,' Ione said. She cast a look round the workshop. 'Nothing more to be said. Matters are quite finished here.'

Cadan she ignored altogether, as if he were a carrier of the family disease. He stepped out of the way as she herded her offspring out of the shop. She was setting off in the direction of her own shop in the air station as the door swung closed behind her.

'Poor lass,' was Jago's comment on the matter.

'What'd you tell her?'

Jago went back into the glassing room. 'The truth.'

'Which is?'

'No one changes a leopard's spots.'

'What about the leopard?'

Jago was carefully peeling some blue tape from the rail of a pintail short board. Cadan noticed how bad his shakes were today. 'Eh?' Jago said.

'Can't a leopard change its own spots?'

'I'll wager you c'n think that one through, Cade.'

'People *do* change.'

'Nope,' Jago said. 'They don't.' He applied sandpaper to the resin seam. His glasses slipped down on his nose and he pushed them back into place. 'Their reactions, p'rhaps. What they show to the world, if you see what I mean. That part changes if they want it to change. But the inside part? It stays the same. You don't change who you are. Just how you act.' Jago looked up. A long hunk of his lank grey hair had come loose from his perennial ponytail, and it fell across his cheek. 'What're you doing here, Cade? Aren't you meant to be at work?'

Cadan preferred not to answer that question directly, so he had a wander round the workshop as Jago continued to sand the rails of the board. He opened the shaping room — scene of his former attempt at employment at LiquidEarth — and gazed inside.

The problem, he decided, was having been assigned to *shaping* boards.

He had no patience for it. Shaping required a steady hand. It demanded the use of an endless catalogue of tools and templates. It asked one to consider so many variables that keeping them all in mind was an impossibility: the curve of the blank, single versus double concavity, the contours of the rails, the fin positions. Length of board, shape of tail, thickness of rail. One sixteenth of an inch made all the difference and bloody hell, Cadan, can't you *tell* those channels are too deep? I can't have you in here cocking things up.

All right. Fair enough. He was wretched at shaping. And glassing was so boring he wanted to weep. It frayed his nerves: all the delicacy required. The fibreglass unspooling from its roll with just enough excess not to be considered wasteful, the careful application of resin to fix the glass permanently to the polystyrene beneath it in such a way as to prevent air bubbles. The sanding, then the glassing again, then *more* sanding.

He couldn't do it. He wasn't *made* for it. You had to be born a glasser like Jago and that was that.

He'd wanted to work in the spray room from the first, applying the paint to his own board artwork. But that hadn't been allowed. His father had told him he had to *earn* his way into that position by learning the rest of the business first, but Lew hadn't demanded as much from Santo Kerne, had he?

'You'll take over the business. Santo won't. So you need to learn things top to bottom,' had been his father's excuse. 'I need an artist and I need one now. Santo knows how to design.'

He knows how to fuck Madlyn, you mean, Cadan had wanted to say. But really, what was the point? Madlyn had wanted Santo employed there, and Madlyn was the favoured child.

And now? Who knew? They'd both disappointed their father in the end, but there was a chance that Madlyn had finally disappointed him worse.

'I'm ready to come back,' Cadan said to Jago. 'What d'you think?'

Jago straightened from the board and set down his sanding block. He examined Cadan before he spoke. 'What's going on?'

Cadan riffled through his brain to try to come up with a good reason for his change of heart, but there was only the truth if he were to stand a chance of getting back into his father's good graces with Jago's assistance. He said, 'You were right. I can't work there, Jago. But I need your help.'

'She got you bad, eh?'

Cadan didn't want to spend another moment on the subject of Dellen Kerne, either mentally or conversationally. He said, 'No. Yes. Whatever. I've got to get out of there. Will you help?'

'Course I will,' the old man said kindly. 'Just give me some time to plan an approach.'

After his conversation in Zennor with the former detective, Lynley had returned to David Wilkie's house, which was no particular distance from the church. There he'd ventured into the attic with the old man. An hour of rooting through cardboard boxes had produced Wilkie's notes on the unsolved case of Jamie Parsons. These notes had in their turn produced the names of the boys who'd been so thoroughly questioned in the matter of Jamie's death. Wilkie had no idea where those boys now resided, but Lynley thought it possible that at least one or two of them still lived in the vicinity of Pengelly Cove. If he was correct, they were waiting there to be questioned.

This questioning occupied Lynley's thoughts as he returned to that surfing village. He gave a great deal of consideration to how he wanted to make his next move.

As it turned out, with Ben Kerne in Casvelyn, one of the boys prematurely dead of lymphoma, and another having emigrated to Australia, only three of the original six still resided in Pengelly Cove, and it was not difficult to find them. Lynley tracked them down by starting at the pub, where a conversation with the publican led him to a car body repair shop (Chris Outer), the local primary school (Darren Fields), and a marine engine maintenance business (Frankie Kliskey) in very short order. At each place of employment, he did and said the same thing. He produced his police identification, gave minimal details about the death under investigation in Casvelyn, and asked each man if could free himself up to talk about Ben Kerne in another location in an hour's time. *The death of Ben Kerne's son Santo* appeared to work the necessary magic, if *magic* it could be called. Each of the men agreed.

Lynley had selected the coastal path for their conversation. Not far outside the village stood the memorial to Jamie Parsons that Eddie Kerne had spoken of. High up on the cliff, it comprised a tall-backed stone bench forming a curve round a circular stone table. In the middle of the table *Jamie* was deeply incised, along with the dates of his birth and his death. Once he arrived, Lynley remembered having seen this memorial during his lengthy walk along the coast. He'd sat in the shelter that the bench provided from the wind, and he'd stared not out to sea but at the boy's name and the dates that marked the brevity of his life. Life's brevity had filled his mind. Along with her, of course. Along with Helen.

On this day he realised once he sat on the bench to wait that, aside from a few minutes upon waking, he'd not thought about Helen, and the recognition of that fact brought her death even more heavily upon him. He found he didn't want *not* to think of her daily and hourly, even as he understood that to exist in the present meant that she would move farther and farther into his past as time went forward. Yet it wounded him to know that. Beloved wife. Longed-for son. Both of them gone and *he* would recover. Even as this was the way of the world and of life, the very fact of his recovery seemed unbearable and obscene.

He rose from the bench and walked to the edge of the cliff. Another memorial – less formal than Jamie Parsons' table and bench – lay here: a wreath of dead and disintegrating evergreens from the previous Christmas, a deflated balloon, a sodden Paddington bear, and the name *Eric* written in black marker pen on a tongue depressor. There were a dozen ways to die along the Cornish coast. Lynley wondered which one of them had taken this soul.

The sound of footfalls on the stony path just to the north of where he stood drew his attention to the route from Pengelly Cove. He saw the three men come over the rise together, and he knew they'd contacted one another. He'd expected as much when he'd first spoken to them. He'd even encouraged it. His design was to lay his cards on the table: They had nothing to fear from him.

Darren Fields was obviously their leader. He was the biggest of them and, as head teacher of the local primary school, he was likely in possession of the most education. He walked at the front of their line up the path; he was the first to nod at Lynley and to acknowledge the selection of meeting site with the words, 'I thought as much. Well, we've said all there is to be said on that subject years ago. So if you're thinking—'

'I'm here about Santo Kerne, as I told you,' Lynley said. 'About Ben Kerne as well. If my intentions were anything more than that, I'd hardly have been so transparent with you.'

The other two looked to Fields. He evaluated Lynley's words. He finally jerked his head in a nod and all of them returned to the table and its bench. Frankie Kliskey appeared to be the most nervous. An unusually small man, he chewed on the side of his index finger – in a spot that was dirty from engine oil and raw from frequent chewing – and his glance shot rabbitlike among them. For his part, Chris Outer seemed prepared to wait for matters to unfold in whatever way they would. He lit a cigarette in the cave of his hand, and he leaned against the bench with the collar of his leather jacket turned up, his eyes narrowed, and his expression reminiscent of James Dean in *Rebel Without a Cause*. Only the hair was missing. He was as bald as an egg.

'I hope you can see this isn't a trap of any kind,' Lynley said by means of preamble. 'David Wilkie – Is the name familiar to you? Yes, I see that it is – believes that what happened to Jamie Parsons all those years ago was probably an accident. Wilkie doesn't think now, nor did he apparently ever think, that what was premeditated among you was his death. The boy's blood showed both alcohol and cocaine. Wilkie thinks you didn't understand his condition and expected him to make it out on his own when you were finished with him.'

They said nothing. An opaqueness had come into Darren Fields' blue eyes, however, and this suggested to Lynley a determination to hold fast to whatever had been said in the past about Jamie Parsons. That made very good sense, from Darren's perspective. Whatever had been said in the past had kept them out of the judicial system for nearly three decades. Why make an alteration now?

'Here's what I know,' Lynley said.

'Hang on, man,' Darren Fields snapped. 'Not a minute ago you were telling us that you'd come about another matter.'

'Ben's kid,' Chris Outer pointed out. Frankie Kliskey said nothing, but his glance kept ping-ponging among them.

'Yes. I've come about that,' Lynley acknowledged. 'But the two deaths have one man in common, Ben Kerne, and that has to be looked at. It's the way these things work.'

'There's nothing more to be said.'

'I think there is. I think there always was. So does DCI Wilkie if it comes to that, but the difference, as I've said, is that Wilkie believes what happened wasn't intentional while I'm far from certain of that. I could be reassured, but for that to happen, one of you or all of you are going to have to talk to me about that night and the cave.'

The three men made no reply although Outer and Fields exchanged a look. One couldn't take a look to the bank, however, not to mention to DI Hannaford, so Lynley pressed on. 'Here's what I know: There was a party. At that party there was an altercation between Jamie Parsons and Ben Kerne. Jamie already needed sorting for any number of reasons, most of which had to do with who he was and how he treated people, and the way he dealt with Ben Kerne that night was apparently the final straw. So he got sorted in one of the sea caves. I believe the object was humiliation: hence the boy's missing clothing, the marks on his wrists and ankles from having been tied up, and the faeces in his ears. My guess is that you likely pissed on him as well, but the urine would have been washed away by the tide whereas the faeces were not. My question is, how did you get him down there to the cave? I've thought about this, and it seems to me that you had to have something that he wanted. If he was already drunk and perhaps already drugged, it can't have been the promise of getting high. That leaves a form of contra-band that he didn't want others at the party – perhaps his sisters who might've grassed to their parents – to see being exchanged. But not *wanting* to have others see him in possession of something that they themselves might have wanted seems out of character in the Jamie I've heard described. Having what others wanted, admired, respected, what-ever, that seems to have been how he operated. Showing these things off to people. Showing off full stop. Being better than everyone else. So I can't see him agreeing to meet in a cave to take ownership of something illegal. That, then, seems to leave us with something more private that was promised him. Which seems to lead us to sex.'

Frankie's eyes did it. Blue, their pupils enlarged. Lynley wondered how he'd managed to keep quiet when questioned by Wilkie away from his friends. But perhaps that had been it: Away from his friends he wouldn't know *what* to say, so he'd say nothing. In their presence, he could wait for their lead.

'Young men, adolescent boys, will do just about anything if sex is part of the picture,' Lynley said. 'I expect Jamie Parsons was no different to the rest of you when it came to that. So the question is, was he homosexual, and did one of you make a promise to him that was meant to be kept when he got down to the cave?'

Silence. They were very good at this. But Lynley was fairly certain he could go them one better.

'It would have had to be more than merely a promise, though,' he said. 'Jamie wasn't likely to respond to the mere suggestion of buggery. I reckon it would have had to be a move of some sort, a trigger, a signal so that he would know it was safe to proceed. What would that be? A knowing look. A word. A gesture. Hand on bum. Stiffie pressed up to him in a private corner. The sort of language that's spoken by—'

'No one here's a poof.' It was Darren who spoke. Not surprisingly,

Lynley realised, as he was a teacher of young children and had the most to lose. 'And none of the others were either.'

'The rest of your group,' Lynley clarified.

'That's what I'm telling you.'

'But it *was* sex, wasn't it,' Lynley said. 'I'm right in that. He thought he was meeting someone for sex. Who?'

Silence.

Finally, 'The past is dead.' It was Chris Outer this time, and he looked as steely as Darren Fields.

'The past is the past,' Lynley countered. 'Santo Kerne is dead. Jamie Parsons is dead. Their deaths may or may not be related, but—'

'They're not,' Fields said.

'—*but* until I know otherwise, I have to assume there may be a connection between them. And I don't want the connection to be that each investigation ends in the same way: with an open verdict. Santo Kerne was murdered.'

'Jamie Parsons was not.'

'All right. I'll accept that. DCI Wilkie believes it as well. You're not going to be prosecuted more than a quarter century after the fact for having been so bloody stupid as to have left the boy in that cave. All I want to know is what happened that night.'

'It was Jack. *Jack.*' The admission fairly burst from Frankie Kliskey, as if he'd been waiting nearly thirty years to make it. He said to the others, 'Jack's dead now and what does it matter? I don't *want* to carry this. I'm that bloody *tired* of carrying it, Darren.'

'God damn—'

'I held my tongue back then, and look at me. *Look.*' He held out his hands. They were shaking, like a palsy. 'A cop comes round and it's all back again and I don't want to live through it another time.'

Darren pushed his body away from the table, a gesture of disgust. But it was also a gesture of dismissal, one that could be interpreted as 'Have it your way, then.'

There was another tight little silence among the men. In it, the gulls cawed and far below, a boat gunned its motor in the cove.

'She was called Nancy Snow,' Chris Outer said, slowly. 'She was Jack Dustow's girlfriend and Jack was one of us.'

'He's the one who died of lymphoma?' Lynley said.

'That would be Jack. He talked Nan into . . . doing what was done. We could have used Dellen – that's Ben's wife now, Dellen Nankervis as she was – because she was always ready for action.'

'She was there that night?'

'Oh aye, she was there. She's what started things. *Because* she was there.' He sketched out the details: an adolescent relationship gone sour, two youngsters each showing the other one up with a willing new partner, Jamie reacting to his sister's becoming openly entangled with Ben Kerne, Jamie's attack on Ben.

'He needed sorting anyway, like you said,' Frankie Kliskey finished. 'None of us liked the bloke. So Jack got Nan Snow to heat him up. End product was, Jamie wanted sex right there in the house.'

'Preferably where everyone could see he was getting it,' Darren Fields added.

'Where *Jack* could see he was getting it,' Chris pointed out. 'That's what Jamie was like.'

'But Nan said no.' Frankie went on with the story. 'No way she'd do it with him where others could watch, especially where Jack could see. She said let's go down to the cave to do it, so that's what they did. That's where we were waiting.'

'She knew what the plan was?'

'Jack told her,' Chris said. 'She knew. Get Jamie down to the cave for sex. Don't meet him there because he's not stupid and he'll smell a rat and won't go down. *Take* him there instead. Act like you want it as bad as he does. We'll handle the rest. So down they came round half past one in the morning. We were in the cave and Nan handed him over. The rest, you can work out.'

'The odds were good. Six of you and one of him.'

'No,' Darren said, his voice harsh. 'Ben Kerne wasn't ever there.'

'Where was he, then?'

'Gone home. He was stupid about Dellen. *Always* stupid. Christ, if it hadn't been for her, we wouldn't have been at the bloody party at all. But he needed cheering up, so we said, Let's go and have his drink and eat his food and listen to his music. Only she was there, that bloody Dellen with some new bloke, so Ben got into the wrong girl's knickers in reaction to seeing Dellen and after that, he just wanted to go home. Which was what he did. The rest of us talked to Nan and Nan went back to the party and . . .' Darren gestured in the direction of the cave.

Lynley carried the story on. 'You stripped him in the cave, and you tied him up. You smeared faeces on him. Did you piss on him? No? What, then? Toss off? One of you? All of you?'

'He cried,' Darren said. 'And that's all we wanted. When he started to cry, we were finished with him. We untied him. We left him to make his way back up the cliff. The rest you know.'

Lynley nodded. The story made him feel queasy. It was one thing to surmise, another to hear the truth. There were so many Jamie Parsons on earth, and so many boys like these men before him. There was also the great divide between them and how that divide was or was not negotiated. Jamie Parsons had likely been unbearable. But being unbearable did not amount to being deserving of death.

Lynley said, 'I'm curious about one thing.'

All of them looked at him: Darren Fields sullen, Chris Outer as cool as he'd likely been twenty-eight years ago, Frankie Kliskey expectant of a psychological blow of some sort.

'How did you manage to hold fast to the same story when the police went after you initially? Before they went after Ben Kerne, I mean.'

'We left the party at half past eleven. We parted at the high street. We went home.' It was Darren speaking, and Lynley got the point. Three sentences only, endlessly repeated. They may have been bloody stupid, those five boys involved, but they had not been ignorant of the law.

'What did you do with his clothes?'

'Countryside's filled with adits and mine shafts,' Chris said. 'That's the nature of this part of Cornwall.'

'What about Ben Kerne? Did you tell him what had happened?'

'We left the party at half past eleven. We parted at the high street. We went home.'

So Lynley thought, Ben Kerne had always been as ignorant of what had happened as everyone else had been, aside from the original five boys and Nancy Snow.

'What happened to Nancy Snow? How could you be sure she'd not talk?'

'She was pregnant by Jack,' Darren told him. 'Three months gone. She had an interest in keeping Jack out of trouble.'

'What happened to her?'

'They married. After he died, she moved off to Dublin with another husband.'

'So you were safe.'

'We were always safe. We left the party at half past eleven. We parted at the high street. We went home.'

There was nothing more to be said. It was the same situation that had existed after Jamie Parsons' death nearly thirty years earlier.

'Did you not feel some sense of responsibility once the police focused their attention on Ben Kerne?' Lynley asked them. 'Someone grassed on him. Was it one of you?'

Darren laughed harshly. 'Not bloody likely. Only person who'd've grassed on Ben would've been someone wanting to cause him trouble.'

22

'She thinks you killed Santo.' Alan didn't make the stunned declaration until they were well away from Adventures Unlimited. He'd man-handled Kerra out of her mother's bedroom, marched her along the hotel corridor and down the stairs. She'd struggled and snarled, 'Let me go. Alan! Let me God damn *go*,' but he'd been obdurate. He'd been strong as well. Who would have believed that someone as wiry as Alan Cheston could be so strong?

He'd taken her out of the hotel entirely: through the dining room door, onto the terrace, up the stone stariway, and along the promontory in the direction of St Mevan Beach. It was too cold to be out there without a pullover or a jacket, but he didn't stop to fetch something to protect them from the rising sea wind. In fact, he didn't look as if he was even aware that the wind was brisk and soon to be biting.

They went down to the beach, and at this point Kerra gave up her struggle, submitting herself to be led wherever he was leading. She didn't give up her fury, however. She would unleash it upon him when they got to where he'd decided to take her.

This turned out to be the Sea Pit, at the far end of the beach. They climbed up its seven crumbly steps and stood on the surrounding concrete deck. They looked down into the sand-strewn bottom of the pool, and for a moment Kerra wondered if he intended to throw her into the water like some primitive he-man taking control of his woman.

He didn't. Instead, he said, 'She thinks you killed Santo,' and then he released her.

Had he said anything else, Kerra would have gone on the attack: verbally, physically. But the statement demanded an answer that was at least marginally rational because the tone of it was both confused and frightened.

He spoke again. 'I've never seen anything like that. You and your mum. That was a *brawl*. It was the sort of thing one sees . . .' He didn't seem to know *where* one would see such a sight, but that would be typical. Alan was hardly the type to frequent locations where women got into hair-pulling, body-scratching, screaming-and-shrieking engage-ments with one another. Neither was Kerra if it came to that, but Dellen had pushed her to breaking point. And there was a reason for what had happened between them. Alan would have to admit to that at least. He said, 'I didn't know what to do. That was so far beyond what I've *ever* had to cope with.'

She rubbed her arm where he'd held onto her. 'Santo stole Madlyn. He took her off me, and I hated him for that. Dellen knows it, so it was easy for her to go from that to saying I killed him. That's her style.'

Alan looked, if anything, even more confused. 'People don't steal people from other people, Kerra.'

'In my family, they do. Among the Kernes, it's something between a knee-jerk reaction and an outright tradition.'

'That's rubbish.'

'Madlyn and I were friends. Then Santo came along and gave her the eye and Madlyn went mad for him. She couldn't even talk about anything else, so we ended up, Madlyn and I, we ended up with nothing because she and Santo . . . God, it was just so typical. He was *just* like Dellen. He didn't want Madlyn. He just wanted to see if he could get her away from me.' Now that she was finally putting it all into words, Kerra found she couldn't stop. She ran a hand through her hair, grasped it hard, and pulled, as if pulling it would cause her to feel something different from what she'd felt so long. 'He didn't *need* Madlyn. He could've had anyone. So could Dellen if it comes to that. She can have anyone. She *has* had anyone, any time she's felt the itch. She doesn't need . . . She *doesn't*.'

Alan stared at her, as if she were speaking a language whose words he understood but whose underlying meaning was foreign to him. A wave hit the side of the Sea Pit, and he flinched as if surprised at its strength and proximity. The spray hit them both, fresh and cold, salty against their lips. He said, 'I'm completely lost.'

'You know perfectly well what I'm talking about.'

'As it happens, I don't. I honestly don't.'

Now was the moment. There was nothing left but to present him with the evidence and to speak the truth as she understood it. Kerra had left the postcard in her mother's bedroom, but the fact of the post-card still existed. She said, 'I went to the cottage, Alan. I looked through your belongings.'

'I know that.'

'All right. You know that. I found the postcard.'

'What postcard?'

'*This is it.* That postcard. Pengelly Cove, the sea cave, Dellen's writing on it in red and an arrow pointing straight to the cave. We both know what that means.'

'We do?'

'*Stop* it. You've been working in that marketing office with her for *how* long? I asked you not to. I asked you to take a job somewhere else. But you wouldn't, would you. So you sat in the office with her day after day and you can't *tell* me . . . You bloody well cannot claim that she didn't . . . You're a man, for God's sake. You know the signs. And there were more than just signs, weren't there?'

He stared at her. She wanted to stamp her feet. He could not possibly be so obtuse. He'd decided this was the way to go: to feign ignorance until she simply threw up her hands in defeat. How clever of him. But she was not a fool.

'Where were you the day that Santo died?' she asked him.

'Christ. You can't be thinking that I had something to do with it.'

'Where were you? You were gone. So was she. And you had that postcard. It was in your room. It said *This is it* and we both know what she meant. She'd begun with red. The lipstick. A scarf. A pair of shoes. When she did that . . . When she does that . . .' Kerra felt as if she would weep, and the very thought of weeping because of this, because of her, because of them, caused all her anger to come roaring back, swelling within her to such an extreme that she thought it might explode from her mouth, a foul effluent capable of polluting whatever remained between her and this man whom she'd chosen to love. Because she *did* love him, only love was dangerous. Love put one where her father was, and that she could not begin to bear.

Alan was apparently beginning to track all this because he said, 'I see. It's not Santo at all, is it? It's your mum. You think that I . . . with your mum . . . the day Santo died. And this was supposed to have happened in that cave on the postcard?'

She couldn't reply. She couldn't even nod. She was working too hard to get back under control so that if she had to feel something – indeed, if she had to *show* that she felt something – that something would be rage.

Alan said, 'Kerra, I *told* you: We talked about the video, your mum and I. I'd spoken to your dad about it as well. Your mum kept telling me about a spot along the coast that she thought would serve our purposes well because of the sea caves and the atmosphere they provided. She handed me that card and—'

'You are *not* that stupid. And neither am I.'

He looked away from her, not at the sea but in the direction of the hotel. From the lip of the Sea Pit the old Promontory King George Hotel could not be seen. But the beach huts could, that neat blue and white line of them, the perfect spot for assignations.

Alan sighed. 'I knew what she had in mind. She suggested we go to the caves and have a look, and I knew. She's not very creative when it comes to innuendoes. But then, I don't expect she's ever had to be creative. She's still a beautiful woman, in her way.'

'Don't,' Kerra said. She found she couldn't bear to hear the details. It was, at heart, the same bloody story with the same bloody plot. Only the leading men altered.

'I will,' Alan said. 'And you'll listen and decide what you want to believe. She claimed the sea caves were perfect for the video. She said we had to go and have a look. I told her I'd have to meet her there, and I used as an excuse the fact that I had errands to run because I had no intention of being in the same car with her. So we met there and she showed me the cove, the village, and the sea caves. And nothing happened between us because I had no intention of *anything* other than nothing ever happening between us.' He'd kept his gaze on the beach huts as he spoke, but now he looked back at her. His expression was earnest, but his eyes were wary. Kerra could not make out what that meant. He said, 'So now you get to decide, Kerra. You get to choose.'

Then she understood. What would she believe: him or her instincts? What would she select: trust or suspicion? She said hollowly, 'They take from me everything that I love.'

He said quietly, 'Darling Kerra, that's not how it works.'

'It's the way it's always worked in our family.'

'Perhaps in the past. Perhaps you've lost people you didn't wish to lose. Perhaps you've let them go yourself. Perhaps you've cut them off. The point is that no one gets taken away who doesn't want to be taken away in the first place. And *if* someone's taken, that's no reflection on you. How can it possibly be?'

She heard the words, and she sensed their warmth. The warmth made her go quiet inside. With what Alan said, Kerra felt a subtle release within her. Something indefinable was giving way, as if a great internal bulwark were dissolving. She also felt the prick of tears, but she would not allow herself to go that far.

'You, then,' she said.

'Me then? What?'

'I suppose I choose you.'

'Just "suppose"?'

'I can't. More than that just now . . . I can't, Alan.'

He nodded gravely. 'I took a videographer with me. That was the errand I went on before Pengelly Cove, to fetch the videographer. I didn't go to the sea caves alone.'

'Why didn't you just tell me that?'

'Because I wanted you to choose. I wanted you to believe. She's sick, Kerra. Anyone can see that she's sick.'

'She's always been so—'

'She's always been so *sick*. And spending your life reacting to her sickness is going to make you sick as well. You've got to decide if that's how you want to live. I, for one, do not.'

'She'll still keep trying.'

'Very likely she will. Or she'll get help. She'll make up her mind or your dad will insist on it or she'll end up out on her ear and she'll have to make a change to survive. I don't know. The point is, I intend to live my life the way *I* want to live my life regardless of what your mum does with hers. Do you want to do the same? Or something else?'

'The same,' she said. Her lips felt stiff. 'But I'm . . . so afraid.'

'We're *all* afraid at the end of the day because there's no guarantee of a single thing. That's just how life is.'

She nodded numbly. A wave broke against the Sea Pit. She flinched.

'Alan,' she said, 'I wouldn't have done anything to Santo.'

'Of course you wouldn't. Nor more would I.'

Bea was alone in the incident room when she logged onto the computer. She'd sent Barbara Havers back to Polcare Cove to haul Daidre Trahair into Casvelyn for a *tête à tête*. If she's not there, wait for an hour, Bea told the detective sergeant. If she doesn't show up, call it a day and we'll lasso her tomorrow morning.

The rest of the team she'd sent to their respective homes after a lengthy postmortem on the day's developments. Have a decent meal and a good night's sleep, she told them. Things will look different, clearer, and more possible in the morning. Or so she hoped.

She considered logging onto the computer a last resort, a giving way to Constable McNulty's fanciful approach to detective work. She did it because, before she and DS Havers had left LiquidEarth earlier that day, she'd paused in front of the poster that had so fascinated the young

constable – the surfer wiping out on the monstrous wave – and she'd
said in reference to it, 'So this is the wave that killed him?'

Both men were with her: Lew Angarrack and Jago Reeth. Angarrack
was the one who said, 'Who?'

'Mark Foo. Isn't this Mark Foo on the Maverick's wave that killed
him?'

'True enough that Foo died at Maverick's,' Lew said. 'But that's a
younger kid. Jay Moriarty. Why?'

'Mr Reeth said this was Mark Foo's last wave.'

Angarrack glanced at Jago Reeth. 'How'd you come up with Foo?'
he said. 'If nothing else, the board's all wrong.'

Jago came to the door that separated the work area from the reception area and show room, where the poster was pinned among others
to the wall. He leaned against the jamb and nodded at Bea. 'Top marks,'
he told her and said to Lew, 'They're doing the job they're meant to
be doing, taking note of everything the way they ought. Had to check,
didn't I? Hope you don't take it personally, Inspector.'

Bea had been irritated. *Everyone* wanted a piece of a murder investigation if the victim was known to them. But she hated anything that
wasted her time, and she disliked being tested in that way. Even more
she disliked the way Jago Reeth watched her after this exchange, with
that knowing look men often adopted when forced to do business with
a female whose position was superior to theirs.

She'd said to him, 'Don't do that again,' and left LiquidEarth with
Barbara Havers. But now alone in the incident room, she wondered if
Jago Reeth had made the misstatement about the poster because he
was in truth testing the strength of the investigation or for another
reason entirely. There were only two other possibilities that Bea could
see: He'd misstated the surfer's identity because he hadn't known it in
the first place which seemed unlikely; or he'd deliberately misstated the
surfer's identity to draw attention to himself. In either case, the question was *why?* and she didn't have a ready answer.

She spent the next ninety minutes floating round the vast chasm of
the internet. She searched out Moriarty and Foo, discovering that both
of them were dead. Their names led to other names. So she followed
the trail laid down by this list of faceless individuals until she finally had
their faces on the computer screen as well. She studied them, hoping
for some sort of sign as to what she was meant to do next, but if there
was a connection between these big wave riders and a seacliff climbing
death in Cornwall, she could not find it, and she gave up the effort.

She walked over to the china board. What did they have after these days of effort? Three pieces of equipment damaged, the condition of the body indicating he'd taken a single heavy punch in the face, fingerprints on Santo Kerne's car, a hair caught up in his climbing equipment, the reputation of the boy himself, two vehicles in the approximate vicinity of his fall, and the fact that he had likely two-timed Madlyn Angarrack with a veterinarian from Bristol. That was it. There was nothing substantial they could work with and certainly nothing upon which they could base an arrest. It was more than seventy-two hours since the boy had died, and there wasn't a cop alive who didn't know that from the time of a murder every hour that passed without an arrest made the case that much more difficult to solve.

Bea studied the names of the individuals who were involved, either directly or tangentially, in this murder. It seemed to her that at one time or another, everyone who knew him had had access to Santo Kerne's climbing equipment, so there was little point going in that direction. Thus, what Bea appeared to be left with was the motive behind the crime.

Sex, power, money, she thought. Hadn't they always been the triumvirate of motives? Perhaps they were not generally obvious to the investigator in the initial stages of an inquiry, but didn't they turn up eventually? Look at jealousy, anger, revenge, and avarice, just as a start. Couldn't you trace each one of them back to a progenitor of sex, power, or money? And if that was the case, how did those three originating motives apply in this situation?

Bea took the only next step she could think of. She made a list. On it she wrote the names that seemed probable to her at this juncture, and next to each she logged that individual's possible motive. She came up with Lew Angarrack avenging a daughter's broken heart (sex); Jago Reeth avenging a surrogate granddaughter's broken heart (sex again); Kerra Kerne eliminating her brother in order to inherit all of Adventures Unlimited (power and money); Will Mendick hoping to make an inroad into Madlyn Angarrack's affections (there was sex once more); Madlyn operating from a hell-hath-no-fury perspective (sex yet again); Alan Cheston desiring a more significant handhold on Adventures Unlimited (power); Daidre Trahair putting an end to being the Other Woman by ridding herself of the man (more sex).

So far, the parents of Santo Kerne didn't seem to have a motive to do away with their own son, nor did Tammy Penrule. What, then, was she left with? Bea wondered. Motives aplenty, opportunity aplenty, and the means at hand. The sling was cut and then rewrapped with Santo Kerne's identifying tape. Two chock-stones were . . .

Perhaps the chock-stones were the key. Since strands of heavy wire formed the cable that made it, it would require a special tool to cut. Bolt cutters, perhaps. Cable cutters. Find that tool and she would find the killer? It was the best possibility she had.

What was notable, though, was the leisurely nature of the crime. The killer was relying upon the fact that the boy would use the sling or one of the damaged chock-stones eventually, but time was not of the essence. Nor was it necessary to the killer that the boy die in an instant since he might have used the sling and the chock-stone on a much simpler climb. He might only have fallen and been hurt, requiring the killer to come up with another plan.

Thus they weren't looking for someone desperate, perpetrator of a crime of passion. They were looking for someone crafty. Craftiness always suggested women. As did the approach that had been used in this crime. Invariably, when women killed, they did not use a hands-on method.

That line of thought shot her directly back to Madlyn Angarrack, to Kerra Kerne, and to Daidre Trahair. Which in turn made her wonder where the bloody hell the vet had taken herself to for the day. That led her inevitably to consider Thomas Lynley and his presence at Polcare Cove that morning, which took her over to the telephone to punch in the number of the mobile she'd given him.

'So what do we have?' she asked when her third attempt to get a connection proved successful. 'And where in God's name are you, Detective?'

He was on his way back to Casvelyn, he told her. He'd made a day of Newquay, Zennor, and Pengelly Cove. To her question of how the dickens this got them to Daidre Trahair whom she *still* wished to see, by the way, he told her a tale of adolescent surfers, adolescent sex, adolescent drugs, drink, parties, caves on the beach, and death. Rich kids, poor kids, and in-between kids, and the cops failing to solve a case despite someone grassing.

'About Ben Kerne,' Lynley told her. 'His friends thought from the first that Dellen was the grass. Ben's father thinks so as well.'

'And this is relevant for what reason?' Bea asked wearily.

'I think the answer to that is in Exeter.'

'Are you heading there now?'

'Tomorrow,' he told her. He paused before saying, 'I haven't run into Ms Trahair, by the way. Has she turned up?' He sounded far too casual for Bea's liking.

'Not a sign of her. And may I tell you how little I like that?'

'She may have gone back to Bristol.'

'Oh please. I don't believe that for a moment.'

He was silent. That was enough of a response.

'I've sent your Sergeant Havers out there to bring her in if she's slithered home.'

'She's not my Sergeant Havers,' Lynley said.

'I'd not be so quick about saying that.'

She'd not rung off for five minutes when her mobile chimed with Sergeant Havers herself ringing.

'Nothing,' was her brief report, mostly broken up by a terrible connection. 'Sh'll I wait longer? Can do, if you want. Not often that I get to smoke in peace and listen to the surf.'

'You've done your bit,' Bea said. 'Shove off home, then. Your Superintendent Lynley's heading towards the inn as well.'

'He's not my Superintendent Lynley.'

'What *is* it with you two?' Bea rang off before the sergeant could work up an answer.

She decided her last task before leaving for the day was to phone Pete and make mother noises about his clothes, his eating, his schoolwork, and football. She'd enquire about the dogs as well. And if by chance Ray answered the phone, she'd be polite.

Pete answered, though, saving her the trouble. He was all afire about Arsenal's acquisition of a new player, someone with an indecipherable name from . . . Had he actually said the South Pole? No. He must have said Sao Paolo.

Bea made the appropriate noises of enthusiasm and ticked football off her list of topics. She went though eating and schoolwork and was about to go on to clothes – he hated to be asked about his underwear but he would wear the same pair of underpants for a week if she didn't stay on top of him about it – when he said, 'Dad wants you to tell him when the next Sports Day is at school, Mum.'

'I always tell him when the next Sports Day at school is,' she replied.

'Yeah but I mean he wants to go with you, not come on his own.'

'He wants or you want?' Bea asked shrewdly.

'Well, it'd be nice, wouldn't it? Dad's all right.'

Ray was making further inroads, Bea thought. Well, she could do nothing about that just now. She said they would see, and she told Pete she loved him. He returned the sentiment and they rang off.

But his remarks about Ray sent Bea back to the computer, where this time she went to her dating site. Pete needed a permanent man about the house, and she believed she was ready for something more than dating and the occasional bonk when Pete was staying the night at Ray's.

She scrolled through the offerings, trying not to scrutinise the photos first, telling herself that keeping an open mind was essential. But quarter of an hour of this topped up her dating despair in ways that nothing else ever could. She decided that if every person who indicated a love for romantic strolls on the beach at sunset actually *took* romantic strolls on the beach at sunset, the resulting mass of humanity would resemble Oxford Street during the Christmas season. It was such rubbish. Whose interests *actually* were candlelit dinners, romantic beach strolls, wine-tasting in Bordeaux, and intimate chats in front of a blazing fire in the Lake District? Was she meant to believe this?

Bloody hell, she thought. The dating scene was bleak. It got worse every year, making her more and more resolved to stick to her dogs for companionship. They might very well enjoy a log fire, those three, *and* she'd be spared the pseudo-intimate conversation that went along with it.

She logged off the computer and headed out. Sometimes going home, even alone, was the only answer.

Ben Kerne completed the cliff climb in good time, and his muscles were burning from the effort. He'd done it as Santo had intended to do it, abseiling down and then making the climb on the return although he could just as easily have parked below in Polcare Cove, and done everything in reverse. He could even have hiked up the coastal path to the top of the cliff and just done the abseil by itself. But he'd wanted to walk in Santo's footsteps, and that required that he park his Austin not in the carpark of the cove itself but in the lay-by not far from Stowe Wood, where Santo had left his own car. From there, he trudged along the public footpath to the sea and he fixed his sling to the same stone post where Santo's own sling had failed him. Everything else was a matter of muscle memory. The abseil down took no time at all. The climb up required skill and thought, but that was preferable to being in the vicinity of Adventures Unlimited and Dellen.

At the end of the climb, Ben wanted to be exhausted. He sought to be drained, but he found that he was as agitated as he'd been when he'd begun the whole enterprise. His muscles were weary, but his mind was rattling along on autopilot.

As ever, it was Dellen he thought of. It was Dellen and the understanding he now had of what he'd done with his life in the pursuit of her.

He hadn't understood at first when she'd shouted 'I told.' And when her meaning began to dawn upon him, he didn't want to believe her. For believing her would mean accepting that the cloud of suspicion under which he'd lived in Pengelly Cove, that very cloud of suspicion that had ultimately driven his final removal to Truro, had been deliberately created by this woman he loved.

So to avoid both belief and its aftermath, he said to her, 'What the hell are you talking about?' and he concluded that she was striking out at him because he'd made accusations of her, or because he'd thrown her pills from the window.

Her face was screwed up with rage.

'Oh, you bloody well know. You *always* believed I was the one who grassed on you. I saw how you looked at me afterwards. I could see in your eyes. And then off to Truro you go and leave me there with the consequences. God, I *hated* you. But then I didn't because I loved you so much. And I love you now. And I hate you and why can't you leave me alone?'

'You're why the cops came back to me,' he said, hollowly. 'That's what you mean. You spoke to them.'

'I saw you with her. You wanted me to see you and I saw, and I knew you meant to fuck her and how do you think I *felt*?'

'So you decided to go one better? You took him down to the cave, had him, left him, and—'

'I *couldn't* be who you wanted me to be. I couldn't give you what you wanted, but you had no right to end things between us because I'd done *nothing*. And then with his sister . . . I saw because you wanted me to see because you wanted me to suffer, and so I wanted you to suffer in turn.'

'So you fucked him.'

'No!' Her voice rose to a scream. 'I did not. I wanted you to feel how I felt. I wanted you to hurt like I hurt, how you *made* me hurt by wanting from me all those things that I could *never* give you. *Why* did you break with me? And *why* won't you leave me now?'

'So you accused me?' There. He'd finally said it directly.

'Yes! I did. Because you're so good. You're so God damn bloody good, and it's your miserable sainthood that I could not tolerate. Not then and not now. You keep turning the other God damn cheek and when you do that, I despise you. And whenever I despised you, you broke with me, and *that's* when I loved you and wanted you most.'

He was left with saying only, 'You're mad.'

He had to get away from her. To remain in the bedroom meant having to come to terms with having built his life on a lie. For when the Newquay police had focused their enquiries upon him for week after week and month after month, he had turned to Dellen for comfort and strength. She made him whole, he'd thought. She made him what he was. Yes, she was difficult. Yes, they had their occasional troubles. But when it was right between them, weren't they better than they could ever have been with anyone else?

So when she'd followed him to Truro, he'd embraced what he decided that meant. When her trembling lips had pronounced the words, 'I'm pregnant again,' he'd embraced this announcement as if an angel had appeared before him in a dream, as if the imaginary walking staff he daily carried had indeed bloomed with lilies upon his waking. And when she got rid of that baby as well, just as she'd done with the babies before it, his and the offspring of two others, he'd soothed her and agreed that she wasn't quite ready, that they weren't quite ready, that the time wasn't right. He owed her the allegiance she'd shown him, he decided. She was a troubled spirit. He loved her and he could cope with that.

When they finally married, he felt as if he'd captured an exotic bird. She was not to be held in a cage, however. He could have her only if he set her free.

'You're the only one I truly *want*,' she would say. 'Forgive me, Ben. It's you that I love.'

Now on the top of the cliff, Ben's breath returned to normal from the climb. The sheen of sweat he wore chilled him in the sea breeze, and he became aware of the lateness of the day. He realised that in making the abseil down the face of the cliff, he'd ultimately stood in the very spot where Santo had lain, dead or dying. And it came to him, that while walking in Santo's footsteps along the path from the road, while fastening the sling to the old stone post, while repelling down and preparing for the climb back up, he'd not thought of Santo once. He'd come to do so, and he'd still not managed it. His mind had been filled, as always, with Dellen.

This seemed to him the ultimate betrayal, the monstrous one. Not that Dellen had betrayed him by casting suspicion on him all those years ago. But that he himself had just betrayed Santo. A pilgrimage to the very spot Santo had perished had not been enough to exorcise the boy's mother from his thoughts. Ben realised tht he lived and breathed her as if she were a contagion afflicting only him. Away from her, he might as well have been with her, which was the reason he'd kept returning.

He was in this, he thought, as sick as she was. Indeed, he was sicker. For if she could not help being the Dellen she was and had always been, he *could* stop being the perversely loyal Benesek who'd made it far too simple for her just to continue.

When he rose from the boulder on which he'd sat to catch his breath, he felt stiff from cooling down in the breeze. He knew he'd pay in the morning for the rapidity of the climb. He went to the stone post where the sling was looped, and he began drawing the rope back up the cliff, looping it carefully and just as carefully examining it for frays. Even in this he found he could not concentrate on Santo.

There was a moral question involved in all this, Ben knew, but he lacked the courage to ask it.

Daidre Trahair had been waiting in the public bar of the Salthouse Inn the better part of an hour when Selevan Penrule came through the door. He looked round the room when he saw that his daily drinking companion was not nursing a Guinness in the inglenook, which Selevan and Jago Reeth regularly commandeered for themselves, and he ventured over to join Daidre at her table by the window.

'Thought he'd be here by now,' Selevan said without preamble, as he pulled out a chair. 'Rang me to say he'd be late, he did. Cops were there talking to him and Lew. Cops're talking to everyone. Talk to you yet?' He gave a sailor's salute to Brian, who'd ventured out of the kitchen upon Selevan's entrance. Brian said, 'The usual?' and Selevan said, 'Aye,' and then back to Daidre, 'Even talked to Tammy, though that was cos the girl had something to tell them and not cos they had questions of her. Well, why should they? She knew the boy, but that was the extent of it. Wished it otherwise, and I don't mind saying that, but she wasn't interested. All for the best as things turn out, eh? Bloody hell, though, I wish they'd get to the bottom of this. Feel sorry for the family, I do.'

Daidre would have preferred it if the old man hadn't joined her, but she couldn't come up with an excuse that would politely communicate her desire to be left in peace. She'd never come into the Salthouse Inn prior to this for the purpose of having a bit of peace, so why would he assume that now? No one would come to the Salthouse Inn for peace as the inn was where denizens of the area gathered for gossip and conviviality, not for meditation.

She said, 'They want to talk to me,' and she showed him the note she'd found at her cottage. It was written on the back of DI Hannaford's card. 'I've spoken to them already,' she said. 'The day Santo died. I can't think why they want to question me again.'

Selevan looked at the card, turning it over in his hands. 'Looks serious,' he told her. 'With them leaving their cards and the like.'

'I think it's more that I don't have a phone. But I'll speak with them. Of course I will.'

'Mind you get yourself a solicitor. Tammy didn't, but that's cos Tammy had something to tell them and not the reverse, like I said. 'S not as if she was hiding something.' He cocked his head at her. 'You hiding something yourself, my girl?'

Daidre smiled and pocketed the card as the old man returned it to her. 'We all have secrets, don't we. Is that why you're suggesting a solicitor?'

'Didn't say that,' Selevan protested. 'But you're a deep one, Ms Trahair. We've known that 'bout you from the first. No girl throws a dart like you without having something tricky in her background, you ask me.'

'I'm afraid that roller derby is as dark as my secrets get, Selevan.'

'What's that, then?'

She tapped his hand with the tips of her fingers. 'You'll have to do your research and find out, my friend.'

Through the windows, then, she saw the Ford as it bumped into the inn's uneven carpark. Lynley got out of it and started to walk in the direction of the inn, but he turned as another car entered the carpark behind him, this one a rather decrepit Mini whose driver honked the car's horn at him as if he were in the way.

'That Jago, then?' Selevan was not in a position to see the carpark from where he sat. He said, 'Cheers, mate,' to Brian who brought him his Glenmorangie, and he slurped down his first gulp with satisfaction.

'No,' Daidre said slowly. 'It isn't.' As she watched the carpark, she could hear Selevan nattering on about his granddaughter. Tammy had a mind of her own, it seemed, and nothing was going to put her off a course she'd set for herself. 'Got to admire the lass for that,' Selevan was saying. 'P'rhaps we're all being too hard on the girl.'

Daidre made appropriate listening noises, but she was concentrating on the action outside, what little there was of it. Lynley had been accosted by the driver of the banged-up Mini. This was a barrel-shaped woman in droopy corduroy trousers and a donkey jacket buttoned to her neck. Their conversation lasted only a moment. A bit of arm waving on the woman's part suggested a minor altercation about Lynley's driving.

Behind them, then, Jago Reeth's Defender pulled into the carpark. 'Here's Mr Reeth now,' Daidre told Selevan.

'Best claim our spot, then,' Selevan told her, and he rose and went to the inglenook.

Daidre continued to watch. More words were exchanged outside. Lynley and the woman fell silent as Jago Reeth climbed out of his car. Reeth nodded to them politely, as fellow pub-goers do, before heading in the direction of the door. Lynley and the woman exchanged a few more words, and then they parted.

At this, Daidre rose. It took her a moment to negotiate payment for the tea she'd had while waiting for Lynley. By the time she got to the entrance to the hotel, Jago Reeth was ensconced with Selevan Penrule in the inglenook, the woman from the carpark was gone, and Lynley himself had apparently returned to his own car for a tattered cardboard box. This he was carrying into the inn as Daidre entered the dimly lit reception area. It was colder here, because of the uneven stone floor and the outer door, which was frequently off the latch. Daidre shivered and realised she'd left her coat in the bar.

Lynley saw her at once. He smiled and said, 'Hullo. I didn't notice your car out there. Did you intend to surprise me?'

'I intended to waylay you. What've you got there?'

He looked down at what he was holding. 'Old copper's notes. Or copper's old notes. Both, I suppose. He's a pensioner down in Zennor.'

'That's where you've been today?'

'There and Newquay. Pengelly Cove as well. I stopped at your cottage this morning to invite you along, but you were nowhere to be found. Did you go off for the day?'

'I like driving in the countryside,' Daidre said. 'It's one of the reasons I come down here when I can.'

'Understandable. I like it as well.' He shifted the box, held it at an angle against his hip in that way men have, so different from the way women hold something bulky, she thought. He looked healthier than he had four days ago. There was a small spark of life about him that had not been present then. She wondered if it had to do with being caught up in police work again. Perhaps it was something that got into one's blood: the intellectual excitement of the puzzle of the crime and the physical excitement of the chase.

'You've work to do.' She indicated the box. 'I was hoping for a word, if you had the time.'

'I'm happy to give it to you – the word, the time, whatever. Let me put this in my room and I can meet you . . . in the bar. Five minutes?'

She didn't want it to be the bar, now that Jago Reeth and Selevan Penrule were within. More of the regulars would be arriving as time wore on, and she wasn't enthusiastic about the prospect of gossip developing over Ms Trahair's intimate conversation with the Scotland Yard detective.

She said, 'I'd prefer some where a bit more private. Is there . . . ?' Aside from the restaurant, whose doors were closed and would be for another hour at least, there was really no other spot where they could meet aside from his room.

He seemed to conclude this at the same moment she did. He said, 'Come up, then. The accommodation is monastic, but I've tea if you're not averse to P.G. Tips and those grim little containers of milk. I believe there're ginger biscuits as well.'

'I've had my tea. But thanks, yes. I think your room's the best place.'

She followed him up the stairs. She'd never been upstairs in the Salthouse Inn, and it felt odd to be there now, treading down the little corridor in the wake of a man, as if they had an assignation of some sort. She found herself hoping that no one would see and misinterpret, and then she asked herself why and what did it matter anyway?

The door wasn't locked – 'Didn't seem to be any point, as I have nothing here for someone to steal,' he noted – and he ushered her within, politely stepping to one side to allow her to precede him into the room. He was right in calling it monastic, she saw. It was quite clean and brightly painted, but spare. There was only the bed to sit on unless one wished to perch on the small chest of drawers. The bed itself seemed vast although it was only a single. Daidre found herself getting hot in the face when she took it in, so she looked away.

A basin was fitted into the corner of the room, and Lynley went to this after setting his cardboard box on the floor, carefully against the wall. He hung up the jacket he was wearing – she could see that he was diligent about his clothing – and washed his hands.

Now that she was here, she wasn't sure of anything. Instead of the anxiety she'd been feeling earlier when Cilla Cormack had brought her the news of Scotland Yard's interest in her and her family in Falmouth, she now felt awkward and shy. She told herself it was because Thomas Lynley seemed to fill the room. He was a good-sized man, several inches over six feet tall, and the result of being in such a confined space with him appeared to be turning her into a Victorian-maiden-caught-in-a-compromising-situation. It was nothing he was doing, particularly. It was, rather, the simple fact of him and the tragic aura that seemed to surround him, despite his pleasant demeanour.

She sat at the foot of the bed. Before she did so, she handed him the note she'd found from DI Hannaford. He told her that the inspector had arrived at her cottage shortly after his own arrival that morning. 'I see you're in demand,' he said.

'I've come for your advice.' This wasn't altogether true, but it was a good place to begin. 'What do you recommend?'

He went to the head of the bed and sat. 'I recommend that you talk to her.'

'Have you any idea what it's about?'

He said, after a revealing moment of hesitation, that he had not. 'But whatever it is, I suggest you be completely truthful. I think it's always best to tell investigators the truth. In general, I think it's best to tell the truth full stop, one way or another.'

'And if the truth is that I killed Santo Kerne?'

'I don't believe that *is* the truth, frankly.'

'Are you a truthful man yourself, Thomas?'

'I try to be.'

'Even in the middle of a case?'

'Especially then. When it's appropriate. Sometimes, with a suspect, it's not.'

'Am I a suspect?'

'Yes,' he told her. 'Unfortunately, you are.'

'So that would be why you went to Falmouth to ask about me.'

'Falmouth? I didn't go to Falmouth. For any reason.'

'Yet someone was there, talking to my parents' neighbours. It was apparently someone from New Scotland Yard. Who would that be if it wasn't you? And what is it you would need to know about me that you couldn't ask me yourself?'

He came to her end of the bed and squatted before her. This gave her more proximity to him than she would have liked, and she made a move to rise. He stopped her: Just a gentle hand on her arm was enough. 'I wasn't in Falmouth, Daidre,' he said. 'I swear to you.'

'Then who?'

'I don't know.' He fixed his eyes on hers. They were earnest, steady. 'Daidre, have you something to hide?'

'Nothing that would interest Scotland Yard. Why're they investigating me?'

'They investigate everyone when there's been a murder. You're involved because the boy died close by your property. Are there other reasons? Is there something you've not told me that you'd like to tell me now?'

'I don't mean why are they investigating *me*.' Daidre tried to sound casual but the intensity of his look made it difficult. 'I mean, why Scotland Yard? What's Scotland Yard doing here at all?'

He rose once again. He went to the electric kettle. Surprisingly, she found that she was both relieved and sorry that he'd moved away from her, as there was a form of safety in his proximity that she hadn't expected to feel. He filled the kettle at the basin and switched it on. When he did speak in answer to her next question, he still didn't look at her.

She said, 'Thomas? Why are they here?'

'Bea Hannaford is undermanned. She should have a murder squad working the case, and she doesn't. I dare say they're spread too thin just now across the district, and the regional constabulary made a request to the Met for someone to assist.'

'Is that usual?'

'To have the Met involved? No, but it happens.'

'Why would they be asking questions about me? And why in Falmouth?'

Silence as he messed about with a bag of P.G. Tips and a cup. He was frowning. A car door slammed outside, and then another. A happy shout went up as fellow drinkers greeted each other.

He finally turned back to her when he made his reply. 'As I said, in a murder investigation, everyone is looked into, Daidre. You and I went to Pengelly Cove on a similar mission, about Ben Kerne.'

'But that doesn't make sense. I grew up in Falmouth, yes. But why ask someone to go there and not to Bristol, where my life is now?'

'Perhaps they've someone else in Bristol,' Lynley said. 'Is it this important somehow?'

'Of *course* it's important. What a ridiculous question! How would you feel, knowing the police were digging into your background for no apparent reason save the fact that a boy fell from a cliff nearby your cottage?'

'If I had nothing to hide, I don't imagine I'd care one way or the other. So we've come full circle. Have you something to hide? Something you wish the police not to know about you? Perhaps about your life in Falmouth? About who you are or what you do?'

'What could I possibly have to hide?'

He gazed at her steadily. 'How could I have the answer to that?'

She felt all on the wrong foot with him now. She'd come to speak to him, if not in high dudgeon, then at least believing that she was in a position of strength: the injured party. But now she felt as if the tables had turned. It was as if she'd thrown the dice a bit too wildly and he'd ever so deftly scooped them up.

'Is there something more you want to tell me?' he asked her again.

She said the only thing she could. 'Nothing at all.'

23

Bea had a new chock-stone on her desk when Sergeant Havers entered the incident room on the following morning. She'd got its stiff plastic sheathing off by using the blade of a new and consequently highly sharp Exacto knife. She'd had to be careful about it, but the operation hadn't taken either skill or much effort. She was in the process of comparing the unsheathed chock-stone to the array of cutting tools she also had on her desk.

Havers said to her, 'What're you on to, then?' The DS had obviously made a stop at Casvelyn of Cornwall on her way to the station. Bea could smell the pasties from across the room, and she didn't need to look to know that Sergeant Havers had a bag of them somewhere on her person.

'Second breakfast?' she asked.

'I skipped the first,' Havers replied. 'Just a cup of coffee and a glass of juice. I reckoned I owed myself a dip into the more substantial food groups.' She carried her capacious shoulder bag and from this she brought forth the incriminating Cornish delicacy, well wrapped but nonetheless emitting its telltale aroma.

'A few of those and you'll blow up like a balloon,' Bea told her. 'Go easy on them.'

'Will do. But I find it essential to sample the local cuisine, wherever I am.'

'Lucky for you it's not goat's head, then.'

Havers hooted, which Bea took as her version of a laugh. 'Also felt the need to give a few words of encouragement to our Madlyn Angarrack,' Havers said. 'You know the sort of thing: Don't worry, lass, buck up, tut tut, tally-ho, and all that, keep your pecker pecking, and it'll all come out in the wash at the end of the day. I found I'm a veritable fountain of clichés.'

'I'm sure she appreciated it.' Bea selected one of the heavier bolt cutters and applied it forcefully to the chock-stone's cable. Nothing but pain shooting up her arm. 'That one's a real non-starter,' she said.

'Right. Well, she wasn't overly friendly, but she *did* accept a wee pat on the shoulder, which was easy enough to give as she was loading up the front window at the time.'

'Hmm. And how did Miss Angarrack take your fond caress?'

'She didn't debark from the pilchard boat yesterday, I'll give her that. She knew I was up to something.'

'Were you?' Bea suddenly took more notice of Havers.

The DS was smiling wickedly. She was also removing a paper napkin carefully from her shoulder bag. She brought it to Bea's desk and laid it gently down. 'Can't use it in court, of course,' she said. 'But there it is all the same for a comparison, if you've the mind for it. Not a regular DNA comparison cause there's no skin attached. But one of those others. Mitochondrial. I expect we can use it for that if we need to.'

It, Bea saw, as she unfolded the napkin, was a single hair. Quite dark, with a slight curl to it. She looked up at Havers. 'You wily thing. From her shoulder, I take it?'

'You'd think they'd have them wear caps or hairnets or something if they're going to be around food, wouldn't you?' Havers shuddered dramatically and took an enormous bite of the pasty. 'I reckoned I needed to do my bit for hygiene in Casvelyn. And anyway, I thought you might like to have it.'

'No one has ever brought me such a thoughtful gift,' Bea told her. 'I may be falling in love with you, Sergeant.'

'Please, guv,' Havers said, holding up her hand. 'You'll have to get in the queue.'

Bea knew that, as Havers had said, the hair was useless in building a crown case against Madlyn Angarrack, considering how the sergeant had got her hands on it. They could do nothing with it save assure themselves through comparison that the hair they'd already found caught up in Santo Kerne's equipment was one belonging to his former girl-friend. But it was something, a shot in the arm that they needed. Bea placed it in an envelope and labelled it carefully for Duke Clarence Washoe to peruse in Chepstow.

'I'm reckoning it's all to do with sex and vengeance,' Bea said when the hair was taken care of. Havers pulled over a chair and joined her, munching the pasty with evident appreciation.

She shoved a wad of it to one side of her mouth and said, 'Sex and vengeance? How've you got it playing out?'

'I was thinking about it off and on all night, and I kept coming back to the initial betrayal.'

'Santo Kerne taking up with Ms Trahair?'

'For which Madlyn either seeks vengeance herself with this—' Bea held up the chock stone in one hand and a bolt cutter in the other – 'and this. Or one of the men does it for her, after she's supplied him with two of the chock-stones, which she's nicked out of the boot of Santo's car. She's already done the business on the sling. That was easy. But the chock-stones require rather more strength than she has. So she needs a helper. She would have known where Santo was keeping his equipment. All she needed was someone willing to be her assistant.'

'That would be someone with a bone to pick with Santo anyway?'

'Or someone hoping to get himself into Madlyn's good graces by helping her out.'

'Sounds like that bloke Will Mendick to me. Santo treats her badly and Will wants to sort him out for her sake; Will also wants to get into Madlyn's knickers.'

'That's how I see it.' Bea set the chock-stone down. 'Have you seen your Superintendent Lynley this morning, by the way?'

'He's not my—'

'Yes. Yes. We've already been through that. He says the same thing about you.'

'Does he?' Havers chewed thoughtfully. 'Not sure how I feel about that.'

'Mull it over later. As for now?'

'He's off to Exeter. Second half of whatever he was up to yesterday, he said. But . . .'

Bea narrowed her eyes. 'But . . . ?'

Havers looked regretful about having to mention the next bit. 'Ms Trahair came to see him. This would be yesterday, late afternoon.'

'And you didn't bring her in?'

'I didn't know, guv. I didn't see her. And since I haven't *yet* seen her anyway, I wouldn't know her if she flew in front of my car on a broomstick. He didn't tell me until this morning.'

'Did you see him at dinner last night?'

Havers looked unhappy before she said, 'Yeah. I s'pose I did.'

'And he said nothing to you then about her visit?'

'He's got a lot on his mind. He might not have thought about telling me.'

'Don't be absurd, Barbara. He damn well knew we want to talk to her. He should have told you. He should have phoned me. This man is walking on very thin ice.'

Havers nodded. 'That's why I'm telling you. I mean, not because I know he's on thin ice, but because I know it's important. I mean, it's important not because he didn't tell you . . . Not that she came to see him. That's not the important bit. What I mean is that it's important that she's resurfaced and I thought—'

'All right, all right! Jesus in a teaspoon. Stop. I see I can't expect you to grass on his mighty lordship, no matter the situation so I'm going to have to find someone willing to grass on you. And it's not like we've the manpower for that, is it, Sergeant? *What*, God damn it?'

This last she said to Sergeant Collins, who'd come to the door of the incident room. He was manning the phones below, for what little good it was doing, while the rest of the team continued with actions she'd assigned them earlier, most of which had them going over old ground.

'Ms Trahair is here to see you, guv,' Sergeant Collins told her. 'She said you wanted her to come by the station.'

Bea pushed her chair back and said, 'Well, thank God. Let's hope we're about to get somewhere.'

An unanticipated hour of research in Exeter provided Lynley with the name of the property management company that, he discovered, was no longer owned by Jonathan Parsons, father of the long ago cave-drowning victim in Pengelly Cove. Previously called *Parsons, Larson, and Waterfield*, it was now *R. Larson Estate Management, Ltd*, and it was located not far from the medieval cathedral. Its director turned out to be a questionably tanned, grey-bearded individual somewhere in his sixties. He appeared to favour jeans, exceptionally good dentistry, and blindingly white shirts worn without a necktie. *R*, Lynley discovered, stood for the unusual non-British name of Rocco. Larson's mother – long gone to her eternal reward – had possessed a devotion to the more obscure Catholic saints, the man explained. It was an equal rights sort of thing. His sister was called Perpetua. Personally, he didn't use Rocco. He used Rock, which Lynley was free to call him.

Lynley thanked the man, said all things being equal he'd prefer Mr Larson, and showed him his Scotland Yard identification, at which point Larson seemed happy enough that Lynley had decided on maintaining a sense of formality between them. Larson said, 'Ah. I suppose you don't have a property you wish to let out?'

'You'd suppose correctly,' Lynley told him, and he asked if Larson had a few minutes to spare him. 'I'd like to talk to you about Jonathan Parsons,' he said. 'I understand you were once his partner.'

Larson was perfectly willing to have a chat about 'poor Jon', and he ushered Lynley into his office. This was spare and masculine: leather and metal with pictures of the family in stark black frames. The much younger blonde wife, two children turned out in neat school uniforms, the horse, the dog, the cat, and the duck. They all looked a bit too professionally polished. Lynley wondered if they were real or the sort of pictures one finds in frames for sale in shops.

Larson didn't wait to be interrogated. He launched into his story, and he needed very little encouragement to carry on with it. He had been in partnership with Jonathan Parsons and a bloke called Henry Waterfield, now deceased. Both of them were older than Larson by ten years or so, and because of this, he'd started out as a junior manager in the firm. But he was a go-getter, if he did say so himself, and in no time, he'd purchased a full partnership. From that point on, it was the three of them until Waterfield's death, at which point it was Parsons and Larson, which was a bit of a tongue twister so they hung on to the original name.

Everything went smoothly until the Parsons boy died, Larson told him. At that point, things began to fall apart. 'Poor Jon wasn't able to hold up his end, and who can blame him? He began to spend more and more of his time over in Pengelly Cove. That's where the accident . . .'

'Yes,' Lynley said. 'I know. He apparently believed he knew who'd left his son in the sea cave.'

'Right. But he couldn't get the police to move on the killer. No evidence, they told him. No evidence, no witness, and no one talking no matter how much pressure was applied. There was literally nothing they could do. So he hired his own team, and when they failed, he hired another and when they failed, he hired another and then another. He finally moved to the cove permanently.' Larson considered a photo on the wall, an aerial view of Exeter, as if this would take him back in time. 'I think it must have been two years after Jamie's death. Perhaps three? He said he wanted to be there to remind people that the murder – he always called it a murder, no matter what – had gone unpunished. He accused the police of botching the matter from start to finish. He was . . . obsessed, frankly. But I can't fault him for that. I didn't then and I don't now. Still he wasn't bringing in any money to the business and while I could have carried him for a time, he began to . . . Well, he called it "borrowing". He was maintaining a house and a family – there are three other children, all of them daughters – here in Exeter, he was maintaining a house in Pengelly Cove, and he was orchestrating a series of investigations with people wanting to be paid for their time and effort. Things got too much for him. He needed money and he took it.' Behind his desk, Larson steepled his fingers. 'I felt awful,' he said, 'but my options were clear: to let Jon run us into the ground or to call him on what he was doing. It's not pretty, but I didn't see I had a choice.'

'Embezzlement.'

Larson held up a hand, palm outward. 'I couldn't go that far. Couldn't and wouldn't, not after what had happened to the poor sod. But I told him he'd have to hand over the business, as it was the only way I could see to save it. He wasn't going to stop.'

'Stop?'

'Trying to get the killer brought to justice.'

'The police thought it was a prank gone very bad, not a premeditated murder. Not a murder at all.'

'It certainly could have been, but Jon didn't see it that way. He adored that boy. He was devoted enough to all the children, but he was particularly mad about Jamie. He was the sort of dad we all want to be and we all wish we had, if you know what I mean. They deep-sea fished, they skied, they surfed, they backpacked in Asia. When Jon said the boy's name, he just blazed with pride.'

'I've heard the boy was rather difficult for the local children in Pengelly Cove.'

Larson drew his eyebrows together. They were thin brows, rather womanly. Lynley wondered if the man had them waxed. 'I don't know about that. He was essentially a good kid. Oh, perhaps he was a bit full of himself, considering the family probably had a good deal more money than the village children's families, and considering the preferential treatment he got from his dad. But what boy that age isn't full of himself anyway?'

Larson went on to complete the story, one that took a turn that was sad but not unusual, given what Lynley knew about families who faced the anguish of a child's untimely death. Not long after Parsons lost the business, his wife divorced him. She returned to university as a mature student, completed her education, and ultimately became head teacher at the local comprehensive. Larson thought she'd remarried as well, somewhere along the line, but he wasn't certain. Someone at the school would be able to tell him.

'What became of Jonathan Parsons?' Lynley asked.

He was still in Pengelly Cove, as far as Larson knew.

'And the daughters?' Lynley asked.

Larson hadn't a clue.

Daidre had spent part of her early morning thinking about allegiance. She knew that some people firmly believed in the principle of every man for himself. Her problem had always been an inability to adhere to that principle.

She considered the idea of what she owed other people versus what she owed herself. She thought about duty, but she also thought about vengeance. She considered the ways in which 'getting even' was merely a questionable euphemism for 'learning nothing'. She tried to decide whether there actually *were* life lessons to be learned or whether life was all a mindless tumble through the years without rhyme or reason.

She ultimately faced the truth that she had no answer to any of the larger philosophical questions about life. So she decided to take the action that was directly in front of her, and she went into Casvelyn to fulfil DI Hannaford's request for a conversation.

The inspector fetched her personally from reception. Hannaford was accompanied by another woman whom Daidre recognised as the ill-dressed driver of the Mini, who had spoken to Thomas Lynley in the carpark of the Salthouse Inn. Hannaford introduced her as DS Barbara Havers. She added, 'New Scotland Yard,' to this, and Daidre felt a chill come over her. She had no time to speculate on what this meant, however, for after a marginally hostile, 'Come with us, then,' from Hannaford, she was led into the bowels of the station, a brief journey of some fifteen paces that took them to what appeared to be the sole interview room.

It was clear that not a lot of interviewing went on in Casvelyn. Past a wall of what seemed to be boxes of toilet tissue and kitchen towels, a disabled card table of three straight legs and one with a bulbous elbow held a small cassette recorder that looked dusty enough to seed vegetables on. There were no chairs to speak of, just a three-step ladder, although an angry shout from Hannaford in the direction of the staircase obviated the necessity of their having to use the boxes of tissue and towels for that purpose. Sergeant Collins – as he was called – came on the run. He quickly provided them with uncomfortable plastic chairs, batteries for the tape player, and a cassette. This turned out to be an ancient Lulu's Greatest Hits, vintage 1970, but, obviously, it was going to have to do.

Daidre wanted to ask the purpose of making a recording of their conversation, but she knew the question would be taken as disingenuous. So she sat and waited for what would happen next, which was DS Havers' digging a small spiral notebook from the pocket of her donkey jacket, which, for some reason, she had not removed despite the uncomfortable tropical temperature in the building.

DI Hannaford asked Daidre if she wanted anything before they began. Coffee, tea, juice, water? Daidre demurred. She was fine, she replied, and then found herself wondering about that response. She *wasn't* at all fine. She was uneasy in the head, weak in the palms, and determined not to appear that way.

There seemed only one manner in which to do that: by taking the offensive. She said, 'You left me this note,' and produced the DI's card with its scrawled message on the back. 'What is it you want to talk to me about?'

'I'd think that was rather obvious,' Hannaford said, 'as we're in the middle of a murder inquiry.'

'Actually, it's not obvious at all.'

'Then it will be, soon enough.' Hannaford was deft about putting the cassette into the tape player although she looked as if she had her doubts on the matter of its properly working. She punched a button, gazed at the turning wheel of the cassette, and recited the date, the time, and the individuals present. Then she said to Daidre, 'Tell us about Santo Kerne, Ms Trahair.'

'What about him?'

'Whatever you know.'

This was all routine: the first few moves in the cat-and-mouse of an interrogation. Daidre answered as simply as she could. 'I know that he died in a fall from the north cliff at Polcare Cove.'

Hannaford didn't look pleased with the response. 'How good of you to make that clear to us. You knew who he was when you saw him, didn't you.' She made it a statement, not a question. 'So our first interaction was based on a lie. Yes?'

DS Havers wrote with a pencil, Daidre saw. It *scritched* against the notebook paper and the sound, normally innocuous, was fingernails on a blackboard in this situation.

'I hadn't got a good look at him. There wasn't time.'

'But you checked for vital signs, didn't you? You were first on the scene. How could you check for signs of life without looking at him?'

'One doesn't need to look at the victim's face to check for signs of life, Inspector.'

'That's rather coy. How realistic is it to check for vital signs without looking at someone? As the first person on the scene and even in the fading daylight—'

'I was second on the scene,' Daidre interrupted. 'Thomas Lynley was first.'

'But you wanted to see the body. You insisted. You didn't take Superintendent Lynley's word for it that the boy was dead.'

'I didn't know he was Superintendent Lynley,' Daidre told her. 'I arrived at the cottage and found him inside. He might have been a burglar for all I knew. He was a total stranger, completely unkempt as you saw for yourself, looking rather wild and claiming there was a body in the cove and he needed to be taken somewhere to make a phone call about it. It hardly made sense to me to agree to drive him anywhere without checking first to make sure he was telling me the truth.'

'Or checking yourself to discover who the boy was. Did you think it might be Santo?'

'I had no idea who it was going to be. How would I have? I wanted to see if I could help in some way.'

'In what way?'

'If he was injured.'

'You're a veterinarian, Ms Trahair. You're not an emergency physician. How did you expect to help him?'

'Injuries are injuries. Bones are bones. If I could help—'

'And when you saw him, you knew who he was. You were quite familiar with the boy, weren't you.'

'I knew who Santo Kerne was, if that's what you mean. This isn't a heavily populated area. Most people know each other eventually, if only by sight.'

'But I expect you knew him a little bit more intimately than by sight.'

'Then you'd expect incorrectly.'

'That's not what's been reported, Ms Trahair. Indeed, I have to tell you that's not what's been witnessed.'

Daidre swallowed. She realised that DS Havers had ceased writing, and she wasn't sure when that had occurred. This told her she'd been less aware than she needed to be, and she wanted to get back on the footing she'd begun with. She said to DS Havers, past the heavy pounding of her own heart, 'New Scotland Yard. Are you the only officer from London here to work on this case? Aside from Superintendent Lynley, I mean.'

Hannaford said, 'Ms Trahair, that's nothing to do with—'

'New Scotland Yard. The Met. But you must be from the . . . What would they call it? The murder side? C.I.D.? Or do they call it something else these days?'

Havers made no reply. She did, however, give a glance to Hannaford.

'I expect you know Thomas Lynley as well, then. If he's from New Scotland Yard and you're from New Scotland Yard and you both work in the same – the same field, shall I say? Would I be correct?'

'Whether Sergeant Havers and Superintendent Lynley are acquainted is none of your concern,' Hannaford said. 'We've a witness putting Santo Kerne at your front door, Ms Trahair. We've a witness putting him inside your cottage in times past. If you'd like to explain how someone you knew only by sight came knocking at your door and gaining admittance to your home, we'd very much like to listen.'

'I expect it's you who went to Falmouth asking about me,' Daidre said to Havers.

Havers looked at her blankly, a good poker face. But Hannaford, surprisingly, gave away the game. She directed her attention suddenly, if briefly, to Havers, and there was speculation in her look. Daidre took this for surprise, and she drew a logical conclusion.

'And I expect Thomas Lynley, not DI Hannaford, told you to do it.' She stated this flatly. She didn't want to dwell on how she felt about the fact, and she had no need of a reply because she knew she was right.

What she did have a need for, on the other hand, was getting the police out of her life. Unfortunately, there was only one way to do this and it had to do with information: naming a name that would take them in a different direction. She found that she was willing to do that.

She turned to Hannaford. 'You want Aldara Pappas,' she said. 'You'll find her at a place called Cornish Gold. It's a cider farm.'

Finding Jonathan Parsons' former wife ate up another ninety minutes of his time once Lynley left Rock Larson's office. He began at the comprehensive, where he learned that Niamh Parsons had long ago become Niamh Triglia and had also, more recently, retired. She'd lived for years not far from the school, but whether she was still at that location, who could say? That was the limit to what they were able to tell him.

From there, he went to an address he unearthed through the simple means of browsing in the public library. As he'd suspected, the Triglias no longer resided in Exeter, but this was not a dead end. Showing his identification and questioning a few neighbours turned up their new place of abode. Like many others before them, they had headed for sunnier climes. Thankfully, this did not turn out to be the coast of Spain but rather the coast of Cornwall, which, while not atmospherically Mediterranean in climate, was the best the mainland of England had to offer in conditions that might be deemed temperate by those who were determinedly sanguine. The Triglias had been among these types. They lived in Boscastle.

This meant another long drive, but the day was pleasant and the time of year had not yet turned Cornwall into an elongated carpark with occasional visual diversions. He made relatively good time to Boscastle, and soon enough he was hiking towards a steep lane of cottages, which wound up from the ancient fishing harbour, an inlet protected by vast cliffs of slate and volcanic lava. The high street came first in his climb – a few shops of unpainted stone that were dedicated to the tourist trade and a few more to meet the needs of the village residents – and after it came Old Street, the location of the Triglias' home. This stood not far from an obelisk dedicated to the dead of two world wars. It was called Lark Cottage, and it was whitewashed like a Santorini hut, with mounds of heather growing in front and primroses planted in window boxes. Crisp white curtains hung at the windows, and green paint glimmered on the front door. He crossed a tiny bridge of slate that spanned a deep gutter in front of the building, and when he knocked, it was only a moment before an apron-wearing woman answered, her spectacles splattered with what seemed to be grease and her grey hair scraped back from her face and springing up from the crown of her head like a hirsute fountain.

'I'm doing crab cakes,' she said, seemingly apropos of her general appearance and her more specific harried demeanour. 'Sorry, but I can't be away from them for more than a moment.'

'Mrs Triglia?'

'Yes. Yes. Oh, do please be quick. I hate to be rude, but they absorb the fat dreadfully if you leave them too long.'

'Thomas Lynley. New Scotland Yard.' As he spoke his full identification, he realised that it was the first time he'd done so since Helen's death. He blinked at this knowledge and the quick but fleeting pain that it brought him. He showed his police i.d. to the woman. He said, 'Niamh Triglia? Formerly Parsons?'

She said, 'Yes, that's who I am.'

'I need to speak with you about your ex-husband. Jonathan Parsons. May I come in?'

'Oh yes. Of course.' She stepped back from the door to admit him. She led him through a sitting room largely given to bookshelves, which were themselves heavily given to paperback books interspersed with family photographs and the occasional seashell, interesting stone, or piece of driftwood. Beyond this, the kitchen overlooked a small back garden with a patch of lawn, neat flowerbeds bordering it, and a leafy tree in its centre.

Here in the kitchen, the crab cakes were managing to produce an impressive disorder. Hot oil splattering onto the cook top largely characterised the chaos, followed by a draining board covered with bowls, tins, wooden spoons, a carton of eggs, and a coffee pot whose liquid was long since gone and whose remaining grounds looked as if they'd been forgotten. Niamh Triglia went to the cooker and flipped the crab cakes, which produced a new burst of splattering. She said, 'The difficulty is getting the breadcrumbs to brown without dousing the entire mixture with so much oil that you feel as if you're eating badly done chips. Do you cook, Mr . . . It was Superintendent, though, wasn't it?'

'Yes,' he said. 'As to the superintendent part. As to the cooking, it's not one of my strengths.'

'It's my passion,' she confessed. 'I had so little time to do it properly when I was teaching, and once I took my pension, I threw myself into it. Cookery courses at the community centre, programmes on the telly, that sort of thing. Problem is the eating bit.'

'Your efforts don't please you?'

'On the contrary, they please me far too much.' She indicated her body, which was largely concealed by her apron. 'I try to cut the recipes down for one person, but maths was never my strong suit and most of the time I make enough for at least four.'

'Are you alone here, then?'

'Mmm. Yes.' She used the corner of the egg turner to lift one of the crab cakes and examine its degree of brownness. 'Lovely,' she murmured. From a nearby cupboard, she took a plate, which she covered with several layers of kitchen towel. From the fridge, she took a small mixing bowl. 'Aioli,' she said, dipping her chin towards the mixture. 'Red pepper, garlic, lemon, et cetera. Getting the balance of tastes just right is the issue with a good aioli. That and the olive oil, naturally. *Very* good e.v.o. is essential.'

'I'm sorry? Evio?' Lynley wondered if this was a style of cooking.

'E.V.O. Extra virgin olive oil. The virgin-est one can find. If there are degrees of virginity in olives. To tell the truth, I've never been sure what it *means* when an olive oil is extra virgin. Are the olives virgins? Are they harvested by virgins? Are they pressed by virgins?' She brought the bowl of aioli to the kitchen table and returned to the cooker, where she began carefully depositing the crab cakes onto the kitchen towels that covered the plate. She took another set of kitchen towels and laid these on top of the cakes, pressing them gently into the concoction to remove as much of the residual oil as she could. From the oven, then, she brought forth three more plates, and Lynley was able to see what she had meant about failing to reduce her recipes to one portion only. Each plate was similarly dressed with kitchen towels and crab cakes. It looked as if she'd cooked more than a dozen.

'Fresh crab isn't essential,' she told him. 'You *can* use tinned. Frankly, I find you really can't tell the difference if the crab is going to be used in a cooked dish. On the other hand, if it's going to be eaten in something *uncooked* – salad or the like – you're best with fresh. But you have to make sure it's fresh-fresh. Caught that day, I mean.' She deposited the plates on the table and told him to sit. He would, she hoped, indulge. Otherwise, she feared she herself might eat them all, as her neighbours weren't as appreciative of her culinary efforts as she'd have liked them to be. 'I've no family to cook for any longer,' she said. 'The girls are scattered to the winds and my husband died last year.'

'I'm sorry to hear that.'

'You're very kind. He went quickly, so it was a terrible shock as he'd been perfectly well up till a day before. Something of an athlete, also. He complained of a headache that he couldn't get rid of, and he died the next morning as he was putting on his socks. I heard a noise and went to see what had happened and there he was on the floor. Aneurysm.' She lowered her gaze, eyebrows drawn together. 'It was difficult not to be able to say goodbye.'

Lynley felt the great stillness of memory settling round him. Perfectly fine in the morning and perfectly dead by the afternoon. He cleared his throat roughly. 'Yes. I expect it is.'

'Well, one recovers eventually from these things.' She shot him a tremulous smile. 'At least, that's what one hopes.' She went to a cupboard and brought out two plates; from a drawer she took cutlery. She laid the table. 'Please do sit, Superintendent.'

She found him a linen napkin and used her own first to clean off her spectacles. Without them, she had the dazed look of the lifelong sufferer of myopia. 'There,' she said when she'd polished them to her liking, 'I can actually see you properly now. My goodness. What a handsome man you are. You'd leave me quite tongue-tied if I were your age. How old are you, by the way?'

'Thirty-eight.'

'Well, what's a thirty-year age difference among friends?' she asked. 'Are you married, dear?'

'My wife . . . Yes. Yes, I am.'

'And is your wife very beautiful?'

'She is.'

'Blonde, like you?'

'No. She's quite dark.'

'Then you must be very handsome together. Francis and I – that's my late husband – were so similar that we were often taken for brother and sister when we were younger.'

'You were married to him for a number of years, then?'

'Twenty-two years nearly to the day. But I'd known him before my first marriage ended. We'd been at primary school together. Isn't it odd how something as simple as that, being at school together, can forge a bond and make things easier between people if they see each other later in life, even if they haven't spoken in years? There was no period of discomfort between us when we first began to see each other after Jon and I divorced.' She scooped some aioli out of the bowl and handed it to him to do the same. She tasted the crab cake and pronounced it 'passable. What do you think of them?'

'I think they're excellent.'

'Flatterer. Handsome *and* well-bred, I see. Is your wife a good cook?'

'She's completely appalling.'

'She has other strengths, then.'

He thought of Helen: the laughter of her, that unrepressed gaiety, so much compassion. 'I find she has hundreds of strengths.'

'Which makes indifferent kitchen skills—'

'Completely irrelevant. There's always takeaway.'

'Isn't there just.' She smiled at him and then went on with, 'I'm avoiding the issue, as you've probably guessed. Has something happened to Jon?'

'Do you know where he is?'

'I haven't spoken to him in years. Our eldest child—'

'Jamie.'

'Ah. So you know about Jamie?' And when Lynley nodded, she continued by saying thoughtfully, 'I suppose we all carry some sort of scars from our childhood for this and that reason, and Jon had his share. His father was a hard man with set ideas about what his boys should do with their lives, and he'd decided that what they should do was science. *Very* stupid to decide your children's lives for them, to my way of thinking, but there you have it. That's what he did. Unfortunately, neither boy was the least interested in science, so they both disappointed him and he never let them forget it. Jon was determined not to be that kind of father to our children, especially to Jamie, and I have to say he made a success of it. We *both* made a success of parenthood. I stayed at home with the children because he insisted and I agreed with him, and I think that made a difference. We were close to the children. The children were close to each other although quite spread out in age. At any rate, we were a very tight and very happy little unit.'

'And then your son died.'

'And then Jamie died.' She set her knife and fork down and folded her hands in her lap. 'Jamie was a lovely boy. Oh, he had his quirks – what boy his age doesn't – but at heart he was lovely. Lovely and loving. And very *very* good to his little sisters. We were all devastated by his death, but Jon couldn't come to terms with it. I thought he would, eventually. Give it time, I told myself. But when a person's life becomes all about the death of another and about nothing else . . . I had the girls to think of, you see. I had myself to think of. I couldn't live like that.'

'Like what?'

'It was all he talked about and, as far as I could tell, it was all he thought about. It was as if Jamie's death had invaded his brain and eaten away everything that wasn't Jamie's death.'

'I've learned he wasn't satisfied with the investigation, so he mounted his own.'

'He must have mounted half a dozen. But it made no difference. And each time that it made no difference, he went just a bit more mad. Of course, he'd lost the business by then and we'd gone through our savings and had lost our home, and that made things worse for him because he knew he was responsible for it happening, but he couldn't get himself to stop. I tried to tell him it would make no difference to his grief and his loss to bring someone to justice, but he thought it would. He was *sure* it would. Just the way people think that if the killer of their loved one is put to death, that's somehow going to assuage their own desolation. But how can it, really? The death of a killer doesn't bring anyone *else* back to life, and that's what we want.'

'What happened to Jonathan when you divorced?'

'The first three years or so, he phoned me occasionally. To give me "updates", he said. Of course, there never were any viable updates, but he needed to believe he was making progress instead of doing what he was really doing.'

'Which was?'

'Making it less and less likely that anyone involved in Jamie's death would . . . would *crack*, I suppose the word is. He saw in this an enormous conspiracy involving everyone in Pengelly Cove, with himself the outsider and them the closed-mouth community determined to protect its own.'

'But you didn't see it that way?'

'I didn't know *how* to see it. I wanted to be supportive of Jon and I tried to be at first, but for me the real point was that Jamie was dead. We'd lost him – *all* of us had lost him – and nothing Jon could do was going to alter that. My focus . . . was on that one fact, and it seemed to me, rightly or wrongly, that the result of what Jon was doing was to keep Jamie's death fresh, like a sore that one rubs and causes to bleed instead of allowing it to heal. And I believed that healing was what we all needed.'

'Did you see him again? Did your girls see him again?'

She shook her head. 'And doesn't that compile tragedy upon tragedy? One child died terribly, but Jon lost all four by his own choice because he *chose* the dead over the living. To me, that's a greater tragedy than the loss of our son.'

'Some people,' Lynley said quietly, 'have no other way to react to a sudden, inexplicable loss.'

'I dare say you're right. But in Jon's case, I think it was a deliberate choice. He was living the way he'd always lived, which was to put Jamie first. Here. Let me show you what I mean.'

She rose from the table and, wiping her hands down the front of her apron, she went into the sitting room. Lynley could see her walk over to the crowded bookshelves where she extricated a picture from among the large group on display. She brought it to the kitchen and handed it over, saying, 'Sometimes photographs say things that words can't convey.'

Lynley saw that she'd given him a family portrait. In it, a version of herself perhaps thirty years younger posed with husband and four winsome children. The scene was wintry, deep snow with a lodge and a ski lift in the background. In the foreground, suited up for sport with skis leaning up against their shoulders, the family stood happily ready for action, Niamh with a toddler in her arms and two other laughing daughters hanging onto her and perhaps a yard from them, Jamie and his father. Jonathan Parsons had his arm affectionately slung round Jamie's neck, and he was pulling his son close to him. They both were grinning.

'That's how it was,' Niamh said. 'It didn't seem to matter so very much because, after all, the girls had me. I told myself it was a man-man and woman-woman thing, and I ought to be pleased that Jon and Jamie were so close and the girls and I were as thick as thieves. But, of course, when Jamie died Jon saw himself as having lost it all. Three-quarters of his life was standing right in front of him, but he couldn't see that. That was his tragedy. I didn't want to make it mine.'

Lynley looked up from his study of the photo. 'May I keep this for a while? I'll return it to you, of course.'

She seemed surprised by the request. 'Keep it? Whatever for?'

'I'd like to show it to someone. I'll return it within a few days. By post. Or in person if you prefer. I'll keep it quite safe.'

'Take it by all means,' she said. 'But . . . I haven't asked and I ought to have. Why have you come to talk about Jon?'

'A boy died north of here. Just beyond Casvelyn.'

'In a sea cave? Like Jamie?'

'In a fall from a cliff.'

'And you think this has something to do with Jamie's death?'

'I'm not sure.' Lynley looked at the picture again. He said, 'Where are your daughters now, Mrs Triglia?'

24

Bea Hannaford didn't like the fact that Daidre Trahair had managed to take control of the interrogation several times during their interview. In Bea's opinion the veterinarian was too clever by half, which made the DI even more determined to pin something on the wily wench. What they ended up with, however, was not what Bea had expected.

Once she'd given the piece of potentially useless information about Aldara Pappas and the Cornish Gold, Ms Trahair had politely informed them that unless they had something to charge her with, she'd be off, thank you very much. The damn woman knew her rights, and the fact that she'd decided to exercise them at that particular moment was maddening, but there was nothing for it but to bid her an extremely less-than-fond farewell.

Upon rising from her chair, however, the vet had directed a question to Sergeant Havers that Bea had found telling. 'What was his wife like? He's spoken to me about her, but he's actually said very little.'

Until that moment, the Scotland Yard detective had said nothing during their interview with Ms Trahair. The only sound she'd emitted was that which came from her steadily writing pencil. At the vet's query, she rapidly tapped that pencil against her tattered notebook, as if considering the ramifications of the question.

Havers finally said evenly, 'She was bloody brilliant.'

'It must be a terrible loss for him.'

'For a time,' Havers said, 'we thought it might kill him.'

Daidre had nodded. 'Yes, I can see that when I look at him.'

Bea had wanted to ask, 'Do that often, Ms Trahair?' but she hadn't. She'd had enough of the vet, and she had larger concerns at the moment beyond what it meant – that Daidre Trahair was curious about Thomas Lynley's murdered wife.

One of those concerns was Lynley himself. After the vet had left them and once Bea had sussed out the location of the cider farm, she placed a call to Lynley as she and Havers headed out to her car. What had he dug up in Exeter? she wanted to know. And where *else* were his dubious wanderings taking him?

He was in Boscastle, he told her. He spun a lengthy tale about death, parenthood, divorce, and the estrangement that can occur between parents and children. He ended with, 'I've a photo I'd like you to have a look at as well.'

'As a point of interest or a piece of the puzzle?'

'I'm not quite sure,' he said.

She would see him upon his return, she told him. In the meantime, Ms Trahair had surfaced and, backed against a wall, had produced a new name for them as well as a new place.

'Aldara Pappas,' he repeated thoughtfully. 'A Greek cider-maker?'

'We're seeing everything, aren't we? I fully expect dancing bears next.'

She rang off as she and Havers reached her car. A football, three newspapers, a rain jacket, one doggie chew toy, and a bouquet of wrappers from energy bars having been removed from the passenger seat and tossed into the back, they were on their way. Cornish Gold was near the village of Brandis Corner, a bit of a drive from Casvelyn. They reached it by means of secondary and tertiary roads that became progressively narrower in the way of all Cornish thoroughfares. They also became progressively less passable. Ultimately, the farm presented itself by means of a large sign painted with red letters on a field of brown, heavily laden apple trees serving as the sign's decoration and an arrow indicating entrance for anyone too limited to understand what was meant by the two strips of stony ground divided by a moustache of grass and weeds, which veered off to the right. They jolted over this for some two hundred yards, finally coming to a surprisingly and decently paved carpark. Optimistically, part of it was set aside for tour coaches while the rest was given to bays for cars. More than a dozen were scattered along a split rail fence. Seven more stood in the farthest corner.

Bea pulled into a space that was near a large timber barn, which opened into the carpark. Within, two tractors – hardly in use, considering their pristine condition – were serving as perches for three stately looking peacocks, their sumptuous tail feathers cascading in a colourful effluence across the tops of cabs and down the sides of engines. Beyond the barn, another structure, this one combining both granite and timber, displayed huge oaken barrels, presumably aging the farm's product. Behind this building the apple orchard climbed the slope of a hill, row after row of trees pruned to grow like inverted pyramids, a proud display of delicate blossoms. A furrowed lane bisected the orchard. In the distance, some sort of tour seemed to be bumping along it: an open wagon pulled by a plodding draught horse.

Across the lane, a gate gave entrance into the attractions of the cider farm. These comprised a gift shop and café along with yet another gate which appeared to lead to the cider-production area, the perusal of which required a ticket.

Or a police identification, as things turned out. Bea showed hers to a young woman behind the till in the gift shop and asked to speak to Aldara Pappas on a matter of some urgency. The girl's silver lip ring quivered as she directed Bea to the inner workings of the farm. She said, 'Watching over the mill,' by which Bea took it that the woman they were looking for could be found at . . . perhaps a grinding mill? What did one do with apples, anyway? And was this the time of year to be doing it?

The answers turned out to be sorting, washing, chopping, slicing, pressing, and no. The mill in question was a piece of machinery, constructed of steel and painted bright blue, attached to an enormous wooden bin by means of a trough. The machinery of the mill itself consisted of this trough, a barrel-like bath, a water source, a rather sinister looking press not dissimilar to an enormous vise, a wide pipe, and a mysterious chamber at the top of this pipe, which at the moment was open and being seen to by two individuals. One was a man wielding various tools against the machinery that appeared to operate a series of very sharp blades. The other was a woman who seemed to be moni-toring his every move. He was wearing a knitted cap that came down to his eyebrows, as well as grease-stained jeans and a blue flannel shirt. She was garbed in jeans, boots, and a thick but cosy looking chenille sweater. She was saying, 'Take *care*, Rod. I don't want you bleeding all over my blades,' to which he replied, 'No worries, luv. I been looking after clobber lots more difficult 'n this lot since you was in nappies.'

'Aldara Pappas?' Bea said.

The woman turned. She was quite exotic for this part of the world, not exactly pretty but striking, with large dark eyes, hair that was thick and shiny and black, and dramatic red lipstick emphasising a sensual mouth. The rest of her was sensual as well. Curves in all the right places, as Bea knew her former husband might have said. She looked to be somewhere in her forties, if the fine lines round her eyes were anything to go by.

The woman said, 'Yes,' and gave one of those woman-evaluating-the-competition sort of looks both to Bea and to DS Havers. She seemed to linger particularly on the sergeant's hair. The colour of this was sandy, the style not so much a style as an eloquent statement about impatience: *Hacked over the bathroom sink* seemed to be the best description. 'What can I do for you?' Aldara Pappas's tone suggested the task was hopeless.

'A bit of conversation will do.' Bea showed her identification. She nodded to Havers to show hers as well. The sergeant didn't look happy about doing so since this required her to conduct an archeological excavation through her shoulder bag, seeking the leather lump of her wallet.

'New Scotland Yard,' Havers told Aldara Pappas. Bea watched for a reaction.

The woman's face was still although Rod gave an appreciative whistle. 'What you get up to now, luv?' he asked Aldara. 'You been poisoning the customers again?'

Aldara smiled faintly and told him to carry on. 'I'll be at the house if you need me,' she said.

She told Bea and Havers to follow her, and she took them through the cobbled courtyard of which the mill formed one edge. The other edges consisted of a jam kitchen, a cider museum, and an empty stall, presumably for the draught horse. In the middle of the yard, a pen housed a pig the approximate size of a Volkswagen Beetle. He snorted suspiciously and charged the fence.

'I could do with less drama, Stamos,' Aldara told the animal. Understanding or not, he retreated to a pile of what looked like rotting vegetation. He stuck his snout into this and flipped a portion of it into the air. 'Clever boy,' Aldara said. 'Do eat up.'

He was an orchard pig, she told them as she ducked through an arched gate that was partially concealed by a heavy vine, to the far side of the jam kitchen. *Private* was fixed onto a sign that swung from the gate's handle. 'His job used to be to eat the unusable apples after the harvest: Let him loose in the orchard and stand aside. Now he's supposed to add an air of authenticity to the place, for visitors. The problem is that he wishes more to attack them than to fascinate them. Now. What can I do for you?'

Had they thought Aldada Pappas meant to make them welcome by leading them towards her house and offering them a nice steaming cuppa, they were soon corrected. The house was a farm cottage with a vegetable garden in front of it, odoriferous piles of manure sitting at the end of raised beds neatly defined by wooden rails. At one side of the garden was a small, stone shed. She took them to this and dislodged a shovel and a rake from its interior, along with a pair of gloves. She brought a headscarf from the pocket of her jeans and used it to cover and hold back her hair in the fashion of a peasant woman. Thus ready for labour, she began to shovel the manure and the compost into the vegetable beds. Nothing had been planted there yet.

She said, 'I'll continue with my chores while we talk, if you don't mind. How might I help you?'

'We came to talk about Santo Kerne.' Bea jerked her head at Havers to indicate that the sergeant's usual brand of ostentatious note-taking was to begin. Havers obliged. She was watching Aldara steadily, and Bea liked the fact that Havers didn't seem the least bit cowed by a decidedly more attractive woman.

Aldara said, 'Santo Kerne. What about him?'

'We'd like to talk to you about your relationship with him.'

'My relationship with him. What about it?'

'I hope this isn't going to be your style of answering,' Bea said.

'My style of answering. What do you mean?'

'The Little Miss Echo bit, Miss Pappas. Or is it Missus?'

'Aldara will do.'

'Aldara, then. If it *is* your style – the echoing bit – we're likely to be with you most of the day and something tells me, you'd not appreciate that. We'd be happy enough to oblige, however.'

'I'm not sure I understand your meaning.'

'The gaff's been blown,' Sergeant Havers' tone was impatient. 'The chicken's flown the coop. The orchard pig's in the laundry. Whatever works.'

'What the sergeant means,' Bea added, 'is that your relationship with Santo Kerne has come to light, Aldara. That's why we're here: to sort through it.'

'You were bonking him till he was blue in the face,' Sergeant Havers put in.

'Not to put too fine a point on it,' Bea added.

Aldara thrust her shovel into the pile of manure and hefted a load of it onto one of the beds. She looked as if she would have preferred hefting it at Havers. 'This is your surmise,' she pointed out.

'This is what we were told by someone who knows,' Bea said. 'She, evidently, was the one to wash the sheets when you didn't get round to it. Now, since you had to meet at Polcare Cottage, may we assume there's a middle-aged Mr Pappas somewhere who wouldn't be too pleased to know his wife was having it off with an eighteen-year-old boy?'

Aldara went for another shovelful of manure. She was working rapidly but barely took a deep breath, and she didn't come close to breaking a sweat. 'You may not assume. I've been divorced for years, Inspector. There's a Mr Pappas, but he's in St Ives, and we see virtually nothing of each other. We quite like it that way.'

'Have you children here, then? A daughter Santo's age, perhaps? Or an adolescent son you'd prefer didn't see his mummy dropping her knickers for another teenager?'

Aldara's jaw hardened. Bea wondered which of her comments had hit the mark.

'I met Santo for sex in Polcare Cottage for one reason only: because both of us preferred it that way,' Aldara said. 'It was a private matter, and that's what each of us wanted.'

'Privacy? Or secrecy?'

'Both.'

'Why? Embarrassed to be doing a kid?'

'Hardly.' Aldara drove her shovel into the earth and just as Bea thought she intended to take a rest, she went for the rake. She climbed into the nearest planting bed and began energetically working the manure into the soil. 'I have no embarrassment about sex. Sex is what it is, Inspector. And we both wanted sex, Santo and I. With each other, as it happens. But as this is difficult for some people to understand – because of his age and my own – we sought a private place to . . .' She appeared to be looking for a euphemism, which seemed completely out of character in the woman.

'To service each other?' Havers offered. She managed to look bored, an I've-heard-it-all-before-now expression on her face.

'To be together,' Aldara said firmly. 'For an hour. For two or three early on, when we were new together and . . . still discovering.'

'Discovering what?' Bea said.

'What pleased the other. It *is* a process of discovery, isn't it, Inspector? Discovery leading to pleasure. Or did you not know sex is about giving one's partner pleasure?'

Bea let that one pass. 'So this wasn't a love-and-heartbreak situation for you.'

Aldara cast her a look. It spoke of both incredulity and long experience. 'Only a fool equates sex with love, and I'm not a fool.'

'Was he?'

'Did he love me? Was this love-and-heartbreak, as you put it, for him? I have no idea. We didn't speak of that. We spoke very little at all after the initial arrangement. As I've said, this was about sex. The physical only. Santo knew that.'

'Initial arrangement?' Bea asked.

'Are you echoing me, Inspector?' Aldara smiled, but she directed the expression to the earth that she was busily raking.

Briefly, Bea understood the impulse investigators often had to smack a suspect. 'Why don't you explain this "initial arrangement" to us, Aldara? And while you're doing it, perhaps you can touch upon your apparent lack of feeling regarding the murder of your lover, which, as you might surmise, certainly looks as if it can be linked rather more directly to you than you might appreciate.'

'I had nothing to do with Santo Kerne's death. I regret it, of course. And if I'm not prostrate with grief over it, that would be because—'

'It wasn't a love-and-heartbreak situation for you, either,' Bea said. 'That's certainly clear as Swiss air. So what was it? What was it *exactly*, please?'

'I've told you. It was an arrangement he and I had for sex.'

'Did you know he was getting it elsewhere at the same time he was getting it from – or doing it to or *whatever* the hell it was – to you?'

'Of course I knew it.' Aldara sounded placid. 'That was part of it.'

'What? The arrangement? What was "it"? A threesome?'

'Hardly. Part of it was the secrecy of it all, the aspect of having an affair, the fact that he had someone else. I *wanted* someone with someone else. That's how I like it.'

Bea saw Havers blink as if to clear her vision, like Alice finding herself down a rabbit hole with a randy bunny when prior experience had led her to expect only the Mad Hatter, the March Hare, and a cup of tea. Bea herself didn't feel dissimilar.

She said, 'So you knew that Madlyn Angarrack was involved with Santo Kerne.'

'Yes. That's how I met Santo in the first place. Madlyn worked for me here, in the jam kitchen. Santo fetched her at the end of the day several times, and I saw him then. Everyone saw him. It was most difficult not to see Santo. He was a highly attractive boy.'

'And Madlyn's a rather attractive girl.'

'She is. Well, of course, she would be. And so am I, if it comes to that. An attractive woman. I find that attractive people are drawn to each other, don't you?' Another glance in the direction of the police made it obvious that Aldara Pappas didn't consider this question to be one that either of them could answer from personal experience. She said, 'We noticed each other, Santo and I. I was at the point of needing someone very like him—'

'Someone with attachments?'

'—and I thought he might do, as there was a directness to his gaze that spoke of a certain maturity, a frame of mind that suggested he and I might speak the same language. We exchanged looks, smiles. It was a form of communication in which like-minded individuals say precisely what needs to be said and nothing more. He arrived early one day to fetch Madlyn, and I took him on a tour of the farm. We rode the tractor into the orchards, and it was there—'

'Just like Eve beneath the apple tree?' Havers said. 'Or were you the snake?'

Aldara refused to be drawn. She said, 'This had nothing to do with temptation. Temptation depends on innuendo and there was no innuendo involved. I was forthright with him. I said the look of him appealed to me and I had been thinking what it would be like to have him in bed. How pleasant it might be for us both, if he was interested. I told him that if he wanted more than just his little girlfriend as a sexual partner, he was to phone me. At no time did I suggest he end his relationship with her. That would actually have been the last thing I wanted as it might have made him rather too fond of me. It might have led to expectations of there being something more that was possible between us. On his part, that is. On mine there were no expectations.'

'I can see it might well have put you in a ludicrous light had he expected more and had you been forced to give it to him in order to keep him,' Bea noted. 'A woman your age going public, as it were, with a teenage boy. Trotting down the aisle in church on Sunday morning, nodding to your neighbours and all of them thinking how . . . well, how *lacking* in something you must be to have to settle for an eighteen-year-old lover.'

Aldara moved to another pile of manure. She fetched the shovel and began to repeat the process she'd followed for the first vegetable bed. The earth within became rich and dark. Whatever she intended to plant within the borders of the bed, it was going to flourish.

She said, 'First of all, Inspector, I don't concern myself with what other people think, as what other people think about me does not rob me of a single eyelash. This was a private matter between Santo and me. I kept it private. So did he.'

'Not exactly,' Havers corrected. 'Madlyn found out.'

'That was unfortunate. He wasn't careful enough, and she followed him. There was one of those dreadful scenes between them – the accosting, the accusing, the denial, the admission, the explaining, the pleading – and she ended their involvement on the spot. That put me in the very last position I wished to be in: as Santo's sole lover.'

'Did she know you were the woman inside the cottage when she turned up there?'

'Of course she knew. There was such a scene that I thought she might do violence. I had to emerge from the bedroom and do something about it.'

'Which was?'

'To separate them. To keep her from destroying the cottage or attacking him.' She leaned on her shovel and looked north, in the direction of the orchards, as if reliving her initial proposal to Santo Kerne and what that proposal had ultimately brought about. 'It was not supposed to be such a drama. When it became one, I had to rethink my own involvement with Santo.'

'Did you give him the old heave-ho as well?' Havers asked. 'Not wanting big drama in your life.'

'I intended to, but—'

'I doubt he would have liked that much,' Havers said. 'What bloke would? Finding himself out of two dolly birds in one fell swoop instead of just one. Being reduced to what . . . wanking in the shower? . . . when before he was getting it on all sides. I'll wager he would've fought you on that one. Maybe even told you he could make things a bit tough on you, a bit embarrassing, if you tried to break it off.'

'Indeed,' she said, without a pause in her labours. 'Had we got to that point, he might have done and said all of that. As it was, we never got to that point. I decided that we could continue as long as he understood the rules.'

'Which were?'

'More caution and a very clear understanding about the present and the future.'

'Meaning?'

'The obvious. About the present, I wasn't going to change my ways to suit him. About the future, there wasn't one. And that was perfectly fine with him. Santo lived largely for the moment.'

'What was second of all?' Bea asked.

Aldara looked at her blankly.

'You said "first of all" before you launched into your lack of concern over what other people think. I'm wondering what "second of all" consisted of?'

'Ah. It consisted of my other lover,' Aldara said. 'As I said earlier, the secrecy of an affair with Santo appealed to me. The affair charged things and I like to have them charged. Actually, I need to have them charged. When they aren't . . .' She shrugged. 'For me, the fire simply goes out. The brain, as perhaps you've discovered for yourself, habituates to anything over time. When the brain habituates to a lover, as the brain will do, the lover becomes less a lover and more . . .' She seemed to consider an appropriate term and she chose, 'more an inconvenience. When that occurs, one disposes of him or one thinks of a way to bring the fire back in the sex.'

'I see. Santo Kerne was doing duty as the fire,' Bea said.

'My other lover was a very good man, and I quite enjoyed him. In all respects. His company in and out of bed was good, and I didn't wish to lose it. But for me to continue to be with him – to please him sexually and to be pleased by him in turn – I needed a second lover, a secret lover. Santo was that.'

'Do all these lovers of yours know about each other?' Havers asked.

'They would hardly be secret if they did.' Aldara moved from the shovel to the rake. Her boots, Bea saw, were becoming encrusted with manure. They looked expensive and would bear the scent of animal faeces for months. She wondered why the other woman didn't care about that. 'Santo knew, naturally. He had to know in order to understand the rules. But the other, no. It was essential that the other never know.'

'Because he wouldn't have liked it?'

'Oh that, of course. But more than that, because secrecy is the key to excitement and excitement is the key to fire.'

'I notice you've been referring to the other bloke in the past tense. *Was* not *is*. Why would that be?'

Here Aldara hesitated, as if she realised what her answer was going to connote to the police.

Bea said, 'May we assume the past is just that?'

'Finito,' Havers added in case Aldara didn't get the meaning.

'He and I are having a cooling off period,' Aldara said.

'And this began when?'

'Some weeks ago.'

'Instigated by whom?'

Aldara didn't reply, which was answer enough.

'We'll need his name,' Bea said.

The Greek woman appeared quite surprised by the request, which seemed a largely disingenuous response, as far as Bea was concerned. 'Why? He didn't . . . He doesn't know.' She hesitated, thinking it over, considering all the signs, Bea concluded.

'Yes, madam,' Bea said to her. 'Indeed. It's very likely he does.' She told her about Santo's conversation with Tammy Penrule, about Tammy's advice to him about being honest. 'As it turns out, Santo apparently *wasn't* asking about whether he should tell Madlyn because Madlyn found out on her own. So it stands to reason he was asking about telling someone else. I expect it's your gentleman. Which, as you can imagine, puts him rather into the hot seat.'

'No. He wouldn't have . . .' But she hesitated again. The fact that she was tossing possibilities round inside her attractive head was obvious. Her eyes grew cloudy. They seemed to communicate all the ways in which she knew he very well could have.

'I'm no expert, but I expect most men don't care much for sharing their women,' Bea pointed out.

'It's a cave-dweller sort of thing,' Havers added. 'My hearth, my fire, my woolly mammoth, my woman. Me Tarzan, you Jane.'

Bea added, 'So Santo goes to him and tells him the truth: "We're both having Aldara Pappas, mate, and that's how she wants it. I just thought you were owed an explanation of where she is when she isn't with you."'

'Absurd. Why would Santo—?'

'Logically, he probably wouldn't have wanted another scene like the scene with Madlyn, especially if it involved a man who might beat the hell out of him in a confrontation.'

'And he *was* beaten by someone,' Havers pointed out, speaking helpfully to Bea. 'At least he was well punched out.'

'Indeed he was,' Bea returned to Havers and then went on to Aldara, 'Which, as you can imagine, does make things look iffy for the other bloke.'

Aldara dismissed this. 'No. Santo would have informed me. That was the nature of our relationship. He wouldn't have spoken to Max.' She stopped herself.

'Max?' Bea looked at Havers. 'Did you note that, Sergeant?'

'Got it in concrete,' Havers said.

'And his surname?' Bea asked Aldara pleasantly.

'Santo had no reason to tell anyone anything. He knew if he did, I would end our arrangement.'

'Which, naturally, would have devastated him,' Bea observed sardonically, 'as it would have done any man. Right. But perhaps the whole of Santo was more than the sum of the parts you saw.'

'That would be the dangly bits,' Havers muttered.

Aldara shot her a look.

Bea said, 'Perhaps Santo actually felt guilty about what you two were up to. Or perhaps after the scene with Madlyn, he wanted more off you than you were giving and he reckoned this was the way to get it. I don't know, although I'd like to find out, and the *way* to find out is by talking to your other lover: former, cooling, or otherwise. So. We're at the end point here. You can give us his surname or we can talk to your employees and get it from them because if this other bloke wasn't your *secret* lover like Santo was, it stands to reason he didn't have to come to you under cover of darkness and you didn't have to slither off to meet him in someone's wheelie bin. So someone here is going to know who he is, and that someone is likely to give us his surname.'

Aldara thought about this for a moment. From out in the courtyard, a whir of machinery started, suggesting that Rod was having success in his efforts with the mill. She said abruptly, 'Max Priestley.'

'Thank you. And where might we find Mr Priestley?'

'He owns the *Watchman*, but—'

Bea said to Havers, 'The town rag. He's local, then.'

'If you think he had anything to do with Santo's death, you're wrong. He didn't, and he wouldn't.'

'We'll let him tell us that himself.'

'You can, of course, but you're wasting your time. If Max *had* known, if Santo *had* told him despite our agreement, I would have known about it. I would have sensed it. I can tell this sort of thing with men. This internal disturbance they have. Any woman can tell if she's attuned.'

Bea observed her steadily before responding. Interesting, she thought. They'd somehow touched on a tender spot in Aldara: a psychic bruise that the woman herself had not expected to be bothered by. There was a tinge of desperation to her words. Worry about Max? Bea wondered. Worry about herself?

She said to Aldara, 'Were you in love with this one? Unexpected for you, I reckon.'

'I didn't say—'

'And you *do* think Santo told him, don't you? Because I believe Santo informed you he was going to tell him. Which itself suggests . . . ?'

'That I did something to stop Santo before he could? Don't be absurd. I didn't. And Max didn't harm him. Neither did *anyone* I know.'

'Of course. Take that down, Sergeant. No one she knows and all the relevant et ceteras you can manage to wring from that.'

Havers nodded. 'Got them in bronze this time.'

Bea said to Aldara, 'So now that we're down to it, let me ask you this. Who's next on the pitch?'

'What?'

'The excitement-and-secrecy-provoking pitch. If you were "cooling off" with Max but still bonking Santo, you needed someone else, yes? Or you'd have had only one and that wouldn't do. So who else have you got, when did he climb on board, and can we assume that he, too, was supposed to know nothing about Santo?'

Aldara drove her shovel into the earth. She did it easily, without anger or dismay. 'I believe this conversation is at an end, Inspector Hannaford.'

'Ah. So you did get someone on board prior to Santo's death. Someone closer to your age, I'll wager. You seem the sort who learns quickly, and I expect Santo and Madlyn gave you a very good lesson about what it means to take up with a teenager, no matter how good he is in bed.'

'What you "expect" does not interest me,' Aldara said.

'Right,' Bea said, 'as it doesn't rob you of a single eyelash.' She said to Havers, 'I think we have what we need, Sergeant,' and then to Aldara, 'save for your fingerprints, madam. And someone will come back later today to rob you of those.'

25

They got caught behind a lumbering tour coach, which made their trip from the cider farm back to Casvelyn longer than Bea had expected. At another time, she not only would have been impatient, leaning on the horn in an aggressive display of bad manners, she also likely would have been foolhardly: Little prompting would have urged her to make the attempt to overtake the coach on the narrow lane. As it was, the delay gave her time to think and what she thought about was the unconventional lifestyle of the woman they'd just interviewed. She did more than wonder how that lifestyle related to the case in hand, however. She marvelled at it altogether. She also discovered she wasn't alone in her marvelling. DS Havers brought the subject up.

'She's a piece of work,' Havers said. 'I'll give her that.' The sergeant, Bea saw, was itching for a cigarette after their talk with Aldara Pappas. She'd taken her packet of Players from her shoulder bag and she'd been rolling a fag between her thumb and her fingers as if hoping to absorb the nicotine epidermally. She seemed to know better than to light it, though.

'I rather admire her,' Bea admitted. 'Truth to tell? I'd bloody *love* to be like that.'

'Would you? You're a deep one, guv. Got a thing for an eighteen year old you're keeping hidden?'

'It's the whole bonding issue,' Bea replied. 'It's how she's managed to avoid it.' She frowned at the coach ahead of them, at the black belch of its exhaust emission. She braked to put some distance between her Land Rover and the other vehicle. 'She doesn't seem to be bothered by bonding. She doesn't seem to bond at all.'

'To her lovers, you mean?'

'Isn't that the very devil of being a woman? You attach yourself to a man, you form what you think is a bond with him, and then, wham. He does something to show you that, despite the longings, stirrings, and absurdly romantic beliefs of your sweet little faithful heart, he isn't the least bonded to you.'

'Personal experience?' Havers asked shrewdly, and Bea felt the other woman studying her.

'Of a sort,' Bea said.

'What sort would that be?'

'The sort that ends in divorce when an unplanned pregnancy disrupts one's husband's life plans. Although I've always found that oxymoronic.'

'What? Unplanned pregnancy?'

'No. Life plans. What about you, Sergeant?'

'I stay away from it all. Unplanned pregnancies, life plans, bonding. The whole flipping package. The more I see, the more I think a woman's better off having a deep and loving relationship with a vibrator. And possibly a cat as well, but *only* possibly. It's always nice to have something living to come home to, although an aspidistra would probably do at a pinch.'

'There's wisdom in that,' Bea acknowledged. 'It certainly keeps one from the entire male-female dance of misunderstanding and destruction, doesn't it? But I do think it all comes down to bonding in the end: this problem we seem to have with men. Women bond, and men don't. It's to do with biology, and we'd probably all be better off if we could simply cope with living in herds or prides or whatever: one male of the species sniffing up a dozen females with the females accepting this as the course of life.'

'They reproduce, while he . . . what? . . . fetches home the dead whatever for breakfast?'

'They're a sisterhood. He's window dressing. He services them but they bond to each other.'

'It's a thought,' Havers said.

'Isn't it just.' The tour coach signalled to turn, which finally freed the road ahead. Bea increased her speed. 'Well, Aldara seems to have taken care of the man-woman problem. No bonding for that girl. And just in case bonding seems likely, let's bring in another man. Maybe three or four.'

'The herd in reverse.'

'You've got to admire her.'

They dwelt on this silently for the rest of the trip, which took them to Princes Street and the offices of the *Watchman*. There, they held a brief conversation with a receptionist cum secretary called Janna, who said of Bea's hair 'Brilliant! That's *just* the colour my old gran says she wants. What's it called?' which didn't endear her much to the DI. On the other hand, the young woman happily revealed that Max Priestley was at that moment on St Mevan Down with someone called Lily, and if they wanted to speak to him, a brief walk 'round the corner and up the hill' would take them to him.

Bea and Havers made the walk. It took them to the top of the town where a roughly shaped triangle of marram grass and wild carrot was bisected by a road that led from lower Casvelyn to an area called the Sawsneck, where the upper crust from far away cities had once come to spend their holidays in a line of grand hotels at the turn of the twentieth century. These were now seriously down at heel.

The aforementioned Lily turned out to be a golden retriever who was joyfully bounding through the heavy-topped grass in delighted pursuit of a tennis ball. Her master was lobbing this as far as he could across the down by means of a tennis racket onto which the dog cooperatively deposited the ball once she'd nosed it out of the copious undergrowth. He was garbed in a green waxed jacket and Wellingtons, with a peaked cap on his head that should have looked ridiculous – so achingly I'm-a-man-in-the-countryside – but instead made him look like a model in *Country Life*. It was the man himself who managed this. He was the sort one had to identify as 'ruggedly handsome'. Bea could see his appeal for Aldara Pappas.

It was windy on the down, and Max Priestley was the only person there. He was calling encouragement to his dog, who seemed to need little enough of it although she was panting rather more heartily than might have been good for an animal her age and condition.

Bea began to stride in Priestley's direction, Havers trudging behind her. There were no paths as such on the down, just trails beaten through the grass and standing pools of rainwater where depressions in the land marked the ground. Neither of them had the proper shoes for a walk in the place, but Sergeant Havers' high top trainers were at least preferable to Bea's court shoes. She cursed as her foot sank into a hidden puddle.

'Mr Priestley?' she called as soon as they were within hearing distance. 'Could we have a word please?' She began to reach for her identification.

He seemed to focus on her fiery hair. 'You'd be DI Hannaford, I presume,' he said. 'My reporter's been getting all the pertinent details from your Sergeant Collins. He apparently holds you in some considerable respect. And this is Scotland Yard?' in reference to Havers.

'Correct on both fronts,' Bea told him. 'DS Havers.'

'I'll need to keep Lily moving as we talk. We're working on her weight.

Getting it off, that is. Putting it on hasn't been a problem as she shows up at mealtimes as regular as a ne-er-do-well brother, and I've never been able to resist those eyes.'

'I'm a dog owner myself,' Bea said.

'Then you know what I mean.' He batted the ball some fifty yards and Lily went after it with a yelp. He said, 'I expect you've come to talk about Santo Kerne. I reckoned someone would be here eventually. Who gave you my name?'

'Is that important?'

'It could only be Aldara or Daidre. No one else knew, according to Santo. The world's general ignorance of the arrangement, he was very good to point out, would prevent damage to my ego should my ego be inclined towards damage. Kind of him, wouldn't you say?'

'Tammy Penrule knew, as things turn out,' Bea told him. 'At least she knew part of it.'

'Did she indeed? So Santo lied to me. Unbelievable. Who would have expected dishonesty from such a sterling bloke? Did Tammy Penrule give you my name?'

'No. Not Tammy.'

'Daidre or Aldara then. And of the two of them, I'd think Aldara. Daidre plays her cards quite close.'

He was so casual about the entire situation that Bea found herself taken aback for a moment. She'd learned over time to have no expectations of how an interview might or might not go, but she was unprepared for Max Priestley's apparent indifference to being made a cuckold by an adolescent boy. She glanced at Sergeant Havers. The DS was making a study of Priestley. She'd taken the opportunity to apply the flame of a plastic lighter to her cigarette, and she narrowed her eyes against its smoke and directed her gaze to the man's face.

It seemed open enough, its expression pleasant. But there was no mistaking the sardonic quality of what Priestley was saying. To Bea's way of thinking, his type of frankness generally meant that either his wounds ran deep or he'd found himself on the receiving end of what he himself had once dished out. Of course, in this current situation, there was the third possibility one had to consider: a killer's attempt to cover his tracks through a show of indifference. But that alternative didn't seem likely to her at the moment, and Bea couldn't say why although she hoped it had nothing to do with his overall magnetism. He was, regrettably, quite a dish.

'We'd like to talk to you about your relationship with Aldara,' Bea acknowledged. 'She's given us bits and pieces. We're interested in your side of the affair.'

'Did I kill Santo when I discovered he was having it off with my woman?' he enquired. 'The answer's no. You'd expect me to say that, though, wouldn't you? Your average killer's hardly going to admit to being one.'

'I do find that's generally the case.'

'Come on, Lil!' Priestley shouted suddenly, frowning into the distance. Another dog walker had appeared at the far edge of the down. Priestley's retriever had noticed and was bounding off in that direction. 'Bloody dog,' he said. 'Lily! Come!' The dog happily ignored him. He chuckled ruefully and looked back to Bea and Havers. 'And to think I used to have such a magic touch with women.'

It was as good a segue as any. Bea said, 'It didn't work with Aldara?'

'It did at first. Right up till the time I discovered her magic was stronger than mine. And then,' he offered them a quirky smile, 'I got a taste of my own medicine, as they say, and the flavour wasn't something I liked.'

At this indication that more was forthcoming, Sergeant Havers did her bit with her notebook and pencil, her cigarette dangling from her lips. Priestley, nodded, said, 'What the hell, then,' and began to complete the picture of his relationship with Aldara Pappas.

They'd become acquainted at a meeting of business owners from Casvelyn and the surrounding area. He was there to do a story on the meeting; the business owners were there to glean ideas for increasing tourism during the off season. Aldara was a cut above the other proprietors of this surf shop and that restaurant or hotel. It was, he said, a tough job not to take notice of her.

'Her history was intriguing,' Priestley said. 'A divorced woman taking on a derelict apple farm and building it into a decent tourist attraction. I wanted to do a story on her.'

'Just a story?'

'At first. I'm a newspaperman. I look for stories.'

They talked both at the meeting and after the meeting. Plans were laid. Although he could have sent the *Watchman's* sole reporter to gather the facts, he did it himself instead. Admittedly, he was attracted to her.

'So the newspaper story was an excuse?' Bea said.

'I intended to do it. It got written eventually.'

'Once you were in her knickers?' Havers asked.

'One can only do a single thing at a time,' Priestley replied.

'Which means . . . ?' Bea hesitated and then saw the light. 'Ah. You bedded her at once. That very day, when you went for the interview. Is that your usual m.o., Mr Priestley, or was this something special for you?'

'It was mutual attraction,' Priestley said. 'Very intense. Impossible to ignore.'

A romantic, he said, would have called what happened between Aldara Pappas and him love at first sight. An analyst of love would have called it cathexis.

'And what did you call it?' Bea asked the newspaperman.

'Love at first sight.'

'So you're a romantic?'

'Looks like I turned out to be.'

His golden retriever bounded up to him. Her exploration of the other dog's pertinent orifices complete, Lily was ready for another throw of the tennis ball. Priestley whacked it to the far edge of the down.

'Something you didn't expect?'

'Never.' He watched the dog for a moment before turning back to them. 'Prior to Aldara, I'd been a player all my life. I had no intention of getting hooked into anyone, and to prevent that—'

'What? Marriage and babies?'

'—I always had more than one woman on a string.'

'Just like her,' Havers noted.

'With a serious exception. I had two or three. Once I had four, but they always knew. I was honest with them from the start.'

Havers said to Bea, 'There you are, guv. It happens sometimes. He brought them the dead whatever.'

Priestley looked confused. Bea said to him, 'But in the case of Mrs Pappas?'

'She was like no one else I'd had. It wasn't just the sex thing. It was the whole package of her. Her intensity, her intelligence, her drive, her confidence, her sense of purpose. There's nothing simpering, soft, or weak about her. There's no manipulation. No subtle manoeuvring. No double message and no mixed or confusing signals. There's nothing at all to be read or interpreted in her behaviour. Aldara's like a man in the body of a woman.'

'I notice you don't credit her with personal honesty,' Bea pointed out.

'I don't,' he said. 'That was my mistake.'

He'd come to believe Aldara Pappas was, at long last in his life, the

One. He'd never thought to marry. He'd never wanted to marry. He'd seen enough of his parents' marriage to be firm in not wanting ever to live as they had lived: unable just to get *on* with each other, to cope with their differences, or to divorce. They'd never been able to manage any option they'd had; nor had they even seen they *had* options. Priestley hadn't wanted to live that kind of life.

'But with Aldara, it was different,' he said. 'She'd had a terrible first marriage. Husband was a rotter who let her think she was infertile when they couldn't have kids. Said he'd been tested three ways to Sunday and found perfectly fit. Let her go to doctors and get all sorts of mad treatments, while he was shooting blanks the entire time. She was dead off men after years with him, but I brought her round. I wanted what she wanted, whatever she wanted. Marriage? Fine. Kids? Fine. A mass of chimpanzees? Myself in tights and a tutu? I didn't care.'

'You had it bad,' DS Havers noted, looking up from her pad. She actually sounded marginally sympathetic, and Bea wondered if the man's magic touch was rubbing off on her.

'It was the fire thing,' Priestley said. 'The fire didn't die out between us, and I couldn't see the slightest sign that it might. Then I dis- covered why.'

'Santo Kerne,' Bea said. 'Her affair with him kept her hot for you. Excitement. Secrecy.'

'I was gobsmacked. I was bloody reeling. He came to me and spilled the whole story. Out of conscience, he said.'

'You didn't believe that?'

'The conscience bit? Not on your life. Not when his conscience didn't take him as far as telling his girlfriend. It doesn't concern *her*, he informed me, as he had no intention of breaking off with her because of Aldara. So I wasn't to worry that he, Santo, might want something more from Aldara than she was willing to give. It was a sex thing between them "You're number one," he told me. "I'm just there to pick up the slack."'

'Good at that, was he?' Havers asked.

'I didn't wait round long enough to find out. I phoned Aldara and broke off with her.'

'Did you tell her why?'

'I expect she worked it out. Either that, or Santo was as honest with her as he was with me. Which, come to think of it, gives Aldara some- thing of a motive to kill him herself, doesn't it?'

'Is that your ego speaking, Mr Priestley?'

Priestley guffawed. 'Believe me, Inspector, I've not much ego left.'

'We'll need your fingerprints. Are you willing to give them?'

'Fingerprints, toe prints, and anything else you want. I've nothing to hide from anyone.'

'That's wise of you.' Bea nodded to Havers who flipped her notebook closed. She told the newsman to come to the station where his prints would be taken. Then she said to him, 'As a point of curiosity, did you favour Santo Kerne with a black eye prior to his death?'

'I would have loved to,' he said. 'But, frankly, I didn't think he was worth the effort.'

Jago's approach, when he revealed it to Cadan, was to employ the man-to-man talk: If Cadan wanted to put distance between himself and Dellen Kerne, there was only one way to do it and that was by facing Lew Angarrack. There was plenty of work at LiquidEarth, so there was no need for Jago to take Cadan's part with his father. All that was necessary, he said, was an honest conversation in which mistakes were admitted, apologies extended, and amends promised.

Jago made it all sound simple. Cadan was hot to do it at once. The only problem here was that Lew had gone for a surf – 'Big swells in Widemouth Bay today,' Jago informed him – so Cadan was going to have to wait until his father's return. Or he was going to have to go out to Widemouth Bay to meet him as he finished up his surf. This second proposal sounded like an excellent idea since, after a surf, Lew's spirits would be high, which would likely translate to Lew's amenability to Cadan's plans.

Jago lent his car to the endeavour. Saying, 'Mind how you go, then,' he handed over his keys.

Cadan set off. Without a driving licence and mindful of Jago's display of trust in him, he took supreme care. Hands at two o'clock and ten o'clock, eyes fixed ahead or flicking to the mirrors, the occasional glance at the speedometer.

Widemouth Bay lay to the south of Casvelyn, some five miles down the coast. Flanked by largely friable cliffs of sandstone, it was much as its named suggested: a wide bay accessed from a large carpark just off the coastal road. There was no town to speak of. Instead, summer cottages were sprinkled across the down east of the road, and the only businesses that served them, surfers, and tourists to the area were a seasonal restaurant and a shop hiring out body boards, surfboards, and wet suits.

In summer the bay was madness because unlike so many bays in Cornwall, it was no difficult matter to get to it, so it attracted day trippers by the hundreds, holiday makers, and locals as well. In the off season, it was left to surfers who flocked to it when the tide was mid to high, the wind was east, and the waves were breaking on the right-hand reef.

Conditions were superb this day, with swells that looked to be five feet. So the carpark was littered with vehicles, and the line up of surfers was impressive. Even so, when Cadan pulled in and parked, he could make out his father easily. Lew surfed the way he did most everything else: alone.

It was largely a solitary sport anyway, but Lew managed to make it even more so. His was a figure set apart from the rest, farther out, content to wait for swells that rose only occasionally at this distance from the reefs. To look at him, one would think he knew nothing about the sport because certainly he ought to be waiting with the others, who were getting fairly consistent rides. But that wasn't his way, and when a wave finally came that he liked, he was on its shoulder effortlessly, paddling with a minimum of effort and the experience of more than thirty years on the water.

The others watched him. He dropped in smoothly, and there he was, angling across the wave's green face, carving back towards the barrel, looking as if at any moment he'd catch a rail or the falls would take him, but knowing when to carve again so that the wave was his.

Cadan didn't need to see a scoreboard or hear a commentary to know his father was good. Lew seldom spoke of it, but he'd surfed competitively in his twenties, harbouring a dream of worldwide travel and recognition before the Bounder had left him with two small children to care for. At that point, Lew had been forced to rethink his chosen path. What he'd come up with was LiquidEarth. From shaping his own boards, he'd gone on to shape boards for others. Thus he lived vicariously the peripatetic life of a world-class surfer. It couldn't have been easy for his father to give up on what he'd hoped to do with his life, Cadan realised, and he wondered why he'd never thought about that before now.

When Lew came out of the water, Cadan was waiting for him. He'd fetched a towel from within the RAV4 and he handed it over. Lew propped his short board against the car and took the towel with a nod. He pulled off his hood and rubbed his hair vigorously. He began to peel off his wetsuit. It was still the winter suit, Cadan noted. The water wouldn't warm up for two more months.

'What're you doing here, Cade?' Lew asked him. 'Aren't you meant to be at work?' He stepped out of the wetsuit and wrapped the towel round his waist. From within the car, he brought out a T-shirt and then a sweatshirt printed with LiquidEarth's logo. He donned these and worked on getting out of his swimsuit. He said nothing else until he was dressed and loading his kit into the back of the car. And then it was to repeat, 'What are you doing here, Cade? How did you get here?'

'Jago let me use his wheels.'

Lew looked round the carpark and spotted the Defender. 'Without your driving licence,' he said.

'I didn't take chances. I drove like a nun.'

'That's hardly the point. And why aren't you at work? Have you been sacked?'

Cadan didn't intend it and didn't want it, but he felt the quick anger that always seemed to be the outcome of a conversation with his father. He said without considering where it would take them, 'I guess you'd think that, wouldn't you?'

'Past history.' Lew stepped past Cadan and went for his board. There were showers at the far side of the carpark, and Lew could have used them to wash the saltwater from his kit, but he didn't do so as the job he could do at home would be more thorough and consequently more to his liking. And it seemed to Cadan that that was his father's way about everything. *To my liking* was the motto Lew lived by.

Cadan said, 'As it happens, I haven't been sacked. I've been doing a bloody good job over there.'

'I see. Congratulations. What're you doing here, then?'

'I came to talk to you. Jago said you were here. And he *offered* his car, by the way. I didn't ask.'

'Talk to me about what?' Lew slammed home the back of the RAV4. From the driver's seat, he rustled through a paper bag and brought out a sandwich encased in plastic. He prised open the lid and lifted out half. He offered the other half to Cadan.

A peace offering, Cadan decided. He shook his head but was careful to say thanks. 'About coming back to LiquidEarth,' Cadan said. 'If you'll have me.' He added this last as his own form of peace offering. His father had the power in this situation and he knew that his part was to acknowledge that fact.

'Cadan, you just told me—'

'I know what I said. But I'd rather work for you.'

'Why? What happened? Adventures Unlimited not to your liking?'

'*Nothing's* happened. I'm doing what you've wanted me to do. I'm thinking about the future.'

Lew looked out at the sea, where the surfers patiently waited for the next good swell. 'I expect you have a plan of some sort?'

'You need a sprayer,' Cadan said.

'I need a shaper as well. Summer's coming. We're behind on our orders. We're competing with those hollow core boards and what we have over them is—'

'Attention to individual needs. I know. But part of the need is the artwork, isn't it? The look of the board as well as the shape. I can do that. That's what I'm good at. I can't shape boards, Dad.'

'You can learn to shape them.'

It always came down to this in the end: what Cadan wanted versus what Lew believed. 'I *tried*. I wrecked more blanks than I shaped properly and you don't want that. It wastes time and money.'

'You've got to learn. It's part of the process and if you don't know the process—'

'Shit! You didn't make Santo learn the process. Why didn't *he* have to learn it, start to finish, like you're telling me?'

Lew gave his attention back to Cadan. 'Because I didn't build the goddamn business for Santo,' he said quietly. 'I built it for you. But how the hell can I leave it to you if you don't understand it?'

'So let me spray first, get that down pat, and go on to shaping afterwards.'

'No,' Lew said. 'That's not how it's done.'

'Jesus. What the hell difference does it make how it's done?'

'We do it my way, Cadan, or we don't do it.'

'That's *always* how it is with you. Do you ever think you might be wrong?'

'Not in this. Now get in the car. I'll drive you back to town.'

'I've got—'

'I won't have you driving Jago's car, Cade. You've had your driving licence taken—'

'By *you*.'

'—and until you prove to me that you're responsible enough to—'

'Forget it. Just bloody fucking *forget* it, Dad.'

Cadan strode across the carpark to where he'd left Jago's car. His father called his name sharply. He kept on going.

He headed back to Casvelyn, burning. All right, he thought. Bloody all *right*. His father wanted proof and he would prove. He'd prove until he was blue in the face, and he knew just the place to do it.

He drove with far less care on his return to town. He blasted over the bridge that spanned the Casvelyn Canal – mindless of the yield to oncoming traffic sign, which earned him two fingers from the driver of a UPS van – and he took the roundabout at the bottom of the Strand without braking to see if he had the right of way. He coursed up the hill and charged down St Mevan Crescent onto the promontory. By the time he reached Adventures Unlimited *in a lather* was the best description of his state.

His thoughts ran circles round the word *unfair*. Lew was unfair. Life was unfair. The world was unfair. His entire existence would be so simple if other people would just see things his way. But they never did.

He shoved open the door of the old hotel. He used a bit too much force, and it hit the wall with a crash that reverberated through the reception area. The sound of his entry brought Alan Cheston out of his office. He looked from the door to Cadan to his wristwatch.

'Weren't you meant to be here this morning?' he asked.

'I had errands,' Cadan said.

'I think errands get done on your own time, not on ours.'

'It won't happen again.'

'I hope not. Truth is, Cade, we can't have employees who don't show up when they're intended to show up. In a business like this, we've got to be able to depend—'

'I *said* it won't happen again. What more do you want? A guarantee written in blood or something?'

Alan crossed his arms. He waited a moment before making a reply and in that moment, Cadan could hear the echo of his own petulant voice. 'You don't much like to be supervised, do you?' Alan said.

'No one told me you were my supervisor.'

'Everyone here is your supervisor. Until you prove yourself, you're rather a bit player, if you know what I mean.'

Cadan knew what he meant, but he was sick to death of proving himself. To this person, to that person, to his father, to anyone. He just wanted to get *on* with things, and no one was letting him. That fact made him want to hurl Alan Cheston into the nearest wall. He itched to do it, to act on the impulse and to hell with the consequence. It would feel so good.

He said, 'Fuck it. I'm clearing out. I've come for my clobber.' He headed for the stairs.

'Have you informed Mr Kerne?'

'You can do that for me.'

'It'll hardly look good.'

'Like I almost care.' He left Alan staring after him, lips parted as if he was about to say more, as if he was going to point out, correctly, that if Cadan Angarrack had some sort of kit he'd left at Adventures Unlimited, it would hardly be on the upper floors of the building. But Alan said nothing, and his silence left Cadan in command, which was where he wanted to be.

He had no kit at Adventures Unlimited. No clobber, no gear, no anything. But he told himself that he would check each room he'd been in during his very brief time in the employ of the Kernes because one never knew where one had left a possession and after this, it would be a bit uncomfortable for him to have to come back and pick up anything he might have left behind.

Room after room. Door opened, a quick look inside, door closed. A quiet 'Hullo. Anyone in here?' as if he expected his supposed forgotten possessions to speak. He finally found her on the top floor, where the family lived, where he could have gone at once had he been practising honesty with himself, which he was not.

She was in Santo's bedroom. At least, Cadan assumed that it was Santo's bedroom by the surfing posters, the single bed, the pile of T-shirts on a chair, and the pair of trainers that Dellen Kerne was caressing on her lap when Cadan opened the door.

She was all in black, jersey and trousers and a band holding her blonde hair off her face. She had on no make up, and a scratch marked her cheek. Her feet were bare. She was sitting on the edge of the bed. Her eyes were closed.

Cadan said, 'Hey,' in what he hoped was a gentle voice.

She opened her eyes. They fixed on him, the pupils so large that the violet of her irises was nearly obscured. She dropped the trainers to the floor with a soft thud. She held out her hand.

He went to her and helped her to her feet. He saw she had nothing on beneath her jersey. Her nipples were large, round, and rigid. He stirred at this. For once, he admitted the truth to himself. This was why he'd come to Adventures Unlimited. Jago's advice and the rest of the world be damned.

He grazed the tip of her nipple with his fingers. Her eyelids lowered but did not close. He knew it was safe to continue. He took a step to be nearer. A hand on her waist and then circling round, cupping her bum while the other hand's fingers stayed where they were and played like feathers against her. He bent to kiss her. Her mouth opened willingly beneath his and he pulled her more firmly against him so that she would feel what he wanted her to feel.

He said when he could, 'That key you had yesterday.'

She didn't reply. He knew she knew what he was talking about because her mouth lifted to his once more.

He kissed her. Long and deeply and it went on and on till he thought his eyeballs might pop from his head and his eardrums might burst. His slamming heart needed somewhere to go besides his chest because if it didn't find another home, he reckoned he could die on the spot. He ground against her. He began to ache.

He broke away from her and said, 'The beach huts. You had a key. We can't. Not here.' Not in the family quarters and certainly not in Santo's room. It was indecent, somehow.

'Can't what?' She leaned her forehead against his chest.

'You know. Yesterday when we were in the kitchen, you had a key. You said it was for one of the beach huts. Let's use it.'

'For what?'

What the hell did she think? Was she the sort who liked it said outright? Well, he could do that. 'I want to fuck you,' he said. 'And you want to be fucked. But not in here. In one of the beach huts.'

'Why?'

'Because. It's obvious, isn't it?'

'Is it?'

'Jesus. Yeah. This is Santo's room, right? And anyway his dad might come in.' He couldn't bring himself to say *your husband*. 'And if that happens . . .' She could see it, couldn't she? What was wrong with her?

'Santo's dad,' she said.

'If he walks in on us . . .' This was ridiculous. He didn't need to explain. He didn't want to explain. He was ready and he *thought* she was ready and to have to talk about all of the whys and wherefores . . . Obviously, she wasn't yet hot enough for him. He went for her again. Mouth on nipple this time, through the jersey, a gentle pull with his teeth, a flicking of the tongue. Back to her mouth and drawing her near and it was odd that she wasn't doing much in turn but did that really matter? 'Jesus. Get that *key*,' he murmured.

'Santo's dad,' she said. 'He won't come here.'

'How can you be sure?' Cadan examined her more closely. She appeared to be marginally out of it, but even so it seemed to him that she ought to *know* they were in her son's room and her husband's house. On the other hand, she wasn't exactly looking at him now and he didn't know if she'd actually *seen* him – as in registering his presence – when she *had* looked at him.

'He won't,' she said. 'He might want to, but he can't.'

'Babe, you're not making sense.'

She murmured, 'I knew what I ought to do, but he's my rock, you see. And there was a chance, so I took it. Because I loved him. I knew what was important. I *knew*.'

Cadan was flummoxed. More, he was fast deflating, losing ground with her and with the moment. Still, he said, 'Dell, Dellen, babe,' to coax her. She'd spoken well of chances because if there was the slightest chance that he could *still* get her down to the beach huts, he was willing to go for it.

He took her hand. He lifted it to his mouth. He ran his tongue across her palm. He said huskily, 'What d'you say, Dell? What about that key?'

Her reply was, 'Who are you? What are you doing here?'

26

When Kerra and her father walked into Toes on the Nose, the café was virtually empty. In part, this was due to the time of day, which was between one meal and the next. In part, this was due to the conditions on the water. When the swells were good, no surfer in his right mind would be hanging about in a café.

She'd invited Ben out for a cuppa. They could have more easily had one in the hotel, but she'd wanted to be away from Adventures Unlimited for their conversation. The hotel was redolent of Santo's death and the recent row she'd had with her mother. For this chat with her father, she wanted to be in neutral territory, in a place that was fresh.

Not that Toes on the Nose was fresh in the true sense. It was instead an inadequate refashioning of what had once been the Green Table Café, a perfect example of if-you-can't-beat-them-join-them, long ago taken over by surfers because of its proximity to St Mevan Beach. The café had recent new owners who'd seen commercial possibilities in putting up posters of old surfing films and playing music by the Beach Boys and Jan and Dean. Their menu, however, remained what it had been when they'd bought the place: cheesy chips, lasagna with chips and garlic bread, jacket potatoes with a variety of fillings, chip butties. One's arteries could clog just reading the menu.

Kerra ordered a Coke at the counter. Her father ordered coffee. Then they took a table as far from the music speakers as possible, beneath a poster for *Endless Summer*.

Ben looked at the *Riding Giants* poster across the room. His gaze went from it to *Gidget*, and he seemed to compare them. He smiled, perhaps nostalgically. Kerra saw this and said, 'Why'd you give it up?'

He returned his gaze to her. She thought for a moment that he wouldn't reply to so direct a question but he surprised her. 'I left Pengelly Cove,' he said frankly. 'There's not much surf in Truro.'

'You could have gone back. How far is Truro from the sea, after all?'

'Not far,' he admitted. 'I could have gone back once I had a car. That's true enough.'

'But you didn't. Why?'

He looked momentarily pensive and presently he said, 'I was finished with it. I'd faced the fact that it had done me no good.'

'Ah, Mum,' she said. 'That's how you met her.' And yet her reply was based solely on assumption, she realised, for they'd never once discussed how Ben and Dellen Kerne had actually met. It was the sort of question children asked their parents all the time once they became aware that their parents were people separate from themselves: How did you and Mummy meet? But she had never asked and she doubted whether Santo had either.

Ben was accepting his cup of coffee with thanks to the café's owner. He didn't reply until Kerra had her Coke. Then he said, 'Not because of your mum, Kerra. There were other reasons. Surfing led me to a place I'd have been better off not going to.'

'Truro, you mean?'

He smiled. 'I'm speaking metaphorically. A boy died in Pengelly Cove, and everything changed. That was down to surfing, more or less. That's why I didn't much like Santo surfing. I didn't want him to fall into a situation that might cause him the sort of trouble I'd seen. So I did what I could to discourage him. It wasn't right of me, but there you have it.' He blew across the top of his coffee and sipped. He said wryly, 'Damn, though. It was daft to try. Santo didn't need me interceding in his life, at least not about that. He took care of himself, didn't he?'

'Not at the end of the day,' Kerra noted quietly.

'No. Not at the end of the day.' Ben turned his coffee cup in its saucer, his gaze on his hands. They were silent as the Beach Boys crooned *Surfer Girl*. After a verse, Ben said, 'Is that why you've brought me here? To talk about Santo? We haven't mentioned him yet, have we? I'm sorry for that. I haven't wanted to talk about him and you've paid the price.'

'We all have things we're sorry about when it comes to Santo,' Kerra said. 'But that's not why I wanted to talk to you.' She felt suddenly shy about her subject. Any discussion of Santo made her look upon herself and her motives and deem them selfish. On the other hand, what she had to say was likely going to lift her father's spirits, and the look of him told her his spirits needed lifting.

'What is it, then?' he asked. 'Not bad news, I hope. You're not leaving us, are you?'

'No. I mean, yes. After a fashion. Alan and I are marrying.'

He took this in, a slow smile beginning to brighten his face. 'Are you, now? That's excellent news. He's a fine man. When?'

They hadn't set a date, she told him. Sometime this year. There was no ring yet, but that was to come. 'Alan insists,' she said. 'He wants to have what he calls "a proper engagement". You know Alan. And,' she put her hands round her glass, 'he wants to ask your permission, Dad.'

'Does he indeed?'

'He said he wants to do things right, from beginning to end. I *know* it's silly. No one asks for permission to marry any longer. But it's what he wants to do. Anyway I hope you'll give it. Your permission, I mean.'

'Whyever would I not?'

'Well.' Kerra looked away. How to put it? 'You may have gone a bit off on the whole idea of marriage. You know what I mean.'

'Because of your mother.'

'It can't have been a pleasant journey for you. I could see how you mightn't want me to take it.'

Ben took his turn at avoiding Kerra's gaze. He said, 'Marriage is difficult no matter the situation the couple finds themselves in. Think otherwise, and you'll be in for a surprise.'

'But there's difficult and there's difficult,' Kerra said. 'Truly difficult. Impossible to accept.'

'Ah. Yes. I know you've thought that: the why of it all. I've been reading that question on your face since you were twelve years old.'

He looked so regretful as he spoke that Kerra felt pained. She said, 'Did you never want to . . .'

He covered her hand with his. 'Your mum has had her trying times. There's no question about that. But her trying times have made her own path rockier than they've made mine, and that's the truth of it. Beyond that, she gave me you. And I have to thank her for that, whatever her faults may be.'

At this, Kerra saw that the moment had arrived when she'd least expected it. She looked down at her Coke, but something of what she needed to say must have shown in her features because he said, 'What is it, Kerra?'

'How do you know?' she asked him.

'Whether to take the leap with another person? You don't know. There's never any certainty about the kind of life you'll have with someone else, is there, but at some point—'

'No, no. That's not what I mean.' She felt the colour come into her face. It burned her cheeks and she could imagine it spreading out like a fan towards her ears. She said, 'How do you know about us? About me? For sure. Because . . .'

He frowned for a moment, but then his eyes widened a little as he took in her meaning.

She added miserably, 'Because of what she's like. I've wondered.'

He stood abruptly, and she thought he might stride out of the café altogether since he looked towards the door. But instead he said to her, 'Come with me, girl. No no. Leave your things where they are,' and he took her to a coat rack, where a small mirror hung within a seashell frame. He stood her in front of that mirror, himself behind her, his hands on her shoulders. 'Look at your face,' he said, 'and look at mine. Good God, Kerra, who would you be if not my daughter?'

Her eyes burned. She blinked the smarting away. 'What about Santo?' she asked.

His hands tightened on her shoulders reassuringly. 'You favour me,' he replied, 'and Santo always favoured your mum.'

By the time Lynley walked into the incident room in Casvelyn, he'd been gone most of the day, traversing Cornwall from Exeter to Boscastle. He found DI Hannaford and Barbara Havers acting the part of audience for Constable McNulty who was expatiating on a topic that seemed dear to his heart. This consisted of a set of photos that he'd laid out on a table. Havers looked interested. Hannaford listened, wearing an unmistakable expression of sufferance.

'He's catching the wave here, and it's a good shot of him. You can see his face *and* the colours of his board, right? He's got good position and he's got experience. He mostly surfs Hawaii and the water's cold as the dickens in Half Moon Bay, so he's not used to it, but what he *is* used to is the size of the wave. He's scared but who wouldn't be? If you're not scared, then you're mad.' He moved to the next picture. 'Look at the angle. He's losing it here. He knows he's going to wipe out and he's wondering how bad it's going to be, which is what you see here, in this next shot.' He pointed at it. 'A midface slap right into the face of the wave. He's moving God only knows how fast and so's the water, so what happens when he hits? Break a few ribs? Get the breath knocked out of him? It doesn't matter which because now he's going the last place anyone would ever want to go at Maverick's and that's over the falls. Here. You can just make him out.'

Lynley joined them at the table. He saw that the constable was talking about a single surfer on a wave the size of a moving hillside the colour of jade. In the photo he was referring to, the breaking wave had entirely swallowed up the surfer whose ghostly figure could be made out behind the crashing white water, a rag doll in a washing machine.

'Some of these blokes live to get their pictures taken riding monster waves,' McNulty said in conclusion to his remarks. 'And some of them die for just the same reason. That's what happened to him.'

'Who is he?' Lynley asked.

'Mark Foo,' McNulty said.

'Thank you, Constable,' Bea Hannaford said. 'Very dramatic, very grim, always illuminating. Now get back to work. Mr Priestley's fingers await your ministrations.' And to Lynley, 'I'm going to want a word with you. With you as well, Sergeant Havers.' She jerked her head in the direction of the door.

She took them to a badly appointed interview room, which seemed to have been used mostly as storage for paper products until the present investigation. She didn't sit. Nor did they. She said, 'Tell me about Falmouth, Thomas.'

Taken up by the events of the day, Lynley was genuinely confused. 'I was in Exeter,' he told her. 'Not Falmouth.'

'I'm not talking about today. What do you know about Daidre Trahair and Falmouth that you haven't been revealing to me? And don't either of you lie to me again. One of you went there and if it's you, Sergeant Havers, as Ms Trahair apparently suspects, then I reckon there's only one reason you took yourself on that little side trip and it doesn't have a damn thing to do with taking orders from me. Am I correct?'

Lynley intervened. 'I asked Barbara to look into—'

'As amazing as it sounds,' Bea cut in, 'I'd already worked that out. But the problem is that you're not directing this investigation. I am.'

'That's not what it was,' Havers said. 'He didn't *ask* me to go there. He didn't even know I was on my way here when he asked me to look into her background.'

'Oh, that's the case, is it?'

'It is. Yeah. He got me on my mobile. In my car. I expect he knew that bit of it, that I was in my car, but he didn't know where I was or where I was going and he had no idea I was going to be able to go to Falmouth at all. He just asked if I would look into a few details concerning her background. As it was, I *could* go to Falmouth. And as it wasn't far out of the way from where I was heading – which was here, of course – I thought I could go there before—'

'Are you mad? It's mile and miles out of the goddamn way. What *is* it with you two?' Bea demanded. 'Do you always go your own way in an investigation or am I the first of your colleagues to be so honoured?'

'With due respect, ma'am,' Lynley began.

'Do *not* call me ma'am.'

'With due respect, Inspector,' Lynley said, 'I'm not part of the investigation. Not officially. I'm not even a—' he sought a term – 'an official official.'

'Are you trying to be amusing, Superintendent Lynley?'

'Not at all. I'm merely trying to point out that once you informed me I'd be assisting you despite my own wishes in the matter—'

'You're a bloody material witness. No one *cares* about your wishes. What did you expect? To go merrily on your way?'

'Which makes it even more irregular,' he said.

'He's right,' Havers added, 'if you don't mind me saying.'

'Of course I bloody well mind. We're not playing fast and loose with the chain of command. Despite your rank,' she said to Lynley, 'I'm running this investigation, not you. You are not in the position to assign activities to anyone, including Sergeant Havers, and if you think you are—'

'He didn't *know*,' Havers said. 'I could have told him I was on my way here when he rang me, but I didn't. I could have told him I was under other orders—'

'What orders?' Lynley asked.

'—but I didn't. You knew I'd be here eventually.'

'Whose orders?' Lynley asked.

'So when he rang, it didn't seem that irregular—'

'*Whose* orders?' Lynley asked.

'You *know* whose orders,' Havers told him.

'Has Hillier sent you down here?'

'What do you think? You could just walk out? No one would care? No one would worry? No one would want to intervene? Do you *actually* think you could disappear, that you mean so little to—'

'All right, all right!' Bea said. 'Retire to your corners. My God. Enough.' She took a steadying breath. 'This stops here. And now. All right? You,' to Havers, 'are on loan to me. Not to him. I can see there were ulterior motives involved in the offer to send you to assist, but whatever those motives were you're going to have to deal with them on your own time, not on mine. And you,' to Lynley, 'will from this moment be straightforward with what you're doing and what you know. Am I being clear?'

'You are,' Lynley said. Havers nodded, but Lynley could see that she was hot under the collar and wanting to say more. Not to Hannaford, but to him.

'Fine. Excellent. Now let's take Daidre Trahair from the start and this time let's not hold anything back. Am I also being clear on that?'

'You are.'

'Lovely. Regale me with details.'

Lynley knew there was nothing more for it. 'There appears to be no Dairdre Trahair prior to her enrolment at her secondary school at thirteen years of age,' he said. 'And although she says she was born at home in Falmouth, there's also no record of her birth. Additionally, parts of her story about her job in Bristol don't match up with the facts.'

'Which parts?'

'There's a Daidre Trahair who's a vet on staff, but the person she identified to me as her friend Paul, supposedly the primate keeper, doesn't exist.'

'You didn't tell me that part,' Havers said. 'Why didn't you tell me?'

Lynley sighed. 'She just doesn't seem . . . I can't honestly see her as a murderer. I didn't want to make things more difficult for her.'

'More difficult than what?' Hannaford asked.

'I don't know. I admit there's something going on with her. I just don't think it has anything to do with the murder.'

'And are you supposing you're in any condition to make that sort of judgement?' Hannaford said.

'I'm not blind,' he replied. 'I haven't lost my wits.'

'You've lost your *wife*,' Hannaford said. 'How do you expect to think straight, see straight, or do anything else straight after what's happened to you?'

Lynley backed away, one step only. He wanted an end to the conversation and this seemed as good a start to that conclusion as any he could come up with. He made no reply. Havers was watching him. He knew he had to make an answer of some sort or she'd answer for him, which he would find unbearable.

He said, 'I wasn't hiding facts from you, Inspector. I wanted time.'

'For what?'

'For something like this, I suppose.' He'd been carrying a manila envelope and from it he brought out the photo he'd taken away from Lark Cottage in Boscastle. He handed it over.

Hannaford studied it. 'Who are these people?'

'They're a family called Parsons. Their son, the boy in the picture, died in a sea cave in Pengelly Cove some thirty years ago. This picture was taken round that time, perhaps a year or two earlier. Niamh the mum, Jonathan the dad. The boy is Jamie and the girls are his younger sisters. I'd like to do an age progression on the picture. Do we have someone who could do it for us quickly?'

'An age progression on who?' DI Hannaford asked.

'On everyone,' Lynley replied.

Daidre had parked on Lansdown Street. She knew her proximity to the police station didn't look good, but she had to see and, in equal measure, she needed a sign that would tell her what she was meant to do next. Truth meant trust and a leap of faith, but that leap could land her directly in the deadly mire of betrayal, and she'd had quite enough of betrayal at this point in her life.

In the rearview mirror, she saw them come out of the police station. Had Lynley been alone, she might have approached him for the conversation they needed to have, but as he was with both Sergeant Havers and Inspector Hannaford, Daidre used this as a sign that the time wasn't right. She was parked some way up the street, and when the three police officers paused in the station's carpark for a few words together, she started her car and pulled away from the kerb. Intent upon their conversation, none of them looked in her direction. Daidre used that as a sign as well. There were those, she knew, who would call her a coward for running just then. There were others, however, who would congratulate her on having sound instincts for self-preservation.

She drove out of Casvelyn. She headed inland, first towards Stratton and then across the countryside. She got out of her car at long last at the cider farm in the fast fading daylight.

Circumstances, she decided, were asking her to forgive. But forgiveness ran in both directions, in every direction if it came down to it. She needed to ask as well as to give, and both of these activities were going to require practice.

Stamos the orchard pig was snuffling round his pen in the centre of the courtyard. Daidre went past him and round the corner of the jam kitchen, where inside and under bright lights two of the jam cooks were cleaning their huge copper pots for the day. She opened the gate beneath the arbour and entered the private part of the grounds.

As before, she could hear guitar music. But this time more than one guitar was playing.

She assumed a record and knocked on the door. The music ceased. When Aldara answered, Daidre saw the other woman was not alone. A swarthy man in the vicinity of thirty-five was placing a guitar onto a stand. Aldara had hers tucked under her arm. She and the man had been playing, obviously. He was very good and, of course, so was she.

'Daidre,' Aldara said, neutrally. 'What a surprise. Narno was giving me a lesson.' Narno Rojas, she added, from Launceston. She went on to complete the introduction as the Spaniard rose to his feet and bowed his head slightly in acknowledgement. Daidre said hello and asked should she come back? 'If you're in the middle of a lesson . . .' she added. What she thought was Leave it to Aldara to have found a male teacher of delectable appearance. He had the large dark eyes and thick eyelashes of a Disney cartoon hero.

'No, no. We've finished,' Aldara said. 'We were at the point of merely entertaining ourselves. Did you hear? Don't you think we're very good together?'

'I thought it was a recording,' Daidre admitted.

'You see?' Aldara cried. 'Narno, we *should* play together. I'm much better with you than I am alone.' And to Daidre, 'He's been lovely about giving me lessons. I made him an offer he could not refuse, and here we are. Isn't that the case, Narno?'

'It is,' he said. 'But you've much more the gift. For me, it is practice continual. For you, you merely need encouragement.'

'That's flattery. But if you choose to believe it, I won't argue. Anyway that's the part you play. You're my encouragement, and I adore how you encourage me.' She put her guitar on its stand and said to him, '*Su talento podría hacer a un ángel llora.*'

'*Tú hablas la tontería. Debo ir.*'

'*Tú debes volver pronto. Jugamos bien juntos.*'

He chuckled, raised her hand, and kissed her fingers. He wore a wide gold wedding band.

He packed his guitar into its case and bade them both farewell. Aldara saw him to the door and stepped outside with him. They murmured together. She returned to Daidre.

She looked, Daidre thought, like a cat who'd come upon an endless supply of cream. Daidre said, 'I can guess what the offer was.'

Aldara returned her own guitar to its case. 'What offer do you mean, my dear?'

'The one he couldn't refuse.'

'Ah.' Aldara laughed. 'Well. What will be will be. I have a few things to do, Daidre. We can chat while I do them. Come along, if you like.'

She led the way to a narrow set of stairs whose handrail was a thick velvet cord. She climbed and took Daidre up to the bedroom, where she set about changing the sheets on a large bed that took up most of the space.

'You think the worst of me, don't you?' Aldara said.

'Does it matter what I think?'

'Of course, it does not. How wise you are. But sometimes what you think isn't what is.' She flung the duvet to the floor and whipped the sheets off the mattress, folding them neatly rather than balling them up as another person might have done. She went to an airing cupboard on the tiny landing at the top of the stairs and brought out crisp linens, expensive by the look of them and fragrant as well. 'Our arrangement isn't a sexual one, Daidre,' Aldara said.

'I wasn't thinking—'

'Of course you were. And who could blame you? You know me, after all. Here. Help me with this, won't you?'

Daidre went to assist her. Aldara's movements were deft. She smoothed the sheets with affection for them. 'Aren't they lovely?' she asked. 'Italian. I've found a very good laundress in Morenstow. It's a bit of a drive to take them to her, but she does wonders with them, and I wouldn't trust my sheets to just anyone. They're too important, if you know what I mean.'

To Daidre sheets were sheets although she could tell these likely cost more than she made in a month. Aldara was a woman who didn't deny herself life's little luxuries.

'He has a restaurant in Launceston. I was there for dinner. When he wasn't greeting guests, he was playing his guitar. I thought, How much I could learn from this man. So I spoke to him and we came to an agreement. Narno will not take money, but he has a need to place members of his family – and he has a very large family – in more employment than he can provide at his restaurant.'

'So they work for you here?'

'I have no need. But Stamos has a continual need for workers round the hotel in St Ives, and I find a former husband's guilt is a useful tool.'

'I didn't know you still speak to Stamos.'

'Only when it suits me. Otherwise, he could disappear off the face of the earth and, believe me, I wouldn't bother to wave goodbye. Could you tuck that in properly, darling? I can't abide rucked sheets.'

She moved to Daidre's position and demonstrated deftly how she wanted the sheets seen to. She said, 'Nice and fresh and ready,' when she was done. Then she looked at Daidre fondly. The light in the room was greatly subdued, and in it Aldara shed twenty years. She said, 'This isn't to say we won't, eventually. Narno will, I think, make a most energetic lover, which is how I like them.'

'I see.'

'I know you do. The police were here, Daidre.'

'That's why I've come.'

'So you were the one. I suspected as much.'

'I'm sorry, Aldara, but I had no choice. They assumed it was me. They thought Santo and I—'

'And you had to safeguard your reputation?'

'It isn't that. It *wasn't* that. They need to get to the bottom of what happened to him, and they aren't going to get there if people don't start telling the truth.'

'Yes. I do see what you mean. But how often the truth is, well, rather inconvenient. If one person's truth is an unbearable blow to another person and simultaneously unnecessary for him to know, need one speak it?'

'That's hardly the issue here.'

'But it does seem that no one is quite telling the police everything there is to tell, wouldn't you say? Certainly, if they came to you first instead of to me, it would be because little Madlyn did not tell them everything.'

'Perhaps she was too humiliated, Aldara. Finding her boyfriend in bed with her employer might have been more than she wanted to say.'

'I suppose so.' Aldara handed over a pillow and its accompanying case for Daidre to sort out while she herself did the same with another. 'It's of no account now, though. They know it all. I myself told them about Max. Well, I had to, hadn't I? They were going to uncover his name eventually. My relationship with Max was not a secret. So I can hardly be cross with you, can I, when I also named someone to the police?'

'Did Max know?' Daidre saw from Aldara's expression that he did. 'Madlyn?' she asked.

'Santo,' Aldara said. 'Stupid boy. He was wonderful in bed. Such energy he had. Between his legs, heaven. But between his ears . . .'

Aldara gave an elaborate shrug. 'Some men, no matter their age, do not operate with the sense God gave them.' She placed the pillow on the bed, and straightened the edge of its case, which was lace. She took the other from Daidre and did the same, going on to turn down the rest of the linen in a welcoming fashion. On the bedside table, a votive candle was nestled in a crystal holder. She lit this and stood back to admire the effect. 'Lovely,' she said. 'Rather welcoming, wouldn't you say?'

Daidre felt as if cotton were stuffed into her head. The situation was so much *not* what she believed it should be. She said, 'You don't actually regret his death, do you? D'you know how that makes you look?'

'Don't be foolish. Of course, I regret it. I would not have had Santo Kerne die as he did. But as I wasn't the one to kill him—'

'You're very likely the reason he died, for God's sake.'

'I seriously doubt that. Certainly Max has too much pride to kill an adolescent rival and anyway Santo *wasn't* his rival, a simple fact that I could not make Max see. Santo was just . . . Santo.'

'A toyboy.'

'A boy, yes. A toy, rather. But that makes it sound cold and calculating and believe me it was neither. We enjoyed each other and that's what it was between us, only. Enjoyment. Excitement. On both parts, not just on mine. Oh, you *know* all this, Daidre. You cannot plead ignorance. And you quite understand. You would not have lent your cottage had you not.'

'You feel no guilt?'

Aldara waved her hand towards the door, to indicate they were to leave the room and go below once more. As they descended the stairs, she said, 'Guilt implies I am somehow involved in this situation, which I am not. We were lovers full stop. We were bodies meeting in a bed for a few hours. That's what it was, and if you really think that the mere act of intercourse led to—'

A knock came on the door. Aldara glanced at her watch. Then she looked at Daidre. Her expression was resigned, which told Daidre later that she should have anticipated what would come next. But, rather stupidly, she had not.

Aldara opened the door. A man stepped into the room. His eyes only for Aldara, he didn't see Daidre. He kissed Aldara with the familiarity of lover: a greeting kiss that became a coaxing kiss, which Aldara did nothing to terminate prematurely. When it did end, she said against his mouth, 'You smell all of the sea.'

'I've been for a surf.' Then he saw Daidre. His hands dropped from Aldara's shoulders to his sides. 'I'd no idea you had company.'

'Daidre's just on her way,' Aldara said. 'D'you know Ms Trahair, my dear? Daidre, this is Lewis.'

He looked vaguely familiar to Daidre, but she couldn't place him. She nodded hello. She'd left her bag on the edge of the sofa, and she went to fetch it. As she did so, Aldara added, 'Angarrack. Lewis Angarrack.'

Which caused Daidre to pause. She saw the resemblance, then, for of course she'd seen Madlyn more than once in the times she herself had been to the Cornish Gold cider farm. She looked at Aldara, whose face was placid but whose eyes shone and whose heart was no doubt beating strongly now as anticipation sent her blood hither and yon, to all the proper places.

Daidre nodded and stepped past Lewis Angarrack, outside onto the narrow porch. Aldara murmured something to the man and followed Daidre out. She said, 'You see our little problem, I think.'

Daidre glanced at her. 'Actually, I don't.'

'Her boyfriend first and now her father? It's critical, naturally, that she never know. So as not to upset her further. It's as Lewis wants it. What a shame, don't you think?'

'Hardly. It's the way you want it as well, after all. Secret. Exciting. Pleasurable.'

Aldara smiled, that slow knowing smile that Daidre knew was part of her appeal to men. 'Well, if it must be that way, it must be that way.'

'You've no morals, have you?' Daidre asked her friend.

'My darling. Have you?'

27

Ultimately on that miserable day, Cadan found himself in a situation in which the chickens of his machinations finally came home to roost: caught in the sitting room of the family home in Victoria Street with his sister and Will Mendick. Madlyn, having just returned from work, was still in her Casvelyn of Cornwall get-up – stripes the colour of candy floss and a pinny with ruffles along the edges. She was slouched on the sofa while Will stood in front of the fireplace with a bunch of lilies dangling from his fingers. He'd shown good enough sense to *buy* the flowers and not bring along rejects from the wheelie bin. But that was the limit to the good sense he was showing.

Cadan himself was perched on a stool near his parrot. He'd left Pooh alone for most of the day, and he'd been intent upon making up for that with an prolonged bit of bird massage, just the two of them with the house – or at least the room – to themselves. But Madlyn had arrived home from work and on her heels had come Will. He'd apparently taken to heart Cadan's bald-faced lies about his sister and her affections.

'So I thought,' Will was saying, with scant encouragement from Madlyn, 'that you might like, well, like to go out.'

'With who?' Madlyn said.

'Well, with me.' He'd not presented her with the flowers yet, and Cadan was hoping fervently he'd pretend that he'd not brought them at all.

'And why would I want to do that, exactly?' Madlyn tapped her fingers on the arm of the sofa. This gesture, Cadan knew, had nothing to do with nervousness.

Will grew redder in the face – he was already blushing like a bloke with two left feet at a foxtrot lesson – and he shot a look towards Cadan that said, *Give us a hand here, mate?* Studiously, Cadan averted his eyes.

Will said, 'Just, perhaps, to get a meal?'

'Out of a bin, you mean?'

'No! God, Madlyn. I wouldn't ask you to—'

'Look.' Madlyn had That Expression on her face. Cadan knew what it meant, but he also knew that Will hadn't the first clue that his sister's detonator was doing whatever detonators did just before the bomb went from UX to X. She pushed herself to the edge of the sofa and her eyes got narrow. 'Just in case you don't know, Will, which you apparently don't, I had a talk with the police. A quite *recent* talk. They caught me out in a lie, and they crawled all over me. And guess what they knew?'

Will said nothing. Cadan urged Pooh onto his fist. 'Hey, what you got to say, Pooh?' The bird was usually very good at providing diversions, but Pooh was silent. If he felt the room's tension, he wasn't responding to it in his normal vociferous manner.

'They knew that I'd followed Santo. They knew what I saw. They *knew*, Will, that *I* knew what Santo was doing. Now how do you s'pose the cops knew that? And do you have any idea how that makes me look?'

'They don't think that you . . . You don't need to worry—'

'That's hardly the point! My boyfriend's having it off with a cow old enough to be his mum and he's *liking* it and this particular cow *happens* to be the cow I work for and all this is going on under my nose with both of them looking like butter wouldn't melt and he's calling her Mrs Pappas, mind you. *Mrs Pappas* in front of me and you can bloody well depend on him *not* calling her Mrs Pappas when he's fucking her. And she *knows* he's my boyfriend. That's part of the fun. She's specially friendly to me because of it. Only I don't know. I even have a cup of tea with her and she asks me all about myself. "I like to get to know my girls," she says. Oh too bloody right.'

'Don't you see that's why—'

'I do *not*. So there they are, those cops, and they're looking at me and I can see what they know *and* what they think. Poor stupid cow, *she* is. Her boyfriend'd rather do some old witch than be with her. And I didn't need that, d'you see, Will? I didn't need their pity and I didn't need them knowing because now it all gets written down for the world to see and *everyone* knows and do you know, have you any *idea*, what that feels like?'

'It wasn't your fault, Madlyn.'

'That I wasn't enough for him? So much not enough that he wanted *her* as well? How could that not be my fault? I loved him. We had something good, or that's what I thought.'

Will said, stumbling, 'No. Look. It wasn't *you*. Why couldn't you see? He would've done the same. He would've walked away, no matter who he was with. Why couldn't you ever see that? Why couldn't you just let him—'

'I was going to have his *baby*. His baby, all right? I thought we would . . . Oh *God*, forget it.'

Will's jaw had dropped with Madlyn's revelation. Cadan had, of course, heard the expression before – someone's jaw dropping – but he'd never imagined how lost it made one look till he saw what Will's face revealed. Will hadn't known about this, then. But of course, how could he? It was a private business held within the family, and Will was not a member of the family or even close to becoming one, a fact which he did not appear to understand. Even now. Sounding numb, he said, 'You could have come to me.'

'*What*?' Madlyn said.

'I would've . . . I don't know. Whatever you wanted. I could have—'

'I *loved* him.'

'No,' Will said. 'You can't. You couldn't. Why won't you see what he was like? He was no good, but you looked at him and what you saw—'

'Don't you *say* that about him. Don't you . . . *don't*.'

Will looked like a man who's spoken a language that he assumes his listener has understood, only to discover she's a foreigner in his country and so is he as a matter of fact and there's nothing to be done about the matter. He said slowly and with dawning knowledge, 'You can still defend him. Even after what you just told me. Because he wasn't going to stand by you, was he? That's not who he was.'

'I loved him,' she cried.

'But you said that you hated him. You told me you hated him.'

'He hurt me for God's sake.'

'But then why did I . . . ?' Will looked around as if suddenly waking. His glance went to Cadan, then to the flowers he'd brought to give Madlyn. He flung these into the fireplace. Cadan rather liked the drama of the gesture, had the fireplace been one that actually worked. But as it didn't work, the act seemed past its sell-by date, the sort of thing one saw in old films on the telly.

The room was filled with a hollow silence. Then Will said to Madlyn, 'I punched him out. I would have done more if he'd been willing to fight, but he wasn't. He didn't even bother to care. He wouldn't fight. Not for you. Not because of you. But I did that. I punched him out. For *you*, Madlyn.'

'*What*?' she cried. 'What on earth were you thinking?'

'He hurt you, he was a first class wanker and he needed teaching.'

'Who asked *you* to be his teacher? I never. I *never*. My God. What *else* did you do to him? Did you kill him as well? Is that it?'

'You don't know what it means, do you?' Will asked her. 'That I even hit him once. You don't know.'

'What? That you're Sir Bloody Whoever in Sodding Armour? That I'm supposed to be happy about that? Grateful? Thrilled? Your hand-maiden forever? What *exactly* don't I know?'

'I could've gone back inside,' he said dully.

'What're you *talking* about?'

'If I so much as trip some bloke on the street. Even accidentally. I could go back inside. But I was willing to do it, because of you. And I was willing to sort him out because he *needed* sorting. But you didn't know that and even now that you *do* know, it doesn't matter. It never mattered. I don't matter. I never did, did I?'

'Why the hell did you think . . .'

Will looked at Cadan. Madlyn looked at Will. And then she too looked at Cadan.

For his part, Cadan thought it was a very good moment to take little Pooh on his walkies for the evening.

Bea was stretching with the aid of a kitchen chair, doing her bit to keep an ageing back more or less pain free, when she heard a key in the front door. The sound of the key was followed by a familiar knock – *bim bim BIM boom BOOM* – and then Ray's voice. 'You here, Bea?'

'I'd say the car's a fairly good indication of that,' she called out. 'You used to be a much better detective.'

She heard him coming in her direction. She was still wearing her pyjamas, but as they comprised a T-shirt and her tracksuit bottoms, she was not bothered by someone's coming upon her in her morning disha-bille.

Ray was done up to the nines. She looked at him sourly. 'Hoping to impress some bright young thing?'

'Only you.' He went to the fridge where she had left a jug of orange juice. He held it to the light, gave it a suspicious sniff, found it apparently to his liking, and poured a glass.

'Do help yourself,' she said sardonically. 'There's always more where that came from.'

'Cheers,' he replied. 'D'you still use it on your cereal?'

'Some things never change. Ray, why're you here? And where's Pete? Not ill, is he? He has school today. I hope you've not let him talk you into—'

'Early start,' he said. 'He has something going on in his science course. I got him there and made sure he went inside and wasn't planning to bunk off and sell weed on the street corner.'

'Most amusing. Pete doesn't do drugs.'

'We are blessed in that.'

She ignored the plural. 'Why're you here at this hour?'

'He's wanting more clothes.'

'Haven't you washed them?'

'I have. But he says he can't be expected to wear the same thing after school day after day. You only sent two outfits.'

'He has clothes at your place.'

'He claims he's outgrown them.'

'He wouldn't notice that. He never gives a toss what he's wearing anyway. He'd be in his Arsenal sweatshirt all day if he had the option, and you know that very well. So answer me again. Why are you here?'

He smiled. 'Caught me out. You're very good at grilling the suspect, my dear. How's the investigation faring?'

'You mean how is it faring despite the fact I've no MCIT?'

He sipped his orange juice and put the glass on the work top, which he leaned against. He was quite a tall man, and he was trim. He'd look good, Bea thought, to whatever bright young thing he was dressing himself up for.

'Despite what you believe, I did do the best I could for you with regard to manpower, Beatrice. Why d'you always think the worst of me?'

She scowled. She dipped into a final stretch and then rose from the chair. She sighed. 'It isn't going far or fast. I'd like to say we're closing in on someone, but each time I've thought that, either events or information has proved me wrong.'

'Is Lynley being any help? God knows he has the experience.'

'He's a good man. There's no doubt of that. And they've sent his partner down from London. I dare say she's here more to keep an eye on him than to help me, but she's a decent cop, if somewhat unorthodox. She's rather distracted by him.'

'In love?'

'She denies it but if she *is*, it's a real non-starter. Chalk and cheese doesn't begin to describe them. No. I think she's worried about him.

They've been partners for years and she cares. They have a history, however bizarre it may be.' Bea carried her cereal bowl to the sink. 'At any rate, they're good cops. One can tell that much. She's a pit bull and he's very quick. I'd like it a bit more if he has fewer ideas of his own, however.'

'You've always liked your men that way,' Ray observed.

Bea regarded him. A moment passed. A dog barked in the neighbourhood. 'That's rather below the belt.'

'Is it?'

'Yes. Pete wasn't an idea. He was – he *is* – a person.'

Ray didn't avoid her gaze or her comment. 'You're right.' He smiled at her in fond if rueful acknowledgement. 'He wasn't an idea. Can we talk about it, Beatrice?'

'Not now,' she said. 'I've work. As you know.' She didn't add what she wanted to add: that the time to talk was fourteen years gone. Nor did she add that he'd chosen his moment with scant consideration for her situation, which was damn well typical. She didn't think what it meant that she let such an opportunity pass, though. Instead, she went into morning mode and got ready for work.

Nonetheless, on her drive even Radio Four didn't divert her enough that she failed to realise Ray had just as good as admitted his inadequacy as a husband at long last. She wasn't sure what to do with that knowledge, so she was grateful when she walked into the incident room to a ringing phone that she picked up from its receiver before anyone from the team could do likewise. They were milling round, waiting for their assignments. She was hoping that someone on the end of the phone was going to give her an idea what to tell them to do next.

It turned out that Duke Clarence Washoe from Chepstow was on hand with the preliminaries about the comparison of hairs she'd provided him. Was she ready for that?

'Regale me,' she told him.

'Microscopically, they're close,' he said.

'Just close? No match?'

'Can't do a match with what we have. We're talking cuticle, cortex, and medulla. This isn't a DNA thing.'

'I'm aware of that. So what *can* you say?'

'They're human. They're similar. They might be from the same person. Or a member of the same family. But "might" is as far as we go. I've got no problem putting myself on record with the microscopic details, mind. But if you want further analysis, it's going to take time.'

And money, Bea thought. He wasn't saying that, but both of them knew it.

'Shall I carry on, then?' he was asking her.

'Depends on the chock-stone. What d'you have on that?'

'One cut. It went straight through without hesitation. No multiple efforts involved. No identifying striations, either. You're looking for a machine, not a hand tool. And its blade is quite new.'

'Certain about that?' A machine for cutting cable narrowed the field considerably. She felt a mild stirring of excitement.

'You want chapter and verse?'

'Chapter will do.'

'Aside from possibly leaving striations, a hand tool's going to depress both the upper and the lower parts of the cable, crimping them together. A machine's going to make a cleaner cut. Resulting ends'll be shiny as well.' He was, he said, expressing this unscientifically. Did she want the proper lingo?

Sergeant Havers came into the room and Bea looked for Lynley to walk in behind her, but he didn't appear. She frowned.

'Inspector?' Washoe said at his end of the line.

'What you've given me is fine,' she told him. 'Save the science for your formal report.'

'Will do.'

'And, Duke Clarence?' She grimaced at the poor sod's name.

'Guv?'

'Thanks for rushing things with that hair.'

She could hear that he was pleased with her expression of gratitude as he rang off. She gathered her team, such as it was. They were looking for a machine tool, she told them and gave them the details on the chock-stone as Washoe had related them to her. What were their options on finding one? Constable McNulty?

McNulty seemed to be feeling his oats this morning, perhaps as a result of the success he'd had tracking down unhelpful photos of dead surfers. He pointed out that the erstwhile air station was a good possibility. There were any number of businesses set up in the old buildings and doubtless a machine shop was going to be one of them.

Car body shop would do as well, someone else suggested.

Or a factory of some sort, came another suggestion.

Then the ideas emerged quickly. Metal worker, iron worker, even a sculptor. What about a blacksmith? Well, that wasn't likely.

'My mum-in-law could do it with her teeth,' someone said.

Guffaws all round. 'That'll do,' Bea said. She gave Sergeant Collins the nod to make the assignments: set out and find the tool. They knew their suspects. Consider them, their homes, and their places of employment. *And* anyone who might have done work for them at their homes or their places of employment as well.

Then she said to Havers, 'I'd like a word, Sergeant,' and she had that word in the corridor. 'Where's our good superintendent this morning? Having a bit of a lie in?'

'No. He was at breakfast. We had it together.' Havers smoothed her hands on the hips of her baggy corduroy trousers. They remained decidedly baggy.

'Did you indeed? I hope it was delicious and I'm thrilled to know he's not missing his meals. So where is he?'

'He was still at the inn when I—'

'Sergeant? Less smoke and more mirrors, please. Something tells me that if anyone on earth knows exactly where Thomas Lynley is *and* what he's doing, you're going to be that person. Where is he?'

Havers ran a hand through her hair. The gesture did nothing at all to improve its state. 'All right. This is stupid and I'll wager he'd rather you didn't know.'

'What?'

'His socks were wet.'

'I beg your pardon? Sergeant, if this is some kind of joke . . .'

'It's not. He hasn't enough clothes with him. He washed both pairs of his socks last night and they didn't dry. Probably,' she added with a roll of her eyes, 'because he's never had to personally wash his socks in his life.'

'And are you telling me . . . ?'

'That he's at the hotel drying his socks. Yes. That's what I'm telling you. He's using a hair dryer and, knowing him, he's probably set the building on fire by now. We're talking about a bloke who probably doesn't even make his own toast in the morning, guv. Like I said, he washed them last night and he didn't put them on the radiator or wherever. He just left them . . . wherever he left them. As far as the rest of his kit goes—'

Bea raised her hand. 'Enough information. Believe me. Whatever he may have done with his pantaloons is between him and his God. When can we expect him?'

Havers' teeth pulled at the inside of her lower lip in a fashion that suggested discomfort. There was something else.

Bea said, 'What is it?' as from below, a courier's envelope was brought up the stairs in the hands of one of the team members already heading out on his assignment. It had just come, the constable told her, two blokes having been working with the relevant software for hours. Bea opened the envelope. The contents comprised six pages, not fixed together. She flipped through them as she said, 'Where is he, Sergeant, and when can we expect him?'

Havers said, 'Ms Trahair.'

'What about her?'

'She was in the carpark when I left this morning. I think she was waiting for him.'

'Was she indeed?' Bea looked up from the paperwork. 'That's an interesting wrinkle.' She handed the sheets to Havers. 'Have a look at these.'

'What are they, then?'

'They're age progressions. From that photograph Thomas handed over. I think you're going to find them of interest.'

Daidre Trahair hesitated just outside his door. She could hear the sound of the hair dryer from within, so she knew that Sergeant Havers had been telling her the truth. It hadn't seemed so. Indeed, when Daidre had confronted the sergeant in the carpark of the Salthouse Inn, asking for Thomas Lynley, the idea that he was drying his socks had sounded like the lamest sort of excuse for his absence from Sergeant Havers' side. On the other hand, the DS from London hardly had a reason to invent an activity for Lynley in order to hide the fact that he might be spending yet another day scouring through the detritus of Daidre's past. For it seemed to Daidre that he'd done as much scouring as he'd be able to do without her own participation.

She knocked on his door sharply. The dryer was switched off. The door swung open. 'Sorry, Barbara. I'm afraid they're still not—' He saw it was Daidre. 'Hullo,' he said with a smile. 'You're out and about early, aren't you?'

'I saw the sergeant in the carpark. She said you were drying your socks.'

He had a sock in one hand and the dryer in the other, proof of the matter. 'I did try to wear them at breakfast, but there's something particularly disturbing about damp socks. Shades of World War I and life in the trenches, I suppose. Would you like to come in?' He stepped back and she passed him, into the room. The bed was unmade. A towel lay in a heap on the floor. A notebook had scribbles of pencil in it, with car keys sitting on its open pages. 'I thought they'd dry by morning,' he said. 'Foolishly, I washed both pairs. I hung them by the window all night. I even cracked it open for air. It was all for nothing. According to Sergeant Havers, I should have had shown some common sense and considered the radiator. You don't mind . . . ?'

She shook her head. He began his work with the hair dryer again. He'd nicked himself shaving, and he'd apparently not noticed: A thin line of blood traced along his jaw. It was the sort of thing his wife would have seen and told him about as he left the house in the morning.

'This isn't the sort of thing I'd expect the lord of the manor to be doing.'

'What? Drying his own socks?'

'Doesn't someone like you have, what do you call them? People?'

'Well, I can't see my sister drying my socks. My brother would be as useless as I am, and my mother would likely throw them at me.'

'I don't mean family people. I mean people people. Servants. You know.'

'I suppose it depends what you think of as servants. We have staff at Howenstow – that's the family pile – and I've a man who oversees the house in London. But I'd hardly call him a servant and can a single employee actually be called staff? Besides that, Charlie Denton comes and goes pretty much at will. He's a theatre lover with personal aspirations.'

'Of what sort?'

'Of the sort involving grease paint and the crowd. He longs to tread the boards but the truth of the matter is that he stands little chance of being discovered as long as he limits his range to what it currently is. He vacillates between Algernon Moncrieff and the porter in *Macbeth*.'

Daidre smiled in spite of herself. She wanted to be angry with him, but he made it difficult.

'Why did you lie to me, Thomas? You said you hadn't gone to Falmouth asking questions about me.'

He clicked off the hair dryer. He set it on the edge of the basin and considered it. 'Ah,' he said.

'Yes. Ah. Strictly speaking, I realise, you were telling me the truth. You didn't go personally. But you sent her, didn't you? It wasn't her plan to go there.'

'Strictly speaking, no. I'd no idea she was in the area. I thought she was in London. But I did ask her to look into your background, so I suppose . . .' He made a small gesture with his hand, a European gesture telling her to complete the thought on her own.

Which she was happy enough to do. 'You lied. I don't appreciate that. You might have asked me a few questions.'

'I did, actually. You likely didn't think I'd check on the answers.'

'To verify them. To make sure—'

'That you yourself weren't lying.'

'I seem so questionable to you? So like a murderer?'

He shook his head. 'You seem as unlike a murderer as anyone I've ever come across. But it's part of the job. And the more I asked, the more I discovered there were areas in your story—'

'I thought we were getting to know each other. Foolish me.'

'We were, Daidre. We *are*. That was part of it. But from the beginning, there were inconsistencies in what you said about yourself, and they couldn't be ignored.'

'You mean *you* couldn't ignore them.'

His expression was frank. 'I couldn't ignore them. Someone is dead. And I'm a cop.'

'I see. D'you want to share what you've discovered?'

'If you like.'

'I like.'

'Bristol Zoo.'

'I work there. Has someone claimed that I don't?'

'There is no Paul keeping primates there. And there is no Daidre Trahair born in Falmouth, at home or elsewhere. Do you want to explain?'

'Are you arresting me?'

'No.'

'Then come along. Get your things. I want to show you something.' She headed for the door but paused there. She offered him a smile that she knew was brittle. 'Or d'you want to phone DI Hannaford and Sergeant Havers first, and tell them you're coming with me? After all, I may push you over a cliff, and they'll want to know where to find your body.'

She didn't wait to hear him reply or to see whether he took her up on the offer. She headed for the stairs and from there out to her car. She assured herself that one way or another it didn't really matter if he followed or not. She congratulated herself on feeling absolutely nothing. She'd come a long way, she decided.

★　★　★

Lynley didn't phone DI Hannaford or Barbara Havers. He was a free agent, after all, not on loan, on duty, or on anything at all. Nonetheless, he took the mobile with him once he'd donned his socks – thankfully far drier than they'd been during breakfast – and gathered up his jacket. He found Daidre in the car park, her Vauxhall idling. She'd gone rather pale during their conversation, but her colour had returned as she'd waited for him to join her.

He got into the car. In closer proximity to her, he could smell the scent she was wearing. It put him in mind of Helen, not the scent itself but the fact of the scent. Helen had been citrus, the Mediterranean on a sunny day. Daidre was . . . like the aftermath of rain, fresh air after a storm. He passed through a fleeting moment in which he missed Helen so much he thought his heart might stop. But it didn't, of course. He was left with the seat belt, which he fumbled into place.

'We're going to Redruth,' Daidre told him. 'Do you want to phone DI Hannaford if you've not already done so? Just to be safe? Although since I've seen your Sergeant Havers already, she'll be able to tell the authorities I was the last one to see you alive.'

'I don't actually think you're a killer,' he told her. 'I've never thought that.'

She changed the car into gear. 'Perhaps I can alter all that for you, then.'

They began with a jerk, bumping over the uneven surface of the carpark and from there out into the lane. It was a long drive, but they didn't speak. She flicked on the radio. They listened to the news, to a tedious interview with a nasally challenged and self-important novelist clearly hoping to be nominated for the Booker Prize, and to a discussion on genetically modified crops. Daidre asked him at last to sort out a CD from the glove compartment, which he did. He chose at random and they ended up with the Chieftains. He put it on and she turned up the volume.

At Redruth, she avoided the town centre. Instead, she followed the signs for Falmouth. He wasn't alarmed, but he glanced at her then. Her jaw was set, but her expression seemed resigned, the look of someone who'd come to the end game. Unexpectedly, he felt a brief stab of regret although put to the question, he couldn't have said what it was that he regretted.

A short distance from Redruth, she turned into a minor road and then into another, which was the sort of narrow lane that connects two or more hamlets. This last was marked for Carnkie, but rather than drive upon it, she stopped at a junction, merely a triangular bit of land where one might pull over and read a map. He expected her to do just that, as they were in the middle of a nowhere characterised by an earthen hedge, partly reinforced by stone, and beyond it an expanse of open land studded occasionally with enormous boulders. In the distance, an unpainted granite farmhouse stood. Between them and it, ragwort and chickweed along with scrub grass were being seen to by sheep.

Daidre said, 'Tell me about the room you were born in, Thomas.'

It was, he thought, the oddest sort of question. 'Why d'you want to know about that?'

'I'd like to imagine it, if you don't mind. You said you were born at home, not in hospital. At the family pile. I'm wondering what sort of family pile it is. Was it your parents' bedroom? Did they share a room? Do your kind of people do that, by the way?'

Your kind of people. A battle line had been drawn. It was an odd moment for him to feel the sort of despair that had come upon him at other moments throughout his life: always reminding him that some things didn't change in a changing world, most of all these things.

He unfastened his seat belt and got out. He walked to the hedge. The wind was brisk in this area, as there was nothing to impede it. It carried the bawling of the sheep and the scent of wood smoke. Behind him, he heard Daidre's door open. In a moment she was at his side.

He said, 'My wife was quite clear about it when we married: Just in case you're considering it, none of this separate rooms nonsense, she said. None of those coy, thrice-weekly nocturnal conjugal visits, Tommy. We shall do our conjugating when and where we desire and when we fall asleep nightly, we shall do so in each other's presence.' He smiled. He looked back at the sheep, the expanse of land, the undulations of it as it rolled to the horizon. He said, 'It's quite a large room. Two windows with deep embrasures look down on a rose garden. There's a fireplace, still used in winter because despite central heating, these houses are impossible to keep warm, and a seating area in front of it. The bed's opposite the windows. It, too, is large. It's heavily carved, Italian. The walls are pale green. There's a gilt mirror above the fireplace, a collection of miniatures on the wall next to it. Between the windows, a demi-lune table holds a porcelain urn. On the walls, portraits. And two French landscapes. Family photos on side tables. That's all.'

'It sounds very impressive.'

'It's more comfortable than impressive. Chatsworth needn't worry about the competition.'

'It sounds . . . suitable for someone of your stature.'

'It's just where I was born, Daidre. Why did you want to know?'

She turned her head. Her gaze took in everything: the earthen hedge, the stones, the boulders in the field, the tiny junction in which they'd parked. She said, 'Because I was born here.'

'In that farm house?'

'No. Here, Thomas. In this . . . well, whatever you want to call it. Here.' She walked over to a stone and from beneath it he saw her remove a card. She brought it to him and handed it over. 'Did you tell me that Howenstow is Jacobean?'

'It is, in part, yes.'

'I thought so. Well, what I had was a bit more humble. Do have a look.'

He saw she'd given him a postcard with the image of a gipsy caravan on it. It was of the type that once embellished the countryside with the flavour of Romany: the wagon bright red, the arched roof green, the wheels' spokes yellow. Since she clearly wasn't of gipsy birth, her parents must have been on holiday, he thought. Tourists had done that in Cornwall for years: They hired wagons and played at being gipsies.

Daidre seemed to read his mind for she said, 'No romance to it at all, I'm afraid. No getting caught short on a holiday and no Romanies in my background. My parents are travellers, Thomas. Their parents were travellers as well. My aunts and uncles, such as they are, are travellers also, and this is where our caravan was parked when I was born. Our accommodation was never as picturesque as this one,' with a nod at the card, 'as it hadn't been painted in years, but it was otherwise much the same. Not quite like Howenstow, wouldn't you say?'

He wasn't sure what to say. He wasn't sure he believed her.

'Conditions were . . . I'd have to call them rather cramped, I suppose, although things improved marginally by the time I was eight years old. But for a time there were five of us shoehorned together. Myself, my parents, and the twins.'

'The twins.'

'My brother and my sister. Younger than I by three years. And not a single one of us born in Falmouth.'

'Are you not Daidre Trahair, then?'

'I am in a way.'

'"In a way?" What way?'

'Would you like to meet my real self?'

'I suppose I would.'

She hadn't removed her gaze from him since he'd looked up from the postcard. She seemed to be trying to evaluate his reaction. Whatever she read on his face either reassured her or told her there was no further point to obfuscation.

'Right. Come along then, Thomas. There's far more to see.'

When Kerra came out of her office to ask Alan's advice on a hiring issue, she was greatly surprised to see Madlyn Angarrack in reception. She was alone and wearing her kit from the bakery, and Kerra had the odd sense that Madlyn had come to make a delivery of pasties. She looked at the reception desk to see if a box with *Casvelyn of Cornwall* written upon it was sitting there.

No box in sight, Kerra hesitated. She reckoned that Madlyn had come on a different sort of errand, and she assumed that the errand might have to do with her. But she didn't want any more harsh words with Madlyn. She felt beyond them now.

Madlyn said her name. She spoke tremulously, as if in fear of Kerra's reaction. That was reasonable enough, their last conversation hadn't gone swimmingly and they'd hardly parted as friends. They hadn't, indeed, *been* friends in ages.

Madlyn had always possessed a glow of health, but that was missing at the moment. She looked as if she hadn't been sleeping well, and her dark hair had lost something of its lustre. Her eyes, however, were still her eyes. Large, dark, and compelling, they drew you in. No doubt they'd done as much for Santo.

'Could I have a word?' Madlyn asked. 'I've asked for a half hour from the bakery. I told them personal business?'

'What, with me, then?' The mention of the bakery made Kerra think Madlyn must have come about a job, and who could blame her? For all the relative fame of its pasties, one could hardly expect to build a career at Casvelyn of Cornwall. Or to have much fun. And Madlyn *could* give surfing instruction if Kerra was able to talk her father into offering it.

'Yes. With you. Could we go somewhere?'

Alan came out of his office, then. He was saying, 'Kerra, I've just had a word with the video crew and they'll be available—' when he saw Madlyn. His look went from her to Kerra and rested with Kerra. His expression was warm. He nodded and he said, 'Oh. I'll speak to you later,' and then, 'Hullo, Madlyn. Fantastic to see you again.'

Then he was gone and Kerra was faced with whatever reason Madlyn had for coming to speak to her. 'I s'pose we could go up to the lounge?'

'Yes, please,' Madlyn said.

Kerra took her there. Outside and below, she saw that her father was directing two blokes who were making something of a mess out of a flowerbed, which edged a lawn that was clipped for bowling. They had containers of shrubbery meant to go at the back of the bed and Kerra could see that the labourers had nonsensically planted the shrubs at the front. She muttered, 'What *are* they thinking?' And then to Madlyn, 'It's to give the less adventurous something to do.'

Madlyn looked confused. 'What is?'

Kerra saw the other girl hadn't even glanced outside, so apparently nervous was she. She said, 'We've made a bowling green over there, beyond the rope climbing set-up. It was Alan's idea. Dad thinks no one's going to use it, but Alan says a gran or granddad might come along with the family and not exactly want to abseil or rope climb or whatever. *I* tell him he's not got the first clue about modern grans and granddads, but he's insisted. So we're letting him have his way. He's been right about other things. If it doesn't work out, we can always do something else with the area. Croquet or something.'

'Yes. I can see how he would be. Right, that is. He seems very clever.'

Kerra nodded. She waited for Madlyn to reveal the reason for this call. Part of her was prepared to tell the girl up front that Ben Kerne wasn't likely to offer surfing so do save your breath in that regard. Part of her wanted to give Madlyn a chance to make her case. Yet *another* part had suspicion this might not be about employment at all, so she said helpfully, 'Here we are, then. D'you want a coffee or something, Madlyn?'

Madlyn shook her head. She went to one of the new sofas and perched on the edge. She waited for Kerra to sit opposite her. Then she said, 'I'm very sorry about Santo.' Her eyes filled, quite a change from their previous encounter. 'I didn't say properly when we talked before. But I'm so very sorry.'

'Yes. Well. I expect you are.'

Madlyn flinched. 'I know what you think. That I wanted him dead. Or at least that I wanted him hurt. But I didn't. Not really.'

'It wouldn't have been so strange if you'd wanted that, at least that he be hurt as much as he hurt you. He was rotten in the way he treated you. I did try to warn you.'

'I know you did. But, see, I thought that you . . .' Madlyn pressed her hand down the front of her pinny. The whole uniform was terrible on her: the wrong colour, the wrong style. It was amazing to Kerra that Casvelyn of Cornwall could keep anyone in their employment, making their girls wear such a get-up. 'I thought it was jealousy, you see.'

'What? That I wanted you for myself? Sexually, or something?'

'Not *that*. But in other ways. In friendship ways. She doesn't like to share her friends, I thought. That's what this is all about.'

'Well. Yes. It was, rather. You were my friend and I couldn't see how you could be with him and still be my friend. It was so *complicated*. Because of how he was. And what would happen when he threw you over? I wondered that.'

'You knew he'd do what he did, then.'

'I thought he might. It was rather his pattern. And then what? You'd hardly want to come round here and be reminded of him, would you? Even being with *me* would remind you of him, put you into the position of having to hear about him when you weren't prepared. It was all too difficult. I couldn't see a way past it and I couldn't put what I was feeling into words anyway. Not in any sensible fashion. Not in a way that would make me sound reasonable.'

'I didn't like losing you as a friend.'

'Yes. Well. There it is.' Kerra thought. What now? They could hardly pick up where they'd left off in the pre-Santo days. Too much had occurred, and the reality of Santo's death still had to be dealt with. His death and the means of it hung between them even now. It was the great unspoken and it would remain so, as long as there was the slightest possibility that Madlyn Angarrack was involved.

Madlyn herself seemed to understand this because she said, 'I'm frightened about what happened to him. I was angry and hurt. Other people knew I was angry and hurt. I didn't keep it to myself, what he'd done. My father knew. My brother knew. Other people knew. Will Mendick. Jago Reeth. One of them, you see . . . Someone might have hurt him, but I didn't want that. I never wanted that.'

Kerra felt a tingle of apprehension along her spine. 'Someone might have hurt Santo to get revenge on your behalf?'

'I *never* wanted that . . . But now that I know—' Her hands balled into fists. Kerra saw her fingernails – those nicely clipped crescents – dig into her palms as if telling her she had said enough.

Kerra said slowly, 'Madlyn, do you know who killed Santo?'

'No!' There was a rise to Madlyn's voice, suggesting what she'd come to say had not yet been said.

'But you do know something, don't you. What?'

'It's only that Will Mendick came round last night. You know him, yes?'

'That bloke from the grocery. I know who he is. What about him, then?'

'He was one of the people I told about Santo and what happened. Not everything, but enough. And Will . . .' It seemed that Madlyn couldn't finish. She twisted her hands in the hem of her pinny and looked miserable. 'I didn't know he fancied me,' she concluded.

'You're telling me he did something to Santo because he fancied you? To get even with Santo on your behalf?'

'He said he sorted him. I don't think he did more than that.'

'He and Santo were friendly. It wouldn't have been impossible for him to get to Santo's climbing kit, Madlyn.'

'I *can't* think he actually . . . He wouldn't have.'

'Have you told the police?'

'I didn't know, you see. Not till last night. And *if* I'd known that he'd even planned it or thought about it . . . I didn't want Santo hurt. Or if I wanted him hurt, I wanted him hurt, not *hurt*. D'you know what I mean? Hurt inside the way I was hurt. And now I'm afraid . . .' She was making a real mess of her pinny. She'd screwed it up and got it hopelessly wrinkled. Casvelyn of Cornwall was not going to like that.

'You think that Will Mendick killed him for you,' Kerra said.

'Someone. P'rhaps. And I *didn't* want that. I didn't ask . . . I didn't tell . . .'

Kerra saw why the girl had come to her, finally. The knowledge dawned upon her and with the dawning came a fuller understanding of who Madlyn was. Perhaps it was the central shift within her that had come about because of Alan. She didn't know. But she did feel *different* about Madlyn at long last, and she could see things from Madlyn's perspective. She rose from her place opposite the other girl and sat at her side. She thought about taking her hand, but she didn't. Too abrupt, she thought. Too soon.

'Madlyn, you must listen to me. I don't believe you had anything to do with what happened to Santo. There was a time when I might have done and I probably did, but it wasn't real. Do you understand? What happened to Santo wasn't your fault.'

'But I said to people—'

'What you said to people. But I doubt you ever said that you wanted him dead.'

Madlyn began to cry. Whether it was from grief too long withheld or from relief, Kerra could not tell. 'D'you *believe* that?' Madlyn asked her.

'I absolutely believe it,' Kerra said.

In the inglenook of the Salthouse Inn's bar, Selevan waited for Jago Reeth in something of a lather, which was unusual for him. He'd phoned his mate at LiquidEarth and asked could they meet at the Salthouse earlier than normal. He needed to talk to him. Jago was good about the matter. He didn't ask could they talk on the phone. Instead, he said, Course, that's what makes mates mates, eh? He'd give the word to Lew and set out soon as he could. Lew was a decent bloke about things deemed emergencies. He could be there in, say half an hour?

Selevan said that would do him fine. It would mean a wait and he didn't want to wait, but he could hardly expect a miracle from Jago. LiquidEarth was some distance from the Salthouse Inn and Jago couldn't exactly beam himself there. So Selevan finished his business at Sea Dreams, packed up the car with everything he would need for the coming trip he'd be taking, and set out for the inn.

He knew he'd carried things as far as he could, and it was time to bring it all to a conclusion, so he'd gone into Tammy's cramped little bedroom, and from the cupboard he'd taken her canvas rucksack, which she'd first brought with her from Africa. She hadn't needed it then and she certainly didn't need it now, because her possessions were few and pathetic. So it was the matter of a moment only to remove them from the chest of drawers: a few pairs of knickers of the overlarge sort an old lady might wear, a few pairs of tights, four vests because the girl was so flat in the chest that she didn't even require a brassiere, two jerseys, and several skirts. There were no trousers. Tammy did not wear trousers. Everything she possessed was black, except the knickers and the vests. These were white.

He'd scooped up her books next. She had more books than clothes and these comprised mostly philosophy and the lives of saints. She had journals as well. Her writing within them was the one thing about her that he *hadn't* monitored, and Selevan was rather proud of this since during her stay with him the girl had done nothing to hide them from him. Despite her parents' wishes, he hadn't been able to bring himself to read her girlish thoughts and fantasies.

She had nothing else except a few toiletries, the clothes she was currently wearing, and whatever she had in her shoulder bag. That wouldn't include her passport, since he'd taken it from her upon her arrival. 'And don't let her keep her bloody passport,' her father had intoned from Africa once he'd put her on the plane. 'She's likely to run off if she has it.'

She could have her passport now, Selevan decided. He went to fetch it from the spot where he'd hidden it, beneath the liner of the dirty clothes bin. It wasn't there. She must have found it straightaway, he realised. The little vixen had probably been carrying it round for ages. And she had been carrying it on her person as well, since he had regularly gone through her bag for contraband. Well, she'd always been a step ahead of everyone, hadn't she?

Selevan had made a final stab that day at bringing her parents round. Ignoring the cost and the fact that he could ill afford it, he'd rung Sally Joy and David in Africa and he'd sounded them out on the matter of Tammy. He'd said to David, 'Listen here, lad, at the end of the day, kids got to follow their own path. Let's s'pose it was some ruffian she decided she was in love with, eh? More you argue against it, more you forbid her seeing the bloke, more she's going to want to do it. It's simple psycho-whachamacallit thingummybob. Nothing more or less'n that.'

'She's won you over, hasn't she?' David had demanded. In the background, Selevan could hear Sally Joy wailing, 'What? What's happened? Is that your father? *What's she done?*'

'I'm not saying she's done anything,' Selevan said.

But David went on, as if Selevan hadn't spoken. 'I'd hardly think it was possible for her to do it, all things considered. It's not as if your own kids were ever able to make you see reason.'

''Nough of that, son. I admit my mistakes with you lot. Point is, though, you made lives for yourself and they're good lives, eh? The girl wants nothing less.'

'She doesn't know what she wants. Look, do you want a relationship with Tammy or not? Because if you don't oppose her in this, you'll not have a relationship with her. I can promise you.'

'And if I do oppose her, I'll have no relationship with her anyway. So what would you have me do, lad?'

'I'd have you show sense, something Tammy's clearly lost. I'd have you be a role model for her.'

'A role model? What're you on about? What sort of role model am I meant to be to a girl of seventeen? That's rubbish, that is.'

They'd gone round and round. But Selevan had failed to convince his son of anything. He couldn't see that Tammy was resourceful: Being sent to England had hardly put her off her stride. He could send her to the North Pole if he wanted, but when it came down to it, Tammy was going to find a way to live as she wanted to live.

'Pack her back home, then,' had been David's final remark. Before he'd rung off, Selevan could hear Sally Joy in the background, crying, 'But what'll we *do* with her, David?' Selevan had said *bah* to it all. He'd set about packing up Tammy's belongings.

That was when he'd phoned Jago. He'd be fetching Tammy from Clean Barrel Surf Shop for a final time and he wanted to do so with someone's good will behind him. Jago seemed the likeliest someone.

When Jago came in, Selevan waved a hello with no small measure of relief. Jago stopped at the bar to have a word with Brian and came over, still in his jacket with his knitted cap pulled over his long grey hair. He shed both jacket and cap and rubbed his hands together as he drew out the stool that faced Selevan's bench. The fire hadn't yet been lit – too early for that as they were the only two drinkers in the bar – and Jago asked could he light it? Brian gave the nod and Jago put match to tinder. He blew on the emergent flames till they caught. Then he returned to the table. He gave a thanks to Brian as his Guinness was brought to him and he took a swig of it.

He said, 'What's the brief, then, mate?' to Selevan. 'You look in a right state.'

'I'm heading out,' Selevan said. 'Few days, a bit more.'

'Are you, then? Where?'

'North. Place not far from the border.'

'What? Wales?'

'Scotland.'

Jago whistled. 'Far piece, that. Want me to keep an eye on things, then? Want me to keep a watch on Tammy?'

'Taking Tammy with me,' Selevan said. 'I've done as much as I can here. Job's finished. Now we're off. Time the girl was let to lead the life she wants.'

'Truth to that,' Jago said. 'I won't be here that much longer myself.'

Selevan was surprised to feel the extent of his dismay at this news. 'Where you off to, Jago? I thought you meant to stay the season.'

Jago shook his head. He lifted his Guinness and drank of it deeply. 'Never stay one place long. That's how I look at it. I'm thinking South Africa. Cape Town, p'rhaps.'

'You won't go till I'm back, though. Sounds a bit mad, this, but I've got used to having you round.'

Jago looked at him and the lenses of his glasses winked in the light. 'Best not to do that. Doesn't pay to get used to anything.'

'Course, I know that, but—'

The bar door swung open, but not in its usual fashion, with someone swinging it wide enough just to enter. Instead, it opened with a startling bang that would have put an end to all conversation had anyone save Jago and Selevan been within.

Two women came inside. One of them had stand-up hair that looked purple in the light. The other wore a knitted cap pulled low on her face, just to her eyes. The women looked around and Purple Hair settled on the inglenook.

She strode over saying, 'Ah. We'd like a word with you, Mr Reeth.'

28

They drove west. They talked very little. What Lynley wanted to know was why she had lied about details that could be so easily checked up on. Paul the primate keeper, for instance. It was a matter of a simple phone call to discover there was no Paul caring for primates at the zoo. Did she not see how that looked to the police?

She glanced at him. She'd not worn her contact lenses on this day, and a bit of her sandy hair had fallen across the top of the frames of her glasses. 'I suppose I hadn't thought of you as a cop, Thomas. And the answers to the questions you asked me – and the questions you had in your head but didn't ask me – were private, weren't they. They had nothing to do with Santo Kerne's death.'

'But keeping those answers to yourself made you suspect. You must see that.'

'I was willing to take the risk.'

They drove for a time in silence. The landscape altered as they approached the coast. From rough and rock-studded farmland whose ownership was delineated with irregular drystone walls patchy with grey-green lichen, the undulations of pasture and field gave way to hillside and combe, and a horizon that was marked with the great and derelict engine houses of Cornwall's disused mines. She took a route into St Agnes, a slate and granite village that tumbled down a hillside above the sea, its few steep streets twisting appealingly and lined with terrace cottages and with shops, all of them leading inexorably and ultimately, like the course of a river, down to the pebbled stretch of Trevaunance Cove. Here, at low water, tractors pulled skiffs into the sea and, at three-quarters tide, good sized swells from the west and southwest brought surfers from surrounding areas to jostle with each other for a place on ten foot waves. But instead of ending up at the cove where Lynley expected, she chose a direction out of town driving north, following signs that were posted for Wheal Kitty.

He said, 'I couldn't ignore the fact that you lied about recognising

Santo Kerne when you saw his body. Don't you see how that threw suspicion on you?'

'At the moment that couldn't be important. Saying I knew him would have led to more questions. Answering questions would have left me pointing the finger . . .' She glanced his way. Her expression was irked, disbelieving. 'Have you *honestly* no idea what it might feel like to be a person who involves people she knows in a police investigation? You're not insensate. There were confidential matters I'd promised to keep to myself. Oh, what am I saying? Your sergeant would have put you into the picture by now. Doubtless you had breakfast with her, if you didn't speak to her last night. I can't imagine she'd keep you in the dark about much.'

'There were car tracks in your garage. More than one set.'

'Santo's. Aldara's. Your sergeant would have told you about Aldara, I expect. Santo's lover. The fact that they used my cottage.'

'Why didn't you just explain that from the first?'

'What, then you would have stopped short of looking into my past, sending your sergeant to Falmouth to question the neighbours, phoning the zoo? What else? Have you spoken to Lok as well? Did you track him down? Did you ask him if he's truly crippled or if I made that up? It does sound fantastic, doesn't it, a Chinese brother with spina bifida. Brilliant but bent. What an intriguing story.'

'I know he's at Oxford.' Lynley was regretful, but there was no help for what he'd done. It was part of the job. 'That's the extent of it.'

'And you discovered this . . . how?'

'It's a small matter, Daidre. There's cooperation between police forces all over the world, let alone in our own country. It's easier now than it ever was.'

'I see.'

'You don't. You can't. You're not a cop.'

'Neither were you. Neither *are* you. Or has all of that changed?'

He couldn't answer that question. Perhaps some things were in the blood and could not be shaken off merely because one desired to do so.

They said nothing more. At one point, in his peripheral vision, he saw her raise a hand to her cheek and his fantasy had her weeping. But when he looked at her directly, he saw that she was merely seeing to the hair that had fallen over the frame of her glasses. She shoved it impatiently behind her ears.

At Wheal Kitty, they did not approach the engine house or the buildings that surrounded it. These sat at a distance and cars were parked in front of some of them. Unlike nearly all of the old engine houses across the county, Wheal Kitty's had been restored. It was now in use as a place of business and other businesses had sprung up round it, these in long, low buildings looking nothing like the period from which Wheal Kitty had come but still built of the local stone. Lynley was glad to see this. He always felt a twinge of sadness when he looked at the ghostly smoke stacks and broken-down engine houses that marked the landscape. It was good to see them put to use again, for round St Agnes was a veritable graveyard of mining shafts, particularly above Trevaunance Coombe, where a ghost town of engine houses and their accompanying smoke stacks marked the landscape like silent witnesses to the land's recovery from man's assault upon it. And the land itself was a place of heather and gorse thriving amidst grey, granite outcroppings, providing nesting spots for herring gulls, jackdaws, and carrion crows. There were few trees. The windswept nature of the place did not encourage them.

To the north of Wheal Kitty, the road narrowed. It became a lane first and ultimately a track, coursing downward into a steeply sided gully. Barely the width of Daidre's Vauxhall, it descended in a series of switchbacks, guarded by boulders to their left and a fast-moving stream to their right. It finally ended at an engine house far more ruined than any they'd seen on the trip from Redruth. This was wildly overgrown with vegetation; just beyond it, a smoke stack shot skyward in a similar state.

'Here we are,' Daidre said. But she didn't get out of the car. Instead, she turned to him and she spoke quietly. 'Imagine this,' she said. 'A traveller decides he wants to stop travelling because unlike his parents and their parents and the parents before them, he wants something different out of life. He has an idea that's not very practical because nothing much he's done has ever been practical, frankly, but he wants to try it. So he comes to this place, convinced, of all things, that there's a living to be had from mining tin. He reads very poorly, but he's done what homework he can on the subject, and he knows about streaming. D'you know what tin streaming is, Thomas?'

'Yes.' Lynley looked beyond her, over her shoulder. Some seventy yards from where they were parked, an old caravan stood. Once white, now it was mostly laced with the colour of rust, which streaked from its roof and from its windows at which yellow curtains printed with flowers drooped. Accompanying this impermanent structure were a tumbledown shed and a tarpaper-roofed cupboard that looked like an outdoor loo. 'It's drawing tin from small stones in a stream and following that stream to larger stones.'

'Lode stones, yes,' Daidre said. 'And then following them to the lode itself but if you can't find the lode, it's a small matter really because you still have the tin in the smaller stones and that can be made into . . . whatever you wish to make it into. Or you can sell it to metal workers or jewellers but the point is you can support yourself, barely, if you work hard enough and you get lucky. So that's what this traveller decides to do. Of course, it takes a lot more work than he anticipated and it's not a particularly wholesome kind of life and there are interruptions: town councils, the government, assorted do-gooders coming round to inspect the premises. This causes something of a distraction, so the traveller ends up travelling anyway, in order to find a proper stream in a proper location somewhat hidden away where he can be allowed to look for his tin in peace. But no matter where he goes, there are still problems because he's got three children and a wife to provide for and since he alone can't provide what needs to be provided, they all must help. He's decided he will give the children lessons at home to save time from their having to be gone for hours to school every day. His wife will be their teacher. But life is hard and the teaching doesn't actually happen and neither does much else in the way of nurturing. Like decent food. Or proper clothing. Jabs for this or that disease. Dentistry. Anything, really. The sorts of things typical children take for granted. When social workers come round, the children hide, and finally because the family keeps moving, they slip through the cracks, all three of them. For years, actually. When they finally come to light, the eldest girl is thirteen years old and the younger two – the twins, a boy and a girl – are ten. They can't read, they can't write, they're covered in sores, their teeth are quite bad, they've never seen a doctor, and the girl – by this I mean the thirteen year old – has no hair. It hasn't been shaved. It's fallen out. They're removed at once. Large hue and cry. Local newspapers covering the story, complete with pictures. The twins are placed with a family in Plymouth. The thirteen year old is sent to Falmouth. There she's ultimately adopted by the couple who begin as her foster parents. She is so filled up by their love for her that she puts her past behind her, completely. She changes her name to something she thinks of as pretty. Of course, she has no idea how to spell it, so she misspells it and her new parents are charmed. Daidre it is, they say. Welcome to your new life, Daidre. And she never goes back to visit who she was. Never. She puts it behind her and she never speaks of it and no one, no one, in her present life knows a thing about it because it is her deepest shame. Can you understand this? No, how could you. But that's how it is and that's how it remains until her sister tracks her down and insists, begs, that she come to this place, the very last place on earth that she can bear to come, the one place she has promised herself that no one from her present life will ever learn of.'

'Is that why you lied to DI Hannaford about your route to Cornwall?' Lynley asked her.

Daidre didn't reply. She opened her door, and Lynley did likewise. They stood for a moment surveying the home she'd left eighteen years earlier. Aside from the caravan – unimaginably once the domicile of five people – there was little else. A ramshackle building seemed to hold the equipment for extracting tin from the stones in which it was found, and leaning up against this were three wheelbarrows of ancient vintage along with two bicycles with rusty panniers hanging from their sides. At one time, someone had planted a few terracotta pots with geraniums, but these were languishing, two of them on their sides and cracked, with the plants sprawled out like supplicants begging for a merciful end.

'My name,' Daidre said, 'was Edrek Udy. Do you know the meaning of Edrek, Thomas?'

He said that he didn't. He found that he didn't want her to go further. He was filled with sadness that he'd unthinkingly invaded a life she'd worked so hard to forget.

'Edrek,' she said, 'means *regret* in Cornish. Come along and meet my family.'

Jago Reeth didn't look the least bit surprised. He also didn't look worried. He looked as he'd looked the first time Bea had come upon him at LiquidEarth: willing to be helpful. She wondered if they were wrong about him.

He said that they could indeed have a word with him. They could join him and his mate Selevan Penrule there in the inglenook or they could ask for a more private location.

Bea said she reckoned they'd have their conversation at the station in Casvelyn if he didn't mind.

He said politely, "Fraid I do mind. 'M I under arrest, madam?'

It was the *madam* that gave her pause. It was the way he said it: with the tone of someone who believes he's sitting in the catbird seat.

He went on with, 'Because 'less I'm mistaken, I don't need to accept your hospitality, if you know what I mean.'

'Is there some reason you'd prefer not to talk to us, Mr Reeth?'

'Not a bit 'f that,' he said. 'But if we're to talk we'll need to do it where I feel a comfort I'm not likely to feel in a police station, if you know what I mean.' He smiled affably, showing teeth long stained by tea and coffee. 'Get all tightened up if I'm indoors too long. Tightened up, I can't speak much at all. And I know this: Inside a station, I'm likely to be tightened permanently. If you know what I mean.'

Bea narrowed her eyes. 'Is that so?'

'Bit of a claustrophobe, I am.'

Reeth's companion was listening to all this agog, his gaze going from Bea to Jago to Bea. He said, 'Wha's this about then, Jago?'

To which Bea replied, 'Would you like to put your friend in the picture?'

Reeth said, 'They want a word about Santo Kerne. 'Nother word. I've spoke to them already.' Then to Bea, 'And I'm dead chuffed to do it again, eh. Often as you like. Let's just take ourselves out the bar. We c'n decide where and when we'll do our speaking.'

DS Havers was about to say something when Bea gave her the look. *Hold off* it said. They would see what Jago Reeth was up to. He was either completely ignorant or wily as hell. Bea reckoned she knew which one it was.

They followed him into the inn's entrance, the bar door closing behind them. They left the barman wiping out glasses and watching curiously. They left Selevan Penrule saying to Jago Reeth, 'Take care, mate.'

When they were alone, Jago Reeth said in a voice altogether different from the one they'd heard him use not only a moment ago but also in their earlier conversations with him, 'I'm afraid you didn't answer my question. Am I under arrest, Inspector?'

'Should you be?' Bea asked. 'And thank you for discarding the persona.'

'Inspector, please. Don't play me for a fool. You'll find I know my rights better than most. Indeed, you can say I've made a study of my rights. So you can arrest me if you like and pray you've got enough to hold me at least six hours. Or nine at the most since you yourself would be doing the review after those first six hours, wouldn't you? But after that, what superintendent on earth will authorise a questioning period of twenty-four hours at this point in your investigation? So you must decide what it is you want from me. If it's conversation, then I must tell you that conversation isn't about to happen inside a lock-up. And if it's a lock-up that you want, then I'll have to insist on a solicitor and I'm likely to employ my primary right at that point, one so often forgotten by those wishing to be helpful.'

'And that is?'

'You know as well as I that I needn't say another word to you.'

'Despite how that will look?'

'Frankly, I don't care how it looks. Now what would you and your assistant here prefer? A frank conversation or my kind and silent gaze resting upon you or the wall or the floor in the police station? And if it's to be a conversation, then I, and not you, will determine where it happens.'

'Rather sure of yourself, Mr Reeth. Or should I call you Mr Parsons?'

'Inspector, you may call me whatever you like.' He rubbed his hands together, the gesture one would use to rid the palms of flour in baking or soil in planting. 'So. What's it to be?'

At least, Bea told herself, she had the answer to wily or ignorant. 'As you wish, Mr Reeth. Shall we ask for a private room here at the inn?'

'I've a better location in mind,' he told her. 'If you'll excuse me while I fetch my jacket? There's another exit to the bar, by the way, so you'll want to come with me if you're concerned I might do a runner.'

Bea nodded to DS Havers. The sergeant looked only too willing to accompany Jago Reeth just about anywhere. The two of them disappeared into the bar for the length of time it took Jago Reeth to fetch his belongings and have whatever word he felt necessary with his friend in the inglenook. They emerged and Jago led the way outside. They'd have to drive to get there, he said. Had either one of them a mobile, by the way? He asked this last with deliberate courtesy. Obviously, he knew they carried mobile phones. Bea expected him to make the requirement that they leave their mobile phones behind, which she was about to tell him was a complete non-starter. But then he made an unexpected request.

'I'd like Mr Kerne to be present.'

'That,' Bea told him, 'is not about to happen.'

Again the smile. 'Oh, I'm afraid it must, Inspector Hannaford. Unless, of course, you wish to arrest me and hold me for those nine hours you have available to you. Now as to Mr Kerne—'

'No,' Bea said.

'A short drive to Alsperyl. I assure you, he'll enjoy it.'

'I won't ask Mr Kerne—'

'I do think you'll find that no asking will be necessary. You merely need to make the offer: a conversation about Santo with Jago Reeth. Or with Jonathan Parsons, if you prefer. Mr Kerne will be happy to have that conversation. Any father who wants to know exactly what happened to his son on the day or the night he died would have that conversation.'

Sergeant Havers said, 'Guv,' in an urgent tone.

Bea knew she wanted a word and that word would doubtless be one of caution. Don't place this bloke in a position of power. He doesn't determine the course of affairs. We do. We're the cops, after all.

But believing that was sophistry at this point. The course was caution, to be sure. But it was going to have to be caution employed in a scenario devised by their suspect. Bea didn't like this, but she didn't see another route to take. They could indeed hold him in custody for the nine hours, but while nine hours in a cell or even alone an interview room might unnerve some people and prompt them to talk, she was fairly certain nine hours or ninety were not going to unnerve Jago Reeth.

She said to him, 'Lead on, Mr Reeth. I'll phone Mr Kerne from the car.'

Only two of them were inside the caravan. A woman lay on a narrow banquette, a furry-looking blanket tucked round her and her head on a caseless pillow whose edges were stained from perspiration. She was an older woman although it was impossible to tell *how* old because she was emaciated and her hair was thin, grey, and uncombed. Her colour was very bad. Her lips were scaly.

Her companion was a younger woman who could have been any age between twenty-five and forty. With quite short hair of a colour and a condition that peroxide encouraged, she wore a long pleated skirt of a tartan pattern heavily reliant on blue and yellow, red knee socks, and a heavy pullover. She had no shoes on and she wore no make-up. She squinted in their direction as they entered, which suggested she either regularly wore or currently needed glasses.

She said, 'Mum, here's Edrek.' She sounded weary. 'Got a man with her as well. Not a doctor, are you? Not brought a doctor, have you, Edrek? I told you we're finished with doctors.'

The woman on the banquette stirred her legs slightly but did not turn her head. She was gazing at the water stains that hovered above them on the ceiling of the caravan like clouds ready to rain down rust. Her breathing was shallow and quick as evidenced by the rise and fall of her hands, which were clasped in a disturbing corpselike posture high on her chest.

Daidre spoke. 'This is Gwynder, Thomas. My younger sister. This is my mother, my mother till I was thirteen, that is. She's called Jen Udy.'

Lynley glanced at Daidre. She spoke as if he and she were observers of a tableau on a stage. Lynley said to Gwynder, 'Thomas Lynley. I'm not a doctor. Just a friend.'

Gwynder said, 'Posh voice,' and continued what she'd been doing when they entered, which was carrying a glass to the woman on the banquette. It contained some sort of milky liquid. She said in reference to it, 'Want you drinking this, Mum.'

Jen Udy shook her head. Her fingers rose, then fell.

'Where's Goron?' Daidre asked. 'And where's your father?'

Gwynder said, 'Your father too, no matter what you like.' Although her choice of words could have carried a bitter undercurrent, they did not do so.

'Where are they?'

'Where else would they be? Daylight.'

'At the stream or in the shed?'

'Don't know, do I. They're wherever. Mum, you got to drink this. Good for you.'

The fingers lifted and fell again. The head turned slightly, trying to pull itself towards the back of the banquette and out of sight.

'Are they not helping you care for her, Gwynder?' Daidre asked.

'Told you. Past the point of caring for her, aren't we, and on to the point of waiting. You c'n make a difference in that.' Gwynder sat at the top of the banquette by the stained pillow. She'd placed the glass on a ledge that ran along a window whose thin curtains were shut against the daylight, shedding a jaundiced glow on her mother's face. She lifted both the pillow and her mother's head and slid herself under them. She reached for the glass again. She held this to Jen Udy's lips with one hand and with the other – curved round her head – she forced her mother's mouth to open. Liquid went in. Liquid came out. The woman's throat muscles moved as she swallowed at least part of it.

'You need to get her out of here,' Daidre said. 'This place isn't good for her. And it isn't good for you. It's unhealthy and cold and miserable.'

'Know that, don't I?' Gwynder said. 'That's why I want to take her—'

'You can't possibly believe that will do any good.'

'It's what she wants.'

'Gwynder, she's not religious. Miracles are for believers. To take her all the way to . . . Look at her. She doesn't even have the strength for the journey. *Look* at her, for heaven's sake.'

'Miracles are for everyone. And they're what she wants. What she needs. 'F she doesn't go, she's going to die.'

'She *is* dying.'

''S that what you want? Oh, I expect it is. You with your posh boyfriend there. Can't believe you even brought him down here.'

'He's not my . . . He's a policeman.'

Gwynder slowly clutched at the front of her pullover as she took in this detail. She said to Lynley, 'We're doing *nought* wrong. Can't make us leave. The town council know . . . We've the rights of travellers. Aren't bothering anyone.' And to Daidre, 'Are there more of them out there? You come to take her? She won't go without a fight. She'll begin to scream. Can't *believe* that you would do this to her. After everything.'

'After what exactly?' Daidre's voice sounded pinched. 'After everything she did for me? For you? For all three of us? You seem to have a very short memory.'

'And yours goes back to the start of time, eh?' Gwynder forced more of the liquid into their mother's mouth. The result was much the same as before. What drained out of her dribbled down her cheeks and onto the pillow. Gwynder tried to sort this out by brushing it off, with little success.

'She can be in a hospice,' Daidre said. 'It doesn't have to go on this way.'

'We're meant to leave her there alone? Without her family? Lock her up and wait till they give us the word she's gone? Well, I won't do that, will I. And if you come to tell me tha's the limit of what you mean to do to help her, you leave with your fancy man. Whoever he says he is. Because he's not a cop. Cops don't talk like him.'

'Gwynder, please see reason.'

'Get out, Edrek. Asked for your help and you said no. Tha's how it is and we'll cope from here.'

'I'll help within reason. But I won't send the lot of you to Lourdes or Medjugorje or Knock or *anywhere* else because it doesn't make sense, there *are* no miracles!'

'Are! And one could happen to her.'

'She's dying of pancreatic cancer. She's got weeks or days or perhaps even hours and . . . is this how you want her to die? In this place? Inside this hovel? Without air or light or even a window to look at the sea?'

'With people who love her.'

'There *is* no love in this place. There never was.'

'Don't you say that!' Gwynder began to weep. 'Just because . . . Don't you say that.'

Daidre made a move towards her but stopped. She raised a hand to her mouth. Behind her glasses, Lynley saw that her eyes filled with tears.

'Leave us to our weeks or days or hours, then,' Gwynder said. 'Just go.'

'Do you need—'.

'Go!'

Lynley put his hand on Daidre's arm. She removed her glasses and wiped her eyes on the sleeve of her jacket, which she still had on. He said to her, 'Come,' and he urged her gently to the door.

'Hard fucking cunt,' Gwynder said to their backs. 'D'you hear me, Edrek? Hard fucking cunt. Keep your money. Keep your fancy boy. Keep your life. Don't need you or want you so don't come back. Hear me, Edrek? I'm sorry I even asked you in the first place. *Don't* come back.'

Outside the caravan, they paused. Lynley saw that tremors ran through Daidre's body. He put his arm round her shoulders. 'I'm terribly sorry,' he said, and he pressed his cheek to the top of her head.

'Who the hell're you lot?' The question came in a shout. Two men had emerged from the shed. They would be Goron and Daidre's father, Lynley decided. They approached in a hurry. 'Wha's this, then?' the older man said.

The younger said nothing. There seemed to be something wrong with him. Openly, he scratched at his testicles. He snuffled loudly and, like his twin in the caravan, he squinted. He nodded at them in a friendly fashion. His father did not.

'What d'you lot want?' Udy asked. His gaze went from Lynley to Daidre and back to Lynley. He seemed to be assessing everything about them but most particularly their shoes for some reason. Lynley saw why when he looked at Udy's own feet. He wore boots but they were long past their prime. The soles were split at the toes.

'Paying a call.' Daidre had stepped away from Lynley's embrace. Face to face with her father, she bore no resemblance either to him or to her brother.

'What you doing here, then?' Udy said. 'We got no need of do-gooders round here. We make it on our own and always have done. So you lot clear out. This's private property, this is, and there's a sign posted.'

It came to Lynley then that while the women in the caravan knew who Daidre was, the men did not, that for some reason Gwynder had sought and found her sister on her own, perhaps knowing at some level that her mission was futile. Hence, Udy had no idea that he was speaking to his own daughter. But when Lynley considered this, it seemed reasonable. The thirteen year old girl who had been his daughter was someone from the past, not the accomplished educated woman before him. Lynley waited for Daidre to identify herself. She did not do so.

Instead, she gathered herself together, fumbling with the zip on her jacket, as if she needed to do something with her hands. She said to the man, 'Yes. Well, we're leaving.'

'You do that,' he said. 'We got a business we're running here and we don't fancy trespassers comin' round on the off season. We open in June and there'll be bits and bobs aplenty for sale then.'

'Thank you. I'll remember that.'

'And mind the sign as well. If it says no trespassing, that's what it bloody means. And it'll *say* no trespassing till we're opened, understand?'

'Certainly. We understand.'

There was actually no sign that Lynley had seen, either one forbidding trespass or one indicating this desolate spot was a place of business. But there seemed little enough reason to point out the man's delusion to him. Far wiser to clear out and to put this place and its people and their way of life behind them. He understood, then, that this was exactly what Daidre had done. He also saw what her struggle now was.

He said, 'Come away,' and he put his arm round her shoulders once again and led her in the direction of her car. He could feel the stares of the two men behind them and, for reasons he didn't wish to consider just then, he hoped they wouldn't realise who Daidre was. He didn't know what would happen *if* they realised it. Nothing dangerous, surely. At least nothing dangerous as one typically thought of danger. But there were other hazards here besides the removal of one's personal safety. There was the emotional minefield that lay between Daidre and these people, and he felt an urgency to remove her from it.

When they returned to the car, Lynley said he would drive. Daidre shook her head. She said, 'No, no. I'm fine.' When they climbed inside, though, she didn't start the engine at once. Instead, she pulled some tissues from the glove box and blew her nose. Then she rested her arms on the top of the steering wheel and peered out at the caravan in the distance.

'So you see,' she said.

Again, her hair had fallen over the frames of her glasses. Again, he wanted to push it away from her face. Again, he did not.

'They want to go to Lourdes. They want a miracle. They have nothing else to hang their hopes on and certainly no money to finance what they want. Which is where I come in. Which is why Gwynder found me. So do I do this for them? Do I forgive these people for what they did, for how we lived, for what they couldn't be? Am I responsible for them now? What do I owe them besides life itself? I mean the *fact* of life and not what I've done with it. And what does it mean, anyway, to owe someone for having given birth to you? Surely that's not the most difficult part of parenthood, is it? I hardly think so. Which means the rest of it – the rest of being a parent – they utterly mangled.'

He did touch her then. He did what he'd seen her do herself: take the hair and tuck it back. His fingers touched the curve of her ear. 'Why did they come back, your brother and sister? Were they never adopted?'

'There was . . . They called it an accident, their foster parents. They called it Goron playing with a plastic bag but I think there was more to it than that. It probably should have been called – whatever "it" was – disciplining an overactive little boy in the wrong way. In any event, he was damaged and deemed unadoptable by people who saw him and met him. Gwynder might have been adopted but she wouldn't be parted from him. So they moved from home to home together, through the system, for years. When they were old enough, they came back here.' She smiled bleakly as she looked at him. ' This place – as well as this story – isn't much like what you're used to, is it, Thomas?'

'I'm not certain it matters.' He wanted to say more but he was unsure how to put it so he settled on, 'Are you willing to call me Tommy, Daidre? My family and friends—'

She held up her hand. 'I think not,' she said.

'Because of this?'

'No. Because this matters to me.'

★　★　★

Jago Reeth made it clear that he wanted Ben Kerne alone with no hangers-on from his family present. He suggested Hedra's Hut for the venue, and he used the word *venue* as if a performance would be given there.

Bea told him he was a bloody damn fool if he expected the lot of them to traipse out to the seacliff where that ancient perch was.

He replied that fool or not, if she wanted a conversation with him, he knew his rights and he was going to employ them.

She told him that one of his rights was not the right to decide where their meeting with Ben Kerne would occur.

He smiled and begged to differ. It might not have been his right, he said, but the fact of the matter was that she probably wanted him to be in a location where he felt easy with conversation. And Hedra's Hut was that location. They'd be cosy enough there. Out of the cold and the wind. Snug as four bugs rolled in the same rug, if she knew what he meant.

'He's got something up his sleeve,' was Sergeant Havers' assessment of the situation once they set off trailing Jago Reeth's Defender in the direction of Alsperyl. They'd wait at the village church for Mr Kerne, Jago had informed them. 'Best phone the superintendent and let him know where we're going,' Havers went on. 'I'd have back-up as well. Those blokes from the station? Got to be a way they can hide themselves round the place.'

'Not unless they disguise themselves as cows, sheep, or gulls,' Bea told her. 'This bloke's thought of all the angles.'

Lynley, Bea found, wasn't answering his mobile, which made her curse the man and wonder why she'd bothered to give him a phone in the first place. 'Where's the blasted man got to?' she asked and then replied to her own question with a grim declaration of, 'Well, we know the answer to that, don't we.'

At Alsperyl, which was no great distance from the Salthouse Inn, they remained in their respective cars, parked close to the village church. When Ben Kerne finally joined them, they'd been sitting there for nearly thirty minutes. During this time, Bea had phoned the station to give the word where they were and phoned Ray to do likewise.

Ray said, 'Beatrice, are you barking mad? D'you have any idea how irregular this is?'

'I've got half a dozen ideas,' she told him. 'I've also got sod all to work with unless this bloke gives me something I can use.'

'You can't think he intends—'

'I don't know what he intends. But there will be three of us and one of him and if we can't manage—'

'You'll check him for weapons?'

'I'm a fool but not a bloody fool, Ray.'

'I'm having whoever's out on patrol in your area head to Alsperyl.'

'Don't do that. If I need back-up, I can easily phone the Casvelyn station for it.'

'I don't care what you can and cannot do. There's Pete to consider and if it comes down to it, there's myself as well. I won't rest easy unless I know you've got proper back-up. Christ, this is bloody irregular.'

'As you've said.'

'Who's with you at present?'

'Sergeant Havers.'

'Another *woman*? Where the hell is Lynley? What about that sergeant from the station? He looked like he had half a wit about him. For God's sake, Bea!'

'Ray. This bloke's round seventy years old. He's got some sort of palsy. If we can't take care of ourselves round him, we need to be carted off.'

'Nonetheless—'

'Goodbye, darling.' She rang off and shoved the mobile into her bag.

Shortly after she finished her phone calls – also telling Collins and McNulty where she was – Ben Kerne arrived. He got out of his car and zipped his windcheater to the chin. He glanced at Jago Reeth's Defender in some apparent confusion. He then saw Bea and Havers parked next to the lichenous stone wall that defined the churchyard and he walked over to them. As he approached, they got out of the car. Jago Reeth did likewise.

His eyes were fixed on Santo Kerne's father. His expression had altered from the easy affability that he'd shown them in the Salthouse Inn. Now his features fairly blazed. She imagined it was the look seasoned warriors had once worn when they finally had the necks of their enemies beneath their boots and a sword pressing into their throats.

Jago Reeth said nothing to any of them. He merely jerked his head towards a kissing gate at the west end of the carpark, next to the church's notice board.

Bea spoke. 'If we're meant to follow you, Mr Reeth, then I have a condition as well.'

He raised an eyebrow, the extent to which he apparently intended to communicate until they got to his preferred destination.

'Put your hands on the bonnet and spread your legs. And trust me, I'm not interested in checking to see what sort of cobblers you've got.'

Jago cooperated. Havers and Bea patted him down. His only weapon was a biro. Havers took this and tossed it over the wall into the church-yard. Jago's expression said *Satisfied*?

Bea said, 'Carry on.'

He headed in the direction of the kissing gate. He did not wait there to see if they were accompanying him. He was, apparently, perfectly certain that they would follow.

Ben Kerne said to Bea, 'What's going on? Why've you asked me . . . ? Who is that, Inspector?'

'You've not met Mr Reeth before?'

'That's Jago Reeth? Santo spoke about him. The old surfer working for Madlyn's dad. Santo quite liked him. I'd no idea. No. I've not met him.'

'I doubt he's actually a surfer although he talks the talk. He doesn't look familiar to you?'

'Should he?'

'As Jonathan Parsons, perhaps.'

Ben Kerne's lips parted, but he said nothing. He watched Reeth trudging towards the kissing gate. 'Where's he going?'

'Where he's willing to talk. To us and to you.' Bea put her hand on Kerne's arm. 'But you've no need to listen. You've no need to follow him. His condition for speaking to us was to have you present and I realise this is half mad and the other half dangerous. But he's got us – that's the cops and not you – by the short and curlies and the only way we're going to get a word from him is to play it his way for now.'

'On the phone, you didn't say Parsons.'

'I didn't want you driving here like a madman. And I don't want you like a madman now. We already have one on our hands, I believe, and two would be overwhelming. Mr Kerne, I can't tell you how far out on a limb we are with this entire approach so I won't even go into it. Are you able to listen to what he has to say? More, are you willing?'

Kerne seemed to search for a way to put it that wouldn't make what he had to say into a fact he might have to accept. 'Did he kill Santo?'

'That's what we're going to talk to him about. Are you able?'

He nodded. He shoved his hands into the pockets of his windcheater and indicated with a tilt of his head that he was ready. They set out towards the kissing gate.

On the other side of this gate, a field provided grazing for cows, and the way towards the sea edged along a barbed wire fence. The path they walked on was muddy and uneven, marked deeply by ruts made from a tractor's wheels. At the far end of the field lay another, fenced off from the first by more barbed wire and accessed through yet another kissing gate. Ultimately, they walked perhaps half a mile or more and their destination was the South-West Coast Path, which crossed the second field high above the sea.

The wind was fierce here, coming on shore in continuous gusts. On these, the sea birds rose and fell. Kittiwakes called. Herring gulls replied. A lone green cormorant shot up from the cliff side as up ahead Jago Reeth approached the edge. The bird dove down, rose, and began to circle. Looking for prey, Bea thought, in the turbulent water.

They headed south on the coastal path, but within some twenty yards, a break in the gorse that stood between the path and perdition indicated a set of steep stone stairs. This, Bea saw, was their destination. Jago Reeth disappeared down them.

She said to her companions, 'Hang on, then,' and she went to see where the stone steps led. She was reckoning they were a means to get to the beach which lay some two hundred feet below the cliff top, and she meant to tell Jago Reeth that she had no intention of putting her life, Havers' life, and Ben Kerne's life at risk by following him down some perilous route to the water. But she found the steps went down only as far as fifteen of them could descend, and they terminated in another path, this one narrow and heavily grown on each side with gorse and sedge. It, too, headed south but for no great distance. Its conclusion was an ancient hut built partially into the face of the cliff that backed it. Jago Reeth, she saw, had just reached the hut's doorway and swung it open. He saw her on the steps but made no further gesture. Their eyes met briefly before he ducked inside the old structure.

She returned to the top of the cliff. She spoke above the sound of the wind, the sea, and the gulls. 'He's just below, in the hut. He might well have something stowed inside, so I'm going in first. You can wait on the path but don't come near till I give you the word.'

She went down the steps and along the path, the gorse brushing against the legs of her trousers. She reached the hut and found that Jago had indeed prepared for this moment. Not with weapons, however. Either he or someone else had earlier furnished the hut with a spirit stove, a jug of water, and a small box of supplies. The man was, incredibly, brewing tea.

The hut was fashioned from the driftwood of wrecked ships, of which there had been countless numbers over the centuries. It was a small affair, with a bench that ran round three sides and an uneven stone floor. As long as it had been in this place, people had carved their initials into its walls so they had the appearance now of a wooden Rosetta Stone, this one immediately comprehensible and speaking both of lovers and of people whose internal insignificance made them seek an outward expression – *any* outward expression – that would give their existence meaning.

Bea told Reeth to step away from the spirit stove, which he did willingly enough. She checked it and the rest of his supplies, of which there were few enough: plastic cups, sugar, tea, powdered milk in sachets, one spoon for shared stirring. She was surprised the old man hadn't thought of crumpets.

She ducked back out of the door and motioned Havers and Ben Kerne to join her. Once all four of them were inside the hut, there was barely room to move, but Jago Reeth still managed to make the tea, and he pressed a cup upon each of them like the hostess of an Edwardian house party. Then he doused the flame on the stove and set the stove itself on the stones beneath the bench, perhaps as a way of reassuring them that he had no intention of using it as a weapon. At this, Bea decided to pat him down again for good measure. Having put the spirit stove in the hut in advance of their arrival, there was no telling what else he'd stowed in the place. But he was weaponless as before.

With the hut's double door shut and fastened, the sound of the wind and the gulls' crying was muted. The atmosphere was close, and the four adults took up nearly every inch of the space. Bea said, 'You've got us here, Mr Reeth, at your pleasure. What is it you'd like to tell us?'

Jago Reeth held his tea in both hands. He nodded and spoke not to Bea but to Ben Kerne, and his tone was kind. 'Losing a son. You've got my deepest sympathy. It's the worst grief a man can know.'

'Losing any child's a blow.' Ben Kerne sounded wary. It appeared to Bea that he was trying to read Jago Reeth and to understand what lay beneath his words. As was she. The air seemed to crackle with anticipation.

Next to Bea, Sergeant Havers took out her notebook and flipped it open. Bea expected Reeth to tell her to put it away, but instead the old man nodded and said, 'I've no objection,' and to Kerne, 'Have you?' When Ben shook his head, Jago added, 'If you've come wired, Inspector, that's fine as well. There are always things wanting documentation in a situation like this.'

Bea wanted to say what she'd earlier thought: He'd considered all the angles. But she was waiting to see, hear, or intuit the one angle he hadn't yet considered. It *had* to be here somewhere, and she needed to be ready to deal with it when it raised its scaly head above the muck for a breath of air.

She said, 'Do go on.'

'But there's something worse about losing a son,' Jago Reeth said to Ben Kerne. 'Unlike a daughter, a son carries the name. He's the link between the past and the future. And it's more, even, than just the name at the end of the day. He carries the reason for it all. For this . . .' He gave a look around the hut, as if the tiny building somehow contained the world and the billions of lifetimes present in the world.

'I'm not sure I make that sort of distinction,' Ben said. 'Any loss of a child, of any child . . .' He didn't go on. He cleared his throat mightily.

Jago Reeth looked pleased. 'Losing a son to murder is a horror, though, isn't it? The *fact* of murder is almost as bad as knowing who killed him and not being able to lift a finger to bring the bloody sod to justice.'

Kerne said nothing. Nor did Bea or Barbara Havers. Bea and Kerne held their tea undrunk in their hands, and Ben Kerne set his carefully on the floor. Next to her, Bea felt Havers stir.

'That part's bad,' Jago said. 'As is the not knowing.'

'Not knowing what, exactly, Mr Reeth?' Bea asked.

'The whys and the wherefores. And the hows. Bloke can spend the rest of his life wondering and cursing and wishing. You know what I mean, I expect. Or if not now, you will, eh? It's hell on earth and there's no escaping. I feel for you, mate. For what you're going through now and for what's to come.'

'Thank you,' Ben Kerne said quietly. Bea had to admire his control. She could see how white the tops of his knuckles were.

'I knew your boy Santo. Lovely lad. Bit full of himself like all boys are when they're that age, eh, but lovely. And since this tragedy happened to him—'

'Since he was murdered,' Bea corrected.

'Murder,' Reeth said, '*is* a tragedy, Inspector. No matter what kind of game of scent-and-chase you lot might think it is. It's a tragedy and when it happens, the only peace available is in knowing the truth of what happened and having others know it as well. If,' he added with a brief smile, 'you know what I mean. And as I knew Santo, I've thought and thought about what happened to the lad. And I've decided that if an old broken down bloke like myself can give you any peace, Mr Kerne, that's what I owe you.'

'You don't owe me—'

'We all owe each other,' Jago cut in. 'It's forgetting that that leads us to tragedies.' He paused as if to let this sink in. He drained his tea and put the cup next to him on the bench. 'So what I want to do is tell you how I reckon this happened to your boy. Because I've thought about it, see, as I'm sure you have and sure the cops here have as well. Who would've done this to such a fine lad, I been asking myself for days. How'd they manage it? And why?'

'None of that brings Santo back, does it?' Ben Kerne asked steadily.

'Course not. But the knowing, the final understanding of it all: I wager there's peace in that and that's what I've got to offer you. Peace. So here's what I reckon was—'

'No. I don't think so, Mr Reeth.' Bea had a sudden glimmer what Reeth intended, and in that glimmer she saw where this could lead.

But Ben Kerne said, 'Let him go on, please. I want to hear him out, Inspector.'

'This will allow him to—'

'Please let him continue.'

Reeth waited affably for Bea to concur. She nodded sharply, but she wasn't happy. To *irregular* and *mad* she had to add *provocative*.

'So here's what I reckon,' Jago repeated, 'Someone has a score to settle and this someone sets out to settle that score on the life of your lad. What sort of score, you wonder, right? Could be anything, couldn't it. New score, old score. It doesn't matter. But a form of accounting's waiting out there, and Santo's life's the means of settling it. So this killer – could be a man, could be a woman, doesn't much matter, does it, because the point is the lad and the lad's death, see, which is what cops like these two always forget – this killer gets to know your lad because knowing him's going to provide access. And knowing the lad leads to the means as well because your boy's an open-hearted sort and he talks. About this and that but as things turn out, he talks a lot about his dad, same as most boys do. He says his dad's riding him hard for lots of reasons but mostly because he wants women and surfing and not settling down, and who can blame him as he's only eighteen. His dad, on the other hand, has his *own* wants for the boy, which makes the boy roil and talk and roil some more. Which makes him look for . . . What d'you call it? A substitute dad?'

'A surrogate dad.' Ben's voice was heavier now.

'That would be the word. Or perhaps a surrogate mum, of course. Or a surrogate priest, confessor, priestess, whatever. At any rate, this person – man or woman, young or old – sees a door of trust opening and he, or she, of course, walks right through it. If you know what I mean.'

He was keeping his options open, Bea concluded. He was, as he had said himself, no bloody fool, and the advantage he had in this moment was the years he'd had to think about the approach he wanted to use when the time came.

'So this person, let's call him or her the Confessor for want of a better term, this Confessor makes cups of tea and cups of chocolate and more cups of tea and more cups of chocolate and offers biscuits but more important offers a place for Santo to do whatever and to be whoever. And the Confessor waits. And soon enough reckons that means are available to settle whatever score needs settling. The boy's had yet another blowup with his dad. It's an argument that goes nowhere like always and this time the lad's taken all of his climbing equipment from where he's kept it in the past, right alongside Dad's, and he's stowed it in the boot of his car. What does he intend? It's that classic thing: I'll show him, I will. I'll show him what sort of bloke I am. He thinks I'm nothing but a lout but I'll show him. And what better way to do it than with his own sport, which I'll do *better* than he's ever managed. So that puts his equipment within the grasp of the Confessor and the Confessor sees what we'll call the Way.'

At this, Ben Kerne lowered his head. Bea said, 'Mr Kerne, I think this is—'

'No.' He raised his head with effort. 'More,' he said to Jago Reeth.

'The Confessor waits for an opportunity, which presents itself soon enough because the lad's open and easy with his belongings, one of which is his car. This is nothing at all to get into as it's never locked and a quick manoeuvre opens the boot and there it all is. Selection is the key. Perhaps a chock-stone or a carabiner. Or a sling. Even the harness will do. All four, perhaps? No, that likely would be – if you'll pardon the expression – overkill. If it's a sling, there's not a problem in the world as it's nylon or whatever and easily cut by shears, a sharp knife, a razor, whatever. If it's something else, things are a bit trickier as everything else save the rope – and rope seems too bloody obvious a choice, not to mention too noticeable – is metal and a cutting device is going to be necessary. How to find one? Purchase one? No. That would be traceable. Borrow one? Again, someone's going to recall the borrowing, yes? Use one without the knowledge of the owner? That seems more possible and decidedly more sensible, but where to find one? Friend, associate, acquaintance, employer? Someone whose movements are intimately known because they've been watched just as intimately? Any of those, yes? So the Confessor chooses the moment and the deed is done. One cut does it and afterwards no sign left behind because, as we've said, the Confessor's no fool and he knows – or she knows, because as we've seen *she* is as possible as *he* when it comes to this – that it's crucial there be no evidence afterwards. And the beauty of it all is that the equipment's been marked with tape by the lad, or even by his father, perhaps, so that it can be distinguished from everyone else's. Because this is what climbers do, you see. They mark their equipment because so often they climb together. It's safer that way, you see. And this tells the Confessor that there's little to no chance that anyone other than the lad will use this sling, this carabiner, this harness, whatever it was that was damaged because, of course, I myself don't know. But I've thought about it, and here's what I've come up with. The one thing the Confessor has to take care with is the tape used to identify the equipment. If he – or she, of course – buys more tape, there's a chance the new tape won't match exactly or can be traced back. God knows how, but there's that possibility, so the thing is to keep that tape usable. The Confessor manages this and it's quite a project because that tape is tough, like electrical tape. He – or she, of course, like I said – rewraps it just so and maybe it's not quite as tight as it once was but at least it's the same and will the lad even notice? Unlikely and even if he does, what he's likely to do is smooth it down, apply more tape on top, something like that. So once the deed is done and the equipment's replaced, all that's left is waiting. And once what happens, happens, and it *is* a tragedy, no one doubts that, there's nothing really that can't be explained away.'

'There's always something, Mr Reeth,' Bea said.

Jago looked at her in a kindly way. 'Fingerprints on the boot of the car? In the interior? On the keys to the car? Inside the boot? The Confessor and the boy spent hours together, perhaps they even worked together at . . . let's say it was at his dad's business. They each rode in the other's car, they were mates, they were pals, they were surrogate father and surrogate son, they were surrogate mother and surrogate son, they were surrogate brothers, they were lovers, they were . . . anything. It doesn't matter, you see, because it all can be explained away. Hair inside the boot of the car? The Confessor's?

Someone else's? Same thing, really. The Confessor planted someone else's or even his own or her own because it can be a woman, we've already seen that. What about fibres? Clothing fibres, perhaps on the tape that marked the equipment. Wouldn't that be lovely? But the Confessor helped wrap that equipment or he or she touched that equipment because . . . why? Because the boot was used for other things as well, a surfing kit, perhaps, and things would get moved round here and there and in and out. What about access to the equipment? Everyone had that. Every single person in the poor lad's life. What about motive? Well, nearly everyone, it seems, had that as well. So at the end of the day, there is no answer. There is only speculation but no case to present. Which the killer probably considers the beauty of the crime but which you and I know, Mr Kerne, is *any* crime's biggest horror: that the killer simply walks away. Everyone knows who did it. Everyone admits it. Everyone shakes a head and says, What a tragedy. What a useless, senseless, maddening—'

'I think that's enough, Mr Reeth. Or Mr Parsons,' Bea said.

'—horror because the killer walks away now he – or she, of course – has done his business.'

'I said that's enough.'

'And the killer can't be touched by the cops and all the cops can do is sit there and drink their tea and wait and hope to find *something* somewhere someday. But they get busy, don't they? Other things on their plates. They shove you to one side and say don't ring us everyday, man, because when a case goes cold, like this one will, there's no point to ringing so we'll ring *you* if and when we can make an arrest. But it never comes, does it, that arrest. So you end up with nothing but ashes in an urn and they may as well have burnt your body on the day they burned his because the soul of you is gone anyway.'

He was finished, it seemed, his recital completed. All that was left was the sound of harsh breathing, which was Jago Reeth's, and outside the cry of gulls and the gusting of the wind and the crash of the surf. In a suitably well-rounded television drama, Bea thought, Reeth would rise to his feet now. He would dash for the door and throw himself over the cliff, having at long last achieved the vengeance he'd anticipated and having no further reason to continue living. He'd take the leap and join his dead Jamie. But this, unfortunately, was not a television drama.

His face seemed lit from within. Spittle had collected at the corners of his mouth. His tremors had worsened. He was waiting, she saw, for

Ben Kerne's reaction to his performance, for Ben Kerne's embracing of a truth that no one could alter and no one could resolve.

Ben finally lifted his head and gave the reaction. 'Santo,' he said, 'was not my son.'

29

The cry of the gulls seemed to grow louder, and from far below them the slamming of waves on rock indicated that the tide was in. Ben thought what this meant and the irony of it: excellent surfing conditions today.

The breathing that had been Jago Reeth's stopped, drawn in and held as perhaps the old man decided whether to believe what Ben had told him. For Ben, it no longer mattered what anyone believed. Nor, finally, did it matter at all that Santo had not been his by blood. For he saw that they had been father and son in the only way that mattered, which had everything to do with history and experience and nothing to do with a single blindly swimming cell that through sheerest chance makes piercing contact with an egg. Thus his failures were every bit as profound as a blood father's would have been towards a son. For he'd made every paternal move out of fear and not love, always waiting for Santo to show the colours of his true origins. Since after their adolescence Ben had never known any one of his wife's lovers, he had waited for Dellen's least desirable characteristics to surface in her son, and when anything remotely Dellen-like had appeared, *that* had been Ben's focus and passion. He as much as moulded Santo into his mother, so great was the emphasis had he had placed upon anything in the boy that had seemed like her.

'He wasn't,' Ben repeated, 'my son.' How pathetically true, he realised now.

Jago Reeth said, 'You're a bloody liar. You always were.'

'I only wish that was the case.' Ben saw another detail now. It fell into place neatly and corrected his previous misunderstanding. He said to Reeth, 'She talked to *you*, didn't she? I thought she meant the police, but she didn't. She talked to you.'

DI Hannaford said, 'Mr Kerne, you've no need to say anything.'

Ben said, 'He needs to know the truth. I had nothing to do with what happened to Jamie. I wasn't there.'

Jago Reeth said abruptly, '*Liar*. You would say that, wouldn't you.'

'Because it's the truth. I'd had a scuffle with him. He tossed me out of his party. But I went for a walk round and then I went home. What Dellen told you . . .' He wasn't sure, then, that he could go on, but he knew that he had to, if only to do the single thing that *could* be done to avenge Santo's death. 'What Dellen told you, she told you out of jealousy. I'd been with your daughter. A snog. We'd got carried away. Dellen saw us, and she had to get even because that's what she and I did to each other. Tit for tat, together and apart, in love and in hate, it never mattered. We were bound by something that we couldn't break free of.'

'You're a liar now. As you were then.'

'So she went to you and she told you I did whatever she told you I did. But what I know about that night is what you know: Jamie, your son, went down to that cave for some reason after that party and that's where he died.'

'Don't you bloody claim that,' Reeth said fiercely. 'You ran off. You left Pengelly Cove and you *never* returned. You had a reason to leave and we both know what it was.'

'Yes. I had a reason. Because no matter what I told him, my own dad, like you, believed I was guilty.'

'With damn good cause.'

'What you will, Mr Parsons. As you wish. Now and forever, if you like. But I wasn't there, so I suppose your job isn't done, is it. Because whatever she told you . . . and *it was* you she told, wasn't it . . . ? She lied.'

'Why would she? Why would *anyone*?'

Ben saw it. The reason, the cause. Beyond the tit for tat and the love and hate, beyond the parry and thrust of what had gone for their relationship for nearly thirty years, he saw. 'Because that's who she is,' he said. 'Because that's simply what she does.'

He left it at that. He got to his feet. At the hut's doorway, he paused, one small matter left unclear to him. He said to Reeth, 'Have you watched me all these years, Mr Parsons? Has that really been the extent of your life? How you've defined yourself? Waiting till I had a boy the very same age as Jamie was when Jamie died and then moving in for the kill?'

'You don't know what it's like,' Reeth said. 'But you will, man. You bloody sodding will.'

'Or did you find me because of . . .' Ben considered this. 'Because of Adventures Unlimited? The purest chance, reading the newspaper somewhere and seeing that story poor Alan worked so hard to arrange.

Was that it? That story in the *Mail on Sunday*? Then dashing here and establishing yourself and waiting because you'd got so bloody good at biding your time. Because you thought – you believed – that if you did to me what you were so sure I'd done to you, that would . . . what? Give you peace? Close the circle? Finish things properly? How can you believe that?'

'You're going to know,' Reeth said. 'You're going to see. Because what I've said here – every word of it, man – is speculation. I know my rights. I made a study of my rights. So when I walk out of here—'

'Don't you see? It doesn't matter,' Ben replied. 'Because I'm walking out of here first.'

He did so. He closed the door behind him and strode along the path towards the steps. His throat ached with the strain of holding back everything he'd been holding back, even without acknowledging that fact, for so many years. He heard his name and he turned.

DI Hannaford joined him. She said, 'He's made an error somewhere, Mr Kerne. They always make an error. We're going to find it. No one thinks of everything. I want you to hang on.'

Ben shook his head. 'It doesn't matter. Will it bring Santo back?'

'He's got to pay. That's how this works.'

'He's already paying. And even if he isn't, he's going to see the only thing there is to see: There's no peace for him in what he's done. He can't scrub it from his brain. None of us can do that.'

'Nonetheless,' Hannaford said. 'We'll be pursuing this.'

'If you must,' Ben said. 'But not for my sake.'

'For Santo's sake, then. He's owed—'

'He is. God, how he is. He's just not owed this.'

Ben walked from her, making his way along the path and up the stone steps to the top of the cliff. There, he followed the South-West Coast Path the short distance to the pastures they'd crossed, and he returned to his car. They could do with Jago Reeth or Jonathan Parsons what they wished to do or, indeed, what they were able to do within the confines of the law and the rights he said he knew so well. For whatever they did would not be sufficient to absolve Ben of the burden of responsibility that would always be his. This responsibility, he saw, went far beyond Santo's death. It was described by the choices he'd made time and again and what those choices had done to mould the very people he'd claimed to love.

In days to come, he knew he would weep. He couldn't now. He was numb. But the grief of loss was inescapable, and he accepted that for the first time in his life.

When he got home, he went in search of her. Alan was in his office, on the phone with someone and standing at a bulletin board on which he'd affixed two lines of index cards which Ben recognised as the plan for the video he wished to make about Adventures Unlimited. Kerra was talking to a tall blond youth, a prospective instructor no doubt. Ben didn't bother either of them.

He climbed the stairs. She wasn't in the family quarters, nor did she appear to be anywhere else in the building. He felt a fluttering in his chest at this, and he went to the wardrobe to check, but her clothes were still there and the rest of her belongings were in the chest of drawers. He finally saw her from the window, a figure in black on the beach whom he might have taken as a surfer in a wetsuit had he not possessed a lifetime of knowledge about the shape of her and the texture of her hair. She was standing with her back to the hotel. As the tide was high, most of the beach was covered, and the water was lapping round her ankles. It would still be frigid this time of year, but she wore no protection against it.

He went to join her. He saw when he reached her that she was carrying a bundle of photographs. She was hollow-eyed. She looked nearly as numb as he felt.

He said her name. She said, 'I hadn't thought of him in years. But there he was in my mind today, like he'd been waiting to get in all this time.'

'Who?'

'Hugo.'

A name he'd never heard before and not one he cared about hearing now. He said nothing. Far out in the waves, five surfers formed a line-up. A swell rose behind them and Ben watched to see who would be in position to drop in. None of them were. The wave broke too far ahead of them, leaving them waiting for the next one in the set and another attempt at a ride.

Dellen continued. 'I was his special one. He made a fuss over me and he asked my parents could he take me to the cinema. To the seal sanctuary. To the Christmas panto. He bought me clothes he wanted to see me in because I was his favourite niece. We've got something special, he said. I wouldn't buy you these things and take you to these places if you weren't *especially* special to me.'

Out to sea, one of the surfers was successful, Ben saw. He dropped in and caught the wave and he carved, seeking what every surfer seeks, the racing green room whose shimmering walls rise and curve and endlessly shift, enclosing and then releasing. It was a beautiful ride and when it was over, the surfer dropped down onto the board and made his way out to the others again, accompanied by the yelps of his mates. Jokingly, they barked like dogs. When he reached them, one of them touched fists with him. Ben saw this and felt a sore place in his heart. He forced himself to attend to what Dellen was saying.

'It felt wrong,' she said, 'but Uncle Hugo said it was love. The special part was being singled out. Not my brother, not my cousins, but me. So if he touched me here and asked me to touch him there, was that bad? Or was it just something that I didn't understand?'

Ben felt her look at him and he knew he was meant to look at her. He was meant to look at her face and read the suffering there, and he was meant to meet her emotion with his own. But he couldn't do it. For he found that a thousand Uncle Hugos couldn't change a single one of the facts. If, indeed, there was an Uncle Hugo at all.

Next to him, he felt her move. He saw she was riffling through the pictures she had with her. He half-expected her to produce Uncle Hugo from within the stack, but she didn't. Instead, she brought forth a photograph he recognised. Mum and Dad and two kids on summer holiday, a week on the Isle of Wight. Santo had been eight years old, Kerra twelve.

In the picture they were at a restaurant table, no meal in evidence so they must have handed the camera to the waiter as they first sat, asking him to snap the happy family. All of them were smiling as required: Look at how we're enjoying ourselves.

Pictures were the things of happy memories. They were also the instruments one used retrospectively to avoid the truth. For in Kerra's small face, Ben could now read the anxiety, that desire to be just good enough to stop the wheel from turning another time. In Santo's face, he could see the confusion, a child's awareness of a present hypocrisy without the accompanying comprehension. In his own expression, he could see the gritty determination to make things right. And in Dellen's face, what was always there: knowledge and anticipation. She was wearing a red scarf twined through her hair.

They gravitated towards her in the picture, all of them slightly leaning in her direction. His hand was over hers as if he'd hold her there at the table instead of where she doubtless wished to be.

She can't help herself, he'd said time and again. What he'd failed to see was that he could.

He took the picture from her and said to his wife, 'It's time for you to go.'

'Where?'

'I'm not sure,' he said. 'St Ives. Plymouth. Back to Truro. Pengelly Cove perhaps. Your family's there still. They'll help you if you need help. If that's what you want at this point.'

She was silent. He looked from the photo to her. Her eyes had darkened. She said, 'Ben, how can you? After what's happened.'

'Don't,' he said. 'It's time for you to go.'

'Please, how will I survive?'

'You'll survive,' he told her. 'We both know that.'

'What about you? Kerra? What about the business?'

'Alan's here. He's a very good man. And Kerra and I will cope. We've learned to do that very well.'

Selevan had found that his plans altered once the police came to the Salthouse Inn. He told himself that he couldn't just selfishly head out with Tammy for the Scottish border without knowing what was going on and, more important, without discovering if there was something he could do to assist Jago. He couldn't imagine *why* such assistance might be necessary, but he thought it best to remain where he was, more or less, and wait for further information.

It wasn't long in coming. He reckoned Jago wouldn't return to the Salthouse Inn, so he himself didn't wait there. Instead, he went back to Sea Dreams and paced in the caravan for a while, taking a nip now and then from a flask he'd filled to see him on the trip to the border, and finally he went outside and over to Jago's caravan.

He didn't go inside. He had a duplicate key to the place, but it just didn't feel right, although he reckoned Jago wouldn't have minded had he entered. Instead he waited on the top of the metal steps, where a wider one played the role of porch and was suitable for his bum.

Jago rolled into Sea Dreams some ten minutes later. Selevan got creakily to his feet. He shoved his hands into the pockets of his jacket and walked over to Jago's preferred spot to park the Defender. He said, 'You all right, then, mate?' when Jago got out. 'They didn't give you aggro down the station, did they?'

'Not a bit,' Jago told him. 'When it comes to the cops, a small measure of preparation is all that's needed. Things go your way, then, instead of theirs. Surprises them a bit, but that's what life is. One bloody surprise after another.'

'S'pose,' Selevan said. But he felt a twinge of uneasiness, and he couldn't exactly say why. There was something about Jago's way of talking, something in the tone, that wasn't altogether the Jago he knew. He said warily, 'They didn't rough you up, mate?'

Jago barked a laugh. 'Those two cows? Not likely. We just had a bit of a chat and that was the end of it. Long time in coming, but it's over now.'

'Wha's going on, then?'

'Nothing, mate. Something went on a long time ago, but that's all finished. My work here is done.'

Jago passed Selevan and stepped up to the door of the caravan. He hadn't locked it, Selevan saw, so there'd been no need for him to wait on the steps in the first place. Jago went inside and Selevan followed. He stood uncertainly just at the door, however, because he wasn't sure what was going on.

He said, 'You been made redundant, Jago?'

Jago had gone into the bedroom at the end of the caravan. Selevan couldn't see him, but he could hear the noise of a cupboard opening and of something being dragged from the shelf above the clothes rail. In a moment Jago appeared in the doorway, a large duffel bag drooping from his hand. 'What?' he asked.

'I asked were you made redundant? You said your work was finished. You been sacked or something?'

Jago looked as if he was thinking about this, which was strange as far as Selevan was concerned. One was made redundant or not. One was sacked or not. Surely the question didn't need consideration. Finally Jago smiled quite a slow smile that wasn't much like him. He said, 'That's exactly it, mate. Redundant. I was made redundant a long time ago.' He paused and looked thoughtful and next spoke to himself, 'More than quarter of a century,' he said. 'A long time in coming.'

'What?' Selevan felt a restless urgency to get to the root of the matter because this Jago was different from the Jago he'd been sitting in the inglenook with for the last six or seven months, and he vastly preferred that other Jago, who spoke directly and not in . . . well, in parables or the like.

He said, 'Mate, has something happened with them cops? Did they do something? You don't sound like yourself.' Selevan could imagine what the cops might do. True, they'd been women but fact was that Jago was an old codger round the same age as Selevan, and he was in poor condition for his years. Besides that, had they taken him to the station, there'd be blokes there, other cops, who could rough him up. And cops could rough one up in places where no evidence was left. Selevan knew that. He watched telly, especially American films on Sky. He'd seen how it was done. Bit of pressure on the thumb nails. Couple of sewing needles screwed into the skin. It wouldn't take much on a bloke like Jago. Only he wasn't acting like a man who'd suffered some sort of humiliation at the hands of the cops, was he?

Jago put the duffel bag on his bed – Selevan could see this much from where he still stood, unsure whether to sit or stand, to go or remain – and he began opening the drawers of the built-in chest. And what came to Selevan then was what should have come the moment he saw the duffel bag in Jago's hands: His friend was leaving.

'Where you off to, Jago?'

'What I said.' Jago came to the door again, this time a small stack of neatly folded shorts and vests in his hands. 'Things're finished here. It's time for me to shove off. Never stay in one place long, anyway. Follow the sun, the surf, the seasons.'

'But the season's here. It's just coming on. It's round the corner. Where you going to find a better season than what you'd get here?'

Jago hesitated, half turned towards the bed. It seemed that this was something he'd not considered: the *where* of his journey. Selevan saw his shoulders alter. There was something less definite about his posture. Selevan pressed the point.

'And anyways, you got friends here. That counts for something. Let's face it, you see a doctor yet for those shakes of yours? I reckon they're going to get worse, and then where'll you be if you set off on your own?'

Jago seemed to think about this. 'Doesn't much matter, like I said. My work is finished. All's left is the waiting.'

'For what?'

'For . . . you know. Neither one of us is a hatchling, mate.'

'For *dying*, you mean? Tha's rubbish. You got years. What the bloody hell did those coppers *do* to you?'

'Not a sodding thing.'

'Can't believe you, Jago. If you're talking of dying—'

'Dying's got to be faced. So's living, for that matter. They're part of each other. And they're meant to be natural.'

Selevan felt a margin of relief when he heard this. He didn't like to think of Jago pondering the idea of dying because he didn't like to think what this suggested about his friend's intentions. He said, 'Glad to hear *that*, at least. The natural bit.'

Jago smiled slowly as comprehension dawned. He shook his head in the way a fond grandparent might react to a beloved grandchild's mischief. 'Oh. That. Well, I could end it easy enough, couldn't I, since I've finished up here and there's not much point in carrying on. There's lots of places to do it in these parts 'cause it'd look like an accident and no one'd know the difference, eh? But if I did that, might end it for him as well and we can't have that. No. There's no end to something like this, mate. Not if I can help it.'

Cadan had just arrived at LiquidEarth when the phone call came. He could hear that his father was in the shaping room and Jago was nowhere to be found, so he answered it himself. A bloke said, 'That Lewis Angarrack?' and when Cadan said no, he said, 'Fetch him, eh. Got to talk to him.'

Cadan knew better than to bother Lew in the middle of shaping a board. But the bloke insisted that this couldn't wait and no, he didn't want to leave a message.

So Cadan went to fetch his father, not opening the door but pounding on it to be heard over the tools. The power planer was switched off. Lew himself appeared, his mask lowered and his eyegear around his neck.

When Cadan told him there was a phone call for him, Lew looked into the glassing area and said, 'Jago not back?'

'Didn't see his car outside.'

'What're you doing here, then?'

Cadan felt that old plummeting of his spirits. He stifled a sigh. 'Phone,' he reminded Lew.

Lew took off the latex gloves he wore for work, and he strode to the reception area. Cadan followed for want of anything better to do, although he peeked into the spraying room and considered the line-up of shaped boards to be painted as well as the kaleidoscope of bright colours that had been tested against the walls. In reception he could hear his father saying, 'What's that you say? No, of course not. Where the hell is he? C'n you put him on the phone?'

He wandered back out. Lew was behind the counter where the phone sat amid the mounds of paperwork on the card table that served as his desk. He glanced at Cadan and then away.

'No,' Lew said to the bloke on the other end of the line. 'I didn't know . . . I damn well would have appreciated it if he'd told me. I *know* he's not well. But all I can tell you is what he told me. Had to step out to speak to a mate in a bit of bother up at the Salthouse. You? Then you know more than I do.'

Cadan clocked that they were talking about Jago, and he did question where the old man was. Jago had been nothing if not a model employee during the time he'd worked at LiquidEarth. Indeed, Cadan often felt that Jago's performance as a stellar worker bee was one of the reasons he himself looked so bad. At work on time, never off for illness, not a complaint about anything, nose to the grindstone, perfectionist in what he had to do. For Jago not to be here now brought up the subject of why and made Cadan listen more closely to the conversation his dad was having.

'Redundant? God, no. I've a pile of work and the last thing on my mind is making anyone . . . Well, then, what *did* he say? Finished? *Finished*?' Lew looked round the reception area, particularly at the clipboard on which the orders for boards were attached. There was a thick stack of them, the mark of longtime surfers' respect for Lew Angarrack's work. No computer design and computer shaping here, but the real thing, all of it done by hand. So few craftsmen could do what Lew did. They were a dying breed, their work an art form that would pass into surfing lore like the earliest long boards fashioned of wood. In their place would come the hollow core boards, the computerised designs, everything programmed into a machine that would belch out a product no longer lovingly shaped by a master who rode waves himself and consequently knew what an extra channel or the degree of tilt of a fin would truly do to a board's performance. It was a pity, really.

'Gone altogether?' Lew was saying. 'Damn. No. There's nothing more I can tell you. You seem to know more than I do anyway. I couldn't say. I've been busy myself. He didn't seem any different . . . I can't say that I did.'

Shortly thereafter, he rang off and he spent a moment staring at the clipboard. 'Jago's gone, then,' he finally said.

'What d'you mean, gone?' Cadan asked. 'For the day? Forever? Something happen to him?'

Lew shook his head. 'He just left.'

'What? Casvelyn?'

'That's it.'

'Who was that?' Cadan nodded at the phone although his father hadn't looked at him to see the nod.

'Bloke Jago lives by in the caravan park. Talked to him as he was packing up but couldn't get much sense out of him.' Lew took off his headphones and dropped them onto the table. He leaned against the counter with its display of fins, wax, and other paraphernalia, his hands supporting him and his head lowered as if he were studying what was inside the case. 'Well, that buggers us,' he said.

A moment passed during which Cadan saw Lew reach up and rub his neck where it was no doubt sore from shaping the surfboard blanks. He said, 'Good thing I came by, then.'

'Why's that?'

'I c'n help you out.'

Lew raised his head. He said, 'Cade, I'm far too tired to argue with you just now.'

'No. I don't mean what you think,' Cadan told him. 'I c'n see how you'd reckon I was seizing my moment: Now he'll *have* to let me spray the boards. But that's not what this is.'

'What is it, then?'

'Just me helping you. I c'n shape if you like. Not as good as you but you can show me. Or I c'n glass. Or spray. Or do the hand sanding. Doesn't matter to me.'

'And why would you want to do that, Cadan?'

Cadan shrugged. 'You're my dad,' he said. 'Blood's thicker than . . . well, you know.'

'What about Adventures Unlimited?'

'That didn't work out.' Cadan saw his father's expression change to one of resignation. He hastened to add, 'I know what you're thinking but they didn't sack me. It's just that I'd rather work for you. We've got something here and we shouldn't let it . . . die.'

Die. There was the frightening word. Cadan hadn't realised just *how* frightening *die* was until this moment because he'd spent his life so focused on another word entirely and that word was *leave.* Yet trying to stay one step ahead of loss didn't prevent loss from happening, did it? The Bounder still bounded and other people still walked away. As Cadan himself had done time and again before it could be done to him, as Cadan's father had done for much the same reasons.

But some things endured in spite of one's dread, and one of them was the blessing of blood.

'I want to help you,' Cadan said. 'I've been playing it stupid. You're the expert, after all, and I reckon you know how I can learn this business.'

'And that's what you want to do? Learn this business?'

'Right,' Cadan said.

'What about the bike? The X-games or whatever they are?'

'At the moment, this is more important. I'll do what I can to keep it important.' Cadan peered at his father closely then. 'That good enough for you, Dad?'

'I don't understand. Why would you want to do it, Cade?'

'Because of what I just called you, you nutter.'

'What was that?'

'Dad,' Cadan said.

Selevan had watched Jago drive off, and he wondered about all the time he'd spent with the bloke. He could come up with no answers to the questions that were filling his head. No matter how he looked at things, he couldn't suss out what the other man had meant and something told him that the entire subject didn't bear too much consideration anyway. He'd phoned LiquidEarth nonetheless in the hope that Jago's employer might shed some light on the situation. But what he'd learned told him that whatever Jago had meant by *finished*, it wasn't connected to surf-boards. Beyond that, he realised he didn't want to know. Perhaps he was being an out and out coward but some things, he decided, were none of his business.

Tammy wasn't one of them. He got into the car with all her posses-sions packed, and he drove to Clean Barrel Surf Shop. He didn't go in at once to fetch her as there was time to kill before she closed the shop for the day. So he parked down on the wharf and he walked from there to Jill's Juices where he purchased a take-away coffee, extra strong.

Then he returned to the wharf where he walked the length of it on its north side, edging along the canal. Several fishing boats nudged the dock here, barely bobbing in the water. Mallards floated placidly near them – an entire family of them with mum and dad and, unbelievably, a dozen babies – and a kayaker paddled silently in the direction of Launceton, taking exercise in the late afternoon.

Selevan realised that it felt like spring. It *had* been spring for more than six weeks now, of course, but that had been a spring of the calendar until this point. This was a spring of weather. True, there was brisk wind off the sea but it felt different as the wind does when the weather shifts. On it the scent of newly turned earth came to him from someone's garden, and he saw that in the window boxes of the town's library, winter pansies had been replaced with petunias.

He walked to the end of the wharf, where the old canal lock was closed, holding back the water till someone wanted to go out to sea in one of the fishing boats. From this vantage point, he could see the town rising above him to the north, with the old Promontory King George Hotel – a place for adventurous tourists now – acting as doorman to a different world.

Things change, Selevan thought. That had proved the case in his life, even when it had seemed to him that nothing was ever going to change. He'd wanted a career in the Royal Navy to escape what he'd seen as a life of unfaltering drudgery, but the fact of the matter was that the *details* of that life had altered in minute ways, which led to big ways, which led to life not being drudgery at all if one just paid *attention*. His kids grew; he and the wife turned older; a bull was brought by to service the cows; calves were born; the sky was bright one day and threatening the next; David moved off to join the Army; Nan ran off to marry . . . One could call it good or bad or one could just call it life. And life continued. A bloke didn't get what he wanted all the time, and that's just how it was. One could thrash about and hate that fact or one could cope. He'd seen that daft poster in the library one time and he'd scoffed at it: *When life gives you lemons, make lemonade.* Bloody stupid, he'd thought. But not really, he saw now. Not altogether.

He took a deep breath. One could taste the salt air in this spot. More than at Sea Dreams because Sea Dreams was way up on the cliff and here the sea was close, yards away, and it beat against the reefs and wore them down, patiently, drawn by the course of nature and physics or magnetic forces or whatever it was because he didn't know and it didn't matter.

He finished his coffee and crushed the cup in his hand. He carried this back to a bin and paused there to light a fag, which he smoked on the way to Clean Barrel. There, Tammy was working at the till. The cash drawer was open and she was counting up the day's takings, alone in the shop. She hadn't heard him come in.

He observed her in silence. He saw Dot in her, which was odd, as he'd never seen the similarity before. But there it was, in the way she cocked her head and exposed an ear. And the shape of that ear, that little dip in the earlobe, it was Dot all right and he remembered that because . . . oh this was the worst of it, but he'd seen that earlobe time and again as he'd mounted her and done his loveless business on her and there couldn't have been a scrap of pleasure in it for the poor woman, which he regretted now. He hadn't loved her, but that hadn't been a fault of hers, had it, although he'd blamed her for not being whatever it was he'd thought she should be in order for him to love her.

He harrumphed because things were dead tight inside him and a good harrumph had always loosened them up a bit. The noise made Tammy raise her head, and when she saw him, she looked a bit wary and who could blame her? They'd been having rather a dicey time of it. She'd not spoken to him other than in polite response since he'd found that letter under her mattress and waved it in her face.

'Shouldn't be in here alone,' he told her.

'Why not?' She put her hands on either side of the cash drawer, and for a moment Selevan thought she was doing it because she expected him to leap on the funds and shove them down the front of his flannel shirt. But then she pulled it out altogether and carried it to the back room, where extra inventory and cleaning supplies and the like were kept along with an overlarge antique safe. She stowed the cash drawer inside this safe, slammed its door home, and twirled the combination lock. Then she shut the back room door, locked this as well, and put the key in a hidey spot that had been created for it on the underside of the telephone.

Selevan said to her, 'Best ring up your guv, girl.' He was aware that his voice was gruff, but it was *always* gruff when he spoke to her, and he couldn't make it any different.

'Why?'

'Time to leave here.'

Her expression didn't change, but her eyes did. The shape of them. Just like her auntie Nan, Selevan thought. Just like the time he'd told Nan that she could sodding shove off if she didn't like the house rules, one of which was her dad deciding bloody who his daughter would see and when she would see him and believe you me, lass, it's not going to be that yob with the motorbikes over my dead body. Five of them, mind you. Five bleeding motorbikes and every time he'd roar up on a new one with his fingernails all gone to grease and his knuckles blacked and who the bloody hell would have thought he'd make a go of it and create those . . . what did they call them? Choppings? Chopped? No, choppers. That was it. Choppers. Just like in America, where everyone was bloody crazy and rich enough to buy just about anything, weren't they. This is what you want? he'd bellowed at Nan. This? *This*?

Tammy didn't argue as Nan might have done. She didn't storm round the shop and slam things about to make a scene. She said, 'All right, then, Grandie,' sounding resigned. She added, 'But I don't take it back.'

'What's that?'

'What I said before.'

Selevan frowned and tried to recall the last conversation which had *been* a conversation and not merely a request to pass the salt or the mustard or the bottle of brown sauce. He recalled her reaction when he'd waved the letter in her face. He said, 'That. Well. Can't be helped, can it.'

'*Can* be helped. But it doesn't matter now. This doesn't change anything, you know, no matter what you think.'

'What's that?'

'This. Sending me off. Mum and Dad thought it would change things as well, when they made me leave Africa. But it won't change a thing.'

'Think that, do you?'

'I *know* it.'

'I don't mean the bit about leaving and the things changing in your head. I mean the bit about what I think.'

She looked confused. But then her expression altered in that quick-silver way of hers. Did every adolescent do that? he wondered.

'S'pose,' he said, 'your grandie's more'n he seems to be. Ever reckon that? I reckon not. So collect your belongings and make that phone call to your guv. Tell him where you'll leave the key and let's shove off.'

Having said that, he left the shop. He watched the traffic coming up The Strand, as townsfolk returned from their jobs in the industrial estate at the edge of town and farther away, as far as Okehampton, some of them. In time, Tammy joined him and he set off back towards the wharf with her trailing at a slower pace that he took as reluctant cooperation with her grandfather's plans.

He said to her, 'Got your passport with you, I take it. How long've you had it out of its hidey place?'

'A while.'

'What'd you mean to do with it?'

'Didn't know at first.'

'But you do now, do you?'

'I was saving up.'

'For what?'

'To go to France.'

'France, is it? You heading for gay Paree?'

'Lisieux,' she said.

'Leer-what?'

'Lisieux. That's where . . . you know . . .'

'Oh. A pilgrimage, is it? Or something more?'

'It doesn't matter. I don't have enough money yet anyway. But if I had it, I'd be gone from here.' She came up to his side then and walked along with him. She said as if finally relenting, 'It's nothing personal, Grandie.'

'Didn't take it that way. But I'm glad you didn't do a runner. Would've been a rough one to explain to your mum and dad. Off to France, she is, praying at the shrine of some saint that she read about in one of her sainty books that's she's not supposed to be reading anyways but I let her read cos I reckoned words's not going to do much to her head one way or 'nother.'

'That's not precisely true, you know.'

'Anyways, I'm glad you didn't scarper cos they'd have my skin for that one, your mum and dad. You know that, don't you?'

'Yes but, Grandie, some things can't be helped.'

'And this is one of them, is it?'

'That's how it is.'

'Sure of it, are you? Because that's what they all say when the cults get hold of them and send them out on the streets to beg money. *Which* they then take off them, by the way. So they're trapped like rats on a sinking ship. You know that, don't you? Some big guru with an eye for girls – just like you – who's meant to have his babies like a sheik in a tent with two dozen wives. Or one of them, you know, polygammers.'

'Polygamists,' she said. 'Oh, you really can't think this is like that, Grandie. You're joking about it. Only I don't think it's funny, see?'

They'd reached his car. She looked in the back as she got in, and she saw her old duffel bag. Her lip jutted out, but she drew it back in. Home to Africa, her expression said, which meant home to Mum and Dad until they thought of another plan to shake her resolve. They'd tick Send Her to Her Grandfather off their list and come up with the next idea. Something like Send Her to Siberia. Or Send Her to the Australian Bush.

She got into the car. She fastened her seat belt and crossed her arms.

She looked stonily forward at the canal, and her expression didn't soften even when she took in the ducklings and how their little webbed feet raised them above the water when they hastened to follow their mother, making them look like tiny runners on the surface of the canal, just the sort of harkening back to a miracle that Selevan reckoned she'd appreciate. She didn't, however. She was concentrating on what she thought she knew: how long a drive it was to Heathrow or Gatwick and whether her plane left for Africa tonight or tomorrow. Likely tomorrow, which would mean a long night in a hotel somewhere. Perhaps even now she was making her plan to escape. Out of the hotel window or down the stairs and then to France by hook or by crook.

He wondered if he should let her think that was where he was taking her. But it seemed cruel to let the poor lass suffer. Truth of the matter was that she'd suffered enough. She'd held firm through everything that had been thrown at her and that had to mean *something* even if it meant what none of the rest of them could bear considering.

He said as he started up the car, 'I made a phone call, I did. Day or two ago.'

She said dully, 'Well, you'd have to, wouldn't you.'

'Truth in that. They said come along. Wanted to talk to you as well, but I told 'em you were unavailable at present.'

'Ta for that, at least.' Tammy turned her head and examined the scenery. They were passing through Stratton, heading north on the A39. There was no easy way to get out of Cornwall, but that had long been part of its draw. 'I don't much want to talk to them, Grandie. We've already said all there is to say.'

'Think that, do you?'

'We've talked and talked. We've rowed. I've tried to explain but they don't understand. They don't *want* to understand. They've got their plans and I've got mine and that's how it is.'

'Didn't know you'd talked to them at all.' Selevan made his voice deliberately thoughtful, a man considering the ramifications of what his granddaughter was telling him.

'What d'you mean you didn't know I'd talked to them?' Tammy demanded. 'That's all we *did* before I got here. I talked, Mum cried. I talked, Dad shouted. I talked, they argued with me. Only I didn't *want* to argue because far as I can tell there's nothing to argue about. You understand or you don't, and they don't. Well, how could they? I mean, Mum's whole way of living should've told me she'd never be able to come on board. A life of contemplation? Not very likely when your real interest is looking at fashion magazines and gossip magazines wondering how you can make yourself into Posh Spice while you're living in a place where, frankly, there's not a whole lot of designer shops. *And* you weigh about fifteen stone more 'n she does anyway. Or whatever she's called these days.'

'Who?'

'Posh Spice. Posh whoever. Mum has *Hello!* and *OK* sent over by the lorryload, not to mention *Vogue* and *Tatler* and whatever else, and that's her ambition. To look like all of them and to live like all of them and it's not mine, Grandie, and it never will be so you can send me home and nothing'll be different. I don't *want* what they want. I never have, and I never will.'

'I didn't know you talked to them,' he repeated. 'They said they'd not talked to you.'

'*What* do you mean?' She flung herself round in the seat so that she faced him.

'The Mother whatever-she-is,' he said. 'The abbot lady. What d'they call her?'

Tammy hesitated. Her tongue came out and licked her lips and then her teeth caught the lower one and she sucked on it in a childlike reaction. Selevan felt his heart twist at the sight of this. So much of who she was was still a little girl. He could see how her parents couldn't bear the thought of watching her disappear behind convent doors. Not *this* sort of convent at least, where no one emerged till they emerged in a coffin. It didn't make sense to them. It was so un-girl-like, wasn't it? She was supposed to care about pointy shoes with tall heels, about lipstick and hair thingummy dandershoots, about short skirts, long skirts, or in-between skirts, about jackets or not, waistcoats or not, about music and boys and film stars and when in her life she should lower her knickers for a bloke. But what she was *not* supposed to think about at the age of seventeen was the state of the world, war and peace, hunger and disease, poverty and ignorance. And what she definitely was *never* supposed to think about was sackcloth and ashes or whatever it was they wore, a small cell with a bed and prayer stand and a cross, a set of rosary beads, and getting up at dawn and then praying and praying and praying and all the time locked away from the world.

Tammy said, 'Grandie . . .' But she didn't seem to trust herself to finish the sentence.

'Tha's who I am, girl. The granddad who loves you.'

'You phoned?'

'Well, that's what the letter said, didn't it? Phone the Mother Whosis to arrange for a visit. Girls sometimes find they can't cope, she said. They think there's a romance to this kind of life, and I assure you there isn't, Mr Penrule. But we offer retreats to individuals and to groups and if she'd like to take part in one, we'd welcome her.'

Tammy's eyes were Nan's eyes once again, but Nan's eyes as they should have been when she looked on her dad, not as they'd become as she'd listened to him rage. 'Grandie, you're not taking me to the airport?'

'Course not,' he said as if it were the most reasonable thing in the world for him to fly in the face of her parents' wishes and drive his granddaughter to the Scottish border to spend a week in a Carmelite convent. 'They don't know and they aren't going to know.'

'But if I decide to stay . . . If I find it's what I think it is and what I need, you'll have to tell them. And then, what?'

'You let me worry about your parents,' he said.

'But they'll never forgive you. If I decide it's best, they'll never agree. They'll never think . . .'

'Girl,' Selevan said to his granddaughter, 'they'll think what they think.' He reached in the side compartment of his door and brought out an *A to Z* for the UK. He handed it over to her. He said, 'Open that up. If we're going to be driving all the way to Scotland, I'm going to need a bloody good navigator. Think you're up for the job?'

Her smile was blinding. It crushed his heart. 'I am,' she told him.

'Then let's carry on.'

The reaction to the day's events that stayed with Bea Hannford the longest was the one that led her towards looking for someone to blame. She began with Ray. He seemed the most logical source of the difficulties that had resulted in a killer's being able to walk blithely away from a murder charge. She told herself that had Ray only sent her the MCIT blokes she'd needed from the very beginning, she would not have had to rely on the TAG team he *had* sent her, men whose expertise was limited to heavy lifting and not to the finer points of a homicide investigation. She also would not have had to rely on Constable McNulty as part of that team, a man whose release of critical information to the dead boy's family had put the police in a position of having virtually *nothing* that was known only to the killer and to themselves. Sergeant Collins, at least, she could live with as he'd never left the station long enough to cause trouble. And as for DS Havers and Thomas Lynley, Bea wanted to blame them for something as well, if only for their infuriating loyalty to each other, but she didn't have the heart to do so. Aside from withholding information about Daidre Trahair, which hadn't turned out to be germane to the case anyway despite her own stubborn beliefs in the matter, they'd only done as she'd requested, more or less.

What she didn't really want to consider was how everything came down to her in the end because she was, after all, in charge of the investigation and she had maintained a pig-headed position on more than one topic, from Daidre Trahair's culpability to her own insistence upon an incident room here in the town and not where Ray had told her it *should* be, which was also where more adequate personnel was stationed. And she'd held firm to *that* desire to work in Casvelyn and not elsewhere simply because Ray had told her she was wrong to do so.

So while it all came down to Ray in the end, it also came down to her. This sort of thing put her future on the line.

No case to present. Were there four worse words? Oh, perhaps, *our marriage is over* were equally bad and God knew enough coppers heard those words spoken by a spouse who couldn't take the life of a cop's partner any longer. But *no case to present* meant leaving a bereaved family in the lurch, with no one brought to justice. It meant despite the long hours, the slog, the sifting through data, the forensics reports, the interviews, the discussions, the arranging of this piece that way and that piece this way, there was nothing left to do save begin the entire process again and hope for a different result or to leave the case open and declare it cold. Only how could it *be* cold, really, when they knew very well who the killer was and that he was going to walk away? That was hardly a cold case. A cold case still shone with a glimmer of hope should something more turn up, whereas this case shone not in the slightest. The regional force might well ask her what she needed to make things right in Casvelyn, but that was more or less in her dreams because what the regional force were far more likely to ask was how she'd cocked this up so badly.

Ray was how, she told herself. Ray had no interest in her success. He was out to get her for fourteen years of estrangement, no matter that he'd brought them about himself.

For want of another direction, she told the team to start sifting through the data again, to see what they could come up with to pin Jago Reeth, AKA Jonathan Parsons, to the wall of murder charge. What, she asked them, did they have that could be handed to the CPS, that could light the fire beneath those Crown prosecutors and set them off? There *had* to be something. So they'd begin this process on the following day and in the meantime they should all go home and get a decent night's rest because they'd not be sleeping much till they had this matter sorted. Then she followed her own prescription.

When she got to Holsworthy, she opened the cupboard in which she kept her brooms, her mops, and also her wine. She chose a bottle at random and carried it to the kitchen. Red, she discovered. Shiraz. Something from South Africa called Old Goats Roam in Villages. That sounded interesting. She couldn't recall when or where she'd bought it but she was fairly certain she'd made the purchase solely because of the name and the label.

She opened it, poured herself a brimming mug, and she sat at the table where her position forced her to contemplate her calendar. This proved to be as depressing as thinking about the last six days, once she considered her most recent internet date, which had occurred nearly four weeks previously. An architect. He'd looked good on the screen and he'd sounded good on the phone. A bit of chit and a bit of chat and nervous laughter and all that rubbish but that was to be expected, right? After all, this wasn't the normal way men and women met, what-ever went for normal these days because she didn't know any longer. A cup of coffee, perhaps? they'd asked each other. A drink somewhere? Certainly, fine. He'd shown up with photos of his holiday home, more photos of his holiday boat, extra photos of his holiday on skis, and additional photos of his car which may or may not have been a vintage Mercedes because by the time they'd got to it, Bea hadn't cared. Me, me, me, his conversation had declared. All me, baby, and all the time. She'd wanted either to weep or to sleep. By the end of the evening, she'd had two martinis and she shouldn't have driven herself anywhere, but the desire to flee had overcome her sense, so she'd puttered care-fully along the road and prayed she'd not get stopped. He'd said to her with an affable smile, 'Hell. Talked only about myself, didn't I? Well, next time . . .' and she'd thought, Won't be a next time, darling. Which was what she'd thought about all of them.

God, how wretched. This couldn't be how life was meant to be lived. And now . . . she couldn't even dredge up his name, just the moniker she'd given him: *Boat Wanker*, which distinguished him from all the other wankers. Was there a way, she wondered, to find a man in her age group without baggage, or a man who might be a person first and a profession leading up to the acquisition of countless possessions second? She was beginning to think not, unless that man was one of a score of divorcés she'd also met, blokes with nothing to their names but a heap of a car, a bedsit, and a mountain of credit card bills. Yet there *had* to be something in between those two extremes of male availability. Or was this how one's remaining years were intended to go when an unmarried woman reached what had once been coyly referred to as 'a certain age'?

Bea downed her wine. She ought to eat, she thought. She wasn't sure if there was anything in the fridge, but certainly she could rustle up a tin of soup. Or perhaps a few of those beef sticks Pete liked for snacks? An apple? Perhaps. A jar of peanut butter? Well, certainly there was Marmite to spread on mouldy bread. This was England, after all.

She dragged herself to her feet. She opened the fridge. She stared into its cold and heartless depths. There was sticky toffee sponge, she discovered, so she could tick pudding off on her menu. And far in the back was an old minced beef and onion roll. This *could* do as a main course. Now for the starter? Perhaps Pot Noodle? In the veg department, there had to be a tin of something. Chickpeas? Carrots and turnips? Bea wondered what she'd been thinking when she'd last done the shopping. Probably nothing, she decided. She'd likely been pushing the trolley along the aisles without an idea in her head as to what she might cook. The thought of proper nutrition for Pete had probably prompted a spontaneous visit to the supermarket but once there, she'd got distracted by something like a call on her mobile and the end result was . . . this.

She took out the sticky toffee sponge and decided to skip the starter, the entrée, and the veg altogether, getting right down to the pudding which, after all, everyone knew was the best part of the meal and why should she deny herself that when she wanted cheering up and this had the best potential to do the job?

She was about to tuck into it when *bim bim BIM boom BOOM* sounded on her front door, followed by the scrape of Ray's key in the lock. He came in talking. He was saying, '. . . spirit of compromise, mate,' to which Pete replied, 'Pizza *is* a compromise, Dad, cos I was set on McDonald's.'

'Don't you dare buy him a Big Mac,' Bea called.

'You see?' Ray said. 'Mum quite agrees.'

They came into the kitchen. They were wearing matching baseball caps, and Pete had his Arsenal sweatshirt on. Ray was in jeans and a paint-stained windcheater. Pete's jeans had a great hole in the knee.

'Where're the dogs?' Bea asked.

'Back at home,' Ray said. 'We've been—'

'Mum, Dad found this wicked paint ball place,' Pete announced. 'It was fantastic. Kapowee!' He mimicked shooting his father. 'Blim! Blam! Bash! You put on these boiler suits and they load you up and off you go. I got him so good, didn't I, Dad? I snuck round—'

'Sneaked,' Bea corrected patiently. She watched their son, and she didn't resist the smile that came to her as he demonstrated the stealth whereby he'd managed to obliterate his father with paint. It was just the sort of game she'd always sworn to herself that her son wouldn't play: a mimicry of war. And yet, in the end, wouldn't boys always be just that?

'*You* didn't think I'd be that good, did you?' Pete asked his father, playfully punching him in the arm.

Ray reached out, hooked his arm round Pete's neck and pulled him over. He planted a loud kiss on his son's head and rubbed his knuckles through Pete's thick hair. 'Go and get what you came for, Paintball Wizard,' he told him. 'We've got dinner to attend to.'

'Pizza!'

'Curry or Chinese. That's the best I'll offer. Or we can have calves' liver and onions at home. Served with sprouts and broad beans.'

Pete laughed. He darted out of the room and they heard him dash up the stairs.

'He wanted his CD player,' Ray told Bea. He smiled as they listened to Pete crashing about his room. 'Truth is, he wants an iPod and he thinks if he demonstrates how many CDs he's got to carry round with him when he *could* be carrying this device the size of . . . what size are they? I can't keep up with technology.'

'These days that's what kids are for. When it comes to technology, I'm utterly out of the loop without Pete.'

Ray watched her for a moment as she spooned up a portion of sticky toffee sponge. She saluted him with it. He said, 'Why do I think that's your dinner, Beatrice?'

'Because you're a cop.'

'So it is?'

'Hmm.'

'Are you in the middle of something? Taking a break?'

'Wish,' she said. 'But that's not the word I'd choose to describe where I am or where the case is.'

She decided to tell him. He was going to learn it all sooner or later, so it might as well be sooner and from her. She gave him all the details and waited for his reaction. 'Damn,' he said. 'That's a real . . .'

'Cock-up?' she offered. 'Generated by yours truly?'

'I wasn't going to say that, exactly.'

'But you were thinking it.'

'The cock-up part, yes. Not the part about you.'

Bea turned away from the expression of friendly compassion on his face. She stared at the window which in daylight would have looked out on a bit of her garden, which, she knew, should have been mulched by this time of the year but was instead offering itself to whatever stray seeds were dropped by skylarks and linnets in flight. Those seeds were germinating into weeds, and in another month or two she'd have a right royal mess on her hands. Good thing all she saw in the window was her reflection and Ray's behind her, she thought. They provided a bit of a distraction from the work she'd created for herself through lack of attention to her garden.

She said, 'I was all set to blame you.'

'For?'

'The cock-up. Inadequate incident room. No MCIT blokes for love or money. There I am, hanging out to dry with Constable McNulty and Sergeant Collins and whomever you deign to send me—'

'That's not how it was.'

'Oh, I know that.' Her voice was weary because *she* was weary. She felt as if she'd been swimming upstream for far too long. 'And I'm the one who sent Constable McNulty to tell the Kernes the death was murder. I thought he'd use sense but of course I was wrong. And then when I'd learned *what* he'd told them, I thought we'd surely uncover something more, some scrap, some detail, it didn't matter what it was. Just something useful as a trip wire for the moment the killer came sauntering by. But we didn't.'

'You may still.'

'I doubt it. Unless you count a remark made about a surfing poster, which isn't likely to amount to anything in the eyes of the CPS.' She set down the container of sponge. 'I've told myself for years there's no perfect murder. Forensic science is too advanced. As long as there's a body to be found, there are too many tests, too many experts. No one can kill and leave not a single trace of himself behind. It's impossible. Simply can't be done.'

'There's truth in that, Beatrice.'

'But what I failed to see is the loopholes. All the ways a killer could plan and organise and commit his ultimate crime and do it in such a way that every bit of it could be explained. Even the most minute forensic bits could be deemed a rational part of one's daily life. I didn't see that. *Why* didn't I see that?'

'Perhaps you had other things on your mind. Distractions.'

'Such as?'

'Other parts of your own life. You do have other parts to your life, no matter your attempts to deny that.'

She wanted to avoid this conversation. 'Ray . . .'

Clearly, he didn't intend to let her. 'You're not a cop to the exclusion of everything else,' he said. 'Good God, Beatrice, you're not a machine.'

'I wonder about that sometimes.'

'Well, I don't.'

A blast of music came from upstairs: Pete deciding among his CDs. They listened for a moment to the shriek of an electric guitar. Pete liked his music historical. Jimi Hendrix was his favourite although in a pinch Duane Allman and his medicine bottle would do just fine.

'God,' Ray said. 'Get that lad an iPod.'

She smiled, then chuckled. 'He's something, that child.'

'Our child, Beatrice,' Ray declared quietly.

She didn't reply. Instead, she took the sticky toffee sponge and tossed it in the rubbish. She washed the spoon she'd been using and set it on the draining board.

Ray said, 'Can we talk about it now?'

'You do choose your moments, don't you?'

'Beatrice, I've wanted to talk about it for ages. You know that.'

'I do. But at the present time . . . You're a cop and a good one. You can see how I am. Get the suspect in a weak moment. *Create* the weak moment if you can. It's elementary stuff, Ray.'

'This isn't.'

'What?'

'Elementary. Beatrice, how many ways can a man say to you that he was wrong? And how many ways can you say to a man that forgiveness isn't part of your repertoire? When I thought that Pete shouldn't be—'

'Don't say it.'

'I have to say it and you have to listen. When I thought that Pete shouldn't be born, when I *said* you should abort—'

'You said that's what *you* wanted.'

'I said lots of things. I *say* lots of things. And some of them I say without thinking. Especially when I'm . . .'

'What?'

'I don't know. Frightened, I suppose.'

'Of a baby? We'd already had one.'

'Not of that. But of change. The difference it would make in our lives as we had them arranged.'

'Things happen.'

'I understand. And I would have come to understand that *then* if you'd allowed me the time to—'

'It wasn't only a single discussion, Ray.'

'Yes. All right. I won't claim it was. But I will say that I was wrong. In every discussion we had, I was wrong, and I've grieved over that wrongness, if you will, for years. Fourteen of them, to be exact. More if you include the pregnancy itself. I didn't want it this way. I *don't* want it this way.'

'And . . . them?' she asked. 'You had your diversions.'

'What? Women? For God's sake, Beatrice, I'm not a monk. Yes, there were women over the years. A whole bloody succession of them. Janice and Sheri and Sharon and Linda and whoever else because I don't remember them all. And I don't remember them because I didn't want them. I wanted to blot out . . . this.' He indicated the kitchen, the house, the people within it. 'So what I'm asking you is to let me back in because this is where I belong and both of us know it.'

'Do we?'

'We do. Pete knows it as well. So do the bloody dogs.'

She swallowed. It would be so easy. But then again, it wouldn't. The stuff of men and women together was never easy.

'Mum!' Pete was shouting from upstairs. 'Where'd you put my Led Zeppelin CD?'

'Lord,' Bea murmured with a shudder. 'Someone, please, get that lad an iPod at once.'

'Mum! Mummy!'

She said to Ray, 'I love it when he still calls me that. He doesn't, often. He's becoming so grown-up.' She called back, 'Don't know, darling. Check under your bed. And while you're at it, put any clothes you find there in the laundry. And bring old cheese sandwiches down to the rubbish. Detach the mice from them, first.'

'Very funny,' he shouted and continued to bang about. He said, 'Dad!

Make her tell me. *Make* her. She *knows* where it is. She *hates* it and she's hidden it somewhere.'

Ray called up, 'Son, I learned long ago that I can't make this mad woman do anything.' Then he said to her quietly, 'Can I, my dear. Because if I could, you know what it would be.'

'That you can't.'

'To my eternal regret.'

She thought about his words, those he'd just said and those he'd said before. She said to him, 'Not really eternal.'

She heard him swallow. 'Do you mean it, Beatrice?'

'I suppose I do.'

They looked at each other, the window behind them doubling the image of man and woman and the hesitant step each of them took towards the other at precisely the same moment. Pete came pounding down the stairs. He shouted, 'Found it! Ready to go, Dad.'

'Are you ready as well?' Ray asked Bea quietly.

'For dinner?'

'And for what follows dinner.'

She drew a long breath that matched his own. 'I think I am.'

30

They spoke little on the drive back from St Agnes. And when they did speak, it was of mundane matters. She needed to stop for petrol, so they'd take a diversion from the main road if he didn't mind.

He didn't mind at all. Did she want a cup of tea while they were at it? Surely there was a hotel or tea shop along the way where they might even have proper Cornish cream tea. Scones, clotted cream, and strawberry jam.

She remembered the days when it was difficult to find clotted cream outside Cornwall. Did he?

Yes. And pasties as well. He'd always enjoyed good pasties, but they'd never had them at home as his father had considered them . . . There he stopped himself. *Common* was the word of choice. *Vulgar* in its most precise usage.

She supplied it for him, using the former term. She added, And you weren't that, were you?

He told her his brother was a narcotics user because that was the truth of the matter. Chucked out of Oxford, his girlfriend dead with a needle in her arm, himself in and out of rehab ever since. He said he thought that he'd failed Peter altogether. When he should have *been* there for the boy – present, he meant, present in every possible way and not just a warm body occupying a sofa or something – he hadn't been.

Well, these things happen, she said. And you had your own life.

As you have yours.

She didn't say what another woman in her position might have said at the end of the day they'd just spent together: And do you think this levels the playing field, Thomas? but he knew she was thinking it, for what else *could* she think at his mentioning Peter in the midst of nothing vaguely related to the topic? In spite of that, he wanted to add more life details, piling them up so that she would be forced to see similarities instead of differences. He wanted to tell her that his brother-in-law had been murdered some ten years earlier, that he himself had been suspected of the crime and had even been carted off to gaol and held twenty-four hours for a grilling because he'd hated Edward Davenport and what Edward Davenport had wrought upon his sister, and he'd never made a secret of that. But to tell her that seemed too much like begging for something that she wasn't going to be able to give him.

He deeply regretted the position he'd put her in because he could see how she would interpret his reaction to everything she'd revealed that day, no matter his declarations to the contrary. There was an enormous gulf between them created first by birth, second by childhood, and third by experience. That the gulf existed only in her head and not in his was something he could not explain to her. Such a declaration was facile, anyway. The gulf existed everywhere, and for her it was something so real that she would ever fail to see it was not equally real to him.

You don't actually know me, he wanted to tell her. Who I am, the people I move among, the loves that have defined my life. But then, how could you? Newspaper stories – tabloids, magazines, whatever – taken up from the internet reveal only the dramatic bits, the heart-rending bits, the salacious bits. Those elements of life comprising the valuable and unforgettable everyday bits are not included. They lack drama even as ultimately they define who a person is.

Not that that mattered: who he was. It had ceased to matter with Helen's death.

Or so he had told himself. Except that what he felt now indicated something different. That he should care for another's suffering spoke of . . . what? Rebirth? He didn't *want* to be reborn. Recovery? He wasn't sure he wanted to recover. But a sense of who he was at the core of who he appeared to be prompted him to feel at least something of what Daidre herself was feeling: caught out in the spotlight, naked when she'd worked so hard to fashion clothing for herself.

I'd like to turn back time, he told her.

She looked at him and he saw from her expression that she thought he was talking of something else. Of course you would, she said. My God, who wouldn't in your position?

Not about Helen, he said, although I'd give nearly anything to bring her back to me if I could.

Then, what?

This. What I've brought you to.

It's part of your job, she said.

But it wasn't his job. He wasn't a cop. He'd walked away from that part of his life because he couldn't bear it a moment longer, because it had taken him away from Helen, and had he known how many hours upon hours he'd *be* away from her and each of those hours trickling through a glass in which the remaining days of her life were contained . . . He would have called a halt to all of it.

No, he said. Not part of my job. That's not why I was here.

Well, they asked you to. She asked you. I can't think you did it all on your own. Came up with the plan, whatever.

I did. He said it heavily and he regretted having to say it at all. But I want you to know that *if* I'd known . . . You see, you don't seem like . . .

Like them? she asked. I'm cleaner? More educated? More accomplished? Better dressed? More well-spoken? Well, I've had eighteen years to put them, that whole terrible . . . I want to call it an 'episode' but it wasn't an episode. It was my life. It made me who I am no matter who I try to be now. These sorts of things define us, Thomas, and that defined me.

Thinking that, he told her, negates the last eighteen years, doesn't it? It negates your parents, what they did for you, how they loved you and made you part of their family.

You've met my parents. You've seen my family. And how we lived.

I meant your other parents. The ones who were your parents as parents are meant to be.

The Trahairs. Yes. But they don't change the rest of it, do they? They can't. The rest is . . . the rest. And it's there as it always will be.

That's no cause for shame.

She looked at him. She'd found the petrol station she was seeking, and they'd pulled into its forecourt. She'd turned off the ignition and rested her hand on the door handle. He'd done the same, ever the gentleman, unwilling to let her pump the petrol herself.

She said, That's just it, you see.

What?

People like you—

Please don't, he said. There is no people-like-me. There are just people. There's just the human experience, Daidre.

People like you, she persisted nonetheless, think it's about shame because that's what you would feel in the same circumstances. Travelling about. Living most of the time in a rubbish tip. Bad food. Second-hand clothes. Loose teeth and ill-formed bones. Shifty eyes and sticky fingers. Why read or write when one can steal? That's what you think and you're hardly wrong. But the feeling, Thomas, has nothing at all to do with shame.

Then . . . ?

Sorrow. Regret. Like my name.

We're the same, then, you and I, he told her. Despite the differences—

She laughed, a single weary note. We are not, she replied. I expect you played at it, you and your brother and your sister and your mates. Your parents may have even found you a gipsy caravan and parked it somewhere quite hidden away on the estate. You could go there and play dress-up and act the part, but you couldn't have lived it.

She got out of the car. He did the same. She went to the pumps and studied them, as if trying to decide which type of petrol she needed. As she hesitated, he went for the nozzle himself. He began to fill the tank for her.

She said, I expect your man does that for you.

Don't.

I can't help it. I'll never be able to help it.

She shook her head in a fierce little movement, as if to negate all that was left unspoken between them. She climbed back into the car and shut the door. He saw that she looked straight ahead afterwards, as if there was something in the window of the petrol station's shop that she needed to memorise.

He went to pay. When he climbed in the car, he saw she'd put a neat stack of notes on his seat to cover the cost of the petrol. He took them, folded them neatly, and put them into the empty ashtray just above the gear stick.

She said, I don't want you to pay, Thomas.

He said, I know. But I hope you can cope with the fact that I intend to do so.

She started the car. They re-entered the road. They drove for some minutes in silence with the countryside passing and evening dropping round them like a shifting veil.

He finally said to her the only thing worth saying, the only request he had that she might grant at this point. He'd asked once and been denied, but it seemed to him that she might reconsider although he couldn't have explained why. They were jouncing across the carpark of the Salthouse Inn where they'd begun their day when he spoke a final time.

'Will you call me Tommy?' he asked her again.

'I don't think I can,' she replied.

$$\star \quad \star \quad \star$$

He wasn't particularly hungry, but he knew he had to eat. To eat was to live, and it appeared to him that he was doomed to go on living, at least for now. After he watched Daidre drive off, he went inside the Salthouse Inn, and he decided that he could face a bar meal but not the restaurant.

He ducked inside the low doorway and found that Barbara Havers had possessed the same idea. She was in the otherwise abandoned inglenook while the rest of the bar's patrons crowded on stools round the few scarred tables and at the bar itself behind which Brian was pouring pints.

Lynley went to join her, drawing out the stool opposite the banquette that she herself occupied. She looked up from her food. Shepherd's pie, he saw. The obligatory accompaniments of boiled carrots, boiled cauliflower, boiled broccoli, tinned peas, and chips. She'd used ketchup on the lot of it, save the carrots and the peas, which she'd moved to one side altogether.

'Didn't your mum insist you eat all your veg?' he asked her.

'That's the beauty of adulthood,' she replied, shoving some of the mash and minced beef onto her fork, 'one can ignore certain foods altogether.' She chewed thoughtfully and observed him. 'Well?' she asked.

He told her. As he did so, he realised that, without anticipating or wanting it, he'd passed into another stage of the journey he was on. One week ago, he'd not have spoken at all. Or if he'd done so, it would have been to make a remark that served to abbreviate the conversation as much as possible.

He finished with, 'I couldn't actually make her see that this sort of thing . . . the past, her family or at least the people who gave birth to her . . . it's not important, really.'

'Course not,' Havers said genially. 'Abso-bloody-lutely not. Not in a bottle. Not on a plate. And specially not to someone who never lived it, mate.'

'Havers, we've all got something in our pasts.'

'Hmm. Right.' She forked up some broccoli doused in ketchup, carefully removing a single pea that had got mixed in. 'Except not all of us have silver serving dishes in ours, if you know what I mean. And what's that big thing you lot have sitting in the centre of your dining room tables? You know what I mean. All silver with animals hopping about it. Or vines and grapes or whatever. You know.'

'Epergne,' he told her. 'It's called an epergne. But you can't possibly be thinking that something as meaningless as a piece of silver—'

'Not the silver. The word. See? You knew what to call it. D'you think she knows? How much of the rest of the world *ever* knows?'

'That's hardly the point.'

'That's *just* the point. There're places, sir, that the hoi polloi aren't going to, and your dinner table is one of them.'

'You've eaten at my dinner table yourself.'

'I'm the exception. You lot find my ignorance charming. She can't help it, you think. Consider where she came from, you tell people. Sort of like saying, "Poor thing, she's American. She doesn't know any better."'

'Havers, hang on. I've never once thought—'

'Doesn't matter,' she said, waving her fork at him. She had chips on it now, although they were barely discernible through the ketchup. 'I don't care, you see. I don't mind. But she does. And that's the bit that gets one into trouble: the minding bit. Don't mind and you can swan round in ignorance or at least pretend to. Mind and you're all thumbs and fumbling with the cutlery. Sixteen knives and twenty-two forks and why are these people eating asparagus with their *fingers*?' She shuddered dramatically. She went for more shepherd's pie. She washed it down with what she was drinking, which appeared to be cider.

He watched her and said, 'Havers, is it my imagination, or have you been drinking rather more than your usual tonight?'

'Why? Am I slurring my words?'

'Not slurring exactly. But—'

'I'm owed. A stiff one. Fifteen stiff ones if that's what it takes. I'm not driving and I should be able to make it up the stairs. Just.'

'What's going on?' he asked her, for it wasn't like Havers to drink to excess. She was generally a one-a-week sort of drinker.

She told him, then. Jago Reeth, Benesek Kerne, Hedra's Hut – which she referred to as 'some mad cabin on the edge of the cliff where we all might've died, mind you' – and the result, which was no result at all. Jonathan Parsons and Pengelly Cove, Santo Kerne, and—

'Are you saying he confessed?' Lynley said. 'How extraordinary.'

'Sir, you're missing the point. He didn't confess. He supposed. He supposed this and he supposed that and in the end he supposed himself right out of that hovel and on his way. Revenge is sweet and all that rubbish.'

'And that's it?' he said. 'What did Hannaford do?'

'What could she do? What could anyone do? If this had been written by the Greeks, I suppose we could hope that Thor would hit him with a bolt of lightning in the next couple days, but I wouldn't count on that.'

'Good grief,' Lynley said, and then after a moment he added, 'Zeus.'

'What?'

'Zeus, Havers. Thor's Norse. Zeus's Greek.'

'What*ever*, sir. I am, we know, one of the hoi polloi. Point is this: the Greeks aren't exactly involved here, so he walks away. She intends to keep after him but she's got sweet F.A. to work with, thanks to that idjit McNulty whose sole contribution appears to be one surfing poster. That and giving out information when he's meant to keep his mug plugged tight. It's a right bloody mess, and I'm glad I'm not responsible for it.'

Lynley blew out a breath. 'Ghastly for the family,' he said.

'Isn't it just,' she replied. She examined him. 'You eating or what, sir?'

'I thought I'd have something,' he told her. 'How's the shepherd's pie?'

'Shepherd's pie-ish. One can't be too choosy, when it comes to shepherd's pie as a bar meal, I find. Let's put it this way, Jamie Oliver's got nothing to worry about tonight.' She forked up a sample and handed it over.

He took it and chewed. It would do, he thought. He started to get up to order himself a plate from the bar. Her next remarks stopped him.

'Sir, if you don't mind . . .' She spoke so carefully that he knew what was coming.

'Yes?'

'Will you come back to London with me?'

He sat down again. He looked not at her but at her plate: the remains of the shepherd's pie and the carefully avoided peas and carrots. It was all so vintage Havers, he thought. The meal, the carrots, the peas, the conversation they'd been having, and the question as well.

'Havers . . .'

'Please,' she said.

He looked up at her. Ill featured, ill dressed, ill shorn. So quintessentially who she was. Behind the mask of indifference she presented to the world he saw what he'd seen in Havers from the first: the earnestness and the truth of her, a woman among millions, his partner, his friend.

He said, 'In time. Not now, but in time.'

'When?' she asked. 'Can you at least say when?'

He looked to the window, which faced the west. He thought about what lay in that direction. He considered the steps he'd taken so far, and the rest of the steps that remained to be taken.

'I've got to walk the rest of the path,' he told her. 'After that, we'll see.'

'Will we?' she asked.

'Yes, Barbara. We will.'

Acknowledgments

I'd like to express grateful acknowledgment to those people who assisted me in gathering the information necessary to write this novel, both in the UK and in the US.

In Cornwall, I'd like to thank Nigel Moyle and Paul Stickney of Zuma Jay's Surf Shop in Bude for the assistance they gave me in understanding what surfing is like in Cornwall, so different from surfing in Huntington Beach, California, where I lived for many years. I'd also like to thank Adrian Phillips of FluidJuice Surfboards in St Merryn and Kevin White of Beach Beat Surfboards in St Agnes for everything they shared with me about shaping boards, both from Styrofoam blanks and from the new carbon hollow core blanks.

Just north of Widemouth Bay, Rob Byron of Outdoor Adventures put me in the picture with regard to cliff climbing and everything related to that sport. I gathered additional details from Toni Carver in St Ives.

Alan Mobb of the Devon and Cornwall Constabulary was good enough to bring me up to date on policing in Cornwall, and he was kind enough to do it twice when I discovered my tape recorder hadn't been working the first time through the information.

I gathered other information at Geevor Tin Mine, Blue Hills Tin Streams, the Lost Gardens of Heligan, the Cornish Cyder Farm, Gwithian parish church, Zennor church, and at the home of Des Sampson in Bude.

Swati Gamble once again proved an invaluable resource in London, cheerfully fielding questions from me on a variety of topics, for which I am extremely grateful.

In the US, longtime surfers Barbara and Lou Fryer were the first people to tell me about Mark Foo's last ride, and they also gave me additional details about surfing so that I could attempt to write my moments in the water with at least a degree of verisimilitude. Dr Tom Ruben was once again my medical consultant, Susan Berner once again graciously consented to read a second draft of the book, giving it her usual fine critical appraisal, and my assistant Leslie Kelly did outstanding research on more topics that I could list here: from roller derby to BMX bike riding.

Perhaps the greatest kindness was done by Lawrence Beck, who managed to unearth for me the one photograph of the late Jay Moriarty that I needed to complete the novel.

Books that I found useful were: *Inside Maverick's, Portrait of a Monster Wave* edited by Bruce Jenkins and Grant Washburn; *Tapping the Source* by Kem Nunn; *Surf UK* by Wayne Alderson; *Bude Past and Present* by Bill Young and Bryan Dudley Stamp, and assorted guides on the South-West Coast Path.

Finally, I thank my husband Thomas McCabe for his consistent support, enthusiasm, and encouragement; my assistant Leslie Kelly for the myriad personal services she performs in order to free my time to write; my editors in the US and the UK – Carolyn Marino and Sue Fletcher, respectively, for never asking me to write something outside my vision of the work; and my literary agent Robert Gottlieb, who pilots the craft and charts the course.

And, of course, those others who gather within the Petri Dish. You know who you are. B—T—. We are one.

Whidbey Island, Washington
August 2, 2007